The Royal Mile

MARY DAHEIM

The Royal Mile

MARY DAHEIM

CAMEL PRESS

Seattle, WA

CAMEL PRESS

Camel Press
PO Box 70515
Seattle, WA 98127

For more information go to: www.camelpress.com
www.AuthorMaryDaheim.com

Cover design by Sabrina Sun

The Royal Mile

Originally printed by Avon Press under the title *Love's Pirate*

ISBN: 978-1-60381-855-1 (Trade Paper)
ISBN: 978-1-60381-856-8 (eBook)
LOC Control Number: 2013954431

Printed in the United States of America

To Jennifer McCord: Publishing brought us together thirty years ago, but what I cherish most is her steadfast friendship and kind heart.

Dear Readers:

Almost 50 years ago, I spent three months in Europe with my cousin, Judy, and two of our friends. We visited Paris, London, Rome, Vienna—just about every major must-see place in Western Europe. They all lived up to expectations, but the city I fell in love with was Edinburgh.

I'm not a Scot, though I've always been a history buff, especially fascinated by British and French history. Of course all the other places I saw in Europe had plenty of their own history, but Edinburgh—especially the High Street or The Royal Mile as it's known—reeked of it.

"Reeked" is an odd word to choose, given that one of the city's nicknames is Auld Reekie, dating from the era when most buildings were heated by coal and wood fires that produced great clouds of black smoke. That's gone now. The evening spent at the annual Highland Games below Edinburgh Castle was in good, clear weather. I can still see the lone piper standing on the castle ramparts, playing his bagpipe as a farewell to the audience.

On the way back to the High Street and our hotel, we climbed up the narrow wynds, flanked by four-hundred-year-old houses that begged to be described on paper. Yet I didn't start writing the book until another six years had passed. I'd already begun a novel set in sixteenth century England, I had a good job in PR, I met Dave, got married, our first daughter was born, and we bought a house on Queen Anne Hill.

Not long after we moved in, I was standing at the kitchen sink, looking at the steep street behind our house and somehow I thought of Edinburgh. I have to write that book, I suddenly thought. The period of Mary, Queen of Scots was as notorious as it was compelling. I researched the period for two years. I even made a huge map depicting how the High Street and its surroundings looked in the 1560s. Six years later, after the births of two more daughters, I finished the 850-page manuscript—and put it on top of the refrigerator.

After a couple of years, Dave got tired of looking at that pile of paper (being six inches shorter, I really couldn't see it) and told me to move it, dust it, or sell it. I opted for the third choice—the other involved housework. After getting a New York agent—Donald MacCampbell, a crusty Philadelphia-born Scot—I made the necessary revisions, a lengthy process pre-computer. Within a month, Donald sold what I'd called The Royal Mile to Avon Books. My editor changed the title to Love's Pirate, somewhat to my dismay. Over thirty years later, I've finally gotten my way. I hope you get as much enjoyment out of reading The Royal Mile as I did from writing this story of love and intrigue in my favorite non-native city.

—Mary Daheim

PART ONE

Chapter One

THE CHURCH BELLS clamored from St. Cuthbert's in the west to the Abbey Kirk in the east. Startled crows flew out of the towers and even the bravest of dogs began to howl. Out in the High Street, crowds of expectant townspeople milled about, jostling one another for the best vantage points. The dismal grey haar that had enshrouded Edinburgh for most of the day finally lifted as shafts of late-day August sun filtered between the tall narrow houses of the Lawnmarket.

Dallas Cameron hesitated for just a moment before she descended the spiraling steps of her family's gabled house in Nairne's Close. Her tumultuous emotions seemed to be echoed in the noisy voices rising up over the roof tops from the High Street. Anger, excitement and, most of all, grief made a muddle of her mind and caused her usual sure step to falter.

The quarrel between Dallas and her sisters had been unseemly. They had stood outside the door of their father's sickroom and railed at each other for a full five minutes before Marthe, the Camerons' aged serving woman, had intervened.

"But Father is dying!" Glennie had protested. "Dallas can't leave now, not even to welcome the Queen!"

The youngest of the Cameron girls, Tarrill, was barely coherent through her tears: "Mary Stuart doesn't know us ... wouldn't care ... we are nobodies!"

Dallas stood straight and proud before her sisters. "Our sire has been well respected as a scholar. Though he never met the Queen, he has waited many years to see Mary Stuart regain her rightful place in Scotland. He would want one of us to welcome her in his stead."

Marthe, exercising a prerogative born out of long years of service and mutual affection for all members of the Cameron family, waved her reddened, pudgy hands and shushed the sisters into silence.

"Cease, lassies, yon good sire would not want ye quarreling. Let Dallas go; she knows what Master Cameron would wish in having his kin greet the Queen in her time of triumph."

So Dallas had finally left the house with its stale smelling sickroom and the aura of impending death. Let Glennie and Tarrill sob over the counterpane, Dallas thought grimly, while I do what Father would wish. But that had always been the way with the Cameron sisters—Glennie and Tarrill would bemoan whatever ill wind blew their way—and wait for Dallas to shift fate in a more propitious direction.

But this time it would be difficult even for Dallas to grapple with fate. The tragedy of their father's death was overwhelming enough. But coupled with it lay the prospect of poverty. Daniel Cameron had been the sole support of his three daughters and two grandsons since Glennie's husband died the previous winter. Even as their father still clung to life, Dallas's practical nature had looked beyond his passing to a bleak future.

Pulling the frayed blue cloak more closely about her slim body, Dallas temporarily put such thoughts from her mind and walked purposefully away from Nairne's Close. She had only gone a few paces before she stiffened as a familiar figure turned a corner and headed her way.

"Dallas!" called George Gordon, quickening his step on the rounded cobblestones. "Are you off to see the Queen?"

Dallas stood her ground and gazed directly at George. It was not easy to face George Gordon under any circumstances; it was extremely difficult to confront him in her time of grief.

"Aye," she answered dully, glancing surreptitiously at the handsome face with its dimpled chin and golden moustache. "You know how my father felt about Her Grace's return."

"My own sire has mixed emotions," George said airily, regarding her from his splendid height. "A Catholic sovereign is well enough—but the Gordons are Highlanders who never have taken well to strong-willed monarchs."

"You needn't remind me how great a lord your sire is," Dallas retorted. She had to bite her tongue to keep from saying that he also needn't remind her that his father was the powerful Earl of Huntly and she was but the daughter of a humble tutor. George Gordon had reminded her of that often enough during his brief stay as a pupil of Daniel Cameron's.

But Gordon was only laughing. "It will be amusing, actually, to see how the Protestant lords vie with the Catholic nobility for Mary Stuart's attentions."

Darkness was descending over the city, but bonfires still burned on the surrounding hills and scarcely a window remained unlighted. Here, below

Castle Hill, the tall gabled houses squeezed together as if for mutual protection. Some of the buildings rose ten stories in height, with dormer windows set at an angle permitting intimate views into neighboring houses. Dallas tried to concentrate on her surroundings rather than on her companion or on the sorrow she had left behind. But George Gordon seemed determined to keep her at his side.

"Queen Mary has been in France since she was six," he was saying, more to himself than to Dallas. "Who could blame her mother, Marie de Guise, for shipping the little Queen off to France instead of letting her fall into the clutches of King Henry the Eighth as a bride for his puny Prince Edward?"

"The French Dauphin was no less puny, since he died within a year after our Queen married him," Dallas pointed out. "But then I marvel you would discuss politics with me, sir. When you were a pupil of my father you seldom cared to talk about much more than court gossip or other frivolous topics."

Gordon chuckled as they walked up the incline, ignoring a bawdy greeting called out by a small group of young men. "It's a night for political speculations," Gordon said. "All Scotland wants to find out if a Catholic queen can rule what has—I fear—become a predominantly Protestant nation. And, of course, how her ambitious—and Protestant—bastard half-brother Lord James will react."

"With all the bastard half-brothers and half-sisters Queen Mary has, she's fortunate to have only one who is so power-crazed," Dallas asserted.

"I've never liked James," Gordon continued as if he hadn't heard her comment. "I think he thought to rule Scotland if Francois had lived and Mary never returned."

The smells of cooking meat, wood smoke and animal dung mingled in the night air. Dallas and Gordon turned down a wynd so narrow that they had to walk single file. They started up a flight of wooden stairs that would bring them almost to St. Giles where the Lawnmarket ended and the High Street began.

"James could prove dangerous," Gordon was saying as they headed towards the Tolbooth. "I hope he never dares pit himself against our clan."

As they approached the Canongate that would lead them to the gates of the city and Holyrood Palace itself, Dallas found herself physically fatigued and even more weary of George Gordon's characteristic self-absorption. "We all have our family problems," she countered as the crowd began to grow in noise and size. "My father is dying."

"My father is unsure of how such a youthful, inexperienced woman will rule," Gordon said. "He prefers to remain in the Highlands until he can judge her performance as a sovereign."

Off in the distance, the skirl of pipes floated down into the Canongate, surmounting the sound of the crowd. Dallas turned and looked at Gordon head-on. "I said my father is dying." She glanced defiantly at her companion, who seemed to have his attention fixed on the warming pans which many of Edinburgh's citizens had lighted on their windowsills as signs of welcome to the Queen.

"You—you said your father is—what?" At last he looked directly at Dallas, puzzled.

"Oh!" Dallas pushed her hands through the jumble of brown hair in frustration. It was always the same with George Gordon; six years had made no difference. He never listened to anyone but himself. He never cared for anyone but himself. Certainly he never had paid any attention to her. "You pay no heed to anything I say, you were always like that! Go play your silly games of intrigue, go bloat yourself on great Huntly's pride and power!"

Gordon looked genuinely puzzled. "My father is a powerful man, everyone knows that. But I still didn't quite hear what you said about your ...."

"You never did—you never will." Dallas whirled away from Gordon and collided with a stout woman, who cursed and waved a fleshy fist in the air.

Dallas was about to retaliate when someone touched her arm and a man's voice spoke low from behind her, "Steady, lass. She's thrice your size."

"Old lard-pot," she bristled.

"She's only caught up in the excitement," said the man at Dallas's side. He was tall, with a dark-skinned face, lean, sharp features and a pair of hazel eyes that looked as if they knew more about this side of heaven than anybody should.

Dallas felt something inside wince. "You can let go of my arm now, sir," she demanded. "I've got two good feet and I'm standing on both of them all by myself."

The dark man lazily ran those all-knowing hazel eyes down from the top of her head to the tips of her toes. "Aye, so you are," he said mildly. "But your shoes don't match."

Dallas regarded her footwear with horror. He was right—somehow, in her distress that morning she had put on two different shoes. She was about to retort that a tutor's daughter was lucky to have shoes at all when she looked up and discovered that the man was gone. No matter—at least he had momentarily taken her mind off George Gordon. George had ridiculed her book learning, rebuffed her girlish attempts to enjoin him in anything but the most trivial of conversations, openly expressed contempt for educated women. Dallas was only a tutor's daughter, and great Gordons married great ladies; George had taken the Duke of Chatelherault's daughter, Anne Hamilton, as his bride.

But that had all happened some years before, and though Dallas had seen George Gordon occasionally in the city, they had scarcely spoken except to bid each other good day. Those incidents were of no importance to him, of course; but each encounter had painfully reminded Dallas of how limited her resources were, simply because she was a woman—and each glance at that handsome, masculine face had made her determined never to let any man take advantage of her.

Dallas reminded herself of that vow as she noted that virtually every window of Holyrood Palace was now illumined with lights. Beyond the royal dwelling stood Arthur's Seat, that stately pile of rock which made the perfect mate for Castle Hill at the other end of the city.

Again the pipes began to play. Somewhere nearby a group of off-key masculine voices sang hymns. A handful of couples danced together in Panmuir Close. Dallas observed them with an envy mingled with annoyance. She would be lucky to have the strength to walk the full mile back to the Lawnmarket, let alone tread any of those light-footed measures the Protestant preacher John Knox railed against in his sermons at St. Giles.

And then, high up on a balcony in the northwest corner of the palace, a tall, slim figure appeared. The crowd let out a single-voiced cheer as Mary Stuart raised her arms to her people. Even from where Dallas stood, the gesture evoked grace, majesty and feminine charm. To her own surprise, Dallas responded with as lusty a cheer as the rest, then watched with fascination as the Queen retreated into the palace. Bonnets were hurled into the air, children who had been hoisted onto shoulders for a better view hooted with joy and the pipes took up their bittersweet serenade.

Dallas kept her eyes riveted on the empty square of light where the Queen had stood. How old was Mary Stuart? Eighteen, nineteen? Younger by at least three years than Dallas herself. Yet, there she had stood, gracious, majestic, like a fairy princess. She was not a witch, as John Knox asserted, but there was something magical about her—some quality, however fleeting, that conquered darkness and distance to reach her people.

Father would approve, Dallas thought as she turned away with others in the crowd. Along the Canongate candles were being extinguished, windows slammed tight, shutters closed. The crowd lessened at every street as handfuls of merrymakers trickled into closes, down the wynds and into the few ale houses which had dared break the Sabbath ban.

By the time Dallas turned into her shortcut to Nairne's Close, several of the polished ashlar and timber-fronted houses were completely dark. In spite of the incline up the side of Castle Hill, she could be home within five minutes, if she hurried; yet the lateness of the hour and the sudden loneliness of the area made her apprehensive. Vexed with herself, she noted that there were footsteps behind her and that she wasn't alone after all. The footsteps were hurrying, gaining on her. Dallas cast a swift glance over her shoulder and thought she recognized the four young men as the same ones who had called out the bawdy greeting shortly after she and George Gordon had headed towards the Lawnmarket.

The young men had noted her glance of apprehension. "Wait up, lass!" one of them shouted. "It's too early to cease our celebrations."

Dallas paid no heed; she kept up her pace but refused to give the youths the satisfaction of seeing her break into a run. Within a few doors they had caught up with her, and one, wearing a leather jerkin and a plaid she didn't recognize in the dark, grabbed her by the upper arm. "Come, refresh yourself with my friends and me."

Dallas tried to pull away but the young man's grip was firm. "It seems to me you've done enough celebrating already," she said archly. Indeed, she noted, he smelled foul from whiskey and his gaze was wavering. Judging his unsteadiness, Dallas relaxed for just a moment, felt his grip do the same, and then she broke free and started to run. One of the more sure-footed of the little group lunged after her, holding her tight by the waist.

"Leave me be!" she shouted, striking out with her arms. A stocky redhead took hold of her wrists, careful to stand back far enough to avoid the kicks Dallas was aiming at him. The fourth and last member of the celebrants was leaning against a stone wall, holding his sides and laughing like a donkey gone berserk.

Dallas screamed and flailed away, but the young men merely seemed amused by her efforts. Panicking, she thought someone would have to hear her, open their shutters or come running down from the Lawnmarket. Yet the narrow little wynd was ominously deserted. It was a night for shouts and shrieks and carryings-on; it was also time for good burghers to be abed.

Her feet suddenly went out from under her as two of the revelers lifted her off the ground. One of them had his hands under her cloak, groping her breasts. Dallas felt a physical revulsion. With her arms suddenly freed, she lashed out, raking the face of the redhead with her nails. But though he jerked away, he only howled with laughter. "A she-cat, a real hellion!" he gasped with delight. "Let's make for Robbie's, lads!"

Breathless from exertion and terror, Dallas was reduced to writhing helplessly in their grasp. They had passed the second row of houses on the hill when a voice that sounded oddly familiar called out behind them, "Kidnappers end up in the Tolbooth, you know."

Drunk as the young revelers were, they recognized authority in that cool, almost casual tone. They stopped in their tracks, dumping Dallas unceremoniously onto the cobblestones. Struggling to her feet, she looked up to see that her savior was the dark man she had encountered near Holyrood

Palace. He stood outlined against a whitewashed house, his hands at his hips, his head to one side.

"We—we're handfasted," blurted the redhead. "We're just having a bit of fun, my mates and I."

"Handfasted?" One dark wedge of eyebrow lifted. "No, I think not." The man took a step forward, and though he moved indolently, there was something menacing in his attitude. His hands remained at his hips but the eyes of all four revelers fastened like magnets on the lethal-looking dirk shoved into the stranger's belt. There was only the briefest hesitation before the four young men took to their heels and scuttled off down the wynd and into the sanctuary of the night.

Dallas had remained huddled against an iron railing while the brief exchange took place. She was still out of breath, her thick brown hair half-covered her face, and a wild trembling had overtaken her limbs. The dark man approached her and gently took her hand.

"You should not have stayed out so late without a proper escort, lassie," he said reproachfully. "Unless," he added with a glint of mockery in his hazel eyes, "it is to your profit to do so."

Dallas pulled her shaking hand away and felt her spirits revive with a jolt. "Pox on you for such impertinence!" she railed. "I go where I please, and never has any man pestered me until this night."

He lifted one shoulder in a gesture of indifference. "As you say. You live nearby?"

"Aye," she muttered. The shaking had stopped and her hands worked at pulling the thick hair from her face.

"Then you won't call out the watch if I walk the remaining distance with you to your door?" He saw a stormy look but went on before she could speak. "My name is Iain Fraser and I live close by, in Mungo Tennant's former home. You know the house in Gosford's Close?"

"Aye, it's a beautiful place," Dallas asserted, trying hard to keep a check on her emotional turmoil. "Though I've heard it said that Mungo Tennant had torture chambers in the cellar and engaged in strange doings to gain his wealth."

Fraser shrugged. "He accumulated sufficient funds to take over the house when the monks were turned out." He glanced at Dallas. "Why do you look so puzzled, lassie?"

"Your name—Fraser ... why is it familiar to me?" But her thoughts were still muddled by the encounter with the drunken youths.

"It's not an uncommon name, even this far from the Highlands," Fraser said lightly. "Is this Nairne's Close?"

"Aye." Dallas paused by the winding stairway to her home and belabored her brain for an appropriate leave-taking. In those anxious seconds, she looked her rescuer full in the face for the first time. He was clean-shaven, with black hair and brows. His mouth seemed to mock even when it was shut tight, and those hazel eyes made her wince inwardly again. He wore heavy riding boots and a dark brown cloak which was held in place by a big silver clasp. On his left hand was a signet ring, a stag's head set in topaz.

"Well," she said at last, "thank you. Thank you very much." She stood poker-stiff, her little chin thrust out like the prow of some doughty fighting ship.

For a fleeting moment, Fraser appeared as if he were going to burst out laughing. But, Dallas noted gratefully, he had turned as serious as she. "You're most welcome, lassie. By the way, I still don't know who I have had the pleasure of rescuing."

"Oh." She shifted uncomfortably on the rounded cobblestones. "I'm Dallas Cameron."

It was Fraser's turn to stiffen. But he relaxed almost at once and grinned crookedly at her. "Then you are Daniel Cameron's daughter—or one of them?"

"The middle daughter," Dallas replied, wishing he'd go away. Now that she had seen the Queen and had begun to recover from her fright with the young revelers, she was extremely anxious to resume her vigil at her father's bedside. She was even more anxious to be rid of Iain Fraser.

Yet as his name crossed her troubled mind a responsive chord suddenly struck. Though she said nothing, Fraser's perceptive gaze seemed to read her thoughts.

"Camerons and Frasers are linked in the most precarious of ways," he said on a serious note. "You'll pardon me if I seem curious about your own kin."

Dallas sighed. "The most important thing about my kin just now is that my dear sire is dying. So if you'll grant me leave ...."

Fraser instinctively reached out his hand to offer physical comfort. But Dallas took a sudden step backwards. "I'm sorry, lassie, I had no idea." He let his hand fall to his side as a frown etched itself on his tanned face. "Is there aught I can do except offer my condolences?"

Confronted with what appeared to be genuine sympathy, Dallas's defenses crumbled slightly; she could not help but make a quick comparison between Fraser's apparent compassion and George Gordon's total indifference. "Nay, though I'm grateful for your offer. Still ...." Her tongue flicked over her full lips, uncommonly dry now. " 'Tis strange I should meet you today .... Father has rambled in his illness, he mentioned the name of Fraser and—let me think ...." Dallas put a hand to her little chin and closed her eyes. "Aye, he spoke of a wrong that should be righted ... and the battle of Blar-na-Leine ...." The big brown eyes opened and looked up at Fraser. She was surprised to see that his own hazel gaze seemed to have kindled into flame at her words.

"Then I must beg a favor." All mockery had fled from his face. He glanced up at the Cameron house, the frown growing ever deeper on his lean features. "I would like to hear what your father says of the past."

Dallas hesitated, torn between her desire to be rid of Fraser and her recognition of the obvious urgency in his attitude. I owe him a debt, she thought, looking away from him to the toes of her unmatched shoes. "Come along then," she said over her shoulder and Fraser followed her up the winding staircase.

Dallas opened the front door and stepped into the entry hall. "This way." She gestured with an unsure hand towards the well-worn wooden staircase. Fraser followed her wordlessly into Master Cameron's bedroom. The family's old friend and physician, Dr. Wilson, sat in the only chair.

Glennie was at the head of the bed, one hand resting gently on her father's shoulder. Tarrill stood by the window with Will Ruthven, who had been one of Daniel Cameron's favorite pupils. Master Cameron's eyes were closed and his breathing was labored. He was the only one who did not turn to stare when Dallas entered with Iain Fraser.

"How is Father?" she asked, removing her cloak as she quickly crossed the small space to his bed.

"He is very weak," answered Dr. Wilson. "He hasn't spoken since you left."

Dallas knelt beside the bed, taking one of her father's pale, veined hands in hers. She let her heavy hair fall over her face so that the others could not read her expression. I went where you wished me, Father. I saw our bonnie Queen; I felt her magic and I rejoiced for your sake. But most of all, I regretted that Mary Stuart will never know what a devoted champion she had in you. She somehow felt better just through this silent expression of her thoughts.

Glennie cleared her throat three times before Dallas looked up. "You have brought a visitor, Dallas." Glennie gave Fraser a ghostly smile.

"Oh!" Dallas reluctantly let go of her father's hand before scrambling to her feet. "This is Iain Fraser, who lives in Gosford's Close. We ... we met during the Queen's appearance at Holyrood. I told him about Father's ramblings ... about someone named Fraser. He thought perhaps ... somehow ...." Dallas floundered, not sure what Fraser did think.

"I had reason to believe your father might know something about my family," Fraser explained just a bit too smoothly. It occurred to Dallas that perhaps he wasn't certain himself about what he expected to learn.

"It's just history," Glennie said as if apologizing for their father's incoherent ramblings. "Everything to him was—is—history."

"No!" Dallas interjected in a voice so loud that the others all were startled. "That's the point—you know as well as I do that though our father loved his

Scots heritage and its history, his real passion was ancient Rome and Greece. If he talks of Frasers and Blar-na-Leine, there must be a reason."

Glennie pursed her prim little mouth and was about to refute Dallas's argument when Fraser intervened. "I think your sister may be right, mistress. If so, the Queen's arrival makes it incumbent upon me to learn what I can. If you'll permit my intrusion, I'd like to bide awhile."

Both Tarrill and Will were staring unabashedly at Dallas and Fraser. How unlike Dallas to bring a man to the house, let alone at such a time! Tarrill would have given vent to her thoughts but an icy stare from Dallas stilled her tongue.

"Where's Marthe?" Dallas asked to break the awkward silence.

"She's with my boys," Glennie replied, referring to her sons, Jamie and Daniel. "The poor bairns have already bade their grandsire farewell. As if they hadn't suffered enough already with their father's passing just a year ago ..." Glennie put a small, plump hand to her face and turned away from the others.

Dallas bit her lip as another silence filled the stuffy little room. Will had taken Tarril's hand. A full ten minutes passed before anyone spoke and then to everyone's astonishment, it was Daniel Cameron.

His once keen dark eyes were open and he was staring at Iain Fraser. "Oh ... 'tis you ... It is fitting that you came ...."

Fraser leaned forward as the others stared at Daniel Cameron who was desperately trying to sit up.

"Nay, nay, Father," protested Glennie, "stay still."

"Fraser?" Daniel Cameron's voice was very weak. The mind that had been so brilliant seemed to be battling through a fog as thick as any Edinburgh haar.

"Aye," replied Fraser and moved around the side of the bed next to Dallas. "Iain Fraser of Beauly."

"So." Daniel Cameron's speech was distorted by the paralysis which had claimed the right side of his body. "Or so you are called. Yet ...." He motioned for Fraser to lean closer. A few whispered words which no one else could hear brought a perplexed and then astonished expression to Fraser's dark face. Dallas leaned forward, straining to hear. "An amulet ... his own name affixed ...." Dallas frowned as the rest of the words eluded her.

In a voice that was fraught with emotion, Fraser spoke low: "Sir, I can't tell you how much this means to me—and to others, as you must know. For almost thirty years I have wanted to know the truth."

"You should have known before now," Daniel Cameron said in an echo of his usually vibrant voice. "But you understand why I could not tell you ...." He clutched at the counterpane with a feeble hand. "You understand the danger?"

"Aye." Fraser was solemn. "A danger which could outweigh the opportunity."

"But ..." Daniel Cameron interposed weakly, "not the responsibility."

Dallas saw Fraser nod. Then her father turned to his favorite daughter and the attempt at a smile was pitiful. "You brought him here .... I should have known you would manage it somehow .... You always do ...." Dallas looked in puzzlement from her father to Fraser. Then Daniel Cameron's dark eyes flickered—and went dim. He slumped back against the pillows, eyes closed, hands slack against the counterpane.

Dr. Wilson felt for a pulse, then bent down to listen to Daniel Cameron's chest. It seemed to take an enormous effort for the elderly doctor to right himself. "I'm sorry," he whispered in a shaky voice, "but Master Cameron is dead."

All except Will Ruthven crossed themselves. Tarrill sobbed aloud and turned to the comfort of Will's arms. Glennie fell down beside the bed, her entire body shaking convulsively. Dr. Wilson rubbed his eyes and sank wearily into the chair. Dallas remained on her knees by the bed, her little chin set resolutely, her gaze fixed on the lifeless features of her father.

Iain Fraser's hazel eyes scanned the mourners. Dr. Wilson and death were old if incompatible companions. Tarrill had Will Ruthven to comfort her. Though Fraser realized that Dallas needed consolation even more than the others, he sensed she would not readily accept any overt efforts on his behalf. So instead, he moved in long, silent strides to Glennie and put an arm around her shaking shoulders.

"Mistress, you've had two cruel blows within the year. Let your grief flow freely, you'll be the better for it as time goes by." He glanced at Dallas, who went rigid at the words she knew were meant for her as well as for her sister.

Glennie sniffed several times and attempted the faintest caricature of a smile. "How ... kind of you, Master Fraser. Your presence is a comfort."

Dallas had positioned herself against the bed so that the others couldn't see that her legs were shaking like reeds in a Highland wind. "I think it best if you would leave us now, Master Fraser—and you, too, Will."

"Will is no stranger here," Tarrill asserted between sobs. She was the tallest of the Cameron sisters and stood almost at eye level with Will Ruthven. "You've known us almost seven years, Will," she declared, squeezing his sturdy hand in her long, tapering fingers. "I don't believe my father would want you to go."

"Pray excuse me," Glennie interjected, gently moving out of Fraser's comforting arm. "I must tell Marthe about Father—and I must let my sons know, too." She sniffed again, straightened her coif and left the bedroom.

Dr. Wilson also got up from his chair and began to gather up his medications. "I shall take my leave then." He nodded at Dallas, Tarrill and Will Ruthven. To Fraser, he made a laborious little bow. "My pleasure, sir.

Though I would have preferred our meeting under different circumstances. I didn't know Master Cameron was acquainted with you."

"He wasn't." Fraser frowned. "But he must have learned who I was, though we never met."

The doctor didn't know what to say; he was too filled with sorrow and fatigue to pursue Iain Fraser's encounter with Daniel Cameron further. Without speaking again, he made his slow-footed way from the bedroom.

After the doctor had gone, Will insisted that Tarrill come away and take some refreshment downstairs. Dallas's mouth twisted slightly as she watched them go, then she turned to Fraser. "Well?"

He had been looking out the window into the empty street below. "I am grateful to your father," he said, his back turned to her, an almost eerie figure in his long black cloak etched against the shadows of the guttering candles. "And," he went on, finally turning to face her, "to you. If it's any comfort, his words must have relieved him of a heavy burden."

"It's one I knew nothing about." Dallas stood stiffly, her fists clenched at her sides. "You are obviously satisfied with what he told you."

Taking note of the hostile, yet remote tone in Dallas's voice, Fraser could not conceal the pity he felt for this strange, prickly, grief-stricken little lassie. "You must take consolation from having known and loved your father," he said slowly. "I have never been certain who my own sire was. Now I may know the truth. It will make a great difference, not just to me, but perhaps to others as well."

Dallas knew the importance of Scottish kinship and family ties but she also knew that her legs were about to collapse. She wanted to be done with Fraser's mysterious family background and with Fraser himself. And she wanted very much to be alone with the body of her father.

"Aye," she said vaguely, and looked not at Fraser but at the crucifix over her father's bed, and finally at his corpse. "Sweet Jesu," she breathed, and had to steady herself by clinging to the bedpost.

Fraser moved silently and swiftly. He put one arm around her waist and his other hand seemed to engulf her face. "You are going to faint, lassie. Sit down."

She did, collapsing on the bed, just an inch or so from her father's feet. Fraser knelt beside her, taking both of her small hands in his. "Lassie, why don't you weep?"

"I—can't." Dallas looked at him in desperation. "I never could—after my mother died."

"I see." Fraser looked away from her to their clasped hands. He sighed, wishing there was something he could do or say to help. At last, she pulled her slim hands out of his grasp and swallowed hard. Their eyes caught and held; it was Dallas who broke the intense silence.

"You'd better go now," she said in a husky tone.

Fraser stood up, looming tall in the little bedroom. "So I had." He paused as if to say something else, found his usually agile mind a blank, reached out to brush the tangle of Dallas's dark hair with his hand, and then was gone.

For a quarter of an hour or more, Dallas remained motionless. Her thoughts were mingled with prayer at first, then memory overcame meditation, sending her back through years of vignettes in which her father teased her over forgetting the date of a Spartan battle or argued about which Roman orator was more eloquent.

But after a while, it occurred to Dallas that the emptiness she felt was not entirely caused by her father's passing. Tarrill had Will Ruthven to comfort her; Glennie had her sons and the memory of a loving husband; even Marthe was probably commiserating with old Dr. Wilson in the kitchen. But Dallas had nobody—nobody, she reminded herself sharply, except for a total stranger of uncertain parentage who had rescued her from rape and then barged into their dying father's bedroom.

I let him touch me, she thought with horrified wonder. No man except George Gordon had ever touched her before—and then only in the most casual sort of way. She had cursed his unresponsiveness at the time but had realized later that any advances could only have been dishonorable and would have brought her grief.

Dallas stared down at her hands: Unlike the groping of the drunken louts in the wynd, Fraser's touch had not been repugnant. It had been a comfort. But, of course, she reasoned, under other circumstances, she would have felt obliged to box his ears.

Slowly, Dallas got to her feet, picked up the stub of candle from the nightstand and made her way to the tiny square of uneven glass which hung above her father's bureau.

The face that stared back at her was hollow-eyed, pale and drawn. As usual, she compared herself to her sisters: plump, pretty Glennie with her sky-blue eyes and sweet little mouth; tall, raven-haired Tarrill with her striking profile and angular grace. Dallas, however, was not as dark as Tarrill nor as fair as Glennie. She was neither tall nor short, and her features never seemed to match. The nose and chin were too small for the wide mouth and the enormous brown eyes. The heavy dark hair tumbled in every direction and the few plain gowns she owned concealed rather than accented the sensuous curves of her body. Indeed, it seldom occurred to Dallas that her body was anything more than the shell which supported her mind. Hadn't her father always told her she was the cleverest of his pupils—and without ever qualifying the compliment by adding that, after all, she was only a girl.

That memory buoyed her momentarily. A fine mind was more rare than beauty, more precious than gold. A pox on George Gordon and his ilk for scoffing at a learned female. So why did the emptiness return, like a savage blow in the pit of Dallas's stomach? She frowned at her image and for one fleeting moment the dark, lean face of Iain Fraser seemed to gaze back at her with that hint of mockery in the hazel eyes.

Dallas blinked rapidly and turned away. Damn the man, she thought, why did he have to intrude upon our lives at such a terrible time? Yet, if he had not encountered Dallas while she was trying to fend off the drunken youths, even now she might be lying in some dark cellar off the Cowgate, battered, mauled, ravished—even dead. She shuddered violently, the memory of those greedy hands making her dizzy. But rather than chide herself as an ingrate for her attitude towards Fraser, Dallas tried to dismiss him from her mind. There was work to be done, sad, terrible work, but only she could—or would—do it.

Willing herself to move, Dallas went to the garderobe to fetch her father's best clothes. Carefully shaking out the long charcoal robe with its lapin trim, Dallas smiled faintly as she pictured her father when he had last worn it at a former pupil's wedding, jesting with the other guests, arguing with a fellow scholar from St. Andrews, paying a pretty compliment to the fresh-faced young bride. Then, with the robe cradled in one arm, she moved to the bed, bent down, and tenderly kissed the lank grey hair which fell over her father's cold forehead.

Chapter Two

DANIEL CAMERON WAS buried with the full rites of the Roman Catholic Church the following Tuesday, two days after Mary Stuart's triumphal entrance into Edinburgh. The burial service was held in the chapel of St. Catherine of Siena's convent at Newington, just outside Edinburgh.

Master Cameron's body was laid to rest next to his wife in the little graveyard at the eastern edge of the Burghmuir. Dallas bowed her head but remained dry-eyed as the priest intoned the final blessing. Tarrill wept openly, clinging to the wheezing Marthe, while Glennie held her sons by the hand and struggled vainly with her own composure. An ardent Protestant, Will Ruthven was not present, but the Camerons' long-time friends, Walter and Fiona Ramsay stood on the opposite side of the grave, their lips moving in silent prayer. Walter, twenty years earlier, had been one of Master Cameron's most beloved pupils.

The little funeral party had returned to the house in the Lawnmarket before noon. It was a clear summer day, with not a trace of the heavy mist that had enshrouded Edinburgh on Sunday.

With Tarrill's help, Marthe prepared a wholesome, if unelaborate meal. Dallas dispensed the port somewhat reluctantly, knowing that it was one of the few remaining bottles in the cellar. Glennie's boys were already wolfing down food in the kitchen where they'd been whisked off by Marthe. Over platefuls of ham and bread and fresh carrots, the mourners talked of Daniel Cameron and his many virtues. Dallas joined in, but privately, she was wishing that those virtues had included a saving nature.

"At least," Walter Ramsay said as he took a pear from the wooden fruitbowl, "your father knew that the Queen was coming back. That must have pleased him greatly."

"Oh, yes," Glennie answered. "He could talk of little else these past few weeks. Though," she added thoughtfully, "he was not overoptimistic about reestablishing the old religion."

"Some of us have remained steadfast," Fiona commented. "And some only follow the new ways to advance themselves."

Walter smiled fondly at his wife. "If you refer to James Stuart, I think his faith is as strong as his ambition. I hope he will use his wits to help, rather than hinder, the Queen. Religious discord is only one problem. An even greater one is that Scotland is a poor country, very poor."

"Poor!" echoed Dallas. "How we fit right in! When our meager savings are gone, we'll be as poor as any Highland crofter."

Glennie regarded her sister with acute embarrassment. "Please," she murmured, "let's not discuss our problems with Walter and Fiona."

Walter waved a sturdy, freckled hand at Glennie. "Now, now, if you can't talk about your difficulties with old friends, who can you speak to? If your purse is a bit thin, Fiona and I can offer you something to help."

It was Dallas's turn to be embarrassed. She'd given the matter much thought, considering a variety of alternatives. Employment for one or all of them had at first seemed the likeliest solution. But Glennie couldn't leave the children and what scant monies she'd earn from taking in mending or such wouldn't help much. Tarrill might obtain a position as a governess, but she'd never command more than enough for her own keep. That left Dallas—she would take up where her father had left off, tutoring young scholars. At first, they might resent a woman—and a youthful one at that—but they'd get used to the idea after a while. Dallas was convinced she could hold the students her father had been teaching at the time of his death and perhaps add a few more.

"Your offer is kind, Walter," Dallas replied with a smile, "but I'm going to continue in Father's place. Tomorrow young Grant and his cousin from Peffermill are coming as usual. I've already sent word that their lessons are not to be cancelled."

Glennie and Tarrill regarded their sister with astonishment, but Dallas had already raised a hand to silence them. "I may not know as much as Father did, but what he taught me, I've learned well. I'll manage just fine," Dallas declared with an air of bravado. "You'll see, what with the Queen and her relations being so well educated and our Scots nobles seldom able to write their own names, I'll have plenty of young scions begging to be taught."

Glennie made a noise in her throat that was half grumble, half-lament. But Walter leaned towards Dallas and smiled encouragement. "You may be right; these laddies who seek advancement will discover they need more than a ready sword and a braw arm."

Buoyed by his comments, Dallas confronted the others. "Of course. Scotland is facing a whole new future and our young men must prepare for it. If they must be taught, why not by me?"

But Tarrill remained unconvinced. "I'll bide and see what happens," she asserted with an ominous stare at her sister. But Dallas stared right back and silently vowed to make her plan work.

That night, after Walter and Fiona had left and the rest of the household had gone to bed, Dallas remained up, ensconced behind her father's desk. A single candle burned on the desk. Outside, the watch went past the house, calling out that all was well.

All might be well with him, but not with her, Dallas thought grimly. The small ledger her father had haphazardly kept for the family accounts lay open on the desk. Glennie had worked on updating it earlier in the evening and there was still sand on the page where she had made the last entries. The funeral expenses had been covered, Dr. Wilson's fee—which he had at first refused—was paid and the masses for Daniel Cameron's soul had been offered by Walter and Fiona.

In the margin, Glennie had made notes indicating that there were sufficient victuals in the house to last a month. The supply of candles, linen, firewood and other household necessities was plentiful. Marthe would make soap as she did every winter, and if somehow they could pick enough berries at the edge of town, they'd be able to put up jam.

The total, not counting the small residue Glennie still had from Jamie's weaving business, came to four marks, three shillings and sixpence. It would not last long, at best into late autumn. The boys would need new clothes, at least young Daniel would; his old ones could be handed down to his younger brother. Glennie needed new shoes, Dallas had noted just that afternoon.

Dallas brushed off the remnants of sand and closed the ledger. At least Marthe didn't have to be paid, having been one of the family for so long that she worked only for her keep and a small allowance. She had come from the Highlands as a sturdy, red-cheeked young wench with the girls' mother, when Eva MacKintosh had been brought to Edinburgh by Daniel Cameron as his bride. And Eva herself, namesake of that famous thirteenth-century heiress to the Clan Chattan, had taken to city life immediately. She retained her old clan loyalty, however, and named each of her daughters after one of the MacKintosh families. When gentle Eva died, her serving woman, Marthe, slipped imperceptibly and unobtrusively into the role of surrogate mother.

Rising from the chair, Dallas went over to the bookshelves. The fine leather spines of her father's cherished collection stood straight and dust-free along the wall facing the fireplace. Plutarch, Ovid, Petrarch—they were all old friends to Dallas.

Glancing over the vacant chair behind the desk, she could almost see her father sitting there, the shock of hair over his forehead, a map of Crete spread out before him, and the wind outside, blowing down between the tall houses. Quickly, she looked away, back to the bookshelves. Sentiment must be overcome, some of the books would have to be sold. It would be one way of securing a bit of extra money to see the family through until she was sure her tutoring project would work out. Despite the brave face she had put on for her sisters and the Ramsays, now that she was alone in the shadows of her father's study, Dallas was uncertain and afraid. But, she lectured herself sternly, there was no reason to dwell on the possibility of failure.

Instead, she thought about her family, about how happy they had all been together until her mother died. The comfortable pattern of their uneventful life was shattered by Eva Cameron's death, and Dallas had reacted more violently than her sisters. She locked herself in her room for two days, weeping inconsolably. For almost ten years now, she had refused to discuss her mother's passing with anyone—not even with her beloved father.

It was very quiet inside the house as she went into the corridor and up the stairs. She undressed rapidly in the dark, careful to hang her mourning dress on a peg by the door. Her room was small, with the bed under one of the eaves and a single gabled window already shuttered for the night.

Sleep, however, proved elusive. For the first time since her father's death, Dallas thought about his last words to Iain Fraser. Dallas knew about the famous Highland battle between the Camerons and the Frasers, for her father had recounted the story on several occasions.

Yet a few months after the battle, Daniel Cameron had made a short trip north, alone, to visit his kinsmen. He was gone for several weeks and when he returned, Glennie and Dallas had begged him for tales of the Highlands and the Cameron kinfolk. Tarrill had been only three at the time, more interested in the pine cone doll her father had brought back for her than in stories of towering mountains and sparkling lochs.

No, there had been nothing extraordinary then in Daniel Cameron's attitude towards his Highland visit. Dallas couldn't dredge up a single recollection which might have accounted for her father's deathbed ramblings and his whispered words to Iain Fraser. She rolled over in bed, tugging at the pillow to make herself more comfortable.

She closed her eyes and immediately conjured up an image of Fraser. But it was not the lean, dark face she had glimpsed in the mirror or even the mocking grin he had displayed upon their first encounter near Holyrood. Rather, she saw him outlined in the wynd on Castle Hill, tall and arrogant, with sufficient authority to frighten off four young men. And to her great surprise, Dallas felt the old emptiness return, accompanied by some other emotion she could not quite identify. Fie on Fraser and his family perplexities, she thought. She laid down, pulling the pillow back into place. But the image of Iain Fraser and the Battle of Blar-na-Leine followed her into sleep and her dreams focused on a swirl of Cameron and Fraser plaids, so alike in their red and green patterns, merging and meeting on a sun-baked hill that turned from green and gold to red, a dark blood red.

THE CELLAR WAS well lighted, for the Cameron house was built entirely above ground. The windows on the west side looked directly into Master Drummond the baker's second story. Mistress Drummond was at one of the bedroom windows, throwing out a pail of slops and shouting, "Get ou' the gait!" No one was in the wynd which separated the Cameron and Drummond houses, but the warning cry was always uttered.

The old trunk was not locked and opened easily. A flutter of dust rose to meet Dallas's nose and she sneezed twice before settling down to sort out the books. Only a handful, she decided, would be worth carting out to the High Street.

She was just shoving the trunk back into its place by the wine and ale casks when she felt rather than heard an odd noise. She paused, her knees on the stone floor, her hands on the battered trunk. The sound was beneath her, not upstairs in the house or out in the wynd. Yet, she told herself that was impossible. It must be rats, rumbling about somewhere, making echoes.

Dallas wiped the dirt from her hands on an old cloth, gathered up the pile of books and started out of the cellar. Halfway up, she heard the noise again, barely perceptible this time, but still coming from the same source.

"Fie," Dallas said under her breath. "I'm turning fanciful." Resolutely she continued up the stairs. Back in the hallway, she packed the books into the now bulging shopping bag, grabbed her old brown shawl from its peg, and hurried out the front door. She had scarcely more than an hour before David Grant and his cousin would arrive for their lessons.

The late summer drizzle had stopped just a few minutes earlier and the sun was struggling to assert itself among the drifting grey clouds. Dallas trudged between the tall houses to the Lawnmarket where Edinburgh's goodwives crowded around the stalls, haggling over heavy bolts of wool, lawn and silk. At the entrance of Beith's Wynd, she saw Lame Angus, the beggar who had lost a leg at Pinkie Cleugh fighting King Henry's men.

Every day for the past fourteen years, Lame Angus had sat on that same spot, his battered tin cup clutched in his hands. Daniel Cameron had always paused for a chat as Angus was a veritable well of information about famous

Scottish battles. Though Cameron had heard each story a dozen times or more over the years, he enjoyed Lame Angus's vivid descriptive powers. At the conclusion of the tale, Dallas's father would discreetly drop some coins into the cup before bidding Lame Angus a fair day. As Dallas had grown older, she, too, would pause to put something in the cup though she was less inclined to linger for the repetitious history lessons.

On this day, Lame Angus greeted her with a mournful shake of his shaggy head. "Poor lass, I've heard of your father's passing. Rest his soul, he was a fine, fine man."

"He was indeed." Dallas smiled wanly at Lame Angus and juggled the shopping bag so that she could reach for her little suede purse. "We are so lonely without him." Lame Angus nodded dolefully. "Many a lively talk we had on this very spot. Flodden Field, that was his favorite. How he liked to hear of King Jamie the Fourth and the dire death which awaited ...."

But Dallas broke in on what was obviously going to be a recapitulation of the tragedy at Flodden over a half century earlier. "Blar-na-Leine, Angus. What know you of that battle?"

"Ah." The beggar leaned back his head, savoring the name as a connoisseur would appreciate a fine wine. "There was a bloody fray! The Field of Shirts, it was called, taking place on a scorching hot day so that the warriors had to strip to the waist."

Dallas nodded her head as the beggar's narrative ran along. So far, she hadn't learned much more than she already knew. Angus, however, was just warming to his tale, and Dallas soon found her mind wandering as the beggar went into great and grisly detail over sword and claymore, pike and broadaxe. At last he came to the conclusion of the battle, with the Frasers' defeat at the hands of the Camerons.

Lame Angus had paused as a goodwife dropped some coins into his cup. "It's a fascinating tale," Dallas said with forced enthusiasm. She dropped two coins into the cup; they had grown sticky in her hand as she waited for Lame Angus to finish his story. And for the first time in her life, she regretted parting with the money. Indeed, she somehow felt cheated, for Angus had not enlightened her in the slightest regarding her father's dying words to Iain Fraser.

Still, she thanked Angus and hurried away, aware that she was going to be late for her first pupils if she wasted more time getting to the bookseller's.

Now, as she approached the High Street, the sun had filtered between the clouds and tall buildings to make steamy patches on the drying cobbles. Many of the dwellings, even the more modest ones, kept small kitchen herb gardens and occasionally Dallas could detect a hint of sage or basil or thyme. But mostly she smelled the peat fires, which sent wreaths of heavy grey smoke swirling from the stone chimney pots. Dallas pulled the shopping bag up over her shoulder as two Protestant preachers, affecting the somber garb of John Knox, walked past her, engaged in solemn discussion.

By Fisher's Close, a young boy with a stout stick drove a gaggle of geese to the market place, a blotchy-faced woman with snow-white hair prodded two Shetland ponies through Liberton's Wynd, and a splendid coach clattered up ahead on the cobbles. The hawkers were already busy parading their wares on the street corners and from somewhere nearby came the tantalizing aroma of fresh-baked bread.

But what Dallas liked best was the city itself, the small, perfect glimpses captured at the end of a wynd or through a gate or between houses: the sun on old mellow brick; a weathervane's cock lording it over the many-turreted chimneys; a sudden, unexpected view of the massive castle wall; a hearth-fire burning merrily behind a mullioned window; a snatch of the silver-blue waters of the Firth of Forth off in the distance; the newer houses with their wooden galleries built out over the High Street.

By Gosford's Close, in a direct line across from King's Bridge, Dallas looked up at the highly decorated front of a house she had often admired. Of course, she thought with a start, this is Iain Fraser's home. And she paused to admire anew the carvings of the Trinity and the Twelve Apostles. Just then the front door opened and two people came out through the close into the High Street. The man was Iain Fraser; the woman who clung to his arm was slender and blonde. Dallas averted her face, hoping Fraser and his companion would stroll right on by.

But they did not. "Mistress Cameron," came the indolent voice, "good morrow. Are you and your sisters faring well enough?"

"All matters considered," Dallas replied crisply. "Our sire taught us independence as well as history."

"But such history," Fraser commented, glancing at the spine of the one visible volume in Dallas's shopping bag. "Don't tell me you've actually read Sallust?"

"I've read his 'History of the Jugurthine War' and 'Conspiracy of Catiline,' " Dallas responded with pride.

Fraser's black brows lifted in frank admiration. "There are only portions of his 'History of the Roman Republic' extant but certain sections are worth reading," he informed Dallas. As he became aware of his companion's hand pressing his upper arm, he turned. "Pray forgive me, ladies," he grinned, "my manners have fled like Pompeii before Caesar. May I present Lady Catherine Gordon, Mistress Dallas Cameron."

Dallas stiffened at the Gordon surname but managed to nod politely at Catherine. "A pleasure," she murmured, wondering if George had ever mentioned her to his blond kinswoman. Probably not; Dallas told herself she didn't care.

"La, Mistress Cameron," exclaimed Catherine, "you look as if you'd been hard at work!"

Dallas was suddenly aware of her black homespun gown, the wild, uncombed mass of brown hair, and the worn shawl. Catherine, by contrast, wore a silk dress of the latest fashion, pale green shot with silver, and her carefully coiffed hair was adorned with tiny seed pearls. She was taller than Dallas, not as full-figured, but graceful as a young larch. Dallas had a sudden fierce desire to take the shopping bag and dump it over Catherine's fair head.

Instead, she answered coolly, "Yes, I work for my keep. Do you?"

Catherine's color heightened as her grasp on Fraser's arm closed fast. "My family provides for me," she answered in a strained voice. "I am a niece to the Earl of Huntly."

George's cousin then, Dallas thought, and decided that must be the reason for her instinctive dislike of Catherine Gordon. "This is as far as I go," Dallas declared, motioning towards the Master Forbes's stall which stood opposite the impressive bulk of St. Giles. "Good day to you both."

Fraser made an exaggerated bow. "It's been a pleasure. Any time you wish to discuss Sallust, don't hesitate to call on me." The mockery was still there, Dallas noted, and wondered if he was being condescending.

"Come, Iain," Catherine urged, her voice now pettish. "We shall be late to Cousin George's soiree." Her hand tugged possessively at his arm.

"Well enough, Cat, I've known George too long and too well to fear his wrath." But Fraser put his big hand over Catherine's smaller one, bade Dallas good-day and headed up the High Street.

Dallas watched them go and wondered why she suddenly had such a sour taste in her mouth. Cousin George indeed, she thought. The overproud Gordon scion could wait until he withered as far as Dallas was concerned. And Iain Fraser was George Gordon's close friend. Two of a kind, Dallas decided—but then all men were alike.

She forced herself to greet Master Forbes with a smile, then realized he already had a customer, a young man wearing the red, blue and white plaid of the Hamiltons. Dallas frowned. She did not need any more reminders of George Gordon—and that included his Hamilton wife.

"A moment, Mistress Dallas," Master Forbes said with a smile. He knew all the Cameron girls well, having sold books to their father for years. He could remember Dallas, just barely toddling, accompanying Master Cameron to the stall some twenty years earlier, her wide-set eyes taking in every new wonder which passed before her. He had always liked Dallas best of the three daughters because she was the most interested in books.

Dallas withdrew to the farthest corner of the shop and put her heavy shopping bag down on a three-legged stool. Browsing through some finely bound volumes of French poetry, she tried to rein in her patience. She didn't have all day, and a Hamilton or not, he seemed to be taking forever over his discussion with Master Forbes.

Unobtrusively, Dallas watched the young man from over the top of a sonnet collection. He was tall, broad shouldered, with brown hair, a full but well-trimmed moustache and a fine Roman nose. She knew that the Duke of Chatelherault had three sons: The eldest, James, was Earl of Arran and said to be mentally unbalanced; the youngest, Claud, was scarcely as old as Dallas. Since the Hamilton she surreptitiously observed above the book binding appeared quite sane and close to thirty, Dallas assumed he was the middle son, John.

So intensely was she staring that she was startled into a little yelp when Master Forbes's cat, Cicero, careened into the shop, a feisty mongrel in hot pursuit.

"Cicero!" Master Forbes bustled from behind the counter as a scrawny youth in tattered clothes came racing after the dog.

Cicero fairly flew through the air, clawing at Dallas's shawl. The dog was at her skirts, barking fiercely. Master Forbes tried to wedge himself between the stool, the bookshelves and Dallas. The youth dove onto the floor, scooping the dog up in his arms just as Dallas managed to extricate Cicero from her shawl.

"Yon filthy cat ate my bird!" the youth shouted as the dog made an abortive attempt to leap out of his master's arms. "See, there are feathers on its face!"

Dallas looked at Cicero; so did Master Forbes. John Hamilton came closer to examine the cat. Indeed, there were two feathers of blue-green hue clinging to Cicero's whiskers.

"What manner of bird?" asked Hamilton, flicking off one of the feathers and holding it up for closer perusal.

"I dinna know," answered the youth petulantly. "I found it lame near Pittenweem one day when I was gathering mussels. But it was glorious colored, like a fairy creature." He glared malevolently at Cicero who had calmed down in Dallas's arms and looked exceedingly smug. "I trained that bird to sit on my shoulder. But yon cruel cat scared him near the Salt Tron. Birdie hopped down—he never did fly so well—and this ... this ...." The youth jabbed an accusing finger at Cicero. "This beastie gobbles him up before I could do aught!"

Dallas held Cicero with one hand and reached out to pet the dog with the other. "Nature must have its way," she said in a soothing tone. "Cats eat birds, dogs chase cats, humans beat dogs. The world can be a harsh place, you know."

Her philosophy was simply stated though the young man seemed to take some time to absorb it. "Aye," he agreed truculently, "harsh be the word for the world. Especially if ye be poor."

Dallas felt a deep pang of compassion for the young man; as shabby as her apparel was, his was much worse. She wished she could give him a few coins, or at least some word of encouragement. "You are very young," Dallas said at last, even though she was probably but four or five years older. "You may yet find a future that is not so harsh."

The youth looked dubious and Dallas wished she herself could believe the brave words. The awkward silence was broken by Hamilton. "Your bird must have been rare," he said in his amiable voice. "I wonder where it came from."

Master Forbes was mopping his brow with a piece of chamois. "Some foreign ship, no doubt. Sailors keep odd pets."

"There be odd ships near Pittenweem some times," the youth said. His dog had begun to growl again, straining to get at Cicero.

"So I've heard," Hamilton said with a smile. "Pirates, perhaps. But in any case, you should be reimbursed for the loss of your bird. Two marks, I should think?" Hamilton opened a small pouch and proffered two gold coins.

"Oh!" The youth flushed deeply, but his thin hand closed over the money. "I'm grateful, I thank ye. But ...." He glanced at Master Forbes and at Cicero. "The cat is yours or ...?"

"It's no matter." Hamilton winked at Master Forbes. "Accounts will be kept straight. Perhaps you may even find another bird some day."

The dog barked, Cicero let out one last meow and the youth backed out of the bookseller's stall with an awkward bow and another thank-you for Hamilton.

"I expect I should credit ye two marks," Master Forbes said a bit ruefully.

Hamilton laughed. "Nay, I'll not drive that hard a bargain." He glanced at Dallas who was still holding Cicero. "In truth, I was sorry for the lad. And I never could stand cats."

"You can't?" Dallas's remark came unbidden; she flushed at her boldness and tried to make amends. "I mean, I'm fond of cats, especially Cicero ...."

"Why should you not be?" Hamilton asked with a smile. "Your affection only shows the depth of your kindliness and the lack of my own." He was still smiling, and Dallas felt as if he were studying her closely behind that veil of pleasant, polite conversation. At last she put Cicero down on the floor. Master Forbes appeared anxious to finish his business with John Hamilton—but Hamilton had now directed his attention to the books in Dallas's shopping bag. "You're selling these to Master Forbes?" he inquired, selecting one of the volumes at random.

"I was considering it," Dallas answered. "My late father had such an extensive library." She regarded him with a pride that matched his own: Damn, she thought, I'll not admit I'm trying to keep us from starving!

But Hamilton's shrewd brown eyes had taken in the worn black gown and the frayed shawl. "Is that Sallust? He's hard to come by, perhaps you'd permit me to make a first offer."

"Oh—well, if you'd wish." Dallas drummed on the cover with her fingernails. "There's an excellent bit of Chaucer here, too. Finely illustrated." Dallas had never liked Chaucer much and she thought the illustrations mawkish.

"Hmmm." The finely molded mouth pursed slightly under the brown moustache. "Yes, they'd both make excellent additions to our family's library. Not," he added with regret, "that either of my brothers care much for reading." Hamilton paused and turned to Master Forbes. "A mark for the two volumes? Is that fair, sir?"

It was more than fair, it was outrageous, since Master Forbes knew how poorly the Chaucer was illustrated. It was also uncharacteristic of John Hamilton to make a bad bargain. But it wouldn't be right to interfere, especially where Dallas was concerned, so Master Forbes merely inclined his head.

"Well done then," said Hamilton, handing the money to Dallas. She was so triumphant over her sale that she failed to notice how Hamilton's hand lingered on her own. But she could not miss the wide smile he bestowed upon her and was somewhat taken aback by its warmth. "Mayhap we'll do business again some day."

"I'm Dallas Cameron, Daniel Cameron's middle daughter," she replied. "And you are Lord John Hamilton, I'll wager."

"And win." The smile grew even wider. "Aye, I've heard of your father, and well regarded he was. I'm sorry about your loss, Mistress Cameron." The smile faded at the more somber words but he bowed deeply before turning back to Master Forbes. It took only a minute or so to conclude their dealings and then Hamilton was gone, but not before he saluted Dallas on his way into the High Street.

"You've bewitched that young man," Master Forbes declared. "Lord Hamilton is no fool, especially where money is concerned."

"Twaddle!" Dallas couldn't help but laugh. "He—he just felt sorry for me, that's all. As he did with the poor youth. Though," she added, all laughter gone, "he got two marks."

"You might get more than you bargained for with that one, Mistress Dallas." Master Forbes eased his bulk from behind the counter. " 'Tis said he's a man of great caution, but once his mind is made up—he'll not change it for aught."

Dallas was anxious to be on her way and disliked the conversation's turn.

"Great Hamiltons don't dally with poor Camerons. Now what think you?" She pointed at the books on the stool.

"I can't be as generous as John Hamilton, ye ken." Master Forbes fingered the volumes carefully. "A shame that it's his brother who is rumored to be a suitor for our Queen. Arran is daft."

"And Protestant," retorted Dallas, wishing this weren't one of Master Forbes's days for gossip. "How much?"

But Master Forbes suddenly metamorphosed from a common gossip into an astute man of commerce. "One mark, a shilling and six-pence."

Dallas met his gaze evenly. "Two marks."

Ordinarily, Master Forbes would have enjoyed haggling to the last penny. But his liking for Dallas and his respect for Daniel Cameron loosened his purse-strings. "So be it, mistress. Ye have done well this day." He counted out the sum and handed it to Dallas. "But mind my words, yon Hamilton found you a comely lass."

"Fie," snapped Dallas but couldn't resist smiling at Master Forbes as she tucked the money away in her tiny suede coin purse. She must hurry or she would be tardy for her first lesson. Dallas cursed herself for permitting so many delays in the course of her errands.

Glennie was just coming into the entry hall with her small sons when Dallas flew inside. "Heaven help me, Glennie, am I late? Where are David and his cousin Oliver?"

Glennie pursed her thin lips and handed Dallas a note. "This will tell you." She stood in silence, a hand on each of her boys' shoulders, while Dallas swiftly read through the message.

"Oh, damnation! They're not coming—ever!" Dallas stared at Glennie for a moment in shock, then crumpled the note and pitched it onto the floor.

"I feared it would be like that," Glennie began, but Dallas interrupted her.

"Nay, nay, these are but two, and certainly the dimmest of father's pupils. Tomorrow Peter MacEachen comes and the next day, the two Maxwells."

"One Maxwell," Glennie corrected her. "Don't you recall? The elder completed his studies this past month and has gone to Italy."

"Oh, I'd forgotten." Dallas put both hands to her temples and rubbed them vigorously. "Fie, I mustn't get so upset. It will work out. There are bound to be a few setbacks."

Glennie gave her sister a sympathetic glance. But all she could say in comfort was, "Perhaps, Dallas. Perhaps." To Dallas's immense relief, Peter MacEachen did show up the following day for his appointed lesson. He was a compactly built young lad of fourteen, the son of a printer who believed in a classical education. Dallas noted at once that Peter seemed uncomfortable but she attempted to put him at ease by going over some of the books she knew he'd read recently. But after a few halting answers, Peter wriggled in his chair and stared at the floor.

"Mistress Cameron," he began nervously, and his adolescent voice broke on her name. "I—I don't think I should be here."

"Why not?" Dallas spoke more sharply than she had intended but Peter would not look up at her.

"Hear the noise outside?" he mumbled.

Dallas turned towards the window. She had been vaguely aware of voices in the wynd but had paid no attention until now. "What is it?"

Peter let out a long sigh. "My friends. They followed me today, making fun of me because I was going to be taught by a lass."

"Ooooh!" Dallas jumped up and tried to keep from shouting angrily at the lad. She stomped about the room for a moment or two, then came to stand directly in front of Peter. "See here," she said, so close that he had to look up at her, "what difference can it make? I'm as qualified as any man. After a while your silly friends will forget who's teaching you."

But Peter looked sheepish and shook his head. "It's no good, mistress. I don't .... I just can't."

Dallas considered reasoning with him further, even pleading. But she recognized that his mind was made up and probably his father would back his decision. Depressed and defeated, Dallas let Peter MacEachen go.

The remainder of Daniel Cameron's students reacted similarly, until after a fortnight, Dallas had no one left to teach. Glennie and Tarrill were too kind to remind their sister they had foreseen the hopelessness of the project but

Dallas knew what they were thinking and rejected their pity.

"We'll just have to think of some other plan," she asserted, praying that they wouldn't realize how desolate she felt. "Perhaps we can get someone to introduce us to court. Surely Her Grace must be seeking good Catholics to serve her."

"What about Will?" Tarrill asked with a touch of diffidence. "Protestant or not, his father, Lord Ruthven, is very influential—I'm sure Will could talk to him."

Dallas rubbed her little chin hard, took a deep breath and decided that her usual candor would have to serve best: "Will Ruthven is betrothed to Dorothea Stuart. I heard the news from Mistress Drummond."

Tarrill gasped as if someone had plunged a dirk between her ribs. "Nay! I would have known .... Will would have told me!" Her shocked gaze darted from Dallas to Glennie and back again.

"I'm afraid Dallas is right," Glennie said with reluctance. "I heard such a tale myself, not long after Father died."

"But ...." Tarrill was on the verge of tears, her tapering fingers clutching frantically at the black skirts of her mourning dress.

"But Dorothea is very rich," Dallas said firmly. "Come, Tarrill, did you ever seriously think Lord Patrick Ruthven's son would offer you marriage? Hasn't it occurred to you that there was some reason why Will stopped coming to our house of late?"

Tarrill wiped away a tear with her shaking fingers. "I—I just assumed it was because we were in mourning and he thought it improper to call on us. And," she added with more vigor, "I do know he's been out of Edinburgh."

"Wooing Dorothea, no doubt. Come, Tarrill, we both know Ruthvens and Gordons don't seriously consider marrying tutors' daughters." Dallas clamped her lips tightly together; she had not intended to mention George Gordon ever again, even to her sisters. They had teased her when she was obviously infatuated with George, and Glennie had warned her not to dream so. But it was Tarrill who had overheard George scoff at Dallas when she quoted Latin to him, and the sound of his derisive laughter had never died away. Dallas stood up abruptly, turned and almost collided with Marthe.

"My poor lassies!" exclaimed the old serving woman, who had just wheezed in from the pantry. "So little left in the larder and winter coming on! Ye'd be better off without my belly to fill, too!"

"Nonsense," Dallas retorted, patting the old woman's bulky shoulders. "You're part of the family."

But Marthe shook her head vigorously, sending the tears rolling onto the heavy linen collar of her plain, worn gown. "Ye've always treated me as such, yet I feel like a leech, draining ye of what wee mite there is these days." Dallas gave Marthe a little shake as she propelled her back to the pantry. "Stop talking drivel! You came with our mother to Edinburgh when she was a bride, you helped raise all three of us and now you're helping with Glennie's boys as well. We'd be adrift without you." She sounded stern but the smile she gave Marthe was tender. "Now hush, and get back to peeling those potatoes. Tarrill and I are going berry-picking—you can put up some of your tasty jam for us when we get back."

The old dame bestowed a rather wet kiss on Dallas's forehead. "Ye be a kind-hearted lassie, whether ye own up to it or not," Marthe asserted, wiping away her tears. "Some day I'll make it up to ye, I promise."

"Oh, fie," Dallas mumbled, embarrassed over Marthe's display of affection, "you've done that a thousand times over." Hastily, she turned away, rummaging through the pantry cupboards, searching for pails. "Don't wait dinner for us, we may be late." She hurried out of the pantry, calling to Tarrill.

Some two hours later as the Cameron sisters were returning from their berry-picking expedition near Kirk o'Field on the edge of town, Dallas indulged in a diatribe against Master Knox and his stiff-necked attitude towards court revelries. "Old curmudgeon," she railed as they entered St. Mary's Wynd on their way up to the High Street. "Spoiling everyone's good time! You'd think it wasn't Christian to smile once in a while."

Tarrill managed a half-hearted smile of her own. The news of Will Ruthven's betrothal weighed her down far more than the buckets of berries. "At least we aren't forced to listen to Master Knox," she said. Dallas merely sniffed at her sister's comment and shifted her mental process from John Knox to jars of jam, trying to calculate how many preserves they would get out of their harvest. She stopped in mid-count as two men came out of a crowstep gabled house just ahead. "I know one of those men," she said to Tarrill, indicating the taller of the two. "It's John Hamilton."

Tarrill looked at her sister with amazement. "Don't tell me you've taken a fancy to a fine lord like John Hamilton. Didn't your infatuation with George Gordon cure you of such notions? What of your words to me about Will?"

Dallas's brown eyes sparked back at Tarrill's flashing black gaze. "It cured me of a lot of notions about men! And you didn't seem to learn from it, I might add!"

Tarrill bit her lip and stared at her berry bucket. "So we both set our sights too high. That doesn't make me hostile to all men—as it has done to you."

"Perhaps I'm more canny," Dallas snapped. "But I'm not pursuing Lord Hamilton for a hold on his heart. He is said to be a good fellow and if we could but speak to him, he might help us get to court." She paused at the Netherbow Port. "Fie, you distracted me so that I've lost him. Where did he go?"

"What difference does it make?" Tarrill scoffed. "You might as well ask John Knox to get us an invitation."

"Speak of the devil," murmured Dallas as they entered the Canongate. "Master Knox is on his balcony, spouting odious heresy."

Knox, attired in the familiar cloth cap and Geneva cloak, was indeed on his balcony, speaking to a gathering crowd of passersby. He frequently indulged himself with such midweek homilies and the good citizens of Edinburgh never failed to gather 'round to listen.

"Frail be the flesh in man, frailer still in woman's weak embodiment," Knox intoned. "The governance of nations must be left only to the strong and righteous. Weakness breeds unto weakness, thereby eroding the spirit until all that is left to eternity is putrefying flesh." Several heads nodded in agreement as a murmur of approbation ran through the crowd.

"Holy Mother," groaned Dallas, "let's get home. I can't bear listening to that drivel!"

At least a half-dozen scandalized burghers turned to stare at Dallas. Tarrill made an effort to smile politely at them but Dallas merely pushed her way through, trying to get to the edge of the crowd. And there, standing just a few feet away from the rapt audience was John Hamilton, proud and somewhat detached.

"My lord," Dallas said in greeting as she shifted the weight of her berry bucket, "what a pleasure to encounter you again. May I introduce my sister, Tarrill."

"I'm delighted to meet you," he said with a little bow. "I've not read the books I purchased from you yet, Mistress Dallas, but I'm looking forward to them."

"I'm so glad," Dallas beamed. "My father would have been pleased to know his treasures had found an appreciative owner. But," she added with an air of desolation, "he was about to find us places at court just before he died. We are quite filled with despair that his plans never came to fruition."

Tarrill shut her eyes for a moment at this piece of fabrication. She considered an attempt at reining Dallas in, but knew it would be useless.

In the background, Knox's sermon finished on a burst about following the Just, "as the children of Israel followed Moses into the Promised Land." The crowd, chattering in agreement, began to break away.

"I'm sorry to hear of your disappointment," Hamilton said as he turned his gaze to the dispersing citizenry. "It's very sad," Dallas said, "yet if only it could be amended by some kind soul. You wouldn't know of anyone who could help us, would you, my lord?" She was smiling again, if wanly, turning her full big-eyed gaze up to Hamilton. Tarrill was amazed, never having seen her sister resort to feminine wiles before. It seemed to Tarrill that she didn't do it very well, but perhaps Hamilton was gullible.

Hamilton, in fact, was more amused than gullible. "I suppose there might be someone who would think it an act of Christian charity to sponsor such charming young ladies," he mused aloud. "I take it you're not friendly with any of the courtiers?"

Dallas had to bite her tongue to keep from remarking that if they had been she certainly wouldn't be making a fool of herself by trying to wheedle an invitation from someone she scarcely knew. Instead, she merely shook her head ruefully, hoping her dark lashes fluttered fetchingly against her skin. "Nay, my lord, we have lived secluded lives, content with family and a few close friends."

Fingering his moustache thoughtfully, Hamilton surveyed the two young women. The younger one was a handsome piece but the loquacious Dallas intrigued him. Her kindness to the youth in Master Forbes's bookstall, the pride that overrode her poverty, and her innate sensuality had captured his interest.

"If that be the case," he said, making an effort to keep his tone serious, "perhaps I might perform the honors myself."

"Oh!" Dallas would have clapped her hands in glee if she hadn't been holding a bucketful of berries. "That's too kind of you, sir!" She stepped back a pace or two as a mother cat slipped past with a tiny kitten in her mouth. "We live off the Lawnmarket, near Naime's Close, anyone there will know how to find us if you ask for the Cameron house. Mayhap you'll want to send a messenger to let us know ...."

Hamilton could no longer control his amusement. The wide-eyed little wench delighted him with the acceptance of what she apparently deemed an easy conquest. First the book sale and now this social coup. Ordinarily, the aggressive, noble ladies he encountered at court put him off; but this lass, with her shabby clothes and inept subterfuge, made him feel anxious to please.

"Stay, mistress," Hamilton protested between bursts of laughter. "You go too fast! There is to be a levee next week and I will see that you learn of the day and the hour. Now truly," he said, getting himself under control, "I must be off. It's been ... a pleasure." He bowed, and with the Hamilton plaid swinging from his shoulder, he moved off down the street.

Dallas, for her part, was fairly jigging with triumph. Despite the weight of the berries, she trotted off up the High Street on cloudlike feet. Tarrill loped behind, calling for Dallas to slow down. But there was no stopping her sister now, for she had won her prize and was convinced that all would be well for the Cameron sisters.

Chapter Three

DALLAS LOOKED UP forlornly at the grey stones of Holyrood Palace. She was about to turn again to the stiff-backed guard but thought better of it and instead moved back to where her sisters were standing, their clothes beginning to soak up the steady drizzle.

"The levee's been cancelled," Dallas announced flatly. "The Queen is abed with sharp pains in her side." Tarrill's reaction almost matched Dallas's for dejection, but Glennie thought first of the Queen. "Poor thing," she said. "That's a frequent complaint, I'm told."

"Nerves," snapped Dallas, kicking the gravel. She sighed deeply and started walking away from the palace. "The fates are frowning on us, we might as well go home."

But home was a dreary place that autumn. By mid-October, drifts of early snow had piled up in the closes, only the most well-trodden tracks in the High Street and the Canongate remained clear, and the steep, narrow wynds made for treacherous footing. Very few coins remained in the stout little metal box and the larder was growing depleted.

"Thank God for neighbors like Master Drummond," Marthe puffed as she put more wood on the fire. They could only afford to keep two fireplaces going, one in the sitting room and the other in the kitchen. Consequently, the family spent most of its waking hours in these two rooms, and at night huddled under as many quilts and comforters as they could find to keep warm.

But Dallas was near despair in her efforts to keep the family fed and clothed. They had cut up her father's few garments for Glennie's boys; Tarrill had spent several days nursing old Master McBain but he had died in spite of her most assiduous efforts; Glennie was doing some sewing for the neighbors but the small amount she earned went for the barest necessities; and at meals there was many a time when Dallas complained of a stomach upset and pushed her plate away, leaving the uneaten food for the others.

Suspicious of her motives, Marthe took her aside one night after supper. “See here, you’re thin as a rail.” She grasped Dallas by the wrist and encircled her upper arm between thumb and forefinger. “I’m wise to ye, lass, stop starving yourself!”

“Fie, Marthe,” Dallas fired back, “I don’t feel like eating much these days. Is it any wonder my stomach is upside down?”

Marthe let go of Dallas’s arm but gave her a look which clearly stated the old dame was not fooled. But it was Marthe herself who gave Dallas another idea for making money. The jams she put up and those lovely little pork pies—why not sell them in the Lawnmarket?

“Like common hawkers?” Marthe was aghast.

“You’d prefer common poverty? By the Mass, nobody around here but me seems to realize we are almost down to our last penny!”

The old serving woman turned redder than ever. “Och, I shouldn’t have spoken so. But the notion of you or your sisters peddling wares in the Lawnmarket fair makes me weep!”

“Weep then,” Dallas responded grimly, “but make the pies anyway. I’ll try my luck tomorrow with them and a few jars of jam.”

And so, on a slushy November morning, Dallas headed out for the Lawnmarket with her pies and jams in a canvas-covered box. She averted her eyes from the curious stares of the neighbors and walked resolutely down the hill. But somehow she could not bring herself to shout at the goodwives and burghers she knew so well from a lifetime in Nairne’s Close. Perhaps further on, up in the High Street where there were fewer familiar faces .... Squaring her shoulders, she marched along, wishing that her worn-out shoes hadn’t already permitted her feet to get wet.

At Beith’s Wynd, she came upon Lame Angus, sitting in his usual spot. She paused for a moment, started to speak and suddenly realized she had nothing to give him. But the old beggar heard every scrap of gossip that filtered through the town and he knew well of Dallas’s predicament.

“Good morrow, mistress,” he said with a sympathetic smile. Before she could respond, he gave a little shake of his shaggy head. “Some other day, mayhap. Pray God your fortunes will change.”

Dallas, who had pitied Lame Angus for so many years, saw that now he was pitying her. She discovered that she could not speak, made a tremulous effort at smiling, and hurried off up the street.

Near Gosford’s Close, she was stopped by a cherrycheeked woman of middle age who expressed interest in Dallas’s wares. After a close examination, she bought one of the pork pies and bade Dallas good-day. Although somewhat encouraged, Dallas still could not bring herself to call out to passersby. Instead, she tried motioning to people who walked by, but a stinging rain began to fall and her potential customers moved quickly off down the street.

Drenched and depressed, Dallas wandered aimlessly along the flagstones, her pies grown cold, her mood black as the rain clouds over her head. Without realizing it, she had come to stand in front of Iain Fraser's town house, magnificent even on such a chill and gloomy day.

Her arms aching from the weight of her wares, her clothes soaked through to the skin, her spirits at the lowest ebb she could ever recall, Dallas looked up at the ornate front of the town house and swore to herself.

"By God and all His holy saints," she murmured to herself through gritted teeth, "it's not fair that a man like Iain Fraser lives so well and I must peddle pies at his doorstep! Fie on him and all his predatory ilk!"

With that she spat in the direction of the town house and was about to whirl away when she saw Iain Fraser riding down the High Street on a fine black stallion.

This time she vowed he would not see her. She all but ran, clutching the canvas-covered box against her bosom. But a loose flagstone tripped her and Dallas went sprawling to the street, jamjars breaking, pies tumbling into the puddles. Slowly and painfully, Dallas started to get up. There was a cut on her left arm from one of the broken jars and red jam mingled with her blood. Dallas wanted to cry but could not; she remained as she was, half-kneeling on the flagstones, wishing for some oblivion to wipe away her living nightmare.

"Good Christ, it's you again, Mistress Cameron." Iain Fraser was pulling Dallas to her feet and eyeing her with genuine shock. "What in God's name are you doing?"

Dallas had an overpowering urge to lean against Fraser and let him comfort her. But despite her misery, the barrier remained intact.

"I fell," she murmured, and wondered why she sounded so petulant.

"You've cut yourself. Come inside and I'll take care of that." He started to lead her back towards the town house but Dallas refused to budge. Many a time she had longed to see the interior of Fraser's home but not now, not feeling as wretched as she did.

"No. I must go home." She backed away a foot or so and almost stepped on one of the pies. For the first time, Fraser noted the canvas-covered box and the wreckage of Dallas's scheme.

"What were you doing? Is that debris yours?" There was no mockery in Fraser's eyes, only puzzlement.

Dallas wanted to lie but couldn't. "Aye." She stared down at the flagstones, waiting for some caustic remark from Fraser. But instead, he turned, called out to his serving man, who was still standing in the street with the stallion, and gave an order to clean up the mess.

"Come," he said to Dallas, "I'll walk you home. I know the way this time."

"Oh, no—you're already almost as wet as I am. Please let me go by myself."

But Fraser was already several strides ahead of her. "I've no mind to have you wander off alone and end up jumping into the Nor' Loch. Somehow I sense you're in that sort of mood."

All resistance gone, Dallas hastened to catch up with Fraser. They completed the short walk in silence just as the rain let up. The house in Nairne's Close was empty and Dallas was grateful that the others were out. She would not have wanted her sisters or Marthe to see her return in such a state of disarray and defeat.

"Change your clothes first," Fraser said as they came through the entry hall. "And tell me where you keep your medications."

"Top shelf, the pantry." Dallas moved up the stairs woodenly, leaving a trail of wet footsteps behind her.

Five minutes later she came into the kitchen wearing her drab but dry brown dress and with her damp hair pinned up on top of her head. Fraser had laid out an old remedy of Marthe's for cuts and bruises, a rag soaked in hot water, and two tankards of ale. The only thing Dallas could think to ask was how Fraser knew which was the right medicine.

"I take it your serving woman is a Highlander. I'd recognize this ancient balm any day." Fraser grinned at Dallas as he took her by the arm and began wiping away the blood and jam. She remained quiet as he ministered to her and it was Fraser who broke the silence after he had finished his task and taken his first quaff of ale. "Well? Do you want to talk about your troubles or not?"

Iain Fraser was the last person on earth in whom Dallas wanted to confide. But there he sat, at ease despite his wet clothes, the topaz ring catching the glow from the fireplace, the lean features displaying a kind of bemused compassion.

"We've no money. Just a few pennies. I only sold one pie."

In spite of himself, Fraser burst out laughing. His reaction snapped Dallas out of her stupor. "You dare laugh at me! You, with your fancy court ladies and a house that must have cost a fortune and ... and a horse that gets more to eat than I do! Oh!" Dallas had to force herself to keep from hurling the ale tankard at Fraser.

"Stay, stay, lassie," he urged, composing his features into a more serious expression. "You've had hard times, I take it, since your sire died."

Dallas clutched the tankard between her hands and tried to becalm herself. Fraser might be the last person in the world with whom she wanted to discuss her troubles, but he also seemed to be the only one who cared to listen. "Aye, terrible hard times." She related all her efforts to avert poverty while Fraser sat quietly, occasionally sipping at his ale tankard. "So there it is," she summed up. "We're going to have to sell this house and move into one of those horrid tenements in the Cowgate. I don't see any other solution."

"Hmmmm." Fraser ran a long finger across his upper lip. "Surely there's another way. Why doesn't one of you marry?"

"Marry?" Dallas regarded him with wide brown eyes. "Marry?" she repeated stupidly, wondering why the idea had never occurred to her before. Not that she wished to wed—but Glennie had enjoyed her married life and Tarrill would have become William Ruthven's bride without a moment's hesitation.

"Both your sisters are bonnie and you're a comely little lass—at least you seem to be when you're not being attacked or falling down or doing some of those other peculiar things for which you have such a propensity. If you and your sisters are willing, you should all find husbands in a trice."

Dallas lifted the ale tankard to her lips to help conceal the blush which she felt spreading across her face. Comely! How could he say that about her? Glennie was pretty, Tarrill was striking, but she, Dallas, had never held any illusions about her own appearance.

As experienced as he was in the ways of women, Fraser seemed to read her thoughts. "You underestimate yourself, Dallas," he said, and neither of them appeared to notice his use of her Christian name. "Your features may not be classic, in fact, I've hardly seen all of them until now when your hair is out of your face, but you definitely make an impression on a man." He was measuring his words, sensing that ordinary compliments would go down ill with Dallas. He was also being totally candid. "Furthermore, I'd wager that if you ever smiled—really smiled—I'd be quite bedazzled. Why don't you try it on me, Dallas?"

But Dallas only glared at him. Fraser began to glare back. They sat thus for more than a minute, unblinking, obstinate and determined. And then Dallas broke out into laughter.

"You see? I'm bewitched." Fraser finished his ale and stood up. "Now it's my turn to go home and dry out. But before I do," he went on, reaching inside his leather jerkin, "let me advance you a little something on your future prosperity."

"Oh, no, I couldn't accept it!" Dallas put her hands up to ward off his donation.

Fraser waved a long forefinger at her. "Look at it this way, Dallas. Under ordinary circumstances I'd be trying to make love to you now." He frowned, wondering if his speculations about Dallas were accurate. Experience or not, there was always a margin for error with women.

For her part, Dallas was regarding him with wide-eyed horror. Surely he didn't expect to buy her favors? "Tell me about your horse," she said suddenly, in a frantic effort to divert him. "He's magnificent, I noticed that today."

Fraser's shoulders slumped in utter disbelief. "He's a Spanish breed, I call him Barvas. Quite unlike the shaggy Highland ponies I rode as a boy." The crooked grin spread across his lean face as he moved around the trestle table. "Jesu, I can't believe you really want to talk about my horse!"

"Oh, but I like horses! I like cats and some dogs and ...." Dallas's voice trickled away as Fraser stood directly in front of her, his hands on his hips, one leg poised slightly in front of the other. She felt trapped; how on earth had she been stupid enough to let Fraser in the house when no one was at home?

"And men?" Fraser's grin stayed intact as he watched Dallas grow pale. "You don't really know the answer to that, do you, Dallas? I'll wager you don't know enough about them to reply."

Dallas backed away and all but fell over her chair. "Fie, I've known men all my life! My father had dozens of pupils, colleagues, friends .... Why shouldn't I know about men?"

Fraser couldn't resist laughing at her again, no matter how much fury it might evoke. "You haven't the faintest notion what I mean. Or at least you won't admit it." He reached out with one long arm and grasped her by the back of the neck. Dallas lashed out at him with her hands but Fraser pulled her so close that her breasts were crushed against his leather vest.

"You're wet," she gasped. "Your jerkin smells like sheep dip."

"So?" Fraser bent down, the hawklike nose brushing her cheek. "You smell like pork pie."

Dallas made another effort to pull away but Fraser's arm held her tight. She put her head down but a firm hand raised her chin. "Iain," she pleaded; desperation quavering in her voice, "please ...."

"I'd like to please," he murmured in that indolent tone, and then his mouth crushed hers and the muffled cry that escaped her lips parted them just enough to let Fraser's tongue explore her own. Dallas knew she had to fight him; she knew, too, that she could not win. Struggling in his embrace, she tried to turn away, but Fraser forced Dallas's head back so far she thought her neck would snap. She tried pounding on his back with her fists, but the leather jerkin protected him well. Indeed, though she felt one of his arms let go of her, he was strong enough to hold her fast with the other. Then Fraser released her mouth and began exploring the curve of her breasts with his free hand.

"Oh, lassie, you are as pitiable as you are enticing," he said into her hair. "Has no man ever tasted your bonnie delights?"

"No!" Dallas cried in panic. She writhed in his grasp as the long, brown hand slowly roamed at will until his fingers pressed the nipple of her left breast. To her astonishment, Dallas felt her own body betray her; something bizarre was happening as her bosom seemed to take on a life of its own and thrust and harden at Fraser's touch. She had to will herself to keep from collapsing against this outrageous assailant who was no better than the drunken louts from whom he'd rescued her on Castle Hill.

And then, to her utter amazement, he released her. Dallas lurched against the table, eyes slightly glazed, hair tumbling down over her shoulders. Fraser just stood there, shaking his head and chuckling as if to himself.

"You not only don't know men, Dallas, you don't know yourself." He glanced at his empty ale tankard. "Did I drain that? Aye, I did. Well," he went on, brushing his dark hair back into place, "as I was about to say, as far as the loan is concerned, you have a choice—my money or my body? Which will it be?"

"Your money," Dallas gasped so swiftly that Fraser couldn't help laughing again. But Dallas shook her head in fierce retraction. "Nay, neither! Not after what you've done! You're a philandering blackguard as I suspected from the start!"

"Probably," he conceded with a grin. "But, lassie, be sensible. After all, that's your byword, isn't it? Come, Dallas, I can afford to be generous and you can't afford to be proud."

Dallas glared at him and made an effort to repin her hair. "But you just tried to ravish me!"

Fraser waved his hand at her. "Nonsense. If I'd actually tried, you'd be quite ravished already. Furthermore," he added with the mockery dancing in his hazel eyes, "you'd be purring like a kitten." He saw the fury renewing itself in her expression and put a finger over her lips to quell the inevitable denial. "Be your characteristically businesslike self for a moment. If not for you, then for Glennie and her bairns."

Dallas stared in open-mouthed awe as Fraser dumped a pile of coins on the table, ten, maybe twelve marks glinting in the firelight. She had to press her hands against the edge of the worn oak table to keep from touching the golden bounty.

"I'm flummoxed," Dallas said, finally turning her gaze from the money to Fraser. "I shouldn't, but you're right, the others have to eat. I'll repay you in like coinage, with interest. But," she added with solemn dignity, "you must know I would never sell myself to you or any man for money."

"Ah, but that's exactly what you're going to do if you plan to get a husband who'll save you from poverty."

Dallas stamped her bare foot. "That's different, wedlock is legal and sanctified. Besides, it won't be me, it'll be Glennie or Tarrill."

Fraser regarded her with exaggerated dubiousness. "We'll see. My wager would be on you, under the circumstances. How's your arm?"

Dallas looked down at the bandage. "It's much better." It suddenly occurred to her that in their scuffling he had managed not to aggravate the scrape. Something akin to awe filled her expression as she looked up at him.

As before, Fraser seemed to sense what she was thinking. "Then I'm not quite the plundering reiver you thought me to be?"

The faintest hint of a smile played at her mouth. "You are ... different," she allowed and wondered why she had a sudden urge to touch the hollow of his cheekbone.

"You are different, too," Fraser said with a smile untouched by mockery. "Take care, lassie, and spend your money wisely."

Dallas had to ask the question, though she doubted he would give her an answer. "Iain ... what did my father tell you before he died?"

Fraser's smile faded at once. "He told me who my father was. Though there is no proof."

"Who was your sire? How did my father know?"

"I can't tell you that." Fraser saw the vexation rekindle in her dark eyes and shook his head. "I'm not being obdurate, it's better that you don't know. But I'm eternally grateful for the knowledge."

"He told me everything!" Dallas realized she sounded like an overindulged child and bit her lip. "That is, I thought he did."

"You're probably right—save in this one matter. On the other hand, I'll wager there were things you never told him." He raised an eyebrow at her. "Such as how you feel about men—and how you felt about George Gordon in particular?"

"Fie!" Dallas blazed at him. "Father didn't need to hear such inanities! And however would you know about George Gordon anyway?"

He shrugged in that manner which was becoming all too familiar to Dallas. "I saw you together the night the Queen arrived, though neither of you noticed me—then. You looked crushed, as if George had inflicted some nearmortal wound. Did he seduce you, Dallas?"

"Oooooh ...." Dallas ran her hands through her hair and again it came tumbling down over her shoulders. "You see too much, you know too much! No! George never did any such thing!"

Fraser's mouth twisted wryly. "Oh. So that was the problem. Women are such touchy creatures—they're outraged when a man tries—and infuriated when he doesn't."

"That's drivel! I would never have let him ...."

But Fraser interrupted her denial. "Ah, hindsight! It's a wonderful mode of self-deception." He was grinning again and reached out to put a finger on her upturned nose. "But it isn't compatible with someone who studies history as you do, lassie."

Dallas batted his hand away. "You speak out of turn! You know nothing about me!"

"You just said I knew too much. That may be an exaggeration, but I do know enough. As for George, he isn't a bad fellow—he's just arrogant and self-centered, like most of the Gordons. But don't judge all men by him. Now," he said, with an indolent wave of his hand, "I must be off. I need a change of gear before I'm attacked by a ram in heat. Or a ewe, I suppose."

Dallas watched him leave the kitchen with mixed emotions. Her stomach was twisted like a tangled skein of yarn, her hands were unsteady as she ran her fingers over the golden coins on the table. The scrape on her arm scarcely hurt but her lips felt bruised. Involuntarily, she brushed her hands against her breasts. Her nipples were no longer taut, but her heart seemed to be thumping far too fast.

"Oh, fie," she breathed aloud and slumped into the chair. Iain Fraser was so accustomed to bedding any wench who came his way that he would have considered it ungallant not to at least try—or so Dallas told herself. But that hardly explained her own reaction. She should have fought more fiercely. On the other hand, she was worn out from her fruitless expedition in the High Street. Yet her honor had been at stake. Well, it was intact—and after all, she was too small to ward off a man as strong as Iain Fraser.

The inner argument raged for at least ten minutes. Best to forget the episode, she finally told herself. Better yet to forget about Fraser's bruising kisses and his hand on her breasts. Dallas felt her cheeks grow hot at the memory. She stood up resolutely and began filling Fraser's empty ale mug with gold coins.

After all, she now faced another problem: How could she explain to her sisters where the money had come from? Dallas poured herself another tankard of ale and sat drumming her slim fingers on the tabletop. She could tell them she'd sold all the pies and jam, of course. But that would only account for a few shillings at most. It would, however, stall them off for a few days, until she came up with a better explanation.

Just as she was about to take the last drink of her ale Dallas heard the front door open. It was Glennie and Tarrill, accompanied by the boys. Dallas swiftly grasped Fraser's tankard and held it close to her body.

"Dallas!" Glennie called out. "You're back already! Did you sell the pies and jam?"

"Oh, aye, all of them." Dallas forced a smile. "A brisk business, despite the rain."

"I feared you'd be caught in that," Tarrill said, helping Glennie get the boys out of their damp clothes. "But I'm glad, Dallas, perhaps I can go out tomorrow with some more."

"Oh, I don't think that's necessary—yet." Dallas didn't want either of her sisters to face the humiliation she had suffered. "Where have you all been?" she asked to change the subject.

"We've been helping Mistress Drummond card wool in exchange for more firewood," Glennie explained. She had her sons stripped down to their threadbare shirts and hose and had stationed them in front of the fire. "Oh, Dallas, what happened to your arm?"

Dallas had forgotten about the bandage. She glanced down at it and shrugged. "Just a scrape. Umm, I brushed up against a rough railing near Gosford's Close."

Something in Dallas's tone made Glennie suspicious. She also wondered why her sister continued to stand by the table, holding her ale tankard with such apparent effort. Then it occurred to Glennie that the bandage was on Dallas's right arm and it had obviously been put on in a very neat manner. Untidy at best, Dallas could never have managed such a feat with her left hand.

"Daniel, Jamie, you're dried off. Run upstairs now." Glennie gave each of the boys a pat as they scampered out of the kitchen, already arguing over which game they would play. "All right, Dallas," Glennie said, seating herself on the opposite side of the table. "What's happened and why is that tankard weighing you down?"

Dallas stood for a moment without moving, then suddenly banged the tankard down on the table, making several of the coins flip out onto the floor. Tarrill gasped, amazed as much by the behavior of her two sisters as by the gold pieces which lay scattered around Dallas's hem.

"I couldn't sell a rope to a drowning man," Dallas admitted bitterly. "Oh, some blowzy goodwife deigned to buy a pie, but it was hopeless. Then I fell down, that's how I hurt my arm. And Iain Fraser offered me this mound of money in exchange for my body. Now are you satisfied?" She glared at both Glennie and Tarrill, daring them to reprimand her. Both stared back, Glennie's blue eyes incredulous, Tarrill's black ones dumbfounded. Taking her advantage, Dallas hurtled on. "You'd rather sell the house and move into the Cowgate? You'd prefer politely starving to death? What about the boys?"

"Dallas, I can't believe my ears!" Glennie was flushed with shock. "You mean—you're telling us you gave yourself to that wild Highlander in exchange for this?" She swept her hand across the table, indicating the gold-filled tankard.

"Wouldn't you rather have me do that than merely accept a loan?" Dallas felt she had regained the upper hand. "Besides, he's not wild, I daresay he even eats with a fork."

"Oh, Dallas!" Glennie blinked several times in a row, a sure sign that she was mightily upset.

Dallas came around to the side of the table where Glennie was sitting. "Nay, I didn't sell my body to Iain Fraser," she asserted, wincing slightly at the recollection of their physical encounter. "It's a loan and we'll pay it back as soon as ... as soon as ...." Suddenly Dallas didn't want to broach the subject of their marriages. Glennie had not sufficiently recovered from the shock of losing both husband and father, and Tarrill certainly wouldn't consider another man until the raw wound of Will Ruthven's betrayal had healed. "Actually, I still have hopes of securing a court appointment for at least one of us," Dallas went on hastily. "Iain Fraser might help us—after all, if we could serve the Queen, he'd get his money back."

"If John Hamilton could exert no more effort than inviting us to a cancelled levee, what will Iain Fraser do?" Tarrill asked sarcastically.

"I've hardly had time to figure that out," Dallas replied haughtily. "What with tutoring lame-witted pupils and peddling pies in the High Street, I've been a bit preoccupied. But it wasn't John Hamilton's fault the levee was cancelled and he isn't the one who made us the loan."

"It all sounds most strange to me," Glennie said with disapproval.

"Strange or not, at least we have ten marks," Dallas replied with an unexpected surge of self-satisfaction. With a brisk swish of her dowdy skirt, she padded barefoot from the room.

EARLY THE NEXT morning, Dallas was in the cellar, checking supplies and calculating precisely how Iain Fraser's loan could be disbursed. Meat was definitely a priority; lard, too, and probably some sugar. But before she could complete her inventory, Glennie was calling to her from upstairs. Dallas replied that she would come up at once and was almost to the landing when she heard a familiar noise. Turning back, she listened intently. Yes, it was the same sound she'd heard in August, coming from under the cellar floor. And suddenly she remembered. Some years ago when she was a child her father had talked about passageways dug out under the city. Smugglers and pirates used them, to carry their illegal booty up from the Firth. The matter was underemphasized, however, lest the girls become apprehensive at the idea of evil men trooping about beneath their very floors. Over the years, most of the pirates and smugglers had been caught and the passages closed off, yet there must be one which was still in use. Not for smuggling, perhaps, but for some secret and probably illicit activity. Dare I? she asked herself, balancing precariously on the edge of the top stair. Could I find a way through our cellar into the passage and see where it leads? Dallas's daring did not quite match her curiosity. Pirates and smugglers alike were said to be ruthless men, without mercy when it came to those who interfered with their livelihood. A whole armada of pirates could run like so many hares in heat under the Cameron house and would never entice Dallas into entering the passageway.

Hurrying up the stairs, Dallas was surprised to hear a man's voice in the entry hall. To her astonishment, John Hamilton stood chatting with Glennie, his body muffled in a dark green cloak, which was held in place by a silver replica of his family crest.

"My lord!" Dallas cried in surprise. "How good to see you! You've met my eldest sister?"

Hamilton smiled broadly. "Aye, a pleasure." He looked down at Glennie who seemed quite undone by a visit from such a great lord. "I was in the neighborhood and remembered you lived in Nairne's Close. I would have come before but I've been on progress with the Queen. I'm sorry the levee was cancelled. Happily, Her Grace's health improved."

"How fortunate," said Dallas, with a touch of asperity. She wished she'd done up her hair that morning and wasn't wearing her dowdy, threadbare mourning gown. "Oh, sir, do come inside by the fire! You must be chilled right through."

"Nay," said Hamilton, stepping inside and stamping the snow from his brown leather boots. "It's not so raw since the wind died down."

Tarrill had appeared in the hallway and Hamilton greeted her in his outgoing manner. She insisted he share ale and collops with them in the sitting room. Dallas winced inwardly at the extravagance but realized they must be hospitable.

After Hamilton had recounted his sojourn north and the Queen's reaction to her countrymen, he put down his tankard and looked at Dallas. "You recall that day in August when you sold me some of your father's books?" Dallas said she certainly did. "Fine volumes, they are, mistress. But Master Forbes confided to me that you kept the best for yourself." The brown eyes twinkled. "Certain histories of Scotland and Edinburgh which are hard to come by. Would I be impertinent to ask if I might buy another one or two?"

"Oh, take them as a gift!" Tarrill exclaimed. "We could not possibly let you pay, my lord!"

Dallas shot Tarrill a murderous glance. Damn her lip, she thought, the chit never did have enough sense to plug up a cat's hole. But Hamilton was insistent. He must not accept such treasures as a gift, no matter how generously bestowed. Would three marks suffice?

Dallas all but gasped. He does feel sorry for us, she decided. He takes in our shabby clothes and the worn furnishings and no doubt has heard rumors of our hardship. He would see to us as he would to Lame Angus or any other poor beggar. Well, three marks were three marks, and along with Fraser's loan would see them through the winter.

When Dallas returned from the library with the books, she found Hamilton, Glennie and Tarrill engaged in conversation about his family background. Hamilton admired the volumes, thanked her profusely, and discreetly handed over a small purse. Dallas was gracious but businesslike, as if she conducted such transactions every day. She turned the conversation back to the old Scots families as tactfully as she could, asking Hamilton not about his own, but of Iain Fraser's ancestors.

"Iain Fraser?" Hamilton eyed her dubiously. "You know him?"

"Oh, aye," Dallas answered nonchalantly. "I see him now and then."

Hamilton set his tankard down on the small sturdy oak table next to his armchair. "He's thought to have a reckless reputation with the ladies, you know."

Dallas shrugged. "I know him but casually. I ask about him because of something my father said shortly before his death." She explained briefly to Hamilton what her father had said while he was dying but did not add that Daniel Cameron had confided something to Fraser which no one else had heard. Hamilton listened attentively and then sat frowning into the fire. "Fraser's history is relatively well known—at least the basic facts."

"If you'd care to relate it, I'd be most interested," Dallas coaxed.

Hamilton stretched his booted legs out towards the hearth. "Well, it all goes back to a house near Inverness, on the River Beauly where Malcolm Fraser brought his bride, Catherine McKim." He linked his fingers behind his head and settled back to tell the tale. The fire snapped in the grate, Marthe padded in to refill the ale tankards, as Tarrill curled up on the settle, her cheek resting on one hand, and Glennie's knitting needles fell into the rhythm of Hamilton's narrative.

"Young Catherine was a sweet lassie and Malcolm was a fine figure of a man though possessed of a violent temper. Soon word was out that Catherine was with child. Yet instead of happily accepting the well-wishes of his friends and family, Malcolm Fraser turned sullen. Everyone thought Fraser must believe Catherine wasn't carrying his bairn. Suddenly she disappeared while rumor swept the countryside that she had died, even that Fraser had murdered her."

Hamilton paused to take a drink from his tankard. The girls sat in rapt attention, waiting for him to resume the story. "Several months passed and the next thing everybody knew, Malcolm Fraser had a fine son—but no wife. The story came out in bits and pieces; he had sent his wife to a convent to bear the child, the child he was convinced had been fathered by another man. He had told her he never wanted to see her or the bairn again. But Catherine died when the child was born and the good sisters were unable to keep him, having no wet nurse at the convent. Fraser at first refused to bring the bairn into his home, but other members of his family insisted. Then, one evening Malcolm rowed out onto Beauly Firth with the bairn. It was a rough, wild night and the boat tipped over. The wet nurse Malcolm had with him—a fact that belies the gossip of his intention to drown the babe—was strong as an Amazon. She saved the child but Malcolm Fraser drowned. Later, she said he was taking the child to some relatives and had no evil intentions. In any event, the bairn did end up with some of his relations at Strath Farrar."

Tarrill murmured something about it all being quite fascinating but Dallas remained silent for some time. Her curiosity was piqued: How had her Cameron father learned who had sired an illegitimate Fraser? It was more than puzzling, it was downright mysterious.

"I know little more of Fraser until he came to court about eight years ago," Hamilton said as Glennie refilled his tankard. "He had gone to the University of St. Andrews. I believe a wealthy clansman provided for his education. Then he served Marie de Guise until she died and after that he left Scotland. He went to France, as I recall, to present himself to Mary Stuart and then he traveled abroad, returning a few months before Her Grace's arrival."

"His fortunes seem to have improved over the years," commented Dallas. "Mungo Tennant's house could not have been bought cheap."

"Perhaps and perhaps not." Hamilton took a deep draught from his tankard. "The rumors about Mungo Tennant may have reduced the price. Not everyone would want a house said to possess a torture chamber. Still, Fraser lives exceedingly well, and frankly, I'm not sure how he manages."

Glennie rose to poke the fire. "Well, I'm glad he does. His early life must have been very sad."

Hamilton shrugged. "No doubt his kinsmen gave him their affection. If not, he's more than made up for it since reaching manhood. Women dote on him, though he's yet to take a wife."

"Neither have you, sir," Dallas put in pertly and then bit her tongue. "Oh, I only meant ...."

But Hamilton astonished her once again. He put out his hand and grasped hers firmly. "Don't fash yourself, mistress. You are quite right. But then I don't make a habit of seducing maids with honeyed words:"

Dallas flushed as Hamilton's brown eyes stayed fixed on her face. Tarrill stifled a giggle from her place by the hearth, but Hamilton was quite serious and did not relinquish Dallas's gaze until he also relinquished her hand. Marthe bustled in again, to offer sesame cakes, and the mood became quite festive. Dallas thought no more of the past that afternoon.

Chapter Four

TWO DAYS LATER Dallas headed out into the wintry November sunlight to see Iain Fraser. She had considered asking John Hamilton about securing an introduction to court again but had decided that as kind and gracious as he seemed, Fraser was a more appropriate choice. Besides, she was now determined to learn what her father had told Fraser; it seemed strange to Dallas that he had ever kept a secret from his favorite daughter. Fraser might have put her off once already, but Dallas felt she had a right to know the truth.

Dallas walked briskly up the well-swept front steps and banged the brass knocker. After what seemed like an eternity, the door swung open and a short, rotund man of about sixty stood before her. He was dressed in servant's clothes and had very small light eyes. His face was quite florid and the veins were broken in his cheeks. Drink, decided Dallas, and hoped he was sober enough now.

"I must see Iain Fraser," she announced imperiously. "At once."

The man grinned at Dallas but shook his head. Two tufts of grey hair danced atop his head. "Nay, lassie, that canna be. Master Fraser is gone from the city."

Dallas was crestfallen. It had never occurred to her that Fraser might not be home. "Oh." She stuffed her chilled hands inside her cloak. "When will he return?"

The man shrugged. "Who knows? What man can say when the rains will fall and the winds will blow? A week, two, a month—I dinna ken." He shrugged again.

Dallas considered for a moment, then reluctantly decided that she would have to come back later and hope to find Fraser at home. But her hesitation had not gone unnoticed by the serving man. "Is it that dire for you to see him, lassie?" For the first time, she caught the reek of whiskey on his breath as he leaned forward confidentially.

"Most certainly not," she snapped, reverting to her imperious manner. " 'Tis strictly business." And with that she turned on her heel, narrowly avoiding a fall off the stoop. "Silly old sot!" she muttered as the serving man cackled gleefully from the doorway.

Dallas did return, twice during the following week. But each time the serving man, whose name was Kennedy, gave her the same information and the same leer.

On her fourth attempt, she left late in the afternoon, having been busy all day with grinding corn for meal and mending worn bedsheets. She had already made up her mind that this trip would be her last—she would leave a note for Fraser and then he could contact her upon his return. Kennedy's attitude had become just too much to bear.

The big handsome house looked the same, with the snow drifting on the solid stone windowsills and the Flemish glass panes reflecting the dying afternoon light. It seemed to Dallas that more candles than usual burned from inside the house, but perhaps that was merely because she had come late in the day.

Once more Dallas climbed the short flight of stone stairs and once more she pulled at the knocker. But this time Kennedy was not the one who opened the door. Instead, a somewhat younger man of medium height and stocky build looked out at her from clear blue eyes. A thatch of bristly red hair fell over his broad forehead and he was dressed not as a servant, but in good yeoman's clothing, topped by a shiny new leather jerkin.

"I've come to see Iain Fraser," she announced, recovering quickly from her surprise.

"I'm sorry, mistress, but he's not at home," he replied politely. Dallas let out a deep breath of disappointment; somehow she had expected the man to have a different answer for her. "But," he continued, before she could respond, "he'll be back shortly. Perhaps you'd care to wait inside?"

Dallas peered beyond the man into the entry hall. Candles flickered from the draught of the open door, a Moorish carpet covered most of the floor, and a Gobelin tapestry depicting the Judgment of Paris hung from one wall. It all looked highly respectable and very elegant. "Yes, I'll wait," she told the man and stepped over the threshold.

They passed through the entry hall and into a small parlor, some sort of supper room, Dallas decided. Damp wood sputtered on the grate and a finely wrought supper table inlaid with mother-of-pearl was set for one. "Be seated, mistress," said the man, indicating a velvet-trimmed chair of intricate design. "May I tell Master Fraser your name when he returns?"

Dallas was absorbed by the room and its rich trappings. She had never been surrounded by so much luxury all at once. "What?" She started from her reverie. "Oh, aye, I'm Mistress Cameron of Nairne's Close. Master Fraser knows me."

The man's gaze wasn't as offensive as Kennedy's, but the reaction was similar. She bristled and was about to add something by way of defending her honor when the man made a little bow of amends: "I'm Cummings, mistress, at your service. I will leave you now, but should you want anything, pray pull this bell-cord." He indicated a long wine-colored piece of fabric by the door.

Dallas nodded as Cummings withdrew. As soon as the door was closed she rose from the velvet chair and began prowling the room. She paused to examine a small gold-leaf clock, an ornate jewel-encrusted crucifix and an almost life-sized marble bust of a Roman emperor. Augustus? Probably, Dallas decided. She moved over by the fireplace where the wet wood had finally caught and now burned evenly in the grate. Holy Mother, Dallas thought, Fraser said he could afford to be generous and it's obvious from all these sumptuous furnishings that he was right. But how has he accumulated such wealth? Dallas wished fervently she could learn his secret and apply it to her own situation.

The little gold-leaf clock had just chimed in with the church bells outside to announce six when Kennedy opened the door. "Cummings thought you might be hungry, mistress," he said with his knowing grin. "Could I bring you aught?"

Dallas's initial reaction was to refuse but her dinner of dried salt pork and boiled potatoes at noon had left her famished this late in the day. Furthermore, she knew Iain Fraser's fare must be considerably more lavish than what poor Marthe was forced to cook. Fraser's loan and Hamilton's payment for the books would not last forever and she hoarded them closely.

"Yes, perhaps I'll have ...." Dallas's voice trailed off as visions of all sorts of delicacies paraded through her imagination.

Kennedy must have guessed her dilemma. "A little capon and honey bread with a side dish of pickled pears might tide ye over, eh, lass?"

Pleasure filtered into Dallas's eyes. "Oh, yes, I should like that very much. And one other thing," she added before Kennedy could disappear into the hall, "could you please send someone to my house in Nairne's Close to tell them I will be detained?"

Kennedy went over to a wall cabinet and pulled out a drawer. He set out writing materials for Dallas and waited as she composed a brief note. "I'm visiting Iain Fraser," she wrote rapidly. "I may be rather late so don't wait up.

I'm quite safe and supping here." She folded the note over twice and gave it to Kennedy.

"I'll send a lad," he said and was gone.

When the food arrived, Dallas ate ravenously. She felt a twinge of guilt when she thought of how Glennie and Tarrill and Marthe and the boys had to make do with the leek soup that had been simmering on the hob all day. But somehow she'd make it up to them, she thought hazily, pushing her plate away and stretching out in the chair. It was after seven now and the full meal, the warm room and the long wait were beginning to take their toll. Briefly, she perused the few books in the room, but they were mostly geography tomes or tracts on the New World, and none of them captured her imagination. At last, tired and bored, she sat down in the velvet-covered chair and in a few minutes she was fast asleep.

She did not hear Iain Fraser come in. Cummings had told him that Mistress Cameron was waiting for him in the supper room, and while he had been surprised enough by that piece of news, he was even more amazed to find her sleeping in his favorite chair. He observed her in silence for a few moments, wryly contemplating the fringe of dark lashes on her cheeks, the slightly parted full mouth, the crazy tangle of brown hair, and the outmoded, crumpled mourning dress. Any other woman in the same place and situation would have tempted him into kissing her awake. Dallas's reaction might prove a bit violent, however, so he merely gave the little supper table a shake, rattling the dishes and silverware just enough to rouse her.

Dallas awoke with a start, momentarily forgetting where she was. She blinked several times as she looked up at Fraser who was standing in front of the chair, his hands on his hips, one foot slightly in front of the other. He was dressed in courtier's clothing, a black slashed doublet trimmed with gold, matching hose and trunks and shiny black boots of Spanish leather. He looks like the devil, Dallas thought dreamily, and the court sword on his left hip heightened the illusion.

"You've got a tail," she murmured, making an effort to sit up straight.

"What?" Fraser turned to see the effect of his shadow, thrown long across the candlelit room. "Oh, aye," he laughed, "like an Englishman. Isn't it said they all have tails?"

"A rumor started by the French," Dallas replied, rubbing her eyes with her fists, and looking like a tousled child. "Oh, I'm sorry I went to sleep—but it was so cozy in here ...." Her voice trailed off as she stretched and yawned. "You have a lovely home. Lord knows I've been here often enough in the last week or two."

"So I'm told," Fraser said, pulling up another chair and sitting down across from her. "And I must say, I'm intrigued by your persistence. Did you come to repay my loan or are you waiting for dessert?"

Dallas's eyes snapped at him. "Fie, sir, I told you I'd not sell myself! I came on business."

"I didn't think it was pleasure," Fraser responded dryly. "Well, if you didn't come to ravish me, do you mind if I eat my supper?" He got up, rang the bell for Kennedy and poured himself a glass of wine. "And you?" he inquired, proffering the decanter.

Dallas shook her head. Kennedy came in with a tray full of food and laid it out on the supper table for Fraser. After clearing away the remnants of Dallas's meal, he winked at her and left the room.

"Impudent," Dallas muttered, but Fraser paid her no heed. She watched him cut up some pieces of pheasant and dip them in a rich brown sauce. Now that she was actually face-to-face with Fraser she wasn't sure how to begin. Her obsession with asking Fraser's assistance in securing an introduction to court now seemed lame; her fixation about making him tell what her father had said on his deathbed was a flimsy pretext since he had already refused; indeed, it suddenly occurred to her that her presence in his house was tenuous at best. Why had she come? She regarded Fraser with apprehension and felt the capon flutter in her stomach.

"Turnip?" Fraser held up a fork to Dallas.

She ignored the gesture but felt somewhat relieved. "What know you of the battle of Blar-na-Leine?" she asked without further preamble.

Fraser paused with the fork in midair. "I was fourteen when that battle took place. I wanted to fight with the rest of my clan, but they said I was too young." His tone was dry, but the hazel eyes had turned frosty. "But after the battle—and the death of three hundred Frasers," and here the bitterness was in his voice, too, "some of the Camerons came north, beyond Loch Ness, to pillage and burn. They went to the house at Strath Farrar where I lived with my aunt. After raping her, they took me captive. Then they stripped the house and set it afire. That's what I know of Blar-na-Leine." He picked up his silver napkin ring and examined it intently. "That is what Highland feuds are like, Dallas; senseless, wasteful things which a poor country like Scotland cannot afford. And yet even here in Edinburgh it's this man against that, one faction ranked opposite another, eternal bickering over some trifle and always in the name of clan or family." He hurled the napkin ring down on the tabletop where it clattered and rolled off onto the carpet.

Dallas had no adequate reply. "I'm sorry for what happened," she said lamely, as if she might offer some sort of recompense for what her clansmen had done to the Frasers. "How did you get away?"

"I escaped, one night when there was no moon. 'Twas simple enough."

He poured himself a second glass of wine. Looking into the glass, he could almost see an awkward, lanky boy of fourteen, dressed in rags, crawling out the window of the crofter's hut where they had kept him, and making his frightened way through the glens and forests to Strath Farrar.

"The Camerons took everything," Fraser went on. "By the time I got back to Strath Farrar my aunt had died and my uncle had been killed in battle." At last, he sat back, pushing the chair away from the table. "You know aught of my history, Dallas, besides what I've told you just now?"

"I've heard a tale or two," she admitted. "About some strange doings near Inverness. I can't help it—I had to ask once more what my father told you before he died." Dallas couldn't look at Fraser; she kept her eyes focused on the wine glass in his hand.

Fraser sighed. "I told you, I can't say. I'm not being whimsical, there are good reasons why you should not know. Especially since what your father told me cannot be proved. At least as far as I can see." He paused and frowned at his empty plate. "It wasn't just a question of being curious about my parentage. As you know, under Scots law, an illegitimate son can neither inherit nor bequeath property. If I could prove who my father was, I could be legitimized. While I ended up with the land at Beauly, my hold on it is tenuous."

"Yet it's yours. That is, no one else has laid a claim to it thus far?"

"True. But the present Fraser chieftain is only a lad and God knows what some of the older clansmen might do. If I had proof of my birthright, I might be entitled to other holdings as well." Fraser paused again. "Some day I may have heirs of my own," he went on, his tone still serious. "I want Beauly for them, too. By Christ, I've earned that property over the years."

Dallas knew well how a Highlander regarded his land, with an almost sacred sense of possession. She wondered if the holdings at Beauly were sufficiently bountiful to make Fraser rich. It was doubtful, she decided, since only an enormous estate could provide the fortune he obviously possessed.

"You spend time there then?"

"Aye, I go there two, three times a year. A widowed cousin cares for the house in my absence."

It was clear to Dallas that Fraser would reveal no more to her. It also seemed clear that if she were ever going to ask him for help in getting to court this was the moment.

"I've been thinking about repaying your loan," she began, but Fraser reached across the supper table and took her chin between his thumb and forefinger.

"Stop fretting over the loan, lassie. Once you've found a handsome husband with a fat purse, you can repay me."

"With my luck, only the husband will be fat," Dallas retorted. The little clock chimed ten and Dallas jumped. "Oh, Holy Virgin, I had no idea how late it was! The lanterns will be extinguished by now!" She looked frantically for her cloak and was about to snatch it up off the floor where it had fallen while she was asleep when Fraser came up behind her. He put one arm around her neck while the other encircled her waist.

"The offer of my body still stands," he said in that indolent tone. "Believe me, Dallas, it would be a fine bargain."

Dallas had gone rigid at his touch. "I'd argue that till Doomsday, Iain Fraser! Now leave me be, I must go home!"

"In time." He brushed the thick hair aside and bent to kiss the nape of her neck. Dallas began to struggle, tugging at his hands, pulling her head away, wriggling to free her body from his grasp.

But his almost effortless strength held her fast. Fraser's mouth strayed to the white flesh just above the high collar of her mourning gown; his hands caressed her breasts, moved to the flatness of her stomach, and then slipped between her legs.

Dallas screamed. Fraser quickly put one hand over her mouth while the other pressed against her thighs. "Oh, hush, lassie! My servants will not interfere with my pleasures. Besides, they'll think you're only protesting for etiquette's sake."

But Dallas's protest had been evoked not just by Fraser's boldness but by the unexpected fire she felt in the pit of her stomach. She tried to keep her legs tightly closed but the effort was making her lose her balance. Nor were her attempts at clawing his arms doing the slightest bit of good. Then she saw the fruit knife on the table; if only she could get just a foot or so closer ... she lunged suddenly, throwing them both off-balance. Fraser's hand fell away from her mouth but he recovered instantly and grabbed Dallas tightly around the hips.

"Nay, lassie, you'll not make mischief with my eating utensils." He kicked at the table, sending it and the fruit knife well out of her reach.

"You savage!" she railed. "Let me go! I don't want your wretched body, I wish I'd never taken your foul money, I'd like to carve you up like that stupid capon!"

"No, you wouldn't." He sounded so calmly self-assured that Dallas was galvanized into renewed vigor. Kicking, biting, scratching, pummeling, she fought with such fury that Fraser began to lose his own temper. "Enough, Dallas!" He grabbed a handful of her hair and dumped her into the velvet-covered chair. Then he fell on top of her and pulled both her arms behind her with one of his hands. Fraser rapidly undid the buttons of her bodice and before Dallas could do anything more than shriek in astonishment, he had freed her white breasts. With her arms held behind her back, the generous curve of her bosom arched forward as if in provocative invitation. Fraser grinned at the horrified expression on her face.

"You are bonnie in other places, Dallas. I've seldom seen such lovely duckies as these." He took his time letting those mocking hazel eyes appraise her breasts. Slowly, his hand began to explore each one, gently at first, then with increasing intensity until his fingers tugged at her nipples and brought them to rigid, pink life. The knee he pressed between her legs sent a shuddering sensation throughout her entire body. Dallas's incoherent protests had turned into moaning gasps, part pain, part outrage—and part something Dallas had never before experienced and was loathe to identify. She could scarcely believe the total helplessness she felt, and the sight of Fraser's dark head bent over her naked breasts seemed utterly unreal. As his mouth covered her right breast and his tongue began flicking greedily at her nipple, she felt dizzy with emotion; she even heard a clamorous sound in her ears which grew and grew until suddenly Fraser stopped abruptly and stood up.

"Christ! The alarm bells! What's happening?" He moved swiftly to the window and pulled open the draperies. Dallas sat as if in a stupor, her breasts still exposed, her hair in even more wild disarray than usual, her arms aching from the awkward position in which they'd been held, and her entire body trembling violently. At least, she thought dully, as the clanging bells continued to sound, I wasn't hearing things ....

"Someone is coming here, on the run." Fraser closed the drapes quickly and returned to Dallas. "There may be trouble, lassie. I'll see that my men get you home safely."

Dallas gaped at him, confounded by the sudden change from passionate ravisher to considerate host.

"Well?" He grinned at her with those mocking hazel eyes. "Though I much enjoy the sight of your delightful body, I'd have thought you too finicky to want my guest to see it half-naked, too."

"Oh!" Dallas flushed crimson. With trembling hands, she began to fasten her gown, conscious of Fraser's amused expression. "Oh, you fiend! I wish I'd killed you with the fruit knife!"

"Don't fash yourself so, Dallas. You enjoyed it far more than you'll admit. Now take some wine and push the hair out of your eyes."

To Fraser's surprise, Dallas did both. Before either of them could speak again, the door to the supper room opened unceremoniously and the Earl of Bothwell hurtled inside. Cummings was on his heels and quickly shut the door behind them.

"An informal entrance, to say the least," grinned Fraser. "And who might be in hot pursuit this time, my lord?" Bothwell grinned back, strong white teeth flashing in the short red beard. He was of average height, with a stocky build and beefy freckled hands. Bothwell paused to get his breath before responding: "Half the town, sir—have you not heard those damnable bells?"

Even as he spoke the alarm died down. The earl sighed with obvious relief, then looked warily at Dallas, as if seeing her for the first time.

"I told him you were not alone, sir," Cummings interposed.

"He seldom is," chuckled Bothwell and bowed as Fraser introduced Dallas. She stared at the Border Lord, remembered her manners and made a quick curtsy. She knew what Bothwell was thinking about her presence in the supper room. With an enormous effort to hide the humiliation she felt, Dallas forced herself to look composed.

But Bothwell had already turned away and was pouring himself a glass of wine. "Such a night!" he exclaimed, draining the glass in a gulp, and going to the window to peer out. "No sign of the watch here. And no sign of ...." He stopped abruptly, eyeing Dallas.

"Oh, come, this is Mistress Cameron and if the watch is pursuing you, there will be no secrets by morning," Fraser asserted. "Besides, I'd hardly let the lassie go home if I thought the entire city might be on the point of violence."

"Scarcely that." Bothwell sat down heavily on the settee and poured himself another glass of wine. "On the other hand, I'm not sure if it's fit for a lady's ears." He eyed Dallas's questioningly and she flushed furiously.

"Well, she is a lady—but she'll hear it anyway, I'm sure." Fraser glanced at Dallas and grinned. She wasn't certain whose discomfiture he was enjoying more—hers or Bothwell's.

The beefy hands set the wine decanter down on the carpet. "A silly thing, really. Alison Craik—you've heard of her?" He saw Fraser and Dallas nod. "Cuthbert Ramsey's ward and a sweet little piece—pardon me, mistress," he said to Dallas, though it was clear he didn't give a fig for her pardon. "She is Arran's mistress—and you know how those Hamiltons loathe me and my border kin. Well," he continued, gulping down more wine, "Lord Johnny Stuart and I decided to kidnap the wench. We'd had some sport"—he paused to see what effect this statement was having on Dallas but she was keeping her eyes riveted on the bust of Augustus—"with her before and she hadn't been unwilling. Lord Johnny is a likeable soul, quite a different sort of bastard half-brother the Queen has in him than in Lord James."

"True enough," commented Fraser, whose own face had turned grim at the mention of James Stuart.

"But I'll admit we went a bit far—we decided on hurrying her leave-taking by tossing her out the window—it wasn't far and Lord Johnny could have caught her easily." Bothwell laughed aloud, apparently quite amused by their nocturnal caper. "But who should appear just as we were about to heave the delightful Mistress Craik through the casement? John Hamilton and some of his men, that's who. Hamilton looked murderous and Lord Johnny and I decided to cut our losses and run for it." He spread his hands in an apparent gesture of supplication. "What could we do? I like a fight as well as any man but we were outnumbered by at least six to two."

Fraser was laughing by now, too, but Dallas still remained rigid with a faint look of distaste on her face. Bothwell and Lord Johnny might be a pair of knaves, but Alison Craik had gotten what she deserved by dallying with any of them, including the allegedly unstable Arran. John Hamilton seemed a cut above such outlandish doings.

Fraser and Bothwell were sharing the last of the wine between them. Dallas gathered her cloak around her and headed for the door. "I must take my leave now," she announced to no one in particular. Fraser looked up from his wine glass long enough to tell her that Cummings would escort her home.

"Good night, Dallas," Fraser said calmly, as if the time she had spent under his roof had been a perfectly ordinary evening.

Dallas murmured a desultory farewell, sketched a curtsy to Bothwell, and was relieved to be in the solid presence of Cummings as they headed out into the sharp night air.

They were just coming out of Gosford's Close when a group of men came hurrying towards them. Cummings paused in midstep and Dallas sensed that his hand had gone to his dirk. She stopped too, both curious and fearful, but as the little band came nearer she recognized John Hamilton in their midst.

"Good evening, my lord," she said, noting with some apprehension that Hamilton and the others were armed.

Hamilton made no effort to conceal his surprise at encountering Dallas at such an unlikely time of night. "You are out past curfew, mistress," he replied. "Is aught wrong?"

"No, no," Dallas replied vaguely. "I supped elsewhere tonight." She shifted from foot to foot, noting that Hamilton recognized Cummings. Standing still made her more aware of the chill winds soughing among the rooftops and up through the wynds.

"I see," said Hamilton in a voice which made Dallas think he saw a good deal more than she would have liked. But Hamilton was motioning for his companions to let Dallas and her escort pass. "Take care," he said in a voice which made Dallas look at him closely. But already he and the other men were moving swiftly away and out of Gosford's Close.

Chapter Five

Glennie and Tarrill had been frantic with worry about Dallas's disappearance. The note had reassured them briefly but when eight and then nine and finally ten o'clock had chimed, they had begun to panic. The alarm bells had further distressed them, for they wondered if Dallas had been involved in whatever strange doings were happening outside.

It was not an easy recital; while recounting the discussion about Fraser's family her mind's eye kept picturing what had happened afterwards. She could almost feel his hands on her breasts and that probing knee between her thighs. It took great effort to keep her narrative going, and when she finished, Glennie expressed displeasure.

"If Father had wanted to tell us about Iain Fraser, he would have done it long ago. As for going to Fraser's house unescorted, well, that was hardly sensible—and most unlike you, Dallas."

Dallas started to make a sharp retort, but instead she turned on her heel and stalked up to bed. Yet sleep proved elusive. Why after such a nerve-wracked evening did she feel wide awake? And restless?

Vexed by her unsettled state, she got up and went to the window. The city lay in darkness, as patches of cloud rolled across the sliver of a moon. "You enjoyed it far more than you'll admit ...." Fraser had said. What unspeakable drivel! She had despised his touch, loathed his kisses, hated the very sight of him turning her into a trifle for his lustful pleasures. Admit that she enjoyed it! Dallas would as soon admit she'd enjoyed a hanging on the Gallows Tree in Liberton's Wynd. Unless it was Fraser who was being hanged, she told herself fiercely.

Resolutely she marched back to bed and tucked the covers under her chin.

After a few moments, her hands strayed to her breasts, the breasts that Iain Fraser had fondled and kissed. Oh, Jesu, she whispered in a shaky tone, I did not enjoy it! She turned over quickly and muffled her face in the pillow. It was well past two when she finally slept, though she woke up several times before the wan winter light broke over the city.

"IS HE REALLY as dreadful as Glennie says?" Tarrill asked in a low voice the next morning as she and Dallas sat munching their bannock cakes.

Dallas shrugged. "I told you, I went to seek information, not to assess Iain Fraser's masculine magnetism." She chewed vigorously on her bannock and wished Tarrill would stop watching her so closely.

"And my Lord Bothwell? Is he as dashing as we hear?" Tarrill's eyes darted towards the hallway where Glennie was busily polishing the oak floor.

"He's not much taller than you," Dallas replied. "And his ears stick out, if you must know."

"Oh." Tarrill was obviously disappointed.

"I'll tell you one thing, though," Dallas added fiercely as she shoved a bannock cake through a small puddle of syrup, "Iain Fraser eats a great deal better than we do."

"Now, Dallas, Marthe does her best ...." But Tarrill was interrupted by the sound of the front door opening and voices drifting into the kitchen. She cocked her head to see if she could make out their visitor's identity. "It's John Hamilton," she breathed, getting up quickly from the table and rushing into the hallway.

Dallas rolled her eyes heavenwards but continued eating her bannocks. Ordinarily, she would be glad to see Hamilton but after the encounter last night in Gosford's Close she was uneasy at his visit.

Both Tarrill and Glennie were in the kitchen doorway. "Lord Hamilton would speak with you," Glennie announced coolly. She was still vexed with Dallas for the previous night's adventure.

"Well, show him in then," Dallas said.

"Not in the kitchen," Glennie hissed. "You can't entertain a fine lord like John Hamilton here!"

"Since there's no fire yet laid in the sitting room, where should I entertain him?" Dallas shot back. "On the front stoop?"

Glennie sighed with annoyance and went back to fetch Hamilton. He bowed as ceremoniously as if he had been in the royal presence chamber and sat down in the chair opposite Dallas.

"I hope you've breakfasted, my lord," Dallas said, polishing off the last mouthful of bannock. "If not, perhaps Marthe can ...."

But Hamilton waved the idea of food away. "Nay, nay, I ate early this morning. But thank you just the same. Ah," he sighed, "bannocks. I haven't tasted those since my old nurse used to make them for me twenty years ago."

Dallas was about to say that if he lived in the Cameron house he'd taste them until he had no taste left, but she decided to behave more graciously. Hamilton cut an exceptionally fine figure this morning, in a dark blue doublet trimmed with white silk and the familiar plaid draped over his broad shoulders.

"You've heard what happened last night?" he asked at last, when he realized Dallas wasn't going to respond to his earlier comment.

But Dallas was slow to reply again; she felt no responsibility to shield the rakish Earl of Bothwell—but for some perverse reason she felt it necessary to protect Fraser. Dallas decided on an uncompromising fib: "Half the city has heard by now. Alison Craik hardly seems worth such a fuss."

Hamilton gave a slight shake of his head. "That may be. But my brother Arran is fond of her and he has vowed vengeance on Bothwell in particular. It is an unfortunate situation. My brother is ...." He paused, searching for the right word. "My brother does not always use good judgment. He ... he tends to be very emotional."

"That's a pity. In the climate of court politics, such reactions may one day get him into serious trouble." Dallas spoke rather stiffly, hoping that the discussion of Arran would divert Hamilton from asking her exactly how she had learned of the episode.

But Hamilton appeared to be as stiff and tense as she. "How true. I've long been afraid that he will undo himself by such rash actions as he now plans."

Dallas was about to offer some words of commiseration when Hamilton swiftly changed the subject: "You were at Fraser's town house last night, weren't you?"

The questioning look in his brown eyes caught Dallas off-guard. Her first reaction, inspired by her customary streak of perversity, was to refuse him an explanation. But he was a kind, decent man; she could not be rude or contrary with John Hamilton.

"I supped there," she replied, twirling the frayed linen napkin and trying to sound as if supping at Iain Fraser's was commonplace to her. And then, seeing the unexpected look of pain on his face, Dallas attempted to extricate herself. " 'Twas an unusual situation—-you may recall that he came here when my father ...."

But Hamilton cut her short. "Everything about Iain Fraser is unusual. I suppose," he went on with an uncustomary note of asperity in his voice, "that's part of his charm."

Dallas spread the napkin taut in her lap, pulling it so hard that the material gave way at the worn centerfold. "It wasn't his so-called charm which induced me to go there," she asserted boldly enough but could not look Hamilton in the eye. "It had to do with a business investment—and another matter." The "other matter" she would not reveal to him; it would sound as if she lacked faith in his ability to help her and her sisters. It also sounded like a very feeble excuse for visiting Iain Fraser.

Hamilton had turned away from her, the proud profile etched against the blackened stones of the fireplace. "Your reasons may have seemed sound enough at the time. Yet going boldly to his town house and supping with a man who ..." He swerved in the chair, leaning forward with the palms of his hands against the table. "Did he ... harm you, Dallas?"

"Harm me!" she burst out. "Why certainly not! You think I'd permit Iain Fraser to take liberties with my person?" Dallas felt herself blushing furiously and decided that the best way of fending off Hamilton's all too prescient queries was to become as indignant as possible. "Really, my lord! You have no right to presume such a dastardly thing!"

Hamilton looked wounded; he also appeared as if he wanted very much to believe Dallas's protestations. "Forgive me," he said, getting up from the chair and putting a hand on her shoulder. "You're quite correct, I have no right to ask such impertinent questions."

"Your concern is not unappreciated." Dallas hoped the prim response would close the issue. She noted that he gave her shoulder a very gentle squeeze before his hand dropped to his side; she also noted with dismay that he was bowing and saying he must be off.

"I must not intrude on your morning any longer," he said in a very formal tone, and before Dallas could speak again, Hamilton strode out of the kitchen. She hesitated a moment, then raced after him, but he was down the steps and into the close before she got to the stoop. Whirling back into the house, she angrily slammed the door with her backside and cursed the footprints John Hamilton had left on Glennie's newly polished floor.

For the rest of the morning, Dallas's mood remained so stormy that both Glennie and Tarrill avoided her. It was only in the early afternoon when a messenger arrived at the door with a small package for Dallas that Tarrill summoned the courage to approach her sister.

"A man brought this for you," Tarrill said, proffering the package to Dallas. "There's a note attached."

Dallas had been washing the sitting room windows, scrubbing with all her strength, heedless of the soap she was wasting. She glanced at Tarrill, wiped her reddened hands, and took the package from her sister. Glennie had come into the room and stood behind Tarrill as Dallas unfolded the note. It was brief: "You must understand and forgive my reticence. You must also forgive the untimely intrusion on our discussion. Perhaps this small token will appease you. Iain." Dallas hesitated, then thrust the note into Glennie's hand.

Glennie's lips moved slightly as she read through the note. "This sounds most strange," she said, daring to ignite Dallas's temper. But she knew her sister well and Fraser scarcely at all. "I'm sorry, Dallas, I spoke unkindly last night."

"You were worried," Dallas grumbled but seemed mollified, though inwardly cursing Fraser for the cryptic reference to his attempt at ravishing her.

"Open the package, Dallas," Tarrill urged, taking the note from Glennie. Dallas unwrapped the parcel so slowly that Tarrill had an urge to snatch it away and undo it herself. Finally Dallas lifted the lid of the little wooden box as her sisters leaned forward to see what was inside.

Perched on a tiny cushion of satin was a dazzlingly wrought silver bracelet. It was worked in the design of King Neptune with mermaids and fishes holding court beside him. Dallas stared as hard as her sisters at the bracelet's artful design and delicate craftsmanship.

"Oh, Dallas," gasped Tarrill, "I've never seen anything so lovely!"

Glennie took the bracelet from Dallas and held it by the window for a better look. "Beautiful," she breathed. "Beautiful!"

Dallas was eyeing the bracelet with a pained expression. "It should fetch a fair price, at any rate."

Her sisters gaped at her. "Dallas!" exclaimed Glennie. "You couldn't sell a gift! It wouldn't be right!"

"Fie," snapped Dallas, "since when can we afford sentimentality? Fraser's loan won't last forever, so I'll augment it with his gift. I'll take it to Master Herriot, the goldsmith, as soon as I can. Put it back in the box, Glennie, before something happens to it."

Glennie obeyed reluctantly and left the room to tend to her sons who were quarreling over a toy drum. Tarrill held the note out to Dallas. "He signed it 'Iain.' Please, Dallas, you can tell me."

"Ninny," her sister scoffed, snatching the note and shredding it into the fireplace. And Fraser was a ninny twice over if he thought to soften her attitude with extravagant baubles.

Master Herriot grudgingly gave Dallas seven marks for the bracelet. She'd had to wrangle, badger, berate and even threaten to get that much; Master Herriot drove a hard bargain.

After leaving the goldsmith's shop, she debated whether or not to buy some Christmas trinkets. They were going to Dunbar for the holidays, to stay with Glennie's McVurrich in-laws, Oliver and Annie. Yes, she must take some presents along, if only as a gesture of gratitude for their hosts' hospitality. And if she had gifts for the McVurrichs then she must have something for her own kin and Marthe. After all, seven marks was not an inconsiderable sum and, along with the remaining marks from Fraser's loan, should last well into spring, if they were cautious.

Two days before Christmas, Donald McVurrich arrived to bring the girls and Marthe and the children back to his parents' home in Dunbar. It hadn't snowed for the past four days in Edinburgh, and Donald, in his laconic manner, had informed them that the road between the capital and Dunbar was passable.

They left the following morning, traveling slowly over the snow-covered roads. The sky was heavy and grey, but they made the day-long journey without running into new snow. By the time they reached the McVurrich cottage, it was dark and the wind was blowing in from the North Sea. Daniel and Jamie, who had each ridden pillion behind Donald and Glennie, were almost asleep when they reached the house, but as soon as their aunt and uncle came outside, their eyes brightened and their voices grew shrill with excitement.

The McVurrichs had worked hard to put their cottage into a festive holiday mood. Pine boughs hung over the door, extra rushlights blazed on the hearth, and a holly wreath adorned the grey stone of the fireplace. Oliver McVurrich had even relaxed his Protestant views enough to permit a wassail bowl for Christmas Eve.

Annie had borrowed enough bedding and straw pallets from the neighbors so that everyone could sleep in the house. It was too cold to put the children in the barn as they had done on previous visits. But Glennie was so insistent that the McVurrichs not give up their own bed that they relented and allowed the three girls to sleep on the floor with Marthe and the children.

On Christmas Day they ate roast goose with a savory stuffing and buttered carrots with dried parsley and freshly baked bread as white as the snow outside the cottage doors. The Cameron girls had not eaten so well in months and all three had hearty appetites. Annie watched them with great satisfaction, not realizing that deprivation as much as her good cooking made them doubly appreciative of their Christmas meal.

"You girls eat like sailors," she laughed, putting bowls of raisin-and-rye pudding before them. "Have ye room for this, too?"

"Oh, yes," beamed Tarrill. "It looks wonderful!"

"Speaking of sailors," Oliver began, "have any of you heard of the strange ship which is said to sail these waters?"

Dallas looked up from her pudding. "Nay, what manner of vessel is she?"

"A carrack," replied Oliver. "I've not seen her myself, but Coltie, the burn-the-wind, says he has, twice. Looked up from his forge and there she was, out on the horizon, in full sail and racing the wind. The second time he saw her from the beach, where he'd gone to gather firewood." He shrugged. "But Coltie has been known to tell a bonnie tale now and again."

"I believe him," put in Donald. The others turned toward the blond-haired youth who was usually so quiet. "Why not?" he challenged, his brown skin growing even darker under his elders' stares.

"Could be other explanations, laddie, mayhap an English spy ship," his mother said, taking her place next to her husband. "The days of the Vikings are long past."

Dallas found the conversation somewhat soporific. The cramped space around the wooden trestle table hemmed her in, the smell of goose fat turning rancid assailed her nostrils, and she felt a sudden urge to get out of the cottage and into the fresh air. She could not walk the familiar streets of Edinburgh here but she could explore the countryside for an hour or so and exercise both her body and her disposition.

She slipped off the end of the long bench where she had been sitting next to the McVurrichs' youngest son, Davie. "Excuse me, all, I'm going to catch a breath of air. Mayhap I'll take one of the horses we brought with us out for a brisk canter."

"You'll not canter much in the snow," Oliver said. "But go, lassie, if you've a mind to it."

Dallas was putting on her cloak when Donald came to join her at the door. "Mayhap you'd prefer company," he said tentatively.

It was the last thing Dallas did prefer, but she smiled at the young man. "Nay, I'd not take you from your family on Christmas Day." Noting the disappointment in his blue eyes, she added, "But come with me to your barn and help me saddle Gala."

They walked the short distance in silence. Once inside Gala's stall, Donald worked quickly and efficiently, pausing only to pat the big grey's neck after he had slipped the bit into her mouth.

"Will you be a weaver like your father?" Dallas asked as Donald led Gala out of the stall.

He gave her a swift, close look. "Nay, I'm no good at the loom. My hands and feet get all a-tangle."

"You might find a place at court, you know. The Queen can use all the loyal men she can find. How old are you, Donald?"

"I'll be twenty in March." He stared down at the mare's heavy hooves. "Is the Queen truly bonnie?" he finally asked.

"Oh, yes, very."

But Donald shook his blond head. "My father'd thump me if I ever went off to serve a Papist sovereign."

"He'd have to catch you first," said Dallas with a wry smile.

That thought had apparently not occurred to Donald. "Aye," he replied slowly, "he would, wouldn't he?" His mouth spread into a grin.

Dallas made no further comment but swung herself up into the saddle and flicked the reins. "Come along, Gala," she urged. The horse ambled out of the barn as Donald stood by the doorway, watching until Dallas and her mount had disappeared over a snow-covered hillock on the far side of the McVurrichs' field.

The going was relatively easy, for the snow had frozen underneath and provided firm footing. Dallas kept Gala to a docile trot, lest they take a nasty spill. She guided the horse along the sea coast, southeast of the town. To the east, she could make out St. Abb's head; behind her was the harbor, where the herring boats lay wintering under heavy canvas. It was rocky going and she had to slow her mount to a walk, but the view of the water was unimpaired. The waves tossed quietly, grey as the sky above, merging on the horizon so that Dallas could not tell where the sea ended and the heavens began.

She felt refreshed already. The chilled air was vivifying, and there was no sign of human habitation after she left the cluster of cottages at Dunbar's edge. Soon, it began to snow with large, wet flakes drifting across her path. Dallas decided to turn back before the snow got too heavy, and reining Gala around, she headed straight for Dunbar and the McVurrich cottage. By the time they had gone about a mile, the flakes were coming down so thick and fast that Dallas could hardly see beyond her horse's head.

She wondered if there was a path down to the shore where the footing would be easier. Proceeding very cautiously, she kept heading in what she hoped was the right direction, and after another ten minutes the snow let up just enough to reveal an opening in the crags which lined the cliff above the shore. Guided by the sound of the waves, she dismounted and led Gala through the rocks. The mare stumbled once and almost went down. Dallas brushed the snow from her face with a shaky hand and patted the horse. "It's all right," she coaxed, "we'll be all right."

She wondered whether the horse could sense the lack of conviction in her voice. Out of breath and unsure of where the path would lead them, Dallas stopped to lean against the mare's heavy sides. Her uneasiness was somewhat dissipated by the horse's solid presence. Dallas stamped her feet and rubbed her hands to keep the circulation going. The northerly wind was blowing the snow in a horizontal direction, thoroughly soaking Dallas's cloak and dress.

They had come out onto a narrow path, some twenty feet above the shoreline. Up ahead, Dallas could make out a steep path which led down to a lagoon. It would be risky but worth trying if she could only maneuver them onto the level footing. But just as she started leading Gala down the path her toe struck a jutting stone and she fell heavily against a small boulder which gave way and plummeted into the lagoon.

Gala shied and neighed shrilly. Dallas scrambled to her feet, unhurt but shaken. She grappled at the reins, then peered into the opening made by the fallen rock. Her eyes widened and her mouth fell open at the sight only a few yards below her: The lagoon led into a large cave, until now completely hidden from sight. And inside the cave, bobbing on the restless waters, was a ship. Her sails were lowered and no flag flew from the topmast. Dallas stared in wonder.

Then she saw the two men who stood at the rail of the half-deck. One of them held a pistol which was aimed directly at Dallas. His voice came over very clear across the water: "Don't move!" he shouted. "Stand as you are!"

Dallas could not have moved if she'd wanted to. Fear, now coupled with astonishment and curiosity, overwhelmed her. She stood motionless as two more men appeared, coming up from the main deck to lower a small boat over the side. Dallas realized they were coming after her and it would not take more than a minute or two to reach the strip of land below her perch on the narrow path. She dared not risk ducking behind one of the rocks, for the man with the pistol still held his weapon on her, ready to fire. Gala stood at her side, nervously pawing the snow-covered path.

The men had already reached the thin strip of shore. They jumped out of the boat and scurried up the short, jagged cliff. A few seconds later they stood in front of her and one of them grabbed her by the arms.

"Who are you?" demanded the shorter of the two in an accented voice.

"Let go!" Dallas demanded, making a vain effort to free herself.

"Nay, the captain takes care of meddlers," the second man countered. He was a Scot, of medium height and wiry build.

They pulled Dallas off the path and half-carried her down the little cliff. As they were putting her into the boat one of the men on the half-deck called out:

"The captain knows about the intruder. Hurry it up!"

The foreigner held Dallas against the side of the little boat while the Scot plied the oars. She did not struggle, for the pistol was still trained on her. Her heart thudded in her breast—would these rough seamen kill her for the unwitting discovery of their ship's hiding place? Better to have frozen to death than to suffer this shame, she thought bitterly.

More men gathered on the decks as the small boat was hoisted back up to the mother ship. Dallas felt their malevolent eyes on her, and as one of them pulled her on the deck another muttered, "Pity to harm such a bonnie wench."

Dallas felt faint. Her feet would not obey her bidding, and the foreigner had to steer her in the direction of the captain's quarters. She stumbled as the ship rolled and would have fallen except for the man's tight grip on her right arm.

Dizzily, Dallas watched the men swing open the hatch. Pirates were said to be vicious, ruthless creatures who dealt as mercilessly with women as with men. If their captain were half as menacing as his crew—but of course he would be the worst of all, the most callous when it came to pillage, plunder, rape and murder. Through a blur Dallas saw the hatch to the captain's cabin swing wide and hazily looked up to see Iain Fraser towering over her.

"Good Christ!" Fraser exploded. To the onlookers clustered in the companionway it was difficult to tell who was more astonished—their captain or their captive.

"Oh, Iain!" Dallas felt the foreigner let go of her bruised arm as she pitched forward in astonishment, catching herself on a fine ebony table.

Fraser was giving angry orders to his crew to disperse. From somewhere behind her, Dallas heard their reluctant footsteps as the cabin door banged shut. To her amazement she realized she was laughing almost hysterically.

Fraser reached down and pulled her towards him, shaking her with a rage that turned her numb, tearing the sodden fabric of her shabby mourning dress with the sheer force of his grip.

"Meddling slut! Have you been paid to spy on me? Is that how you plan to make your fortune?"

Dallas made an effort to deny his accusation, but the violent shaking motions rendered speech impossible. At last she went limp and fell against him. The vile oaths stopped at once and she felt herself being picked up and carried somewhere soft and warm. When she tremulously opened her eyes, Fraser was standing over her, holding out a cup of wine.

"Here," he said, the anger still flashing in his eyes, "drink this."

Though her teeth had begun to chatter, Dallas did as she was bidden, then sank back onto what she recognized as the captain's bunk. Forcing her eyes to focus, she took in the rest of her surroundings.

The cabin was small but lavishly appointed, much in the style of Fraser's town house. A Turkish carpet covered the deck but the furniture seemed to have been acquired from all over the civilized world, including a latten and mahogany Italian writing desk, a French armoire, a Flemish sea chest, and wall hangings which Dallas thought might have come from Araby.

She took another drink from the cup and then sank back onto the furs. The shaking was beginning to ease up but her head ached furiously. "I feel sick," she said in a voice she scarcely recognized.

"You ought to," Fraser snapped. "By God, I can't believe this has happened." He paced the cabin deck, his hands clenched tightly behind his back.

"Iain, I'm going to be sick!"

"Oh, Christ!" he exploded, but hurried to fetch a basin from the nightstand. "Here, I'll hold your silly head." But Dallas didn't lose her stomach after all. Somehow, with Fraser kneeling beside her and his big hand firmly supporting her forehead, she felt much improved. At last she waved both him and the basin away, collapsed again onto the furs and let out an enormous sigh.

"So this is how you've acquired your wealth, Iain Fraser," she said finally, and though her voice sounded normal, there was wonder in her tone.

"Aye," he replied shortly, putting the basin away. "Why not? As an orphaned bastard, I had to make my fortune some way."

"You've fared right well," Dallas said. "By what sanction do you plunder?"

Fraser sat down opposite her in the Spanish armchair. He was dressed as a sailor, in a white cambric shirt with a black leather vest and black hose. He wore long calfskin boots and the ever-present dirk. "None, now. But my original expeditions were approved by Marie de Guise." He spoke more naturally now, but Dallas could tell by the tenseness of his jaw muscles that he was still angry.

She allowed him to pour her another cup of wine after he had poured one for himself. The history of his adventures interested her very little in comparison with her own predicament. In less than ten minutes, Dallas had experienced terror, relief and an intense physical reaction. Though her stomach had calmed down, her head still ached and her arms hurt. She was afraid again, but it was a different kind of fear. The horror of being raped by a dozen sailors and condemned to death by their captain was gone. For all his faults, Fraser would hardly murder someone he knew, especially, Dallas reasoned somewhat illogically, someone who owed him money.

But Fraser's hawklike gaze was unflinching and Dallas's anxiety increased. Abruptly he stood up, flinging his wine cup onto the ebony table, sloshing the remaining contents over the dark wood's gleaming finish. "Good God, why did it have to be you, Dallas?" He shook his head several times and resumed pacing the cabin. The ship gave another lurch, sending the wine cup clattering to the deck. Fraser, who kept his balance without apparent effort, paid no heed.

"Would it be so dreadful if people knew you were a pirate?" Dallas asked.

He turned on his heel and stared at her, a faint smile tugging at the corners of his mouth. "I mislike the idea of hanging, if that's what you mean. Oh, the Queen might be lenient, but her half-brother, James Stuart, and his ilk would give her little opportunity to display any kindness. This isn't a game, Dallas," he went on, the cool hazel eyes watching her steadily. "Do you know what they do to pirates? They hang them in chains, along the water's edge at Leith. It's an ugly death and I've no mind to end that way."

"Jesu," Dallas murmured, but he appeared not to hear her. They were both silent for several moments until Dallas asked, "Why would a powerful man like James Stuart want to destroy you? He has his own wealth secured."

Fraser's mouth clamped shut in a long, lean line. Frowning deeply, he came back to sit by the bunk. "It's the old story of Scots rivalries and one I greatly detest." He paused, seemed about to say something, apparently changed his mind, then continued. "Look at Bothwell—now the Hamiltons are after his hide."

Dallas sat up, her legs dangling over the edge of the bunk. "Where did you get this ship?" She had decided it was wise to play for time, since each passing moment seemed to have a pacifying effect on Fraser.

"Three years ago I went to the Continent to pay my respects to Mary Stuart in the event that she would one day return to Scotland. From France, I went to Italy and in Venice I saw this ship. I won her at dice." He smiled at her astonished look. "Oh, it was not as casual as it sounds. I had long thought that piracy would be a lucrative career, so I sought out the ship's owner, discovered that he was a man who gambled and drank, usually at the same time, and determined that when the stakes got high enough I'd demand his ship instead of money. I won."

"You sailed her back to Scotland then?"

"Nay, I had repairs made in Venice and then hired a crew primarily made up of Italians—that was one of them, Corelli, who brought you aboard. We sailed to the Isle of Lewes where I have some property."

"Barvas," murmured Dallas.

"What? Oh, aye, that's how I named my horse. It's a spot little visited by anyone, much like this cave—until now." He sighed. "Dammit, Dallas, you make decisions difficult for me."

"If you really intend to do away with me, you could just let me sit here in these soaked clothes and I'll die on my own, thank you." She had regained her self-confidence and with it, her temper.

"I've got the crew to think of, too, Dallas," he declared. "What assurance have I that you won't babble? I've not noticed discretion as one of your strong points."

"Does your ship have a name?" Dallas asked, ignoring his last remark.

"I christened her *La Richezza*." He was beginning to sound impatient. "That's Italian for riches."

One of Dallas's mad, wild plans was starting to take root. She wondered if she could live up to her own daring. "What manner of ship is this?" she asked, stalling for yet more time to pluck up her courage.

"A carrack. Fast enough to outmaneuver any merchant ship and most man-of-war vessels but sufficiently sturdy to sail these heavy North Seas. Now listen, Dallas, if you're keeping me occupied in the hope that someone is going to race to your rescue, think again. It would take a small army to capture this ship—-and they'd never discover her in the first place."

He rose and poured himself more wine. All his life he'd faced various crises with a reasonable amount of aplomb, but this one was fraught with extraordinary complexities, not the least of which was Dallas herself. The ship swayed again but less violently this time. He glanced at Dallas and frowned at the outline of her breasts under the wet gown and the bare flesh of her shoulders where the fabric had torn. "Damn all," he cursed under his breath.

"Not all women babble," Dallas said quietly. "I know all about your secret passageway, but I've never told a soul." It was a reckless move, but it hit home. He reached out as if to grab her by the arm but instead let his hand fall back to his side. "There's no torture chamber under your house, Iain, and I'll wager there never was," she went on, taking advantage of her surprise tactic. "Mungo Tennant was probably a pirate or a smuggler, too, and circulated that rumor to divert suspicion from his real activities. Until recently, I'd forgotten the old stories about the secret passageways and the noises we used to hear in our cellar. But why have I just begun to hear them again in the past few months?"

Fraser had recovered his equanimity. "Because I've only lived there since the spring. It took some time to shore up the old tunnel and make it safe for transport. Although at one time the whole north side of Edinburgh was honeycombed with such passages, Mungo Tennant's house was the only one on the south side with a tunnel clear through to the Nor' Loch. I'd learned that somewhere, and had waited for over two years to buy that place." He paused to gaze somberly at Dallas. "We've conversed long enough. How can I make certain you won't betray me?"

Dallas was acting totally on instinct. She propped herself up on one elbow and met Fraser's stare head-on. "It's quite simple. We will strike a bargain, you and I."

She saw his shoulders tense. "You think you're in a position to bargain with me, Dallas?"

The fear came back, but she fought it down. Yet she could not help glancing at his long, brown hands, realizing that he could, in an instant, snap her neck like a chicken's and leave her lost to the world forever. Still, she had to plunge forward and take the chance that she had judged him rightly. "I will never give your secret away, Iain—if you agree to wed with me."

Iain Fraser would have looked no more stunned if she had asked him to sail the *Richezza* straight to the moon. Then his expression changed as he threw back his head and roared with laughter. Dallas pulled herself to a full sitting position, clutching the furs to her breast while her cheeks turned hot.

"You're the one who put the idea of a rich husband into my head in the first place! Is wedding me such a mirth-provoking suggestion?"

He shook his head, helpless with laughter. "Nay, nay," he finally gasped. "But it's not the way I imagined you'd pay off your debt. Your calculating little mind works in swift steps, lassie." The laughter subsided and he looked at her in disbelief.

Dallas hadn't even thought about the debt. She could demand its cancelation and nothing more. But permanent security dangled temptingly before her. "I'd prefer not to be the one to wed. But we can't live forever on your loan. It's quite simple, Iain—your secret will be safe and my sisters and I will be provided for."

The practical tone employed by Dallas evinced admiration from Fraser. The wench had courage and common sense. It was his turn to stall for time. "You sold the bracelet, of course."

"Aye." Dallas inadvertently glanced at her wrist as if she could picture Fraser's gift adorning her flesh. But all she saw was the faint scar from her tumble on the flagstones in Gosford's Close.

Fraser stood up, fingering the dirk at his side. "So you'd wed with me to ensure your family's future." He went over to the ebony table and poured himself yet another cup of wine.

"We can live separately," Dallas was saying in reasonable tones. "You can keep your mistresses and go your own way. If I have my income and perhaps a place at court to help my sisters find suitable husbands, I shall be quite content."

Fraser was silent for a long time. Dallas watched him drink his wine and make circular patterns with his finger on the tabletop. Have I gone too far? she asked herself. Why would he agree to my bargain when he could so easily solve the problem by silencing me forever?

Apparently, Fraser was sharing her thoughts. "I have alternative choices, Dallas." He stood just out of the lantern light so that his eyes were in shadow. "I can arrange it so you never leave this ship alive." Though his voice lacked inflection, he paused just long enough to let the renewed threat sink in. "I can buy your silence without marriage. Or I could even sail away from Scotland and never return."

"You'd not do that. A Highlander always comes home." Dallas's reflex response caught Fraser off-guard, though she could not see his expression clearly. But his momentary silence gave her the courage to continue. "Nor would paying me to keep quiet guarantee either of us what we want. If Glennie or Tarrill marry well, I could betray you at will. As for my part, if anything should happen to you, my income ceases forthwith."

Fraser was pacing again. "You've not alluded to my first option."

Dallas licked her lips and stifled a sneeze. "You wouldn't harm me, Iain. I know you wouldn't."

He strode the length of the cabin twice before coming back to the bunk. For the first time, Dallas noted that he was so tall his head just missed touching the top of the cabin. "If there's one thing I can understand, it's survival," he said, holding out a big hand to Dallas. "You have your bargain, lassie."

PART TWO

Chapter Six

IAIN FRASER PROVIDED his betrothed with an escort back to Dunbar. The foreign sailor, Corelli, and a Welshman named Evans were chosen for the task. Their attitude, along with that of the other crew members, had changed greatly towards Dallas. When their captain had brought her up on deck and introduced her as his future bride, the initial reaction was sullen. But they respected Fraser, many of them almost worshiped him for his bravery and daring. He was shrewd, he was fair, and above all, he was a superb seaman. And a man ought to take a wife; a different wench in every port was well enough but it was good to come home to the same woman.

So they cheered their captain and the bedraggled girl who stood at his side. Not exactly a fine lady, but no doubt comely enough under the grime and shabby clothes. Oh, she had surprised the captain, but wenches enjoyed doing that sort of thing. No need to worry about her giving their secret away—if their captain's identity were revealed, his wealth would be forfeit to the Crown, leaving the little lass a penniless widow.

When Dallas arrived at the McVurrich cottage, just as the pale sun was setting, she was greeted with great tumult. Corelli and Evans had left her on the other side of the hillock which bordered the McVurrich farm. It would be easier to explain her prolonged absence if they were not around.

But the truth would not do. "When the storm came, Gala and I happened to be by an abandoned croft. We just waited until the snow stopped."

"But the storm didn't last more than half an hour," Glennie pointed out. "Why did it take you so long?"

"I got lost," Dallas replied glibly. "Finally, a couple of young men came by and set me aright."

Glennie appeared satisfied. But she made Dallas promise not to go off alone during the remainder of their visit. The next two days passed pleasantly enough, with Oliver commandeering a neighbor's sleigh for a ride through the snow-covered fields. On the morning of the twenty-eighth, the McVurrichs waved them off with a mixture of tears and laughter. Donald accompanied them again, and by the time they reached Edinburgh that evening, a freezing rain was slashing down on the city. Wearily, the little group carried their belongings into the Cameron house. They set about lighting candles and building a fire in the kitchen grate while Marthe tucked the boys into bed. Donald spent the night, but although Glennie and Tarrill pressed him to stay over for another day, he refused. His parents would fret, he said, and by nine o'clock the next morning, he was on his way home.

"A good lad," Glennie said after his departure. "But he must get away from Dunbar. Neither weaving nor farming suits him."

"Happily, they have three other boys," Tarrill commented as she poured water over the breakfast dishes. "No doubt one of them will stay on to help Oliver."

"I hope so. Of course my Jamie never liked it on the farm, either. That's why we moved to Edinburgh," Glennie said in a reminiscent tone.

Dallas had been sitting in silence at the table while her sisters cleaned up the kitchen. "Glennie, Tarrill," she called out, interrupting their amiable family discussion. "I'm going to wed Iain Fraser."

Dishes clattered in the sink as Tarrill whirled around. Glennie gripped a meal sack so hard that the weave was impressed on her palms. Then they were both exclaiming at once, dashing across the kitchen to ply Dallas with questions.

Dallas remained calm and would say no more until her sisters quieted down. "The wedding is set for January twenty-eighth, the feast of St. Thomas Aquinas. Iain is of the old faith and somehow we'll find a priest to wed us."

When Dallas paused, Tarrill and Glennie again began chattering simultaneously. "But you sold his bracelet," Tarrill cried. "You don't know him well enough," Glennie objected.

"We've seen each other several times," Dallas said matter-of-factly. "And I sold the bracelet before I knew we were to be wed."

Her sisters were silent for a moment. Then Glennie reached out and took Dallas's hand. "Do you love him?"

Glennie felt Dallas flinch. " 'Tis not always a matter of love where marriages are concerned." She gazed at Glennie and then at Tarrill. "We will not be poor again, and that's what matters. Now let's speak of other things."

ON THE SECOND Monday of January, Iain Fraser formally called on his bride-to-be. Marthe watched fretfully as Fraser made conversation with his future in-laws. Tarrill seemed diffident and Glennie appeared ill-at-ease. The two boys, however, were delighted by their prospective uncle and reveled in his teasing. At last, the family tactfully withdrew to give the couple a few moments alone.

Although Dallas had been busy with preparations for the wedding, she had not given much thought to the groom. Indeed, she had found it much easier not to think about him at all. But as they faced each other in the faint January light of the parlor Dallas had to admit that she was very nervous.

"So the happy couple can now dither in privacy over the nuptials," Fraser said, settling himself into a chair by the fireplace. "Are you dithering, Dallas?"

Dallas turned defensive. "I'm making the appropriate plans, if that's what you mean."

Fraser rubbed at the bridge of his hawklike nose. His silence made Dallas even more nervous. But when he finally spoke, his words were matter-of-fact: "I understand you've been out shopping. Is there anything left on the shelves of Edinburgh's merchants?"

Dallas tossed her head and smoothed the new yellow gown she'd purchased only that morning. "Our late father would not want us to go on wearing black before such a momentous occasion as my marriage. And, of course, I have to arrange some sort of trousseau in keeping with your status."

"My status is not that of Holy Roman Emperor, however," he reminded Dallas caustically. Seeing the fire banking in her eyes, he grinned. "Stay, lassie, I've no mind to spoil your fun. Just don't push too far. Cummings will see to the bills. Meanwhile," he went on, taking a small leather pouch from his doublet, "in case you've spent all my loan, here's a little something for your household expenses."

Dallas took the purse, gingerly weighing its contents. The gesture was not lost on Fraser. "What's your family's old war cry?" he asked. " 'Sons of the hounds, come here and get flesh.' You've got yours, Dallas. Don't gloat so."

"I'm not gloating!" Dallas stood up with an outraged swish of yellow silk. "You're the one who keeps making me sound greedy!"

Fraser stood up, too, one long finger brushing the end of her nose. "I'd like to tarry longer and listen to you shriek at me, but I must be gone."

Though Dallas had pulled back at his touch, she refused to let him have the last word. She followed him out to the doorway, searching for an appropriate parting sally. "You mentioned family mottoes," she called after him. "You were right about our family's, but mayhap you don't recall my clan's byword: 'Touch not the cat without a glove.' You'd best remember that, Iain Fraser."

His hand was on the latch, but he turned his level gaze on her. In two easy strides he was in front of Dallas, his arms stretched out, the palms of his hands resting on the wall behind her. He leaned down so that his face almost, but not quite, touched hers. And he remained thus for a full minute while Dallas stared helplessly up into his eyes.

"I'm remembering," he said, and suddenly withdrew his hands from the wall and wheeled around towards the door. He had not touched her, yet Dallas felt as if the whole weight of his body had come crushing down upon her.

FOR THE NEXT hour, she put her betrothed out of her mind. Alone in her bedroom, Dallas sorted through her trousseau for the third time. The splendid silks, rich brocades, handsome lawn and delicate laces delighted her. Never had Dallas owned one dress half as fine as the least of these. She smiled to herself as she twirled a garnet-encrusted cap in her hands. Clever, her father had called her—and so she was, to contrive such an ingenious way of saving her family from an uncertain future. Not only would she be admitted to the court circle but under her agreement with Fraser, Dallas could maintain her independence. An ideal situation for them both—Fraser could dally with his paramours while Dallas would have all the financial security of a well-married woman without the conjugal responsibilities.

She put the little cap down on her bureau and picked up a pair of dark green calfskin shoes with the daintiest of heels. From some far chamber of her mind she could hear Fraser's voice saying, "Aye, lassie, but your shoes don't match." That had been their first encounter. Well, Dallas vowed, she'd never wear unmatched shoes again. But Fraser's voice continued to intrude; so did his lean, dark image. A sudden fear gripped her: What if he didn't intend to live up to his part of their bargain? Twice he had all but attacked her, plundering her mouth with his ferocious kisses, exploring her body with his hands and tongue—she dropped the shoes in agitation as that unaccustomed fire began to bank in the pit of her stomach.

But he had scarcely touched her aboard his ship. And heaven only knew, he could have ravished her on the spot and none of his crew would have lifted an eyebrow. Dallas frowned. The man was an enigma—perhaps in his way, as practical as she. Yes, that must be it, she decided, he was basically a shrewd, canny Scot like herself who knew how to separate business from pleasure. Satisfied with her rationale, Dallas immersed herself in her trousseau once more. Yet her delight had diminished; the fire in her stomach had turned to something else, something very like the familiar emptiness she had known too often and too well.

DALLAS AND IAIN Fraser were married shortly after midnight in an ancient stone chapel at the edge of the city. The clandestine rites were held in the presence of the immediate family, along with Marthe, Cummings and the Earl of Bothwell, and Walter and Fiona Ramsay who had traveled to Edinburgh for the occasion. The priest who conducted the traditional ceremony was old and frightened, but well rewarded by Fraser for his efforts.

Afterwards, the wedding party proceeded under the cover of darkness to Fraser's town house. They were stopped once by the watch at the city gates, but a sizeable bribe gained them reentry. A sumptuous wedding supper awaited them, laid out on a long oak trestle table in the formal dining salon.

As they feasted on venison, pheasant, roast pig and a variety of side dishes, the conversation flowed as freely as the wine. Dallas felt quite confident and infinitely proud of herself. She sat at the long table between her new husband and the Earl of Bothwell, who frequently leaned across her to make good-natured gibes at Fraser's newly married state. Caught up in her own euphoria, Dallas paid little heed to comments which might normally annoy her.

"Your envy in seeing me wed must reflect your own desire to attain marital bliss," Fraser commented to the Border Earl. "I marvel that you've remained a bachelor so long."

Bothwell chuckled and waved a wine bottle at Fraser. "There was a certain lady in Denmark some years ago—but that's a long and complicated story."

"It sounds most fascinating," Tarrill said from her place on Bothwell's left. She seemed quite intrigued by the dashing earl.

Bothwell lifted one square shoulder. "But not fit for your sweet ears, lass. When I do wed, she'll be the perfect wife, docile and mild, loving and sweet." He turned to Tarrill and pinched her cheek. "Does your sister here possess those qualities?"

This remark roused Dallas. "Fie, sir," she laughed, "I'd not care to be such a milksop as you describe. You don't want a wife, you want a pet pup."

The earl grinned at both Dallas and Fraser. "Your lady seems to have a mind of her own, Iain. I trust you'll know how to handle such independence."

Fraser said nothing. He merely smiled enigmatically and motioned for Kennedy to serve the burnt sugar cakes dipped with honey.

At last, as the candles dipped low in their silver sconces and Marthe dozed in her chair with Glennie's boys asleep at her feet, Fraser rose. "No need for you to escort us to our nuptial bed, good friends," he announced. "I know the way in my own house. Besides, it is very late and you must be as exhausted as yon laddies." He gave Dallas his arm and bowed to the company. The others did follow them, but only as far as the foot of the stairs where they lifted their glasses in one last toast. As Dallas preceded her husband up the winding staircase she heard Glennie call out: "God bless you, God bless you both!"

ONCE INSIDE THE bedroom, Dallas sank into a chair by the fireplace and kicked off her shoes. Her wedding gown was made of white satin with a stiff lace collar and matching lace at the cuffs. Glennie had piled her sister's hair high, in shining dark coils, and the transformation had evoked a smile of pleasure from Dallas when she had looked at herself in the mirror earlier that day. Indeed, she had discovered that her new affluence had a beneficial effect on her appearance. The trousseau on which she'd lavished Fraser's money created an effect which even Dallas had to admit was more than satisfying.

But except for one last admiring glance at herself in the dressing table mirror, Dallas's new wardrobe was not uppermost in her mind. It had been a long, eventful day and she was weary, if still exhilarated. She reached up absently to unpin the wispy veil from her hair and relaxed, studying the room itself. It was furnished comfortably, like the rest of the house, with touches of Continental elegance which Fraser had doubtless acquired through piracy. Her own belongings had been moved into the house that morning and had already been unpacked by Flora Campbell, the maid Fraser had hired to serve his new bride.

" 'Twas a wonderful meal," Dallas sighed, glancing at the big canopied bed which took up at least a third of the room. Its covers were turned down to reveal white sheets of the purest linen. Stifling a yawn, Dallas decided that the bed looked most inviting. "Oh, Lord, I am tired! I suppose you had best send for Flora."

Fraser had been poking at the coals in the fireplace grate. He looked up. "Flora? Why? Think you I can't undo the hooks of your gown myself?" He stood up, replaced the poker, and idly brushed a few stray crumbs from his dark blue doublet.

Dallas's hand froze on the gauzy veil. Surely he was teasing her, of course he understood this was no marriage in the true sense. She looked at the bed again, then hastily averted her eyes. "What do you mean? If Flora is asleep, I can undress myself."

"But I have no intention of letting you do that. Have you forgotten that we are now husband and wife?" The hazel eyes gleamed in the firelight as his indolent gaze surveyed Dallas from the top of her head down to the bare feet peeking out from under the satin hem.

Dallas took a deep breath and then forced herself to stay calm. He wasn't jesting, he was quite serious, she could see that in the set of his jaw. A sense of panic began to overtake Dallas as it dawned on her that the situation might be out of her control.

"Fie, Iain, we've gone through the ceremony, and that's that." Dallas stood up, turning back to the dressing table where she began brushing out her hair. The thick coils tumbled down over the lace collar onto her back. "We made a bargain, remember?" she said to the image in the mirror. "We agreed not to meddle with each other after the wedding. Perhaps you've had too much wine to recall the terms."

"I've had enough to drink," he conceded lazily, "but not overmuch. I know the bargain. Yet a marriage isn't a legal marriage unless it is consummated. You wished to bind us together and so we shall be. You thought me gallant or virtuous aboard the *Richezza*? Nay, lassie, I took no chances of you naming me a pirate and a ravisher. I'll brook no loopholes that you can later squirm through when it suits your fancy."

Dallas whirled about so quickly that the hairbrush and several cosmetic jars flew a-tumble onto the carpet. "Blackguard!" she cried, panic turning to horror. "You'd be more likely than I to walk out on this marriage."

"Marriage?" Fraser echoed the word with supreme mockery. He stood very still, his dark form long and threatening in the firelight. He stared at her for a long time, as if he were waiting for her to understand what she had done to both of them.

Suddenly Dallas was more afraid than she had ever been. Mute and motionless, she watched her husband remove his doublet and pull off his boots. He reached for his dirk but stopped before putting it on the bureau.

"I don't imagine you'd be above sticking me with this, would you?" he asked dryly, tossing the dirk atop the canopy, well out of Dallas's reach. "I do recall a certain episode involving a fruit knife." Then he pulled off his white shirt and tossed it on the floor. He was lean, but hard-muscled, and seemed broader of shoulder without doublet or cloak to conceal his torso.

As Fraser moved deliberately towards her, Dallas backed away until she came up against one of the clothes chests. He stood a scant six inches from her but kept his hands at his sides.

Dallas still couldn't quite believe what was happening to her. The customary strong-willed obstinacy with which she usually met difficult situations seemed no defense at all against the man who stood in front of her with that mocking grin on his dark face. Surely there must be some way out of all this, if only her wits were working half as hard as her thudding heart.

"Oh, lassie," he said musingly, "you are the first woman I've ever met who said, 'Don't touch me'—and meant it. For what purpose do you build this barricade around yourself?"

Dallas put her hand to her mouth and shook her head. "You would never understand .... I can't ...." She was whimpering like a piteously frightened kitten.

Though Dallas was determined not to cry, she saw that the threat of tears moved Fraser not an inch. Nor did he look as if he cared much about any explanation she might offer. She was legally his, he was going to take her, and there was absolutely no way she could stop him. For a brief, wild second, she considered running away—but his back was to the only door in the room, he could catch her easily, and it was his house and his servants. Dallas felt almost physically ill at the thought of her own helplessness.

Fraser put out his hands to grasp her by the upper arms. Slowly he pulled her away from the clothes chest and gazed down into the enormous dark eyes. He bent to kiss her mouth, leisurely at first, then with a growing intensity until Dallas felt his teeth against her lips. His hands had already slipped around her back and were working expertly at the hooks of her wedding gown. She tried to pull away, felt her fingers claw ineffectually at his chest as her bare feet glanced harmlessly off his shins.

He moved away just enough so that he could look again into her frightened face. "No, no, Dallas. It's useless for you to act the outraged virgin. I have no intention of hurting you any more than I have to—but if I must, I will."

She closed her eyes as the tears trembled against her lids. Dallas knew he was right. Clever! She had not been so clever after all; indeed, she had been extremely stupid to think that there was anything in life for which she would not have to pay a price. But the price of surrendering herself, even just once, to this philandering pirate was terrifying. Instinctively, she made one last effort to pull away.

"Dallas!" Fraser's voice was sharp, even angry. "Are you willing or not?"

Dallas could see that his patience had run out. But from somewhere in the back of her mind came Lord Bothwell's description of the docile, perfect wife; she could not be such a one, she had come into this marriage on her own terms, she was as determined as any Cameron Highlander to yield no ground to a marauding Fraser.

"No!" Dallas lurched sideways, momentarily catching Fraser off-balance. He cursed under his breath and yanked her back into his arms. One hand grasped both her wrists, the other pulled the satin from her shoulders as the sleeves gave way with a soft ripping sound. Dallas bent to bite the fingers which held her prisoner, but Fraser let go for an instant. It was Dallas's turn to be caught off-guard; Fraser took advantage of her hesitation to scoop her up in his arms and dump her none too gently on the bed.

"I had hoped to make love to you as a man should love a woman," he declared in a strange growl that was so unlike his usual indolent voice. "But now you've made that impossible."

His knee had come down hard on her thighs. She felt his hands wrench away the rest of her gown and the fine lawn shift. Though her fingers clawed at the bare flesh of his back, it was only a few seconds before she was completely naked. With horror, she watched his eyes slowly appraise her body as the faintest hint of a smile touched his lean mouth. For an instant, she thought she saw something else in his face—regret? It was such a fleeting expression that she couldn't be sure.

She was sure of one thing, however: Fraser would not have the satisfaction of thinking for one moment that she was willing. Dallas grabbed a handful of Fraser's dark hair and pulled with all her might. His head jerked back and this time he swore out loud. As she tried to gain enough leverage to budge his knee he took both her wrists and pulled them taut above her head.

"Iain!" Dallas gasped as she saw the fierce, angry look in his eyes and the set line of his mouth. The pirate in him had never been so visible.

It appeared he hadn't even heard her cry. "Christ! I've never had a woman so obstinate! Why would it have to be my wife?"

The genuine note of frustration in Fraser's tone made her wonder if there was still time to reason with him. But he was already pulling off the rest of his clothes, and without even looking at her face, he spread Dallas's legs apart.

As if transfixed, Dallas stared at his nakedness, at that hard, threatening ultimate weapon which he was about to use to defeat her. He had let go of her wrists; it crossed her mind to claw him in one last desperate effort of token resistance. But before she could translate thought into deed, he was upon her and she felt him probing between her thighs, felt the lunging sensation that was more strange than painful, and then a deep, hard thrust that made her gasp. Before her senses could recover, he plunged again—and again—and now Dallas cried out in pain and shock. Still Fraser did not stop and Dallas felt as if she would die from hurting—or from humiliation.

Then the pain began to recede and she was conscious only of his incessant thrusts until at last, with one great effort, he let out a long, deep sigh and relaxed his body against hers. Dallas lay very still, her shaking somewhat abated, the sensation of Fraser's manhood feeling so foreign, so astonishing, and yet so—what? She dared to open her eyes, but all she could see was the outline of Fraser's dark head buried in her shoulder. He had defeated her; he had forced her surrender; he had invaded her very being and caused her pain and yet—the emotional drain was just too much to make comprehension possible. She wished Fraser would move.

He did, slowly withdrawing himself from her and getting up on his knees. Then he glanced at the counterpane and frowned. "Damn, you've stained it. I bought that two years ago from an Oriental trader in Tripoli."

Dallas gaped at him. The man had violated her and now he was fretting over his damnable counterpane! Dallas felt rage rebuild and began to sputter incoherently.

"Look, Dallas," Fraser said, tracing the outline of delicate silken embroidery, "these are oranges and this is some sort of melon and those are pomegranates. At least I think they're pomegranates," Fraser added, looking slightly bemused.

"Pomegranates!" Dallas exploded. "You—you fiend! You care more for your silken pomegranates than for what you've done to me!" She snatched at the counterpane and pulled it around her body to hide her nakedness. "A pox on your pomegranates! I hate you!"

Fraser stretched his tall, lean frame and shrugged. Dallas wished to heaven he'd either put on his clothes or go away. The sight of his naked body made her nervous. But instead, he came to the bed and pulled back the covers. "Don't fash yourself so, lassie. The bargain's sealed and from now on you'll have it your own way. But for Christ's sake, let's get some sleep."

It took Dallas several minutes to resign herself to slipping between the sheets next to Fraser. But the silken counterpane was little protection against the winter night and Dallas reasoned that there was no point in adding illness to her other problems. She lay rigid on her back, careful not to touch Fraser. But he was already asleep.

Even in Dallas's extensive vocabulary, there were not enough invectives to describe her new husband. Still, she had to be fair—her native Scots inclination for legality made her appreciate Fraser's firmness concerning consummation. She also had to admit that if she had not been determined to fight him off, he might have behaved more civilly.

And there was something else, too—something that she had experienced after the shock and pain, while he remained inside her—what was it? She rummaged through her mind to bring back the feeling and associate it with a similar sensation .... Yes, she was beginning to put her emotions back in some sort of order, which permitted her to think rationally. That feeling she had had in the supper room when Fraser had attempted to make love to her ... the fire banking in the pit of her stomach, that's what she had felt again, but in the turmoil of resisting him, she had not recognized her own response.

Slowly, she turned over on her side and looked at her husband. He was sleeping flat on his stomach, his head turned away from her. Dallas frowned into the darkness; surely that strange fire was not born of desire? Or pleasure? Dallas had read enough love poems and folklore to know that women could derive as much joy from mating as men. But such carryings-on were not for her; had she not already surrendered far more of herself than she had ever intended?

And even if the pleasure could be worth the price, certainly a man such as Iain Fraser, who worried more about his Oriental counterpane than his terrified bride, wasn't the kind to offer more of himself than just carnal satisfaction.

Dallas turned again to look at her husband. He shifted in his sleep, the dark hair ruffled slightly against his neck, one, long, sinewy arm lying on the much-maligned counterpane. She stared at him for some time, observing his rhythmic breathing, the lean hardness of his shoulder, the outline of his hand with the signet ring.

Dallas buried her head in the pillow and wept soundlessly, letting the tears flow for the first time since her mother had died.

Chapter Seven

WHEN DALLAS AWOKE the next morning, Fraser was gone. There was no sign of his clothes and even the dirk had disappeared from atop the canopy. A small French clock on the mantel indicated it was almost noon. Dallas lay alone in the big bed, wishing her head would stop aching and wondering where Fraser had gone. After a few minutes had passed, she decided it was just as well he had risen before she did. She wasn't sure she could face him just yet, not in broad daylight, in this very room where .... Abruptly, she turned her thoughts away from last night. What was done was done, and she might as well get up and face her new life.

Her trousseau was stored in one of the clothes chests. She took out a lapin-trimmed dressing gown and put it on quickly, for it was very cold in the bedchamber. As soon as she had slipped into a pair of mules she rang for Flora.

The tall, gaunt maid appeared promptly, looking efficient and alert.

"I'd like a light breakfast, just eggs and bread," Dallas ordered. "And maybe a slice of ham and some hot chocolate. Oh, bring honey for the bread, please." She sat on the edge of the bed, frowning at her fingernails. One of them had been broken in the tussle with Fraser.

Flora stared at Dallas for a moment longer than was necessary, then said, "Yes, madame," and closed the door.

"Prune," Dallas said aloud, and wished she'd asked Flora to lay a fire in the empty grate. Of course, she could do it herself; she'd certainly had sufficient practice over the years. But if she was supposed to be a lady, she'd have to learn to act like one. It suddenly occurred to her that she didn't really know what ladies did. How did they spend their days? What would she do to occupy her time now that there were no floors to scrub or beds to change or bargains to search for in the marketplace? It was too soon to go back to the house in Nairne's Close and visit her sisters. People would wonder at her haste to be reunited with her family. Grimly, she forced herself to face the empty day.

Flora returned just as Dallas had finished filing her nails. The maid set the tray down on the bed and, without being asked, began to build a fire from a bundle of wood which was stored in a small cupboard by the hearth.

"What time did Master Fraser say he'd return?" Dallas asked casually as she spread honey on a thick slice of bread.

"He left no word, madame," Flora replied coolly. "I understand he seldom does."

Dallas said nothing. She shivered suddenly and was glad that Flora's back was turned. The fire crackled brightly as the maid got up from her knees and swept some bits of wood and ash from the hearth. "Do you wish me to wait until you are ready to dress, madame?" she inquired.

"No," said Dallas, carefully picking up the mug of steaming chocolate from the tray. "I shall dress myself this morning."

Flora's eyebrow raised almost imperceptibly. Dallas felt as if she were under surveillance from this bony, sharp-eyed woman. Was Fraser paying the maid to watch his wife?

But Flora merely said, "As you wish, madame," curtsied perfunctorily and withdrew from the bedchamber.

THE CHEERLESS JANUARY day droned on. Dallas straightened up the room, sorted through her wardrobe, wrote a letter to Fiona and Walter Ramsay to thank them for attending the wedding, and read for a while from a collection of Du Bellay's poems which Iain Fraser kept next to the bed on a shelf with several other books. She had a small supper about six and some time later she heard the clatter of hooves outside in the street. A muffled command to one of his servants informed her that the master of the house had returned.

Dallas sat in the armchair by the fire, anxiously gripping her book. At any moment she expected to hear Fraser's tread on the stairs. But the little French clock ticked away the minutes and there was no sign of her husband. Over a quarter of an hour passed before she heard the distinctive sound of a coach rattling over the cobbles and creaking to a halt outside the house.

Hurrying to the window, Dallas peered between the draperies into the street. Torches blazed on each side of the coach while the driver scratched himself vigorously and muttered at the four big horses. Then the front door of the house banged open and shut as Iain Fraser sprinted down the four steps and crossed the close to the coach.

A masked woman, her hair covered with a furred hood, leaned out from one of the coach's windows. She called out something Dallas could not hear and then laughed as Fraser climbed into the conveyance. The driver stopped scratching himself long enough to start the horses moving through the High Street.

Dallas picked up the object closest to her hand—an Italian porcelain statue of Venus—and smashed it against the wall. It was one thing to keep a mistress or two in some discreet place he could visit secretly—but it was something else again to flaunt his whore in front of her and his household the day after their wedding! She stalked the room from wall to wall until she felt her headache returning. At last she sat down on the edge of the bed and covered her face with her hands. But she would not cry again, not for any reason he might ever give her.

DALLAS WAS AWAKE early the next morning. She would have preferred sleeping late again, for the prospect of another long, boring day stretched before her. She would not spend it sequestered in the bedchamber, however. After all, this was her house, too, and although Cummings had shouldered that responsibility in the past, it was a wife's duty to take over.

Yet when she broached the subject with Cummings later that day, he seemed strangely indifferent to the idea. "We have our routine, madame. The house is well run, as I'm sure you can tell."

"Certainly it is," Dallas responded amicably enough. "But you must have a great many responsibilities besides the house. As Master Fraser's wife, I have an obligation to relieve you of some of them and make your tasks easier."

Cummings shrugged but appeared rather amused in his dry way. "As you say, madame. I shall mention it to Master Fraser when he returns."

Inwardly Dallas fumed. Mention it indeed! Was there nothing she could do in this house on her own? She wasn't used to being restricted; until now her life had been relatively free, to come and go as she pleased, to accept responsibility, to make up her mind for herself.

She was still steaming with indignation when Kennedy brought her a message. It was from Fraser and couched in formal terms: "You will be pleased to learn that I have secured for you an appointment at court as one of the Queen's ladies. Your official summons to join Her Grace at Holyrood will arrive shortly."

The message was simply signed, "Iain." Dallas was pleased at the content but annoyed that Fraser hadn't told her in person. Where was the man? Obviously, he was still in Edinburgh. He must be at court already, she decided, and vowed that she'd greet him with a rebuke for his neglect.

But as she headed upstairs with the note clutched in her hand it occurred to her that it wasn't neglect on his part. It was the bargain, after all. They were to go their separate ways, and that was precisely what Fraser was doing. Well and good, Dallas thought savagely, for I've no desire to see him anyway. And she stomped up the rest of the stairs and into the deserted bedchamber.

DALLAS MET THE Queen of Scotland on a chilly February afternoon as the drizzling rain splattered the windows of the royal audience chamber. Iain Fraser's bride was received by the Queen in the presence of her four Marys, the lifelong attendants who had lived in France with their sovereign.

Mary Stuart was not beautiful in the classic sense but her flawless white skin, her innate grace and the radiance of her smile set her apart from other women. She wore a honey-gold gown of taffeta and a heart-shaped cap with a flowing veil which covered most of her auburn hair.

"We bid you welcome, Mistress Fraser," Mary Stuart said as Dallas made a deep if somewhat awkward curtsy. "I'd hoped your husband would be able to join us but he is away from Holyrood with my brother, Lord Robert."

As Dallas had not seen her husband since their wedding night, she was hardly surprised that he was absent upon her formal presentation at court. Indeed, she was relieved, since his presence would have made her doubly nervous.

The Queen, however, was exerting her charm to put Dallas at ease. "Your late father was a well-known tutor and scholar, I'm told. I also understand that he never veered in his support of my mother. It pleases me to greet the daughter of such a loyal subject."

"And it pleases me to meet the Queen he so wanted to see." Dallas's nervousness had abated; Mary Stuart was younger than she, after all, and though she wore her royal demeanor as gracefully as her taffeta gown, Dallas perceived a vulnerability in her sovereign's character. "Even though my father died the day you came to Edinburgh, I went out that night to watch you on the balcony at Holyrood." Dallas thought back to that August evening and how mesmerized she had been by Mary Stuart's brief appearance. Now, seeing the Queen at such close proximity, the magical quality was less potent, but the personal charisma made it clear why Mary Stuart could win such steadfast devotion from her adherents.

YET NOT ALL the courtiers reacted as graciously as their Queen. Dallas was snubbed by some, excluded by others and gossiped about by most. Who was this little chit who had come from nowhere to marry Iain Fraser? A tutor's daughter? How strange! But then Fraser himself was enigmatic.

In the excitement over her summons to Holyrood, it had not occurred to Dallas that she was no better equipped to be a lady-in-waiting than to be mistress of a wealthy man's home. For the first time in her life, Dallas was discovering that she had a lot to learn—and none of it to be found in a book.

The first week of March had turned unseasonably warm. Although the casement windows in the Queen's antechamber had been thrown open, no breeze ruffled the heavy velvet hangings. Dallas was seated at her embroidery frame with the other attendants, concentrating on a figure of Apollo who was beginning to look slightly crosseyed as her stitches grew more erratic.

The Queen was not present but her four Marys—Fleming, Beaton, Livingstone and Seton—were plying their needles along with Dallas, Barbara Hamilton and Dorothea Ruthven. Dallas felt awkward in their company, an outsider looking in.

As Dallas plucked out Apollo's eyes and started afresh her ears were half-tuned to the continual gossip exchanged by the ladies-in-waiting.

"It's a year of brides," Mary Livingstone was saying as she bit off a piece of thread with her strong white teeth. "The Queen's half-brother, Lord Johnny, will soon marry Bothwell's sister, then her other half-brother, Robert, will no doubt take my lord Cassilis's sister to wife. And even James Stuart may finally wed with the Earl Marischal's daughter, Agnes Keith."

"Agnes!" Mary Beaton made a face. "She's sour as week-old milk, but perhaps she and James are well suited."

"Now, now," clucked Mary Livingstone, "the Queen dislikes criticism of Lord James. In terms of political matters, he is the most reliable of her bastard half-brothers."

"And the most ambitious," Mary Beaton retorted. Dallas said nothing but inwardly agreed. James Stuart had impressed her as arrogant, pompous and capable of great ruthlessness. His appearance at court functions always seemed to throw a pall over the occasion.

"Don't forget we have two brides right here," put in Barbara Hamilton, who was John Hamilton's sister. Barbara was somewhat older than the others but she was still a handsome woman.

The four Marys looked up at Dallas and Dorothea Ruthven. For Tarrill's sake, Dallas had been prepared to dislike Will Ruthven's bride. Upon their first meeting, she had decided that the dislike was both real and mutual.

"Will and I have been married much longer than Dallas and Iain," Dorothea said in her wispy little voice. "Tell me, Dallas, do you still feel that wonderful shortness of breath when your husband comes into the room?"

"I've never had asthma," Dallas replied, giving such an abrupt pull on her thread that it broke in two.

Dorothea giggled in mock delight. "How witty you are, Dallas! It must be all those books you've read. Is that why you've never had time to learn to dance or play the virginals?"

Dallas was growing used to such snide comments. The four Marys were invariably kind, even the Queen's rather cynical half-sister, Jean Argyll, had not been outwardly rude, but the taunts of others made it extremely difficult for Dallas to keep her tongue in check. But she did so for the Queen's sake, since Mary Stuart disliked contention among her courtiers; a recent quarrel between the Countess of Morton and Barbara Hamilton had sent the Queen to bed with stomach cramps.

So Dallas merely shrugged and tried to concentrate on rethreading her needle. But Dorothea wasn't finished with her prey. "I suppose," she went on, deftly working gold thread into Helen of Troy's tresses, "that being a tutor's daughter, you never had the luxury of time for life's finer things. You seem to be struggling with your needlework, too."

The other ladies had all paused to watch Dallas and Dorothea. After more than a month at court, Dallas felt what little patience she possessed begin to unravel like her embroidery thread. "I've spent the last ten years taking care of my family. My sisters and I were taught many things but none of them were intended to merely pass away idle time."

Mary Fleming suppressed a smile; she found Dorothea Ruthven cloying. But Barbara Hamilton frowned at Dallas. "Any skill, whether it be art, music or whatever, is worth learning. Your background is no excuse for not attempting to improve yourself."

The rebuke made Dallas bristle. "If that's the case, would you like me to teach you how to empty a chamberpot, Lady Hamilton?"

"Lady Fleming," Barbara corrected her. With dignity, she lowered her eyelashes. "I've been a widow these past three years."

The quiet response silenced Dallas momentarily. She had forgotten that Barbara was Mary Fleming's sister-in-law. The complexities of court relationships still baffled Dallas. But that particular maze wasn't what vexed her now. The reason for Dorothea's hostility was obvious. But Barbara's attitude puzzled Dallas, since John Hamilton had always been so friendly.

But the awkward silence was broken by a knock at the door. It was David Rizzio, the young Italian court singer, who bowed his way into the room.

"Come in, Davie," Mary Beaton said, relieved at the diversion. "We'll teach you to stitch if you'll teach us to sing."

The swarthy little man with the homely face and wavy black hair grinned at the three ladies. "Alas, I could never stitch as well as you can already sing. I thought perhaps the Queen was with you. I've composed new songs for next week's masque."

Mary Livingstone informed him that the Queen was in a council meeting. "You could sing them for us," she urged.

Rizzio shook his head in an exaggerated way. "Oh, no, no, no. She must hear them first, they are in her honor."

Mary Beaton pressed her lips together to keep from smiling at the young man's obvious devotion to Mary Stuart. Rizzio had arrived a short time earlier in the train of the ambassador from Savoy. He had found his niche at once in the Scots court, enthralling his noble audience with a rich bass voice and a heart-rending style. Although some said his love songs were directed only at Mary Stuart, none could doubt his genuine talent.

Teasing Rizzio out of his obvious disappointment, Mary Livingstone jabbed playfully at his midriff with her needle. "If you won't let us hear your songs, why not go serenade Master Knox under his window in the Netherbow. He is quite the connoisseur of music, I'm told."

But Rizzio had been in Scotland long enough to know all about Master Knox. "Signor Knox knows only solemn, ugly Protestant hymns," he replied with disdain. "Lah, lah, loh, loh," he intoned in a purposely off-key voice. "Dio mio! Such music is the real sin against God!"

All the ladies laughed and Rizzio joined them with his deep guffaw. They were still chuckling when the door flew open and the Earl of Arran charged into the room.

"Where's my lute?" he demanded of Rizzio, grasping the smaller man by the front of his doublet. "You took my lute!" Arran was fairly jigging with wrath.

Rizzio was both astonished and perplexed. He tried, with some respect, to disengage himself but Arran held tight. "I did take it last night, but only to hand it to Her Grace. She still has it, I am quite sure."

Barbara Hamilton had stood up and glided over to her brother's side. "Becalm yourself, Jamie. Master David has done you no wrong."

Arran let go of the doublet and stood gaping at Rizzio. Dallas had not yet seen him up close and noted that he was neither as tall nor as good-looking as his brother John. His brown hair was parted in the middle and longer than was fashionable. He wore a small moustache and a short beard and his full lower lip seemed to be in a perpetual state of pout.

"Perhaps the lute is in the Queen's chamber," Barbara said in a soothing voice. "Shall I look?"

Arran appeared not to hear her. He aimed a kick at Rizzio's shins, missed, muttered, "Cur!" and bolted out of the room.

"Is he all right?" Dallas asked in wonder after Arran had banged the door shut.

"He is highly excitable," Barbara answered calmly.

"Where is your middle brother, John, these days?" Dallas asked as Rizzio curled up on a cushion at her feet. "I've not seen him since I came to court."

"He keeps to himself at his home in Arbroath," Barbara replied. "He would prefer to disassociate himself from Arran's quarrel with Bothwell."

"Prudent," Dallas said but thought fleetingly that court life might prove more congenial if John Hamilton were present.

Chapter Eight

THE GREAT HALL at Falkland Palace was festooned with as many spring flowers and as much greenery as could be found in late March. Sprigs of fresh evergreen, bunches of daffodils, bowls of crocus, and nosegays made from primroses enlivened the grey palace walls.

The Queen's ladies looked like a spring bouquet in their identically cut but variously colored chiffon gowns. The other women glittered in court dresses trimmed with jewels, furs and exquisite laces. Even the men had burst out of their somber Scots cocoons and cut dashing figures in the glow of the thousand candles which lined the long walls.

Mary Stuart looked exceptionally lovely that night. The white gown set off her complexion and auburn hair. If she was under a strain, only those who knew her intimately could detect it in the faint shadows which appeared under her amber eyes. James Stuart was at her side, and though he was not dressed as gaudily as the others, his dark visage was set off to good advantage in a well-cut grey velvet doublet slashed with cloth-of-silver.

The masque had been a great success and the courtiers cheered Rizzio's new compositions. Afterwards, the musicians plied their instruments while the company danced the evening away on the great hall's shining tiles.

Dallas had been dancing with Maitland but was now chatting in a group which included Mary Fleming, Kirkcaldy of Grange, George Seton, Jean Argyll and a titian-haired woman Dallas didn't recognize.

From behind her hand Dallas asked Jean Argyll, "Who is that?"

"Delphinia Douglas, some kin to Morton," Jean whispered. "She's a widow just out of mourning so doubtless you've not seen her at court before."

At that moment Delphinia appeared to catch Dallas's eye. She was very tall, with a full, blooming figure and strong facial features. “I don’t believe I’ve met the lady in red,” she announced in a husky voice to George Seton.

Seton, who was the Queen’s dancing master, introduced the two women. Dallas was polite but wondered why Delphinia looked at her in such a knowing manner. Does she, too, look down on me because I’m only a tutor’s daughter? she wondered. There was no time for further speculation, however, for the Earl of Morton had joined the group and was taking great pains to greet each of the ladies in a deliberate, if, it seemed to Dallas, unctuous, manner.

“It’s good to see you back at court, Delphinia,” he declared, his small, squinting eyes appreciatively taking in her voluptuous body. “I hear you’ve found some consolation to alleviate your bereavement.” Delphinia’s generous mouth curved into a half-smirk, half-smile, but before she could respond, Morton had glanced at Dallas. “I also take it you’ve been introduced to Mistress Fraser?”

“Indeed,” Delphinia purred, squaring her broad shoulders so that her awesome bosom strained invitingly at the fine damask of her gown. “I’d been about to tell her how sorry I was that her husband is not in attendance tonight. Pray tell us, Mistress Fraser, how is it that we so seldom see you in your bridegroom’s company?”

The exchange between Delphinia and Morton had left no doubt in Dallas’s mind as to who was consoling the obviously unaggrieved widow. Catherine Gordon, Delphinia Douglas—how many women was Fraser dallying with? Keeping her fists clenched tightly at her sides lest she submit to the impulse to grab a handful of Delphinia’s titian hair, Dallas forced herself to sound as sweet as honey mead: “I never discuss my husband’s activities with others, his business and court duties being a man’s sphere, after all. And,” she added, sweeping an insinuating look at Delphinia from under her dark lashes, “since he’s precisely what I’ve always desired in a spouse, I’d never dream of criticizing him.”

Delphinia allowed herself a husky little laugh. “How charming! Iain is a fortunate man to have such an accommodating bride. Doubtless you fulfill all his needs in the same way he does yours—assuming, of course, such needs coincide.”

An impatient grunt issued from Kirkcaldy of Grange’s throat. Renowned as a fighter, he had little time for word battles, especially where women were concerned. But neither Dallas nor Delphinia appeared to notice his displeasure. “Needs, like tastes, vary,” Dallas said in the same dulcet tone. “Take food, for example—some savor a dainty partridge—while others prefer the haunch of a big fat cow.”

Morton’s round little mouth grew even rounder as Mary Fleming put a hand to her lips to suppress her mirth. As for Delphinia, the statuesque body had gone rigid though her expression remained fixed. She had no opportunity to retaliate, however, for the Queen was signaling to her ladies that she wished to retire. Dallas excused herself, and with Mary Fleming and Jean Argyll, hurried off to join their mistress.

As the ladies chattered their way to the Queen's chambers, Lord Johnny Stuart came hurrying after them. "Your Grace," he called to his half-sister, "James has the Earl of Arran with him. He's bringing him to you now."

Mary Stuart brushed an auburn curl from her forehead. "I shall await him in my chambers," she said, and asked that all her ladies remain until the audience was over. Once inside the chamber, she pulled off the pearl and gold tiara which suddenly seemed to weigh down her entire body.

"By Our Lady," the Queen murmured fretfully, "I'd like to be done with this quarrel of Arran's and Bothwell's." Though a fire burned low in the grate, the March winds had put a chill in the night air. Mary Stuart asked Dallas to fetch a robe, as the chiffon gown suddenly seemed inadequate.

"Thank you, Dallas," she said with a tired smile. She was adjusting the feathered bodice when Mary Fleming admitted the Queen's two half-brothers and the Earl of Arran. James had the earl by the arm, but when Arran saw the Queen, he broke free and flung himself at her feet.

"Mercy!" he shrieked, burying his face in the folds of her robe as a terrible fit of sobbing consumed his thin shoulders.

The Queen looked down at Arran with mingled distaste and compassion. "Why are you here at Falkland, my lord? We understood you to be at your father's place."

Arran lifted his head. "Ah," he said softly, suddenly looking well pleased with himself. "My father wanted to keep me confined, but I outwitted the old fool. I tied my bedsheets together and climbed out the window. Try though he may, he cannot keep us apart, sweet wife-to-be."

Mary Stuart tried to hide her revulsion. "You are very clever," she soothed. "Now do get up, my lord."

Though he struggled to his feet with some difficulty, Arran's smile remained fixed. "Some say I would harm you—that's vile calumny. 'Tis not I who would endanger you, 'tis Bothwell! The man's a sorcerer!" Arran's eyes began to roll and his spindly arms flailed at the air.

The spectacle was both frightening and embarrassing. Mary Fleming clasped her hands in a prayerful attitude, James Stuart scowled ferociously, and Dallas had a terrible desire to laugh aloud. But the Queen sat calmly, and when the pathetic earl seemed to have regained his composure, she smiled. "I think perhaps my brother should see that you get some rest. It's been a trying day for you, my lord." She glanced at James. "Will you take my lord to a quiet room where he can feel secure?"

James Stuart nodded and grasped Arran firmly by the shoulder. The earl started out docilely but turned at the door. "We'll wed soon then, sweet Queen?" he whispered.

Mary Stuart stiffened but managed to keep her smile in place. "You may be assured that I'll see to your future," she said softly.

Arran sighed with contentment as James Stuart led him away into the darkened passage.

"Your Grace," Jean Argyll urged, "you must retire at once. This incident has been most distressing."

Mary Stuart sat motionless for a moment, her skin almost transparent. But before she could reach out to take her half-sister's hand, Iain Fraser strode into the room and dropped down on one knee in front of the Queen. He was dressed in riding clothes and there was a deep cut under the hollow of his left cheekbone.

Dallas stiffened, her thoughts racing back to the last time she had seen him, on their wedding night. Fraser, however, did not acknowledge her presence.

"Iain!" cried Mary Stuart, giving him her hand. "How good to see you! But you are hurt—what happened?" Fraser dismissed the cut with an offhand gesture. "Nothing serious. But it may be a cause for concern to you. May I speak with you privately?"

The Queen nodded, then asked her ladies to withdraw. Dallas hesitated; was she to be sent away with the others while her husband conferred with Mary Stuart? But both the Queen and Fraser stood motionless, obviously waiting for complete privacy.

Dallas trudged after the others, aware that her husband had not given her so much as a glance. Bastard philandering pirate, she cursed under her breath as she stalked down the hall. She had not seen him in weeks, not since their wedding night, and the cur couldn't even greet her with courtesy. But the Queen—oh, that was different! There was an obvious intimacy between them, an affection which Dallas detected in just those brief moments. Mary Stuart's concern for the cut he had suffered, his nonchalant response, the warmth with which she welcomed him ....

Dallas paused in mid-step; the others were a few yards ahead of her in the passage and paid no heed. Iain Fraser was a pirate. Of course, he was a courtier, too. In fact, that was all he was to the rest of the world—only she and his crew knew of his other guise. It was puzzling. Fraser had no real political power or influence. He wasn't a Hamilton or a Gordon or a Douglas or a Stuart. He was no diplomat like Maitland or soldier like Bothwell. So why was Mary Stuart so eager to seek his counsel?

Whipping the folds of her scarlet skirt around her, Dallas turned and all but ran back towards the Queen's chambers. There was a small dressing room on one side, with a separate entrance which no doubt had been used over the years by the mistresses of amorous Stuart kings. If the door was unlocked, Dallas could slip inside and discover why Iain Fraser meant so much to Mary Stuart. Surely even Fraser would not be bold enough to woo the Queen of Scotland?

Surely he might, Dallas told herself grimly, and put her hand to the dressing room latch. It opened easily and she tiptoed inside. The door between the little chamber and the Queen's room was solid oak. Dallas had to strain to catch the muffled words.

"Arran … erratic," she heard her husband say. "Bothwell ... assassination of James Stuart and William Maitland ...."

The Queen's silver voice carried more clearly: "If I were to be taken captive, then Arran and Bothwell would rule Scotland."

Dallas strained to catch Fraser's reply. "But Arran says Bothwell would betray him and thus bring down the Hamiltons." Fraser must have turned away because the next words were totally incomprehensible.

Again, Dallas could hear the Queen without too much difficulty. "Is Arran so insane that he thinks his tale about Bothwell will make me grateful enough to marry him?"

"Yes. But I don't believe ...." There was a pause before Fraser continued and this time Dallas could only catch an occasional phrase: "... Take Bothwell and Arran into custody .... James won't believe Bothwell's innocent ... you must keep James as your ally ...."

"But you are Bothwell's friend," Mary protested.

Dallas could not hear Fraser's answer at all. But she did hear Mary agree that she probably needed her half-brother James more than any other ally in Scotland. And then she heard something which riveted her to the worn floorboards:

"Still, Iain, I need you almost as much as I need James—you're the only trustworthy emissary I have to keep contact with foreign Catholic powers."

Fraser's laugh was muffled. "But in secret ... profitable, too, since I can ply my trade at the same ...."

Someone was in the passage, lifting the latch of the dressing room door. Dallas remained motionless, certain that whoever was about to enter was doing so for the same purpose she had slipped into the little room. As the door swung slowly open she turned quickly and pulled a dove-grey gown from a wooden peg.

James Stuart stared into the gloom at Dallas. He was of medium height, with dark hair, a luxurious beard and hooded grey eyes which concealed all but the most fleeting expression of surprise.

Dallas knew from what Fraser had told her aboard the *Richezza* that James was no friend to her husband. The animosity between the two men made it imperative for Dallas to prevent James from overhearing the conversation in the adjoining room. It would be calamitous for the Queen's half-brother to learn of Fraser's piracy; it might be even worse if he were to discover that Fraser was acting on behalf of Mary Stuart's Catholic interests.

"My lord!" Dallas spoke too loudly and her smile was overly bright. She made a deep curtsy. "May I assist you?"

James Stuart's countenance was bland. "I merely wished to see if I had left my cloak and gloves here before I went to the masque. I also wish to bid my royal sister goodnight and assure her that Arran is well taken care of."

The explanation was so smooth that Dallas could almost believe it. "Let me look for your cloak, my lord. But first let me put back Her Grace's gown." Dallas accompanied her words with a great rustling of silk and a clatter of slippers which she managed to topple from a shelf. "Oh, fie, how clumsy I am!" She giggled, pressed her hands to her cheeks, and looked apologetically at Lord James. "I'm still new at court and so ...." Her voice trailed off in feigned embarrassment.

The hooded eyes might have been suspicious; on the other hand, they might have been merely disapproving. It was difficult to tell with Lord James. But Dallas was already busying herself with a pile of petticoats. "I shall attend Her Grace," James announced, turning back to the door which led into the passage. "I must have left my cloak and gloves in her chamber."

"Actually," said Dallas, dumping the petticoats into a heap, "I believe she's asleep. Lady Jean insisted she retire."

But James was already out of the dressing room. Dallas followed him, aware that she was about as welcome at his heels as a flea-plagued mongrel. Without so much as a backward glance, James pounded twice on the Queen's door. It opened immediately, catching James off-guard as he faced a vexed Jean Argyll.

"Hush, James," Jean whispered to her half-brother. "Our poor sister is asleep. If you wish to see her, you'll have to wait until morning."

James frowned at Jean, glanced quickly past her, but saw nothing except a darkened chamber. "As you will," he muttered, bestowing a brief look of displeasure on Jean and ignoring Dallas altogether. Both women watched in silence as he walked briskly down the corridor.

After he was out of sight, Jean turned to Dallas: "Don't worry, Iain is gone, safely out of the palace."

Dallas sighed with relief and started back to her own quarters. Flora Campbell was dozing in a chair when Dallas returned to her room. The maid jumped as her mistress entered, but got quickly to her feet and appeared as alert as ever. Dallas decided to dismiss her for the night, since she was too weary to answer questions or engage in conversation.

After Flora was gone, Dallas disrobed quickly and slipped into her nightdress. She was about to climb into the big bed when she heard a knock at her door. Damnation, Dallas thought, one of the other ladies wants to gossip into the night about Arran and the Queen. She considered ignoring the knock but finally gave in, slipped on her robe and went to the door.

Standing there with one hand leaning on the door frame was John Hamilton. By the light of her candle, Dallas saw that his riding clothes were rumpled and there was dust on the dark plaid that was flung over one shoulder.

"I'm sorry to disturb you, Dallas, but may I come in for a moment?" He waited for her response but it was clear that he was in a great hurry.

"If you must, my lord," Dallas said, stepping aside to let him in. She felt uncomfortable receiving Hamilton in her nightclothes but she had little choice.

"You are alone?" Hamilton inquired, glancing swiftly around the room. When Dallas nodded, he seemed to relax a bit. "Is it true that my brother is in the palace?"

Dallas placed the candle down on the lacquered table. "He is. He came to see the Queen. He acted ... unbalanced."

Hamilton flicked the riding crop he was carrying against his thigh. "By heaven," he muttered, "I should have guessed he'd make more mischief. I couldn't find Barbara anywhere. Dallas, what happened? Where is Arran now?"

"The Queen told James to take charge of him."

"James! He'll not treat my brother kindly, I'll wager that." Hamilton moved anxiously around the room, apparently trying to determine his next move. "If Bothwell's true intent was to undermine our family, he's succeeded. And if my brother invented all this himself, then the result is the same." He stood behind an armchair, his hands resting on its brocaded back. "Unlike most other courtiers, I am not an ambitious man, Dallas. But I have great pride where my family is concerned. I will not stand by and let anyone destroy the Hamiltons."

"It's a pity you weren't born the eldest," Dallas said quietly. "You would have made a much more suitable match for Her Grace."

Hamilton eyed her speculatively. Then he moved around in front of the chair to where Dallas was standing. Without warning, he took her in his arms and kissed her lips. It was a tender, probing kiss and Dallas was too surprised to resist.

But Hamilton released her at once and shook his head. "I should either have done that a long time ago or not at all," he said, as if to himself.

"You're quite right, my lord," Dallas said in a shaky voice. "I'm a married woman now."

"You went through a marriage ceremony, you mean," Hamilton said bluntly. "But you don't sleep with your husband."

Dallas hoped he couldn't see that she was flushed. John Hamilton was the first person to say aloud what many must be thinking—that her marriage was one of convenience, and something of a sham to boot. Barbara must have told him, Barbara, whose antipathy towards Dallas had seemed so puzzling. Nor did Dallas still understand unless Barbara thought her brother had been spurned for Iain Fraser.

"Whatever arrangement my husband and I have, it's none of your business, my lord," she said with a haughty toss of the thick brown hair. "Now if you please, I'd rather you would leave. No doubt your brother needs you."

Hamilton had stepped closer and Dallas feared he would take her in his arms again. "And you don't?" he asked softly.

"Not in the least," said Iain Fraser. He was sitting in the window embrasure with one long leg draped over the casement.

"Jesu!" whispered Dallas, whirling around to see Fraser swing his other leg over the sill and drop into the room.

"I hate to break up this intimate discussion," Fraser said lazily, standing with his thumbs hooked in his belt, "but isn't it past our bedtime, wife?"

"Lord John is concerned for his brother," Dallas explained in an unsteady voice. "He'd like to know what is happening."

"So would we all," remarked Fraser. "I'd suggest, then, that Lord John go ask James. After all, the Queen's half-brother usually knows where each sparrow falls—and why."

"Your husband is probably right," Hamilton conceded. He moved uneasily towards the door, as if he were torn between getting away from Fraser and leaving Dallas alone in what he was certain could be a dangerous situation. His innate gallantry got the better of him, however, and he turned to face Fraser squarely. "I came here uninvited, and with no intention of compromising your wife. To my knowledge, she is as virtuous as she is fair."

"You need not categorize my wife's attributes to me," Fraser replied quietly. "I know her much better than you do. But my patience is wearing thin. In view of the fact that your younger brother, Claud, attacked me tonight and since your presence here compromises Dallas regardless of your intentions, you may consider yourself very fortunate that I haven't already killed you." Fraser's words were bland enough to match his smile, but his eyes held a menacing threat.

Hamilton's hand had moved by reflex to his dirk but he stopped and stared back at Fraser. The two men glared at each other, in a brief but eloquent exchange of pride, anger and enmity. Dallas had the feeling that an imaginary gauntlet had been tossed down between them and that this was only the first scene of a dangerous drama.

Finally Hamilton turned on his heel and headed for the passage. He paused briefly to look over his shoulder at Dallas, as if to assure himself that she would be all right without his protection. Then he slammed the door and left them both staring after him.

Dallas decided to wrest the advantage from Fraser by attempting a frontal assault. "Will you explain how you happen to be jumping through windows in Falkland Palace at midnight?"

Fraser had sunk into the armchair where he was munching at some sweetmeats which Flora had placed in a crystal bowl. "Marchpane," Fraser said appreciatively. "A great favorite of mine." He put another piece in his mouth and offered the bowl to Dallas.

"Fie, I've no mind to sit around in the middle of the night eating sweetmeats and talking nonsense!" Dallas stood in front of him, her hands on her hips. "What in heaven's name are you up to?"

"I was up to the windowsill before I realized you had a guest," Fraser retorted amiably. "A guest, I might add, you ought to avoid." Noting that she was on the verge of an explosive response, he put up a hand. "No, not just for the obvious reason. The Hamiltons are in disgrace. They will not be welcome at court for some time. Don't get involved in their troubles."

"And you?" she countered. "What of you and my lord Bothwell? Is he not in trouble, too?"

"Aye, and that's why I made my unorthodox entrance just now. Bothwell did not go into the borders as I had thought he would. He remained, bold as brass, in Edinburgh. Don't ask me why, he can be as unpredictable as April weather. But he will no doubt be arrested and so may I, as his accomplice."

"But you haven't done anything," Dallas protested. Fraser put the comfit bowl aside and brushed some crumbs from his cloak.

"That would hardly matter to James Stuart. If he thought he could get the Hamiltons, Bothwell and me out of the way in one blow, he'd do it. I may still get away in time—but if I do I'll have to stay away, perhaps for months. So whether it's imprisonment or self-imposed exile, I won't see you for a while. Consequently, I thought I'd better make certain you were paid up in advance. I'd hate to have a wife suing me for her allowance in addition to my other problems." He pulled a heavy pouch from his shirt and tossed it to her. "There, that ought to keep you and your relations for a bit."

Dallas took care not to measure the pouch's contents this time. "Thank you," she said petulantly.

"Your gratitude is overmuch, wife," he grinned, getting up from the chair.

"Do you realize how long it would take a High Street whore to earn that sum?"

"I don't but I'm sure you do," she replied tartly. "How much do trollops like Delphinia Douglas and Catherine Gordon cost you?"

The grin faded slightly from Fraser's mouth. He shrugged. "Catherine's family has more wealth than Croesus. As for Delphinia, she's a lusty willing wench who makes only an occasional mercenary demand. Which reminds me," he said, glancing out the window to make sure no guards were yet combing the grounds for him, "I must make a demand of my own." He paused just long enough to watch Dallas's eyes widen. "Nay, lassie, nothing of that sort—Johnny Hamilton has no doubt already drained you of passionate emotion. I had in mind something less exciting—food."

"I'll summon Flora," Dallas announced without expression. The maid appeared promptly, making Dallas wonder if she had been listening at the antechamber door. Fraser requested beef, bread and whiskey. After Flora had departed on her errand, Dallas moved restlessly about the room, placing the money pouch in a drawer, adjusting the drapes which Fraser had disarranged, and fidgeting with the remaining pieces of marchpane in the crystal comfit dish. Fraser watched her with detachment, standing with his back to the small fireplace, his elbows resting on the mantelpiece.

"How," he asked at last, "did you end up in that dressing room to foil little Lord Jamie's eavesdropping attempt?"

Dallas dropped a prayer book she had picked up from the small lacquered table. "Fie," she breathed, bending to retrieve it. "I was curious, I wanted to know why you had come to Falkland and ...." Dallas looked surreptitiously at Fraser, then fixed her gaze on the prayer book. "Well, I wanted to know how you had gotten hurt."

Fraser brushed at the cut on his cheekbone. "Oh, this? Claud Hamilton and some of his cronies set upon me thinking I might know where Bothwell was. Luckily for me, they drink better than they wield a sword." He paused, waiting for Dallas to respond, but she did not. "Well, now at least you know why the Queen wanted to speak with me privately. At least I assume you heard enough." He hooked his thumbs in his belt and regarded her levelly.

"I did." Dallas met his gaze then and it was impossible for her to mask the concern she felt. "Piracy is dangerous enough—but acting as a secret emissary—what happens if you are caught?"

Fraser rubbed the bridge of his nose and shifted his stance from one booted leg to the other. Before he could speak, Flora came into the room bearing a linen-covered tray. Ever discreet, she sensed that a private conversation was taking place and immediately withdrew. Fraser seated himself in a chair next to the small lacquered table and began to cut up his beef.

"Queen Mary made it very clear from the start that she could offer me no personal or political protection," he said matter-of-factly. "If I am discovered in either guise, as pirate or envoy, she is impotent to help me."

He paused to let this sink in fully on Dallas. She sat down on a footstool next to Fraser's chair and pressed her fingers against her chin. "Who knows this besides you and the Queen?"

"My crew guesses—but they are unquestionably loyal. Cummings knows—and you." Fraser's gaze was now almost as solemn as Lord James's. He and Dallas stared at each other for a long, silent moment; each recognized that Dallas held his fate in her hands in ways that neither of them had ever fully fathomed until now.

Dallas stood up abruptly, smoothing the folds of her night-robe. "Well, I have no intention of betraying you, Iain. Though I wonder why the Queen must have such secret dealings in the first place."

Fraser broke off a piece of oatmeal bread and smeared it with butter. "For purposes of military alliance against Queen Elizabeth and England, to find a suitable Catholic consort, to keep in contact with the Pope. Her reasons are sound—but unacceptable to Lord James and his Protestant adherents."

"I see." Dallas was quiet for a moment. She needed time to consider her husband in this new light. And husband he was, a fact which had somehow eluded her in the past hour of tension and surprise. Dallas dropped back onto the footstool and asked Fraser if he had tended to the cut on his cheek.

"I did. But," he went on, pushing aside the now empty tray and draining the last of his whiskey, "it's touching to know you're concerned about my welfare."

"Stop mocking me!" Dallas had a sudden desire to grab Fraser by the shoulders and shake him. But her husband only laughed, got up, and moved with pantherlike grace to the window where he gazed down at the man-made lake and beyond, to the ancient kingdom of Fife.

"A fine view you have," he commented in his usual drawling, indolent voice. "You've done right well as a married woman. No wonder you won't betray me."

His remark made her want to shake him more than ever. But though she rose from the footstool, she made no further move. How could he even think she would betray him when .... Dallas's mental process seemed to bog down in confusion. She would lose her income, of course, that was the bond, that was her side of the bargain. How ridiculous of him to even consider her betrayal!

But instead of bargains and betrayal, Dallas's words surprised them both. "You left me after our wedding night. You hauled your whore right up to the front door and never bade me a by-thee-well!"

Fraser turned from the window and stared at her with a raised eyebrow.

"Ah, so you noticed. I thought you'd be too busy going over my ledgers to care."

"I never touched your damnable ledgers!" Dallas realized she was shrieking and put a hand over her mouth. "Well, I didn't," she amended in a much quieter voice.

Fraser shrugged and came to stand in front of her. "No matter, we've both kept our sides of the bargain and that's what matters, eh, lassie?" He gave her that uneven grin and one finger flicked at her chin. "Now I must be off."

Dallas blinked rapidly. It seemed there were so many other things she ought to tell Fraser. Surely he would want to know how she'd fared in her weeks at court, surely she should ask where he had been all this time, surely they ought to talk more about this business with Arran and Bothwell and the Hamiltons ....

But Fraser was already at the windowsill. "Thank you, Dallas," he said with a wave. "You acted bravely tonight. If Lord James had been successful in his eavesdropping, I might be on my way to the Tolbooth." One last grin and he was gone.

For a brief moment Dallas felt uncommonly pleased by his words; perhaps he was beginning to realize that she was a clever woman. But very soon the old emptiness returned and Dallas wondered why being considered clever didn't seem as important as it had in the past.

THE QUEEN AND James Stuart dealt swiftly with Arran and Bothwell. Both men were imprisoned in Edinburgh Castle and it was generally conceded that Arran would never be released. Bothwell, however, was a different matter. Though James urged an even stiffer penalty for the Border Earl, the Queen was adamant. Bothwell might prove too useful to keep permanently incarcerated.

John and Claud Hamilton and their cousin Gavin were banished from court. Even Barbara left, though the Queen made her a private and affectionate farewell. Iain Fraser, however, was not found, and despite James's urgings, Mary Stuart did not press for his detainment.

Spring blossomed into summer. Queen Mary allowed her half-brother to assume more and more responsibility for running the government. The arrangement suited them both: James quenched his lust for power and Mary satisfied her youthful penchant for enjoying herself. The court moved from palace to palace during the summer, to Stirling, to St. Andrews, to Falkland, to Holyrood, to whichever residence provided the most attractive hunting or the best weather.

Fraser had rejoined the court at the end of July. Since he was accepted back warmly by Mary Stuart, no one questioned his part in the Arran-Bothwell affair. Arran had been confined to St. Andrews, while Bothwell had recently escaped from Edinburgh Castle and had fled into his border sanctuary.

On the whole, it had been a damp, dreary summer. But the last three days of July turned warm enough to dry out the long grasses on the golf course at St. Andrews. The Queen and her courtiers laid wagers whether Lord Fleming and Iain Fraser or George Seton and Johnny Stuart would win the match. Lord James, who decried golf as ungodly, sulked in the distance.

"The Queen should play," David Rizzio fretted to Dallas. "She is most excellent at golf."

Dallas was stroking two mangy Manx cats she had found in the stables. "Her side aches again. She played too much tennis yesterday."

Rizzio emitted one of his melodious, dramatic sighs which seemed to convey passion, sympathy and yearning all in a single breath. "Our poor sovereign lady! She needs the strength of a loyal man to help support the weight of her crown."

"Mayhap," Dallas replied absently. She was examining the cats closely. They were ill fed and suffered from obvious neglect. She made up her mind to adopt them. "I should fetch some curds," she said, more to herself than to Rizzio.

"You are kindhearted, like our Queen," said Rizzio, beaming at Dallas as George Seton blasted his way out of a sand trap.

"Not really, Davie, not like Her Grace at any rate." She gave Rizzio a warm smile. They both shared similar experiences at court, being outsiders and the objects of frequent derision. Dallas turned to watch her husband drive the ball a hundred yards or more above the long grass. She had scarcely seen him since his return to court. Like the other players, he was in his shirtsleeves; but unlike the others, and despite the heat of the day, Fraser had not yet broken a sweat.

"Ugh," said a husky voice behind Dallas. "What are those dreadful animals doing here?" Delphinia Douglas stood tall and magnificent in a richly embroidered gown of cream-colored silk.

Dallas glared defiantly at Delphinia. "They've been abandoned, poor things. I intend to take them under my care."

Delphinia's laugh was low and contemptuous. "How charming. But then I find it touching that you have those creatures on which to bestow your affection."

Rizzio stopped watching Johnny Stuart's swing from behind an oak tree. He scowled at Delphinia; in the past, many of her barbs had been aimed at him.

But Dallas didn't rise to the bait immediately. She picked up one of the cats and watched Iain Fraser line up a short putt. " 'Tis the last hole, I believe," she said mildly.

"You don't golf, I take it?" Delphinia asked, giving Fraser a little wave as the ball dropped into the hole.

"Nay," Dallas answered politely. "But Davie has offered to teach me tennis."

Delphinia raked Rizzio with her glance. "How kind. It is always a fine thing for a man to teach a woman skills that she lacks."

Dallas compressed her lips tightly and turned away to watch Lord Fleming's good-natured argument with George Seton. The courtiers were spurring the men on as the match reached its conclusion.

"There's an archery competition tomorrow, I understand," Delphinia went on in her husky voice. "I don't suppose you've tried that sport yet either, Mistress Fraser." Dallas, still trying to remain calm, admitted that she hadn't. "I enjoy it," Delphinia asserted, catching at her tawny veil, which a sudden breeze had blown askew. "Though I have had a problem with my stance—-I must practice tomorrow." She smiled widely and applauded lustily as Fraser and Lord Fleming were proclaimed victors. "Bravo, Iain," she called, waving her long white hand in a victory salute.

Fraser grinned back but approached the Queen as etiquette demanded. Dallas could no longer contain her tongue. She picked up the other cat and stood at Delphinia's elbow. "If you're having trouble with your stance, I suggest you spread your legs further. I understand you always score better that way, Mistress Douglas." And with that sally, Dallas stalked off, a cat under each arm, leaving Delphinia looking aghast and Rizzio unable to control his mirth.

THE AUGUST SUN glinted off the windowpanes of the little houses which clustered around the town square as Iain Fraser strolled the high street of Linlithgow. Small children tumbled with each other along the side of the dusty road and Fraser paused to retrieve a ball which a chubby red-haired boy of about five had tossed into a horse trough. Fraser lobbed it back to the child, who seemed fascinated by the tall, dark man with the deep suntan and the hint of the sea around his eyes.

Fraser was feeling exceptionally well this morning. His self-imposed exile had proved most profitable. Two Flemish barks, an English caravel, and several other lesser foreign vessels had yielded sufficient booty to keep him and his crew affluent for the next few months. In addition, he had visited with King Philip of Spain at Cadiz. It had not been a prearranged interview; the *Richezza* had needed some minor repairs after the encounter with the English caravel. Cadiz had been the nearest port, and flying the flag of Scotland, Fraser had sought refuge there. As the King happened to be staying in the city while on pilgrimage, Fraser deemed it politic to present himself to the austere Spanish monarch. Naturally, Mary Stuart's future had been discussed along with the possibility of marriage with Philip's son, Don Carlos. Fraser was not impressed by the tales he had heard of the young man. Indeed, he sounded as unstable as Arran. But it would do no harm to play with the possibility, and such marital maneuverings kept other royal powers guessing, especially Elizabeth.

But as Fraser continued on his way back to Linlithgow Palace, he felt the first faint hint of apprehension disturbing his sense of well-being. He had been in danger too often both on land and sea not to know when trouble was a-brewing. He moved along purposefully, the only change in his manner being the proximity of his right hand to his dirk. Ahead of him was a small inn, the King's Corbie. He decided to test the daring of his pursuer and stepped inside.

The common room was filled with the smells of dry rushes and frying meat. Two men lounged in a corner, drinking from heavy tankards. A serving wench came through a side door, a basket of eggs over one arm. She set the basket down on a table and walked with a deliberately swaying motion towards Fraser.

"I'll have four of those," he said, indicating the eggs. "And some bread and ale."

She dimpled at him and curtsied, low enough to reveal the deep cleft between her full breasts. Fraser absent-mindedly patted her generous bottom as she turned towards the kitchen. He waited with his legs stretched out on the wooden bench, his eyes on the door. At least five minutes went by before he was rewarded by the entrance of a small, wiry man in a canvas jerkin and mismatched riding boots. The little man looked wary but determined. He high-footed it over to Fraser, who was stroking his hawklike nose and eyeing the new arrival speculatively.

"Let's see—you began following me just after I passed the horse trough, correct?" Fraser asked.

The little man's mouth opened wide to reveal several gaps in his teeth. "Canny," he said with an appreciative grin. Then he leaned down and whispered into Fraser's ear. "My lord James Stuart wishes to see you, sir, at once. He's at an inn down the road, The Sword and Shieling."

"A pity I'm headed in the other direction." Fraser looked indolent but his right hand was never far from his dirk. He'd be damned if he'd go traipsing off to The Sword and Shieling and fall into James's neat little trap. "Why don't you ask Lord James to join me for breakfast? The eggs here were collected just minutes ago."

"He said you must meet him at the other inn," the man repeated doggedly. "Right away. It's urgent."

"All things are urgent with James." Fraser looked up as the serving wench, her breasts jiggling provocatively, came towards him with the platter of eggs, bread and a tall tankard of ale. She bestowed another dimpled smile on him and brushed his arm with her thigh. Fraser reached out to caress one of her breasts, winked, and then set about eating his breakfast.

"Lord James is not a patient man," the messenger warned. He waited for a response but Fraser was stuffing half an egg into his mouth.

"Salt!" he called out and the serving wench hurried back to the table. After she had gone and the eggs were seasoned to Fraser's taste, he turned back to the little man. "On the contrary, Lord James is infinitely patient. That's part of his game, to wait and wait and eventually outlast his opponents. However," he added, quickly turning on the bench to grasp the messenger by the jerkin, "I am not patient at all. Have you no manners? I'm eating!" With one hand, he shoved the man away, sending him sprawling onto the rushes. The two men in the corner looked up from their ale with mild interest. The serving wench's mouth formed a small little circle of admiration. But the messenger stared venomously at Fraser, got to his feet, and stalked from the inn. Fraser turned back to his breakfast and speared another egg.

AN HOUR LATER, when Fraser returned to his quarters at the palace, he was surprised to find James Stuart waiting for him. Lord James sat at a small escritoire, the hooded eyes regarding Fraser with unconcealed animosity.

"So you declined my invitation," James said by way of greeting. "That was most thoughtless, sir, in fact downright impertinent." Fraser did not reply immediately. "Well?" James demanded. "Have you lost your usual glibness?"

"I'm so overwhelmed by your visit that I can't think of an appropriate comment. I considered 'Get out,' but it sounded so boorish."

James, who was well known for his self-control, bristled in spite of himself. "You go too far, Iain. I should have you arrested this very moment."

"On what grounds, James? Or do you need any since you hold the reins of Scotland so firmly in your hands these days?" Fraser's tone was hard as flint, but a smile played at his mouth.

"In your case, I could find ample grounds. I'm not convinced you had no part in Bothwell's escape. And now you meddle in foreign affairs!" He had raised his voice and had to check himself to keep from pounding his fist on the escritoire.

Fraser was somewhat taken aback. But of course the Queen would have told her half-brother about King Philip's offer of Don Carlos as a possible bridegroom. If the two countries were about to enter negotiations, then James would have to be informed. No doubt the Queen had somehow made Fraser's reasons for being in Cadiz sound quite innocuous. She could no more afford to betray his role to James than he himself could.

"I'd hardly call it meddling to deliver a message from the King of Spain to the Queen of Scots," Fraser declared. "Come, come, James, what would you have done in my position?"

"What I'd like to know is how you got in that position in the first place," James growled. The heavy dark brows came together in the familiar frown. "I don't like it, taking such matters into your own hands. You're not on the council, you have no official position at court, you possess no title. In fact," James added slowly, "you don't even know who your father was."

"Oh?" The dark wedge of eyebrow lifted. "Do I not? How can you be so sure, Jamie?"

The room grew ominously quiet. James's eyes were wide open, staring at Fraser with an incredulity that was tinged by fear. "You were never able to learn anything, I've heard tales of how you tried, even back when we were both at the university."

Fraser shrugged. "I didn't—then. But that was over ten years ago. I know now."

"I don't believe you." James's tone was brusque, one hand cut at the air as if in dismissal of such an obvious falsehood. "It could have been anyone, a tinker, a shepherd, one of your father's own clansmen."

"But it wasn't." Fraser moved slowly to the escritoire and drew himself up to his full height, towering over James. "My mother was no less discriminating than your own, Jamie. Though yours was inclined to make her indiscretions public."

James's grey eyes held a chilling, icy light—and then the heavy lids shrouded any further expression. "You talk. You pretend, perhaps. It makes no matter—you have no proof."

Fraser did not answer. He just stared at James for a long moment and knew without the slightest doubt that Daniel Cameron had been right.

"So," James finally said to break the silence, "it makes no difference what you think you know." He picked up his serge bonnet and clapped it on his head. "You are still a bastard, Iain Fraser."

Fraser stood with his arms folded across his chest, making no motion to open the door for Lord James. "Aye," he said lazily, "and so are you, Jamie. So are you."

THE EARL OF Bothwell had sent for Iain Fraser, who set out the following dawn for the Border country. It would mean a full day's ride to Hermitage Castle, but Fraser knew Bothwell would not have sent for him unless there was an urgent reason.

THE COURT WAS due to leave Linlithgow the following day, August eleventh. Fraser had planned to travel with the Queen's party but now he would have to catch up with the royal entourage somewhere along the way, at Stirling, perhaps, or Perth.

It was close to midnight when Fraser sighted Hermitage. The structure stood on a little slope above a small copse and a rolling burn. It was an ancient castle, around whose walls many a battle had been waged. Fraser appreciated its strength and position as he noted that light shone from two slits in the stone. The earl must still be awake, he thought as he dismounted and led Barvas up the hill to the moat.

Six of Bothwell's moss-troopers appeared virtually from nowhere, their pikes gleaming in the moonlight. Fraser identified himself and after a brief discussion among themselves, the retainers ordered the drawbridge let down.

Fraser found Bothwell sprawled by the fire in the dining hall, an empty wine cup in his hand. "You made good time, Iain," the Border Earl said.

"I assumed you had ample cause to summon me here," Fraser responded, settling himself onto a deerskin rug near Bothwell. "I haven't eaten since late this afternoon. Is there anything left in your larder this time of night?"

Bothwell banged the wine cup on the hearth and two serving men came running. Fraser asked for meat and cheese and bread, with ale to wash it down. Then he pulled off his boots, peeled away his cloak and stretched himself. "Well? What's afoot?"

"How's your wife?" Bothwell poured himself another cup of wine from a leather jug. He wasn't drunk, but he wasn't quite sober, either. When Fraser didn't reply, Bothwell chuckled. "All right, all right," he sighed, propping himself up on one elbow. "I'm off to France. I want you to go with me."

"Christ," muttered Fraser. "Why should I want to sit around kissing the French King's arse for the next few months? I'm not about to be put to the horn." He kicked at a bone Bothwell's hounds had left on the hearth and one of the dogs let out a low rumbling noise in his throat.

"I can't stay here forever, like some secluded monk," Bothwell declared. "James will get to me somehow, even if he has to bribe one of my servants into putting something unsavory into this." He brandished his wine cup, slopping some of the contents onto his shirt. "And then James will go for you next. This progress is no ordinary sojourn. The Queen aims for a showdown with the Gordons. If you go north, you'll regret it."

A serving man was setting a tray of food down by Fraser. "Finally—I was well nigh weak from hunger." He took out his dirk and began cutting the big slab of beef. "You mean well, I know, but I've got to take my chances."

"Think it through, Iain," Bothwell urged. "There will be a confrontation, if not all-out war. Dammit, man, this is serious!" Bothwell kicked at one of the hounds making a play for Fraser's supper. "James knows you're a friend of the

Gordons and he'll find some way to bring you down with the rest of them. So you're better off out of Scotland for a while."

Fraser shook his head, pausing to swallow a mouthful of goat's cheese. "I've been out of the country, remember? I've no mind to leave again so soon. Besides, I'd rather keep my eye on James than sit around Chenonceaux or Amboise wondering what he's up to next."

Bothwell swore under his breath. "You're an obstinate man, Iain. Have it your way, but don't say I didn't warn you."

Fraser shrugged and threw some scraps to Bothwell's hounds who scrambled ferociously in the rushes for their prize. He'd made up his mind, he would leave again in the morning and by nightfall would be in Stirling, the court's first stop on its way to the north and Gordon country.

Chapter Nine

THE SEPTEMBER MISTS settled over the Highlands, protecting the wooded mountain glens from the human eye. This was lonely land, with only a few scattered cottages and a handful of poor farms. Food was scarce, the corn had not ripened, and the weather was as wet and dreary as it had been the previous year.

On the hillsides, mountain sheep grazed on the tough grasses. Occasionally, a few shaggy Highland cows wandered across the rutted roadway, forcing the royal cavalcade to halt. The animals gazed suspiciously at the intruders, with almost the same look that many of the human inhabitants displayed when the courtiers came by.

The royal caravan traveled into the foothills of the Cairngorms, whose majesty was captured only in fleeting glimpses of cloud and mist. Across the Spey, through Buquhane, Grange, Balvaney and Elgin they went, their numbers now augmented by a sizeable army.

Neither the foul weather nor the dismal harvest could dispel Iain Fraser's pleasure in being back on his native terrain. The special feel of the rocky ground beneath his horse's hooves, the damp smell which blew in from the sea, the sudden lush green specter of a wildwood glen seemed to make his blood run just a little faster.

But the Highlands stirred the blood of others in a different way. Mary Stuart had ordered the Earl of Huntly to meet her in Aberdeen. He came as requested but brought some fifteen hundred Gordon troops with him. The Queen was furious at Huntly's bold show of military strength and spurned the earl's offer to stay in his home at Strathbogie.

In retaliation, she gave her bastard half-brother, James Stuart, the title of

Earl of Moray—a title which had belonged to the Gordons for years. As far as Huntly was concerned, such an inciting gesture equaled a declaration of war.

ON THE EVE of the court's departure for Inverness, tempers were raw throughout Darnaway Castle. Tension seemed to drip from the stone walls as the soldiers made ready to march and the courtiers warily watched each other.

Iain Fraser's mood was no better than the rest. He had been ill pleased when James had been given the Moray earldom. As James strutted about the castle accepting the deference of the other courtiers, Fraser found his arrogant posturing insufferable.

Restless, tense and unable to sleep, Fraser prowled the corridors of Darnaway. He despised the idea of fighting Huntly and his Gordons. George Gordon had been his friend for years, Catherine had been his mistress for some time, and all of Huntly's brood were closely linked in some way. Fraser cursed the heritage of clan rivalries and wondered for the dozenth time if he should not have sailed the *Richezza* away from Scotland and its ominous atmosphere.

So deep in thought was he that it took a moment to recognize the woman coming towards him in the gloomy passageway: It was Dallas, carrying a lone taper in one hand and a decanter in the other. As she drew closer and he saw her face in the candlelight he noted that she looked weary.

"You're up late," he said, stopping in the middle of the narrow passageway so that she could not brush quickly by him as had become her habit since the progress began.

"Her Grace's stomach is all astir over what may happen tomorrow when we arrive at Inverness. I brewed some barberry bark and white wine for her," she said, indicating the decanter. "She is also upset because Queen Elizabeth refuses to release Lord Bothwell."

"It was bad luck for Bothwell that his ship got caught in that squall off the English coast." Fraser spoke in a conversational tone, but Bothwell's plight was another source of deep concern; when he reached shore, English soldiers had arrested the earl on piracy charges. The incident had made Fraser realize how precarious his own position was.

But Fraser said nothing for a long moment. Dallas watched the hazel eyes that seemed to spark in the light of the taper—and then the flame was extinguished, leaving them in virtual darkness. "Why did you blow out ...." Before Dallas could say more, he had taken both taper and decanter from her and set them on the ledge of a small window embrasure. She could hardly make out his expression as his arms went around her, and she felt her face pressed against the fine cambric of his white shirt. Dallas stiffened, waiting for what she assumed to be the inevitable assault upon her body. She would resist him, if for no other reason than that a passageway in Darnaway Castle was hardly an appropriate place for Iain Fraser to gratify his lust. There were other reasons, of course, but somehow they seemed to evade Dallas at the moment. Fraser was holding her close, not too tightly, only enough to keep her from bolting without a bit of effort.

"Dallas?" Fraser murmured into the mass of heavy hair.

"Yes?" Her voice was muffled against his chest; she could hear the steady beat of his heart.

"Are you all right? You look peaked of late."

She was surprised at the genuine note of concern in his voice. "Aye, I'm fine. Weary, of course, and upset." She managed to pull away enough to look up at him. "But we all sire these days."

"Aye." He sighed and one hand moved to smooth the hair from her forehead. "You now have cats, I'm told."

"I brought them from St. Andrews." She wondered what to do with her hands; they hung limply at her sides, feeling awkward. She reached up and traced the faint scar on Fraser's cheekbone. "You healed nicely. I'm glad."

His grip tightened just a bit. "I also heard you put Delphinia in her place."

"What?" She frowned and saw he was grinning at her. "Oh—well, I couldn't help it, she baited me in the most insufferable ways."

"Hmmmm." He leaned down and rested his cheek on the top of her head. "We quarreled because of that, you know."

"No. I mean, I knew you'd quarreled. Why because of that?" Dallas felt herself leaning against Fraser, felt her arms actually holding onto his shoulders.

"She complained to me about your remark—I would not endure her bad temper regarding my wife."

Dallas could hear her own heart beating, too—a very rapid rate at that—and she was unnerved by Fraser's words. "She does have dreadful manners," Dallas said at last, in a voice that was low and breathless.

"And an even worse temper. Worse than yours."

"Iain!" The comment momentarily broke the spell. She pulled back again to look into his face. He was laughing very softly. At her? At Delphinia? At himself? He looked so human, Dallas thought, so unlike a ravaging pirate or a cynical philanderer or even the dashing courtier. "I must go to the Queen—truly, I must."

The note of desperation made Fraser waver. But she was right—she had her own obligations, and service to the Queen of Scotland was one he could readily accept. He released her reluctantly; Dallas was astonished to discover that she was just as unwilling to leave him. But already he was handing back her taper and decanter.

"I can't relight it for you, lassie. Can you see well enough?"

She assured him she could. Bidding him a somewhat formal good-night, she resumed her walk down the passageway. But after a few yards, she paused to look back. Fraser stood where she had left him, watching her. He raised his hand in salute and Dallas had a sudden, overpowering urge to drop taper and decanter and rush back to the sanctuary of his arms. But she could not surrender to such a whim, she told herself sternly, and began to walk briskly towards the Queen's chamber.

INVERNESS CASTLE WAS more fortress than dwelling place. It stood on a rise above the River Ness, and commanded a splendid view of the surrounding Highland country. But when the Queen's company arrived at the castle gates on a September afternoon with the sun breaking through grey clouds, there was no sign of greeting. Huntly's son, Alexander, was keeper of Inverness Castle. While it was a royal establishment and not officially connected to the Gordons, Alexander was in charge, and he brazenly refused the Queen admittance. He was promptly taken captive and hanged from the battlements.

Dallas was appalled at the Queen's show of cruelty. But Mary Stuart was a monarch, after all, and had to assert her authority over rebellious subjects. And, once ensconced at Inverness, the Queen put this grim incident behind her.

She was intrigued by the Highlanders, their strange garb and their stranger tongue. "I had no idea they were so different," she confided to Fraser as she sat outdoors on a mild September night to receive the Fraser clan's allegiance. Mary had dressed in the Stuart plaid for the occasion, with a velvet bonnet on her head.

"They think you a fairy queen," Fraser said. He himself wore the dark red and green plaid of his clan. "See now, Your Grace, here come the Frasers, led by their young chief, Lord Hugh of Lovat."

Dallas stood apart from the others, watching Lord Hugh bow to the Queen. The Highland dusk settled down over the sharp-faced hills as haunches of venison were roasted over an open pit. Dallas ate heartily, savoring both the tangy flavor of the meat and its accompanying aroma.

To Dallas's surprise, Fraser left the Queen's company and strolled over to join her beneath the tall pines where she stood alone watching the others. He handed his empty plate to a servant and paused to listen as the sweet notes of a clarsach sounded in the distance. "My aunt used to play the harp like that when I was a lad," Fraser said with a nostalgic smile. "Well, Dallas, what think you of my native ground?"

"It's wild but beautiful in places," she conceded. "I prefer the city, I was raised there, after all."

Off to their right, several Fraser clansmen had begun a traditional Highland dance. The clarsach song died away, replaced by the heartier music of a half-dozen bagpipers. "Yet your own parents came from the north," Fraser pointed out. "I'm surprised you aren't drawn to this country in spite of your citified rearing."

"It's too untamed, too uncivilized," she replied firmly. "I don't feel at home here in the slightest."

The courtiers who had been eating and talking nearby now moved forward to watch the dancers. Dallas took a step as if to join them, but Fraser put a hand on her shoulder.

Fraser moved his hand to the back of her neck. She wore her hair piled high, crowned by a jaunty crimson hunting hat with a black feather. "I'm sorry to hear that, lassie," he said, running his fingers up and down behind her ear. "I'd hoped it might appeal to you."

"It does not," Dallas asserted, pulling away from his touch. "Corpses hanging from battlements, war about to break out, and a possible ambush in every copse—I find the place downright barbaric."

"And what token will you give this barbarian when I ride away to offer my life in the Queen's service?" Fraser's mouth mocked her, but the hazel eyes seemed unusually still.

"Token?" she blinked at him, telling herself she ought to turn on her heel and stomp away, yet somehow unable to do so. "Do you mock me?"

"Nay. But if you can think of nothing suitable, I'll take one of my own choosing." With startling swiftness, he pulled Dallas into his arms and brought his mouth down roughly on hers. She felt his tongue force her lips open, felt his body pressing hard against hers, felt as if she'd fall over backwards if he weren't holding her. But her own arms had gone around him, and she wondered hazily why she didn't try to wrench away. He finally lifted his mouth from hers. "Oh, lassie," he grinned, "I chose well. I've a mind to try for more."

"Don't be greedy," she whispered shakily, wondering vaguely what had happened to her hat. "You'd presume upon my generosity."

"I would indeed." In the distance, the clarsach played a haunting melody. The laughter of the courtiers seemed very far away and the wind flirted with the tall pines as the autumn moon hung like a wedge of gold in the cloudless night sky.

Fraser sought her lips again, and Dallas realized that he had not had to force her mouth open this time. She seemed to melt against him, feeling that lean, hard body pressing into the softness of her own flesh. The consuming hunger of Fraser's kisses touched off that not-quite-forgotten fire in the pit of Dallas's stomach. She was clutching at his back, her fingers digging into his plaid-draped shoulders.

Dallas actually felt dizzy as Fraser released her mouth long enough to let them both catch their breath. "Iain ...." She had virtually collapsed against him, her arms still holding him tight.

But another voice was calling Fraser's name. The Earl of Morton, accompanied by young Lord Hugh, had come barreling towards Dallas and Fraser. Lord Hugh looked embarrassed at the sight of his clansman holding a rather disheveled but obviously willing young lady in his arms. The Earl of Morton, who recognized Dallas at once, was astonished. Iain Fraser making love to his own wife? The earl's porcine features puckered as he spoke:

"The Queen has been searching all over for you, Iain. She commands you to join Lord Hugh in teaching her the Highland dance steps."

Fraser suppressed a terse oath. Dallas felt herself being carefully set upon her feet. Her husband put an arm around her waist and began to lead her towards the Queen. "Morton," he called over his shoulder, "would you mind retrieving my lassie's hat? She seems to have lost it in the heat of the evening's excitement."

DALLAS WAITED A long time for Fraser to return. But the Queen kept him at her side for the remainder of the festivities. At last, feeling weary and depressed, Dallas headed back towards the castle, telling herself that she didn't really care whether Fraser rejoined her or not.

But once in the quarters she was sharing with Mary Seton, Dallas realized she had no desire for sleep. In fact, she knew she would not be able to sleep. After putting the crimson hunting hat away and removing her dark blue velvet jacket, she stared out the slitted window at the revelers below. Several others were leaving, too; Mary Seton would no doubt be back shortly. Dallas did not want to talk to Mary—she considered undressing and feigning sleep, changed her mind, and headed out into the corridor. Walking aimlessly, she encountered only an occasional servant or courtier and one of the Queen's terriers seeking its mistress.

After ten minutes or more, Dallas realized she was lost. The passageway ahead was in total darkness. Apparently the torch had been blown out by a draught. She was about to turn back when someone called her name very softly. Startled, she looked around to see a hooded figure in the window embrasure.

"It's me, George Gordon," came the low voice. "Don't say anything, Dallas, or these priestly robes will be my shroud."

Dallas hurried towards Gordon and peered at him incredulously. He was indeed attired as a priest and only the blond moustache made him recognizable. "What on earth ...?" Dallas began, but Gordon signaled for her to be silent.

"Where is Iain's room?" he whispered. "Just show me."

But Dallas had no idea where her husband was quartered. And she refused to admit this to George Gordon. But the fact that Gordon had dared risk his life by appearing within Inverness Castle made Dallas realize that his presence signaled an utmost urgency, not only for himself but perhaps for Fraser as well. Fear overcame pride and Dallas started down the corridor with Gordon following noiselessly at her heels. Perhaps a servant could tell her where Fraser's room was located.

But it was not a servant whom Dallas encountered as she reached the west wing; it was David Rizzio, carrying his lute and looking at Dallas and her companion with large, curious eyes.

"I'm lost, Davie," Dallas said with a forced smile. "This priest has come to hear the Queen's ladies' confessions on the morrow. I thought perhaps he could bide with Iain tonight, but now I can't find my way back to his room."

Rizzio still looked puzzled but graciously gave directions. "Strange, ma donna," he added with his infectious grin, "your lord was just looking for you."

It was Dallas's turn to stare. But she recovered quickly, bade Rizzio goodnight and led George Gordon towards Fraser's quarters.

"You and Iain seem to have problems keeping track of one another," Gordon murmured. "How is it that you two ever married?"

"That's hardly your business, sir," Dallas snapped. She gave Gordon a swift, sharp look over her shoulder. Muffled as he was, his features were difficult to distinguish. But Dallas suddenly realized that his presence had made no emotional impact on her. She could regard him dispassionately, without feeling or regret. She could not, however, help from making a scathing comment: "As far as our marriage is concerned, I might point out that Iain doesn't suffer from superficiality as some men do."

"Ah!" Gordon couldn't suppress a chuckle. "Well, I must confess, the wedded state appears to agree with you. You've become bonnie as a May morning. You also seem to hold a grudge against me. I often wondered."

"I'll wager you never wondered at all," Dallas retorted, discovering she had gone one door too far and had to reverse herself, almost colliding with Gordon in the process.

Iain Fraser answered her knock immediately. The room was dark, however, and Dallas assumed he had just returned.

"Lassie!" he grinned at her, "I've been ...." But he stopped at once as he saw the hooded figure behind her. "What's this? Have you brought a cleric to shrive me?" Gordon all but pushed both Dallas and Fraser into the room, then quietly but quickly closed the door. He threw back the hood and began speaking before Fraser could do more than utter an oath of astonishment.

"I must talk to you alone." Gordon turned to Dallas. "I appreciate your help, but both Iain and I will appreciate your silence even more."

Dallas looked from one man to the other. Fraser was lighting a candle and regarding Gordon quizzically.

"I haven't much time, Iain," Gordon said impatiently. "Truly, I can't speak in front of your wife."

Fraser sighed and turned to Dallas. "George is probably right. Although you do keep a secret well, lassie." He bent down and brushed her lips with his. "Good night, wife—and be careful."

Dallas looked at him wistfully, then glanced at George Gordon. Instead of going directly to the door, she put her arms around Fraser's neck and kissed him hard on the mouth. "Good night, Iain. You be careful, too." With one last stare at Gordon, she swept out of the room.

"You—and the Cameron!" Gordon shook his blond head. "Astounding! Why, Iain? She's as poor as she is prickly."

"Never mind my domestic affairs," Fraser replied rather testily. "What in Christ's name are you doing here?"

Gordon turned serious. "I'm on my way to my father-in-law's country house. I had to see you before I left."

Fraser raised his eyebrows. "You? Run from a fight and hide in the bosom of your Hamilton in-laws? That's not your way, George."

The other man sat down heavily on the bed. "True enough. But I'm my father's heir and he's already lost one son in this war of wills ...." Gordon stopped, shook his head in an abrupt, jerky motion and looked away for a moment.

"Here." Fraser handed Gordon a cup of whiskey, poured some for himself, and gestured for his visitor to continue.

Gordon drained his cup in two gulps and handed it back to Fraser for refilling. "The Gordons know this terrain far better than the Queen's troops. Her men are growing restless waiting and that's bad for soldiers. And maybe you've noted that they aren't as loyal as they might be—surely the sprig of heath which many wear in their helmets hasn't eluded you with its significance. Those men secretly support the Gordons."

"I've considered that." Fraser placed one knee on a chair and leaned across its back. "Does James know?"

"He suspects, or so our spies tell us. That's why he has divided the soldiers into two companies. The first into battle will be made up of ones he isn't certain are loyal. The second wave will be those whose support is without question."

Fraser set both feet down on the floor and a loose board creaked beneath his heel. "So why risk your life to see me, George?"

Gordon put down his whiskey cup and tucked his hands up inside his flowing black sleeves. He suddenly looked very pious and Fraser couldn't suppress a grin. "The second company will be led by Lord James." Gordon cleared his throat and looked quickly around the room as if eavesdroppers might be lurking in the shadows. "I think you should command the first."

The grin died quickly on Fraser's face. "Good God, man!" Fraser exploded. "You talk treason! You'd have me lead disloyal troops in mutiny against the Crown?"

Hastily Gordon signaled for Fraser to keep his voice down. "I'm taking the longer view, Iain. Victory for the crown is victory for Lord James and the Protestant religion. Victory for the Gordons is ultimate victory for the Queen—and the old faith. Can't you see where your real loyalties lie?"

"Don't play on religious sentiments which don't exist," Fraser declared in an annoyed tone. "I've never joined the Lords of the Congregation and I never will, but I'm no ardent Papist. I worship God in my own way and have no desire to slaughter my fellow human beings for the sake of kirk or clan."

"You'll slaughter us." Gordon's blue eyes regarded Fraser with genuine pain. "What's the difference?"

"The difference is I've vowed to serve the Queen." Fraser sighed, his anger turning to regret. "God knows I mislike Lord James as much as you do, George. You know what these Protestant fanatics have done to the Highland customs, the language, to things that have no bearing whatsoever on religion. They've plundered more than churches and convents with their harsh, artless hands—they've tried to change a way of life treasured for centuries by a race of poor but proud people." He shook himself and banged his fist against the casement. "Christ, I sound as fulsome as Knox himself!"

Gordon said nothing for a long time. When he finally spoke, it was with a sigh of resignation. "But you're still saying no. I'm sorry, Iain, I'd hoped for a different reply."

"I'm sorry, too, George." Fraser put out his hand to the other man. "Most of all, I'm sorry that this battle has to be fought in the first place. Now for God's sake, get the hell out of here before your poor sire loses yet another son."

THE AUTUMN HAARS faded early on the morning of October twenty-second, 1562. At the Earl Marischal's house in Aberdeen, Mary Stuart waited anxiously with her women. At Corrichie Moor, her troops waited for the Gordons.

A tumbling burn separated the royal army from Huntly's men, who had gathered on the Hill of Fare. The sky was a pale grey, the sun an ineffectual white globe. Broadswords and axes stood ready and a few of Huntly's men clung to their bows. Across the burn, Lord James had augmented his forces with 120 expert harquebusiers.

As Huntly moved to the head of his men, James Stuart cantered not to his own position of command, but to where Iain Fraser stood beside Barvas at the edge of the burn.

"A fair enough day for victory, eh, Iain?" James called out, reining in his mount. The Queen's half-brother seemed uncharacteristically jaunty.

"It's not raining, if that's what you mean," Fraser answered back.

James chuckled into his dark beard. He and Fraser had scarcely spoken since their tense meeting at Linlithgow in August.

"I'm trying to be optimistic. I think I have reason to be, don't you?" He gestured with a gloved hand towards the troops which were poised a hundred yards or so beyond Fraser. "You will lead the first van, Iain, along with Lord Forbes and Lord Hay."

Fraser did not react visibly, but inwardly, his whole being revolted at the order. It was a trap, clever and deadly. He would be in command with two men whose loyalty was questionable, whose troops were ready to bolt in Huntly's favor. If that happened, Fraser would either be abandoned to the Gordons or, if he survived, charged with treason along with the other rebel soldiers. If he'd accepted George Gordon's suggestion in the first place, he would at least have had the advantage of a well-defined tactical plan. But being forced into the situation at the last minute, uncertain of what either Forbes or Hay intended, Fraser was at a dangerous disadvantage. The alternative, however, was equally perilous—if he refused, James would denounce him as a traitor.

"I'd be honored to share the leadership," Fraser replied without inflection. "I had no idea you put such faith in my abilities."

James forced a smile. "I'm a good judge of men, Iain. Even you must admit that."

Fraser caught the irony in James's tone and merely laughed. He watched the other men salute and gallop away, then turned to three of his Fraser clansmen. "Keep close by me, to my rear," he commanded in a low voice. "The enemy may be in more places than we suspect." The Highlanders glanced around, noting the soldiers who wore sprigs of heath in their helmets. They, too, had heard rumors of possible defection and were no more anxious than Fraser to take a blade in the back.

Swinging up into the saddle, Fraser scanned the second company to make sure James's harquebusiers were well out of range; a bullet would be no more welcome than a sword thrust. As a final precaution, he would see to it that Forbes and Hay rode out ahead of him. "Well, Barvas," he murmured, patting the big stallion's neck, "we are about to have our mettle tested."

The pipers began to play the old, familiar war songs that raised the men's blood to feverish fighting pitch. The horsemen and foot soldiers stirred. Across the glen, Huntly's men held their ground, waiting for their chief to give his signal.

Fraser knew the battle plan. Despite Huntly's good position on the hill, the royal troops were to make their charge straight across Corrichie Moor and through the glen. Fraser glanced at Forbes and Hay who nodded their assent to move out. Lifting their broadswords, all three commanders cried out, "A Stuart!" The waiting game had ended.

The first van moved out, down through the heather and the wet earth. Across the burn they marched, horsemen following foot soldiers. The cloud cover held and the air was cold and damp.

The first company reached the Hill of Fare without difficulty. Though a few rocks proved slippery, the footing was generally firm enough. Crowding up the slope, the men kept their eyes fixed on the sea of blue and green plaid which lined the summit.

At last Huntly gave the orders to advance. His son, John Gordon, raised his sword and their followers moved off the crest of the hill in a swirl of pipes and a rattle of chain mail.

From halfway up the hill, Fraser saw them advance. He reined up on Barvas for a brief moment to assess the situation. Huntly had remained on the hilltop. One phalanx was led by John Gordon, and Fraser spurred Barvas on just as the first contingent of rebel forces collided with the royal troops.

Swinging his sword at the first man who approached him, Fraser knocked his opponent flat with one blow. The man wasn't dead but would fight no more that day. Wheeling Barvas around, he fended off a second soldier whose horse went out from under him. Then a commotion from behind diverted his attention. Turning cautiously, he saw what he had feared to see: The royal troops were flinging down their weapons, some of them rushing to embrace the enemy

"Whoresons!" he shouted, though no one could hear him over the din of clattering weapons and charging horses. Two Gordon supporters stood very near, not attacking, apparently waiting to see if he intended to give up the fight, too.

"You think I'll run like a craven coward?" he yelled, and this time he was heard, his three Highlanders keeping close behind him. Lashing out with his sword, Fraser caught one opponent in the arm. The other man struck at Fraser with his axe, but the thrust was neatly parried.

Fraser whirled for the next onslaught, but instead of a charging enemy, he saw the Earl of Huntly sitting atop the hill, watching the battle rage 'round him. Fighting his savage way through the earl's supporters until he finally faced the Gordon chieftain, Fraser was shocked to see how wretched the proud old nobleman looked, with his red eyes and corpulent body and the sprig of heath wilting in the sun.

"Iain," Huntly said in almost pleasurable surprise. And then the proud old earl plunged forward and crashed onto the marshy ground.

Fraser jumped down from his horse and knelt beside Huntly. "He's dead," Fraser said in a sharp voice. "His heart was not as great as his valor." Other troops from both sides gathered around them in a tight little circle. They stared at the crumpled figure and some of the Gordon soldiers crossed themselves.

Straightening up, Fraser did not hear the cries of victory from the royal troops as they moved quickly up the Hill of Fare, unimpeded by the Gordon defenders. He took Barvas's reins and led the stallion away as the stunned soldiers parted ranks to let them pass. Somewhere during the confusion, he'd been separated from the three Highlanders but that no longer mattered, the battle was over. Fraser's sword was still clutched in his hand and a sudden weariness overtook him. Down the hill he went, as soldiers rushed by him, shrieking in wild jubilation, waving bloodied scraps of Gordon plaid like victory banners.

In the glen, it was relatively quiet. Fraser walked with Barvas to the burn and let the horse take a few measured drinks from the rippling water. The dead and wounded lay about them, but the battle had not been heavy with bloodshed, for the burn still ran clear. When Barvas was done, Fraser threw himself onto his stomach, cast off his helmet, and drank freely. He was just putting his hands down on some rocks for leverage to raise himself when he felt the blade go deep into his back. The last thing he remembered was how his chain mail had been rent to permit the thrust and that his old instinct for danger had finally failed him.

Chapter Ten

MARY STUART GREETED her half-brother, James, with a warm embrace. But her eyes grew misty when he described Huntly's death. "I would rather he had died in battle," she said. "What of his sons?"

Brusquely James stated that John and Adam had been taken captive. "Neither should be spared," he asserted. "It's bad enough that George is safely tucked away with those damnable Hamiltons."

The Queen shook her head. "No—at least not Adam. He's but seventeen." She turned to Maitland. "What think you, master secretary?"

Maitland, still attired in his chain mail, inclined his head. "I think you should make the most of your victory, madame."

"Maitland is right, of course," James said swiftly, not wanting to allow his half-sister time to think the situation through. "John should be executed immediately and I'd not show mercy to Adam, either, young as he is. As for Huntly, you must try his corpse, as tradition dictates."

The Queen glanced away from James to her ladies. Dallas, Jean Argyll and Mary Fleming all looked as revolted by the idea as did the Queen herself. "I don't know—I must have time to think this out." She pressed her hands to her head and sat stiffly in a carved armchair. "Perhaps you should leave me now, gentlemen. I thank you most heartily for your efforts on my behalf this day. Oh, and I must thank Iain, too. Where is he?"

Maitland glanced quickly at James who cleared his throat more loudly than was necessary. The Queen looked at them both questioningly but neither seemed willing to speak out. It was Dallas who finally broke the silence.

"Well, my lords," she demanded, fighting back a surge of panic. "Where is my husband?"

It was Maitland who stepped forward to take her hand, which she immediately snatched away. Further disconcerted, the usually suave secretary broke into a stammer: "I'm s-sorry, madame. Your husband received a grievous wound. I'm afraid he will n-not recover."

From somewhere in the room, there were gasps and whimpering noises, but Dallas didn't hear them. She brushed past Maitland and went directly to Lord James. "Where is he?" Her voice was hoarse, the words coming out through clenched teeth.

Lord James shifted uncomfortably. "I believe he was taken to a crofter's hut near Corrichie Moor. But you'll be informed when ...."

"Get me an escort! Now!" She was blazing with emotion and the others watched her, transfixed.

Recovering from his astonishment at being ordered about like a potboy, Lord James stood his ground. "I'm afraid that's impossible. No woman could go near that battlefield today. The wounded are still being removed and it would be nightfall before you got there." His icy demeanor had returned, but he could not conceal a glimmer of triumph behind the hooded eyes.

"I'll do as I please!" she announced and turned back to Maitland. "You'll see that I have an escort immediately, sir, if this unfeeling piece of granite here won't come to my aid!"

Maitland looked from the rigid James to a sobbing Queen and back to Dallas. Inwardly, he cursed Dallas for putting him in such an awkward position but knew he could not refuse. "If you'll permit me," he said to the Queen who nodded in assent, "then come along, Mistress Fraser, and I'll see what I can do."

Dallas followed him hurriedly from the room but not before she had given James one last look of utter contempt.

FIFTEEN MINUTES LATER, Dallas was attired in her riding habit and in the company of four men, including Will Ruthven. Except for the most formal greetings at court, it was the first time she had spoken to him since the night of her father's death.

"I'm sorry to hear about Iain," Will said diffidently as the horses were readied in the Earl Marischal's stables.

Dallas scarcely heard him. She swung up into the saddle without aid and was the first one down the gravel path.

The sun was beginning to set as they headed towards Corrichie Moor, but Dallas never paused to consider the scenery. Will now led the way since Maitland had told him exactly where Fraser had been taken.

It was not far to the crofter's hut, and by the time they reached the battle site, all of the men, living and dead, had been removed. Only the scarred ground, a discarded weapon or some shreds of plaid gave witness to the day's momentous events.

"A quarter of a mile further," Will called out to Dallas. She nodded grimly and spurred her horse to keep up the pace.

A half-dozen black-faced sheep grazed atop the Hill of Fare where earlier that day Stuart and Gordon troops had joined in combat. They ignored the intruders and continued munching at the few tough little patches of grass left intact by the soldiers.

The little party found easy going on the downside of the hill. Just beyond, in a narrow hollow, a small stone farmhouse lay huddled against a copse of larch and pine. Dallas pulled ahead of the others, and within five minutes she had reined in, dismounted and was banging on the cottage door with her riding crop.

A grey-bearded man with a heavy limp came out to stare at her. He would have been more surprised to see an expensively dressed young lady of the court at his door if he had not already watched what had seemed like half of Scotland conduct a raging battle in front of his farmhouse earlier that day. To further disturb his unvaried pattern of life, a nobleman now lay gravely wounded inside on a straw pallet.

"I'm Mistress Fraser," she announced, all but pushing him aside. "Where is my husband?"

The man jerked with his thumb in the direction of the pallet, but Dallas was already hurrying across the room. A pitiful peat fire smoldered on the hearth, providing the only light inside the poorly furnished croft. A stoopshouldered woman was stirring something in a pot which hung over the fire. She looked up when Dallas came in but said nothing.

On the pallet, under the watchful, anxious eyes of Cummings, lay Iain Fraser. He was stripped to the waist, and a dirty bandage covered most of his chest and back. His eyes were closed and his face was dirty from blood and sweat.

"Mistress Fraser!" cried Cummings, low and relieved. The usually composed and efficient Cummings had lost his aplomb. He had never thought he could be so glad to see his lord's wife. And the last place he'd expected to see her was in this miserable crofter's hut.

Dallas had knelt down by the pallet. "Cummings, tell my escort to stay outside. And get me some plantain weed, I saw some by the corner of the house."

Cummings jumped to his feet, glad to be doing something useful. Dallas had thrown her cloak onto the dirt floor. She looked at the taut, lean face of her husband, deathly pale beneath its tan. His breathing was slow and painful, but at least he was still alive. She got to her feet, took off the brown riding hat with its elegant trim of pheasant feathers, and turned to the woman who had continued stirring her pot.

"I need fresh water. Is this the only bandage he's had on so far? Has he taken anything to eat or drink? Has he been conscious at all?"

The verbal barrage was too much for the old woman. She stared at Dallas, trying to remember the first question. "I've water in this bucket, mistress, drawn today. Aye, that's the only bandage. 'Twas his shirt—we had naught else." She stopped and gazed phlegmatically at Dallas.

"Very well," said Dallas, deciding she'd heard enough. It was all too clear that Fraser had not opened his eyes since being wounded. Working briskly, she pulled up the brown serge of her riding habit and ripped at the fine taffeta petticoat. She should have had sense enough to bring bandages, but the question of whether Fraser lived or died had blotted all else from her mind. Very carefully, she began to undo the old bandage and found that she could not budge Fraser without help.

"I'll have to wait for Cummings," she said to herself, then turned back to the old woman. "Get me a bowl. And have you any mouldy bread?" She remembered Marthe's old cure for a variety of skinned knees, bruises and scrapes.

The woman had gotten out a much-chipped piece of crockery and a pestlelike mixing implement. "Mouldy bread?" She wrinkled her brow. "Aye, I save the crusts for the birds and such." She didn't need to add that every other crumb which hadn't turned stale was saved for herself and her husband.

Cummings returned with the plantain which Dallas mixed in the bowl with some ash from the peat fire. The woman had rummaged through a cupboard to find the mouldy bread. Dallas had Cummings help her raise Fraser up from the pallet, and soon the ragged, blood-stained bandage was removed.

But Dallas was perplexed. "Where's the wound?" she whispered.

Cummings bit his lip. "In the back, madame," he informed her, almost as ashamed as if he'd struck the blow himself. Carefully, he turned Fraser over onto his stomach.

Dallas stared at the oozing red hole. Her eyes met Cummings's unhappy gaze. "In the back?" she breathed.

He nodded. "I found him facedown in the burn." He spoke very low so that the woman could not hear. "It was after the battle. He would have drowned in another minute."

Her mouth set in a tight line. "If I could ever be sure who had committed such treachery .... Cummings, do you know?"

He shook his head. "Like you, madame, I can only harbor my suspicions."

She made no further comment but set about cleansing the wound. Rubbing the ash and plantain mixture gently onto Fraser's flesh, she then applied the mould and finally had Cummings help her wrap the fresh bandage around her husband's body. Soon Fraser lay back on the pallet, his face wiped clean, the dark hair brushed back from his forehead. Dallas sat back on the dirt floor and prepared to take up her vigil.

SOME TIME LATER, after Dallas had asked Cummings to send Will and the other men back to Aberdeen, the old woman spoke hesitantly. "I have some barley broth, madame, if he wakes."

"He will," Dallas replied staunchly. "But it may not be until the morrow." She glanced back at Fraser, noting that his breathing seemed easier.

Dallas was not conscious of sleeping that night, but she must have, for just as the first light of dawn crept in between the cracks in the hut's walls she found herself curled up on her cloak. Cummings snored softly in the corner, and over by the hearth the old couple slept side by side.

Later, after the early morning mist had begun to clear, she ate some broth and a corncake at Cummings's insistence. She must have dozed again, for the next thing she knew, Cummings was walking through the doorway with a pail in his hand. The crofter and his wife were nowhere to be seen.

"I was watering the horses," he explained. "Barvas is stabled out back with your mount and my own. Our hosts are outside, counting their sheep and chickens to make sure the soldiers didn't steal anything."

Dallas only half-heard what Cummings said. She was watching Fraser closely, noting that his forehead was still beaded with sweat. "We must change the bandage again." She stood up and launched another assault on her petticoats while Cummings politely turned the other way. Once the old bandage was off, Dallas saw that the wound was beginning to pucker around the edges and that the swelling had gone down some. Reaching for more of her plantain and ash mixture, she was startled when Fraser stirred in Cummings's arms.

"He's moving," she whispered.

Cummings looked down at his master's face. "Aye, madame! Sweet Christ, his eyes are opening!" Fraser's lids flickered for just an instant and then he fell back as limp as before.

Dallas clamped her mouth shut to hide her disappointment. Then she resumed ministering to the wound and putting on another bandage. Though they watched hopefully throughout the next hour for a further sign of recovery, Fraser remained motionless.

"Stretch your legs out a bit, Cummings," Dallas said. "You've been here longer than I have."

"I've already been out once or twice today, madame," Cummings replied. "You had better get some air yourself."

Dallas shook her head. "Not yet. I'll go after you get back." Cummings hesitated but then agreed. In his absence, Dallas rummaged through the cupboards, looking for something to eat. She had no real appetite but felt vaguely weak and knew she should take some food to sustain herself. The larder was pitifully low, revealing only a couple of eggs, some black bread and a few apples, one of which she took out and rubbed against her skirt.

Munching on the apple, she went to the door and looked out. The sun was high in the sky; it must be close to noon. She could see Cummings across the hollow, exercising Barvas. The crofter and his wife were digging for something in a little garden patch about a hundred yards away. Potatoes, Dallas decided, and turned away from the door to toss her apple core onto the dead ashes in the hearth. She was wondering whether or not to use the remaining water in the wooden bucket for washing her face when she heard a noise. She turned quickly and saw Fraser struggling to lift himself from the pallet.

"Iain!" She flew across the room, dropping down on her knees beside the pallet. "Don't move! You're very ill!"

He was still feverish but his eyes were alert. "Dallas? Where in Christ am I?"

She pushed at him gently, moving him back onto the straw. "You're in a crofter's hut near the Hill of Fare. You were wounded during the battle, remember?"

His eyes flickered darkly. "Not during," he breathed. "After." And his eyes closed again as he fell back into a deep sleep.

Dallas and Cummings kept up their watch for the rest of the day, but Fraser did not wake again. In the morning his fever seemed to be gone. Stiff and sore, Dallas got to her knees, noting that the others still slept. Then, Fraser rolled over onto his side and opened his eyes. "What the devil are you doing here, Dallas?" he asked quietly, and she was astonished to see a hint of the familiar mocking smile.

"I—I was told you were wounded," she whispered back. "You think I'd let you die here by yourself?"

"So you had to protect your investment, eh, lassie?" he grinned.

Dallas was too relieved to be angry with him. Yet his initial question was well put: Why had she come? There were many women at court, trapped into marriages of convenience, who would not have ridden like a whirlwind and nursed a wounded husband in the meanest of circumstances. They would have wept ostentatiously, wondered what they had to wear for mourning, and sent a servant to handle the situation.

But compelled by both fury and fear, Dallas had flown to Fraser's side.

Why? The question could not be put aside. And the answer was as clear as it was startling: Dallas loved her husband.

It had been one of those discoveries which she had managed to avoid confronting in her typical, practical approach to life. In the first place, it simply wasn't possible. Dallas had vowed never to face rejection again—and never to love any man. What she had felt for Fraser—even in the beginning, and finally under that golden Highland moon at Inverness—she had dismissed as foolishness, misplaced romanticism or a too-active imagination.

It had been relatively easy to deny her feelings as long as she and Fraser were apart. Even after Inverness, she told herself those impassioned moments had meant nothing to him; she had merely been convenient and surprisingly willing. In the weeks which followed, she had scarcely seen Fraser as he joined the other men in preparing for battle. Indeed, it had almost appeared as if he were trying to avoid her.

So if she had given her heart away, she had managed to keep her pride. Dallas would not let Fraser know how she felt. Why, she thought, looking at those lean, sharp features and the hazel eyes, he would probably have a relapse from laughing at her!

So she merely shrugged. "I shouldn't wish you dead, certainly. All in all, you've been most conscientious in living up to our bargain."

Fraser fingered the black stubble of beard on his chin. "Oh, aye, we've both done our part in that." He sighed and laid back with his hands behind his head, wincing from the pain such a movement caused him. "I could eat something. In fact, I may be starving to death. How long have I been here?"

"Two days. The old woman made up some fresh okra soup last night. I'll heat it for you." She started to rise but Fraser reached out to put a hand in her hair. Dallas was astonished by the firmness of his grip. He started to say something, changed his mind, and shook his head. "You look a fright, Dallas."

"You don't look so grand yourself, sir," she threw back at him. Then as he dropped his hand she put her head down on his chest. The thick, uncombed hair tumbled across the bandage as she felt his arms go around her. "Fie, Iain, I'm so glad you're better! You frightened me witless when I first came here!"

He said nothing for a long time, savoring her softness and the faint smell of jasmine which still clung to her hair. Dallas felt an odd sense of being at peace. She had no urge to offer Fraser resistance, and though she would not confess her love, his arms made her feel contented. The important thing, she told herself, was that her husband was alive. Her long vigil was over and she was so weary ....

Fraser continued to hold her quietly and listen to the steady rhythm of her breathing. It had, in fact, grown a little too steady. "Dallas, are you asleep?" he whispered.

"What? No, no, truly ...." She raised her head, moving slowly out of his arms. "Well, I am tired, what would you expect, sleeping on this damnable dirt floor when I've slept at all?" She stood up and looked at him peevishly. In the corner, Cummings let out one final snore before he began to awaken.

He was overjoyed to find his master conscious and in full command of his faculties. The two men spoke together in low voices while Dallas stepped over the old couple to stoke the dying fire.

Later, after Fraser had eaten the broth and some bread, he slept again. That pattern continued for the rest of the day, short periods of wakefulness, a bit of food and then an hour or so of sleep. Dallas busied herself by trying to comb her hair and straighten out her clothes. She went outside for a while, helping the old woman gather eggs and pick some late vegetable marrow from the garden patch.

The following morning Dallas awoke to find Fraser sitting up on the pallet, scratching himself vigorously. "Where in God's good name can a man take a bath around here? I seem to have attracted some companions in this place." He crushed two of the offenders beneath his bare heel.

"The burn, I suppose," Dallas replied drowsily and saw her husband's eyes harden. "I'm sorry, Iain, but you can't walk that far anyway. Maybe they have a tub some place around here."

"Never mind. And I could walk that far, if I had to." As if to prove it, he stood up, carefully flexing his leg muscles. "A trifle weak, but not as bad as it could be." He began to walk slowly around the small hut. "Later today, I'll test my strength on Barvas. Will you join me, madame?"

"You're daft, Iain. You mustn't ride so soon. Besides, it's going to rain."

But he did go out that afternoon and Dallas went with him, marveling at the pleasure she found in his company. Clever! she had chided herself. How could I have been so stupid! But, still, she would keep the truth to herself, no matter how difficult it might prove.

The rain held off during the hour they rode through the hollow and over to the burn between Corrichie Moor and the Hill of Fare. Cummings had insisted that Fraser wear his shirt, since his master's had been used for bandages.

They kept their horses to no more than a canter. Fraser did not sit as easily in the saddle as usual, but his endurance seemed quite remarkable to Dallas. When they reached the spot by the burn where he had been attacked, Fraser reined Barvas in. "See, that is where I stopped to drink." He stared down at the rocks as if they could reveal to him the identity of his assailant. "It was a clever plan, at the start," he said, as much to himself as to Dallas. "By placing me in command of that traitorous first company, they were sure I'd be killed either by Gordon or Stuart men. When that didn't happen, and when James discovered he'd have to force the rebel troops to resume fighting or lose the day entirely, he devised yet another method of getting me out of the way."

Dallas shivered. "What will you do when you get back to Aberdeen? Will you confront James?"

Flicking the reins, Fraser turned Barvas around to head back towards the hut. "I'm not going back to Aberdeen. Much as I'd enjoy being there in person to show James that his scheme failed, I'm off to Beauly. It'd be pointless for me to return to court for a while. From Beauly, I'll join my crew on the Isle of Lewes and make ready to sail as soon as I'm recovered. And," he said with his crooked grin, "I may make some inquiries about my parentage."

Dallas felt strangely hollow inside. "You aren't fit to travel for days yet. We could go somewhere else nearby, there must be a Fraser house that would give you hospitality."

He smiled to himself at her use of the word we. "Nay, Dallas, I'm better off away from here just now. And you must return to court. I need you there to look after my interests." He slowed Barvas so that she could bring her mount alongside his. "James may try something else, perhaps to put me to the horn or confiscate my lands. You might not be able to stop him, but I know you'd try." He grinned at her as they wound their way around the Hill of Fare.

"I don't think James likes me any better than he likes you," Dallas responded. "He all but gloated when he told me you were dying and, I must admit, I wasn't very gracious about it." She bristled at the memory of Lord James actually refusing to get her an escort. "The weasel-faced little arsehole," she breathed. "When will you leave?"

They could see the hut now, with its curl of peat smoke rising from the stone chimney. The old woman was out in the front, chasing her chickens. "On the morrow," Fraser said.

"No! That's too soon!" Dallas protested. "You can't go so far alone!"

Fraser's tone was reasonable. "Oh, yes, but I won't go the whole distance at once and I know this country like the back of my hand. Cummings will escort you back to Aberdeen. In fact, it might be best if you went this afternoon."

Dallas's mouth set in a stubborn line. "I won't go. If I can't go with you, then at least I'll stay here until you're ready to leave."

He knew it was useless to argue with her, as useless as it was for Dallas to try talking him out of leaving in the morning. And, of course, he was pleased that she wanted to stay with him. The rest of the day passed quietly, with Fraser making what few preparations he could for his journey, and in the evening he told Dallas about Beauly and the surrounding countryside. When it was finally time for bed, he offered her the pallet.

"I'll stay where I am, thank you," she replied, spreading her cloak out on the floor. "I've no mind to take up with those infernal lice."

Once again, he didn't argue. Cummings was already bedding down in his accustomed corner while the old couple finished cleaning up from the sparse evening meal. Fraser stretched himself out on the pallet. "Actually, Dallas," he whispered so that the others couldn't hear, "there's room for two."

Dallas hesitated. "I'm fine," she whispered back at last. "Besides, you ramble about in your sleep since you started to get better."

"As you will." He was silent for a moment while the old couple began to settle down by the hearth. "Give me your hand, Dallas," he commanded in a low voice.

Dallas obeyed, reaching out to let him take her fingers in his. Soon they were both asleep, their hands still clasped together.

DRESSED IN A fresh bandage, his chain mail and Cummings's too-small shirt, Fraser went outside to where Barvas was tethered. It was raining, a steady cool drizzle which brought the clouds in low above the surrounding hills.

"You'll have to pay these people for their kindness," Fraser said as he checked Barvas's saddle and girth. "You have money?"

"Nay, I never thought to bring any. What about Cummings?"

"Not enough on his person to make adequate recompense." He frowned as Barvas whinnied softly, apparently impatient.

"My rings," Dallas said, holding out her hands, now red and scratched from her labors. "They could sell them, couldn't they?"

He pointed to her right hand. "That sapphire will do nicely, a full year's livelihood for these poor folk. You weren't considering your wedding band, were you?"

Dallas's right hand flew to her left, covering the wide band of beaten gold set with emeralds. "Oh, no, I wouldn't do that!"

Her genuine horror delighted him. He took her chin in his hand and bent down to kiss her firmly on the mouth. She felt her lips part under his and wished he would never stop kissing her. But he released her almost at once. "Take care, lassie," he said, and swung up into the saddle.

IT RAINED HARDER as Fraser rode west. He traveled slowly, as he had promised Dallas, and spent the night in a shieling outside of Strathdon. When he arrived at Inverness the following evening, the first thing that struck him was the subdued atmosphere which hung about the city like the rain itself. The Gordon stronghold was feeling the effects of its clan's defeat at Corrichie Moor. Great Huntly was dead and their new chieftain was somewhere in the south, hiding out with the Hamiltons.

Wearily, Fraser clattered over the stone bridge which crossed the River Ness. The old high kirk, built on a knoll once called Michael's Mound, stood to his right, its stones a brooding grey in the waning October light. In another hour, he should reach Beauly, and he spurred Barvas into a trot. They set out through a gentle green valley. Beyond the tree-covered ridges lay the gaunt mountains of the west, waiting for their first cap of snow.

He reined in at Beauly just after dark. The wound in his back was throbbing and his skin was soaked with rain and sweat. The members of his clan would welcome him, though at Corrichie some had taken up arms for the Gordons. No matter, he thought, I'm alive. I'm safe for now—and I'm home.

Chapter Eleven

DALLAS WAS ALONE in the royal chambers at Aberdeen. The preliminary packing for the return south was all but accomplished, and as she glanced out the window towards the sloping drive she saw a half-dozen royal retainers piling a baggage cart high with trussed crates. These, she knew, contained the priceless vestments from St. Matchar Cathedral which had been entrusted to the Gordons and now had been confiscated by the Crown. An even larger crate still lay on the ground, monstrous in size, grisly in content. Inside rested the disemboweled body of Great Huntly, destined to be tried in the ancient way, in front of Parliament with the Queen sitting in attendance.

Shuddering, Dallas turned away to fasten the clasps of a leather-bound trunk. The Queen and the other courtiers had left the Earl Marischal's house a few hours earlier, headed for the town square to witness Lord John Gordon's execution. Mary Stuart had persevered in her efforts to spare young Adam's life, and George Gordon was still safe with the Hamiltons. But James Stuart would not relent in John Gordon's case; he would die at noon, with the Queen looking on.

After the hanging of Alexander at Inverness Castle and the subsequent victory over the Gordons at Corrichie Moor, Mary Stuart had lost her blood lust. She had protested vehemently when James insisted upon her being present for John Gordon's beheading. James, however, asserted that many people felt she had encouraged him in his alleged plans to wed with her and that only by attending the gruesome event could she prove her own innocence. Trembling noticeably, she had left for the execution site with James holding firmly onto her arm.

Dallas, however, had no such compelling motives for being present. She simply refused to budge from the Earl Marischal's residence and the Queen was in no condition to insist upon her attendance. So she had passed the long morning by supervising the packing and had just finished giving instructions to a page for moving out the leather-bound trunks when the Queen returned with her ladies.

The Queen was barely able to walk, her white skin a deathly grey, her body supported by Jean Argyll and Mary Livingstone. With barely a glance at Dallas, the royal attendants half-carried their mistress into the bedchamber and closed the door. Five minutes later Jean Argyll returned, her own countenance pale and wretched.

"It was horrible," she murmured, sinking onto a large teakwood box. "Lord John called out that Her Grace's presence gave him comfort and that he died for love of her. Then the executioner set about his task and proved—inept." Jean's tongue flicked over her lips as she closed her eyes at the memory of the bloody spectacle. "I never saw the like, butchery is what it was, and our poor Queen weeping hysterically."

Dallas put a tight rein on her imagination, trying not to visualize the tortured demise of the once handsome John Gordon. Nor could she help but spare a pang of compassion for his brother, George. "I'll be glad to be gone from here," she asserted, flinging a pair of the Queen's slippers into a carton. "It's a barbarous place, encouraging barbarous deeds."

"You've suffered here yourself," Jean said sympathetically. "I'm still astonished at how you nursed your husband back to life."

Dallas lifted a shoulder. "Iain's strong as an ox, he'd probably have survived without my ministrations."

"That's not the point," Jean said gravely. "You went there at considerable risk to yourself. You must have gone without sleep and decent food. It seems to me you made a great sacrifice."

Avoiding Jean's gaze, Dallas gathered up an armload of chemises and began sorting and folding them. She was aware that many of the courtiers had been gossiping about her flight to the farmer's croft and her unusual diligence in caring for her lord. For a wife who seemed virtually indifferent to her husband, Dallas had behaved in an inexplicable manner. Jean, in particular, estranged from her own spouse for several years, considered Dallas's actions quite bewildering and yet somehow admirable.

"I reacted on impulse," Dallas said without expression. "Often, such instincts prove right." Carefully, she laid the chemises one on top of the other in the box. It had been over a week since Fraser had ridden away from the croft. Dallas had spent much time contemplating her love for him and the tenderness he'd shown her. Gratitude motivated her husband, she told herself sternly. So she argued with herself, cursing the ill fate of loving a man who could not possibly love her. If he did—even a little—why had he not sought her out in the weeks before the battle? Surely he could not have been that immersed in preparation.

And now he was gone, probably for months. Dallas looked into a grim future of loneliness and unrequited love. It was a prospect she could never have imagined facing—but it was as real as it was disturbing.

DALLAS TOSSED HER ivory fan onto a table, narrowly missing a bowl of scented water. "I suppose you have no money, no references, nothing to offer save your hulking body?" She turned to Donald McVurrich who stood haplessly downcast before her. He said nothing, just stood with his arms at his side, in a shirt he had long ago outgrown and breeches that had been patched at least a dozen times. Dallas had not seen him in almost a year and a half, since that fateful Christmas at Dunbar. Her sisters had visited the McVurrichs the previous summer but Dallas had been with the court on the progress north. In that time, Donald's shoulders had broadened, his blond beard had grown out and his voice had deepened. He was no longer Oliver McVurrich's young laddie, but a full-grown man.

For all that, he still looked boyishly chagrined as he hung his head in front of Dallas. He was a good fellow, after all, she reasoned, and felt repentant. "Oh, sit, Donald, you must be tired and hungry. I'm just fretful these days, forgive my rampant tongue."

As Donald sat down awkwardly in a dainty French chair, Dallas summoned Flora. In a few moments, the maid had moved brusquely out of the room to fetch food. Dallas pulled up a footstool and sat down by Donald. "I can't present you today—you've heard that the Queen's half-brother, Lord Johnny, died last night?"

Donald looked surprised. "I noted the mourning but thought it was for her two uncles in France who passed on recently."

"For them, too, but Johnny's death was a terrible shock. 'Tis a most unhappy time at court."

"Mayhap I shouldn't have come," Donald muttered. "Mayhap I don't belong here. 'Tis all so fine." He indicated the small room with his hand, the Flemish tapestries, the finely crafted furniture, the mirror edged in gilt.

"Nonsense. Holyrood is much more elegant. Stirling is a barn by comparison." Dallas sniffed disdainfully as she kicked at a worn place in the Persian carpet. "My husband's house in Edinburgh is furnished with things too grand for this old fortress." And she thought to herself, it has been more than a year since I've been there, six months since I've seen Iain. Oh, her allowance arrived on schedule, but why didn't the man send some word with it? If the money hadn't come, she wouldn't even know he was alive. "You'll grow accustomed to court life," she went on, thrusting aside the depressing matter of her husband's prolonged absence. "I have done so, though Lord knows it wasn't easy."

Flora came in then with a heaping platter of food. Donald ate eagerly, spilling bits of bread and chicken onto the carpet Dallas had scorned but now regarded somewhat ruefully. "We'll have to get you some decent clothes," she said, pilfering a chicken wing from the platter. "Let's see, after the funeral we go to Falkland. Then perhaps I can introduce you. Meanwhile, you'd best remain with me. You can help me with the move to Falkland."

"I'd be as honored to serve you as the Queen herself," Donald blurted, and flushed deeply.

Dallas turned away so he could not see her roll her eyes in annoyance. She did not need an infatuated country dolt to complicate her life. "You won't say that after a few days in my service," she snapped. "I'm not nearly as patient nor as kind as the Queen."

Donald sensed instinctively that he should protest and wished he knew some of the flattering phrases which must come so glibly to the courtiers' tongues. But instead, he silently cursed himself for his lack of eloquence and concentrated on wiping his plate clean with a piece of honeyed rye bread.

IT HAD BEEN years since Iain Fraser had traveled through Cameron country. Now, fully recovered from his wound, he cantered along the east side of Loch Lochy, unable to keep from marveling at the distance he had traveled on bare feet some eighteen years earlier. How far? he asked himself, smiling wryly at the memory of the dark, gangling youth, hungry and tired, often falling down in his struggle to get home to Beauly.

He had spent the month of October there this past year, regaining his strength and seeing to his lands. Then, feeling fit except for occasional twinges of pain brought on by excessively damp weather, he had gone to the Isle of Lewes to rejoin his crew. They had sailed on December second, braving severe storms en route, but had made port at Genoa just before Christmas. Fraser had gone on to Rome to see the Pope but could elicit no promise of the loan Queen Mary wanted. Returning to Genoa, he spent the remainder of the winter aboard the *Richezza*, harassing foreign ships in the Mediterranean.

By early April, he was back in Scotland. After devoting the next few weeks to his properties, Fraser headed south to accomplish something he had wanted to do ever since Dallas's father had confided the secret knowledge on his deathbed: Fraser would search among the Camerons to see if he could find any further evidence proving his real father's identity.

His own tight-lipped Fraser kin had never told him anything helpful. They probably didn't know, he had finally concluded. For a long time he wished he could find Moireach, his old nurse. She would know if anyone did. But the courageous woman who had saved his life that night on Beauly Firth had long since disappeared, perhaps even died.

So here he was, back in Cameron country. He could not recall precisely where he had been held captive. Great stands of gloomy pine and a careening waterfall had been close by, but such sights were common in this part of the Highlands.

It was on his second day in the saddle that Fraser found the cottage he was seeking. Although he did not think he could recall the face of his captor, he recognized it at once. The beard and hair were almost white and the skin was deeply furrowed, but Fraser knew he'd finally found the right Cameron.

"What do you want?" the old man asked suspiciously, his roughened hands holding the door open a crack.

"I'm Iain Fraser. Do you remember me?"

The lifeless brown eyes revealed nothing. "Nay," the man answered. "I know no Frasers."

"You knew me once, from Blar-na-Leine." Fraser spoke in conversational tones, but the man's head lifted slightly.

"Blar-na-Leine," he repeated without inflection. "That was nigh on twenty years past."

"Aye, I was but fourteen. You remember now?"

The man nodded slowly. He seemed faintly impressed but neither curious nor frightened. If he had considered that Iain Fraser had come to wreak vengeance for his captivity, the idea did not outwardly disturb him.

In the woods which surrounded the cottage, the skylark had commenced its evensong as a stately stand of foxgloves swayed in the evening breeze. The sun had slipped halfway behind the western hills, bringing dusk to the Highlands.

Fraser was growing impatient with the man's unresponsiveness. "I'm wed to your kin now, to Daniel Cameron's middle daughter. May I come inside?"

At last the man reacted with some kind of emotion. "A Fraser wed to a Cameron? Nae such a thing!" He shook his head violently, the beard tumbling from one side of his chest to the other.

"City ways are different." From inside the cottage came the sound of a kettle boiling over onto the peat fire. The old man turned around slowly.

"I must tend to yon kettle. I'm all alone here. My woman passed on two years ago or more." He shrugged away the time, he could not really remember. Fraser wondered if he remembered very much of anything.

The old man motioned for Fraser to come in. The little place reeked of peat and overcooked vegetables. An aging, gaunt hound lay on the hearth, barely stirring as his master took the kettle off the hob. The ceiling was so low that Fraser had to stoop to keep from hitting his head.

"Leeks and a bit o' mutton," the old man said, ladling the kettle's contents onto a wooden plate. "Will ye eat?"

Fraser sat down at the table, aware that the invitation signified acceptance. A Highlander who offered hospitality never went back on his word.

"I never knew your Christian name," Fraser said as the old man got out a second plate.

"Griogair," the man replied, handing the full plate to Fraser. He sat down on the hut's only other chair and began eating with his fingers. They ate in silence, save for the rustling of the pines, the faint echo of the waterfall and the labored breathing of the hound on the hearth. It was almost dark inside the cottage.

Cameron had gotten up to place his almost finished meal next to the hound. The animal raised its head with great effort and began lapping up the contents. Its master, meanwhile, poked at the fire, sending an eerie light across the pokey little room. "You remember the hound, Iain Fraser?" he asked.

"The whelp. It's the same dog, then?" He did recall a frisky puppy, the only comfort he'd had during his captivity. It seemed hard to believe that this pathetic hound, like the old man, were the only remaining links to the past. Fraser gave the remnants of his own meal to the hound and then pushed his chair back from the rickety table. "You held me for ransom. Why?"

Cameron shuffled his feet and looked down at the hound. "Och—I'm not sure." He scratched his thatch of white hair. "There was some tale about you, aye, your father, Malcolm—nae, it was not Malcolm who was your real father." He paused, as if waiting for Fraser to verify this.

"So I've been told. Go on."

"Your true sire, he was—Huntly? Argyll? Who? I've forgotten."

Fraser tried to keep the impatience out of his voice. "I was never told—then. That's why I'm here. I thought you might help me."

Cameron gaped at Fraser. "Och, so that's it!" He chuckled as he let out the hound, which was making for the door on shaky legs. "A man ought to know from whose loins he's sprung. But all I remember is ...."He shook his head, the recollection eluding him. "But there was the bauble, a bonnie thing with writing on it. None of us could read, that's why we sent for Daniel Cameron. A learned man, was Daniel, though too refined for my tastes."

"What bauble?" Fraser had moved closer, leaning forward on the table so that its legs creaked beneath his weight. He felt the tension building up inside him and could scarcely keep from grabbing Cameron by the shoulders and shaking the facts from the old man.

"Well," his host began, fingering the strands of his beard, "we took some things from your house at Strath Farrar, not that there was much to take, but pilfering is part of clan warfare, ye ken?" He paused, vaguely apologetic, but trusting in Fraser's worldly wisdom. "Among the loot was a necklace of sorts, gold with some bonnie stones set in it. Tucked away in a wall, it was, and then there was this writing. That seemed odd, so we thought it might be important." He stopped then, maddeningly, and waited for Fraser's reaction.

"Was it important? What did Daniel Cameron say?"

The old man shook his head slowly. "Nothing. Not to us. Daniel paid us for the bauble, a fair sum, he was a fair man, and told us the writing was not meant to be bruited about. Then he went back to Edinburgh. We were pleased enough, since you had run away before he got here. And that," he concluded as he got up to poke again at the fire, "is all I ever knew."

Fraser silently cursed Griogair Cameron for his ignorance. Daniel Cameron must have given the "bauble" to someone for safekeeping. But whom? Fraser could guess, but the knowledge helped him little and what had become of the bauble since might forever remain a mystery. His journey into Cameron country had not been in vain, but he was mightily disappointed.

Standing up, Fraser took out a pouch and dumped some coins onto the table. "I believe you've told me all you know and I'm grateful," he said in a constrained voice. "Accept this as a sign of my gratitude." He saw the old man's eyes glint at the sight of the money. And suddenly Fraser wanted to get out of the cottage as quickly as possible.

Griogair Cameron followed him outside. "Wait up, man. It's pitch dark. Bide here this night."

"Nay," Fraser replied, untethering Barvas. "I must be elsewhere in an hour or so." It was the truth: He had to be anywhere else, save under Griogair Cameron's roof.

MARY STUART'S SPIRITS revived at Falkland. It was a favorite hunting place, with great stags leaping through the enclosed woods and an occasional wild boar set loose for the Queen's pleasure.

But John Gordon's execution and the deaths of her French uncles and her half-brother, Johnny, had been hard to bear. She missed Bothwell, she missed Fraser, she missed John Hamilton. For once, she became adamant with James: If the first two could or would not rejoin the court, at least Hamilton must be permitted to return. Considering him the least of three evils, and alarmed by his half-sister's faltering health, Lord James relented.

Hamilton had been at court for several days when Dallas saw him for the first time. She had reluctantly joined the other courtiers in a boar hunt and was thinking that the animal which now hung by its feet from a strong yew branch looked a great deal like the Earl of Morton. But when the slain beast was laid before the Queen, and Lord Robert Stuart plunged a knife into its belly to remove the entrails, Dallas turned away, nudging her mount towards a small glen tufted with newly unfurled bracken. Just beyond her a small spring gurgled up through watercress and a throstle cock flew out of the reeds towards the sanctuary of a hazel tree.

"Turn back!" called a voice from behind Dallas. "That ground grows soft under the bracken!"

Shifting in the saddle, she saw John Hamilton reining in his bay gelding just a few yards away. He had been in the company of the Queen most of the morning and Dallas had glimpsed him only from a distance, purposely avoiding him. Hamilton had always seemed a most agreeable sort, kind and decent, yet the unexpected kiss he'd bestowed on her that night in her room made her remember the comments of Master Forbes about her effect on him at their first meeting. It would probably be unwise to encourage any familiarities on Hamilton's part.

But she could hardly avoid him now. Carefully, she guided her horse in his direction, noting that the animal's hooves were already covered with mud. "Thank you, John," she said somewhat stiffly. "I'd not noticed how marshy it was here."

"I saw you go off alone in this direction," he explained, placing a steadying hand on his horse's neck as the animal moved nervously, "and feared you might not realize the hazard." The brown eyes regarded her with warmth. "I'm glad to see you again, Dallas."

"And I'm glad to see you," Dallas said, thinking her reply vapid, yet realizing she spoke honestly. She was glad to see him, to note his solid presence next to her, the wide-shouldered body attired in a light brown hunting costume edged with black. He was as handsome as ever, perhaps even more so since the days of his exile had given him a new maturity, reflected in the scattering of prematurely grey hairs at his temples and in his moustache. His face was somewhat leaner, the brown eyes a trifle sadder. No doubt he grieved for the pitiful state of his brother, Arran, whose madness seemed irreversible.

They walked their horses out of the glen but away from the other courtiers who were readying their javelins for the next kill. Hamilton spoke of his months at Arbroath, of long days passed in hunting and fishing, of supervising the old abbey's renovation, of watching the winter storms blow up out of the North Sea, of wondering if he and his family would ever be restored to favor.

"And you, Dallas?" he asked at last as the turrets of Falkland rose up above the budding plane trees. "I heard your lord was wounded at Corrichie Moor."

Dallas felt her grip tighten on the reins. "He recovered."

Hamilton's full mouth twitched slightly. "But though returned to health, not to court, I understand."

"No." Dallas felt her terse answers gave away more than she wished.

She went on, trying to sound casual instead of defensive. "His estates in the Highlands require attention. Highlanders love their land."

Sensing her embarrassed manner, Hamilton let the matter drop, but in the weeks that followed, Dallas frequently found herself in his company. He never made an improper advance, never uttered a word that went beyond commonplace court flattery. If his hand lingered a bit too long on her waist when he helped her up into the saddle or if his fingers strayed occasionally to her bare throat when they danced, well, that was his way. Yet, Dallas knew that the others were watching them with amused curiosity.

"If Lord John demonstrated as much devotion to the Queen as he does to you, I think she might wed him forthwith," Mary Fleming teased Dallas one warm afternoon in early June as the two women arranged huge bouquets of spring flowers for the evening's banquet. The feast was in honor of Secretary Maitland's return from London.

"Lord John is an old and trusted friend," Dallas replied coolly, thrusting an iris into a bowl of ruby cut glass. She paused for a moment, astonished at herself for describing Hamilton as a friend. He was, she realized, the first friend she'd ever had. To cover her surprise, she plunged ahead. "We enjoy each other's company, nothing more. No doubt he'll wed someone soon, if not the Queen. He's over thirty, you know."

Mary Fleming mopped up some water she had spilled on the shining beechwood table top. "That's what puzzles me," she said. "He is rich, his family is royal, he possesses great personal charm and good looks—yet, he's never married. Oh, he's had his mistresses, at last count he'd acknowledged at least two bastards, but ...." She shrugged in that Frenchified way all the Marys had acquired during their stay on the Continent.

"Bastards?" Dallas blinked and promptly impaled her thumb on a rose thorn.

"The man's no monk. But it's said his mistresses are always well provided for and whatever issue—as long as he's convinced the bairns are his—will be recognized and supported." Mary Fleming worked as she talked, creating a wonderfully imposing arrangement of tulips, peonies, narcissus and syringa massed against a background of pink rhododendrons with their shiny green leaves. "There! What do you think?"

"Lovely," murmured Dallas, sucking at her thumb, and thinking something else entirely. So no man was different from another, as far as women were concerned. John Hamilton and his mistresses, Iain Fraser and Catherine Gordon and Delphinia Douglas and Lord only knew who else. She picked up a bunch of marigolds, thrust them into a tall Chinese vase and wondered why her flowers always looked woefully displaced instead of gracefully arranged as Mary Fleming's did.

Chapter Twelve

Dallas had to admit that Donald McVurrich looked splendid in his guardsman's livery. She had secured the post for him as soon as Mary Stuart had recovered from her initial period of mourning over Lord Johnny's death. The new position in Her Grace's household gave Donald not only a sense of belonging but a new eloquence as well. He had fairly strutted before Dallas in his new attire, regaling her with a long list of his duties. She had listened patiently, glad to see the young man so well pleased with himself.

During the banquet for Maitland, Donald was posted at one of the doors, tall and expressionless. Dallas waved at him from her place between Hamilton and Lord Erskine. Donald had darkened just a bit but otherwise remained motionless.

"Your protege looks suitably imposing," Hamilton said as he offered Dallas a bit of partridge from his own plate. "Any number of ladies are chattering about the transformation."

Dallas allowed Hamilton to pop the partridge into her mouth. "No doubt he'll break a heart or two before he's much older," she said after she'd swallowed the succulent fowl.

The Queen, however, was not eating at all. Dallas noted that Mary Stuart looked unusually pale and petulant as she refused a steaming dish of mussels.

Lord Erskine saw Dallas's puzzled gaze. "Perhaps you have not heard the latest, madame," he commented, dabbing his fingers in a bowl of rose water. "The Queen is much vexed this night, having received a message Maitland brought back from Elizabeth."

"Surely Her Grace is resigned to Elizabeth's whims by now," Hamilton put in.

"It's not that," Erskine said, keeping his voice low. "The English Queen has had the arrogance to suggest her former lover, Rob Dudley, as a suitor for our sovereign lady's hand."

Both Dallas and Hamilton were genuinely shocked. "The cheek!" Dallas cried. "To offer an infamous discard as husband for our Queen!"

"That's assuming she's actually discarded him," Erskine replied. "Some say Elizabeth and Dudley are still thick as thieves."

"Then she's not serious, but merely insulting," Hamilton declared, turning sympathetic brown eyes towards the Queen, who was disdaining a glass of white wine proffered by Lord Fleming. "I scarcely blame Her Grace for being so galled."

Servants were moving discreetly among the tables, removing empty plates and uneaten food. At one end of the banquet hall, musicians tuned up their instruments.

"A pavane," Hamilton said into Dallas's ear. "Will you dance?"

Dallas would have preferred to remain where she was but didn't want to hurt Hamilton's feelings. Rising from her chair, she let him lead her onto the floor.

"You look exceptionally lovely tonight," he said. "Black becomes you."

Dallas, along with the rest of the court, wore mourning for Lord Johnny Stuart. Her black silk dress was cut low in the bodice but filled with delicate white lace which floated up to her shoulders and formed a graceful frame for her face. Her hair was piled high, held in place with silver combs, and the only jewelry she wore besides her wedding ring was a pair of dangling pearl eardrops. The dress was cut away at the waist to reveal a great flounce of white lace petticoats, edged in silver.

"You're flattering me," Dallas said absently, well aware that he wasn't. She knew she looked well tonight, but somehow it didn't seem important. If Iain Fraser didn't return soon, Dallas had decided to leave the court. Pining away from loneliness might be easier in less crowded surroundings. The stately dance continued, with Hamilton making occasional comments about the other courtiers. Dallas listened with half an ear and, when the music stopped, announced she was feeling rather warm and preferred to sit.

Hamilton took her by the arm and steered her over to a window embrasure. "It's the warmest night of the year," he said, sitting next to her on the cushioned seat. "See, the casement is open and yet I don't feel a breath of air."

"Aye," Dallas sighed, wishing she hadn't left her fan at the table.

Before either could speak again, they both became aware of a distraction near the main doors to the banquet hall. A group of courtiers had congregated, apparently welcoming a newcomer. "What's going on?" Dallas asked, craning to see between the black and white wave of dancers. Already several couples had moved off the floor to join the group at the door. When their numbers finally parted, Dallas saw Iain Fraser striding up to the Queen's dais.

Hamilton let out a deep sigh of regret, which Dallas did not hear. She was on her feet, ready to move across the banquet hall floor, when Hamilton put his hand on her black-clad arm. "Stay, Dallas. You'd run to him after he's left you alone for all these months?"

Dallas regarded him quizzically. He was right, of course. Had he guessed all along what she was thinking? Dallas plopped back down on the cushions and adjusted an eardrop. "It's the first of June," she explained pettishly, "and I haven't received my allowance for the month."

Hamilton gave her a sidelong glance, then turned his attention back to the royal dais. Lord James stood rigid beside the Queen, keeping tight rein over his careening emotions. Mary Stuart was smiling and speaking with animation for the first time that night. Several of her ladies, including the odious Delphinia Douglas, were fairly fawning over Fraser. Dallas felt her excitement turn to ash.

The musicians had ceased their playing and the whole room seemed to be riveted on Fraser and the Queen. Dallas shifted on the windowseat and pushed the casement open even further. She felt a great need for more air.

At last, Mary Stuart signalled for the music to begin again. Her fair skin flushed, she allowed Fraser to lead her onto the dance floor. In a rush of excited chatter, the other courtiers chose up partners and resumed dancing.

"The blackguard!" Dallas had sprung to her feet in a flurry of black silk and white lace. "Almost seven months he's been gone and he dares dance the coranto before greeting his own wife!"

Hamilton frowned. "Etiquette demands ...."

"Etiquette be damned! Don't you dare defend Iain to me, John Hamilton! I'm leaving," she went on, quickly lowering her voice as a curious Earl of Morton plodded by with Jean Argyll on his arm. "You've been most gallant this evening and I'm grateful, but I refuse to stay here while my husband humiliates me in public."

Hamilton was torn: He wished to detain Dallas but she was right—he would not, could not defend Fraser further. His only option was to leave with Dallas. Cautious as ever, he speculated briefly over the repercussions. Before he could make up his mind, the dance ended and Iain Fraser was standing in front of them, bowing low.

"May I intrude or is this a private party?" The hard gleam in the hazel eyes belied the indolent tone of his voice.

Dallas pointedly kept her hands folded in front of her to ward off the obligatory kiss of her fingers. "Your intrusion appears welcome by most," she replied archly. "Some of us, however, are more amazed than thrilled."

"Amazed?" Fraser's gaze turned blandly innocent. "How so, wife?"

Dallas winced at his form of address. "Your comings and goings are so unpredictable, sir. Especially since you go so much more than you come."

A tight little smile played at the corners of Fraser's mouth, but Hamilton intervened before the other man could speak. "I'm surprised that you came back to court at all," he said in a controlled voice. "I thought you'd settled down in the Highlands to tend your sheep and till the fields."

Fraser shrugged. "I stayed there for a time, as you did at Arbroath. But I daresay that whatever compelled you to remain within the fastness of your family compelled me to do the same." He continued without changing inflection, "Just as what drew us back to court may have been the same."

"The Queen sent for me," Hamilton declared with a touch of asperity. "And did she do so with you?"

Fraser chose to ignore this barb. He turned to Dallas and extended his hand. "Are you still overcome by amazement or will you dance with me?"

"I think not." Dallas stood as erect as she could, well aware that both men towered over her, but determined to salvage as much dignity as possible from an awkward situation. "I was about to withdraw. So if you'll both excuse me ...."

But Fraser's patience was overtaxed. "I think not." He grasped Dallas by the elbow and propelled her onto the dance floor. Hamilton made as if to stop them, considered the consequences, then resigned himself to discretion.

"You whoreson," Dallas hissed at Fraser, her dark eyes blazing with wrath. "You've no right to force me to dance with you!"

"I've every right, since you're my wife," Fraser responded, as incensed as she. "What kind of homecoming is this after seven months?"

"That's the point," she retorted, hoping the other dancers couldn't hear them. "Not a word from you, not a message of any kind, except the damned allowance, which you probably arranged in advance to send me through Cummings!"

"You knew I had matters to tend to, you knew I would go to sea. I do have a wife to support after all, and I notice that her tastes are far from simple." Fraser eyed the silver-edged lace and the eardrops. "Are those pearls or plover eggs?"

"They cost less than you'd imagine," she snapped back. "My upbringing taught me how to drive a shrewd bargain."

The hazel eyes turned hard. "So it did. But your 'bargains' are costly to everyone."

They had both stopped dancing, though the music played on. Several courtiers slowed their own pace and began to stare.

"I must attend the Queen," Dallas announced with a haughty lift of her head. "I forgot, I'm to spend the night in her chambers." With a swish of silk and lace she marched off, heading for the royal dais where Mary Stuart was chatting amiably with Lord Patrick Ruthven and Gavin Hamilton, who had been reinstated with his cousin, John.

The Queen, however, was not yet ready to retire. Buoyed by Fraser's arrival, she was enjoying herself and declared that she'd dance until the candles burned themselves out. "But there's no need to wait for me, Dallas," she said with a knowing smile. "Mary Beaton will take your place tonight. I've already made the arrangements."

Dallas looked questioningly at the Queen. "Then if you don't mind, Your Grace, I'll take my leave. I'm rather weary."

Mary Stuart's smile widened. "No need to make excuses, my dear, by all means, take to your bed."

Turning away to leave the banquet hall, Dallas heard Patrick Ruthven snicker behind her back. Dim as his son, Will, she thought, and could not help scanning the room for a glimpse of Fraser. Sure enough, he was dancing with a radiant Delphinia Douglas, totally unaware that his wife was making her exit. Damn, she cursed to herself, he cares no more for me than for any other trifle who falls into his arms. Let him dally with his Delphinias and Catherines and whomever else; I'll be hanged if he'll ever know I care a jot about him.

Hamilton, however, caught up with her at the door. "Surely you haven't let your husband's return spoil your evening, Dallas?" he asked, putting a hand on her arm. "Bide awhile, I'll get us something to drink."

Dallas hesitated; perhaps it would serve Fraser right to see how she could enjoy herself with another man. But that was childish, she had no reason to think he'd care about what she did or didn't do. Nor did she want to use Hamilton in such a selfish way.

She could not resist, however, putting a hand over Hamilton's. "Nay, John, my mood is sour as week-old milk tonight and I am tired."

Forcing a smile, Dallas let him kiss her fingertips and then left the banqueting hall, eyes straight ahead so that she could not look back at either Hamilton or her husband.

FLORA, AS USUAL, was waiting up. Dallas dismissed her peremptorily, and since Flora had grown accustomed to her mistress's unpredictable ways during the last year and a half, she glided out of the room with only a curt goodnight.

Dallas pushed open the room's one window; how could Flora keep from suffocating on such a night? she wondered. The faintest hint of a breeze was blowing up from the man-made lake down in the deer park. She didn't bother with a candle but undressed by moonlight. Her hair freed from the confining combs, her bare feet sinking into the carpet, she was wondering whether to trouble with a bedgown on such a night when someone rapped at the door.

Grabbing the first robe she could lay her hands on, Dallas wrapped the garment around her and called out: "Who is it?"

"Flora, madame, come quick!"

Dallas pulled the door open. "What's happening? What's wrong?"

Flora's usual impassivity had fled. "It's the Queen, madame! Come at once!"

Dallas started protesting that she had no slippers and was wearing just her robe but Flora was already down the hall. What now, Dallas thought, another sudden attack of nerves? Or mayhap Arran has gotten loose and is harassing the Queen.

The two women raced through the hallways, the stone walls illuminated only by a few guttering torches. They flew at such a speed that Dallas didn't realize they had passed the turn to the Queen's chambers until they stopped in front of a heavy oak door at the end of the passageway. Instead of knocking, Flora opened the door and all but shoved Dallas into the room.

She was in the music gallery, now lying in shadow and apparently deserted. "Flora!" Dallas whirled around to discover that her maid had disappeared. The door was closed, the woman must have fled into the hallway. "Flora!" she cried out, suddenly apprehensive. Then a big hand clamped over her mouth as someone stepped out of the darkness.

"Hush, lassie, you'll rouse the guard!" Iain Fraser turned her around to face him.

"You! What's going on here?" she demanded. "Where's the Queen?"

"Still dancing her dainty feet off and no doubt laughing at what a clever fellow am I."

"I don't understand," Dallas said, but of course she did. Her breath seemed constricted and she felt a vaguely familiar ache in her stomach. "Iain ...."

He had her by the hand, half-leading, half-dragging her along the music gallery. At the far end stood two French doors. They opened at a touch and Fraser pulled her along down the terrace and out to the lawn.

"Where are we going?" Dallas asked, stumbling along behind him.

"To the lake," he threw over his shoulder.

Five minutes later, they stood at the edge of the quiet water, moonlight reflected against the far shore. The trees rustled slightly above them and the night scent of roses was heavy in the air. The sound of laughter and music from the castle was just a dim hum.

Dallas noted that Fraser was as barefoot as she, and he had removed his black doublet. The white shirt gleamed in the moonlight as he stood, hands on hips, looking into the water. She pulled her robe more tightly around her, and though she wasn't cold, she shivered.

"Iain ..." she said in a low voice. "Iain?"

He turned slowly but, instead of walking towards her, moved a few paces along the edge of the lake. There, by some rocks, lay a bundle Dallas couldn't identify. Fraser bent down and began taking the bundle apart. He pulled out a blanket and spread it on the grass, then arranged two pillows on the ground and pushed a second blanket aside. He stood up to look at her. "Our bower, madame," he declared with a courtly bow.

"You're mad," she whispered and shivered again.

He had walked over to where she stood. "Nay, sweetheart, I'm not mad, save with wanting you." She felt his arms go around her, pulling her close. Fraser's kiss was gentle at first, then grew harder, fiercer, until Dallas realized she was answering him with a hunger as deep as his. Slowly, carefully, he brought her down onto the woolly Highland blanket. She felt Fraser's lips seek her bare throat and travel searchingly to the opening of her robe.

In one quick motion, he undid the single tie and pulled the robe aside, freeing her arms from the sleeves. Dallas felt herself tense slightly as she lay naked on the ground before him. "Don't be afraid, lassie," he whispered. "I've thought about your lovely body all these long months, ever since our wedding night."

Dallas felt his hands on her breasts, and under his exploring fingers, her nipples turned as taut and firm as the first time he had touched her. The trembling was replaced by a shudder of delight and from somewhere in the pit of her stomach the almost forgotten fire returned. Fraser's hands moved to caress her thighs and the curve of her back. She arched towards him, her arms clutching at his shoulders. Fraser broke free just long enough to strip off his own clothes which he tossed in the direction of the rocks. Dallas stared at the hard, brown body and felt the fire in her stomach kindle into inferno proportions.

Sweet Jesu, she thought, is it possible that I can want this man so much? Fraser was beside her on the blanket, kissing her lips again, her forehead, her ears. His hand slid down her hip and came to rest between her legs. Tentatively, she touched his hand with hers; then, as if involuntarily, she pressed his fingers into the soft, throbbing flesh of her most intimate being.

Yet Fraser hesitated, and Dallas wondered if her reflex action had somehow been wrong. Confused by her new emotions and her husband's reaction, she gazed wonderingly at the face which was only an inch or so away from hers.

"There is something you must know, Dallas," he said in a quiet voice. She looked at him questioningly and was somewhat relieved to see him smile ever so slightly. "I love you, Dallas, I've loved you for a long time."

Her confusion was replaced by astonishment. "You? You love me?" Dallas was wide-eyed and incredulous.

"You silly little goose, why else would I have married you?" Now the half-smile was transformed into the familiar grin and his hand tightened between her legs.

"I made you marry me, we had our bargain ...." It all seemed so long ago, and Dallas was having trouble concentrating on anything but Fraser's touch and that raging fire which was demanding to be quenched.

He laughed delightedly and nipped her nose with his teeth. "I knew you'd say that. Nay, Dallas, I didn't have to marry you—I could have pensioned off your whole family, found suitable husbands for you and your sisters, too. You were so obsessed by poverty that you would have settled for anything as long as it came in cold, hard coinage."

His admission was almost too much for Dallas to take in. But she, too, had her own confession to make, words which she had once thought she would never utter: "I love you, Iain, I love you more than anything in the world!"

Unlike Dallas, Fraser expressed no surprise. "I know, I knew it long before you did. That's why I've waited so long to make love to you."

Now that they had made their mutual pledges, there were no further restraints between them. Fraser's fingers explored her intimately; her hands clutched at his back, pausing only momentarily as she felt the scar from his wound. At last, he raised himself above her and gazed deep into the dark eyes. "This time it will not hurt," he promised her. Dallas felt that strange sensation she had experienced on her wedding night as Fraser entered her body. But now she welcomed the probing hardness, she arched towards him, she felt the fire consuming her as Fraser thrust more deeply. Their bodies surged together, moving in an impassioned rhythm that seemed to overwhelm the darkness and blot out everything but the two of them. The fire engulfed Dallas, at first blurring her senses, then sharpening them suddenly in a devastating flash of ecstasy as Fraser plunged for the last time and then seemed to swallow her up with his own body.

"Oh, lassie," he breathed into her hair, "you were well worth the wait."

Dallas was too stunned to say anything at all. So this was what the waiting had been for, she thought with awe, and wished that Fraser would stay entwined with her forever.

PART THREE

Chapter Thirteen

WHILE THE MOON shifted in the clear sky and the breeze began lifting little waves on the glistening lake they slept in each other's arms beneath the second blanket Fraser had brought. They were awakened shortly after dawn by a noise in a nearby thicket. Looking sleepily over their pillows, they saw a handsome doe with two speckled fawns staring at them. The animals stood in a motionless montage for a few moments, then sprung back into the thicket, long legs flashing out of sight.

Dallas lay down again, nestling back against Fraser. So this was why women did all sorts of foolish things at a man's urging, she thought dreamily, why a Delphinia Douglas or a Catherine Gordon would shamelessly pursue a man like Fraser without even the faintest hope of marriage. But, she smiled to herself, he is mine. And he loves me! She purred as deeply as one of her Manx cats as Fraser began stroking the cleft of her buttocks. Dallas waited for a few moments, then rolled over to face him and wound her arms around his neck to kiss him fiercely on the mouth. She pushed her body against his until her breasts ached with pleasurable pain. It was as if once the dam of her emotions had been unlocked, she had become obsessed by her need for him.

But it was Fraser who demurred. "Dallas, I could lie here and make love to you until All Saints' Day, but in case you haven't noticed, it's raining."

During the night, the breeze had brought in a heavy cloud cover and big drops were beginning to splatter onto the lake and the surrounding greenery of the park. He got up and retrieved his clothes, dressed quickly, and then handed Dallas her robe. "Hurry, lassie, this is going to be a downpour."

The French doors were open; in fact, the breeze had blown one of them ajar. Their feet made wet prints on the parquet floor as they hurried towards the passageway. No one in this part of the castle was astir yet. They slowed their pace as they moved down the silent corridor to Dallas's room. Flora was not there; she had followed Fraser's instructions perfectly.

Dallas folded up the blankets and laid them on a heavy oak chest at the foot of the bed. A small clock on the nightstand told her it was just after six. Fraser, shirtsleeves rolled back to the elbows, was washing up in a pewter basin. "I'm famished, lovey," he declared, toweling off his face. "When do the kitchens start up here?"

"About now." She was plumping up the damp pillows they had brought in from outdoors. Dallas turned to face him, her brows wrinkled with curiosity. "Why there—out by the lake?"

He tossed the towel onto the back of a chair. "Why not? Can you think of a more romantic site? Nor were we likely to be disturbed, with the revelry going on inside the palace." He did not add that he would never have made love to her, not this special, precious time, in a bedroom which might have reminded her of their wedding night. During all the time he had waited for Dallas to acknowledge the depth of her feelings and desire for him, he had known that he would take her in some unlikely place. During the wait, he had also come to understand himself and his love for her.

The days which followed were the happiest Dallas had ever spent. Fraser took up quarters in her room where they made love each night in the too-narrow bed. Dallas would have requested a change in their living situation but knew that within a few days the court would be moving on. She also knew the courtiers were whispering about her marriage; that unconventional liaison which had caused so much gossip now appeared to have changed.

One night, as the late spring mists settled down on the Kingdom of Fife and Falkland Palace, Dallas asked a question which had puzzled her for some time: "Last fall at Inverness ... why did you avoid me after we'd ... after the Highland revels?"

Fraser was half-asleep, one arm flung across Dallas's breasts. "Hmmmm?" He frowned slightly into the darkness before propping himself up on his elbow. "Oh, aye. George Gordon brought me fateful news that night. Afterwards, I had to face the fact that I might not survive the battle. As it turned out, I damned near didn't—but not in the way I'd expected. Still," he went on, his voice very serious, "I had no mind to leave you a pregnant widow. I kept my distance so I could keep my self-control."

Dallas threw herself against his chest. "Holy Mother, I'd no idea you could be so noble!" She nuzzled against him, her hands caressing his back. "But later, at Corrichie Moor—you were so determined to leave in such a rush."

Fraser kissed her bare shoulder. "That was hardly the proper place to consummate our passion," he said dryly. "As I recall, you complained about my other wee bedmates—and the old couple stumbling over our writhing bodies would have dimmed even my ardor."

"No doubt we would have shocked Cummings," Dallas put in, lifting her face to kiss him soundly on the mouth.

"Hmmmm. Cummings," Fraser said between kisses, "isn't easily shocked. However," he added, cupping her breasts together and kissing each one in turn, "you must remember that I wasn't a well man."

Dallas reached down to feel the renewed firmness of Fraser's manhood. "I have a feeling you were well enough," she declared, suddenly rolling over on top of him so that she could capture him between her thighs. "You were just hell-bent to go to sea again."

"Not so," replied her husband. He grasped her by the buttocks and squeezed hard until she let out a little yelp of pleasurable pain. "But if I had tarried with you then, I'd have never been able to leave. And I had to, if only to keep from murdering James Stuart."

The words sounded well and Dallas savored them as they savored each other. But she wondered—how strong was her hold on this restless man? As much as he professed to love her, would Iain Fraser ever be content to stay in the circle of her arms?

ON THE LAST night at Falkland, the Queen gave a lavish supper and afterwards stunned the entire court by knighting Iain Fraser. As she lifted the sword of state she looked defiantly at Lord James and declared that Fraser was being honored "for his right, honorable and valorous service unto the Crown at Corrichie Moor." James, as Dallas put it later, looked fit to spit.

But, as far as Dallas was concerned, the triumph was short-lived. The knighthood meant more than just a title for Fraser; it also meant the Queen had a task for him. Disappointed in Maitland's mission to England, she was sending Fraser southward, not by sea, but by land. Fraser suspected the journey was not entirely Queen Mary's idea; Lord James obviously wanted the newly made baron as far from court as possible.

Dallas stormed about their chamber when she heard the news. "How can you leave me? We've ... we've had so little ...." She faltered, her hands twisting at a long rope of pearls which hung almost to her waist.

Fraser looked up from the saddlebags he'd been packing. "I'm going not because I want to. Only you and the Queen know in what special capacity I can serve her. And James no doubt is dithering because now he's afraid to turn his back on me." There was no point in burdening Dallas with the details. Mary Stuart wanted him to press for Bothwell's release; she also wanted inquiries made about other possible suitors. The less Dallas knew, the better for her and everyone else.

“How long?” she asked, signifying her reluctant acceptance by folding some of his shirts and placing them in the saddlebags.

“A month or so, no longer,” Fraser answered. “I expect the court to be up north by then, maybe at Ellerig.” Fraser inspected a favorite pair of calfskin boots to see if they would survive the journey south. “What of your own packing? Aren’t you due to leave shortly?”

Dallas held up a black doublet slashed with cloth-of-gold, worn by Fraser for only the most important court functions. She could picture him sauntering about Whitehall or Greenwich in it, with the English ladies swooning over his hawklike profile and mocking grin. She rolled the doublet up in a big wad and flung it into the saddlebag.

“I packed last night while you were with the Queen,” she replied, pouting ferociously. She could not stop him from going, but she’d be hanged if she’d be gracious about it.

Flora came then to tell Dallas that the Queen awaited her. A page had come with the maid to fetch their baggage. Dallas indicated three trunks, eight hatboxes and two satchels for herself. There was one small carton for Flora.

After the page and the maid had left, Dallas picked up a dark grey cape trimmed with seed pearls and jet. She held on to her wide-brimmed hat with the grey ostrich feather and turned to her husband. Fraser had finished his packing and was making out a list of instructions for Cummings, who would remain in Edinburgh.

“I must go,” Dallas said, still sulking. Damn the man, he seemed more interested in his infernal list than he did in her.

Fraser finished off one more item, then rose to put his arms around her waist. “Try not to be too angry with me, lassie,” he implored. “You’ll be busy, the time will pass quickly.”

With the moment of departure upon them, Dallas forced herself to smile. “It’s a strange thing, that having gone so long without your love—at least without your lovemaking—that now I cannot imagine enduring the days to come without it.” She laughed wryly, as if at her own folly.

Fraser realized that he was placing Dallas in an unfamiliar and difficult situation. “As I said, it won’t be for long. Just don’t let Johnny Hamilton try to make some well-bred effort to console you.” The grin he gave her was but a ghost of his usual mocking manner. From somewhere he felt a sense of alarm, and held her tight.

“My hat! You’ll crush it!” But she lifted her face for his kisses and had to force herself to break from his embrace when Flora knocked once more at the door.

“Come, my lady, they are gathering in the courtyard!”

Dallas was at the door, adjusting her hat brim. "I love you, Iain," she said and hurried into the passageway.

ON A HAZY June morning, Fraser and his two retainers trotted through Bishopgate into London. The first thing that struck Fraser were the crowds of people. Soldiers, prentices, housewives, merchants, street vendors and children jostled each other along the narrow streets. House upon house pressed against each other and all but shut out the daylight. Once a city of open spaces, greenery and pleasant vistas, London had grown overcrowded and seemingly airless.

Maneuvering Barvas through the congested streets was no easy task. Fraser's patience had worn thin by the time they reached The Strand, which was wide enough to permit less encumbered travel. He had made up his mind to stay at an inn near the river where he would not feel so hemmed in.

Turning south at Charing Cross, where a stout woman extolled the virtues of her eel pie and two prentices from rival cabinetmakers threatened each other with table legs, they rode toward the Thames. Fraser found a respectable-looking inn near the river's edge, The Lamb and the Staff. No doubt he would be invited to stay at court once he had presented himself, but until then, the timber-fronted hostelry would do nicely.

The innkeeper, a burly man who shaved his head, was as garrulous as he was efficient. Being a cosmopolitan fellow whose livelihood was at least partially provided by foreigners, he had none of the prejudices Fraser found in most Englishmen. While his guest dined on leg of mutton and green beans the innkeeper rattled off the latest London news.

"The court has gone to Windsor, we've had plague here, you know." The innkeeper picked his teeth thoughtfully with a splinter. "No need to worry, the disease has run its course."

Fraser drank deeply from his tankard of English ale. He didn't like it as well as the Scots variety, but he was thirsty. He and the innkeeper were in a secluded inglenook as the common room began to fill up with the noon trade. "So when will the court return?" he asked.

"Hard to say, our sovereign lady being unpredictable, as her fair sex often is, bless 'em. But I've heard she'll be back soon to welcome the new Spanish ambassador. De Quadra, poor soul, Papist that he was, succumbed to the plague."

Frowning, Fraser silently considered this unexpected turn of events. De Quadra had been a known quantity, which was always helpful when it came to affairs of state. His replacement would have to be studied carefully before Fraser could proceed with any negotiations for a Spanish marriage.

The innkeeper kept on talking but his guest was deep in thought. Whatever else he needed to know, he could learn at the source, the court itself. Besides, he was intrigued by the idea of meeting Elizabeth, that enigmatic, imperious redhead who considered Mary Stuart not just a political rival, but also her chief competition as a woman. Aye, he'd like very much to see Elizabeth Tudor face-to-face. He would leave for Windsor at dawn.

AS SECRETARY OF State, William Cecil had direct access to Queen Elizabeth's ear with no overbearing half-brother to interfere. Cecil may have been no more clever or resourceful than his Scots counterpart, William Maitland. But Cecil and Elizabeth worked as a team; Maitland and Mary had always to contend with James Stuart.

"Who is this Highlander?" Elizabeth demanded of Cecil as they conferred in her chamber the day after Fraser's arrival at Windsor. "He's no Melville or Maitland with some official diplomatic capacity."

"He's a special emissary, Your Grace, come to discuss certain matters of concern to your royal cousin." Cecil spoke smoothly as he carefully adjusted the white linen collar of his severe black doublet. "He served Marie de Guise some years ago and has been at court off and on since Queen Mary's return."

Elizabeth's long, tapering fingers strayed to the tiny scars still left on her face from the previous autumn's bout with smallpox. "Alexander Fraser's son?"

Cecil cleared his throat delicately. "No, madame, he's a bastard, claiming the name of Malcolm Fraser, to whom his mother was married at the time of his birth. His sire is not known."

The Queen's pale brows drew together. "So my dearest cousin would send me an emissary who might have been spawned by some wandering tinker or the local Gaberlunzie man? Is this her way of showing gratitude for the sacrifice I would make to give her Rob Dudley as a husband?" Elizabeth bristled as Cecil wondered if he were in for one of her awesome temper tantrums.

"Since she is said to place great faith in Fraser, I can only assume she intends to do you honor. After all, her closest advisor is her bastard half-brother, James of Moray."

Elizabeth swung her fan at an errant fly. Discussions of legitimacy tended to make her nervous when they struck too close to home. Elizabeth could never forget that many people believed that her own parents' marriage had never been valid, thus making her as much of a bastard as James himself.

"God's teeth," she exclaimed, squashing the fly on the tabletop, "I'll see this ignoble Highlander. Have him come to me this afternoon, in my audience chamber."

Fraser appeared promptly at three. He had assumed that the Queen would be alone, with Cecil perhaps, but essentially a private audience. He was not pleased to discover the Queen of England seated among a rollicking group of courtiers which included Rob Dudley.

She did not wait upon ceremony. "Ah, Master Fraser—or is it now Baron Fraser? Come sit, we were just listening to one of Surrey's new poems."

Fraser strode up to the Queen and dropped on one knee. He had rehearsed an appropriately gallant speech but quickly abandoned it in light of his surroundings. "It's a pleasure to meet the Queen of England face-to-face," he said quietly. "I'm delighted to know that Your Grace can find ample opportunity for self-indulgence."

Though his tone was courteous and the kiss he implanted on her fingertips was impeccable, the insolence of his words could not be missed. Only one man at court could speak to her in such a way and that was Rob Dudley. The other courtiers held their breath while Elizabeth and Fraser took their measure of one another.

Even seated, she was a tall woman, Fraser noted, though probably not quite as tall as Mary Stuart. Her red hair was curled tightly about her face and her skin was a dazzling white. She was not beautiful, but her features were strong and her hazel eyes had a certain regal allure. She lacked Mary Stuart's charm and femininity but made up for it with the sort of fascination that only a very powerful and self-confident woman can exude. She wore a gown of peach-colored brocade, too heavy for the warm June day, and every fold of the material displayed small clusters of jewels. A pearl and emerald necklace hung down her slight bosom, there were emeralds in her ears, and a net of pearls over her hair. A fan-shaped ruff stood almost as high as her head and her fingers winked with jewels. The effect was overdone, yet somehow it suited her. He thought of what Dallas had once said about a similarly overdressed lady—that she looked as if she'd taken the contents of her closet, thrown them up in the air and then run under them. Fraser was both impressed and amused.

Angered though she was, Elizabeth could not easily dismiss Fraser's indolently arrogant bearing nor the clear hazel eyes which seemed to take in so much. His dark blue doublet and hose with a matching short cape were well tailored if somewhat plain by English court standards. In fact, she thought wryly, Cecil would approve of such attire.

But, she had to admit, this rude Highlander possessed a powerful animal attraction. Too dark, of course, his features too sharp for her tastes—but all the same, a formidable man.

She decided not to rebuke him, not just yet. Elizabeth never liked doing the obvious. So while her courtiers expected a sharp reprimand or even immediate dismissal, the Queen smiled coolly. "Surrey is a fine poet, it runs in his family. Now do sit, Baron Fraser." She nudged Rob Dudley playfully with her fan. "Rob, move over a space and make room for our Scots visitor."

Dudley obeyed, but not until he had given Fraser a long look of sheer malice.

THAT AFTERNOON, WHILE the English Queen and her courtiers extolled the virtues and condemned the follies of Surrey's poetry, two apparently unrelated occurrences took place, one far to the north in Edinburgh, the other just a few hundred yards away from the audience chamber.

The first was the discovery of Kennedy's body in the Nor' Loch. He had floated ashore late that afternoon and was found by some young boys who had gone for a swim. Fraser's serving man had been dead for several days and it was all too obvious that he had been tortured before he died.

The second occurrence was the arrival of a letter, addressed to William Cecil. The messenger who brought it had ridden hard and long but would not be satisfied until he saw Cecil in person. The Queen's secretary had finally allowed the messenger a brief audience. After he read the letter and had stared hard at the signature to make sure it was authentic, he folded the parchment slowly and grew very thoughtful.

THE DEER DRIVE at Ellerig would be the highlight of the summer progress. There, in the heavy woods of Glen Shira, the court would spend more than a week pursuing the magnificent creatures with bow and arrow. The Queen could hardly control her anticipation and spent many hours at practice shooting.

Dallas wrote letters instead. She wrote to Fraser, of course, trying not to dwell too long on how miserable she was without him, and she also wrote to Tarrill and Glennie. Now that she had been with the court for well over a year, the constant moves from castle to castle and great house to great house had lost their charm. She yearned for a more stable existence and especially for the familiar wynds and closes of Edinburgh. Even when the court was in residence at Holyrood during the winter months, there was little opportunity to explore the city as she used to do.

She missed her sisters, too, and Marthe and the boys. The failure to get husbands for Tarrill and Glennie rankled her. But when Dallas considered the men at court as possible suitors, they were already married, too highborn or of such disreputable character that she wouldn't dream of letting them near her kin. Sighing, she sanded the letter and called to Flora.

"It is the fourteenth, isn't it? That's what I put on the letter."

"Aye, my lady," Flora replied, looking up from a pile of mending. "Over five weeks now."

"I suppose he could be back any day. He said he'd probably join the court at Ellerig." At least he had written—twice, in fact. He mentioned little about state matters or the progress of his mission, but his letters were full of vivid details about Elizabeth and life at court. The second letter, dated July third, had arrived at Ellerig the previous morning. Fraser had said the court was moving back to London where Elizabeth would welcome the new Spanish ambassador.

"I need a messenger, Flora," Dallas said. "I must get this letter off to my sisters today so it reaches them before they go to visit the McVurrichs at Dunbar."

Flora nodded and got up. But when she opened the door, John Hamilton was just lifting his hand to knock. Flora greeted him courteously, then continued on her errand.

Hamilton was dressed in riding clothes. "We're off for a gallop," he said in his usual amiable way. "Are you joining us?"

"Nay, John, not today, I have a headache." She smiled wanly at him, grateful for his continued kindness to her.

Hamilton frowned and lowered his voice. "I'm worried about you, Dallas. Are you all right? Nay, I don't mean the headache—I mean, well, otherwise?"

Dallas had to tell someone, and Hamilton's sympathetic gaze invited her confidence: "I think I'm going to have a child, John."

His handsome face turned pale under the summer tan. But he forced a wide smile and stepped forward to hug her tight. "Why, Dallas, that's wonderful news!" He held her close for several moments, then stepped back, his hands on her shoulders. "Does your—husband know?"

She shook her head. " 'Tis not something I want to tell him by letter." Somehow she looked smaller and younger to Hamilton, even more waiflike than the first time he'd met her in the bookseller's shop. "Of course," she went on with a spark of her usual self-assurance, "he will be back soon."

"Yes, he may be on his way north even now," Hamilton said with what he hoped sounded like conviction. He would have added further words of consolation, but Flora came into the room just then, Secretary Maitland on her heels.

"My lady," the maid began, but Maitland smoothly stepped in front of her. He, too, was dressed for riding, in a debonair outfit of blue serge trimmed with miniver. Despite his patented aloofness, Dallas had warmed to him since he had begun courting Mary Fleming.

But Maitland spoke before Dallas could offer a greeting. "My lady, I have distressing news." As a reflex action, he glanced at Hamilton, remembered that the other man and Dallas were friends, and decided he could speak freely. "Your husband has been arrested by Queen Elizabeth for piracy."

The room seemed to move in great waves, the floor actually felt as if it were shaking under her feet, and the three other people turned into a great blur. Dallas did not feel Hamilton's arms catch her as she fell, and the next thing she knew, she was lying on the bed with a cold cloth over her forehead and Flora was holding smelling salts under her nose.

"Oh!" She choked and sneezed at the same time. "Get that out of here, Flora!" She put her hands over her face and lay back on the pillows. The cold cloth had fallen onto the floor and Hamilton picked it up, proffering it to Dallas. "Nay, I don't need that, either. Maitland, tell me, why? What happened?"

"A message arrived just a few minutes ago," he explained, his carefully cultivated diplomat's voice tinged with genuine sympathy. "Iain had gone to London with the rest of the court. Just as the retinue entered the city the Queen's men arrested him and took him to the Tower. He was charged with at least fourteen individual acts of piracy against English vessels and their crews."

Dallas felt sick, enraged, weak, desperate and stupefied, all at once. But she forced herself to remain rational. "Why? On what grounds? I don't understand." At all costs, she must protect Fraser, even—maybe especially—from his own countrymen.

Maitland shrugged. "I don't know. Queen Mary is mightily upset. Though just after your husband's arrest, the Earl of Bothwell was released."

Hamilton frowned quizzically at Maitland. "Hold on, William, this begins to sound rather strange. One Scot for another? How do you figure that?"

"I don't," Maitland replied candidly. "Not yet, at least. If Bothwell returns to Scotland, mayhap he can enlighten us."

Sitting up on the bed, Dallas spoke fiercely: "If it's ransom they want, I'll pay it. If it's politics, then you, Maitland, must secure his release. If it's something even greater, then the Queen must act."

Maitland smoothed his trim moustache. "It's not ransom, Dallas. And I cannot act without the Queen's sanction, though God knows she wants Fraser returned almost as much as you do. But then she wanted Bothwell's release, too. We must consider Elizabeth's reasons, obscure as they may be, and—other factors."

Dallas knew all too well what Maitland meant: James. The Queen's half-brother would not want Fraser back in Scotland any more than he had desired Bothwell's return. And without James's support, both Maitland and Mary Stuart were stymied.

But Dallas would not openly acknowledge the powerful grip in which James held them all. She rose from the bed to face the others. "A pox on Elizabeth and such 'other factors.' Iain will be released, I've no doubt of that."

Yet for the rest of the day her imagination dwelt on the sinister fate of prisoners condemned to the Tower, of pirates hanged in chains on the strand at Leith, and of the gallows tree in Liberton's Wynd.

Chapter Fourteen

THE DEER DRIVE was a great success. Armed with bows and arrows, javelins, and even a few stout clubs, the courtiers galloped through Glen Shira in a great state of excitement. Several hundred of the local inhabitants had been commandeered to flush the animals from the woods. They chased the deer in large herds towards the royal party while the Queen watched with sparkling eyes and cries of delight.

Dallas did not join them. It wasn't just her horror of watching the magnificent animals killed and then skinned before her very eyes which kept her away; she had plans to devise, decisions to make. She had seen the Queen, of course, who had lamented Fraser's arrest most deeply.

With little hope that he would ever receive the letter, Dallas wrote to Fraser. But frustration gnawed at her. Surely there was some more positive action she could take. It was Donald McVurrich who finally helped make up her mind. He had come to visit while he was off-duty; naturally, he was sorry to hear about Fraser's arrest.

"I scarce spoke to him more than once or twice," Donald said, "but he seemed like a braw enough fellow."

Coming from Donald, that was high praise. Dallas was lying on a mound of goose-down pillows while Flora did her hair. A glass of red wine stood on a table within reach and the two Manx cats were curled up by Dallas's feet.

"I wish I knew what to do," Dallas fretted as she reached for the wine glass. "I've spoken to Maitland, to the Queen, to Ambassador Randolph. I could see James, but it would do no good and I'll be damned if I'll go a-begging to that snake."

Donald remained silent, his big, bony hands incongruous under the ruffled cuffs. Dallas remembered to offer him wine, but he refused. "I'd write to Elizabeth herself, if I thought it would help," Dallas went on, "but she'd probably laugh her nasty head off at my naivete." She grimaced as Flora combed a snarl out of the thick dark hair. "Oh, I'm so frustrated, just lying here like a lump!"

Shifting awkwardly in the too-small armchair, Donald reached down to pet one of the Manx cats which had leaped onto the carpet. "Well," he began slowly, "if I were you, and my spouse were in prison somewhere, I know what I'd do."

Dallas eyed him curiously. "And what's that, Donald?"

He gave a slight lift of his broad shoulders, as if to indicate that the answer was so simple it almost wasn't worth mentioning. "I'd go there," he said matter-of-factly.

ACCOMPANIED BY DONALD, Dallas set out for Edinburgh on July twenty-third. When they arrived at the house in Nairne's Close, Dallas was distressed to discover it was shut tight. She had completely forgotten about her sisters' proposed trip to Dunbar.

"We'll just have to go to my husband's town house," Dallas announced as she gazed fondly up at her family home.

Donald was about to mount the cart again when Mistress Drummond appeared in the wynd. She made a great fuss over Dallas, exclaiming at the finery of her riding costume and the amount of baggage stowed into the cart.

"Your sisters left day before yesterday," Mistress Drummond said, "fetched by one of the McVurrich lads. Your brother, is that not so?" she asked, pointing to Donald. "Aye, I remember you. They were to go even sooner but—" and she dropped her voice in that familiar tone of a great confidence about to be bestowed. "They had a visitor, Walter Ramsay—his Fiona passed on just a week ago." She waited for Dallas's reaction, which came swiftly and genuinely.

"She'd been ill for some time," Dallas said sadly. "I'm sorry she's gone, sorry for poor Walter."

Dallas endured a few more minutes of Mistress Drummond's unfettered tongue and then made her excuses to be off. The little group reached Fraser's town house a few minutes later, just as the sun began to slip down over the Nor' Loch. The house looked the same, Dallas noted, but there was an air of emptiness about it. Was no one at home here either, she wondered?

Cummings came to the door almost at once, but Dallas noticed that he had peered out warily. When he saw his master's wife, he broke into a wide smile. "Come in, Lady Fraser! Have the baggage brought around to the side, I'll send a servant right away."

Dallas, with Flora at her heels, went into the handsome entry hall. The baggage was unloaded, Flora set about readying a hot bath for Dallas, Donald took care of the horses, and Cummings ordered supper for everyone.

At last, bathed and fed, Dallas sat with Cummings in the supper room. Naturally, the subject of Fraser's arrest was uppermost in both their minds. "I could not believe such effrontery when I heard the news," Cummings said, shaking his head. "Imagine, arresting an emissary of the Queen's!"

"But why the charge of piracy, Cummings? That upsets me greatly." Dallas propped her feet up on a stool and wished the ashiette of pork, new potatoes and fresh peas hadn't made her feel so queasy.

Cummings gazed at Dallas bleakly. "I guess you couldn't have heard, mistress. About Kennedy, I mean." When Dallas said she certainly had not, Cummings went on: "A fortnight ago, more or less, some young laddies found Kennedy's body washed up at the Nor' Loch's edge. He'd been tortured."

Dallas stared at Cummings, as understanding filtered quickly through her mind. "You think that's how Elizabeth—knew?"

"I'm only guessing," Cummings sighed as he poured himself a glass of sherry. "Kennedy liked his drink, you know. He'd often go to a tavern for some libation, staying until curfew, hobnobbing with his friends. But on this particular night, he never came back. I wasn't unduly concerned, I figured he'd drunk himself into a stupor. But when he didn't come back the next day, I sent two servants to find him. Kennedy had been seen in The Black Sheep, drinking with two men nobody recognized. Later, when he was in his cups, he left with them. And that's the last time he was seen alive."

Dallas pushed her hands through her disheveled hair. "So you think those men tortured Kennedy and forced him to admit Iain is a pirate?" She watched Cummings nod slowly. "But who hired them—the English or James Stuart?"

"Either. Perhaps someone else." Cummings used a napkin to blot up some drops of sherry which he'd spilled on the supper table. "But my money is on that blackguard James."

"What of Bothwell? Is he in Edinburgh?" Dallas poured herself a drink, for the queasiness had left her parched.

"He came and went like a summer wind," Cummings replied. "To France, I hear. He stayed just long enough to find out what kind of welcome he'd get at court. When he learned that James still considered him a criminal for escaping after the Arran affair, Bothwell decamped."

Dallas swore under her breath. "A lot of help he is!" She stood up, holding onto the supper table to steady herself. These passing spells of dizziness and nausea would certainly slow her journey to London. Should she tell Cummings of her plan? She thought not, at least not yet; better to send him a letter from Dunbar. Nor would she tell him—or her sisters—of her pregnancy lest they try to dissuade her from going at all.

Dallas thanked Cummings for everything, bade him good-night, and walked purposefully up the stairs to the chamber where she had spent her wedding night.

THEY REACHED DUNBAR before sunset the next day. Glennie, Tarrill, Marthe and the rest of the family were all surprised to see her ride up to the cottage with Donald and Flora. While they greeted Dallas warmly, there was noticeable constraint between Donald and his father. The two men scarcely spoke to each other during the first part of supper, but Annie McVurrich finally broke the barrier by asking Donald about his life at court. Though he reverted to his taciturn manner at first, Donald opened up after Dallas remarked how well he was thought of by several of the staunchest Protestant lords; at last Oliver McVurrich chimed in with a few questions on his own.

Dallas, however, did not speak of her own plans until after the McVurrichs had retired and she sat outside in the mild summer night with her sisters. Both women reacted with horror.

"You can't go to London!" Glennie exclaimed. "Even with Donald, it's too dangerous."

"Nonsense," Dallas retorted. "Women travel in England all the time. And I can imitate a London accent quite well."

Even as her sisters tried to stop Dallas, they knew their cause was lost. They sat outside for almost an hour, until a stiff breeze came up from the sea. Finally, Glennie got up to check on the boys, who were sleeping with the younger McVurrich lads in the stable.

"I wish I could go with you, Dallas," Tarrill said wistfully. "Your life seems so exciting compared to mine."

"Exciting? I hardly consider my husband's imprisonment a subject of envy."

But Tarrill went on as if Dallas hadn't spoken. "You once said your position at court would help Glennie and me find husbands."

The resentment in Tarrill's voice made Dallas both angry and guilty. "I've seen to it that you and Glennie are provided for," she replied defensively. "Tell me, Tarrill," Dallas asked with genuine sympathy, "are you so unhappy?"

Tarrill leaned against the trunk of a sycamore tree and stared off into the summer night. "Nay, not unhappy—it's just that I'd like to find someone to love, who would love me. I'm not sure you'd understand, Dallas, your own marriage to Iain was one of convenience, though I assume you feel something for him or else you wouldn't be racing off to London ...."

"Yes," Dallas broke in abruptly, "I feel something." She wondered if Tarrill had caught the irony of her words. "Don't fash yourself, you'll find a husband.

Perhaps the longer you wait, the better your chances that he'll be right for you."

A faint smile touched Tarril's mouth. "I hope so, Dallas. It seems as if I've waited a long time already."

Dallas turned away so that Tarrill would not see the pity in her eyes. Nor did she want her to see the love for Fraser, not now, when she might be on the verge of losing him forever.

In the morning, Dallas's sisters sent her on her way with admonitions to take care and the promise of frequent prayers. Donald and his father exchanged a salute which Dallas hoped might signify a reconciliation, and by eight o'clock the little party was headed for the border.

IAIN FRASER WAS imprisoned in the Beauchamp Tower. His quarters were cramped but not without comfort. He had a bed, a chair, a table and a view of Tower Green. The lieutenant of the Tower, Sir Reginald Stanley, had brought him books with which he passed most of his waking hours. But he was allowed no correspondence and so far he had been permitted no visitors, though Queen Mary's ambassador, Sir James Melville, had tried to see him on several occasions.

For a man of Fraser's restless temperament, the month-long incarceration was nerve-wracking. The only thing that kept him from attempting to tear down the walls with his bare hands was the certainty that somehow he would get out very soon. He had little faith in lawful methods of attaining his goal, but each day he dwelled upon a variety of plans for escape. In fact, he had come to the conclusion that time was as much his ally as his enemy: If he could lull his captors into thinking he was resigned to his fate, they would eventually relax their guard. He had engaged in combat too often not to know that any opponent will ultimately make a mistake through either overconfidence or tedium.

There was time, too, to speculate on why he had been arrested in the first place. He had overheard the news that Bothwell had been released. Had some plan been afoot all along to substitute one supporter of Mary Stuart for another? Or had James intended all along to have Fraser shut away in an English prison? Certainly that was possible. If his conjectures about James's enmity were indeed correct, then the Queen's half-brother would much prefer Bothwell's presence in Scotland to Fraser's.

So the drowsy summer days slipped by, with Fraser absorbed in the intricacies of politics and the difficulties of escape. He thought of Dallas, of course, and wondered how she'd taken the news of his arrest. He hoped she had not done something wildly reckless, such as a head-on confrontation with James. But then she could not be certain that James was behind this particular plot. No, he decided, Dallas would rant and fret and curse, but she would not subject herself to possible danger.

Dallas was, in fact, less than a mile from the Tower of London. It had taken over two weeks to make the journey, since she felt unwell much of the time, and there had been at least two days when she hadn't been able to travel at all. But she had finally reached London on August twenty-fourth, where the little party put up at a recently completed inn not far from Whitehall.

As Fraser had done before her, Dallas set about discovering where the Queen was. In the Midlands, she was told, where Elizabeth was visiting several noble families. She would not return until September.

"Fie," Dallas exclaimed when Donald brought her the news. "And Sir James Melville is with them." She paced her chamber, contemplating the next move. "Cecil, too, I suppose?"

Donald said he was, though suffering mightily from gout. Dallas could not suppress a small smile of satisfaction at this scrap of information. "Well, then, I must go directly to the Tower. I can't spend a fortnight lolling about here."

Neither Donald nor Flora attempted to dissuade her. If Dallas were rebuffed in her efforts to see Fraser, they'd prefer her wrath to pent-up frustration.

The next morning Dallas and Donald set off for the Tower. With its massive bulk and flying pennants, the grim stonework looked formidable and menacing; Dallas felt her heart turn to brick.

When they reached the entrance at Petty Wales off Thames Street, the guards seemed more puzzled than officious. "You cannot be admitted without some sort of pass or letter," a blond young man half a head shorter than Donald told them. "Even though your husband is here, madame, we cannot permit it."

"I've not traveled all the way from Scotland to be told I have to obtain some diddling scrap of paper before I see my own husband," Dallas snapped. "Make way, and let me speak with the lieutenant of the Tower."

The guard was somewhat put off by Dallas's aggressive manner. He was used to women who wept and begged and lamented but not to one who appeared ready and mayhap eager to use her riding crop on him. Besides, he had caught sight of the lady's husband when he was exercising on the Tower battlements. The young guard had instantly recognized the prisoner as the type of man he wouldn't care to cross.

"Sir Reginald is not at his residence today. But he will return tomorrow and I'll tell him about your visit," the young guard said, hoping to soothe Lady Fraser's temper.

Dallas narrowed her eyes at the young man. "Very well. I'll be back tomorrow morning, before eleven." And Dallas swished away towards Thames Street, with Donald right behind her.

Sir Reginald was a reasonable man who often wished he had never been appointed to the lieutenancy of the Tower. He and Lady Stanley had a fine house with a private garden and even a small orchard and the pay was good enough, but the responsibilities frequently overwhelmed him. Oh, most of the poor wretches imprisoned there deserved their fate and maybe worse. But now and then, the Tower received a victim whose punishment Stanley secretly questioned—such as Iain Fraser—and though Stanley, like most Englishmen, had little love for the Scots, he had grown to admire and respect the man.

So when Sir Reginald received word that Lady Fraser was in London demanding to see her husband, he reluctantly granted her an interview. His first impression enchanted him—the big dark eyes, the rich, thick hair done up in a gold mesh net, the full, firm figure dressed in a dark red riding habit with a flurry of white lace at the throat. A charming little thing, he thought, and no doubt a fit mate for the dark, lean pirate who was imprisoned nearby in the Beauchamp Tower.

"After all," Dallas was saying demurely when Sir Reginald had poured her a glass of wine, "I've been married to Iain for almost two years, and if anyone knew he was involved in piracy, it would be me. But, sir, I find the accusation laughable!" Dallas plied her fan and fluttered her lashes.

"Yes, well, of course, these things happen," Sir Reginald said, noting the trim ankle below the red hem of Dallas's skirt.

" 'These things'?" Dallas's eyes grew round. "I don't understand. You mean a mistake?"

"Uh, well, I can't say that, and then there's been no trial yet," Sir Reginald said, shifting uncomfortably in his chair as Dallas pulled off her white kid gloves. "But in truth, madame, I can't give permission for you to see your husband until I have word from the Queen or Cecil."

Dallas's eyes sparked for just an instant, but she maintained her guise of a demure young wife. "But who would know, sir? Just you and me—and Iain, of course. It would be our little secret. Oh, I do love secrets, don't you?" She leaned forward and gave a breathy little laugh.

Sir Reginald reminded himself that he was a hardened soldier who'd served his country bravely in France some twenty years earlier. Drawing himself up to military posture in his high-backed chair, he shook his head. "Nay, madame, as delightful as it might be, rumors would run amok in this place before you ever got back outside. But," he added more gently, "I'll send a letter with your request to Master Cecil as soon as the court is back in London."

Dallas hesitated between resignation and fury. But the lieutenant of the Tower seemed to be a decent sort, and ultimately she might gain more by keeping to her original pose. As hateful as the prospect was, she'd have to give in. Thanking Sir Reginald effusively, she cast one last lingering look at him over the rim of her fan.

THE FIRST RUSSET leaves of autumn had drifted down outside the inn's narrow windows before Dallas heard from Sir Reginald. On the twentieth of September he wrote to inform her that his request on her behalf had been refused. Fraser was allowed no visitors and that dictum included his wife. He apologized profusely and added, as if to placate her somehow, that Fraser was well and in apparent good spirits. He had not, however, told his prisoner of Dallas's presence in the city.

"I would not have raised his hopes unduly, since I feared his anticipation at seeing you might be dashed by Master Cecil's decision."

So, Dallas thought, Sir Reginald had felt all along that her request would be denied. She gave orders to Donald and Flora that she would leave immediately for Whitehall.

The palace had been reconstructed on the site of Cardinal Wolsey's magnificent York Place. It was set on the river's edge and had been a favorite residence of Elizabeth's parents, King Henry and Anne Boleyn.

Dallas corralled a page and announced imperiously that she wished to see Sir James Melville, the Scots ambassador. The page glanced at the other petitioners waiting in the antechamber, compared their unstylish attire with Dallas's turquoise blue finery, and informed her that she would be next. Five minutes later, he ushered her into Melville's chamber.

Sir James was just over thirty, with receding red hair and a close-trimmed beard. He had met Dallas at Holyrood the previous year and had thought her tongue oversharp, though she obviously possessed an unconscious physical allure. He was not, however, pleased to see her at Whitehall.

"Madame," he began, after hearing her out, "I regret your husband's arrest as much as anyone, but I've spoken to Queen Elizabeth several times and she is closed as a clam about her intentions. Furthermore, I've tried to see Iain myself, with no success. Until the Queen reveals what game she's playing, we'll just have to wait."

Dallas pounded her fists on Melville's desk. "Wait, wait, wait! I've been in London almost a month and that's all I've done! Pox on Elizabeth and her harebrained whims! Must I go to her myself and tell her what I think?"

That was the last thing Melville wanted Dallas to do. At best, she'd create a terrible scene, which would do no good for relations between England and Scotland; at worst, she'd find herself in the Tower, a prisoner like her husband. "Nay, madame, that you must not do," Melville asserted. "You'd only make it harder for Iain. The Queen can retaliate in many ways—further deprivation, torture, even—death." He let the last word fall heavily between them to impress upon Dallas the possible consequences of her folly.

His ploy worked. Dallas agreed to keep away from Queen Elizabeth but insisted Melville make another effort on Fraser's behalf. At last he promised to do so, though he knew his efforts would be in vain.

BY THE END of September Dallas had decided to move out of the inn. The quarters were too confining and the bills were mounting. She had contacted the Countess of Lennox, who responded graciously with an invitation for Dallas to stay at her London residence.

The Countess was a full-bodied woman of forty or so with auburn curls and an overbearing manner. Though a Stuart by ancestry, she was an English subject by birth. Her husband, Matthew, was also a Scot but owned more land in England than in Scotland. His political intrigues in his native land had earned him exile across the border. Together, the Lennoxes formed the most important and formidable Scots alliance in London.

"Certainly I'll speak to Elizabeth about your husband," the Countess asserted in her usual brisk manner. "She's a tartar, but no one ever put the fear of God into Margaret Lennox."

Dallas felt braced by the Countess's words. They weren't mere bluster, either. Margaret Douglas Lennox had a claim of her own to the English throne through her grandfather, Henry the Seventh. She had never considered herself anything less than Elizabeth's equal.

But even Margaret Lennox's methods took time. It was late October, damp and foggy, before the Countess won her first round. Sir James Melville would be allowed to see Iain Fraser.

On the day Melville was scheduled to visit the Tower, Dallas prowled her bedroom all morning. Outside, rain pummeled the Lennox gardens, drowning the last chrysanthemums in puddles of mud. The Lennoxes' elder son, Lord Darnley, who had been mentioned as a possible husband for Mary Stuart, had stopped by earlier to show off his newest creation from the tailor. He had admired Dallas's own taste in clothes and wanted her opinion. She had regarded the preening youth without much enthusiasm, for she found him spoiled and self-indulgent, but had finally declared he looked splendid and sent him on his way.

The bouts of nausea were past now, but Dallas was faced with a new dilemma: Very soon she would have to add panels to her gowns. Already there were only three dresses in her travel wardrobe which she could still squeeze into. She and Flora began altering Dallas's gowns and making clothes for the baby. It helped pass the time but Flora worried whether or not Dallas would be back in Edinburgh in time to give birth.

"Of course," Dallas declared more vehemently than she felt. The months of waiting had undermined her confidence. "It will be February before the bairn is due."

Just then the Countess of Lennox entered with Sir James Melville following in her wake, looking not unlike a pet terrier. "He's seen your husband, my dear, and Iain is quite hale if not exactly hearty. He has books and is allowed outside occasionally and the food is quite passable—but let Sir James tell you himself."

Melville was beginning to think he'd never get the chance. "He seems to be resigned to a lengthy stay in the Tower," Melville said, "though he's unable to conquer his native restlessness. His gaolers play cards and dice with him to help pass the time. Once a week or so he dines with Sir Reginald and Lady Stanley in their quarters. There's an enclosed garden area on the river side of the tower grounds where he can take the air."

Dallas was relieved. At least Fraser wasn't penned up in some tiny dark hole shut off from the world. "What did he say when you told him I was here?" she asked.

Melville could not meet her eager gaze. "Ah, no, madame, I didn't mention your presence in London." As Dallas began to explode with recrimination he waved a hand to silence her. "Please, don't you see, if he knew you were here, he might do something reckless, try to escape. His current perquisites—for which you may no doubt thank the Countess here—give great hope that the Queen may be ready to show leniency."

"You mean I can't even write to him?" Dallas's voice was thin and forced. She wanted so badly for him to know she was close by. Just seeing Melville here in her room, so soon after he had actually been with Fraser and spoken to him, made her heart ache more than ever with longing.

"Nay, not yet," Melville cautioned soothingly, "bide awhile, it's the only way."

Dallas slumped into a chair, feeling the babe turn over in her womb. She uttered a brief, foul oath and started to make a motion of dismissing Melville but remembered her manners. She thanked him with forced courtesy, said good-day to both him and the Countess, and took to her bed for the rest of the afternoon.

YOUNG DARNLEY'S SULKY face followed Dallas all the way out into The Strand. When she'd announced her intention of taking advantage of the fine autumn weather to visit the shops and stalls of Cheapside, Darnley had insisted upon going along.

"You'd be bored," Dallas had told him. But Darnley had persisted, asserting that shopping amused him, that he enjoyed perusing ladies' fripperies or sniffing scents at the perfumers'.

"Donald is going, why can't I?" he'd whined, as peevish as a puppy whose biscuit has been taken away.

"Donald isn't going," Dallas had informed him, though she had originally planned it that way. But if Donald went, Darnley would, too. "Flora is accompanying me, and that's that!"

So she'd trudged out of Lennox House with Flora walking briskly at her side, while Darnley leaned in the doorway, mumbling to himself. Flora was mumbling, too, declaring that Dallas's real mission was as harebrained as it was hazardous.

"You know what Sir James told you, if your husband finds out you're in London, he'll do something foolish. This whole scheme, right down to deceiving the Lennoxes, is much too rash!"

"Hush!" Dallas threw Flora a withering glance. "Melville and the Lennoxes can dredge up a hundred reasons why I shouldn't see Iain. I only need one to tell me I should."

Sir Reginald Stanley welcomed Dallas cordially to his lodgings in the Tower. The demure manner she had adopted for her previous interview had vanished, however. It had gotten her nowhere and she'd decided on a more direct approach.

"As you can see, Sir Reginald, I'm with child. My husband has a right to know and you have a duty to let me see him."

Sir Reginald stifled a sigh. He thought Melville had taken care of Lady Fraser and her importunate demands. "I'll write to Her Grace again and explain your condition," he said, not without sympathy. "It's possible she may change her mind."

"It's possible she may not." Dallas waved her gold-tasseled purse at the lord lieutenant. "I'll not be put off another moment! Take me to my husband or I won't budge from this place!"

Rubbing his close-cropped beard in vexation, Sir Reginald ground his teeth together. "I can't, really I can't. If need be, I'll have to order my men to carry you out bodily."

Dallas made a sweeping gesture over her abdomen. "You'd do that to an expectant mother? You'd have your minion churls mishandle me so?"

It was best not to tell Lady Fraser exactly how men—and women—could be ill handled in the Tower. Yet Sir Reginald felt ill-at-ease. What had happened to the charming, enticing little lady who had visited him some weeks earlier? "Please, madame," he entreated, "you'd best leave at once. I'm helpless to accede to your request."

Hurling Sir Reginald a scalding glance of contempt, Dallas whirled around to where Flora stood in motionless disapproval. Without another word, Dallas flung out of the room, down the corridor and through the lodging house doorway. Flora flapped along beside her mistress, her mouth set in a prim, angry line.

Once outside on Tower Green, it was only a short distance to Fraser's prison site Dallas raced across the open area as fast as her increasing girth would permit, pulling up short in front of the Beauchamp Tower. With a sharp clang of steel, the two guards on duty crossed their halberds, blocking her passage. One of them ordered her to halt, the other stared in astonishment at her boldness.

"Let me pass! I must see my husband, Baron Fraser!" Dallas was shrieking at the top of her lungs, one hand fending off Flora's attempts to restrain her.

"Stay where you are," the first guard commanded. "No one enters here except with the lord lieutenant's permission!"

"Don't stop me! I'm carrying my husband's babe! Let me by!" Dallas darted forward, trying to slip under the halberds. But Sir Reginald was already halfway across Tower Green, with two other soldiers following close behind him.

The halberdiers had moved their weapons down far enough to keep Dallas from getting inside. The other two guards were now upon her, each grabbing an arm, halfcarrying, half-dragging her back towards the Tower gateway. Dallas screamed like a madwoman, swore, bellowed and cursed all the way onto the Lion's Gate Bridge. Flora's disapproval of Dallas had turned to indignation with the guards, and her own reproaches rent the brisk autumn air. Then the Tower entrance clattered shut behind them as Dallas struggled to her feet from the rough stones where the guards had unceremoniously dumped her.

"Iain must have heard me," she gasped, leaning in exhaustion against the bridge's cold masonry. She glanced across the moat to gaze at the outline of the Beauchamp Tower. "Oh, God, he's so near ...." The babe moved wildly in her womb and Dallas's hand flew to her stomach, fear flooding her face. "Sweet Virgin! What have I done?"

Flora rushed to put her arms around her mistress. "I warned you of such foolhardiness! You'll lose the bairn, too!"

But the child quieted down in a few moments. Still shaken, but no longer frightened, Dallas extricated herself from Flora's grasp and began walking slowly away from the Tower. She had made one last desperate attempt to see Fraser. Now Dallas realized that she was as much a prisoner of her body as he was of the English Queen. At least she had not failed completely—he must have heard her, must know she carried his babe, must realize that she was near.

SOME DISTANCE FROM the Beauchamp Tower, in the enclosed garden area between the Jewel House and the decaying ancient hall of the royal lodgings, Iain Fraser lounged on a small stone bench and threw bread crumbs at the ravens. The damp, dying smell of autumn came off the river and somewhere in the distance he heard shouts. Bargemen quarreling over a fare, no doubt, he thought lazily, and winked back at the one-eyed sparrow he'd made into a pet.

Chapter Fifteen

THE COUNTESS OF Lennox was irate when Melville told her about Dallas's outrageous behavior in the Tower precincts. He warned the Countess that if such a thing happened again he could not restrain Elizabeth from wreaking vengeance on everyone involved.

His threat turned the Countess's anger from Dallas to Melville himself. "I refuse to let you permit that harridan to menace me! You tell Elizabeth that I'm protecting Lady Fraser out of compassion for her situation, out of Christian charity for a fellow human being! That barren twig of an illicit union can't possibly understand a loving wife's need for her husband at such a time!"

Intimidated by the Countess, Melville did not point out that Dallas's behavior had gone beyond the boundaries of acceptable conduct. There was no need for him to do so, of course, since despite her tirade, Margaret Lennox fully understood that Dallas would have to be watched more closely in the future.

THE WALLS OF the Beauchamp Tower were scarred by the scribblings of previous prisoners. Iain Fraser refrained from leaving his own mark in the masonry but spent many hours contriving fantasies about the various names, dates, snatches of verse and pithy sayings. It was as good a way as any to pass the time when the guards had other duties or the light was too poor for reading.

During the first few weeks of his imprisonment he'd paced the floor so much that he'd worn a path through the rushes. Realizing that such exertion was as fruitless as it might prove unnerving, he had forced himself to stop and turn his mind, if not his body, to other methods of enduring the endless days.

But every so often he'd catch himself straining at the bars of the tower's one small window or heaving his weight full-bore against the unyielding iron door of his prison. Such vain efforts were followed by an anger with himself which always brought him back to instant rationality.

Had he known what Melville had told Dallas, Fraser would have scoffed. The ambassador was dead wrong on two counts: First, Elizabeth had made no move to release Fraser during the month which had followed—or the next. Melville's second error in judgment pertained to Fraser himself. Not only was he unresigned to his captivity, he was making ready to escape.

During the last week of November, a candle had been overturned in Fraser's cell, setting fire to the rushes and causing considerable damage to the walls. Fraser himself avowed that he'd no idea how the accident had occurred, being asleep at the time. His gaolers thought it providential that he hadn't been overcome by smoke or burned to death before they unlocked the door. But fate had been kind to Fraser, since he'd awakened in the nick of time to call for the guards who rushed in to save him.

Naturally, it was impossible for Fraser to remain in the Beauchamp Tower until repairs were made. Sir Reginald, thankful that his prisoner hadn't died in the fire, a tragedy for which he himself would be blamed by both the Scots and English governments, felt he owed Fraser a favor. He asked his prisoner if he'd prefer a change in scenery, perhaps a view of one of the gardens?

"I stayed at an inn overlooking the river when I first came to London," Fraser had said upon apparent reflection. "I enjoyed the bustle of the river traffic then, perhaps it would be a pleasant distraction."

Sir Reginald had agreed and ordered that Fraser be moved to the Cradle Tower, which provided a view of both the river and the Queen's privy gardens. His cell there was somewhat larger, but more importantly, it was separated from the Thames by a mere fifty yards, the narrow moat and a relatively low stone wall.

That had been the first part of Fraser's plan. The second was to find an accommodating gaoler. Many hours of dice and cards were passed that autumn and much ale and whiskey were consumed before Fraser decided on his man. He was one Octavian Goolsby, a native Londoner, who'd tried many a trade in his time, liked none of them, and was employed as a gaoler only until he'd saved enough to go to Italy, where he could spend his days in the sun.

"Full o' Papists, Italy is, but I say, so what?" Goolsby had expounded one night when he and Fraser had diced and drunk the hours away. "Weren't we all Latin-mumblers fifty years ago or less? Besides, I don't have to kiss the Pope's arse or ask him to dinner."

"Passage to Italy doesn't come cheap, though," Fraser mused. "How long will you have to work?"

"Oh, a year at least." Goolsby laughed good-naturedly as he noted the pile of coins in front of Fraser. "Maybe two, if you keep winning."

"Maybe not more than a few weeks, if I'm released," Fraser said mildly.

Goolsby's eyes, which had been rather glazed by drink, suddenly came into focus. "How so? You mean you'd bribe me?" He bristled indignantly, but without conviction.

"Not at all. I just know someone with a ship. I could arrange your passage—without charge."

That was how it began, and by mid-December Fraser had gotten word to Cummings with full instructions for an escape attempt. There would be no moon on the night of January eighteenth, which would give the *Richezza's* crew sufficient time to sail from the Isle of Lewes and anchor off the mouth of the Thames. Corelli would take the land route and secure a skiff in which he'd wait in the river by the Tower Wharf. Goolsby would supply the rope and both he and Fraser would climb out of the Cradle Tower and make for the stone wall. As the momentous night grew near, Goolsby displayed more excitement than Fraser.

"What a joke!" he exclaimed. "A gaoler escaping from the Tower! But damme, I've felt as much a prisoner here as you, I feel like that whenever I've worked in the same place very long."

Goolsby, of course, knew every move of the night watch. At precisely twelve-thirty they threw the thin but sturdy coil down from the Cradle Tower's window. It was raining and quite chilly but there was no wind. Goolsby went first, slipping a bit, but reaching the moat without mishap. Fraser followed, hoping that his expert seaman's knots would hold for the second descent. He slipped smoothly down the rope and dropped into the murky water. They waited for a few seconds against the tower itself, then swam to the stone wall. There was just enough space in the masonry to provide hand and footholds. The men scrambled up to the top quickly, but as they were about to leap down onto the wharf Goolsby lost his footing on the slippery stones and toppled backwards into the moat.

Fraser froze on the wall. Down below, Goolsby was treading water. The splash had attracted two guards who came at the run along the Tower battlements. Goolsby might make it back up the wall before the guards got down to the bridge by the gate, but Fraser doubted it. If he waited for Goolsby, they were both lost. Instead, he shouted loudly, "Goolsby, you fool, you'll never catch me now! You're lucky I didn't kill you!" As he leaped onto the wharf he saw his accomplice swimming towards the bridge, apparently ready to join the guards in pursuit.

At first, he couldn't make out Corelli or the skiff in the darkness. But after a suspenseful moment he sighted Corelli, waving from just a few yards down the river. Fraser ran to the skiff, getting in quickly but carefully, so as not to overturn the little craft. Corelli said nothing but plied the oars expertly. They were a quarter of a mile down the Thames, moving with the current, before the Tower guards had their own boat away from the wharf. Ten minutes later they had reached Wapping Wall where horses awaited them. Miraculously, one of the mounts was Barvas, secured by Corelli earlier that day from the retainers who had waited patiently all these months for Fraser's release. The two men joined Fraser and Corelli, and together they galloped away from London and off towards the coast.

IT WAS ALMOST dawn when Fraser and his companions reached the coast beyond Gravesend. A lone beacon aboard the *Richezza* signaled to the four men and their exhausted mounts. A longboat had pulled up along shore to take the party out to the mother ship.

Once aboard, Fraser found his crew assembled on deck. He saluted them with a warm sense of camaraderie and gratitude as they cheered his arrival. After a brief speech of thanks, Fraser gave orders for the ship to set an easterly course and then retired to the sanctuary of his cabin. MacRae, his first mate, was waiting for him. Corelli had joined them and an early breakfast was served by one of the cabin boys.

"There were times when I thought not to see this again," Fraser declared, making a sweeping gesture to include the entire ship as well as the handsomely appointed cabin. "Now I must make a decision—whether to head for France, as Bothwell did, or go back to Scotland."

"We'll abide by your decision as always, captain," MacRae said as he spread marmalade on a crust of brown bread. "But if I may venture an opinion, the men have been land-bound too long."

Fraser chewed thoughtfully on a piece of salt pork. "True. But a few more weeks won't kill them, should I decide to go to Edinburgh. I'm not in the same position as Bothwell, I'm not considered a criminal in Scots eyes. Lord James is another matter, but I should have no legal worries about being in Scotland."

He paused to drink down a big swallow of Scots whiskey, the first he'd had in months. Grinning at his two crewmen, he went on: "You gentlemen also seem to forget that I've a bonnie wife I haven't laid eyes—or hands—on since June and she's probably either pined away or bought up half of Edinburgh by now."

Corelli blinked at his captain. "But no, your wife is not in Edinburgh. She's in London!"

Very slowly, Fraser laid down the knife he'd been using to cut off another piece of bread. He stared at Corelli for a long moment before he spoke, and when he did, his voice was hard as stone. "By God, man, I hope you're not telling me the truth."

"But it's so, captain," Corelli cried, his black eyes wide. "I thought you knew, she has been there for months!"

Fraser grasped the knife and plunged it into the tabletop. "Good Christ, I never knew! We must go back!" Corelli and MacRae exchanged quick glances. "You can't, sir, you know that. London will be crawling with men searching for you. If you're caught, it will certainly mean your death!" MacRae spoke fervently, his hands folded tightly together as if in supplication.

"Not only that," Corelli went on hurriedly, "but your lady, sir—I was told yesterday while in London that she is in no condition to travel now. She has not been seen outside of Lennox House for the past month or so."

Fraser had risen from his chair to tower over the two men. "What in Christ's name are you talking about now? Is Dallas ill?"

There had been two or three other occasions in Corelli's life when he had wanted to disappear magically, but they had all occurred in the heat of battle aboard ship when he was cornered by the enemy. Yet now, confronted by the fearsome rage of his captain, he wished he were anywhere but aboard the *Richezza*.

"She is about to have a baby," he replied at last, his accent suddenly as thick as it had been when he first sailed with Fraser from Venice.

Fraser's hands covered his face in anger and despair. Why had that damned fool Melville not told him? Had Sir Reginald known all along, too? He realized Dallas had probably written to him and that her letters had been intercepted. But he'd never dreamed she would come all the way to London, that she was with child, and now about to give birth alone in a strange country, with only the Lennoxes for companionship. Fraser had never gotten the opportunity to meet them or the son Mary Stuart had charged him to study as a possible consort.

But there was no point in being angry with his crewmen. As always, they had acted in his own best interests, convinced that their only goal was Fraser's freedom. Dallas would have encumbered them severely, and the flight might even have touched off premature labor, endangering both her and the child.

But such reasonableness did not comfort Fraser in the slightest. His wife was about to give birth to his bairn and she was in danger. As soon as his escape was made known to Queen Elizabeth, there was no telling what revenge she'd seek.

"Damn all," he breathed, looking up at MacRae and Corelli. "Turn back. I can't leave my lassie."

Pale dawn filtered across the Thames's broad mouth as the *Richezza* dropped anchor. Fraser and six of his men would go ashore north of Tilbury as soon as the tide changed. Silently, they stood at the ship's rail, waiting to lower the longboat. Corelli's fingers strayed nervously to his dagger. MacRae chewed his lip and wondered if there wasn't some final, compelling argument he might offer that would dissuade his captain from committing certain folly.

It was not words which finally changed Fraser's mind, however. As the wan winter sun rose up behind them, their eyes were attracted by the gleam of steel. Ringed along the shore, as far as they could see, were helmeted soldiers. Fraser swore, grasped his telescope, scanned the half-mile, and swore again.

"Crafty bitch," he snarled. "Elizabeth knew I'd probably have a ship waiting." Swinging around, he pointed the telescope up river. Sure enough, a trim caravel was sailing past Tilbury, cannon protruding from the bulwarks. "Lift anchor!" Fraser scowled at both Corelli and MacRae, silencing the sighs of relief which had sprung into their throats.

Slowly, too slowly, it seemed to the crewmen, the *Richezza's* sails unfurled and lifted under the morning breeze. A sudden explosion off the bow rocked the ship, sending several crewmen to the deck and slamming Fraser against the rail.

Righting himself, Fraser ordered his crewmen to return the fire. The English vessel was gaining on them and he had little doubt that the second volley would find its mark. Counting on the *Richezza's* maneuverability, he shouted to turn the ship to starboard, and nodded his head in grim satisfaction when the cannonfire struck some one hundred yards off the port side.

Then the *Richezza's* own guns opened up. The English vessel was not hit but slowed down. Now, moving with the wind, Fraser noted that his ship was pulling away. Elizabeth wasn't foolhardy enough to risk one of her vessels being sunk in vain pursuit of an alleged pirate, Fraser reasoned. She had probably counted on a surprise attack or the possibility of the Scots ship being unarmed. Even more likely, she must have reckoned that Fraser would either not make it as far as the river or else be caught by the soldiers if he tried to return.

But as the *Richezza* sailed smoothly towards the mouth of the Thames and the open waters of the North Sea, Fraser received no gratification from their narrow escape. He had no choice now but to go north, to Scotland, and leave Dallas to fend for herself.

THE LENNOXES, HOWEVER, were doing their best to help Dallas in her dangerous predicament. The news of Fraser's flight from the Tower reached them at the breakfast table, brought in person by a distraught Melville. Dallas, along with the two Lennox boys, was also present when the ambassador rushed in.

"I don't blame your husband, madame, for wanting to escape," Melville declared as he refused the offer of eggs and ham, "but I fear it may go ill with you. Queen Elizabeth knows you're here and within a very short time, she may send men after you. Is there some place you can go?"

It was one of those rare moments in Dallas's life when she felt totally devoid of spirit. She was glad Fraser had gotten away, but if only he could have taken her with him! Did he know now that she was in London? Would he risk coming back after her? She hoped not, though suddenly she was so overcome with yearning for him that she actually felt weak.

The Countess, however, was taking matters into her own hands. "Lady Fraser can go to Chelsea. I have a former maid there who recently married a quite respectable clockmaker. They are kind and discreet."

"And indebted to you, Mother dear, since you gave her fifty guineas as a wedding present," Darnley smirked.

"Now, now, Henry," his mother said in mild reproof. "It's a smart girl who knows which side of her bread gets the butter. Yes," she went on, turning to Dallas, "have Flora and Donald pack your things at once. You should be gone within the hour."

The Earl of Lennox had risen from his chair. "You just sit, Dallas, and I'll tend to that. Eat up, it's not a long journey but it's a miserable day."

Dallas was grateful for his kindness but her appetite was gone. She glanced outside at the steady rain and hoped it wouldn't turn to snow before the day was out. Melville was making his excuses to be gone. It was clear he was nervous about his presence in Lennox House. It simply would not do to have the Queen's men find him there.

And Melville had only been gone about ten minutes when the soldiers arrived. Dallas was upstairs, making sure Flora and Donald had packed everything, when the Countess rapped frenziedly on her door. "They're below," she whispered as if the soldiers could hear her through the thick floors. "Quickly, get Flora and Donald out the back way with your things."

"But I'd better go with them," Dallas protested.

"My dear, there's no time. Besides, they aren't looking for a middle-aged maid and a young lad. And there's no mistaking your condition." The Countess chewed at her thumbnail. "Ah, I have it! Come with me!"

Dallas stumbled along as quickly as she could down the passageway to the portrait gallery. The Countess propelled her through the door and into a room Dallas had seen many times before, with its walls covered by portraits of Tudors, Douglases, Stuarts and other illustrious ancestors. Rummaging in a cupboard, the Countess extracted a painter's smock and a large beret. "Hitch up your skirts, slip this smock on and put your hair under the beret," she commanded Dallas. "There, that's the easel where Master de Vroot has been working on our son's portrait. Take these brushes and try to look as if you knew what you were doing."

"But surely they'll see I'm not a man, even in this huge smock!" Dallas cried.

"Not with your back turned," the Countess replied, helping Dallas tuck her skirts and petticoats inside the smock. "They'll see what they think they're seeing, a rather small, rotund Dutchman hard at work."

Both women froze as they heard the thud of footsteps in the corridor. "They're here," the Countess breathed, hurrying briskly to the door. "Hold on, good fellows," she called out to the Queen's men. "Now what is this? Have you talked to my husband?"

There were six men, attired in the Queen's livery. Yes, they had seen the earl. He had told them Lady Fraser had escaped with her husband, had, in fact, left two days earlier. But they had their orders: Lennox House must be searched.

The Countess was still standing in the doorway. She shrugged her plump shoulders. "If you must, though I resent this intrusion very much and will certainly tell the Queen about it when next I see her." She made an expansive gesture towards the portrait gallery. "Look where you will, but don't disturb Master de Vroot. He's finishing our darling son's portrait and is extremely temperamental. You know these Dutchmen," she added in a low, conspiratorial tone.

Two soldiers came inside the gallery, opened one or two of the cupboards, decided they were too small to hide anyone, glanced fleetingly at the alleged Master de Vroot whose back was to them and who appeared absorbed in touching up Lord Darnley's eyebrows.

"Very well, we'll take the bedchambers next," one of the soldiers said. The Countess followed the men out of the room, warning them not to disturb Master Tucker either, the expert craftsman who was refinishing the molding around the fireplace in the Count's bedroom. "He's being paid by the hour, you see," Dallas heard the Countess say before the door closed.

They had left not a minute too soon. Dallas suddenly felt the first spasms of labor flash across her back and into her midsection. She put a hand to her mouth to stifle a cry and had to sit down on the floor. Holy Mother of God, she thought, has all this upset made the baby come early? The spasm having passed, she clumsily pulled herself to her feet and took off the beret. Her skirts had already tumbled back down about her ankles and she wondered how long it would take for the Countess to get rid of the soldiers.

As it turned out, they were in the house nearly an hour. They found nothing, however, except the irascible Master Tucker, who insisted they had destroyed his inspiration for the day and ought to be put on the rack. He had stormed from Lennox House in a fury, telling the Countess he would never return. "You will," she said matter-of-factly, and went back inside to hurry the Queen's men along.

When she went to tell Dallas that it was safe to come out, she found her writhing on the portrait gallery floor.

THE BABY WAS born late that night, delivered by the expert hands of the Countess's own physician. A sizeable fee would keep the man quiet, should he guess that the new mother was not the kitchen maid she was purported to be. Dallas had suffered a great deal, but her child, though premature, was healthy and of good size. It was a boy, and the exhausted mother was convinced he looked exactly like his father.

"I've no name for him," she lamented when the little bundle had been put at her breast. "I didn't want to name him without consulting Iain. What shall I call him?"

"At this juncture, I'd call him Trouble," the Countess snorted, but could not resist a smile for both mother and babe. After all, she remembered well the many infants she had borne in this same bed, though only two sons had survived. "Now, sleep, my dear, we'll worry about getting you to Chelsea later."

But Dallas did not sleep. After the baby had been placed in a tiny cradle the Countess had resurrected from somewhere, she laid in the bed, wondering where Fraser was and if he had gotten away safely. All she knew was that he had fled the Tower and gone down the Thames in a skiff with another man. Where was he? When would she see him again? Finally, overcome by self-pity and weariness, she dozed off into a fretful sleep.

THE NEXT NIGHT, Donald, Flora and two of the Lennox retainers helped move Dallas and the baby by litter to Chelsea. Word of their imminent arrival had been sent ahead. The Countess had not wanted to move Dallas so soon but feared the soldiers might come back. She had already taken too many risks for this worrisome if amusing Fraser chit. Oh, she was fond of Dallas in her way; in fact, her determination reminded the Countess of herself in younger years. But she simply couldn't take more chances. When Dallas told the Countess she could never repay her, her hostess had smiled enigmatically.

"Life is strange," the Countess had said before she closed the curtains on Dallas's litter. "There may come a day when you can show your gratitude in a way beyond our wildest dreams." The last glimpse Dallas had of the Countess was of that lady's benign smile being bestowed on her tall young son, Lord Darnley.

WITHIN A WEEK, the furor over Fraser's escape died down. Elizabeth had first taken out her wrath on both Sir Reginald Stanley and Sir James Melville, but once Fraser had gotten out of the Tower and sailed down the Thames, it was fruitless to expend men and money on further pursuit.

As for Dallas, the Queen wasn't convinced she had flown with her husband. The wench was supposed to be well gone with child, and while Elizabeth deplored being outwitted by Margaret Lennox, Fraser's wife wasn't worth further effort. A Queen of England had more important things to think about than a passel of crazy Scots who ought to stay on their own side of the River Tweed.

So Dallas was left in peace at the little house in Chelsea. During the next three weeks she began to regain her strength. The baby did not fare as well, however, for Dallas had no milk. A wet nurse was found, and Dallas was relieved to see the child fill out.

"As soon as he's sturdier we'll go home," Dallas declared one frosty February morning as she sat rocking the child while Donald mended Gala's saddle. The couple who had so generously taken them in were gone for the day, Alicia to market, and her husband, Tom, to his shop at the other end of the road. Though the house was cramped with their guests, both Alicia and Tom remained cheerful and complacent. They found the newcomers a diversion, and the baby thrilled Alicia, who was expecting her first child in the summer.

"The roads may not be fit for travel just yet," Donald said to Dallas. He had been a pillar of quiet strength during the last months and they had grown closer, much like an older sister and a younger brother.

"Fie, Donald," Dallas said as she bounced her tiny son on her knee, "I don't care if we have to push through blizzards from here to Dunbar. I must get home!"

"Queen Mary's been abed all winter, I hear," Donald remarked, ignoring Dallas's outburst. "The cooper down the way said she's upset because her plans to wed with Don Carlos have gone amiss."

"While you're gathering gossip, I wish to heaven you'd find out if Iain is safe," Dallas grumbled. "He could be in a dungeon somewhere for all I know! He's been gone well nigh a month."

"I'll ask the smithy," Donald said. "He has a cousin who travels to Edinburgh as a courier ...." But Donald broke off and gaped past Dallas to the small parlor's doorway.

John Hamilton stood on the threshold and Dallas felt as if her deliverance were at hand.

Chapter Sixteen

As long as Iain Fraser lived, he would never forget the glint of pure hatred which had surfaced in James Stuart's eyes. Schooled as he was at dissimulation, James had attempted to conceal his dismay over Fraser's return to Scotland, but his true feelings had been apparent for one swift, revealing moment. Fraser had no doubt who had arranged his imprisonment in the Tower.

Mary Stuart, on the other hand, was delighted to see Fraser. But, she lamented to him in private, he would have to stop his work as a secret emissary. "Elizabeth's charge of piracy makes it too dangerous for you to continue. It doesn't matter that nothing can be proven, James must know something."

Fraser had to agree. The men who had tortured and murdered Kennedy must have been in James's hire. Kennedy's death was yet another sin James must some day atone for, Fraser thought to himself.

But neither revenge nor intrigue were uppermost in Fraser's mind when he first arrived in Scotland. Dallas and the baby must be brought home as quickly as possible. Within two days of his return, a half-dozen Fraser retainers were sent south to London.

For almost three weeks, Fraser heard no word from his men. He had learned something about patience during his stay in the Tower and knew that Dallas might not yet have borne their child. So he resumed his life at court, affecting a show of unconcern, but inwardly distressed by the lack of news. In answer to the courtiers' curious questions, Fraser merely replied that his wife was awaiting the babe and would not return until she was well enough to travel. Such was actually the case, he kept telling himself, yet nagging doubts persisted.

To help pass the time, he resumed his liaison with Delphinia Douglas, who had aggressively pursued him as soon as he returned to court. Bedding Delphinia did not seem wrong to Fraser. Despite his love for Dallas, he realized that if they were destined to be separated for long periods he could never remain completely faithful to her. It never occurred to him that Dallas might think otherwise.

During his stay in the Tower he had tumbled only two women, a buxom if over aged laundress and an eager virgin who worked in the Tower kitchens. Both had fallen far short of his usual standards, but he'd hardly been in a position to be choosy. It had never occurred to him to feel guilty about them, either.

"So negotiations with Spain have gone awry," Delphinia was saying as she stretched luxuriously in front of the mirror-topped dresser. "I can't say I'm sorry—Don Carlos sounds like a wretched sort." She preened a bit, her full figure straining at the folds of her magnificent satin peignoir. "As for Elizabeth still backing Rob Dudley's suit ...." Delphinia paused to watch Fraser's image in the mirror. He was prowling around the room, the firelight casting dark shadows on his bare back. "You're still too thin, Iain. And you haven't heard a word I said."

"Aye, I heard you, Delphinia." He turned towards her with a faintly sheepish grin. "You were speaking of the Queen's potential suitors."

"So I was." Delphinia piled her hair on top of her head, flipped the titian strands this way and that, then let them tumble back over her shoulders. "Poor Mary, over twenty and still no man to keep her warm at night. I was scarcely sixteen when I first wed. Of course, he was much older, but as he'd had two wives before me, he certainly knew what he was about." She paused; Fraser was prowling again. "Which, I might add, is more than you seem to these days. Whatever is wrong, Iain?"

For a brief instant, Fraser had a desire to throttle Delphinia. But he controlled himself, came to take her in his arms and buried his lips against her bosom. But when he finally possessed Delphinia, it was Dallas's face that he saw in the recesses of his mind.

As John Hamilton stood in the parlor of the clockmaker's house in Chelsea he was uncertain about how much to tell Dallas. Anxious for her safety ever since she had left the court at Ellerig, Hamilton had used every possible means at his disposal to find out what had happened to Dallas in London. When he learned that she was staying with the Lennoxes, he was greatly perturbed. It was Lennox, after all, who had pitted himself against Hamilton's own father, the Duke of Chatelherault, in a struggle for power some twenty years earlier. Lennox had fled to England and Chatelherault had won not only the Dowager Queen's support but the Lennox lands as well.

Now there was talk about Lennox's son Darnley being offered as a possible suitor for Mary Stuart. If the young whelp was accepted as a prospective bridegroom, Lennox would demand restoration of his properties. As nominal head of his great house, Hamilton must devise some means of opposing the courtship—or work out a compromise with the earl.

So, when Fraser returned to Scotland without Dallas, Hamilton told himself it was time he went to London in an attempt to find out what was on Lennox's mind. When Fraser appeared indifferent to his wife's fate, Hamilton felt obliged to act on Dallas's behalf while in London. And when Hamilton discovered that Fraser was bedding Delphinia Douglas, he ordered his servants to be ready to leave for England within twenty-four hours.

"I came to London on business with the Lennoxes," Hamilton explained to Dallas, sparing her any upsetting details. "You know how it is between our families, the old rivalry." He spread his hands in a familiar gesture. "But the important thing was that they told me where you were. Show me your babe, Dallas. My God, I'm relieved to see you!"

Dallas held out the child for Hamilton's inspection. "He's putting on weight now. John!" she exclaimed. "What of Iain?"

Hamilton was smiling at the babe, rubbing his fingers gently along the tiny cheek. If he had not paused for just an instant in reaction to Fraser's name, Dallas would not have felt the sudden stab of fear.

"He's in Edinburgh," Hamilton answered evenly, turning to look her in the eye.

"Ahhhh." Dallas handed the infant to Donald, who held him awkwardly. "Put him in the cradle in the other room, Donald." She did not speak again until he was gone. "I'm so thankful Iain's safe," she said, collapsing into a chair. "Do sit, John. For a moment you frightened me. I thought something was wrong."

Hamilton did not sit down but moved about the room, his riding cloak swinging from his shoulders. "Something is wrong, if you ask me." He spoke angrily, the handsome face dark with wrath. "A man who leaves his bonnie wife and wee bairn to sit at table with Queen Mary and her courtiers ...." He stopped, aware he'd said too much, but angry enough not to care. "Make no mistake, Dallas, I've never liked your husband, but I always respected him until now. But this, his desertion of you and the babe is too much! I wish to God I'd slit his throat before I left Scotland!"

Dallas shuddered at the vehemence of his words. She had listened to his seething declarations in astonishment. Surely Hamilton was mistaken. Fraser would never abandon her. Mayhap he still didn't know about the babe. He couldn't come back to England to get her, it was too dangerous. And yet ....

She twisted her wedding ring around her finger several times before she spoke. "I think you misjudge Iain, John. He has his reasons for doing whatever—whatever it is he's doing."

Hamilton's rage had subsided somewhat, though he was still not himself. In a flurry of riding cloak and a flash of sword at his hip, Hamilton dropped down in front of Dallas. "Forgive my errant tongue, Dallas. I've come for only one reason, to take you home!"

Dallas argued feebly, but she wanted to go, with Hamilton or whoever could get her safely back to Scotland. At last she gave in, agreeing to leave in the morning. Hamilton would spend the night in London; there was simply no more space in the little house and his serving men were quartered in the city anyway.

He got to his feet as Dallas rose from the chair. "Don't worry. I made certain I wasn't followed here," he assured her. "I'll be careful in the morning, too. I trust neither Elizabeth nor the Lennoxes." He started for the door, turned back, and put her face between his hands. "My God, Dallas," he breathed, his own face almost touching hers, "I've been through hell these past months. I nearly started for London a hundred times." And then he let his hands fall to his sides and walked quickly out of the parlor.

HAMILTON HAD MANAGED to hire a coach for the journey north. During the first ten days of travel, the weather was kind. That false spring which February often displays for a few deceptive days permitted them to make good time as far as Durham. But then nature turned whimsical and brought snow down in large flakes to smother the eager daffodils, which had just begun to bud.

"A day or two of delay, that's all," Hamilton said as he and Dallas shared supper in her room at The Fox and Hare near Durham's great cathedral. Many people had been stranded and the common room was filled with complaining travelers whose plans were disrupted by the sudden change in weather.

"At least we have rooms," Dallas said, getting up to comfort the babe who had begun to fuss in his makeshift crib. The original wet nurse had not come with them, having a family in Chelsea. But another girl had been found on short notice, a young widow with a babe only a few weeks older than Dallas's child. Nan, as the girl was called, had been anxious to leave her in-laws, who treated her harshly. Her own parents had been dead for years, and traveling all the way to Scotland with a dazzling noblewoman and a handsome lord was an adventure beyond her wildest dreams.

So Nan was ensconced with her own babe and Flora next door to Dallas. Hamilton was crowded in with his serving men and Donald a few yards down the hall. At present, the others were enduring the common room's hubbub while they ate. Dallas, however, had declared she couldn't put up with such a commotion and insisted on having a harassed serving wench bring up supper for two. It was an uninspired meal and served lukewarm, but she and Hamilton were both hungry.

"If we can't dine well, we can at least drink," Hamilton said, pulling out a leather canteen of whiskey. "I thought we might be glad of this somewhere along the way."

"I've never liked the taste, but there are times when the effect is downright welcome," Dallas commented, pushing away the remnants of boiled pork hock and undercooked potato.

Hamilton poured whiskey into tumblers for both of them. The baby was sleeping soundly now, occasionally making little snuffling noises into the blankets. Dallas had kicked off her shoes and removed her shawl after the first tumbler of whiskey. The drink had warmed her and the fire was finally burning cheerfully on the grate.

Hamilton poured more whiskey and stretched his legs out on a small bench. They chatted comfortably for an hour or more, about Dallas's experiences in London, the birth of the babe, her flight from the Lennoxes, and of Hamilton's life at court. They never mentioned Fraser. Indeed, Hamilton had not once spoken his name since they left Chelsea. Yet Dallas had thought of little else. What if Fraser did not love her anymore, what if he never had? God only knew it had been almost impossible for Dallas to believe he had loved her all along and had actually wanted to marry her.

"You're dreamy-eyed, Dallas," Hamilton said. "Are you weary?"

"Oh, a bit, John. But each day I feel stronger." She stretched and yawned, shaking her head at his offer of more whiskey. "Nay, it makes me drowsy and Lord knows another tumbler would make me drunk as well."

"I'd best leave you," Hamilton said, rising from his chair. The two candles had almost guttered out in their lead holders. Outside the wind blew the snow against the windows, sealing the inn off from the world.

"Don't forget your canteen," Dallas said, rising to pick the vessel up from off the little bench. "Great heavens, it's empty!" She giggled and tossed the canteen to Hamilton, who caught it neatly with one hand. Unexpectedly, the other hand reached out and grasped Dallas by the wrist. She stopped giggling immediately and met his gaze head-on.

Hamilton's moods of good humor, kindliness, annoyance, anger and affection were all familiar to Dallas. But she was unprepared for the sudden flare of passion which enveloped his features. The canteen thudded onto the bare floor as Hamilton pulled Dallas to him and kissed her mouth. Fleetingly, she recalled the first time he had kissed her, at Falkland. Ages ago, it seemed. It had not been unpleasant, but she had felt nothing in response. Now, awakened to sensuality by Fraser and denied his or any man's touch for nine long months, she felt herself answering Hamilton, kiss for kiss, caress for caress.

But for all his unleashed desire, Hamilton was a different man than Fraser. Dallas recognized this instinctively: On those occasions when Fraser exhibited tenderness, she could always sense his ever-present animal intensity. The brute male did not dominate Hamilton's lovemaking; even in passion, his innate gentleness touched Dallas's heart as much as it fired her senses.

"John ...." She pulled away to look up at him. "John, please don't ...." Her words withered away as she saw the look of love and vulnerability in his brown eyes.

But Dallas recognized her own weakness as well. She clutched at his hands as he pulled away the little velvet jerkin.

"Sweetheart," he said softly, "don't deny me. I love you."

"You can't!" she breathed, trying to free herself from the arm which held her fast while his other hand undid her cream-colored blouse. "I'm a married woman, truly married, with a child!"

But Hamilton seemed not to hear her protests. She felt the soft fabric of her blouse slide off her shoulders, heard the deep sigh of pleasure as he looked at her naked breasts, and was dazedly aware that he had pulled her down on top of him on the bed.

"You are so lovely! Stay, sweetheart, let me taste your sweet body." Hamilton held her with one hand under her buttocks, the other lifting her torso just above his face. The pride, worldliness, authority and power of the House of Hamilton had been replaced by the most helpless of all creatures—a man in love and afraid of rejection. Dallas felt herself melt into his embrace and leaned down to let him kiss her breasts.

He seemed to smother himself in the firm, ripe flesh, and Dallas experienced an exquisite sensation of pleasure, which she dimly told herself should not be happening.

Hamilton was tugging at her riding skirt, pulling it and her undergarments down over her hips. Dallas reached behind her to push at his hands but her efforts were ineffectual. As her naked thigh lay between his legs, any doubts Dallas might have had about Hamilton's intentions were quickly dispelled.

"John!" Dallas jerked away from him, shivering with both cold and emotion. "We must not! Please leave now, before ... before we ...."

Hamilton merely smiled and pulled her over onto her back. "Before we do what fate intended us to do?" Even as he spoke he had begun to take off his own clothes. "Nay, Dallas, you'd cheat both of us out of tonight while your husband dashes from Delphinia Douglas's bed to Catherine Gordon's, to God knows whose? If he loves you," Hamilton added as he finished undressing, "he has strange ways of making it known. And by the Cross, he can't love you as I do!"

Dallas winced at the condemnation of Fraser but her efforts to defend her husband were doomed as she saw Hamilton's powerful, naked body looming over her at the edge of the bed.

"Sweet Jesu," she whispered, "why couldn't you look more like your wretched brother Arran?"

Hamilton laughed outright and fell beside her on the lumpy mattress. He kissed her lips gently, two, three times before his mouth claimed hers with an unquenchable hunger, his hands roaming lightly over her thighs. Then he was kissing her stomach and Dallas moaned softly as she let her fingers run through his hair and caress his neck.

This is wrong, she told herself in a voice that seemed to come from very far away; even if John loves me this is wrong .... But she could picture Fraser laughing with Delphinia or Catherine, exchanging intimate glances, making love to them as if his wife didn't exist. She could see it all almost as clearly as she could see John Hamilton's head buried between her thighs, igniting the fire she had thought only Iain Fraser could spark.

But when he finally penetrated her body, she saw nothing at all. The tender passion of his possession evoked no memories of Fraser but only the deepest fulfillment of her pent-up desires.

IT WAS STILL snowing when Dallas awoke the next morning. Her baby was beginning to fuss but she didn't dare summon the wet nurse until Hamilton left. He still slept, sprawled on his stomach, looking younger and even more vulnerable in repose.

Dallas crept out of bed and picked the babe up, rocking him to and fro, trying to keep him quiet a bit longer. Donald and the serving men would no doubt wonder where Hamilton had spent the night, but under such crowded conditions, they might assume he had found lodging elsewhere. At least she hoped so; she didn't want Donald to know about last night.

No one must ever know about last night, she thought as she kissed the fine black hair of the baby's head. Guilt was setting in, but not shame. There was nothing shameful in Hamilton's love for her. It was her own feelings which puzzled her. Whatever Fraser had done, even if he didn't really love her, she still loved him. Justified or not, she was angry with him and resentful. But it had taken her too long to realize that she loved him for her not to know that she always would, intensely, passionately, almost obsessively.

Yet here she was, cuddling Fraser's child and standing beside this sleeping man with whom she had committed adultery just a few hours ago. Was it possible that she loved Hamilton, too, in a different way? It was not mere lust, since she and Hamilton had spent many pleasant hours together before last night. Dallas had to admit to herself that she didn't know the answer. She shivered under her nightrobe and put the baby back in the crib. Hamilton was moving in the bed, one hand reaching out to grope at the now empty place beside him.

"Dallas?" He was awake, regarding her with a sleepy smile.

"I'm here, I had to tend the babe. John, you'd better go. I must summon Nan."

"He's quiet now," Hamilton said, rolling over onto his back and yawning. "Why don't you come back to bed, sweetheart?"

"Nay, you must leave. The babe will be screaming his head off in a minute. I'm surprised he's been good this long, he hasn't eaten in hours." Dallas deliberately turned her back on him and began to sort out her clothes.

Hamilton slipped out of bed to stand behind her, his arms around her waist, his hands reaching inside her nightrobe to caress her thighs and attempting to part her legs. "Dallas," he murmured, his lips in her tumbled hair, "I love you so much. Why don't you just take the babe into the nurse's room?"

With a sudden move, she pulled free from his grasp. "Because we can't spend the day in bed, that's why. John, you must understand, what happened last night must never happen again." She was frowning at him, trying hard to look severe.

She didn't convince him, but he relented anyway. "All right," he sighed, picking up his own clothes. "But we won't leave Durham today and I don't really think you'll fight me off with a poleax tonight. Besides," he went on as he dressed hurriedly, "I've been thinking."

"Thinking?" Dallas snorted. "When have you had time to think?"

"Never mind," he laughed, "but I have. When we do get out of here, we're not going to Edinburgh. We're going to Arbroath."

"Arbroath!" Dallas stopped in the middle of fastening her riding skirt. "Certainly not! Why would we go to your country home instead of to court?"

Hamilton was adjusting the cuffs on his shirt. "Because you're going to live with me at Arbroath while we wait for your marriage to be annulled. I'm taking no chances of letting you get away from me this time."

Dallas stood motionless, her hands clutching her blouse and jerkin. "Nay, John! I don't want an annulment! Iain and I have a child, it wouldn't be right!"

"Dallas, if you must argue, please put your blouse on. The sight of your delectable breasts is most distracting." Hastily, she pulled the blouse around her and fastened the pearl buttons. "I'm not arguing, I'm just stating facts. Don't cite me precedent of other papal annulments, I would never consent. Unless," she added uncertainly, "Iain wanted it."

Hamilton paused just long enough to let Dallas consider this possibility.

"It's my fault you made such a strange marriage in the first place. I was a fool not to ask you to be my wife when you were still free. I loved you even then, but I have a terrible habit of taking too long to make up my mind."

"And proud Hamiltons don't marry poor Camerons, eh, John?" Dallas could not resist the barb but was immediately sorry when she saw how her remark had wounded him.

"You must remember how things were with my family then. Poor Arran thought the Queen might wed ...."

But the babe had begun to howl again and Dallas went to pick him up. "Never mind, what's done is done. Now you must leave so this poor mite can be fed."

Hamilton gathered up the rest of his belongings, including the leather canteen, which still lay on the floor where he had dropped it the previous night. It was useless for him to pursue the matter of the annulment just now. He had implanted the idea in Dallas's mind—-and she had not said she wouldn't go to Arbroath.

"If the snow lets up we'll visit the cathedral," he said, pausing to kiss her cheek. " 'Tis a wondrous sight, I'm told."

Dallas nodded as she jiggled the screaming infant up and down in a vain effort to quiet him. Hamilton looked at the tiny contorted face and decided the babe was just as obstinate and demanding as his father. As he went out into the corridor he wondered which would prove the greatest obstacle in winning Dallas—the sire or the son.

TWO MORE DAYS in Durham, mostly trapped in the teeming inn, but the snow stopped long enough for Dallas and Hamilton to visit the cathedral. Soaring triumphantly above the River Wear, the majestic church was almost five hundred years old, yet showed scant ravages of time. Inside, Dallas marveled at the huge Norman columns, and Hamilton paused to read the inscription denoting the burial place of the Venerable Bede.

"Think of it!" Dallas exclaimed later back in her room at the inn. "All the years of toil which went into that magnificent structure! I've never seen its like in Scotland, though it grieves me to admit it."

"A poorer, smaller country must build to fit its own perspective," Hamilton remarked vaguely, his mind on matters other than English architecture. "Well, Dallas," he said with an imploring smile, "do we dispense with argument over whether or not you'll bed with me tonight?"

Dallas laid aside the slim volume of the Venerable Bede's writings which she'd purchased at the Cathedral. "You sound rather sure of yourself, John," she chided.

Hamilton traced her jawline with his finger. "I'm sure of only one thing, that you and I find great happiness in each other."

Averting her gaze, Dallas fumbled with a small gold locket she wore around her neck. "That scarcely makes it right," she murmured, thinking it would be much easier to state her case if he hadn't moved his hand down to her thigh. "I know you've had other mistresses, John, women who've borne you children. How can I be sure I'm not just another such as they?"

"I told you once, a long time ago, that unlike—" he paused, obviously loath to bring Fraser's name into the conversation. "Unlike other men, I've never been the kind to seduce women on a mere whim. The mistresses I've known over the years have always come to my bed of their own free will and not until now have I ever offered marriage—or my heart."

Unable to avoid his direct, candid gaze, Dallas sighed. "Why must you be so damnably convincing?" She smiled ruefully, leaning forward to put her arms around his neck. They kissed once, long and deep, before he lifted her in his arms and carried her to the bed.

Chapter Seventeen

THE FOLLOWING DAY it snowed fitfully, allowing them to explore the city more thoroughly but preventing them from leaving it. That night Dallas and Hamilton made love again; secure in his arms, satisfied by his ardor, Dallas thrust aside her doubts and completely abandoned herself to Hamilton. If Donald and Flora seemed to eye them with speculation, she ignored it. They didn't really know, she told herself, and mayhap she was only imagining their suspicious stares.

On the morning of the fourth day, the snow had turned to rain and a rapid thaw had set in. As soon as the slush began to run off the cobbled streets the party set out for Hexham, hopefully their last stop before crossing into Scotland.

The road had turned to mud, forcing them to stop several times to free the mired coach wheels. Potholes, ruts and occasional rocks made for a jarring ride. Hexham was not reached until very late.

As they sorted themselves out in the village's only inn, Hamilton glanced at Dallas. "You'll dine in your room tonight?"

The question had become their byword during the stay in Durham, but tonight Dallas shook her head. "I don't think I'll dine at all. In truth, John, I'm not feeling well. Those jolts and jerks today upset both my head and my stomach."

At first, Hamilton thought she was putting him off. But as he peered at her closely, he saw she was very pale and almost white around the lips.

"Sweetheart," he said low, so that the others could not hear, "you're not well. Let me carry you up to bed."

"Nonsense, I can walk. I'll be fine, it's just a passing indisposition." As

Flora carried the babe, Dallas led the way upstairs. She had almost reached the top when she halted, her head swimming dizzily.

"Mistress!" Flora cried. "Let me get Lord Hamilton!"

Dallas held fast to the bannister, trying desperately to make the world stop spinning. "I'll manage, our room's just two doors down." With a tremendous effort, she mounted the last three steps and negotiated the twenty paces or so to the door. Once inside, Dallas fell onto the bed and groaned aloud.

Flora laid the baby down and raced to her mistress. "What is it, are you going to retch?"

But Dallas was too weak to answer. She let Flora loosen her clothing and make her as comfortable as possible. Soon she slept, deeply for a few hours, waking after midnight to feel somewhat better. She went back to sleep again, and when she woke up next, the faint morning light was making patches on the worn oak floor.

Flora was already up, holding Nan's baby, while Nan nursed Dallas's child. Both women turned anxiously when Dallas called to them. "What time is it?" she asked, sitting up in bed.

"Just past seveny madame," Flora answered. "Rest now. Lord Hamilton says we'll stay here today."

But Dallas insisted she felt recovered. Since it was a fine day, they should take advantage of it. Hamilton came in shortly, his face etched with concern, but when he saw Dallas dressed and determined to travel, he smiled with relief. "I'm not sure you're wise, but I won't argue. Perhaps you ate something disagreeable at that vile hostelry yesterday in Newburn."

Dallas allowed for the possibility but still thought the effects of the jostling coach ride were a more likely explanation. The important thing, however, was that they reach Scotland by nightfall.

By noon they were just west of Falstone, deep in the wild border country of England, where many a Scots raider had killed or been killed over the centuries. With such a heritage of blood, it was wise for the little party to keep its nationality secret.

But Dallas was puzzled. "I know little of England," she called out the coach window to Hamilton, "but aren't we headed away from Berwick?"

Hamilton drew his horse up to the coach. "We're not going that way, I learned this morning that the road is washed out at Tweedmouth." It was true, but Hamilton had not planned to take that route in any event. Though Arbroath lay on the eastern coast north of Dundee, it could only be reached overland by a westerly approach through Hawick, Stirling and Perth. It was at least a four-day journey from the border by coach but that was as well. The extra time would give Hamilton more opportunity to convince Dallas he was right about their future together.

Dallas was dozing when they crossed the Cheviot Hills into Scotland at dusk. Great sweeps of dormant heather, the riotous River Liddel, rough shadowy crags and the ghosts of moss-troopers dogged their passage north. The road here was as uneven and rutted as the one between Durham and Hexham. And except for a few miserable crofters' huts, there was no place to put up for the night.

"How much longer, my lord?" Donald asked Hamilton as their horses moved slowly into the night. Donald, like Dallas, had been perplexed when their party had turned northwest instead of northeast. But then he had seldom ventured more than ten miles from his father's farm at Dunbar until the last year or so.

Exhausted, they finally came to the village of Teviothead, where a tavernkeeper agreed to take them in. Impressed by the obvious quality of the travelers, and even more overcome by the handful of coins Hamilton produced, the proprietor scurried around to prepare adequate accommodations. But it was after ten o'clock before Dallas and the other women carried the babes and their belongings into a draughty, sparsely furnished room. By that time, they were grateful for any kind of comfort after the excruciatingly long day. The men were weary, too, and Hamilton made no effort to ask Dallas if she were supping in her room.

HAD THEY BEEN heading for Edinburgh, they would have gone due north from their midday stop at Galashiels. But instead, they took the road west to Peebles.

"John," Dallas inquired for the second day in a row, "why this route? Don't tell me the road is washed out between Galashiels and Edinburgh."

"I'll explain when we stop to rest at Peebles," Hamilton replied, smiling down into the coach. Then he put spurs to his horse and galloped on ahead through the fine mist, which had been falling all morning.

Dallas was uneasy. She was certain now that Hamilton was determined to take her to Arbroath. She would not go; if he confirmed her suspicions when they reached Peebles, she would simply refuse and go on to Edinburgh with Donald as escort. They could reach the capital by night, unless the weather worsened.

But when they got to Peebles about three, Dallas was feeling ill again, as wretched as she'd been at Hexham. When Hamilton came to fetch her from the coach, she was lying down among the cushions, with Flora holding her clammy hands.

"She's taken sick again, my lord. Mayhap we should bide here at Peebles." Flora eyed Hamilton with disapproval. She'd always admired the man and been grateful for his many kindnesses to Dallas, but at the moment she blamed him for her mistress's indisposition.

Hamilton calculated quickly. His cousin, Gavin, had a small house, Strathmuir, just south of Lanark in Hamilton country. It was about fifteen miles away; they could get there in about two hours. He made the suggestion to Dallas, who nodded feebly. Once more, the coach began to rumble along the rough road which ran parallel with the River Tweed.

Less than half an hour from their destination, Dallas awoke from a fretful sleep to feel a damp sensation between her legs. With great effort, she raised her head from the cushions and saw that her brown travel gown was stained with blood. Flora, who had been gazing out the window of the coach, turned to look at her mistress. She screamed, waking Nan and the babes, who all began to shriek at once. Hearing the outcry, Hamilton ordered the driver to stop.

"What is it?" he called, wheeling his horse around.

Flora hurled the door open. "It's Lady Fraser, my lord! She's bleeding to death."

Hamilton leaped from his horse and looked inside the coach. Dallas was lying unconscious in a pool of blood, her skin as white as fine linen.

"Jesus God," Hamilton muttered. He paused for just an instant, his heart weighed down in his chest. Then he gave orders for two of his men to ride ahead to Strathmuir House and make sure the servants were ready to receive them. To Donald, he gave instructions to race on to Lanark and get the local physician, reputed by Gavin to be a learned man. Donald, grim faced with worry, was the first to gallop off down the road and out of sight.

Hamilton ordered the driver to move the coach as carefully as possible. He was sick at heart, cursing himself for Dallas's alarming condition. He should not have forced her to travel so soon after the babe's birth, he should never have bedded her, he should have stayed in Durham and waited until the roads were repaired.

As the coach creaked slowly over the last four miles Hamilton vowed he'd do anything Dallas ever asked of him if only she'd get well. He'd give her up, he'd turn Papist, he'd make peace with Iain Fraser—whatever her wish, he'd grant it.

It occurred to him then that it had been her wish to leave Chelsea as soon as possible. She'd argued, of course, but Dallas always argued. She'd not rebuffed his lovemaking, either, at least not very seriously. As for changing their destination, in his heart he felt she'd go with him to Arbroath, to stay there at least until she'd sorted out her feelings about her marriage.

But his logic comforted him little as he glanced inside the coach to see Dallas lying motionless against the cushions. Both babes were quiet now, taking turns suckling at Nan's bountiful breasts. Hamilton sighed with relief as he sighted the rooftops of Strathmuir nestled among a grove of plane trees.

The servants were waiting in the hallway. Gavin Hamilton visited Strathmuir seldom but kept a half-dozen people in permanent residence to maintain the house and grounds.

Hamilton carried Dallas inside, placing her gently on a settee in the drawing room. The bedrooms were all upstairs and he didn't want to move her any further than necessary until the doctor arrived. Flora stayed with him, her composure regained, but her face was almost as white as Dallas's.

It seemed like hours before Dr. Crawford arrived with Donald, but it was actually less than twenty minutes. He was a sparse-looking man, dressed in garments a generation old. The first thing he did was send Hamilton, Flora and Donald out of the room.

Dr. Crawford remained alone with Dallas for over an hour. As darkness crept over Strathmuir he finally emerged, his thin face expressionless. "She is still alive," he announced, "but you must not move her for at least two days. I have done what I could. I don't believe in tying string around the patient's thumb to stop the bleeding and hold the soul in the body as so many so-called physicians do. I have my own methods, based upon years of research. And I don't discuss them with anyone except my most trusted colleagues." With that remarkable speech, he made straight for the door.

Hamilton moved to intercept the doctor. "Wait up, man, you've not been paid. Besides, I'd like you to stay here, at least overnight."

"I never stay overnight with patients, no matter how important or how ill. I've slept in the same bed every night for twenty-three years. If you wish, I'll return in the morning." He paused just long enough to accept a hefty purse from Hamilton, then went out into the night.

Donald and Flora lingered by the drawing room door while Hamilton went in to see Dallas. She was undressed, lying under a heavy comforter. Her skin was still white and there were blue smudges in the hollows under her closed eyes. Even the jumble of brown hair seemed lifeless.

Hamilton watched her for a long time, until he felt his eyes wet with tears. At last, he turned to Flora and Donald, his hands spread in a helpless gesture. "We can pray—I know naught else to do."

But Flora had already thought of something else. Later that night she wrote a letter to Iain Fraser and sent Donald out into the mist, headed posthaste for Edinburgh.

GLENNIE WAS STILL in her nightrobe when she opened the door to Donald McVurrich. She was both astonished and relieved to see him, not having heard from Dallas since receiving a brief letter about the baby's birth. But one look at Donald's stricken face told her he did not have good news.

She ushered him inside and, along with Tarrill and Marthe who had come downstairs into the hallway, listened to his distressing tale. "I went to Fraser's town house but he wasn't there and I could rouse no one," Donald said as the women led him into the kitchen. "Do you know where he is?"

"Oh, I'm so upset, I cannot think!" Glennie exclaimed in distraction. "This is the sixth of March, I believe the court left yesterday for Craigmillar. Iain must have gone with them."

Donald rubbed his forehead with a weary hand. "Then I must ride there at once," he said, "though I ought to have a fresh mount to keep up my pace."

"You must eat something first," Tarrill insisted. Marthe was already building up the fire, readying ingredients for breakfast. "Master Drummond keeps a horse, mayhap you can borrow it."

"When you go back to Strathmuir, should one of us come with you?" Glennie asked, her trembling hands smoothing the long plaits of her hair.

Donald considered the suggestion for a few moments. "I'll save time if I ride straight from Craigmillar with Fraser. If—when Dallas is better, we can send for you."

Glennie nodded; she was too disturbed to think for herself. Marthe was stirring up the bannock batter and Tarrill rose to get out some eggs and ham. While Donald ate they plied him with questions. Why had Dallas not waited to travel until she was fully recovered from childbearing? What was Hamilton doing in England? Why didn't they come straight to Edinburgh? Donald answered as best he could, but he knew little more than they. He kept his speculations to himself.

By the time he finished his meal, the light rain had changed into a downpour. Tarrill suggested that he wait, but Donald was determined to leave as soon as he had borrowed Master Drummond's horse. Yet after he had secured the fresh mount and endured Mistress Drummond's endless questions about Dallas, the wind had whipped up from the Firth, blowing the storm into a genuine March gale. Reluctantly, he told Tarrill and Glennie that he would have to bide awhile after all.

It was one of those wild late winter storms, which hung over the city for twenty-four hours, sending water flowing through the streets like Highland burns and blowing down several trees in the vicinity. Even after the rain subsided to a drizzle and the wind died away to a whisper, Donald knew it was pointless to leave Edinburgh. It would take at least a day or more before the roads dried out and became something other than impassable troughs of mud. He returned Master Drummond's horse and settled in to wait.

BY THE TIME Donald left Edinburgh, the fears for Dallas's life had receded at

Strathmuir House. She had been conscious, if not entirely lucid, for three days when Dr. Crawford predicted a certain recovery.

"Under my treatment, they either die within the first day or so, or else are totally well in a fairly short time," he told Hamilton. "If you don't mind, there's no need for me to see her again." He refused Hamilton's offer of another purse, though this was his third visit to Strathmuir. It was obvious that large fees meant little to him in comparison with the solitude he craved in which to carry on his research.

During the early stages of Dallas's illness, Hamilton and Flora had taken turns keeping a constant vigil by the settee. Hamilton's color had drained and Flora had taken on a pinched look as a result of those long, anxious hours, but both were revived in spirit after Dr. Crawford's final visit.

"Sweetheart," Hamilton said after the physician had left, "I'm so relieved you're going to be all right." He sat in a chair by Dallas's bed, for the doctor had given permission to move her upstairs to the master bedroom.

"You've said that fifty times since I came 'round last night," Dallas reminded him with a wan smile. "And I won't listen to you blame yourself for what happened. Even that pickle-faced doctor said such things can occur for no reason." He'd also said that the jarring trip north had probably caused Dallas to hemorrhage, but she blamed herself as much as Hamilton for the precipitous flight from Chelsea.

But Hamilton's expression was implacable. "I asked too much of you—in many ways."

Dallas put a small, limp hand on his arm. "You asked no more than I was willing to give. And you gave me a great deal in return."

His strong fingers gently stroked the back of her hand. "Mayhap." Her words buoyed him somewhat, but this was no time to discuss their future. Later, when she was feeling stronger, they could face those decisions together.

BY THE FOLLOWING day, Dallas was sitting up in bed, fending off Flora's exotic concoctions designed to restore strength. "Some decent meat and vegetables are all I need," Dallas declared. "This last potion practically gave me the swoons. Fetch me some beef, rare as can be, and bring me my babe."

Amid much fuming, Flora did as she was bade. When the child was brought to her, Dallas exclaimed to Hamilton that she was certain he had grown during her illness. "Do you think he missed me? See, he's trying to hold my finger!"

Hamilton experienced the familiar bittersweet pang of seeing Dallas with her baby. But he smiled and patted the child's dark head. "He's cried enough, if that proves anything. Now don't hold him too long and tire yourself out. Dr. Crawford insisted you rest a great deal."

"Fie, I feel well enough to dance the galliard at Holyrood," Dallas laughed. It was an exaggeration, of course, but she was feeling stronger all the time. Flora had washed her hair that morning and it fell in thick masses over her shoulders. She was still very pale, however, and somewhat thinner. To Hamilton, her pallor only made her more desirable and he had almost cursed aloud when Dr. Crawford had insisted that she not make love for at least six weeks. It had been presumptuous of the doctor to make any such allusion, but he was not a totally unworldly man and had felt the caution necessary.

As Dallas cooed to her babe, a serving man tapped on the door, announcing visitors below. Hamilton rose, wondering if Donald had returned with Dallas's sisters. But as he descended into the entry hall, he saw Donald standing beside Iain Fraser.

Both men were wet, for the rain had started in again that morning. Both looked strained and tired, too, after the hard ride from Craigmillar. But while Donald appeared merely distressed, Fraser looked thunderous.

"Where is my wife, Hamilton?" he demanded before the other man had even reached the bottom of the stairs.

"She's upstairs and recovering rapidly," Hamilton replied, trying to hide the shock he felt at seeing Fraser. "She has been very ill, but a local physician has worked wonders."

Fraser pulled off his cloak and threw it at Donald. "If he hadn't, you'd be a dead man. You damned near killed my wife!" Fraser was blazing with anger, taking menacing steps towards Hamilton, who was searching desperately for an honorable way to handle this explosive situation.

"You know I would never do anything to harm Dallas," he asserted with a forced calm. "Even the doctor said that what happened to her was probably without cause."

"Keep your excuses for yourself! Why in Christ's name you take it upon yourself to haul my wife and child back to Scotland, I can't think! By God, man, I ought to skewer you right now!" Fraser's hand flew to his dirk.

Hamilton's composure broke. "I brought her to Scotland because you wouldn't! You left her and the poor bairn alone in London, at the mercy of that vixen Elizabeth! You didn't care one whit if she ever came back!"

"I sent my own men to get her. They were waylaid by thieves and barely escaped alive. Now I'm beginning to wonder if those thieves wore the Hamilton badge!" Fraser's eyes had narrowed, his hand tight on the dirk. "Get your weapon, you son of a swine. I'll not have it said I killed an unarmed man!"

Donald made a move to restrain Fraser, thought better of it, and backed out of the way. Hamilton called to him. "You have a dirk, McVurrich. Throw it to me."

Donald did, and Hamilton caught it by the handle. The two men took each other's measure carefully. Fraser was an inch or so taller, but at least a stone lighter than Hamilton. The entry hall was long enough, though narrow. There would not be much room for maneuvering. From somewhere beyond them, agitated voices could be heard as the servants gathered to watch the excitement.

"I'm telling you now," Hamilton said low, "I intend to marry Dallas. I want her to get an annulment."

Fraser lunged at Hamilton, just missing his left shoulder. "That's for your dung-assed annulment!" The two men stood toe to toe, the eight-inch blades grinding together so hard Donald thought they'd make sparks. "Dallas wouldn't have your overproud carcass on a silver plate!"

"Hypocritical bastard!" Hamilton exploded. "How well do you know your wife?"

With a lightning move, Fraser brought his arm up under Hamilton's right wrist, sending the other man reeling backwards. "What are you saying?" Fraser was amazed at the implication; had Dallas succumbed to Hamilton? It seemed utterly impossible, yet Fraser knew that if he had been in Hamilton's place, he would never have wasted the opportunity to bed her. But Dallas was not like other women; furthermore, she was his wife.

Consumed by rage, he threw himself at his enemy, knocking over a pedestal vase. Both men banged to the floor, grappling in mortal combat. Darkness was setting in and no candles had yet been lighted in the hallway. Donald still stood to one side, his hands clutching Fraser's cloak until his big knuckles turned white.

Fraser's dirk lashed out, hitting home between Hamilton's ribs. The pain blinded him for a moment, but with great effort, he forced Fraser off of him, momentarily pinning him against the wall. Fraser grasped the other man's right wrist, wringing it harder and harder until the dirk clattered away onto the stonework. Fraser cast it well out of reach, then laid his own blade against Hamilton's throat.

"Now tell me, John Hamilton," he said slow and low, "did you bed my wife?"

There was total silence in the hallway, no sound from the cluster of servants gathered in the dining room opposite, and only the wind soughed through the plane trees outside. Hamilton looked up into the cold, furious hazel eyes of Iain Fraser and knew that the truth would doom him and a lie would do the same. Through a mist of agony from the wound in his side, Hamilton heard a voice from the top of the stairs:

"It's true, I have lain with John. It wasn't his fault, it was mine." Dallas spoke, standing shakily with one hand on the newel post, the other clutching her babe. Her dark eyes were huge and she looked as if hell had opened up beneath her feet.

Fraser watched her as if under a spell. Suddenly, he leaped up from Hamilton and mounted the stairs three at a time. He stood two steps below Dallas, so that their eyes met evenly. "Jesu!" he whispered. "I would never have thought you culpable of such wantonness!"

If Dallas had not felt so weak or so frightened she would have lashed out at him, told him how she'd felt abandoned by him, how he'd betrayed her by his infidelity, how she'd spent months in London trying to help him, how she'd borne the child without him by her side. But she just stood there, miserable and defenseless, with the child crying against her shoulder.

He took the babe from her then. "You'll keep no bairn of mine, you slut," Fraser spat at her. "That's assuming he is mine and not Hamilton's whelp." The baby was crying lustily now as Fraser held him cradled against his chest with one arm. He still gripped the dirk in his other hand and brought it up to Dallas's bare throat. "I should kill you, madame, as I hope I've killed your paramour. But for the love I've borne you, I will not." He dropped his hand to his side, turned away and walked down the stairs. Pausing to take his cloak from Donald, he went from the house, the babe still crying loudly as the door closed behind them.

Chapter Eighteen

HAMILTON DID NOT die. He was unconscious by the time Dallas and Donald reached him, but though the wound was serious, it was not fatal. Dr. Crawford was summoned again, arriving in a testy mood and warning that he would not come to Strathmuir again, no matter what terrible predicaments befell its inhabitants.

"He's young, strong, healthy," he told Dallas and Donald. "Lord Hamilton will be up and about in a few days. Just don't let him overdo for a while." When Dallas tried to give him a ruby and diamond bracelet as recompense, he all but sneered. "My wife's been dead these past five years. I'd never bother to sell it so what good is it to me? Keep your baubles, madame."

That rebuff was the least of Dallas's worries. She was still numb from Fraser's repudiation and his usurpation of their babe. For three days, she kept to her bed trying to figure out what to do next. It occurred to Dallas that the tribulations of the last week or more had stemmed from the betrayal of her marriage vows. While she could not honestly regret bedding with Hamilton, her feelings for him faltered when compared with her need for Fraser and their son.

She calculated that within another week she'd be strong enough to go to Edinburgh by coach. If Fraser and the babe were in the city, she'd do everything in her power to win them back. From that moment on, she'd live one day at a time, until she was reunited with her husband and her son.

On the same day that Dallas got out of bed, Hamilton was also on his feet again. He was a bit weak and heavily bandaged around the ribs, but well on his way to recovery. When he came into Dallas's room and saw her combing her hair in front of a mirror, he approached her tentatively.

"I suppose it's pointless to tell you how sorry I am about all that has happened," he began, pulling up a chair to sit next to her.

She smiled tremulously at him in the mirror. "Don't blame yourself. The important thing is to go on from here and put the past behind us."

He gave a little laugh. "Hamiltons always build the future on the past. I would have assumed we could do the same."

She turned to look at him directly. "Nay, John, we cannot. I must get my babe back. And, if I can, I'll get Iain back, too." She saw the protest forming on his lips, and put a hand on his arm. "Now, wait, John—I know what you're going to say, and even if you're right, I've got to try. You and I sinned, and see what it's brought us. You might have died, I might have, too, and I've certainly lost the child, for now at any rate. So you see why I must leave you as soon as I can travel?"

He rubbed his forehead in a desolate gesture. "Oh, Dallas, I know how you feel. But I think you're making a mistake. Unless Iain changes his mind, your marriage is ended. If you'd get your annulment and marry me, we could find much happiness together."

"I still wouldn't have my child," she put in, wishing Hamilton would stop looking so forlorn.

"We could have our own, dozens, if you'd like. I could give you everything you'd ever want, but most especially," he added gently, touching her cheek, "my love."

She took his hand and kissed the palm. "I know," she sighed. "And don't think I take your offer with anything but a grateful heart. Yet I have to do what I think right."

He was gracious enough not to press her further. Besides, Dallas might change her mind when she had time to realize that Fraser's rejection of her was final. Hamilton smiled sadly as he stood up. "I made a vow while you were so ill, back along the road to Strathmuir. I swore that if you got well, I would do whatever you asked of me. I just never thought it would be so hard."

He walked slowly out of the room, the wound in his side hurting far less than the wound in his heart.

SPRING HAD COME to Edinburgh, at least by the calendar. But rain fell on the city and a chill wind blew up from the Nor' Loch as Dallas arrived with Donald at the Cameron house in Nairne's Close. The last weeks of her stay at Strathmuir had been uneventful, for Hamilton had chosen to keep as far from her as possible. He had not explained, and didn't need to, for Dallas understood. On the last day of March, when she left with Flora and Donald, he had arranged to be away at Hamilton Castle, visiting his father.

The day's journey to Edinburgh was made by coach, as Dallas was not yet able to ride. Nan and her babe accompanied them, since the wet nurse was now Dallas's responsibility. A position at court, perhaps, or in some well-to-do household would be sought for Nan—unless, of course, Dallas got her son back.

Glennie, Tarrill and Marthe were overjoyed when Dallas arrived. They had, however, heard rumors through the ever-vigilant Mistress Drummond. When Dallas confirmed the tale and gave the details, all three women were struck dumb.

"You might as well know the truth from me," Dallas declared, "since most of Edinburgh must have heard it already." Fraser himself would never have talked about that awful afternoon but tradesmen, peddlers and other visitors had stopped at Strathmuir since; doubtless they had picked up the story from the servants.

"I don't know what to say," Glennie repeated for the third time. "John Hamilton is a fine man, but you should never have—never have ...." she faltered, unable to give Dallas's behavior a name.

"Well, by heaven, I did," she retorted defiantly, "though I still can't make out the difference between my liaison with John and my husband's escapades with half of Edinburgh!" She stood up and plunged a hot poker into the mulled wine Marthe had prepared for them. In the past few days Dallas had gone beyond guilt to outrage. If Fraser had been in the room, she'd have used the poker on him.

"It's different with men," Glennie mumbled inadequately, glancing at Donald who was rambling uneasily about the parlor. Nan and Flora had fled upstairs to unpack and tend to Nan's babe, who had turned colicky overnight.

Donald, in fact, was getting on Dallas's nerves. He had scarcely spoken to her since Fraser's arrival at Strathmuir. He had held her in special esteem, different from the frivolous court ladies, and more like a sister than anyone he had ever known. But when his suspicion about her and John Hamilton had been revealed as fact, he had remembered all his father had told him about Papist whores and their insatiable carnal appetites. He had even begun to wonder if the Queen herself were as virtuous as she was purported to be. As for Glennie and Tarrill, he thought speculatively, they *seemed* like decent women, but who could really tell?

Naturally, his attitude had not gone unnoticed by Dallas. As Tarrill handed him a mug of steaming wine, Dallas spoke her mind: "Since you've been acting lately as if you were in the employ of Queen Jezebel, I've wondered if it wouldn't be best for you to return to court. No doubt Her Grace would be delighted to welcome back such a model of moral rectitude."

The bite in Dallas's words stung Donald, but he merely nodded. "It is where I belong. I'll leave tomorrow."

An awkward silence followed Donald's decision. Marthe wheezed out of the room to fetch food while Tarrill fidgeted with a cream pitcher she was trying to mend and Glennie sorted out her latest knitting project, a muffler for Walter Ramsay's birthday present. Dallas's rocking chair creaked as she sat scowling into the fire while the wind whipped through the chimney, sending patterns of bright sparks against the bricks.

"Mayhap I should have stayed in Chelsea," Dallas said at last. "At least all I had to worry about there was being thrown into the Tower."

Tarrill put down the broken pitcher and hurried over to sink down by Dallas's side. "Dearest sister, it's just that everything is all a-jumble! So much has happened to you and it confuses us!"

Dallas patted Tarril's dark head rather absently. "Yes, I suppose." She gazed for a long time into the dancing fire. "Sometimes I wonder where it all began. Was it here, in this room, the night our father died?"

Tarrill raised her head slowly, as Dallas's hand dropped away. Glennie's knitting needles clicked together and then stopped in midair. They both stared at their sister. They had, after all, allowed her to be their self-appointed savior. For a time, it had seemed to work out in a satisfactory, if unorthodox fashion. Yet now, the path that had led them to physical comfort and financial security had also led Dallas to heartbreak and disgrace. They were both ashamed.

Glennie also got up to come stand by Dallas. She hugged her sister's shoulders tenderly. "We've behaved very badly towards you, Dallas. Can you forgive us?"

"Fie, don't fawn over me so! I'm weary and out of sorts." As Marthe huffed into the room carrying a platter full of food, Dallas squeezed her sisters' hands and then pushed them firmly away from her chair.

DONALD LEFT THE next morning for Craigmillar where the court was in residence. His farewell to Dallas was brief but somewhat warmer than his manner had been during the past few weeks. She thanked him for all his help during the previous months and insisted that he accept a pouch of coins in recompense. Donald demurred but when Dallas pointed out brusquely that he had well earned it and that if he hadn't gone with her to London, he would have received his regular wages as a Queen's guardsman, he finally relented. Dallas was pleased that he did, but her reaction was tempered by the fact that the money was the last she had managed to put aside since leaving Scotland the previous summer.

That was not the main reason she headed out an hour later for Fraser's town house, however. She had to know if her husband was in Edinburgh and if the babe was with him. Wearing her plainest dark green dress and a brown cloak, she headed through the rain for Gosford's Close. For once, she hardly noticed the sights and sounds of her beloved city. Intent upon her mission, she did not pause to reacquaint herself with Edinburgh's sooty, colorful, dingy, raucous, dank, secret charms. Later, perhaps, when she had found out where Iain had taken their son.

The town house looked much the same, though the upstairs windows were shuttered. He's not here, Dallas thought with a heavy heart, but then she really hadn't expected him to be. She tugged at the knocker and waited for a response. As rain trickled down her forehead, she pulled her hood up more securely and tucked her hands inside her cloak. She'd forgotten her gloves. "Fie," she said under her breath, just as Cummings opened the door.

"My lady!" He drew in his breath, obviously disconcerted by her presence on the front stoop.

"I gather my husband is not here," she said, irritated by Cummings's punctilious look. "But I must know—where is the bairn?"

Cummings did indeed alter his expression, not to pity, nor sympathy, nor even compassion—yet Dallas felt some sort of understanding pass between them. He seemed to waver about inviting her inside but must have remembered his orders. "You're right, my lady, Baron Fraser is not in residence. Nor is wee Magnus."

"Magnus!" Dallas shrieked the name. "He calls our babe *Magnus*?"

Cummings took a step backwards. "Aye, a woodcutter he much admired as a lad in the Highlands was named Magnus. A fine man, wise and strong, he told me."

"Magnus," Dallas repeated the name to herself, trying to reconcile it with her tiny babe. "Well? Where then is Magnus?"

"I cannot say," answered Cummings, managing to look simultaneously self-righteous and shamefaced.

A gust of wind blew Dallas's hood off. She snatched it back over her hair and shook a finger at Cummings. "Don't think I won't find out! If Iain thinks I'll give up my child without a fight, he's much mistaken! I'll not rest until I've got him back!"

Before Cummings could respond, Dallas had whirled away and was heading back towards the High Street.

LATER THAT DAY a messenger arrived for Dallas. Cummings had sent money and a note which read: "My lady, our conversation was terminated so abruptly this morning that I had no chance to give you your monthly allowance, this being the first day of April. As you are aware, Baron Fraser had been in arrears due to his detention in London and your own absence from Scotland. The sums covering the past ten months are included as my master did not want you to be out of pocket. He wishes in no way to violate the tenets of your matrimonial agreement."

Dallas flung the note into the fire and threw the pouch onto the dresser without counting its contents. Then she sat down at her small, worn oak desk to begin a letter to the Queen. She would not be rejoining the court for a while, Dallas wrote in her big sprawling hand, but would appreciate it if the Queen could find a place for a reliable wet nurse. She hoped Her Grace was pleased to have Donald McVurrich back at court. She had heard Her Grace had been unwell for a time but understood she was recovered, for which Dallas thanked God most gratefully.

Tapping the end of the quill against her teeth, Dallas mulled over how to phrase the all-important next few lines. At last, since she assumed the Queen knew the whole sordid story anyway, she wrote with complete candor: "As my husband has taken away our son and I know not where either of them may be, I beseech Your Grace to tell me if you know of their whereabouts. If ever I pleased you in any act or deed, I pray to God you will assist me in this most heart-rending matter." Signing her name with something less than the usual flourish, Dallas blotted the page and sealed it with hot wax.

When the Queen's reply was delivered a week later, it was no comfort to Dallas. Mary Stuart had not seen Fraser since the first week of March. She was deeply distressed by the problems the Frasers had encountered, Mary wrote discreetly, and would keep them both in her prayers. Dallas crumpled up the fine parchment and consigned that missive to the fire, too.

"Where would you take a bairn not yet three months old if you were Iain?" Dallas asked Tarrill that night as the two sisters filled a large oak tub with hot bath water.

"If he's not at his town house and not with the court, then mayhap he went north to Beauly."

"That's possible," Dallas said, dumping a pitcher of steaming water into the tub, "but I don't know any of his relations there. He mentioned names now and then, but I'm not sure who is who."

Tarrill tested the water with her fingers, withdrawing them quickly. "Oooh, that's hot! What about the Fraser chieftain? Wouldn't he know which members of his clan lived where?"

Dallas considered this idea for a moment. "He's but a lad, I met him two years ago on that dreadful progress north. But he is well spoken and takes his responsibilities seriously." She picked up a cake of Marthe's lye soap and rubbed it thoughtfully between her hands. "Aye, Tarrill, you may be right. I'll send a letter to Lord Hugh tomorrow."

IT WAS LATE May before Dallas received a reply from the Fraser chieftain. As he himself was unlettered, an old priest at Beauly Priory penned the message from him. Regrettably, he had not seen his kinsman, Iain, since the Queen had held court almost two years ago at Inverness. But if the child were in the Highlands, Fraser's widowed cousin, Sorcha MacSymond, might know where. He wished Lady Fraser well and hoped she would soon find her babe and her husband.

Frustrated, Dallas reread the letter several times. Sorcha—she had heard Iain mention the name. At least it was another possibility. And Lord Hugh had replied, as she had feared he might not. Her own letter had been phrased to make it sound as if her husband and child had disappeared under mysterious circumstances. True enough, she'd decided at the time, and hoped fervently that the real story hadn't yet reached the Highlands. She sat down to write to Sorcha MacSymond at Beauly.

AS SPRING MERGED into summer, Dallas became more and more immersed in the old, familiar routine of her childhood home. Walter Ramsay was a frequent visitor, no longer concealing his courtship of Glennie. Both Dallas and Tarrill were pleased. Their older sister had always been genuinely fond of Walter but was becoming increasingly coquettish in his presence. The two boys already treated him as they would a stepfather and he responded in kind.

For Dallas, that was the only bright spot of a lonely, depressing season. While her family was a comfort, they were no substitute for husband or child. Nan had joined Lord Erskine's retinue in Musselburgh, which was a relief to Dallas since the presence of the other babe only served as a constant reminder of her own. Flora, of course, stayed on, frequently meeting head-on with Marthe in domestic matters. Dallas and her sisters would have been distressed at the bickering if they hadn't finally realized that the two women often sat up late into the night exchanging gossip over mugs of ale.

In early August, Dallas finally got a reply from Sorcha MacSymond. With trembling fingers, she opened the battered letter which looked as if it had suffered a hard passage in its course from the Highlands. It became clear at once that Dallas's ruse had not worked with Fraser's cousin as it had with Lord Hugh:

"I have delayed writing because I felt that Iain would not wish me to have any correspondence with you. While he did not completely open his heart to me during his stay last spring, I was made to understand that you were to have nothing more to do with wee Magnus. I myself was never blessed with a child so I cannot fully understand how it is with a mother's heart. Yet since Iain brought Magnus to me, I have learned something of maternal feelings and now realize the anguish you must be suffering. So if God and Iain will forgive me, I am writing to let you know that the babe is safe and well with me here at Beauly."

Dallas covered her face with the letter and fell onto the bed. At last, she thought numbly, I know where he is! All the months of waiting and wondering were finally over. She rolled off the bed, dropped to her knees and fervently thanked God for letting Sorcha act so mercifully.

Naturally, she would go to Beauly. This time she would not ask Donald to escort her. He might refuse, and although he had seemed to have thawed a bit on his last two visits to the Cameron house, she thought it best to seek someone else to accompany her north. But who? She couldn't ask Cummings to lend her any of Fraser's retainers—he'd refuse outright.

She was still racking her brain over the matter two days later when John Hamilton came to call. When Marthe brought him into the parlor Dallas stared in astonishment. "John! You shouldn't have come! I heard you were with the court on progress!"

"I was, I left at Linlithgow." Hamilton shifted his weight uneasily, while Marthe stood in the doorway like a squat, red-faced sentinel.

Dallas gestured for the serving woman to leave. Marthe hesitated, shot a disapproving glance at Hamilton's broad back, and huffed away indignantly.

"Sit, I'll fetch wine." Dallas fluttered uncharacteristically about the room, momentarily forgetting where the decanter was kept.

"Never mind, Dallas, I dined with Gavin an hour ago," Hamilton said. "See here, sweetheart, I didn't mean to disconcert you. But I had to make one last attempt to reason with you."

Dallas sat down in the rocking chair opposite him. "Oh, please, I can't go through that again!" She clenched her fists and shook her head.

He rubbed thoughtfully at the thick moustache, deep creases lining his forehead. "I know I vowed to do what you wished, but now we've both had time to think, to distance ourselves from that wretched day at Strathmuir. Obviously, you have not reconciled with Fraser. Nor do you have your child back."

"Not yet," Dallas responded, her chin jutting. "Such things take time."

Hamilton leaned forward, the clan plaid slipping from his shoulders. "Don't build walls of words between us, Dallas. Tell me this—do you love me?"

She looked away from his level gaze, down to the tips of her shoes. "I don't know," she breathed, "I have never known what I feel for you."

He sighed, his hands on his knees. "All right. I can try to accept your ambivalence. But surely after all these months you can't hold out hope for your marriage to Fraser?"

Living one day at a time as she had promised herself, she had not looked too far into the future. She had always found it difficult to believe that Fraser truly loved her. Pursued by court beauties, great ladies and women in half the ports of Europe, it had seemed unlikely that his choice should have fallen on her. If he had never loved her, then her chances of getting him back were hopeless. She had given him a lawful heir; perhaps that was all he had wanted from her. Yet Dallas stubbornly refused to give up.

"I don't know." She raised her eyes to look at Hamilton. "The smallest scrap of hope can sustain me for a long time. You see, John, I may love you in a very special way I can't explain. Looking back, I would have married you if you'd asked me before I married Iain. I think I could have gone to your bed more willingly than I first did to his. You didn't frighten me, you were always kind and good. I liked you from the beginning, though I was afraid of men. If we had wed, I know I would have learned to love you. And maybe I do anyway. But I still love Iain. Can you understand that?" Her words held a pleading note, for she had to make him see what was going through her mind.

He adjusted the plaid as he considered her explanation. "God only knows I'd like to. Maybe some day I will." He stood up, turning away to absently pick up a pewter candlestick on the mantel, and he seemed to hesitate before he spoke again. "I'll be going away then, Dallas, I'll be gone for some time."

In spite of herself, Dallas felt a dull sensation in her chest. "Where? For how long?"

He turned back to face her. "I'd made up my mind before I came that if you rejected me I'd go abroad to Italy. I'd prefer not leaving the Queen at this juncture, I'd rather wait until she'd found a suitable husband and is completely out from under James's thumb. Since Patrick Ruthven joined the council, James's influence has waned, yet I mislike Ruthven, too." He put the candlestick down and passed his hand over his forehead. "On the other hand, I must do right by myself. I cannot stay here, where I'd see you and ache with wanting you. So after I have my business affairs in order, I'll sail to the Continent to see if I can bury my memories there."

He looked so defeated that Dallas could hardly refrain from taking him in her arms. "Oh, I wish you wouldn't do that on my account! I can't bear to think of you so unhappy!"

He smiled faintly. "I'll survive. It's not your fault, not really. Without you, there's no real future for me here just now. Some still say the Queen should marry a Hamilton, since we stand next in line to the throne. But while my brother Arran lives, God help him, there is no chance that Mary Stuart would wed with me. Nor am I sure I want that particular honor."

"You'd make an excellent consort, John," Dallas insisted, thinking that the crown of Scotland should more than make up for losing her. "Stay, there must be some way to set your brother aside since he's clearly mad. Besides, I'm leaving Edinburgh for some time. My son is at Beauly, and I'm going there as soon as I can find an escort."

"You found out where the bairn is?" Hamilton was momentarily distracted from his own problems. "Dallas, do you think you should venture into Fraser country under the circumstances?"

"The circumstances are that Iain has taken our son to Beauly," Dallas said with asperity. "And that's where I'm going."

Hamilton fretted for a few moments over her plan. But he knew she had made up her mind. "Who will escort you? Donald?"

"No, not this time," Dallas shrugged. "I'll find somebody. I'm not concerned about that," she lied.

"If you must go on this mad excursion, let me do you one last favor. I have two men in Edinburgh with me, MacPherson and Chisholm, who are both from the Highlands. You must permit them to go with you."

Though she smiled with relief and gratitude, Dallas wished Hamilton hadn't shown her yet another example of his kindness. Why, she asked herself, did he have to be so damnably *good*? She started to thank him, but he motioned to cut her short.

"Send a note to Gavin's house when you're ready to leave. And for God's sake, take care." He stepped towards her, started to take her in his arms, then let his hands drop to his sides. "Now I must leave, Dallas. You will think of me from time to time?"

The lump in her throat made it hard to speak. "Oh, yes, yes," she answered low. "I could never forget you, John. Never. You have given me great joy."

"And sorrow." He lifted one hand to touch her hair, let his fingers linger there for a moment as he gazed into her eyes, and then murmured, "Farewell, my own dear love," and was gone.

Chapter Nineteen

THE HIGHLANDS IN late summer revealed their wonders to Dallas in a ceaseless panorama of green, brown and blue. The country through which she traveled with MacPherson and Chisholm was different from the Gordon lands she had visited with the court two years earlier. Along Loch Lochy, crested mountains fringed the horizon, casting morning shadows on the undulating blue water. Some of the burns ran a clear brown and occasionally Dallas would catch the silver flash of a salmon cutting against the current. So this was Cameron country, she marveled, and felt an atavistic stirring of her blood.

In late August the heather was beginning to ripen, making brilliant claret splashes against the hillsides. Often Dallas would glimpse a peaty waterfall, tumbling down between huge round boulders to disappear among great stands of pine and birch.

Occasionally they would meet a Cameron, startling him as much as they startled the grouse which flew nervously up from the moors. But as Dallas knew no Gaelic and the natives knew little Scots, she never spoke directly to any of her kin. Once, Chisholm managed to engage one of the Highlanders in a conversation when they paused for the night at one of the few hostelries along the route. He told the man that Dallas was a Cameron by birth.

"Hard to believe," the man had replied in his native tongue, "so fancily got up. She'd not survive long in the Highlands."

Most nights they slept under the stars, grateful that the weather remained warm and clear. They had taken the longer route on their journey to Beauly, since Cameron country itself was primarily high, rocky ground. By traveling along Loch Lochy and Loch Ness, they were able to keep to a lower, more level elevation.

At last, into Fraser country, on the eighth day of their expedition, they rode past the red sandstone bulk of Beaufort Castle, home of the Fraser chieftain. Fording the River Beauly, they asked a passing herdsman for directions. Warily, the man gave up the information after being proffered a coin by MacPherson.

As the late August sun dropped behind Beauly Manor, the sky turned from blue, to lavender, to crimson and then to a golden glow. The house itself was two-storied, of a tawny stone quarried nearby at Strathpeffer. Not quite half a century old, it had been built by Malcolm Fraser's father. Set among yew and beech trees, clusters of rhododendron bushes flanked the exterior and the scent of honeysuckle hung on the evening air.

When Dallas announced herself to a retainer who was outside rounding up a litter of collie pups, she received the first hint of what her reception might be like. The servant said nothing but merely shooed the dogs inside and left the new arrivals standing on the flagstone walk.

"Doesn't he speak Scots either?" Dallas asked in exasperation. She was weary, dirty and more than a little anxious about seeing her son for the first time in almost six months.

Chisholm, the shorter and more loquacious of her companions, just shrugged. "Hard to say, my lady. Highlanders are a strange breed, and as I'm one myself, I can rightly say so. They're as independent as any great lord, having never known master nor serfdom. A law unto themselves, as my sire always said."

Dallas silently agreed with that statement. It fitted her husband perfectly. She thought she understood him a little better after these past few days of traversing the Highlands. The restlessness, the arrogance, the intensity that went into Fraser's personality all seemed to emanate from these hills and glens, the mountains and forests. Yet there was one other thing she knew about the Highlander: He always returned home.

The heavy door opened and a slim woman with prematurely white hair stepped outside. She was half a head taller than Dallas and about fifteen years older. Eyes as blue as any Highland loch gazed out from under straight, silver brows.

"My lady," she said in a husky voice, "I could scarce believe my ears when Niall told me you were here. Oh, but you should not have come!"

It was the last thing Dallas wanted to hear, but the first thing she'd expected. "You are Sorcha MacSymond?"

The other woman nodded, worrying her lower lip with her upper teeth. "Truly, I cannot ask you in. Your—Iain would never approve!"

Dallas considered several options, including a swoon at Sorcha's feet, a heartfelt plea on behalf of motherhood, an enormous bribe, and threatening to kill herself on the spot. Instead, she drew upon the oldest Highland tradition of all:

"So you'd refuse a Cameron hospitality, Sorcha Fraser MacSymond? And how many times has that meant bloodshed along The Aird?"

Sorcha flushed to the roots of her white hair. "So you are a Highlander after all? Very well. But just this one night." She turned away and led them into Beauly Manor.

MAGNUS WAS ASLEEP by the time Dallas had supped and washed. He lay nestled in a sturdy birch cradle, under the lightest of lambswool blankets. Dallas could hardly refrain from picking him up and holding him tight against her breast.

"He has two teeth and is beginning to crawl," Sorcha whispered with great pride. "See his hair, is it not black as the night corbie?"

Dallas was too overcome to reply. The hair was dark as Iain's but beginning to thicken in a way which reminded her of her own heavy mane. One little fist lay outflung on the blanket and the change from infancy to babyhood made Dallas grieve for the months of separation.

After the two women had watched the babe in silence for at least five minutes, Sorcha led Dallas from the nursery. "He is a wondrous bairn," she said as they walked down the hall to the room where Dallas would spend the night. "Mayhap I should not have let you see him, but Iain did not so specify."

"What *did* Iain specify?" Dallas asked, unable to suppress a note of asperity.

"That you would never take him from Beauly," Sorcha replied, opening the door of a plainly furnished but comfortable corner bedchamber. "I suspect he never thought you'd come here."

Dallas sniffed at how badly Fraser had underestimated her. But she decided it would not be wise to speak disparagingly of him in front of Sorcha. His cousin must be handled carefully if Dallas was to attain her goal. "I love my child very much," Dallas said simply. "What mother wouldn't?"

It was Sorcha's turn to hold her tongue. "If you'd like to bathe, I'll have water sent up. Meanwhile, the servants are taking care of the horses so they'll be ready when you set out in the morning."

"We're most grateful," Dallas said with what she hoped was a diffident smile. "Yes, a bath would be most refreshing." As for the horses and the morrow, Dallas thought to herself, she'd keep to her promise of living one day at a time.

THE SIMPLEST RUSE, of course, was a minor illness. When informed that Lady

Fraser had kept to her bed that morning, Sorcha hurried upstairs to inquire about her unwanted guest's welfare.

"It's nothing serious, I'll be fine by tomorrow," Dallas said with a brave smile. "I was very ill last March, I almost died. So on occasion, I have these bouts of passing weakness."

Sorcha MacSymond had as natural a curiosity as most women. "Truly? What happened?" She shuddered and pulled a chair up next to the bed.

Dallas was relieved that she could speak in honesty. "Oh, aye, it was ghastly! I was fleeing England with the babe, and the roads were all but impassable due to a late winter storm at Durham. I nearly bled to death before we reached Strathmuir. Thank the good Lord for a wonderfully enlightened physician from Lanark!" Dallas sank back into the pillows with a great sigh only partially feigned at the vivid recollection. But she was watching Sorcha closely to see how much the other woman knew of those terrible days in March.

"Great heavens, it sounds dreadful!" Sorcha fanned herself with her hand, for this last day of August had turned very close. Somewhere off in the western hills, a thunderstorm was brewing. "I knew you had been in England, but nothing of your illness. Iain—well, Iain did not say a great deal while he was here."

"I see," Dallas said without inflection. She let her eyelids droop down to indicate drowsiness. "Oh, mistress, I'm so weary!"

Sorcha got up immediately. "Forgive me, I'll let you sleep. I had no idea you'd been so ill!" As Dallas began breathing deeply, Sorcha tiptoed from the room.

ABOUT NOON SORCHA returned, opening the door very cautiously so as not to waken Dallas in case she was still asleep. Dallas had in fact slept for an hour or so, but more from boredom than weariness. Although she had been awake since midmorning, she feigned several yawns and a sleepy-eyed expression when Sorcha returned.

"I'm much refreshed, don't fash yourself. I just awakened," Dallas said with a tremulous smile. "Sit there, by the bed, I don't want you waiting on me."

Sorcha MacSymond found her guest quite disconcerting. When she had learned that Iain had married a Cameron, her Highland blood had reacted in traditional fashion: No good could come of such a union. Yet when he had come to Beauly after being wounded at Corrichie Moor, Iain had seemed well content with his bride. He had not spoken of her in detail, but when he mentioned Dallas's name, it was usually accompanied by a smile or fond reference. Then, when he had arrived in late March with the babe, his attitude was totally changed. He had not talked about his wife at all except to tell Sorcha that he no longer wanted the baby to remain with his mother.

Naturally, Sorcha's worst fears had been confirmed: Bringing a two-month old bairn to the Highlands in inclement weather was risky, and Sorcha had been convinced that only the direst of circumstances would have compelled Iain to behave in such a manner.

Yet during the month he had stayed at Beauly, Iain had never explained his reason for bringing the child north. He'd talked about his adventures in London, his imprisonment in the Tower, his escape and return to Scotland—but never about his wife. He spent considerable time with the babe, however, and it had touched Sorcha's heart to watch the tall, dark arrogant man cuddle the tiny bairn and try to make him smile.

When at last he had made ready to ride from Beauly to the Isle of Lewes, he had seemed reluctant to bid Magnus farewell. Sorcha had had to reassure him at least a dozen times that she and the wet nurse Fraser had engaged would see that no harm befell the babe. She had also promised that Dallas would never be permitted to take the child away from Beauly.

Now that Sorcha had met Dallas, she was puzzled. Iain's wife seemed deeply fond of the babe. She appeared to be kindhearted and considerate. She was bonnie, too, in an unruly, unusual way. Sorcha's curiosity, which had merely been ignited by previous speculations, now flamed to inferno proportions.

"Perhaps," Dallas was saying from among the pillows, "I can hold Magnus before I leave. Surely Iain wouldn't be so cruel as to deny me that?"

Sorcha felt mesmerized by the big dark eyes. "I—well, no, I can't imagine any objections." But she could, knowing Iain's capacity for anger when his wishes weren't obeyed. Still, what harm in it, since Dallas would be gone from Beauly by morning? "Will you return to Edinburgh?" she asked.

The sigh which Dallas emitted conveyed both despair and sadness. "Aye. I have two sisters there whom I've supported for some time. The eldest is a widow with two young boys. They depend on me—but of course, I'm thankful I can help When our father died three years ago and left us all alone—but forgive me, I don't wish to bore you with such pitiful recollections."

At Beauly, there were seldom any women of Sorcha's own station and education to help pass the days. True, she kept busy as chatelaine of the manor house, but it had been a lonely task these past five years since her husband's death.

"I'm not bored at all, I've often wondered about you." Sorcha's husky voice was friendly and encouraging. "I'll not pry, but never think I'm not interested."

Dallas warmed to her tale. "We were almost starving, the boys so thin and peaked, my younger sister, Tarrill, broken-hearted after being jilted by a young man who felt she was beneath him. Then one night I was almost raped by some drunken youths and Iain happened to come by. It was the Lord's own doing, I've always been convinced of that ...."

Sorcha listened raptly as Dallas spun out her story. She never lied, but she omitted some rather pertinent facts, such as attempting to blackmail Fraser into marriage and their peculiar matrimonial bargain. But later she got to the difficult part: Dare she tell Sorcha the truth about John Hamilton and risk alienating her? Better now than later, after she'd won the older woman's trust.

"At the time, it didn't seem so wrong," Dallas said, all pretense now gone. "Iain had left me and the babe, and even though his reasons may have been faultless, I couldn't see that then. John had loved me for a long time. He's a truly fine man and wished to marry me. It was wrong, but it happened. I never considered how Iain would react. In fact, I'd begun to believe that he wouldn't even care." Dallas was no longer acting but speaking from the heart. Sorcha sensed as much and felt greatly moved by the other woman's experiences. Though she loved and admired Iain, she knew his faults. He was basically a just man, but capable of great rashness and incalculable obstinacy. And as far as Sorcha knew, he had never been in love in his life—unless with this tumble-haired creature of Cameron ancestry.

" 'Twas a serious sin," Sorcha replied somewhat stiltedly. She rose to pull the heavy drapes, shutting out the bright afternoon sun. The storm had passed over during the night, blowing out to sea. "While I understand Iain's wrath, I sympathize with your dilemma." Sorcha stood thoughtfully with one hand on the bedpost. "Such irony, his own mother sinned in the same way."

Dallas fell back among the pillows. "True. Sorcha," she said, relying on instinct, "may I stay a few days? I can't leave my babe just yet. God only knows when I'll see him again."

The decision was difficult for Sorcha. Though Iain was several years her junior, she had deferred to him since he had reached manhood. He was not due to return to Beauly until midautumn. It was now the first day of September, so if Dallas stayed a fortnight or so, she'd be gone before he came back. But he'd find out she'd been there; would he be infuriated if Sorcha let Dallas stay on? Or would he come back at all—there was always that terrifying question whenever Iain went to sea.

"I can't refuse you," she answered, squeezing Dallas's hand. Besides, she reasoned, Iain had only insisted that Dallas not take the babe away from Beauly …

FROM THAT POINT on, Dallas began to hone her scheme for getting Magnus out of Beauly Manor. The wet nurse would have to be taken along, either by bribery or force. Chisholm and MacPherson would act as Dallas's accomplices. They would leave by night, some time within the next two weeks before the weather began to turn foul. If Sorcha retained any suspicions, they would be put to rest by then.

The stables were close to the house, Dallas noted as she strolled the grounds one bright late summer day with just the faintest whiff of autumn damp in the air. As far as Dallas could tell, there were only about a dozen servants at the manor house.

Chisholm and MacPherson were out by the kennels, playing with some of the collie pups. Dallas decided this was as good a time as any to approach Hamilton's men and broach her plan to them. She assumed they'd be willing to join her.

But they were not. Chisholm, in particular, was dismayed by the suggestion. "Mother you may be, my lady, but as a Highlander, I'd never take it upon myself to help steal a Fraser bairn from a Fraser house."

Dallas was momentarily nonplussed. "Don't be daft, man. My husband stole my babe from me in your own master's house!"

But Chisholm shook his head and MacPherson backed him up. "That was different. See here," Chisholm went on kindly but firmly, "I would not speak out of place, but we know how it was at Strathmuir. Lord Hamilton is always honest with those who serve him. You want your bairn—and your lord. If you take the son, you'll never win back the sire."

One of the dogs began to bark, setting off several others. Dallas stalked off several paces, the better to think. She was not used to the Highland code, sometimes it seemed as foreign as the ways of Araby. But most of all, it was Chisholm's words about Fraser which disturbed her. Hamilton had known what she would try to do and had arranged to thwart her. Though he might be far off in Italy, and she in the furthest fastness of Scotland, it seemed to Dallas that his generous heart was still guiding her in some strange fashion.

And Hamilton was right, of course. If she disobeyed Fraser's orders so blatantly, he would never forgive her. It would be better for both of them if she remained at Beauly until they could face each other and try to overcome the past. So she remained at the manor house, tending the babe, marveling at his efforts to crawl, delighting in his smile. Not mocking yet, she told herself with a pang, but oh, so heart-wrenchingly like his father.

She became familiar with the house and its surroundings. As much as Dallas loved city life, she found the comparative isolation a welcome retreat for her bruised heart and troubled mind. Her first impression of the Highlands, garnered under the threat of war and later blurred by Fraser's near death at Corrichie Moor, were now somewhat altered. Yet though Dallas responded to the untamed majesty of her surroundings, she felt no sense of belonging as she did in Edinburgh.

Salmon were coming up to spawn in the River Beauly and the leaves had begun to turn amber gold. The house itself was comfortable, if not as lavishly appointed as Fraser's residence in Edinburgh. She and Sorcha had slipped into friendship, bound together by the babe, by kinship and by Iain himself. Sorcha often told Dallas stories of Fraser as a youth, of his prowess with the dirk and claymore, his expertise at Highland sports, his fondness for animals, in particular a shaggy Highland pony he called Muc.

"It means pig, in Gaelic," Sorcha explained. "He named the pony that because it ate so much."

Dallas listened to the stories avidly, but never without an ache in her heart. Sorcha's recollections made Fraser seem closer and at the same time further away. Dallas might be learning more about him now, but if she never got him back, the loss would only seem the greater.

Indeed, her emotional state seemed to change from day to day, sometimes almost from hour to hour. Rocking her son in the nursery, she could imagine Fraser returning to embrace them both and assure her of his love. Then, when the rains pelted the mullioned windows of her bedroom and the sky turned a moribund grey, Dallas could visualize her husband raging into the manor house, cursing her temerity, turning her out into the storm.

Frustration was the worst of it, for Dallas could do nothing to alter Fraser's true reactions. She prayed, she thought, she walked the hills around the manor house, and everywhere she looked, she could imagine her husband having passed that way before her. The way he stood, thumbs hooked in his belt, one long leg slightly braced in front of the other, the twisted, mocking grin, the black hair just brushing the neck of his shirt, the hazel eyes glinting with amusement or blazing with anger—but most of all, the lean, hard, brown body pressed next to her, arousing responses she'd never imagined she possessed.

There were times when she could have sworn that if she turned around, Fraser would be standing behind her, cloak blowing in the north wind, gazing intently out toward Beauly Firth. She would stare at the place where her eyes had sought his phantom spirit and ache with loneliness. But despite her unhappiness and inner turmoil, Dallas never once blamed Hamilton. She could no more fault his love for her than she could damp down her own feelings for Fraser.

The fortnight stretched into a month. Neither woman mentioned the passage of time. Dallas would never voluntarily leave Magnus, and Sorcha found the other woman's company too welcome a break in the lonely routine. Yet it was October now, with the heather darkening on the moors and the beeches shedding their crimson leaves. Fraser would soon be home.

The first frost had silvered the rooftops of Beauly Manor when Father Beathan came to the door, asking to see Lady Fraser. Niall, the serving man, admitted the old priest, leading him upstairs to the nursery where Dallas and Sorcha played with Magnus.

"Father!" Sorcha cried in greeting. "I've not seen you for so long! To what honor do we owe this visit?"

An arthritic finger pointed at Dallas. "If that be Lady Fraser, 'tis honor enough."

Dallas confirmed her identity. Both women helped the old cleric into a chair and Sorcha hastily brought wine, for Father Beathan was overexerted by his trip up the stairs. "I come from the priory," he said after he'd regained his breath. "Some months ago I wrote a letter to you for Lord Hugh. Later I heard you'd come to Beauly."

Dallas nodded as she rocked her baby against her breast. Suddenly, she was overcome by guilt. "Father, has my child been baptized?"

The old man looked puzzled, but Sorcha broke in. "Aye, Father Dughall baptized him when Iain first came. He assumed you'd found no priest in London—under the circumstances."

Dallas smiled with relief. "You understand, Father, it's only in isolated places like this that priests can be found to perform the sacraments."

Bitterness flickered in the watery grey eyes. "I understand too well. But I've come on another matter." He turned to Sorcha. "Child, what I say is confidential, but you can be trusted. Did I not marry you long years ago to Lucais MacSymond?"

Sorcha smiled at the memory. "Oh, yes, in the chapel. More than twenty years ago, Father."

"A good man, Lucais." He paused in recollection, his mind appearing to travel through time to happier days. "But now my own course is almost run. I know, I've had dreams .... Before Advent, I shall join our blessed Lord." The women accepted this statement of faith in silence. Father Beathan had the look of a dying man, and one who wasn't particularly concerned about the prospect. Dallas noted that Magnus was asleep but didn't wish to interrupt the priest by putting the babe in his cradle.

"For over thirty years I've held a secret," the old man was saying, his gnarled hands resting against his gaunt chest. "I swore I'd keep it always, but such vows must be tempered by human needs and God's will. I see it as both that I should break my silence now before I die." He coughed then, deeply, rackingly. Sorcha offered more wine, but he refused.

"I was summoned to the convent one night while Iain's mother lay dying. Her child, she told me, was no seed of her husband's but of another man, far greater than Malcolm Fraser. Her lover didn't know she was with child when he left Beauly, but before they parted he gave her an amulet." Father Beathan paused to cough again. "He had two amulets made, one for Catherine Fraser and one for himself. But he was called away precipitously; the amulet he would have kept for himself was left within the Fraser house. It was, I heard later, stolen by the Camerons after Blar-na-Leine."

Dallas grimaced, ashamed of her kinsmen's crime. "I'm sorry for their villainy. But what happened to the amulet?"

Father Beathan's grey eyes looked faintly perplexed. "But I thought you would know, Lady Fraser. A tinker—no, it was a Gaberlunzie man—came to the priory several months later and said someone named Daniel Cameron from Edinburgh had come north and taken the amulet away from his kinsmen."

Dallas frowned deeply. She felt the stares of both Father Beathan and Sorcha; but she could remember nothing of importance surrounding her father's long-ago visit to the Highlands. "I don't recall anything about an amulet. In truth," she said on a sigh of frustration, "I know nothing of Iain's parentage. My father told Iain the truth the night he died. But my husband would not share the knowledge with me because there was no proof."

"Ah." Father Beathan nodded slowly. "But there is proof somewhere. The amulet *is* the proof. You are certain you recollect no hint at all as to what your father might have done with it?"

Magnus was beginning to squirm in his sleep. Dallas caressed his back to quiet him. "No, I've thought about it before. Even though I was but a child at the time, I remember his return vividly. He never spoke of an amulet or mentioned any Frasers."

"Could the amulet be hidden in your family home?" Sorcha asked.

Dallas considered the suggestion for only a brief moment. "My sisters and I know every nook and cranny of that house. What few hiding places there are we've used over the years for games. So have my sister's boys. No," Dallas assured them, "I would swear the amulet is not in the house."

Silence fell on the little group, broken only by an occasional small noise from Magnus. "If Iain's father was a great lord," Dallas finally said, as much to herself as to the others, "my father might have entrusted the amulet to the man himself. Or his kin."

Both Father Beathan and Sorcha mulled this idea over for a few moments. "That's very likely," Sorcha declared. "Yet why would the man not then acknowledge Iain as his son?"

Father Beathan lifted a frail hand. "Lady Fraser may be correct in part. But other conjectures are ... irrelevant."

Dallas gave Father Beathan a puzzled look. "Father, you sound as if you know more than you told us. Am I right?"

The old priest fumbled at the cross on his chest. "Aye. I know who your husband's father was. But," he continued quickly as Dallas leaned forward in eager anticipation, "the knowledge was given me in Catherine Fraser's dying confession. I cannot reveal his name."

Dallas stifled an oath. The one man alive who could bear witness to Fraser's parentage sat before her—-and his vow of silence was inviolable. Yet the old priest's very presence indicated that there must be some urgency about resolving the question. Dallas's rocking motion had become so jerky that the babe awoke and began to cry.

Father Beathan got up on uncertain legs. "I'd best leave you to tend the bairn. I am glad to have told my tale. It is one more burden shed before I leave this world. And remember, there were two amulets. If the wet nurse who tended Iain could ever be found, she might well answer all your questions."

"Moireach?" Sorcha's fine silver brows drew together. "She went away years ago, when Iain was a wee laddie. No one knows what happened to her."

"A pity." Father Beathan was raising his hand to give a blessing before his departure. But Magnus had begun to cry and Dallas handed him to Sorcha.

"Thank you, Sorcha, I must beg a favor of Father Beathan before he leaves."

The old priest's gaze was steady. "Yes, my child?" he asked softly.

"Please, Father," she entreated, "let me confess. It has been such a long time since I made an account of my sins."

Father Beathan took the request in stride; he was accustomed to performing the sacraments on an impromptu basis these days. Easing himself slowly back into the chair as Sorcha left the room, he bowed his head for a brief, silent prayer.

Dallas knelt down on the floor. She crossed herself and then began: "Bless me, Father, for I have sinned ...."

ALL HALLOWS' EVE was appropriately stormy, with rain pummeling the rooftops and the wind bending the trees behind the manor house. Dallas and Sorcha sat by the fire, making baby clothes for Magnus. The child was growing rapidly, requiring a new wardrobe every few weeks, or so it seemed to the two women.

The wild night outside had made Sorcha uneasy. She muttered to herself and began plucking out a two-inch row of uneven stitches. "This gloom hampers my sewing," she complained. "Perhaps I should light more candles."

"A good idea," Dallas agreed with a smile. "They'll frighten off the witches, too."

Sorcha took a taper and held it to the fire, then lighted several candles on the table by her chair. "That's better, it's not so dreary now." But she stood motionless, wrapped in indecision, until Dallas looked up from her own stitchery.

"Sorcha, are you all right?"

The other woman raised a hand to her breast. "I'm afraid, I should not mention it, but I'm worried about Iain."

"He's due to return about this time," Dallas commented reasonably. "Surely you can't pinpoint any particular day under the circumstances." Then a new thought occurred to her: "Sorcha, are you upset about Iain's return or about me being here?"

Sorcha twisted the plain gold chain at her neck. "Aye, he'll be angry, I'm sure of it." She came over to put a hand on Dallas's shoulder. "I can bear his wrath, I've endured it before, but I don't want him to hurt you again. I've grown fond of you, Dallas—you're like a younger sister or a daughter to me."

Dallas patted Sorcha's hand. "I'll risk his anger," she said simply. Then she turned away and stood for a moment, looking out into the night, watching the trees make eerie patterns against the darkened sky and wondering if indeed there were witches riding the night wind over the moors.

THE ROOFS OF Naples shone dully in the pale December sun. Housewives carried their purchases home from the marketplace on their heads and workmen pounded desultorily at the walls of a new church just off the piazza. On a balcony overlooking the wintry grey Mediterranean, Iain Fraser sat on a stone bench and watched the view with disinterest. His feet were propped up on the railing, his left arm in a sling. He balanced a thick copy of Petrarch on his knees but his mind was not on the book. He was not even thinking about the wound in his shoulder which still plagued him. At least he had taken the Spaniard's thrust cleanly during the fight off Barcelona; but MacRae had taken command during the return voyage to Naples. Two crewmen had been killed and it was cold comfort to Fraser that the Spanish vessel had at last been sunk with all hands lost.

They had been in Naples for almost a month. MacRae had rented a house near the harbor where Fraser could watch his crew make repairs on the *Richezza*. But Fraser's mind was not on his ship that morning. Instead, he was thinking of the previous evening.

Bored by the weeks of convalescence, he had gone out into the city to a taverna where a dark-eyed dancer had caught his fancy. Her full figure, the mass of dark hair and the sensuous mouth had all beckoned until he realized how much she reminded him of Dallas. When the dance ended and she came to straddle his knee, he had given her a handful of coins instead of an invitation to his bed. Cursing him over her shoulder, the dancer had flounced away to seek a more willing partner.

Fraser had been about to leave when a scuffle in the corner caught his attention. Ordinarily, he would have ignored such a brawl but an English oath made him pause. A crew member? No, he would have noticed the man earlier. Yet the voice was oddly familiar. He waited by the door until the melee broke up to reveal Octavian Goolsby holding an Italian by the scruff of his neck.

"An' yer Pope can put this up his holy arse!" He picked up a large salami and thumped it over his adversary's head.

"Goolsby!" Fraser called out, grinning at the Englishman. "Get out, before these folks figure out what the devil you're saying!"

Astonished, Goolsby stepped over the sprawled bodies of two other men and rushed for the door. He and Fraser were out into the night before anyone realized what had happened.

Later, on the balcony above the harbor, Goolsby related how he'd gotten to Italy. On the night of Fraser's escape from the Tower, the other guards had not believed Goolsby's story, but he'd bargained with them, said he knew where the prisoner would hide out, and led them to a deserted building west of Tower Wharf. Once inside, he'd overpowered the one holding a torch and plunged them all into darkness. He alone knew the layout of the building, having worked there unloading cargo some years before.

"I left in a rush, while they cursed and stumbled over each other," Goolsby recalled with a chuckle as he hefted Fraser's wineskin over his shoulder. "An old friend at Smithfield took me in that night and the next day I rode to Dover. The Queen's men were so busy looking for you and your wife that they didn't bother with small change like m'self."

At Dover he'd found a Portuguese caravel ready to sail.

Offering himself as crew, he'd worked his way to Lisbon, and eventually to Genoa.

"Been in Italy since August," Goolsby declared with self-satisfaction. "Sun, wine, women, just like I planned. I came to Naples last week, after a month in Rome. Sorrento next, I'll keep moving south till winter is over." He took a deep swig from the wineskin. "But about yerself, how come you be here and what's the decoration?"

Fraser glanced at his sling. "Oh, aye, this. A souvenir from the Spanish."

"Ah, so you were the one with the ship. I thought so," Goolsby said with a wink. "The piracy charges weren't so wrong then. You must have some hair-raising tales to tell."

Perfunctorily, Fraser recounted the battle with the Spanish ship. Ordinarily the telling of such a story would amuse him enough to make a quiet evening pass pleasantly. But tonight the episode seemed of little interest and Fraser's audience sensed the lack of enthusiasm.

"You got other things on your mind, Baron Fraser," Goolsby commented, squeezing the last of the wine between his lips. "I'd best leave you, 'tis late anyway." He raised himself with an effort, then turned to Fraser for one last question. "Your wife, did she get back to Scotland? I never even knew she was in London till I heard the Queen's men were on her heels."

Fraser was peeling a peach with his dirk. He looked up briefly. "Aye, she got back."

Goolsby felt the curtain fall between them. He decided to change the subject quickly. "By the way, you're not the only important Scot in Italy these days. Lord John Hamilton is in Rome, somebody pointed him out to me just before I left."

Fraser's hand tightened on his dirk. "Hamilton," he echoed, the hazel eyes flickering up at Goolsby. "In Rome?"

"Come to live, I hear," Goolsby replied, wondering what he'd say wrong next. "I'm on my way, Baron Fraser. Good luck to ye."

Rising, Fraser tried to shake the shadows away. "I'm glad you escaped. I've often wondered how you fared that night. God knows I didn't like leaving you. I take it you never got the money I'd left behind?"

"Money?" Goolsby's squat nose wrinkled in recollection. "Nay, I'd no chance to take that. No matter, as long as my neck's still the same length."

But Fraser was already counting out a large number of coins from a leather pouch. "I don't recall exactly how much I had in prison, but it was meant for you in case you didn't get away. Take this, you earned it."

The coins clinked together in Goolsby's square hands. "God's teeth, you're a generous man! Hearty thanks to ye, sir!" Goolsby's gap-tooth grin beamed up at Fraser. "Who knows? Some day I might want to go back to England. Maybe I'll sign on with your crew next time." He chuckled richly and headed somewhat uncertainly down the stairs.

Between them, the tavern dancer and Goolsby had made for an unsettling night. Fraser slept poorly, at first trying to convince himself that his wound was bothering him, at last admitting that his unease came from quite a different source.

That morning Fraser gazed down on the masts of the *Richezza* and contemplated his future. So Hamilton had exiled himself to the Continent. Dallas must have rejected his offer of marriage and any attempt to get a papal annulment. The news jarred Fraser. During the months since he'd left Scotland, his revised opinion of her had begun to fit comfortably with his own behavior: Dallas was as faithless a slut as any other, using her wiles to make one advantageous marriage, then using her body to make an even better one. It was not difficult to understand, he'd told himself. Dallas was not well born, she had faced poverty. He himself was a bastard, unrecognized and left to make his own way in the world. Both of them were determined to rise above their humble origins, to stand as equals with any man or woman in Scotland. But in betraying him with Hamilton, Dallas had gone too far.

Or so he'd thought. Ironic, that Hamilton was probably mooning around some Roman villa, thinking about Dallas, too. Damn the wench, damn those brown eyes the color of a peaty burn at sunrise, the crazy, tangled hair that reminded him of a wild spring waterfall, the untamed yet calculating essence that combined the Highlander's spirit with the Lowlander's soul. Of all the women he'd ever met, only Dallas possessed such honest earthiness and mysterious femininity at the same time.

The morning breeze from the Bay of Naples made his shoulder throb. Sometimes he still thought he felt a twinge in his back from the thrust at Corrichie Moor. He thought of James then, and that he still had scores to settle with the Queen's half-brother. But most of all, he thought of Dallas, the way she'd been in the little croft with her thick hair against his chest and the surprising skill she'd manifested in nursing him back to health. He remembered that night at Falkland, too, the look of wonder in her eyes as she waited for him to take possession of her body and the sumptuous feel of her flesh beneath his.

"Dammit," he shouted as MacRae came up the stairway. "When can we sail from this pestilential place?"

MacRae paused on the top stair. "Within the week, sir, if the winds are favorable." He eyed his scowling captain warily. "Shall I convey the orders to the crew?"

Fraser looked down into the street below, apparently absorbed in a fracas between two peddlers who were about to come to blows over whose mule cart had the right-of-way. "Aye," he muttered, "we're going home."

BY JANUARY, SORCHA's earlier concern about Fraser's safety had become an obsession shared by Dallas. Christmas had passed quietly at Beauly Manor, with a few Fraser kin trudging through the snow to share presents and the wassail bowl. Glennie had written to Dallas earlier in the month, urging her sister to come home.

Dallas wrote back, saying she could not—the roads weren't fit for travel yet, the Hamilton retainers had been sent back long ago, and besides, she was waiting for her husband. No matter how infuriated he might be when he found her at Beauly Manor, she would face him.

At the beginning of the third week in January, visitors arrived at the manor house. The clatter of horses on the flagstone walk sent Dallas racing to the nursery window. Was Fraser home at last? But she did not recognize the three riders, and neither did Sorcha when she joined Dallas at the casement.

But after the two women had hurried downstairs, Dallas felt her heart turn over with apprehension. All three men wore the badge of Lennox, and instinctively, she knew her debt had come due.

Touching his cap, one of the men asked for Lady Fraser. Identifying herself, Dallas accepted a folded piece of thick parchment bearing the Lennox seal.

"My lady," the letter began, "I have been unable to write you until recently, not being apprised of your whereabouts for many weeks. I came to Scotland in September, while my wife, the Countess, remained in London. We were both most thankful that you reached your homeland without mishap, and many times gave heartfelt thanks to God that we were able to assist you during your time of trouble." Dallas frowned at the wording, thinking how little the Lennoxes knew or pretended to know about her journey home, and how the earl had made sure that she was reminded of her great debt to them.

"As our son, Henry, is coming to Scotland for a visit, I fervently hope you will join me in making him welcome at court. The men I have sent with this humble correspondence will be honored to accompany you back to Edinburgh." The earl's firm signature was etched at the bottom of the page.

"Here," Dallas said dully, handing the paper to Sorcha. "Read for yourself." She eyed the three retainers with distaste. She didn't doubt for a moment that they were instructed to use physical force, if necessary, to bring her back to Edinburgh. It was pointless for her to refuse; indeed, the Lennoxes had probably saved her life or at least spared her imprisonment in the Tower. Whatever scheme they were hatching involved high stakes, and if they wanted her help, she would have to go.

Not waiting until Sorcha finished the letter, Dallas announced that the men could bed down in the servants' quarters for the night. "I will leave in the morning," she said in a toneless voice, her thoughts back up in the nursery with the babe. Dallas did not look at Sorcha but went straight up the stairs to pack.

MAGNUS WAS TRYING to walk. He took two or three tentative steps before plopping down among the rushes. Dallas picked him up, trying not to hold him so tight that she frightened him. "Sweet bairn," she murmured, "I'll not leave you for long." Magnus nuzzled her cheek and pulled at her hair, a favorite pastime of his.

"I don't know how I'll manage when you're gone," Sorcha was saying, wiping away her tears with a linen handkerchief. "You should wait awhile, the roads will be very difficult ...."

"We've been through all that," Dallas reminded her. "If Lennox's men could get here, I can get to Edinburgh. Oh, Sorcha, please don't cry! I will be back, I promise!"

Dallas gave the babe a quick kiss and handed him over to Sorcha. The three Lennox servants stood stolidly in the hallway, apparently detached from the scene. Dallas gave Sorcha a brief hug, then turned away. "I'm ready," she said and marched ahead of the men through the open doorway.

THE FOLLOWING DAY Iain Fraser returned to Beauly Manor.

PART FOUR

Chapter Twenty

ALONG THE SLOW, wintry route to Edinburgh, Dallas learned many things from the Lennox retainers. In November, James of Moray and Secretary Maitland had met at Berwick with Lord Randolph and the Earl of Bedford. The two Scots and their English counterparts had earnestly discussed the prospects of marriage between Mary Stuart and Rob Dudley, whom Elizabeth had recently named Earl of Leicester. The advancement in title was not sufficient to placate Queen Mary.

Meanwhile, negotiations for a Spanish marriage had foundered. The match was not quashed by Elizabeth or Philip, but by Queen Mary's French uncles, who finally decided they opposed an alliance between their Scots niece and the power of Spain.

Into all this matrimonial intrigue and disappointment had ridden the Earl of Lennox, visiting Scotland for the first time in over twenty years. Observers were puzzled by his arrival but soon understood when his eligible young son was invited to join him.

Dallas remembered Darnley well. Petulant, spoiled, with a touch of spite, but maybe he had grown up. Queen Mary's matrimonial ventures troubled her not a particle compared to her own.

SORCHA HAD BOLDLY come out with the truth while Iain Fraser took his first meal inside Beauly Manor. Then she waited for his angry recriminations. But they never came.

"I should have known she'd come here, once she learned where I'd taken the bairn," Fraser said calmly. "I'm just surprised she didn't try spiriting him away."

"She'd no mind to disobey you, Iain," Sorcha asserted, thinking he seemed very subdued since his arrival.

He gave her a hint of the familiar twisted grin. "I wonder." Picking up a piece of mutton, he chewed thoughtfully. "She must have used everything but witchcraft to win you over, Sorcha. By God, I'm a bit amazed at that, too."

"She's a fine woman, Iain," Sorcha said with unaccustomed spirit. "She told me everything, and I hold none of it against her."

Fraser lifted a dark eyebrow at his cousin. "You don't have to. She didn't take holy vows to be faithful to you."

"Oh? And your part of those vows was omitted?" Sorcha's own silver brows raised and the cousins glared at each other over the trestle table.

"Sweet Christ," Fraser said at last in low, angry tones, "I believe the wench has turned you against me!"

Sorcha made a supplicating gesture. "Nay, Iain, I care too deeply for you to let anyone do that! But I learned to care for her, too, and she's suffered greatly at your hands, whether it was your fault or not. Dallas loves you very much."

He wiped his hands with a napkin and threw it onto the table. "I have thought much about her while I was away," he said, the anger subsiding. "I considered what she'd do, I thought she might stay with Hamilton, but he has gone to live abroad."

Sorcha's unaccustomed assertiveness had unnerved her. To cover her emotions, she began scraping their plates and fussing with the cutlery. "A sorry state for everyone," she murmured, dropping a fork among the rushes. As she stooped to retrieve it, she suddenly remembered Father Beathan's visit.

Fraser heard her out with rapt attention. When she said that the priest had actually known his father's identity, his whole body tensed, one hand on her arm. "Is he still at the priory? Are you sure he heard the name only in confession?"

Sadly, Sorcha shook her head. "He died in November, just as he foretold. That secret went with him to the grave. Yet you know the name, Dallas told me so."

Fraser leaned back again. "Aye, but without proof or witnesses, it does me no good. Nor can I tell you who he was. I could not tell Dallas, either."

"I understand that. I'm not sure why that must be so, but I won't pry. Father Beathan mentioned two amulets," Sorcha went on, hoping that news might somehow help. Fraser listened closely but shook his head when his cousin finished her tale.

"Daniel Cameron said nothing about the amulets." Fraser paused, the dark brows drawn close together. "Perhaps he would have done so—if he had had more time—or strength."

"Yet both must be somewhere," Sorcha pointed out. "Daniel Cameron took the one which belonged to your father—your mother must have kept the other."

Fraser gave a brief shake of his head. "No, the Camerons would have taken both of them had they been in the house at Strath Farrar. And I didn't even know about the one which was there until that old thieving Griogair Cameron told me."

Sorcha put her long, slim hand across the table and touched her cousin's fingers gently. "Do you know what I think, Iain? I would wager that your mother—for whatever reason—entrusted that other amulet to Moireach."

Fraser patted Sorcha's hand absently. "Perhaps. She certainly wouldn't have given it to her husband. It's possible that she gave it to the sisters who had cared for her at the convent but I doubt it. She would have been able to give them money instead. And somehow, though I never knew her, I can't envision my mother giving her lover's gift away in recompense for anything."

"I did know her—and you're right." Sorcha was silent for a moment, then shook her head and sighed. "I still think Moireach must have taken it with her."

"Which does me no good since no one knows what became of her. I've made inquiries, you know. They've led me nowhere."

Sorcha regarded her cousin with mingled compassion and affection. She knew more than anyone how much his lands at Beauly meant to him. And how ironic that though he now knew who his father was he could neither share that knowledge nor use it to secure his future. "Iain," she said in a quiet, almost diffident voice, "can I fetch you wine, a sweet?"

But Fraser was on his feet. "No," he answered, "I want to see my son."

SINCE LORD DARNLEY had not yet arrived in Scotland when Dallas got to Edinburgh the first week of February, she insisted upon visiting her sisters before going to court. She arrived in time to see Walter Ramsay kissing Glennie good-bye. They were to be married in April, just after Easter. Dallas hugged Glennie, kissed Walter's cheek, and joined in Tarrill's congratulations.

The sisters' reunion lasted just four days but gave Dallas sufficient time to catch up on the wedding plans and the local gossip. When Tarrill told her that John Hamilton had sailed for Italy at the end of autumn, Dallas felt a deep sense of loss matched by a faint pang of relief.

On her last day at home, Dallas spent a few hours shopping, hoping the venture would take her mind off her troubles. She had bought virtually nothing in months and couldn't possibly appear at court in her outmoded wardrobe. During her absence from Edinburgh, Cummings had sent the monthly allowance to Glennie and Tarrill. Dallas jammed her share into a beaded pouch and set off to plunder the High Street.

In the Upper Bow, Dallas found several of the latest gowns from Paris; in the Lawnmarket she selected cloth for costumes of her own design; between the Bell-House and the Tron Church, she visited the hatmakers; by the time she reached Forrester's Wynd, she'd run out of money to pay for the six pair of new shoes which had caught her fancy.

"I assume my credit is good," she said with more confidence than she felt. Assured that it was, she sailed off to the leather craftsmen in Dalrymple's Yard. At least, she thought with a small sense of satisfaction, the rest of the world still regarded her as Iain's wife.

But the euphoria of acquiring new things faded when she reached Gosford's Close. Iain Fraser's town house loomed above her, the carved facade seeming to mock her as much as its owner ever did. What if Iain never came back? She started for the front stoop, stopped, and headed down the nearest wynd. She'd walk off her fears, as she had done so often in the past.

Dallas wandered the south side of the city for over an hour, through High School Wynd, past the old Dominican Monastery, beyond Kirk o' Field. Stepping over puddles, horse dung and an occasional drift of melting snow, she avoided the impoverished neighborhoods near Horse Wynd and St. Peter's Close, preferring instead to admire some of the fine tenements which belonged to Edinburgh's wealthier citizens. One house in particular caught her eye, a timber-fronted stone structure she had always considered particularly elegant. Three large dormer windows were set off by scallop shell carvings, and the finely molded doors showed evidence of inspired workmanship.

One of the doors opened as Dallas was contemplating the double row of small windows along the first- and second- story galleries. Delphinia Douglas appeared, carrying a large ermine muff and a small monkey which was dressed in a miniature guardsman's costume.

Dallas moved out of the way just as a coach drew up to the door. But she wasn't quick enough to avoid Delphinia's notice. "My lady Fraser," Delphinia called in her rich voice, "your feet must be soaked, you're standing in a pile of slush."

"I didn't know you lived here," Dallas said, momentarily taken off-guard. " 'Tis a handsome house."

Delphinia paused to give instructions to her maid, who had appeared with several boxes and bundles. "Yes, I like it well," she replied with a smirk. "It suits my needs when I'm not with the court. Naturally, being a widow, I could never afford such a place on my own, but—a friend helped me with the payments." She gave Dallas a smug, self-satisfied look.

Dallas blinked hard but kept her outrage in check. "How good to know generous people," she smiled. "I've just returned from spending the autumn at my husband's home in the Highlands. Such a charming, snug little manor house, though I'd like to make some changes in the decor when next I visit there."

The fine titian eyebrows lifted slightly. "Oh? You've seen your husband recently?"

Dallas had built the trap for herself. "Off and on," she answered vaguely, then gestured towards Delphinia. "Oh, take care, I do believe that monkey is doing something nasty on your muff." She nodded pleasantly to the other woman and tried to move with as much dignity as possible through the slushy street.

MARY STUART RECEIVED Dallas back at court warmly. The Queen was in good spirits, looking forward to Lord Darnley's arrival. She was residing at Wemyss Castle, high above the Firth of Forth in Falkland. Only patches of snow remained on the ground and Mary was able to hunt on all but the most inclement days.

No mention was made to Dallas of either her husband or her son. She felt the curtain of discretion come down whenever her prolonged absence was alluded to, but was well aware that behind her back the courtiers whispered with avid curiosity.

The Earl of Lennox welcomed Dallas heartily. Her reaction was restrained, though she tried to conceal the resentment she felt over being separated from her child. When they were alone for a few moments while the other courtiers pursued a six-point stag, Lennox came straight to the point: "The Queen is fond of you and thinks you have a fine mind," he declared, fingering the row of lace at his wrist. "Like most ladies, she listens to her companions' opinions, particularly when it comes to matters of the heart."

"She might listen but then go her own way," Dallas pointed out. "Indeed, she's not had much opportunity to find out what her heart truly wants."

Lennox nodded in agreement. "Exactly. That's why I'm so pleased my son is coming here. He's a handsome young man who can well please any lady. The Queen needs a suitor, why not our wellborn and courtly son?"

Dallas could think of a number of reasons why not, most particularly the spoiled petulance Darnley had often exhibited during her stay at Lennox House in London. Furthermore, he was almost four years younger than Mary. The Queen needed a man, not a boy. But Dallas made no comment.

"So, when he arrives, I trust you'll speak well of him to the Queen. There may be many who will not—'tis natural enough, any prospective husband of Mary Stuart will have enemies. But if you would consent to help us make sure he gives a good impression, the countess and I will be most grateful." Lennox smiled kindly enough, but the meaning in his words was unmistakable: You owe this to us. And to be fair, Dallas had to admit he was right.

She straightened her hunting hat and nodded slowly. After all, it was up to Mary Stuart to choose her own husband. If Darnley proved unsuitable, surely the Queen would be wise enough to reject him. "I'll do what I can, I promise you that."

Lennox was well pleased. "As I told the countess before I left London, Lady Fraser will be one person we can count on in Scotland."

AT FIRST GLANCE, Dallas thought Henry Darnley had changed since she'd seen him last. The year-long interval had given him added confidence, the rough edges of his charm had smoothed over, and his very height seemed to add maturity. His good looks remained rather boyish but he was impeccably gallant, especially in the presence of the Queen.

And Mary Stuart responded like any love-starved young woman. She delighted in his excellent dancing, his expertise at the hunt, his flowery efforts at verse. The romantic mood of the court was heightened by preparations for Mary Livingstone's marriage to Jon Sempill. The Queen was determined to make the nuptials as lavish as possible, and even insisted upon paying for the wedding gown and bridal banquet. Whatever time she spent away from Darnley, Mary devoted to preparing for her lady-in-waiting's great day.

The court had returned to Holyrood, where Rizzio conducted rehearsals of the music for both the ceremony and the banquet. During the winter, he had taken over the post of Queen's private secretary, a promotion which many begrudged him because of his foreign birth. Mary Stuart ignored the criticisms and continued to treat Rizzio with great affection.

"Davie," she called to him as the courtiers sat listening to a boys' choir go through a Latin hymn for the twentieth time, "mayhap you've scored the piece too low. They're not basses like yourself, you know."

Rizzio glowered in feigned exasperation. "They're not singers either, I begin to think." He raised his hand to the restless group of twelve-year-olds. "Now, think of the angels, of heavenly wings and golden-edged clouds!" Two boys sneezed, several scratched and all burst into full-throated if unsynchronized song.

Maitland shook his head at Mary Fleming. "A soloist might fare better," he remarked. "By the time these boys learn the music, their voices will have changed."

Mary Fleming tapped Maitland on the nose with her fan. "Now, William, you know that if anyone can make them sound well, it will be Davie." Maitland gave Mary a besotted smile; the middle-aged, suave secretary of state's infatuation with the ebullient, sparkling young lady-in-waiting had changed him considerably.

The twenty-second attempt sounded infinitely better. Mary Stuart was listening with approval when Jean Argyll rustled up to tap her on the shoulder. "Your Grace," she whispered, "Baron Fraser awaits you in the audience chamber."

The Queen's face brightened. "Praise our Holy Mother! I thought he'd never come back!" She got up quickly, nodded for Rizzio to let the singing continue and hurried out of the gallery.

Dallas had overheard Jean's words. She plied her fan rapidly. He was alive, he was safe, he was *here*. Relief, apprehension and elation flashed over her, making her knees feel weak. In spite of the cool March day, perspiration began to trickle down her brow. She eased away from the others to stand by a window, which she opened surreptitiously. She was reminded sharply of that other encounter at Falkland, when she and John Hamilton had watched Fraser make his entrance into the ballroom. But Hamilton wasn't with her now, and Fraser did not return to the gallery with the Queen. She came back with Jean Argyll a half hour later, just as the rehearsal ended. Mary Stuart looked pleased and happy, pausing to exchange a few words with several courtiers who were obviously inquiring about Fraser. Dallas slipped out a side door, unnoticed and distraught.

THE CONFRONTATION TOOK place that evening at supper, a private party just off the Queen's bedchamber. The Queen had not yet entered when Fraser arrived with Catherine Gordon on his arm. He greeted the four Marys, Jean Argyll, Patrick Ruthven, William Maitland, Jon Sempill, Robert Stuart and Lord Erskine, in turn. Dallas stood in a corner of the small narrow room, hoping she didn't look as miserable as she felt.

Fraser appeared fit, tan and arrogant as ever. Or so it seemed to Dallas at first glance. But as he approached with Catherine clinging to his sleeve, she noticed the deeper lines in his face and the strain around his hazel eyes.

Her initial reaction was to bolt, to race from the room and hide somewhere in the deepest recesses of the palace. But she was trapped in the corner, knees weak as water, hands clenched so tightly that the gold and emerald wedding band cut into her flesh.

So absorbed was Dallas in her own anxiety, she did not notice that Fraser's tension almost equaled her own. Indeed, for several seconds, it appeared he would not speak to her at all. The expression in his eyes was speculative, wary; then he stopped, regarding Dallas as if she were someone he had met but casually.

"So, my lady, you are at court again," he said with studied nonchalance. "You've managed to flee the creditors of Edinburgh?"

Dallas was hardly in the mood for banter, especially when she observed the coldness of his eyes. "You'd have me attend the Queen in rags, sir?" she replied, surprised at the hollow sound of her own voice.

His gaze swept her from head to foot, not missing a detail of the crimson gown with its high-standing lace collar, the underskirt of black trimmed in gold thread and the white egret plumes in her hair. Mary Seton had told Dallas how comely she looked earlier in the evening, but the compliment had fallen on deaf ears.

Fraser, however, did not flatter or banter. "Nay, madame, I'd never want you to bring dishonor to someone you cared about." He bowed formally, put an arm around Catherine's shoulders and moved away just as the Queen arrived with Lord Darnley.

During the meal, Dallas picked at her food, veered between rage and despair, and tried to maintain some sort of civil conversation with Jon Sempill and Lord Erskine. Fraser, sitting between Catherine and Mary Beaton, seemed to be keeping both ladies highly entertained. Somewhere during the endless evening, Dallas realized that one place was vacant: James Stuart had not joined the royal party. Pox on James, Dallas thought venomously, pox on all of them—-Fraser was there ignoring Dallas, displaying a total indifference that was far worse than outright anger.

Throughout the next five days, the wedding preparations for Mary Livingstone and her Jon reached fever pitch. Later, Dallas wondered what she would have done if she'd not been so busy. She glimpsed her husband from time to time but never exchanged more than a curt nod. He was usually in the company of Catherine Gordon, the Queen, or one of the other court ladies.

It was bearable during the daylight hours of unceasing activity, but at night Dallas could hardly bring herself to blow out the last candle. She slept fitfully, suffered from nightmares she could never recall upon awakening, and wondered if it was really true that a person could die from a broken heart. But there had to be something she could do to resolve the situation. Was Fraser waiting for her to crawl to him and beg forgiveness? If necessary, she'd do it, but she held back, fearing blatant rejection and the shattering of her final, fragile hope.

Mary Livingstone and Jon Sempill were married in the Chapel Royal at Holyrood on March sixth. The radiant couple presided over a sumptuous banquet in the dining hall and no guest was merrier than the Queen of Scots. By contrast, Dallas sat glumly in her place between a Livingstone she'd never met before and Secretary Maitland. Fraser had partnered a series of women during the evening, and only because she refused to let him see how downcast she was did Dallas consent to dance at all.

Maitland was a more sensitive a man than most. Years of diplomacy, however, had schooled him in subtlety. "There are times like this when the future is all that matters," he said during a pavane. "Mary and Jon can put the past behind them to start anew. They can forget all previous pain and unhappiness, if they try."

Dallas executed a slow turn, then faced Maitland again. "Aye, they can. Some of us cannot."

IT WAS VERY late by the time the courtiers had made their raucous way to the bridal chamber. Wearily, Dallas broke away from the group as Mary Livingstone prepared to throw the bridal stocking to the eager unmarried ladies of the court. Dallas went alone to her room that until now had been shared with Mary Beaton. But tonight Mary had assumed the new bride's duties with the Queen, and Dallas was grateful to be alone.

Lighting a taper by the dressing table, she began to take the pins from her hair. She stopped for a moment to stare at her own reflection: She looked tired, anxious, bereft of her usual vibrancy. This can't go on, she thought savagely, or I'll turn into a bitter old hag. Standing in deep thought for nearly five minutes, Dallas made her decision.

Taper in hand, she marched resolutely into the corridor. Snatches of laughter and talk could still be heard from various parts of the palace. At last she came upon a sleepy-eyed page, swallowed her pride and asked where Baron Fraser was quartered. The lad seemed puzzled at first, then gave her vague directions. Dallas decided she'd probably have to ask someone else the precise room, but at least she was headed towards the right part of the palace.

But she didn't need to inquire again. No sooner had she crossed into the east wing than she heard Fraser's laughter behind the door to her right. She paused as a woman's voice echoed in response. Dallas rubbed at her forehead, started to turn away, tried to fight off the all-consuming rage which had begun to overtake her and then grabbed at the doorknob. She was too angry to be surprised when the door flew open.

Catherine Gordon was curled in Fraser's arms on the bed. They were both bared to the waist and Catherine's high, pointed breasts gleamed in the candlelight.

Fraser stared at Dallas. "It seems we should have locked the door, Cat. Our visitor forgot to knock."

Catherine huddled against Fraser in a vain effort to hide her nakedness. Dallas had kicked the door shut behind her, set the taper down, and stood with her hands on her hips, the dark eyes blazing. "You dared revile me for what I did! You dared to shame me, to take away our bairn!" Something glinted on the dresser next to Dallas. It was Fraser's dirk. She grasped it in her hand, advancing upon the entwined couple. "You dared attack John Hamilton!" Catherine cringed and averted her face from Dallas's wrath.

"Dallas, would you mind putting the dirk down and leaving peaceably?" Fraser said in a tightly controlled voice. "You can't seriously equate your infidelities with mine. Nor, I might add, is this the place to do it."

"And why not?" Dallas demanded, heedless of the menace in Fraser's eyes. "It seems the most likely place to me, under the circumstances."

Fraser had carefully disengaged himself from Catherine's arms. He stood up, moving slowly towards Dallas. "Nay, Dallas, it's not the same, a woman can't behave as a man, it's not like that, you know."

But Dallas wasn't being diverted by words. She moved in a flash to the bed, grabbing Catherine by the arm. The dirk glinted against Catherine's bare breast. "You tried to kill John, why shouldn't I do the same with your whore?" Catherine had begun to whimper, struggling to pull away from Dallas's viselike grip, and beseeching Fraser to help her.

"You couldn't kill anybody if you tried," Fraser said reasonably, trying to keep control of himself and the situation. "You couldn't even bear watching the deer drive at ...." The astonishing quickness of his fist caught Dallas completely by surprise. One second she had been standing with the dirk poised against Catherine's flesh, the next thing she knew she was lying on the floor with a viciously throbbing jaw. Catherine was gone and Fraser was standing over her, toying idly with the dirk.

She tried to get to her feet, failed and then did something Fraser had never seen her do before: She began to weep, in great convulsive sobs that wracked her entire body. Fraser frowned, fingered the dirk, and placed it back on the dresser. He watched Dallas as if hypnotized, but when the sobbing showed signs of turning into hysteria, he dropped down on one knee beside her.

"Stop it, lassie, or I'll have to hit you again!" He shook her, none too gently, and waited until the sobs began to subside into gulps. Finally, she pulled herself up, just enough so that her head was resting against his knee.

Fraser wrestled with his own special demons: This was the moment he'd been waiting for, ever since that fearful day at Strathmuir House almost precisely one year ago. For months, he'd postponed the inevitable confrontation by staying as far away from Dallas as possible. But finally, that morning in Naples, he'd known he could no longer put off making his choice. The next move was his, and he knew that it would either salvage or destroy their life together.

His hand came down to touch her hair. "Dammit, Dallas, why did you bed with Hamilton?"

Dallas could not look up at him. One shaking hand brushed at her tears, the other clutched at his leg for support. "I thought you'd abandoned me—and our bairn." She swallowed hard, trying to steady her voice. "I heard you were in Edinburgh, carrying on as if you had no wife or child. There was no word from you, nothing at all."

He put an arm around her shoulders, pulling her into a less awkward position next to him on the floor. Cupping her chin in his hand, he forced Dallas to look at him. "I didn't know you were in London until I was aboard the *Richezza*. We turned back but Elizabeth had sent a company of men and a ship as well. I had no choice, short of suicide, but to sail north. As soon as I reached Scotland, I sent my men to bring you home, but they were attacked shortly after crossing the border."

Dallas shielded her eyes with her hand. Though only two candles burned in the room, it seemed unbearably bright. "I never knew what happened to you after you got out of the Tower—so little news reached Chelsea where the Lennoxes had sent me. Oh, Jesu, if I'd known then that you ...." She began to sob again, burying her head against his chest.

"Neither of us knew much of the other," Fraser said grimly, "in many ways." He felt the warm tears against his bare flesh and absently stroked her hair. Distraught and disheveled as she was, he was reminded of the night they had met. He'd rescued her then, and in a sense he could rescue her now. For Fraser realized he had the power to destroy Dallas, as surely as he could have killed her with his dirk at Strathmuir. By denying his love for her, he would crush the bright side of her spirit and cast her back into the lonely, isolated abyss she'd dug for herself before their marriage. Fraser had helped her climb up out into the light of love. But by opening her heart, he'd awakened her body—and it had betrayed them both.

"We'll not speak of blame or guilt," he said quietly as Dallas's sobs began to subside again. "Whatever we've done to each other, we're still husband and wife, bound now by our child."

Jaw aching, eyes burning, utterly depleted by emotion, Dallas drooped against Fraser. "I love you, I never stopped loving you even when I ...." Her voice broke, one limp hand trailing aimlessly down Fraser's bare arm. The taper she had brought with her guttered out on the table; the lone candle by the bed was almost burned down. For a long time they sat in silence on the floor, Dallas's head on Fraser's chest, his arms supporting her body. Somehow, they would survive the dark night together.

LATER, WHEN THE guards drowsed at their posts and the other palace inhabitants slept, Fraser carried Dallas to the bed. He was not sure he wanted to make love to her, he was almost afraid of how he'd react, knowing that Hamilton now knew her body as intimately as he did.

But the slit of moon which had risen over the Firth cast Dallas's face in a faint, ghostly light. The dark eyes were so sad, the expression so forlorn, the yearning for him so open. And, with an unaccustomed pang of conscience, he remembered how he'd been about to take Catherine Gordon just a few short hours before in this same bed. Catherine was sweet, she was willing, she fancied herself in love with him—but Fraser couldn't imagine her going from the High Street to the Canongate to help him, much less to London or Corrichie Moor as Dallas had done.

Fraser pulled Dallas close into his arms and kissed the cheek that wasn't bruised. "Oh, lassie," he murmured into her ear, "you've walked all over my heart with those little feet of yours."

"My feet belong to you, all of me is yours," Dallas said on a shadowy breath. "Love me, Iain, as you did before."

Their profiles almost met against the pillow. "Not as before, it can't be the same. But I love you nonetheless." Fraser buried his face in the curve of her throat and tried to blot out the mental images of Dallas and John Hamilton together.

Dallas, however, was thinking only of Fraser and how very long it had been since she'd held him in her arms. More than a year and a half of lonely, aching anxiety had dragged by; despite his words of reassurance, could she still stir his senses?

But Fraser was already unfastening her dark green court dress. Dallas moved so that he could reach the hooks more easily. Yet she noted that the usual intensity seemed absent from his manner and as much as she yearned for him, her own emotions were too drained to permit any show of aggression.

When they were finally undressed, Fraser's eyes scrutinized Dallas in the faint moonlight. "Childbearing has only enhanced you," he said in an oddly wistful voice.

His remark could not help but bring back the memory of those terrible months waiting for the babe and waiting for him. Dallas shuddered slightly as Fraser leaned down to kiss her mouth. "We'll talk about what happened to you in London—later." He kissed her again and this time Dallas did feel a hint of the old intensity. Then his lips moved down to the valley between her breasts while his fingers circled her nipples. Despite her physical and mental exhaustion, Dallas drew her legs up and wrapped them around Fraser's thighs. He began to kiss her breasts and one hand cupped the crown of her womanhood.

Dallas responded with a moan of desire which turned to short little gasps of pleasure as Fraser plied her tender flesh with his long fingers. Wordlessly, each explored the other in a renewal of the passion they had first discovered at Falkland. When Fraser penetrated between Dallas's thighs, she felt her world turn 'round and 'round, until at last sublime fulfillment gave them the peace both had craved for so long.

Chapter Twenty-One

THE NEXT DAY Fraser moved Dallas back to Gosford's Close. Cummings had concealed his surprise when Fraser arrived at the town house with Dallas. The serving man was pleased to see the couple back together, though he'd never thought the reconciliation would actually occur. Flora was sent for, the closed-off rooms were opened up, and Baron and Lady Fraser settled down into unaccustomed domesticity.

Rekindled passion was no talisman against disagreement, however. When Dallas told him she'd promised to help the Lennoxes in their efforts to wed Darnley to the Queen, Fraser responded with annoyance.

"He's callow, easily led, one of the last suitors I'd ever choose for our Queen." Fraser was in the process of shaving while Dallas sat in bed, a breakfast tray on her knees.

"What could I do? They saved my life," she pointed out, sipping at a mug of hot cocoa. "Besides, he seems the model of a young princeling."

Fraser wiped the razor off with a towel. "Naturally, since that pose is his only attribute befitting a potential consort." He turned toward the bed, the towel flung over his bare shoulders. "Have you in fact sponsored him?"

Her husband's lean, hard body momentarily distracted Dallas. "What? Well, no, all I've done is say such things as, 'Oh, yes, madame, he has wonderfully long legs,' or 'Certainly, Your Grace, he dances better than any man at court.' As you may have noticed, Queen Mary doesn't need much encouragement."

He sat down on the bed, munching at a piece of toast Dallas had left uneaten. "Aye, that's the crux of the matter," he sighed. "Unless Elizabeth demands Darnley's return, I'm afraid our bonnie sovereign will play the giddy girl and wed the young fool. I wish I knew of a better match than Darnley. The

Queen's husband can be a problem for all of us, for all of Scotland."

Dallas had managed to let the bedgown slip over one shoulder, all but exposing her breast. "It's my husband I'm thinking of now," she declared with a toss of her tangled mane.

He leaned down to kiss her mouth. "Don't detain me, lassie. I'm off to make arrangements for fetching Magnus. Then I must see Maitland, and after that there's tennis with Lord Robert."

"Mmmmm," murmured Dallas, nipping at his neck with her teeth. "You do keep busy!" She let the bedgown slip all the way down, pulled the towel from his shoulders and tauntingly rubbed the tips of her breasts against his chest. Fraser gathered her into his arms, cursed and laughed at the same time, and marveled anew at how Dallas had changed since their wedding night in this same bed so long ago. But then, he thought wryly, so had he.

WHEN FRASER RODE to Dunbar the following week, Dallas begged to go along, but he was firm: His crew was as superstitious as any and would balk at having a woman aboard, even the captain's wife. So while Fraser began his journey to bring their son back from Beauly Dallas joined the court at Stirling.

Her mind now capable of entertaining matters other than her own, she sought out Donald McVurrich, whom she had not seen at his guardsman's post when she returned from Beauly. As it turned out, Donald had resigned his post in favor of a position with the Queen's almoner. Quite by accident one day he had gotten involved in helping with the ledgers. Though Donald had never learned to read, he had a veritable genius for numbers and the almoner had asked him to stay on at a substantial increase in salary.

"That's marvelous, Donald," Dallas declared. "Since you enjoy the work, it's an ideal situation for advancement."

"But it would help if I could read," Donald replied. His attitude towards Dallas had warmed since her arrival at Stirling. In his methodical, plodding way, Donald had reflected upon the events which had led to her affair with Hamilton. Though he could never condone what she had done, he was beginning to understand why she had done it. And, he reasoned in his pragmatic fashion, if Fraser could forgive her, he ought to be able to do the same.

Donald's remark had given Dallas an idea. She picked up one of her Manx cats—carefully tended during her long absence by Mary Beaton—and stroked the animal's fur. "For some time now, I've been thinking of securing a place for Tarrill at court. Since Glennie is marrying Walter Ramsay within a fortnight, it might be well if Tarrill moved out." Though Dallas knew Walter and Glennie would have no objection to Tarrill remaining with them, she thought the change would benefit her younger sister. Certainly, she had neglected Tarrill's future for too long. "If Tarrill comes to court, she could teach you to read and write."

Donald mulled over the suggestion. " 'Tis strange, a lassie to teach me letters ...." He picked up a catnip ball from among the rushes and threw it across the room. "But I need to learn, if she'd have time."

Dallas assured him that Tarrill most certainly would. He left her then, just as Mary Beaton entered. She halted in midstep as both cats careened in her direction, sending the ball skittering into a corner.

"See how ungrateful they are after all I did for them while you were away!" Mary Beaton exclaimed. "They're ignoring me." She watched the cats romp for a moment, then turned to Dallas. "Darnley is ill," she said, fine creases lining her high forehead. "Nothing serious, a cold, but Her Grace is behaving as if he had some grave disease."

Dallas said nothing. In her position of self-promised advocate for Darnley, she exercised unwonted discretion when his critics attacked him. Though Mary Beaton was the least outspoken of the four Marys, Dallas knew she liked him as little as did the other three.

"She's making a fool of herself," Mary Beaton declared, tugging fretfully at the chain of a dainty looking glass which hung from her waist. "She's in and out of his sickroom constantly. Why, she visited him last night after midnight!"

"The Queen has never been in love before," Dallas said pleasantly. "She did not love Francois, he was like a brother."

"Her own brothers certainly take different positions where Darnley is concerned." Mary Beaton went on in the same peevish vein. "Lord Robert is his boon companion, but Lord James stays away from court more and more."

As far as Dallas was concerned, that was welcome news. The lengthier James's absences, the less likely he and Fraser were to have a fatal confrontation. Though Dallas knew deep down that eventually her husband would call James to account for his misdeeds, she wanted desperately to protect their newly found happiness.

"If the Queen truly loves Darnley, there's nothing any of us can do to discourage her," Dallas pointed out, knowing full well that her reasoning, however sound, excused her from joining with the others to enumerate the young suitor's drawbacks as a future consort. As she watched Mary Beaton's classic profile pucker with contempt, it occurred to Dallas that the Queen's present mood would lend itself nicely to a request for Tarrill to come to court.

AS DALLAS PREDICTED, the favor was granted. Tarrill would join the Queen's entourage by the end of April. When Dallas returned to Edinburgh at the beginning of Holy Week, she told her sister of the appointment. Tarrill was thrilled; her happiness for Glennie and Walter had been marred by self-pity. The invitation to court came at a most propitious time.

The following day, just after Dallas had interviewed a half-dozen candidates for the position of nurse to Magnus, Fraser returned with the babe. Mother, father and child engaged in a joyful reunion, truly together for the first time.

"Not seasick for an instant," Fraser boasted as they watched their son toddle about the nursery, which Dallas had had redecorated during her husband's absence. "He drinks from a cup now. Sorcha taught him."

"How is Sorcha?" Dallas asked, putting out her arms to Magnus, who promptly decided he'd rather climb up on top of a table.

Fraser retrieved the child and held him high over his head. "She was awash with tears when we left Beauly, but most pleased that you and I were reunited."

Fascinated, Dallas watched her husband go through a series of rather peculiar acrobatics with Magnus. Both father and son laughed inordinately at the exercise until Magnus reached out and grabbed his mother by the hair.

"Ah!" cried Dallas, "he hasn't forgotten me!"

"There's not a male alive who could forget you, lassie," Fraser said, finally putting the child down amid a pile of toys Dallas had purchased the previous afternoon. "He's had a long ride this morning, though we broke the journey from Dunbar near Haddington. I think he needs a nap."

"Oh, let him enjoy his new toys for a bit," Dallas urged. "See, he especially likes that little ship."

Fraser put his arm around Dallas's waist. "He can play with them later. Even if he's not ready for bed, I am."

GLENNIE AND WALTER were married in a quiet ceremony at St. Andrew's Church on Castle Hill. As James's influence dwindled, the Catholic clergy became increasingly bold in performing the sacraments. Rumors filtered through the city that, before long, adherents of the old faith would be permitted to practice their religion as openly as they had in the past.

Other rumors made the rounds as well. Darnley was still sick, now having contracted measles. The Queen nursed him with a devotion that enraged Darnley's opponents. Elizabeth was enraged, too, and sent a spate of messages north, demanding that both Darnley and Lennox return to England at once. When neither budged, the English Queen sent Margaret Lennox to the Tower.

By the third week of May, Darnley was up and about. Ague had followed the measles, or so it was said. There were many who thought Darnley was simply prolonging his ill health to keep the Queen by his side. Fraser was one of these, and had purposely put off seeing the Queen until she had emerged from the sick room and could put her mind on something other than Darnley's physical state.

When Fraser rode through the magnificent gatehouse of Stirling Castle, the first thing he saw was Darnley himself, preening against the battlements, soaking up the admiration of a half-dozen courtiers. Fraser reined Barvas in, frowned at the miniature spectacle, and decided he simply couldn't stomach greeting the overproud youth. If Darnley had seen him and reacted to the snub, Fraser paid no heed. The spoiled stripling wasn't consort yet, he thought grimly.

Outside of the Queen's chambers, Fraser saw Tarrill hurrying along the corridor with a huge basket of spring flowers. After an exchange of greetings, Tarrill told her brother-in-law that she and some of the other ladies-in-waiting were going to make perfume.

"Her Grace is more interested than ever in her feminine attractions," Tarrill explained. "Her wardrobe, her hair, her scents, her cosmetics must all be given special attention."

Fraser grimaced slightly and changed the subject. "And you? It seems to me that you're well suited to court life. Those black eyes are full of sparkle these days, Tarrill. Tell me, have you met any prospective suitors?"

Tarrill blushed slightly but looked up to meet his gaze. "Gallants, yes, suitors, no. But then it's only been a few weeks." She smiled at Fraser pleasantly, though her mind had gone back to the first meeting with Will Ruthven after her arrival at court. Despite all the time that had passed since his marriage, she had felt a pang of yearning when he had walked into the audience chamber at Holyrood. Maturity had enhanced his looks, as did the finely tailored court garments. Tarrill had tried to ignore him but a few days later he had sought her out and attempted to apologize once more for his arranged marriage. Inwardly distressed but outwardly composed, Tarrill had insisted that he speak no more of the past; he was a married man, they must never meet alone, he must always behave as if there had never been anything more than friendship between them. Will had gone away downcast, but since that time he had behaved discreetly and if she still felt her heart turn over a little whenever he was near, she would just have to get over such girlish fancies.

Before Fraser could pursue the subject of Tarrill's marriage prospects further, Jean Argyll emerged from the Queen's chambers.

"Tarrill, where have you ...." She stopped abruptly as she saw Fraser. "Iain, I didn't know you were at Stirling! Pray come in, Her Grace will be pleased to welcome you."

An ironic grin twisted Fraser's mouth. He didn't doubt that Mary Stuart would greet him warmly; it was what might happen afterwards which concerned him. But he kissed Jean Argyll's tapering hand, gave Tarrill a brotherly hug around the waist, and followed the two women into the royal quarters.

MARY STUART WAS more radiant than Fraser had ever seen her. The fair skin glowed, the amber eyes sparkled, the gestures were more animated than ever. She didn't seem to walk so much as lilt; even her auburn hair seemed to take on a new luster. Fraser knew he was beaten before he began.

The Queen was gracious enough to inquire about Lady Fraser and the babe, however. When Fraser had assured Mary that Dallas was fit and Magnus was most accomplished for his age, he plunged into more serious matters.

"You are extraordinarily vivacious, Your Grace," he declared. They were alone as Mary had dismissed her ladies. "I understand the cause is yon long laddie I espied outside the castle."

Mary flushed, giggled and flicked a finger at her pearl eardrop. "Oh, yes, Iain! I am so happy these days! I can't tell you how truly alive I feel since Henry came to Scotland!"

Fraser made an effort to smile. "First love can be intoxicating," he said mildly. "Sometimes it can also be deceptive."

The Queen's giggle faded. "That's a strange thing to say! I might almost believe you're trying to spoil my happiness."

Fraser put one foot on a petit-point chair and rested his arms across his knees. "You know all the clichés about love being blind and the lover unable to see the faults of the beloved. The only problem with such old saws is that they're usually rooted in truth."

The Queen's amber eyes were tinged with hurt and the faintest stirrings of anger. "You *are* trying to damp down my joy. Don't tell me you disapprove of Henry Darnley?"

The question had come, as Fraser knew it would. He also knew his answer would not change the Queen's intentions one jot, but it could make a great deal of difference to him. Yet he could never stifle his candor, regardless of the consequences.

"That's precisely what I'm telling you, Your Grace," he declared bluntly. "I find Lord Darnley most unsuitable. He is not worthy of you."

Mary Stuart drew herself up to her full regal height. The pearl eardrops swung like danger beacons. Until now, she had always found it difficult to become angry with Fraser, but this time he had gone too far. "Baron Fraser," she said stiffly, "I'll not allow you to speak of Henry in such a manner. Henceforth, you are no longer in my employ in any capacity and you are not welcome at court."

Fraser planted both feet on the floor and folded his arms across his chest.

He had expected tears, rage, argument—but not this. Fleetingly, he thought of Dallas, back in Edinburgh, no doubt romping in the nursery with Magnus or serving honey cakes to Walter and Glennie. Just when his life seemed to have dropped anchor in a peaceful cove, the overbearing fop of a Darnley had ruined everything. He wanted to shake Mary Stuart until her teeth rattled, but instead he shrugged lazily. "So be it, madame. But remember, when you bed with a cur, you wake up with fleas." He did not wait to be formally dismissed but turned on his heel and strode from the room.

WHILE FRASER RECOUNTED his interview with the Queen, Dallas could not suppress her anger. She stood by the dressing table, a pair of green silk slippers in her hand, an expression of wrath vivid in her eyes. "You actually told her that! You insulted Darnley! And her as well!" Dallas whirled on Fraser, spitting words like a shower of sparks. "Just once, why couldn't you have kept your damned mouth shut? What difference did it make, she'll wed the silly fool anyway! Oh! I can't believe you could ruin it all!"

"Enough, Dallas," Fraser said reasonably. "It's not I who ruined all, it's Darnley and the Queen. I might add, it's also people like yourself who didn't point out from the beginning what an impossible person he is."

"So now it's my fault! And what good would it have done to tell her the truth? You know the position I was in." Dallas stormed about the bedroom, kicking at a chair that got in the way, knocking over a bottle of perfume which stood too near the edge of her dressing table.

"While I was in London I heard many sordid stories about him," Fraser asserted. "You lived under the same roof with him, surely you must have guessed what he was like."

"Spoiled, petted, selfish, vain—but he was still a lad, burdened with a set of doting, ambitious parents," she allowed, "but not mad like Don Carlos, not some other woman's castoff like Rob Dudley, not diseased like Francois. In fact, with her love and guidance he might turn out well enough yet. But that's not the point, you should have held your tongue!"

Fraser's patience had finally trickled away. He grabbed Dallas by both wrists and pulled her up so close to him that their toes touched.

"You make it sound as if I deliberately set out to destroy myself and our happiness. Now stop acting like an unreasonable child and try to realize that I did what any honest man would."

Dallas was hardly placated by rationality. "And where did it get you? What will you do now?"

He let go of her wrists and moved back a pace or two. "I thought about that on the way back from Stirling. I have no choice, I'll leave Edinburgh for a bit. It's possible that Mary will see reason eventually. She may even decide she's not as angry with me as she thinks she is."

"I knew it! I knew it!" Dallas stamped her feet, picked up one of the slippers and hurled it at Fraser. "You'll leave us—I think you were just looking for an excuse!"

The calm which Fraser had started to recover fled quickly. "By God, Dallas, you know that's not so!" He grabbed her by the hair and swung her around to face him. "I never make excuses, I do what I want and nobody, not wife, not child, not Queen, not the Pope himself, could ever put me in that position!"

"You arrogant churl," Dallas shrieked, "let go of me, you're pulling my hair!" She swung wildly, catching him on the shoulder. Fraser grasped her arm and twisted it behind her as Dallas brought her knee up into his groin. He winced, put pressure on her arm until she gasped with pain, and shoved her halfway across the room where she thudded against the bed.

"You just don't learn, do you, Dallas?" Fraser breathed as she reached for a book from the nightstand. Before she could aim it properly, he was beside her, clipping her wrist with the side of his hand. He pulled her down onto the floor, in a tumble of legs, skirts, petticoats and leather boots.

Dallas squirmed on the carpet, her hands pushing against his face. Fraser snatched her arms away, holding her wrists above her head with one hand. Infuriated by him and her helplessness, she bit hard into his shoulder; Fraser's free hand lashed out to strike her cheek.

"Swine!" Dallas gasped in pain. "I'll pay you back for that!" She arched her back, trying to free herself but his knees pinned her hips to the floor.

The hand he'd hit her with moved down to hold her chin in an immobilizing grip. "Say you love me," he commanded fiercely. "If we quarrel, we quarrel out of love, not malice."

"You struck me!" she wailed. "That makes twice!" Fraser had still not released her wrists, but he let go of her chin, his hand moving down to her breasts. None too gently, he pressed through the material of her gown, feeling her nipples grow hard at his touch. "The first time I hit you didn't count. You were trying to commit mayhem, as you may recall. This time you bit me. You know full well I wouldn't hurt you unless I was sorely provoked."

Dallas had moved up against him so that her thigh pressed between his legs. "I won't endure being hit," she said half-angry, half-tantalizing.

"You haven't answered my question," he reminded her, giving her wrists a little twist. "Do you love me?"

She closed her eyes and went limp under the pressure of his body. "Oh, fie, Iain, I love you more than life! Now either get up or make love to me. You've made a shambles of my gown."

The mocking grin spread across his face. "At least you've given me a simple choice. Assuming, of course, that your knee hasn't permanently emasculated me."

"It would take more than my knee to do that," Dallas retorted. He had gotten up and she had rolled over onto her stomach to let him undo her gown. "Oh, Iain, if you must leave, can't I come with you?"

"Not to sea, which is always the best place for me when I must get away," he replied as she wriggled free of her clothes. "If I must go, I might as well make it a profitable absence. James can sulk at Wemyss, but I prefer to be more active."

"I never thought I'd see you side with James over anything," Dallas said, rubbing her sore arm. She was still on the floor, naked, waiting somewhat impatiently for Fraser to finish taking off his own garments.

"Nor I," he answered, slipping down beside her. "I can't think of a less likely accomplice than that conniving whoreson." He placed his hands between her thighs and put his head down against the warmth of her stomach. "I think I like fighting with you, lassie. You have the quaintest way of making a man forget whether he won or lost."

Chapter Twenty-Two

FRASER HAD BEEN gone for three days when Dallas returned to court. She had wondered if the ban on her husband applied to her as well but had been assured by Tarrill that it did not. "You've always supported Lord Darnley," Tarrill had pointed out, "and the Queen is not angry with you."

The reminder of her opposition to her husband's feelings irked Dallas, but she had not admitted it to her sister. Though she was not anxious to resume her place at court, she hoped to soften the Queen's attitude toward Fraser. Mary had always been fond of him, Dallas reasoned, and if the Queen's giddy state changed soon, Fraser's candor might be excused.

Magnus remained at the town house in the care of a husky, affable middle-aged woman named Ellen MacRobie, a widow who was kin to Mistress Drummond. She'd raised six children of her own, and while good-natured, indicated that her charge could push her only so far and no further. She appeared to have no desire to exercise authority outside the nursery, which would eliminate any possible friction with Flora.

On a rainy afternoon in late June, Dallas disinterestedly watched a billiards match at Holyrood between the Queen, Darnley, Lord Randolph and Mary Beaton. Dallas had joined Tarrill, Rizzio, Mary Fleming and Lord Erskine, but drifted away from them when the old Duke of Chatelherault entered the room. She had not seen him for some time and could not refrain from inquiring about his son's welfare.

Chatelherault knew of the scandal involving his favorite son, Johnny, and Lady Fraser. He knew that John had almost been killed over this dark-haired, voluptuous little chit, but in spite of that, he had a soft spot in his heart for her.

Indeed, he'd never met a mistress of John's that he hadn't liked, and this one must have been special if his son had wanted to marry her.

But Hamilton had lost her and now had exiled himself to Italy, a state of affairs which Chatelherault lamented. His eldest son, Arran, was still imprisoned at St. Andrews, and his youngest, Claud, was constantly involved in petty intrigues.

And now here was the wench responsible for John's long absence from Scotland, asking how he was getting on and looking as if she actually cared. "He enjoys the climate, the change of customs, most of the food," the old Duke replied, kindly enough. He would like to have added that Hamilton had taken a Roman marchesa as his mistress, but decided to spare Dallas that piece of news. "He was going north this summer, to the Italian lakes to fish and hunt."

"I'm glad he's faring well," Dallas replied with sincerity.

Chatelherault nodded as Darnley expertly sent a half-dozen balls ricocheting into the side pockets. The Queen squeezed his arm and praised his play. Darnley seemed to inflate with pride, glancing at the others to make sure they offered their own plaudits.

"While I don't like Johnny being away," the Duke said in a low voice, "there are times when I'm glad he's not here to see all this. The Darnley pup would surely turn his stomach."

Dallas was surprised at how freely Chatelherault spoke to her. But of course he'd heard that Fraser had quarreled with the Queen over Darnley. And everyone at court knew that Darnley had actually cuffed the old Duke and called him a fool.

"I hear the Queen has applied to Rome for a dispensation so they can be wed," Dallas commented, trying to steer the conversation onto more neutral ground. "Being cousins, they need the Pope's permission."

Chatelherault snorted. "She'll not tarry for Pope nor any man, save that puling laddie. Now that her French blood's running full spate, Her Grace won't wait much longer to have him in her bed." His weary eyes looked down at Dallas as he compared the Queen's impetuosity with the procrastination of his middle son. If Johnny had acted more impulsively, if he'd married the pert little Cameron before Fraser stole her away, maybe it would have been a good thing after all ....

CHATELHERAULT'S PREDICTION ABOUT Mary Stuart was on the mark. The Queen did not wait for the dispensation but married Henry Darnley on Sunday, July twenty-ninth. Garbed in black to symbolize her widow's status, Mary Stuart was escorted to the Chapel Royal at Holyrood by her future father-in-law, the Earl of Lennox.

Dallas and Tarrill knelt together in the second pew as Darnley entered to join his bride. He appeared jaunty and actually giggled when he had difficulty placing one of the three rings on Mary's finger. When the marriage service was concluded, he kissed his new wife rather breezily and left the chapel. Though he had agreed to be wed according to Catholic rites, he'd have no part of the mass which followed. Mary remained with her ladies, her face transfigured during the holy sacrifice.

"I'll wager her mind isn't on her prayers," Dallas whispered with a nudge in her sister's ribs.

"Pray that she'll be happy," Tarrill whispered back.

Dallas nodded half-heartedly and tried to direct her attention to the altar. It was scarcely six o'clock in the morning and she resented rising so early, even for a royal wedding. Wearing her heavy gown of brocade and suffering from the early heat haze which penetrated even the stone walls of the chapel, Dallas was feeling dizzy. She was almost certain she was pregnant again.

Somehow she endured, sufficiently recovered to help the other ladies undress the Queen and array her in the most sumptuous of gowns to indicate her step towards a happier life. Threads of gold shimmered against creamy satin, a diamond tiara nestled in the auburn hair and a fabulous assortment of jewels sparkled at throat and wrists. Mary Stuart entered into her nuptial festivities like a goddess sailing the high tide of heaven.

The following day, Mary announced that henceforth her husband would be known as. King of Scotland. When the proclamation was nailed up on the Mercat Cross, only one voice shouted, "God save His Grace!"

It was the Earl of Lennox.

DALLAS LAY ON a divan in the rooms she shared with Tarrill and fervently wished the waves of nausea would pass. She was two and a half months gone with child, and just as miserable as she had been with Magnus. Just as alone, too, she told herself savagely, cursing her husband for the hundredth time.

"I'd consider it most thoughtful of Iain if he could stay around long enough to help me get through bearing his babes," Dallas grumbled.

Tarrill giggled. "Well, at least he stayed around long enough so that you can have them in the first place."

"That's not funny," Dallas snapped. "Why don't you go teach Donald to spell 'consideration' or some such helpful word a man ought to know?"

"Donald is doing very well," Tarrill replied. "He seems slow, but it's not because he's stupid, he's just careful."

Dallas eyed her sister speculatively. "Oh? Well, I never thought he was stupid. Tarrill, fetch me some aqua vitae, I'm perishing of thirst."

Tarrill was pouring the liquid into a crystal tumbler when the door flew open. Darnley swayed into the room, obviously drunk. "Where's m'wife?" he demanded, looking fuzzily at the two women.

"Her Grace is next door in her chambers," Tarrill responded, aghast at the consort's condition so early in the day. Rumors of Darnley's drinking habits had abounded in recent weeks, but neither Dallas nor Tarrill had actually seen him intoxicated.

"Pah," he expostulated, "m'wife must be here, 'tis her room, is it not?" He looked about, apparently trying to convince himself he couldn't possibly be mistaken.

With effort, Dallas got up to face Darnley. "Nay, Your Grace, you came to the wrong door. My sister and I have the chamber adjoining the Queen's."

Darnley's eyes focused on Dallas. "Wait—I know you now, you're Lady Fraser, the one who almost caused my parents to be arrested. My mother is in the Tower now, is that your doing?"

Dallas tried to conceal her contempt and annoyance. "Certainly not. Queen Elizabeth was displeased with your marriage plans. When you refused to return to England, she arrested your mother."

"Elizabeth!" He literally spat out the name. "Cunning bitch! Who cares if she didn't want me to wed Mary!" He laughed and hiccuped at the same time, then his eyes narrowed. "But Elizabeth isn't the only one who disapproved. Your husband didn't want me to marry the Queen either, is that not so? Eh?" He jerked a long arm in the air where it dangled while he awaited Dallas's reply.

"I let my husband speak for himself," Dallas said crisply.

The arm flopped to Darnley's side. "Arrogant bastard," he mumbled. "He liked to tell m'wife what to do, she used to listen—but," he added maliciously, "not anymore! Now she listens t'me."

"I'm sure she does," Tarrill said with a forced smile. She had moved next to Dallas, standing protectively by her pale sister. "Perhaps you'd best go to her and offer your counsel now."

"I know what to offer," Darnley retorted with a lascivious giggle. He patted his codpiece and started to walk away uncertainly. But he paused at the door, steadying himself with a groping hand. "I don't like your husband, Lady ...." His beardless face puckered at the effort of recalling Dallas's name. "I don't know where he is, but I'll see to it that he stays away." And with that, the King of Scotland staggered out into the hallway, leaving the door open behind him.

THE FOLLOWING DAY, James, Earl of Moray, and Baron Iain Fraser of Beauly were put to the horn. The proclamation was spread through the Canongate, down the High Street and into the Lawnmarket. Both men were declared outlaws and their properties forfeit to the Crown. Henry Darnley had disposed of his two most outspoken opponents in one stroke.

Immediately upon hearing the shattering news, Dallas raced to see the Queen. Mary Stuart and some of her ladies were working on the royal doll collection. Swatches of brightly colored fabric lay scattered on the bedchamber floor and the crimson counterpane was covered with dolls of every size and shape.

The Queen's page Bastien admitted Dallas. Mary Stuart looked up from her work to see Dallas rush across the room and drop into a deep curtsy.

"Your Grace," Dallas implored, remaining at the Queen's feet, "please, may I speak to you alone?"

Mary Stuart glanced uncomfortably from Mary Fleming to Jean Argyll to Mary Seton. "You know the others well," the Queen said stiffly. "Say what you will."

Dallas was sure she saw sympathy on the faces of the three ladies; all the Marys had been recently reproached for their lack of enthusiasm over the royal marriage. "Your Grace," Dallas began, "I am horrified to learn Iain has been outlawed. He has served you well for many years. Even," she added pointedly, "at considerable risk to his personal safety."

The Queen plucked at the thick strands of a tiny raven-tressed wig. "He was loyal to me for a time, yes." Her tone was measured, her gaze averted from Dallas, who still knelt at her feet. "But he chose to withdraw support when I needed it most. The same holds true for my half-brother, James. The Crown cannot tolerate dissent which flirts with treason."

"Treason!" Dallas shot to her feet. "My husband would never countenance treason! All he did was give you his honest opinion. And though I argued with him at the time, he was right!"

"Sweet Virgin!" The Queen's trembling hand dropped the little wig, which fluttered to the floor like a wounded bird. "You dare to speak so bold, too!"

"Though tardily," Dallas retorted. She sighed unhappily, noting the tears in Mary Stuart's eyes. "Fie, madame, neither Iain nor I wish you ill. Every effort he's ever expended has been for your own good and that of Scotland. And I, in my small way, have tried to be your loyal servant."

But the Queen was beyond reason or apology. She turned her back on Dallas, reaching out blindly for Jean Argyll. "Leave me," the Queen sobbed, falling into her half-sister's arms.

With great effort, Dallas clamped her mouth shut and swept out of the royal presence.

"YOU'LL LEAVE THE court, then?" Tarrill broke the nub of her quill in her agitation. She and Donald were working on his penmanship in the garden at Holyrood.

Dallas plopped down on a cushion next to her sister. It was a lazy August afternoon, heavy with the scent of marigolds and phlox. "I don't know ... the Queen didn't actually dismiss me .... Mayhap I would serve Iain's purposes better by staying on. Yet I don't know if I can bear to watch that wretched Darnley gobble up his new power like a spoiled brat stuffing himself on too many sweets." She stared off in the distance to the hilly mound of Arthur's Seat, which stood sentinel above the palace.

"What of your husband's properties?" Donald asked, as down-to-earth as ever.

"I'd like to know," Dallas said bitterly. "I can't think how they'll take Beauly Manor away without a battle from the Fraser clan. As for the town house, I'll fight for that myself."

"Dallas, you must be careful. You can't wage war against the Crown by yourself, especially now that you're ...." Tarrill flushed, but her sister interrupted.

"Fie, Tarrill, Donald isn't an innocent. I care not if he or anyone else knows I'm pregnant."

Donald lifted his fair head slowly. "That's fine news, Dallas. My good wishes be with you." He smiled and reached out to touch her hand.

She gave his fingers a quick squeeze. "You're a good fellow, Donald, thank you." Across the garden, moving towards the rear entrance of the palace, a tall figure caught her attention. "By Our Lady, that's George Gordon." Dallas hadn't seen him since the night he had smuggled himself into Inverness Castle. He appeared somewhat heavier, less quick of step and—as always—so totally self-absorbed that he paid no attention to Dallas or her companions. The lack of reaction did not disturb Dallas; she merely gazed at him bemusedly and asked when Gordon had returned to court.

"Today, in fact," Tarrill answered. " 'Tis said he'll be restored to his father's lands and titles. And," she went on, adjusting the nub of her quill, "Bothwell is rumored to be en route to Holyrood."

Dallas broke off a tuft of ageratum and brushed its purple bloom against her cheek. "Hmmmm, that's interesting. One Catholic lord reinstated, one Protestant lord reinstated. And in exchange, one of each faith outlawed. How delicately our monarchs play their game." She tossed the ageratum aside and stood up. "But, by heaven, I've decided I'll stay at court to fight for my husband, even if I have to learn how to wield the claymore to do it!"

THE WHITE AND yellow roses glowed with vibrant beauty against the grey stone marker which designated the resting places of Daniel and Eva Cameron.

Four years since her father's death, Dallas thought as she got up from her knees and turned to where Flora was standing with a wicker basket over her arm. Sometimes it seemed to Dallas as if her father had been gone forever; sometimes it seemed as if he were with her still. She never opened a book without hearing his voice make some pungent comment; she never entered the house in Nairne's Close without half-expecting to see him emerge from his study to greet her warmly. And she never thought about her husband's ancestry without wondering what her father had told Fraser but had never confided in his favorite daughter.

"The nuns tend this graveyard well," Flora commented, her critical gaze appraising the haphazard placement of tombstones and markers. "They were fortunate not to be turned out."

Dallas only half-heard Flora's remarks. Her mind was still on her father, and she wished that Glennie and Tarrill had come, too. But her younger sister was in attendance on the Queen, and her eldest, having forgotten that it was the anniversary of their father's death, had been immersed with Marthe in putting up pear preserves for the winter. So, as it was a fine August day, Dallas and Flora had walked the short distance from Edinburgh to Newington, carrying the basket of roses and intending to stop for supper at the town house in Gosford's Close.

Two grey-clad nuns were gathering herbs in the convent garden as Dallas and Flora came out of the graveyard. Beyond, where the road dipped out of sight, dust swirled in brown billows as a coach rumbled towards the capital. Both women stepped well off the road as four horses cantered towards them and stopped.

"Lady Fraser," called a voice from inside the coach, "may I offer you a ride?"

Dallas saw the Earl of Morton's face framed by the coach window. "It's a fine day for walking, thank you just the same." Morton, she noted, looked as porcine as ever, the heavy jowls sagging slightly under the red-brown beard.

"It's clouding over, we'll have rain within the hour," Morton said, looking skyward. "You'll not make it to Holyrood without getting drenched."

Morton was right, dark clouds were gathering on the northern horizon, settling down over the Ochil Mountains. Dallas had been so absorbed during her half-hour in the graveyard that she had not noticed the sudden shift in weather.

"I'm going to my own house for the evening," Dallas replied, wavering slightly in her refusal. Much as she disliked Morton, there was no point in catching cold, especially now that she was pregnant. "If you could let us off in Gosford's Close ...."

The coach door swung open. "Certainly, pray get in." Dallas and Flora sat opposite Morton, the maid rigid with disapproval. The earl spoke of inconsequential matters, though his words were slow and measured as ever. Dallas answered him cordially, but her thoughts were still shaded by her father's memory. A quarter of an hour later, the coach pulled up in front of the town house, where Cummings was standing on the stoop, ordering some tradesmen to go around to the rear entrance.

"It's the fabric for your new gowns, madame," Flora said, quickly opening the coach door. "I'd best see to it at once." The maid stepped down onto the cobbles without waiting for the footman to assist her.

Morton chuckled. "I don't think she cares for my company," he commented, leaning over to close the coach door. "But then I was hoping for a moment's privacy with you, my lady."

Dallas sat up straight, hands folded in her lap. The ride had made her queasy and the air had turned humid as the rain clouds pressed in upon the city. "To what purpose?" she inquired.

The earl leaned forward, elbows resting on his knees. "Ladies in distress move me deeply," he said in a confidential tone. "Your husband's predicament must put you under great duress."

With effort, Dallas refrained from making a nasty retort. If ever a man was not touched by "ladies in distress," it was Morton, who had a reputation for outright cruelty where defenseless women were concerned. "Iain's plight upsets me, of course," Dallas said calmly, "but the winds of politics change. I'm sure he will be permitted back soon."

Morton's pudgy thumb gestured towards the coach window and the town house beyond. "How sad it would be for you to lose such a charming residence. Have you thought of selling?"

"*Selling!*" Dallas made the word sound obscene. "Sweet Virgin, neither of us would ever do that."

The piglike eyes squinted at Dallas. "You may lose it anyway. I have kin who've often admired the house."

"It's well worth the admiration, but definitely not for sale," Dallas asserted, making a move to get up from the cushioned seat. The coach seemed confining, overly warm, and outside the rain pelted the cobblestones. "Many thanks for ..."

Morton's hand grasped Dallas's knee in a firm grip. "You're a brave little wench. You ought not bear the burden of defending your lord's properties alone. A man, one with influence at court, could help you in your husband's prolonged absence."

Dallas jerked her knee away from Morton's touch. "I need no help," she avowed, standing up so abruptly that her head struck painfully on the low roof of the coach.

The earl's small eyes gleamed with amusement. "How spirited of you! Yet I recall you have not disdained the protection of at least one other powerful lord in the past."

"You're impertinent, sir!" Dallas put out an unsteady hand to open the coach door but he grasped her by the wrist.

"With James outlawed, I'm in a position to intercede with the Queen on your husband's behalf. Think, madame," he went on, giving her wrist a little squeeze, "even if Darnley won't allow your lord's return, I can see to it that when Parliament meets, his properties are kept out of the Crown's hands."

Dallas's head was throbbing from where she'd struck it, but she'd never yield an inch to him, not for all the threats or promises he could muster. Her eyes glared defiance, evoking a curt little nod from the earl. "Have it your own way, Lady Fraser," he said in an ugly voice as he let go of her wrist. "You'll be the sorrier for it."

Dallas didn't waste time replying; she shoved the carriage door open and jumped down onto the wet cobbles. Before she could get inside the house, Morton had shouted to his driver and the horses began to trot out of Gosford's Close.

DALLAS HAD COLLAPSED on the settee in the little supper room. "The man's a swine," Flora sniffed, using a perfumed handkerchief to wipe her mistress's brow. "I should never have left you alone with him."

"He's a loathesome opportunist." Dallas closed her eyes, tried to relax, and gave Magnus a hug before he jumped out of her arms and headed for the silver comfit dish. "I'll not tell Iain about this incident. He has enough enemies as it is."

"I should have guessed what Morton was up to," Flora said in self-reproach. "I saw him watching you all the way from Newington, lust-filled as a wild bull."

Dallas took a sip of whiskey and gingerly touched the bump on her head. "No wonder the Douglases are detested by so many, if Morton is like the rest."

Flora snorted in agreement but said nothing. Dallas drank again, more deeply this time, and felt herself reviving. Morton's odious proposition would have to be put out of her mind. But she could not erase the fact that Fraser was far away and that she was very much alone. In a moment of uncustomary bleak despair, Dallas wondered how she could go on battling for her husband and herself, for Magnus and the tiny being she carried in her womb. She took another drink, squared her shoulders, and then felt her lips tremble as she saw Fraser's empty armchair across the room.

SOME FORTY MILES east of Scarborough, on an unusually placid North Sea, the men of the *Richezza* had fired a signal volley to the English frigate which lay several hundred yards off the port side. Dipping the ensign, orders were given to bring the two ships side-by-side. It was common practice, since vessels often rendezvoused at sea to exchange supplies or information. It was also a common ruse used by pirates.

The battle was short and decisive. Piracy was not unusual and all but the most stout-hearted crews had learned it was wiser to yield their cargos than their lives. MacRae had taken command of the *Richezza's* men and, following his captain's orders, made a cursory check of the frigate's bounty. As Fraser had predicted, there was little of interest, since the English crew had recently sailed from Leith, ladened with wool, whiskey and a few unexceptional trinkets to sell in the London markets. MacRae appropriated several casks of whiskey but let the rest of the goods remain aboard. The English captain, however, was another matter: Bound and blindfolded, MacRae and Corelli led him across the gangplank and onto the *Richezza*.

Fraser, who ordinarily would have been the first to board an enemy vessel, waited indolently in his cabin. Since his purpose was not loot but information, he had wanted to take no chances of being recognized by the English crew.

"Sit him down there," he commanded MacRae, indicating a carved armchair. "Welcome, Captain, have we been made rich by our plunder?"

The Englishman sat awkwardly with his hands trussed behind him. His blindfolded eyes turned in the direction of the deep voice. "Scarcely. I fear you've wasted your time, sir."

"A pity." Fraser poured himself a cup of wine. "If you can't make me wealthy, perhaps you can amuse me instead." He picked up the pistol from the table and cocked it. The click made the other man jump and Fraser smiled slightly. "Your name, sir?"

"Richard Miller of Portsmouth, captain of the *Sea King* these past four years," he replied, feeling the sweat break out on his forehead.

"Ah." Fraser still held the pistol aimed at Miller, knowing that if he set it down the other man would hear the sound and relax. "Let me see how you might amuse me best … You look too clumsy to dance and I doubt that you can sing, so why not tell me some entertaining yarns? You sailed from Leith?"

Captain Miller licked his dry lips. "Aye, two days ago, the twenty-eighth of August."

Fraser used his free hand to take another drink of wine. "That's hardly hilarious," he said dryly. "What news of Edinburgh, then? Oh, I know you must have figured me for a Scot by my accent and you're quite right. Perhaps you can give me the latest gossip from home."

The English captain snorted. "Gossip consists mostly of speculating how long your Queen can put up with that oaf she married." He stopped abruptly, wondering if he had offended his captor. "At least, it seemed to me that the people of Edinburgh care little for their new sovereign lord."

Fraser rubbed his finger along the bridge of his nose. So the Queen had actually married the simpering fop after all. He'd hoped against hope that at the last minute she might have seen Darnley for what he was. And the Englishman had referred to the "new sovereign lord"—the silly lass must have conferred kingship on Darnley. Fraser's lean mouth drew into a taut line. "Interesting enough in itself," he said mildly. "What else?"

Captain Miller was racking his brains. What in Christ did the man want to hear? And why? Was he just a homesick sailor, eager for news? "George Gordon has returned to court, complete with his father's Huntly earldom. Bothwell's back, too. The Queen's half-brother, James, has been put to the horn and has led the Queen a merry chase about Edinburgh."

Fraser leaned forward. So James had turned rebel. In spite of himself, his opinion of his old adversary went up a notch. "Who caught whom?" he asked in a noncommittal tone.

"It's undecided," the captain replied, somewhat relieved to note that his captor was at least sufficiently diverted to go on talking. "James Stuart flirts about the edges of the city with his troops, while Queen Mary and her men give chase. Old Chatelherault and Argyll were informed that they would be outlawed, too, if they helped Lord James."

Miller felt the perspiration trickle into the blindfold as he grimaced in an effort to recollect any other scraps of information which he hoped might save his skin. "Yes, and one other, Baron Fraser, was also outlawed along with Lord James. Apparently he was out of the city when the proclamation was read."

Fraser's fist clenched so hard against the table that his signet ring left a dent in the wood. "My, my," he said lightly, after a pause to regain his composure, "it sounds as if being at sea is more peaceable than being in Scotland these days. All those poor lords falling into disgrace over a lassie's wedding."

The Englishman had gained confidence through gaining time. He began to recall all sorts of items, suddenly spewing them out in a rush of words: "Though Lord Argyll is out of favor, his wife remains with the Queen—but they've been estranged for years. James Stuart announced his intent to turn his rebellion into a religious war, but the Queen would have none of that. Lennox tried to convince the Queen that James wanted to kidnap the earl and his son and ship them both back to England, and now James is rumored to be seeking help from Queen Elizabeth. Fraser's lady is with child, but said to be at court, pressing for her husband's reinstatement ...."

Miller blathered on, but Fraser had ceased listening. He put both the wine cup and the pistol down on the table very slowly, his shoulders suddenly slumped. MacRae and Corelli, who still stood behind their captain's chair, watched him with compassion. But he rallied quickly, to cut the Englishman off.

"Enough, I grow bored with politics. You're short of plunder, short of entertainment, Captain. You'd best return to your dull English dogs and take your trinkets on to the Thames." He signaled to MacRae. "Unbind him, but leave the blindfold in place. At least we'll get something decent to drink out of this miserable expedition."

Captain Miller, now sweating with relief rather than fear, was trundled out of the cabin by Fraser's two crewmen. When they were gone, Fraser poured himself more wine and stared into his cup. Somehow, he'd get back to Dallas, at least for a while. Outlawed or not, he could never abandon her again as he had while she carried Magnus. That folly, however unwitting at the time, had nearly lost her to him. Then he grinned, recalling what the Englishman had said. He could envision Dallas struggling up from bouts of nausea, sailing into battle on his behalf. If ever a lassie was worth risking all, it was his wife, he decided, and left the cabin to give orders for sailing north.

Chapter Twenty-Three

EVERY YEAR IN early September, horse races were run on the sands at Leith. Though the Protestant leaders decried the sport as unholy, all but the court's most ardent adherents of the new religion came to the races. The most splendid animals, Arabians imported from Spain, were entered in the competitions, and betting ran high among the onlookers.

The straightaway course was six furlongs and lined with stalls, tents and banners. Riders generally came from the wealthier families or the Queen's household. When Will Ruthven had sprained his ankle two days earlier, he'd asked Donald McVurrich to take his place on the chestnut gelding, Scorpio.

"I'm not used to these foreign breeds," Donald complained to Dallas and Tarrill, "but I vowed to do my best."

"Just don't fall off and get hurt," Dallas admonished. She fanned herself briskly, for the late summer sun was warm. Hawkers plied the crowd, selling a variety of refreshments and souvenirs. The Queen stood nearby, disdaining the comfort of a hastily erected dais set up close to the finish line. Darnley lounged at her side, looking bored.

Tarrill avoided looking at Will Ruthven, who was hobbling along with Jon Sempill. Instead, she scrutinized some notes she'd made on a little pad which dangled from her waist. "Let me see, two bays, a black and a grey have won so far. I've gleaned forty royals on two winners already; shall I wager it all on you, Donald?"

He studied the big chestnut, which was being soothed by a stable boy. "Horse looks willing, but I'm not sure about the rider." He grinned shyly at Tarrill. "If you put up all your money, I'll have to win."

"Your only serious competition is Lord Robert and one of the Douglases,"

Dallas pointed out. "The rest are either drunk already or out of condition."

Donald acknowledged her observations with a nod, heard the call to saddle up, and turned to Tarrill. "I need a talisman," he mumbled, his skin turning dark. "Like the knights of old."

Tarrill looked up at him from under her black lashes. "Oh—mayhap my handkerchief, no, wait." She unfastened the little note pad from her waist. "Here, take this, it signifies our work together on your letters."

He took the trinket in his big hand and stuffed it inside his shirt. "Thank you. When I give it back, I hope you'll be able to write down that a chestnut won this race." He bowed to both women, then turned towards his mount.

Tactfully, Dallas decided not to tease her sister about the exchange. They moved away from the riders' area towards the royal entourage. Darnley happened to look in their direction as they approached. He glared at Dallas and spat into the sand.

"Whoreson," Dallas murmured without breaking stride.

"Please, Dallas," Tarrill begged, "have a care. I'm so afraid he'll make the Queen dismiss you."

Dallas snorted with contempt as she elbowed her way to a better viewpoint.

The horses and their riders were being led down along the sands to the starting place. Dallas shielded her eyes from the sun, noting the masts of several ships out in the harbor. She wondered, as she did almost constantly, where Fraser was.

Tarrill, however, was wondering if she'd lose her forty royals. She placed wagers for herself and her sister with one of the oddsmakers just as David Rizzio edged up beside them. "*Buona fortuna*," he greeted the sisters. "Which do you choose?"

"Scorpio," Tarrill answered. "I've already won twice."

Rizzio's wide eyes displayed admiration for her acumen. "Excellent, but I am not so fortunate. Already I've lost ten times that much this afternoon!" He made an exaggerated grimace and raised his hands to heaven in mock despair.

A pistol shot sent all heads craning towards the starting place. Far down the sands, they could see the horses thundering up the course in a cluster of color and speed. At the end of the first furlong, three of the riders had spurred their mounts ahead of the others.

"Donald is up there!" Tarrill cried excitedly.

"You can't see that far back," Dallas objected.

"I can so!" Tarrill shouted, for the crowd noise was growing louder as the horses approached the halfway point. "He's the only fair-haired rider in the race!"

Unable to argue that point, Dallas fell silent until she could make out Donald and his mount. Sure enough, he was in second place, behind Lord

Robert. The third horse, ridden by the Queen's page Bastien, was losing ground to an outsider, spurred on by the Douglas lad.

"Go, Donald, come on, Scorpio!" Tarrill was shrieking, clenching her fists and all but falling over the ropes which separated the observers from the race course. Just as Scorpio moved to pass Lord Robert's mount, the Douglas horse drew even with them both. Thundering across the finish line, Tarrill announced in a shrill voice that Donald had won by a nose.

The crowd grew silent, uncertain of the result. Then a rumble of contention began to swell as the riders cantered along the sands to cool off their mounts. Maitland had been chosen as presiding judge and he stood next to the royal dais, fending off a group of courtiers who were anxious to give him their expert opinions. Waving them aside, he mounted the three steps and held up his hands for quiet. "The winner is Scorpio, ridden by Donald McVurrich of the Queen's household!"

Cheers mingled with hoots of derision. Maitland smiled dryly as he descended the dais, thinking he'd rather face the most dangerous and intricate of foreign negotiations any day than a partisan group of racing enthusiasts.

Tarrill hugged Dallas and squealed with delight. "I told you! He did it!"

Rizzio was smiling at the women. "Congratulations, dear ladies," he said gallantly, kissing their hands in turn. "I should have followed your lead—my own money was on Lord Robert."

"I think Donald had an extra incentive," Dallas smiled as her sister slipped through the crowd towards the riders' area. "Oh, Davie, I'd like to see my sister happily married. What do you think?" She nodded her head towards Tarrill and Donald, who were greeting each other jubilantly.

Short as he was, Rizzio had to stand on tiptoe to see the couple. "He's a fine young man, I've heard good things of him from the almoner. But he lacks confidence with women."

Dallas had respect for Rizzio's perceptions. Not much passed by the little man. "That's so," she agreed. "Mayhap I should have a little talk with him."

"Mayhap you won't need to, mayhap I was wrong," Rizzio said, pointing to the couple. They were easing their way from Donald's admirers, moving out of the crowd towards one of the refreshment tents. Donald's arm was around Tarrill's shoulders.

"His victory has probably done more for him than my talk would," Dallas laughed. "I suppose I should assume the guise of discreet sister and disappear for a bit. Good luck on the last race, Davie." She allowed Rizzio to give her hand another kiss before she wandered off down the sands.

Dallas had not won a race until Donald's victory, but the sum she'd wagered on him made up for her losses. The final contest did not interest her much, since she knew none of the riders except Delphinia Douglas's brother, and Dallas certainly wasn't going to waste her money betting on him.

Away from the crowd, she felt the salt air on her cheeks and a soft breeze in her hair. No more nausea now, but her gowns were beginning to feel tight around the waist. She strolled on, the sound of the crowd growing fainter with every step. Up ahead, a strange formation caught her attention. Curious, she walked a little faster but the sun was still in her eyes. Some fifty feet away from the curious object she stopped and gasped. It was a gibbet and a half-naked man dangling in chains, with much of his flesh pecked away by sea birds. Though she could not read the lettering at the top of the gallows, Dallas knew the man had been a pirate.

Covering her eyes with her hands, Dallas fled blindly away from the grisly sight. Collapsing against some old pilings, she discovered her nausea had not left her after all and became violently ill.

She didn't know how long she sat there, shivering and weak. But when she glanced back down the beach, the crowd was dispersing, the sun was beginning to set and a heavy mist was rolling in over the harbor. She could never catch up with the others, she must have walked close to a mile.

One arm clinging to the piling, Dallas fretted over what she ought to do. There was no one headed in her direction nor did she see any fleet-footed youth who might race off with a message. Picking up her skirts to mount some rickety wooden stairs which led up from the sands to the town, Dallas tried to blot out the image of the executed pirate and concentrate on more practical matters. Tarrill and Donald would figure she had simply been tactful and left them alone. If they asked, Rizzio would confirm the notion, and everyone would naturally assume that Dallas was returning to Holyrood with some of the other courtiers. Since it was only a little over a mile from the town up through Leith Wynd to the Canongate, Dallas reasoned that she ought to be back at the palace shortly after the others arrived.

Her step was slow, however, as she moved along the narrow street which ran parallel to the harbor. A few local citizens glanced at her elegant mauve gown and Flemish lace shawl, but since they all knew of the court's presence at the races that day, she attracted a minimum of attention.

Wearily, she trudged away from the harbor and into Leith. Still shaken by the sight of the corpse on the gibbet, she paused near an ale house, wondering if she should go inside and purchase a tankard of ale to quiet her shattered nerves. No, she decided, certainly not unescorted in a town frequented by rough seamen. She'd have to keep walking until she reached Holyrood.

But Dallas had not counted on the encroaching darkness or the heavy mist filtering into the wynds of Leith. She didn't know the town well and soon realized she wasn't entirely certain how to reach Leith Wynd. She also had the vague feeling that someone was following her.

Turning to look unobtrusively over her shoulder, she was almost sure she saw a man's outline in the mist. Being the supper hour, there were few others abroad now and Dallas was suddenly reminded of the night when the young roisterers had tried to attack her after Mary Stuart's entry into Edinburgh. Forcing herself to walk faster, she heard nothing but her own footsteps echo over the cobbles.

But when she turned a corner which she hoped led out of the town, the unmistakable footfall of booted feet assailed her ears. She didn't dare turn around now and the fog had grown so thick she couldn't see for more than a foot. Whoever it was had almost caught up with her; panicky, she vacillated between flight and confrontation. Before she could do either, an arm went around her neck and a hand closed over her mouth. Dallas kicked, pummeled with her fists and strained against the steel grip, but in vain. Her feet were off the ground and she was being lifted into a darkened, mist-filled close.

Her assailant had put her back on her feet but kept his hand over her mouth and her arms pinned to her sides. Dallas began to renew her struggle but went rigid when she felt her captor's hand move down to feel the outline of her swelling stomach. Then the familiar voice sounded low in her ears and she slumped against her abductor's chest: "Hush, lassie," he whispered, "it's just your husband. I thought you might fancy dining out this evening."

"Ooooh ...." Dallas groaned as he withdrew his hand from her mouth but kept one arm around her shoulders lest she fall. She turned slowly to face him. He wore a heavy cloak with the hood pulled up to conceal his sharp features. "You fiend, you frightened me so!" She wanted to be angry but began laughing instead.

He signaled for her to be quiet. "Whisper, lovey. I've gone to a lot of trouble to keep you from giving me away. Now come along, there's an inn just a few doors down where we can talk. Corelli is posted outside to keep watch."

He took her hand and they hurried along the street, now completely swathed in fog. A few feet from the inn's entrance, another man muffled in a cloak made an almost imperceptible nod to Fraser.

Inside, noisy voices argued over the outcome of the day's racing event. Heavily Protestant though Leith might be, it seemed as if half the town had been wagering that afternoon down on the sands. Fraser propelled Dallas between the crowded tables to an inglenook which he had kept waiting for them.

After they were seated, Dallas sat with her chin on her hands, feasting on her husband's presence. "I'm so glad to see you—how did you find me?"

Fraser beckoned for a serving wench to bring ale. "We dropped anchor last night in Leith Harbor so Corelli and I could row ashore. I learned this morning that the court was coming down for the races so I watched from a place nearby, hoping to see you. It wasn't until you left the others just before the last race that I could single you out. I followed you, hoping you might stop to rest so I could tell you I was here."

Dallas accepted a tankard from the serving wench who was winking boldly at Fraser. He pretended not to notice and kept his gaze on Dallas, who was drinking thirstily. "Saucy," she muttered as the girl left them. "I was so frightened—there was a pirate hanging in chains. I remembered what you told me a long time ago ...." Her lips trembled as her voice trailed away.

Fraser covered her hand with his own. "Don't fash yourself, Dallas. I'm here in one piece, though I can stay but a few hours." He glanced around them to make sure no one was listening. "I know about being declared an outlaw, about James, too. I also know," he said, smiling and squeezing her hand, "about the babe."

Dallas squeezed back but couldn't resist a bit of sarcasm: "I'm so pleased you've shown up at least once while I'm bearing these bairns of yours. I was beginning to think you believed I purchased them in the Lawnmarket."

"Why not? You've bought everything else they have to offer." He grinned as she kicked him under the table. "Now let's eat something before I have the misfortune of being recognized."

They asked for stewed beef, bread and boiled potatoes, the most sophisticated offerings of a meager kitchen. Dallas wanted to know how Fraser had kept so well informed about events at court. He told her of his informative exchange with Captain Miller. Fraser, in turn, wanted to know what had happened since. Though he had gleaned some scraps of news that morning in Leith, Dallas brought him up-to-date, including her own efforts on his behalf.

"The Queen won't budge to reinstate you yet," she said, cutting up a piece of stringy beef. "But I have written to Sorcha warning her that your properties there might be confiscated. I also wrote to Lord Hugh Fraser, discreetly suggesting he might marshal the clan on your behalf, if need be. So far, there's no problem with the town house, though Cummings is prepared to have all the booty in the cellar moved on a moment's notice through the passageway to my former home." Dallas took another drink of ale as she tried to recall what else she'd accomplished in her husband's absence. "Oh, yes, Cummings is considering the possibility of deeding the town house over to Walter Ramsay temporarily so that it would be in his name instead of yours and therefore safe from confiscation. I've practiced your signature and can reproduce it almost precisely—I've always had a knack for that sort of thing.

Now the same ruse might work for the lands at Beauly and Inverness, but that's a more complicated situation ...."

Fraser was laughing helplessly. "I should have known you'd not sit idle and let the family fortune be spirited away! But forgery?" He shook his head at her ingenuous lack of scruples.

"Oh, fie, Iain, it's hardly forgery under the circumstances. If we truly belong to each other as we've vowed, then your signature is as much mine as yours, correct?" Dallas looked so sincere that Fraser began to laugh again. Unable to think of an answer to Dallas's peculiar logic, he dumped some coins on the table and stood up. "I don't think I can stand any more devious intrigues this evening from you, Dallas. Since I have so little time, I suggest we spend the remainder of it doing something less cerebral."

Dallas carefully pulled her skirts free of the splinters in the aged inglenook. "You chose this place well, Iain, we're fortunate that no one from the court has come here."

"They have better taste." Steering Dallas towards a narrow stairway, he let her proceed him up to the room.

"Now," he said when they were inside the homely little chamber to which the innkeeper had ushered him earlier in the day, "let's see how you look with my bairn inside you."

"Fat," Dallas declared as she let Fraser unfasten her gown. "You may hate the sight of me."

A rushlight burned low on a shabby bureau. The room's only window was uncurtained and the heavy mist trickled down in uneven paths on the warped, dirty panes. Outside, two angry cats squalled at one another.

"Oh, lassie," Fraser asserted as Dallas's garments dropped to the floor, "you are bonnie and bountiful. See how rounded you are," he said as his hands caressed the swelling abdomen. "And your breasts—they are fuller and finer than ever." He cupped each one in his hands, jiggling them experimentally.

"I feel uncomely," Dallas replied in an almost diffident tone. She was surprised by her own shyness; though this was the second child she would bear her husband, he had never before seen her pregnant body. She could not help but think that he must be comparing her to the flawless beauties he had known—and even to her own usual lithe, slender self.

But Fraser never took his eyes off her as he undressed. She had moved to the bed where she pulled a worn blanket around her shoulders as much as to hide herself as to ward off the cold.

"How could I hate the sight of seeing you filled with me?" he asked as he sat beside her. "No man should ever despise the proof of his manhood." Fraser held her face between his hands and kissed her mouth. Dallas clung to him, keenly aware of her hunger for his lovemaking. Diffidence overcome by her husband's assertions and her own desire, she fell back on the bed, pulling him down with her. Fraser's kisses covered her body, from her throat to her breasts, to the soft, firm mound of her belly and at last between her thighs.

Dallas moaned with pleasure and pressed his dark head even more closely. At last he entered her, but more cautiously than in times past, and though his thrusts were deep and sure, there was a sense of cherishing as well as passion in his embrace. Dallas almost wept with joy as her husband brought them both to the pinnacle of ecstasy. Afterwards, he stayed inside her for a long, lingering moment, and his kiss seemed to draw the very life from her soul.

"To think I ever fought you off!" she said when he finally released them both and was stroking the curve of her shoulder. "Perhaps I should have read less of history and more of love."

"No matter, lovey," Fraser said with a grin as he pulled the blankets around them. "You learn your lessons very well."

LATER, SHE SLEPT dreamlessly, curled up against her husband. But long before dawn, he was awake, dressing quietly in the darkness. Dallas had sensed his departure from the lumpy bed. Half-asleep, she rolled over to feel the patched blanket still warm from Fraser's body. "Iain?" Anxiously, she peered into the gloom.

"I'm here, lovey," he answered low. "I'd have awakened you before I left, but it's best I go while it's still dark. In the morning, you'll be safe to join the usual traffic up Leith Wynd to Edinburgh. Go west from here, to the fowler's stall, then past the fishmonger's and you're in the wynd."

Her eyes had grown accustomed to the darkness. She could make out her husband's form, already covered by the heavy cloak. "I won't ask when you'll come back. I don't want to coax you into disaster."

Fraser stuffed his leather gloves into his belt, then came to take Dallas in his arms. "You're cold, lassie. Keep warm and well." He kissed her mouth, her eyelids, the tip of her nose. She held him close, hating to surrender his touch, yet knowing she mustn't detain him any longer. "Take care of Magnus and this new one," he admonished, stroking her stomach. "I promise I'll be with you when the bairn is born." He kissed her one last time, grinned with sheer pleasure at the look of love in her big eyes, and then moved quietly out into the corridor.

DELPHINIA DOUGLAS AND Catherine Gordon were two of the last people on earth with whom Dallas cared to spend an evening. Yet she was flanked by both women, playing a game of Sept-et-Un with George Gordon, Lord Bothwell and David Rizzio.

Naturally, Delphinia and Catherine liked each other only slightly better than they liked Dallas. Catherine not only loathed her former lover's wife but had grown fearful of her since the night in Fraser's rooms. For months, she'd worried about poison or a chance encounter with Dallas in a deserted palace corridor. Though she had spoken to Fraser since that terrifying night, and he had assured her his wife was not a potential murderess, Catherine could never look at Dallas without feeling afraid.

Delphinia's attitude was quite different. Far shrewder than Catherine, Delphinia knew that Dallas was obsessed with love for her husband and therefore vulnerable. The besotted little chit was swollen with another babe; if she kept that up, she'd eventually look like a sow. With any real luck, Dallas might even die in childbirth. Delphinia had no intention of giving up.

"My trick," Bothwell asserted, slapping his card on top of Gordon's. "Your play, Catherine, or are you woolgathering?"

Catherine blushed prettily as she turned a knave face up. "My luck is poor tonight. Perhaps I should quit while I'm ahead."

"Except you're not ahead, sweet Cat," George Gordon pointed out. "I can't afford to go on staking you unless your fortunes change soon."

"At least," Rizzio put in, grimacing comically at Dallas, "we don't have to play your sister tonight. The lovely Tarrill is uncanny with the cards."

"She's with the Queen," Dallas said. Tarrill, in effect, had taken over Dallas's post with Mary Stuart these past months. Only on rare occasions, when the Queen required her full complement of ladies, was Dallas asked to join the retinue. Though she was annoyed by this treatment, she continued to stay on at court. As long as Mary Stuart didn't formally dismiss her, Dallas felt it best to remain near the center of events.

And recently she had seen the first glimmer of hope. Darnley was finally beginning to exasperate even the infinite bounds of Mary's love. His liking for low company, his excessive drinking, his neglect of duty and his increasingly callous attitude towards Mary herself had all begun to turn spring's passion into winter's disenchantment.

But Darnley had one monumental accomplishment to shore up his position: The Queen was pregnant. No matter how odious he had become to his enemies, he had sired the future heir to the throne.

It was Dallas's turn to be caught unprepared for the next round of play. Rizzio tactfully drew her back into the game, but she made a stupid blunder and lost the trick to Gordon.

"Dallas, I'm amazed," Gordon remarked with a lift of his golden eyebrows. "Your keen mind seems to have deserted you."

Dallas's eyes narrowed. "You know the saying, George," she said, glancing at Catherine as well. "Lucky at cards, unlucky at love. Still, I like to win—at both."

Gordon smirked, Catherine blushed and Delphinia chuckled in her throaty manner. Dallas now concentrated fully, raking in the next two tricks and was almost certain she had the last one—and the game. Triumphantly, she put down her king, only to have Delphinia slowly and smugly play the ace.

"Fie," Dallas grumbled, "I thought all the aces were gone!"

"Nay, madame," Delphinia purred. "I always keep something in reserve." She scooped the pile of coins in the direction of her magnificent bosom and gave Dallas a sidelong look. "Never fear, I'm not one to throw my hand in until the final game is over."

Later, after the others had gone, Dallas remained with Bothwell, taking a last cup of mulled wine. "I should have thrown the cards in her face," she sighed, "but I wouldn't give her such satisfaction."

Bothwell leaned back, putting both feet up on one of the empty chairs. "Pah, no need to concern yourself, Dallas. You're Iain's wife, you hold all the real cards."

Dallas had kicked off her shoes and was massaging one of her feet. She felt at ease with Bothwell, he was Fraser's friend, even if he had gotten her husband into numerous scrapes in the past. Dallas felt she could trust him and, unlike so many other women at court, could admire his rough-hewn physical charm without being personally attracted by it.

Bothwell, on the other hand, had found Dallas much changed since the night he'd witnessed her marriage to Fraser some four years earlier. Nubile but frigid, bonnie but independent, that had been his opinion at the time, and he'd frankly wondered why Fraser had taken her to wife. But upon getting better acquainted with her since his return to court, he perceived the difference the years—and no doubt Fraser—had made in Dallas, and now found her company stimulating.

"You're right, I suppose," Dallas conceded. "But then I'm easily upset these days, with Iain gone for so long and the babe due in just two months. Does the Queen ever mention him?"

Bothwell poured more wine for himself but Dallas refused another cup. "Yes. But she refuses to reinstate him."

Dallas pulled her fox-trimmed shawl more closely about her shoulders to ward off the late-night January draughts of Linlithgow Palace. "She is threatening to attaint the dissident nobles when Parliament meets. I keep hoping that as Darnley falls from favor she'll change her mind."

"She may yet," Bothwell said. "James still plays his waiting game in Newcastle, hoping his royal half-sister will relent."

"I'd like to see James attainted—but if he is, Iain will be, too," Dallas fretted. "I wish to God I could do more for Iain. I feel so helpless." She sighed and turned to Bothwell. "What do you want, now that you're back in the Queen's good graces?"

The Border Earl chuckled as he riffled through the deck of playing cards, which still lay on the table. "A rich wife, for one thing, but I'm assured of that. Plans are underway for my marriage to Jean Gordon next month."

"George's sister?" Dallas shifted in her chair, for the babe had begun to stir strenuously in her womb. "I'd heard some gossip linking your names, but I'd also heard Jean Gordon's heart beat in a different direction."

"That's the lady. Oh, it's no love match, but she'll do as she's told, and since George is now Earl of Huntly, his wishes are to be obeyed."

Dallas leaned forward, elbows on the table, slim fingers pressed together under her chin. "You and George will make a strong alliance. As friends of Iain's, can you not bind together to reinstate him?"

Bothwell frowned. "I told you, I've made certain hints to the Queen, but she seems implacable ...."

"You made them alone," Dallas pointed out, "but if you and George both press for his return, you might succeed."

The heavy dark-red brows lifted slightly. "Mayhap. But I wouldn't count on it in our sovereign's present mood. Pregnancy has weakened her, physically and emotionally. There are undercurrents I much mislike these days. I would to God I could take these cards and foretell the future."

Dallas understood what Bothwell meant. "Maybe it's well that we can't know the future," she said at last. "If we did, we might not be able to face it."

Chapter Twenty-Four

THREE WEEKS LATER Tarrill lay ill at Holyrood with a raging fever and severe stomach cramps. The Queen's physician had been called, diagnosed the disease as a form of influenza, and assured Dallas that her sister would recover. "But," he warned Dallas, "in your condition, I'd stay away from her until she is well."

Dallas was loath to take his advice but did. She summoned Donald to look after Tarrill, packed a boxful of belongings, and had a coach take her to the town house where she spent several days playing with her son and teaching him his ABC's.

Donald McVurrich's visits to Tarrill during her week-long illness had created yet another bond between them. On her first day out of bed, he had finally plucked up the courage to kiss her. To his surprise, she kissed him back. Donald began to wonder if his hopes might aspire to his heart's ambition.

Dallas noted the change between them when she returned to Holyrood. Tarrill, however, was not all that pleased to see her sister come back. "You're less than a month away from being due," she reminded Dallas. "You ought to stay at the town house where Flora and Dr. Wilson can tend you."

But Dallas shook her head. "Nay, Tarrill, the days drag by so now, and with Iain still away, I think I'd go mad just sitting around. I can't get down on the floor to play with Magnus, I can't hold him in my lap, it's most frustrating. At least here, something is always happening to stir my interest."

"If you call one pregnant woman watching another interesting," she said with some asperity. "The Queen moans and groans all the time, smiling only at Rizzio. And don't think there aren't any number of people who find that irksome!"

"I wouldn't think you'd be one of them," Dallas commented mildly. "You've always seemed to like Davie well enough."

"I still do, it's the situation I don't like. I've never cared for intrigue or politics." She rubbed her fingers along her temples and gave Dallas a faint smile. "I still have headaches from my illness, maybe that's what makes me irascible. Thank heaven Donald comes by to cheer me every day."

Dallas made no comment but was almost as grateful as Tarrill for Donald's attentions to her sister.

MARY STUART EMERGED from her cocoon of pregnancy to take part in the Bothwell-Gordon nuptials. Once again, she played the royal patroness, paying for Jean's wedding gown, giving advice on the festivities, and refraining from criticism of Bothwell's insistence on being married according to Protestant rite.

Dallas did not attend the wedding but managed to find an elegant silver-edged mirror in the secret cellar which she dispatched as a gift. Impatient for the babe's birth and extremely uncomfortable, Dallas spent that twenty-fourth day of February watching Magnus build a fort on the nursery floor. Later, while he was taking a rare nap, she wrote again to Lord Hugh Fraser, this time boldly asking for his clan's assistance in the event Parliament moved to attaint her husband.

The following week, Dallas discovered she had acted none too soon: Parliament was to convene on March seventh; James Stuart and Iain Fraser were to be attainted on March twelfth. Dallas was back at Holyrood when she heard the shattering news. She immediately sought an audience with the Queen but was turned away by David Rizzio.

"Her Grace is unwell again," he said, his huge eyes sympathetic, though for the Queen or herself, Dallas could not tell. "She must rest, if she is to open Parliament on Thursday."

"Davie, you know how imperative it is that I see her," Dallas implored, wishing the babe would stop churning in her womb. "If there is any chance at all that she'll grant me an interview, you'll let me know, won't you?"

This time Dallas was certain Rizzio's compassionate gaze was meant for her alone. "I will, I promise. Now rest yourself, *madonna mia*, you are pale as ash."

Dallas did rest, that day and the next. By Thursday she felt somewhat better, though Rizzio had sent no summons. From her window, Dallas watched the procession form in the courtyard before heading to the new Tolbooth where Parliament would assemble. She saw Bothwell, George Gordon and several other nobles surrounding the magnificently gowned Queen, but Darnley was nowhere in sight. Sulking no doubt, Dallas decided, as she turned away from the window in disgust.

Two days later, Tarrill came into their chambers just before suppertime. "Oh, Dallas," she moaned, her hands pressing her temples, "I have one of those wretched headaches! Could you take my place with the Queen?"

Dallas laid aside the little bedgown she'd been sewing for the new babe. "Don't be absurd, you know the Queen won't want me in attendance. I've been waiting a week to see her and she's ignored my pleas for an audience."

Tarrill was wringing out a cloth in cold water. "Then I'd think you'd jump at this opportunity," she said querulously. "Knowing I'm not well, she could hardly turn you away."

"That doesn't mean she'd consent to let me speak," Dallas pointed out. "Besides, I can scarcely move. Go find someone else to take your place."

But Tarrill was already on the bed with the cloth over her forehead. "I can't get up again, I have to lie still. If you won't go, do be quiet!"

Dallas complied, for at least five minutes. Maybe Tarrill was right, maybe in that intimate atmosphere the Queen would listen to her entreaties, maybe if the pregnant Queen saw Dallas so close to giving birth, she'd relent. There was so little time before Parliament would act. Clumsily, Dallas struggled to her feet and trudged slowly but quietly from the room.

THE LITTLE SUPPER closet off the Queen's bedchamber was lighted with a dozen candles, casting an amber glow on the party already assembled at the long narrow table. Dallas hoped her entrance would be unobtrusive, but her unwieldy condition made such a wish impossible. As Dallas attempted a futile curtsy, the Queen looked faintly dismayed, nodded abruptly and gazed down at her plate.

Dallas sat at Tarril's place between Lord Robert and Arthur Erskine. Once again, Dallas noted that Darnley was not in his wife's company. Rizzio was helping Jean Argyll to a plate of breaded oysters. Anthony Standen, the Queen's page, was pouring white wine for his mistress. Later, perhaps, Dallas tried to console herself, when they played cards or listened to music, the Queen might unbend and hear her out.

They were just finishing the first course when the door to the privy staircase opened, revealing the elongated figure of Lord Darnley. The Queen's surprise was more obvious this time, but her welcome was almost as chilly.

"I thought you'd be in the town, as is your wont," she said pointedly. The Queen turned to Standen. "Anthony, fetch His Grace a chair." She turned her attention back to her food while Darnley edged nervously up to the table.

Dallas felt what little hope she'd had melt away. The evening was going to be a disaster. With Darnley lurking about, there would be no opportunity for her to plead Fraser's case. All appetite vanished, she pushed her plate aside, and wondered if she should excuse herself and leave.

Before she could make up her mind, the privy staircase door opened for a second time. This time the others were as startled as the Queen, for Patrick Ruthven stood in the doorway, the glint of armor showing under his court gown.

Looking around Erskine's shoulder, Dallas noted that Ruthven's eyes were wild and his skin was dead white. Will Ruthven had confided recently to Jean Argyll that his father was mortally ill. Dallas wondered if the man were in a delirium and had wandered by accident into the supper room.

But Ruthven's voice was coherent when he finally broke the sudden silence: "Your Grace," he said with a curt nod to the Queen, "let yon David come out; he's been here too long."

The Queen gasped; Lord Robert's hand went to his side, but he wasn't armed. Darnley looked down at the table, unable to meet his wife's angry gaze. "Is this your doing?" she demanded of her husband. "What impertinence do we have now?"

"It's—it's for your own good," he mumbled in reply.

The Queen was about to upbraid Darnley further but Ruthven broke in: "Madame, you have relied too long on this foreign secretary of yours—his arrogance is insufferable, his influence is insupportable, and his familiarity with your person is beyond contempt."

Rizzio had scrambled from his chair and backed down along the table to cower by the room's only window. Ruthven pushed his way past the others but was momentarily diverted by Arthur Erskine. Jean Argyll cried out, Lord Robert leaped up to aid Erskine, and the Queen reeled against the table.

"Lay no hands on me!" Ruthven shouted. And then the room was filled with hurtling bodies as several men rushed through the privy staircase door. One or two of the Douglases, Ker of Fawdonside, Will Ruthven, and at least three others Dallas didn't recognize, were charging in Rizzio's direction. Chairs overturned, plates crashed to the floor, one of the velvet wall hangings was ripped loose and fell in green and crimson waves across the carpet. Jean Argyll just managed to grab a single taper as the candelabra toppled over the table's edge.

Somehow, the Queen had reached Rizzio's side, where he knelt, clinging to her skirts. Ker and one of the other men held pistols, while the rest of the intruders brandished long, gleaming daggers. Someone reached out to wrest Rizzio away from the Queen, their shadows dancing grotesquely off the wall like so many writhing bats. In a confusion of motion, noise and terror, the little secretary was dragged from the supper room, out through the bedchamber and into the adjoining room above the main stairway. His frantic cries echoed back to the immobilized supper party: "*Justizia, justizia!*" he screamed. "*Sauvez ma vie, madame, sauvez ma vie!*" Scuffling sounds, more cries—then silence.

"Jesu!" Dallas whispered, leaning against the wall. A vague pain fluttered across her back but there was no time to think of that now. People seemed to come racing in from all directions, Mary Stuart's attendants through one door, the assassins' accomplices through the other. Somehow, the Queen's people managed to disperse the assailants who retreated into the bedchamber.

"Miserable cur!" Mary Stuart screamed at Darnley. "You are the guilty party, more so than the others! Oh, God help me, I'm surrounded by traitors!"

Just then Ruthven staggered back through the door and collapsed into a chair. He was sweating profusely and gasping for breath. Grabbing the decanter of white wine, he sloshed some into a glass and drank greedily.

"And you, Patrick Ruthven," the Queen cried, whirling on the shaking nobleman, "you'll suffer for this, I swear it by the babe I carry in my womb!" She pressed a hand to her side and ordered Jean Argyll to find out what had befallen the pathetic Rizzio. Darnley was at the window, calling down to the townspeople who had heard the commotion and were beginning to assemble in the courtyard. Mary moved towards him, but Lord Lindsay, who had just entered the supper room, roughly pulled her away.

"Keep your distance, madame," he commanded, "or I'll cut you into collops!"

The look of hatred which Mary Stuart cast upon him would have withered a more sensitive man. Jean Argyll burst through the door. "Davie is done to death," she shrieked hysterically, "butchered by these madmen!"

The Queen swayed, caught herself on the table and made a stupendous effort to regain her composure. Ruthven and Darnley were slinking away, but Mary made no move to stop them. She muttered something in French, put an arm around Jean Argyll, and turned her face away. Lord Robert came to comfort both his sisters, telling them that they had best retire before the evening's terrible events did serious mischief to the Queen and her child.

Throughout these exchanges, Dallas had been frantically pondering what could be done to help the Queen. Was Rizzio the only intended victim? Would the assassins return to slay their sovereign? Or did they hope that the tragedy would trigger a miscarriage and possibly eliminate both mother and child in one blow? Dallas was sure of only one thing: She must find Lord Bothwell. He'd know what to do, he'd take decisive action.

Dallas stumbled out through the bedchamber and into the adjoining room. She paused, eyes riveted on a pool of blood near the top of the stairs. Rizzio must have been murdered there, then dragged down the steps and out of the palace. Repelled by the brutal imagery, she picked up her skirts to avoid the crimson stain. A third of the way down the staircase, she stopped suddenly as the flutter of pain assailed her lower back once more. This time there was no mistaking the cause: Dallas knew her labor had begun.

After the spasm passed, she moved slowly but resolutely down the stairs. Certainly Bothwell wouldn't have been involved in the ghastly plot. And surely he'd want to help the Queen. She moved cautiously, struck by the ominous calm in the immediate vicinity. Outside, she could still hear a few shouts from the citizenry and somewhere off in the distance, horses clattered off over the cobblestones of the Canongate.

Dallas had just entered the east wing when a figure moved out of the shadows. It was one of Morton's Douglases, wearing chain mail and a steel cap. She stopped, wondering if he'd bother to detain her.

But he recognized her from the supper room and moved to block her way. "Lady Fraser?" His cold blue eyes surveyed her from under dark brows which grew almost together over the bridge of his nose. "Go to your chamber. Stay there until you're released."

"I'm no prisoner here," Dallas retorted. "I'll go where I please. Now step aside." She made a clumsy gesture to push his arm away but one hand shoved her backwards.

"You heard me. Go to your rooms. This is no night for gallantry." His voice was rough, faintly slurred with drink.

Angry as she was, Dallas realized she had to comply. But the pain came again and she was paralyzed by it, unable to either move or speak. Douglas mistook her frozen state for disobedience and slapped her hard across the face.

"Bitch! Go now, or suffer the same fate as Rizzio!" Dallas didn't doubt that he meant the threat. One hand touched her stinging cheek, the other clutched her abdomen. "Nay ...." she murmured, "I cannot—the babe ...."

"No tricks!" Douglas grabbed her by the shoulder, a knife held menacingly in his other hand.

"Please ...." She saw Douglas fuzzily before her, the knife raised in mid-air. She saw something else, another man, a flash of steel, and then Douglas thudded facedown onto the floor.

"Dallas!" Fraser scooped her up in his arms and moved as quickly as possible back towards the staircase. "Where are your rooms? Please, lassie, try to tell me!"

"Up the stairs … left … third door, there's a torch outside." As the pain ebbed once more, Dallas's mind and eyes began to come back into focus. "Let me walk, I must weigh ten stone! Oh, Iain, I can't believe you're here, it's a miracle!"

"A lucky guess," Fraser grunted. "No talking, no walking, I'll manage." But his bulky burden didn't make for an easy task. He finally reached the room and kicked the door open with his foot. Tarrill and Donald were standing close together, astonished and afraid.

Fraser waved their cluster of questions aside and laid Dallas on the bed. "Do you know how to deliver a baby, Tarrill?" he asked, loosening the hooks of Dallas's gown.

"I helped Marthe when Glennie gave birth to Jamie," she answered hesitantly. "But 'twas a long time ago."

Fraser turned grimly to Donald. "And you?"

"Nay," he replied, horrified at the prospect of being pressed into service, "I know nothing about bairns. Farm animals are all I ken."

"Fie, Donald, I'm not a sow or a ewe. Why don't you fetch the court physician?" Dallas was sitting up, clutching her loosened gown around her bosom. The pains appeared to have subsided temporarily and the shocks of the last hour had not yet taken their toll.

Tarrill sat down gingerly on the edge of the bed. "Dr. Arnault is not here, Dallas, he's with a sick relation in Restalrig. I know, because Mary Fleming was here to tell us about poor Rizzio and she had already tried to find the doctor to attend the Queen. There's no midwife in the palace, either."

Dallas swore under her breath, then shook her head in ironic dismay. "By heaven, I'd like to bear a babe some day in relative peace! My deliveries seem to take place at the most inopportune times!" She turned to her husband who was standing beside her, frowning at the bulge of her abdomen. "Iain," she commanded, "if you don't tell me how you really happened to have materialized from nowhere, I'll burst with more than just the babe."

Fraser eased himself onto the bed, his hand on her shoulder. "I knew approximately when the baby was due. I promised to be with you this time." He gently pushed her back against the pillows before launching into the rest of his story. "We sailed the *Richezza* to the Isle of Lewes, then I rode to Beauly where Sorcha told me about your letter to Lord Hugh." He stopped, aware that Dallas had gone as white as the pillowcase. "What is it, lassie? Another pain?"

"Nay," Dallas gasped, clumsily shifting her bulk in the bed. "My water broke."

Fraser looked up helplessly at Tarrill. Donald looked away, embarrassed and ill at ease. "It's all right," Tarrill soothed. "It just means that real labor should begin now. Come, Dallas," she went on, helping her sister move over to the edge of the bed, "we'll put a blanket over the wet spot so you don't take a chill."

" 'Tis easier with ewes," Donald murmured to Fraser, who had gotten up from the bed while Tarrill tended Dallas.

"Sweet Christ," Fraser muttered to nobody in particular. It occurred to him that though he may have been a father more times than he would ever know, he'd never actually seen a baby born. A new sense of guilt assailed him as he thought of the women who had borne his children and of how Dallas had gone through all of this before without him.

"Don't stop talking, Iain," Dallas commanded as she settled back down in the middle of the bed. "It keeps me distracted."

Fraser came back to sit gingerly beside her. "Where was I?" He took her hand and brushed the tip of her nose with his lips. "Oh, aye, I went to the town house, Cummings told me where you were, and then I sent a message to Bothwell so he could get me into Holyrood. A few minutes after we sneaked up to his rooms, all hell broke loose ...."

But Fraser was interrupted again as Dallas clutched at his hand and writhed in pain. Transfixed, he stared at his wife until the spasm passed. "Go on, go on." She was grimfaced and breathless but insisted that Fraser keep up his narrative.

"Before we could decide what to do, one of Bothwell's men came flying into the room, crying that Rizzio was murdered and that the conspirators were coming after Bothwell and probably intended to kill George Gordon, Fleming and Livingstone as well. We could hear the tramp of boots and rattle of steel somewhere close by, and when the door burst open again we thought we would have to fight for our lives, but it was George, fleeing the assassins."

This time Fraser recognized the anguish in Dallas's huge eyes before her body began to tense with the next pain. He stopped, felt her fingernails bite into his flesh, pressed his lips together in a tight, grim line and waited. Without urging, he took up his tale as Dallas slumped back against the pillows. "I told Bothwell and George to jump out the window, it was only a few feet to the ground. They wanted me to come with them but I couldn't leave you here, lassie, with murderers crawling all over the place. You can imagine how astonished I was when I found you with that cur of a Douglas waving his dirk at you."

Shakily, Dallas reached up to touch her bruised cheek. "It was a nightmare. I can hardly take it all in."

Tarrill stared at Dallas and Fraser. "One of the Douglases threatened you with a knife? Oh, Dallas!"

"I hope to God I killed the whoreson," Fraser asserted as Dallas began to groan again. This time the sound grew more high-pitched and its intensity made Fraser grind his teeth. He found himself speechless when the pain finally passed.

"Why did they kill Davie?" Tarrill asked, knowing that silence would serve her sister ill. "Was it just resentment?"

Fraser rallied enough to reply. "He was a symbol of many things, I suppose—lowly birth, foreign intervention, the old faith. And Darnley was crazed with jealousy." Donald shook his head. "Poor little Davie. He was a good-hearted fellow."

"He was one of the few who was kind to me when I first came to court," Dallas said in a shaky voice. It was the last coherent sentence she would speak for the next hour; the room became a bedlam with her cries as Tarrill mopped the sweat from her sister's brow with one hand and forced whiskey down her throat with the other. Fraser held his wife by the shoulders, to keep her from rolling off the bed. Donald busied himself with emptying a bureau drawer and lining it with soft linen for the baby's arrival. At one point he went to the door when a guard knocked loudly to demand what all the commotion was about. Donald shouted back that Lady Fraser was giving birth and to mind his own business.

For Fraser, Dallas's agony seemed to go on forever. Duels to the death, battles on the high seas, lethal political intrigue, imprisonment and exile—all were situations he could master. But his pain-wracked lassie filled him with helpless frustration.

And then Dallas let out one final ear-piercing shriek as the bairn's head appeared between her thighs.

"Thank God," breathed Tarrill, and the next few minutes were spent in a frenzy of bringing the new babe into the world.

The church bells chimed midnight as Dallas lay exhausted and Fraser cradled his second son against his chest.

"Another boy, lovey," he grinned in spite of himself. "You'll have to wait until next time for your lassie."

"Next time!" Dallas gasped. "Don't speak to me of next time!"

Fraser looked shame-faced. "I'm sorry, Dallas, my poor sweet mite, I swear to God I suffered as much as you did just now."

"Then you have the lassie," Dallas said and drifted off into a deep sleep.

Chapter Twenty-Five

Fraser slept beside Dallas that night, the bairn slumbered in the makeshift cradle by the divan where Tarrill was stretched out, and Donald sprawled under a big quilt on the floor. None of them, not even the new babe, stirred before eight o'clock.

Tarrill was the first one up, rousing Donald with instructions to beg, bribe or barter his way out of the palace and return with a wet nurse. She herself would go down to the royal kitchens to fetch some breakfast.

Their departure awoke Fraser who got up just as the babe began to squall. He carried the bairn about the room, hoping the little cries wouldn't wake Dallas.

They did, of course. Looking ghostly and feeling weak, she moved her head to watch Fraser and the babe. "Bring him here, Iain. I haven't really seen him yet."

As Fraser placed the little bundle in her arms she gasped with astonishment: The child had bright red hair and looked like neither of his parents. "By heaven," Dallas gasped, "I just assumed he'd look like Magnus! Who has red hair in your family?"

Fraser's mouth twisted wryly. "My mother was dark, I'm told. I would guess my father's side of the family has passed the red hair on to the bairn."

Dallas touched the tiny pink cheek with her forefinger. "Whoever he takes after, he's sweet as honey. But I think he's hungry. I have no milk yet and probably never will, if I'm dry as I was with Magnus. Maybe he'd be content to suckle anyway."

Fraser watched Dallas put the babe to her breast. "I think I'm jealous. It's been a long time since I've had any taste of you, lovey."

She smiled at him over the fuzzy red head. "I'll not be fit for much for a while, I'm afraid."

"I'll wait," he asserted in a tone which made Dallas think he actually might. "But right now we've got to name the little scamp. I've been thinking, up in the Highlands I knew a wonderful old poacher named ...."

"Oh, no, not this time! It's my turn—I still haven't recovered from Magnus." Dallas shifted the babe from one breast to the other as her chin jutted out. "This one's to be called Robert, after the Bruce. He was a great hero of my father's."

Fraser rubbed at the dark stubble on his chin. "Robert. Well, it's unexciting but solid. If you insist, lassie."

Dallas did. After the newly named Robert had satisfied himself, she handed the child back to Fraser. "What are we going to do now?" she asked as her husband strolled around the room with his son propped against his shoulder. "Eventually they're bound to find out you're here."

Fraser hadn't had much time to contemplate his next move. The events of the previous night had thrown his earlier plans into confusion. He had intended to see the Queen and use his considerable powers of persuasion to change her mind. He knew he might fail, but continued exile from Scotland—and from Dallas—had become intolerable.

But if the Queen was being held captive, she was powerless to help him. Bothwell had told Fraser that he thought one of the motives for Rizzio's murder had been the banishment of the Protestant lords. Fraser, however, was no Protestant, and he certainly had no desire to throw in his lot with the likes of Patrick Ruthven, the Douglases and their ilk. As for James Stuart, where did he fit in?

At least one of his questions was answered when Tarrill returned a few minutes later carrying a hamper of food. "The Queen's under guard, sequestered with Darnley. Lady Huntly, George Gordon's mother, is with them. Her Grace is said to be well and calm. You can't help but admire her courage."

"I've never doubted Mary Stuart's pluck," Fraser commented, helping himself to a fresh-baked roll and sausage. Despite the terrors of the previous night, life was apparently going on in some sort of routine fashion at Holyrood.

"Imagine, Will Ruthven being part of such a horrible crime! To think I ever cared for him!" Tarrill spoke with fervor as she dished up boiled eggs for Dallas. "Lord Lindsay has been most callous with the Queen," she went on, plumping up the pillows behind her sister. "It's said he threatens to lock her away at Stirling while Darnley rules in her stead."

"Jesu," Dallas exclaimed, "I heard such rumors weeks ago but never thought anyone would be foolish enough to set Darnley up as king in his own right. The conspirators must be daft."

"Or uncommonly canny," Fraser pointed out. "Darnley would make an admirable puppet."

Donald returned just then with a bedraggled-looking wench no more than a child herself. The engorged breasts, however, indicated that she was no maid but a mother.

"I found her in the Grassmarket," Donald said somewhat apologetically. "Her name is Meg and her own bairn died aborning just a few days ago."

Dallas eyed the girl skeptically. "She needs a good scrubbing, if you ask me. Have you any family, Meg?"

Terrified blue eyes blinked rapidly at Dallas, then looked down at the floor. She was pitifully thin, with stringy blond hair and an angular face which might have been presentable with proper attention. A nervous garbled account finally explained her plight: Unwed, Meg had been thrown out of her parents' house when they learned she was with child. She had lived with her sister in Potter Row Port, but there were too many mouths to feed and Meg had decided to leave when her baby was born dead.

Pity overcame repugnance, and Dallas smiled at the girl. "You'll be better off with us," she said kindly, knowing full well that if left on her own Meg would end up starving to death or selling her body for a few coins. "We're a bit, uh, unsettled just now, perhaps you've heard what's been happening at the palace. Tarrill, can you see that she gets a bath?"

Her sister obliged, while Donald insisted on escorting them. The mood of the palace was still tense and he didn't want Tarrill walking unescorted through the corridors.

"A nuisance for Tarrill and Donald," Fraser commented after they'd left. "I could have given the lassie a bath myself."

"Fie, Iain, you can't be that desperate!" Dallas made as if to throw a crust of bread at him, felt too weary to bother, and collapsed back against the pillows. "Well? Have you figured out what we're going to do?"

Fraser paused by the makeshift cradle to be sure little Robert was all right. "Aye, I have. You'll stay here until you're well enough to go back to the town house. As for me, I think I may have figured out a way to gain the Queen's pardon."

Dallas eyed him warily. "How?" she inquired.

"Simple enough," Fraser responded, hooking his thumbs in his belt .... "I'm going to help her escape."

ANDREW KER OF Fawdonside stood outside the door of the Queen's chamber, his pistol balanced in his hand. Two guards lounged nearby, vaguely curious about the tall, dark-haired woman with the tiny bairn in her arms.

"I tell you, Her Grace would want to see the babe as proof that her lady-in-waiting has been delivered safely in spite of last night's events." Tarrill spoke with authority. Little by little, her youthful diffidence and nai'veté were giving way to a new confidence and self-assurance.

But Ker had already weathered several plots to get Mary Stuart out of the palace that day. The resourceful Lady Huntly had connived at most of them, but so far Ker and his confederate Lindsay had thwarted her. "I can relay the message," Ker asserted. "In truth, the Queen has other things on her mind just now."

"How little you know of women!" Tarrill exclaimed as Robert began to cry. "The Queen will have her own babe soon, yet you think she'd not be interested in my sister's newborn! Oh, sir, you underestimate maternal instincts, whether they be in the heart of a Queen or a ...."

It had been a long day preceded by a longer night, and Ker was weary. The cries of the infant and the relentless voice of Tarrill weakened his obstinacy. "Enough, mistress." He gestured to the guards. "Search her."

Tarrill juggled Robert as she submitted to the guards. Apparently the child armed her against overfamiliar pawing and a minute later, she was ushered into the royal bedchamber.

The Queen was reclining on a divan, a fur throw over her lap. Darnley stood by the window, gazing distractedly out at the March mist. Lord Lindsay sat in an armchair, picking his teeth with his dirk while the indomitable Lady Huntly chased one of the Queen's terriers away from Tarrill's skirt.

Mary Stuart was surprised to see Tarrill and her tiny bundle. She had not yet heard about Dallas's delivery and, indeed, had forgotten all about the other woman's advanced state of pregnancy in her anxiety over the welfare of her own unborn royal babe. "He's adorable," she cooed, pulling the blanket aside for a better look. "And red hair! Tarrill, I treated your sister badly last night. I regret my behavior very much."

"As matters turned out, I'm sure Dallas will not think unkindly of you, Your Grace." Tarrill noted that the Queen was pale but composed. Her eyes were reddened and fatigue lines showed around her mouth, but otherwise she was concealing the ravages of the previous night remarkably well. Glancing discreetly around her, Tarrill made sure that Darnley was still looking out the window and that her back was turned to Lindsay. "See, madame," she said, pulling aside the blanket, "how long he is! And touch his hand, it's soft as gosling fluff."

Only the twitch of a muscle next to the Queen's mouth revealed her surprise as she saw the rolled-up piece of paper tucked between Robert's small arm and chest. She made as if to touch his hand but palmed the paper instead. "A delightful babe," she agreed as her hand slipped beneath the fur throw. "Newborn children are sent to us like welcome messengers from heaven."

"True enough." Tarrill smiled as the two women's eyes locked together in understanding. "And such messengers need not be answered but only accepted as they are."

Darnley swung away from the window, regarding Tarrill and the baby with a petulant expression. "You'll tire Her Grace, she's been through a strenuous time."

Tarrill had to hold her tongue in check; how could Darnley play the hypocrite so blatantly? She curtsied to the royal couple, murmured her farewells, and acknowledged Mary Stuart's dismissal.

WHEN DONALD MCVURRICH had left the palace that morning, he'd taken the simplest and most direct route: Several of the guards on duty were from the royal household but had been ordered, under pain of execution, to serve the conspirators. Donald had selected two he knew well from his own service as a guardsman, explained his mission, and after a minimum of indecision, the men had let him out of the palace. Donald, they reasoned, was an honest man.

But getting Iain Fraser out of Holyrood was a different matter. Not even Donald's staunchest friends would have permitted the outlawed baron to leave the palace. So, well after dark, Fraser and Donald crept downstairs to one of the rear entrances. They waited in the shadows until they heard a crash outside, then Donald raced to the door. The lone guard, whom Donald recognized but did not know well, stood uncertainly at his post, trying to determine from which direction the noise had come.

"Over there!" Donald called in a low voice, all but pushing the smaller man over in his effort to move him away from the door. "It's some knave who tried to assault Mistress Tarrill! He must have jumped out the window!"

Both men ran towards the arbor Donald had indicated. Quick as a cat, Fraser slipped out the door and made for a tree some thirty feet away. He grabbed the lowest limb and swung himself up into the concealing branches.

Donald and the other man searched the area by the arbor carefully. "He must be here," the guard said. "I heard him land."

"Maybe he broke his leg and is unconscious," Donald suggested, making sure his body barred the sight of the bolster Tarrill had thrown out the window. "Or maybe he's slunk away. I'll go around this way, you go back by the trees over there."

The man hesitated, then agreed. A few moments later he was wishing for moonlight or at least a torch when something hit him from straight out of the sky. Fraser had dropped down from the tree, and one blow to the skull knocked the guardsman unconscious. Knowing his luck was running thin, Fraser fled through the palace gardens and into the sanctuary of the misty night.

Donald saw him go, rushed back to retrieve the bolster, and carried it upstairs. He paused just long enough to nod in reassurance to Tarrill and hurried back to the rear entrance in time to see the guardsman trying to sit up.

"What happened, man?" Donald exclaimed as two other guards came cautiously around the corner from another part of the palace grounds.

The man's eyes were still glazed. "I dinna know .... Someone jumped me from yon trees .... Did ye see him?"

"Nay, I was over by the lion pit. Damn," Donald moaned, "he must have run off."

The other two guards were strangers to Donald and eyed him suspiciously. Lindsay's men, Donald decided, judging from their badges. "Who?" one of them asked. "Who got away?"

Donald shrugged. "One of those Frenchy cooks. No loss, I'd say, their food's too rich anyway." He saluted the other men and loped off into the palace.

"I don't like it," the Lindsay retainer said, watching the door swing shut behind Donald. "It may be a trick."

The man Fraser had attacked struggled to his feet and snorted. "It's a love brawl, not politics. Mistress Tarrill is involved and now that Master McVurrich has risen in the world, he'd like to think he owns her. Christ, my pate hurts—have you anything to drink?"

RELIEVED THAT FRASER apparently had gotten away safely, Dallas slept well that night. The following morning she awoke refreshed and wanted to sit up for a while.

But Tarrill reacted with firmness. "You know what happened last time. I'm going to make sure you don't overdo."

Dallas protested but knew Tarrill was right. There'd be no jostling coach rides, no frantic flights, no exertion of any kind for many weeks. No love-making either, she realized with a pang, but put that unhappy thought aside when Meg placed Robert in her arms.

Late that afternoon, a visitor arrived. Donald, who had gone to open the door just enough to see who the newcomer was, found himself staring into the haughty countenance of James Stuart.

"I'm here to see Lady Fraser," James declared, as if his sudden appearance in Holyrood Palace was not in the least out of the ordinary.

Donald hesitated, glancing back to look at Dallas who was reading a history of the Punic Wars. "It's my lord James Stuart of Moray," he told her, seeing her own look of amazement.

Laying the book aside and adjusting the ties of her nightrobe, Dallas instructed Donald to let James in. Striding briskly across the room, the Queen's half-brother allowed Tarrill to pull up a chair for him beside the bed.

"Congratulations, madame," he said with a curt bow. "I understand you've provided your husband with a second heir."

"How kind of you to pay your respects," Dallas said dryly. "Show my lord the babe," she commanded Meg, who was clearly undone by the arrival of such an illustrious personage. "It seems that you and Lady Agnes have some catching up to do," Dallas added smugly.

James glanced with disinterest at little Robert. "All in good time, madame," he said coolly. "If you will, I'd like to speak privately."

Dallas twirled a lock of thick hair around her finger. "Well—under the circumstances my companions are not free to entertain themselves just anywhere. Have you a suggestion, sir?"

"The situation has changed somewhat," James said impatiently. "They may go where they wish, as long as they stay in the palace."

Dallas shrugged. "Very well. Tarrill, why don't you and Donald show Meg how to get to the kitchens?"

The trio trooped from the room while James examined his blunt fingernails. He was dressed in riding clothes which were somewhat rumpled and soiled, and he had aged a bit since Dallas had last seen him.

"Where is Fraser?" James asked without further preamble.

Dallas was still toying with her hair. "Great heaven, I wish I knew. Iain is so unpredictable, such a restless sort." She gave James the most cloying of smiles.

"Madame," James intoned without changing expression, "I know he has been at Holyrood within the last forty-eight hours. He was seen the night Rizzio was murdered."

It was probably true, Dallas reasoned, several people could have glimpsed Fraser while Bothwell and George Gordon were leaping out of windows and general chaos reigned. But James's insinuation about her husband's presence in connection with Rizzio's death was going too far.

"I won't deny Iain was here," Dallas retorted. "Would you deprive a husband the privilege of being with his wife when their child is born?"

James ignored the question. "I've met with the Queen. She is behaving most reasonably and has spoken with the lords who saw fit to dispose of Rizzio. I've personally urged her to act with clemency, but there will be limits to such mercy."

The threatening tone served only to rile Dallas. "I don't understand. You're making no sense, sir."

With a sigh that indicated he felt he was dealing with a particularly obtuse child, James pulled a sheet of parchment from inside his jerkin. "This was entrusted to me earlier today. It's signed by the conspirators who agreed to kill Rizzio."

As James held the parchment up by one corner Dallas scanned the names. Sure enough, between Ruthven's and Morton's signatures was Iain Fraser's. Incredulous, Dallas looked more closely. She had practiced her husband's signature too often not to be familiar with every nuance. For one thing, the two r's in his last name were always dissimilar. And, she noted with relief, the ones etched on the bond were exactly alike.

"Twaddle," Dallas scoffed, flicking at the parchment with her fingernail, "that's a forgery!"

If James was taken aback by her assurance, he didn't show it. "You'd say that, of course. But most people would accept it as proof of your husband's complicity."

"Has the Queen seen this?" she asked, pointing to the parchment.

"Not yet, but she will." James was putting the bond back inside his jerkin. "She might forgive the others since they weren't outlaws to begin with—but for your husband to compound one offense with another even more heinous...." He shook his head dolefully as if he could hardly fathom such evil doings.

To his amazement, Dallas burst out laughing. "Fie, my lord, no wonder Protestants hate playacting. They're so inept at it!" She saw the hooded eyes regard her warily. "Don't feel bad," she went on with mock amicability, "you just made one mistake." She paused but he said nothing. "You put Iain's name on the bond but left off your own."

James's withering glance would have made a less brazen person than Dallas cringe. "Really, madame, such allegations are groundless. I've been in England for months."

"Quite so," Dallas replied. "And only a man who knew something was going to happen could have gotten from Newcastle to Edinburgh so quickly. I've made that trip and I know it can't be done at this time of year within thirty-six hours as you claim. I daresay, James, you must have set out well before the first lunge was ever made at poor Davie! I marvel that no one else has figured that out—yet." James started to interrupt but Dallas was just warming up. "And who has benefited most from Rizzio's death? Not Darnley, who's back cringing at his wife's side. Not Lord Ruthven, who looks ready to drop dead at any moment. As for the others, I can't imagine they'll reap great rewards. But you—you come galloping into Holyrood as the compassionate brother and Mary falls into your arms! It's all very cunning, now it's my turn to congratulate you!"

At this point, Dallas was actually out of breath. She sat back in bed, her arms folded across her bosom. James looked as if he had declared war on himself in a titanic struggle to retain his self-control. At last he stood up, the hooded eyes as expressionless as ever. "Your recent delivery has made you prone to the wildest fancies, madame. I trust you'll get over them quickly. If not," he added in a chilling tone, "I'll make certain that a remedy is provided for you."

STUART OF TRAQUAIR, the Captain of the Royal Guard, had sensed nothing amiss until he felt the cold menace of steel at his throat.

"Keep your cries to yourself and you'll keep your life," a low voice commanded Stuart in a not unpleasant tone. "You and I have business to conduct, in the name of the Queen."

"Fraser?" Stuart turned slightly in the unyielding grip but dared not move further.

"Aye. Are you loyal to the crown of Scotland?" The words were whispered, but intense. The two men stood locked together in the cloister just outside the Chapel Royal at Holyrood. Darkness had set in a bare five minutes earlier and Fraser had been relieved that Stuart had been late in making his evening rounds. He was equally relieved that Donald's information about the captain's routine had been accurate.

But Stuart had not yet answered Fraser's question. "Well?" Fraser pressed his dirk against Stuart's neck. "Speak, dammit, I haven't got all night."

"I could talk better if you'd take away that damnable dirk. My head's a-spin with all that's gone on these past two days."

Fraser considered the matter, decided to trust Donald's opinion of Stuart's devotion to the Queen, and released the other man. Stuart turned around slowly, adjusting the collar of his uniform and trying to assess Fraser's intentions.

"I have a personal loyalty to the Queen, yes. But my men and I have been acting under a certain amount of duress and ...." He chewed his full underlip as his forehead wrinkled in consternation.

"And a house divided?" Fraser's face was half-mocking, half-sympathetic. "Never mind, from now on will you serve the Queen?"

Stuart considered Fraser's question for a moment; it was clear that he was not an impulsive type. "Aye, I will."

"All right. I've not much time to waste," Fraser said, looking into the darkness to make sure they were still unobserved. "Arthur Erskine, Anthony Standen—both are indisputably loyal?"

Another pause. From somewhere in the distance, Fraser heard the sound of heavy footsteps. "I'd say so, yes."

"Others?" Fraser moved deeper into the shadows as the footsteps came closer.

Stuart had heard the noises by now. He peered nervously into the night. "I don't know. I can only vouch for these two."

"Go with them to the Queen. Do as she commands, she knows how to get out of the palace if you will help her." Fraser was already moving away, keeping close to the walls of Holyrood, making sure his boots made as little sound as possible.

There was no response from Stuart, who could make out the forms of the approaching men by now. "Who goes there?" he shouted, very much the Captain of the Guard. Fraser was out of earshot by the time the men replied.

THE ELEMENT OF risk in getting Mary Stuart out of Holyrood was high, but the escape plan was simplicity itself. The scheme hinged on two critical factors—securing Darnley's cooperation so that Mary could get past the sentries on the privy staircase, and making sure that her rescuers waiting in the grounds remained undetected. The success of the first half of the plan lay entirely with the Queen and her ability to win over the unstable Darnley. The second part was up to Fraser.

In the four hours that passed between Fraser's encounter with Stuart of Traquair and the planned escape of the Queen, Holyrood Palace appeared moribund. Scarcely half of the windows showed candlelight behind them and virtually no one went in or out. Fraser remained hidden on the grounds, moving only once, when his retainer, Simpson, came to join him at their appointed rendezvous.

It was only a few minutes before midnight when the two men heard someone walking nearby. Fraser glanced up over the thick yew hedge but could not identify the newcomer in the darkness.

"He's pacing," Simpson whispered. "He keeps going back through the cemetery where Her Grace is supposed to come out."

"Christ." Fraser edged along the ground, stopping at intervals to see if he could recognize the intruder. At last the man stopped by the chapel door, his restless form exuding an air of impatience.

"It's young Ruthven," Fraser said in a low voice. "Damn the whelp, what's he doing out here?"

"Do we skewer him?" asked Simpson, who never balked at bloodshed in a worthy cause.

Fraser didn't reply at once but kept his eyes riveted on Will Ruthven's outline. If all went as planned, the Queen and Darnley would enter the Chapel

Royal from the south door, which provided private access from the palace. They would proceed across the south side to the great west entrance and then out into the cemetery.

Just as Simpson unsheathed his dirk, the figure of a woman appeared along the north side of the chapel. She was moving quickly, her skirts fluttering in the night air.

"Tarrill!" Will called out, his hands turned upwards in a pleading gesture. "Thank God you came!"

"It's madness," she said, out of breath and clearly out of patience as well. "I got your note, I wasn't going to come, but ...."

"I know, I promised a long time ago I'd never approach you again. But I had to explain how I got involved in this dastardly affair, I couldn't spend the rest of my life thinking that you'd condemn me as a murderer."

Fraser and Simpson both knelt motionless by the hedge. Time was running out, it must be almost midnight. Stuart of Traquair and the others should be arriving at any moment. Tarrill knew the escape plan, it had been written out in the note she'd smuggled to the Queen with wee Robert. Why didn't she get Will Ruthven out of the way?

"We can't talk here," Tarrill said, as if in answer to a prayer. "Come, we can go to my sister's room. She's sleeping." She'd already turned away from Will and was moving hastily along the side of the chapel. Will hurried to catch up, already launched upon his explanation.

"Families must support each other, my father always said, and when he told me how much harm Rizzio was causing the Queen with his baseborn ways and self-aggrandizement ...." His voice trailed away as he and Tarrill rounded the corner of the chapel.

At that moment Mary Stuart and Darnley stepped out through the great west entrance into the cemetery. Fraser and Simpson watched as the royal couple paused for just a moment, staring down at a freshly turned mound of earth.

"Rizzio," they heard Darnley say and then saw the Queen shudder.

Close by, four other figures moved quietly in the darkness. Stuart of Traquair, Arthur Erskine, Anthony Standen and another loyal member of the Queen's household had arrived with the horses just as the church bells pealed midnight.

Fraser was the first to reach the Queen. "Thank God you made it safely!" He grinned and grasped the Queen's hand. "Quickly, you'll ride with Erskine."

"Iain," Mary Stuart began, "I'm so grateful ...."

He signaled for her to be quiet. "Later, we've no time." Fraser had pointedly ignored Darnley, who was looking hopelessly ineffectual. Anthony Standen indicated a mount for the consort and within seconds, the little party was moving quietly away from the chapel and out of Edinburgh.

After the city lay behind them, they rode at breakneck speed, sparing neither horses nor riders. They stopped once, at Seton, to permit George Gordon and Lord Bothwell to join them.

Despite her advancing pregnancy, the Queen made no pleas to slow down. Darnley, in fact, urged them all to ride even faster. "Come on, come on! By God's blood, they will murder both you and me if they catch us!"

"We're not being followed," Mary shouted back. "If Erskine rides any harder, we'll damage the babe."

"Never mind!" Darnley yelled frantically. "If this one dies, we'll make more!"

Appalled, the Queen could not reply but clung all the tighter to Erskine. Fraser, however, had pulled Barvas up alongside Darnley. "Have a care, man," he said mildly. "You speak to a mother and a Queen."

Darnley threw Fraser a look of sheer malevolence. "You! The Queen may be grateful, but expect no fawning praise from me!"

The contempt in Fraser's eyes made Darnley look away. "Don't worry, Your Grace," Fraser said, spurring Barvas to move ahead, "I've never expected anything from you yet."

Dawn was spreading across the horizon when they reached Dunbar Castle. Pale shafts of light trailed above the North Sea as the morning mists hovered over the water. In a clatter of horses' hooves and booted feet, the party dismounted at the castle entrance.

Some hours later, after the Queen had eaten and rested, she asked to see Iain Fraser alone. Their old intimacy was badly strained and the interview was one of those rare occasions when Mary Stuart's poise deserted her.

"Your plan worked wonderfully well," she told him, twisting at a plain linen kerchief. "If it hadn't been for your help, I might be a prisoner in Stirling Castle by now."

"You behaved with great flair and daring," he said, thinking how vigorous she looked in spite of her recent ordeal. "Winning Darnley over was vital to the plan and you managed that alone."

She looked at him squarely for the first time since he'd entered the room. "He bends like a sapling in the breeze. I was a fool, swept away like a milkmaid mooning for her sheepherd." The amber eyes grew overbright. "But in spite of all that, I can't reinstate you, Iain. I'm sorry."

Fraser propped one booted leg on the opposite knee. He regarded the Queen with compassion, sensing the genuine misery she was experiencing in her rejection of him. "If it's not Darnley, it must be James. Correct, lass?"

The auburn lashes dipped against her cheeks. "Yes, he's adamant. I don't understand why he hates you so, Iain, but he does. Why, he's even willing to reconcile with Bothwell! Yet when I mention your name, he becomes intransigent."

Fraser thoughtfully rubbed the bridge of his nose. "It doesn't make much sense, does it? James and I were put to the horn at the same time—yet he did more than merely criticize Darnley, he fomented a rebellion. Now you'll pardon him and retain the charges against me. I ask you, is that just?"

Mary Stuart swept out of her chair and moved agitatedly around the room. "Of course not! Nay, don't get up!" She gestured nervously at Fraser. "It makes no sense, but what does in this world of madness? I need James more than ever if I'm to keep my crown. Oh," she went on in a voice tinged with tears, "I need you, too, but I have to choose—and James is my brother."

Now Fraser did stand to gently place his hands on the Queen's forearms. "Enough, don't upset yourself, you've been a brave lassie so far. I don't like it, I won't pretend I do, but I appreciate your dilemma. You must do what is right, not just for yourself, but for Scotland."

Mary looked up at him through misty eyes. "You realize that if James weren't my blood relation, I'd choose you?"

Fraser gazed at her for a long moment, the half-grin twisting his wide mouth. Then he held the Queen close and felt her lean limply against him. "Don't cry, you'll upset the bairn." But Mary didn't cry, she just stayed for a long time in the sanctuary of his arms. Fraser was glad the Queen couldn't see his ironic expression. Dammit, he thought, the lassie needs me, she cares for me, she ought not be torn so. As always, she was more than just a lovely woman in distress; to Fraser, she was Scotland.

At last, she eased out of his arms. "The hardest part is that I have a favor to ask," she said with a wry little smile. "If you refuse, I'll understand."

Fraser folded his arms across his chest. "Well?"

The Queen resumed her long-legged walk about the room. "I've told you how I feel about Darnley. I know he was up to his silly neck in Davie's murder. I can't endure him much longer, I haven't been able to let him touch me for months ...." She swallowed hard at the revelation but plunged onward: "I can't act officially until after the babe is born, I mustn't put the child's legitimacy in jeopardy. But in the meantime, I want you to go to Rome and start proceedings for my divorce."

Fraser appeared to be contemplating the room's furnishings. Indeed, some corner of his mind registered the slightly shabby wall hangings, the worn chairs, the rushes which needed their annual spring replacement. Dunbar Castle was a far cry from the Queen's usual residences. Its very tawdriness reinforced Mary's desperate situation.

"I'll go," he said simply. "I can't remain in Scotland for long."

Mary put her hands on his shoulders. "Oh, Iain, you are too good to me! I promise, your lands won't be confiscated! When you return, your properties will be waiting for you!"

Fraser felt little confidence in Mary's declarations, but he held his tongue. Slipping his arms around the Queen's waist, he stared into the amber eyes. "One other thing you must promise, lassie. You'll see that no harm befalls my wife or my children. Fair enough?"

"Certainly, of course, I've not done right by Dallas. I'll make amends, I swear!" The Queen was flushed, smiling, grateful, and seemingly submissive. Fraser leaned down, brushed her cheek with his lips, and wished to God he could put more faith in her promises.

Chapter Twenty-Six

IF THE *RICHEZZA* had been anchored at Dunbar, Fraser would have sailed immediately for the Continent. But since the ship was up north, off the Isle of Lewes, he would have to travel overland to join his crew. The temptation to see Dallas and his children was too much; he would risk stopping in Edinburgh.

Dallas, meanwhile, had left Holyrood for the town house. When the royal couple's escape had been discovered Tuesday morning, a great hue and cry went up all over the palace. More frightened by James Stuart's threat than she would admit, Dallas decided to take refuge in her own home. Tarrill could protest all she liked, but the mile ride in a litter to Gosford's Close was hardly hazardous. And in the ensuing consternation over the Queen's flight, nobody was much interested in Lady Fraser's departure with her new babe, her sister, a wet nurse and a minor member of the royal almoner's staff.

Once out of Holyrood, Tarrill was as relieved as Dallas. The note from Will Ruthven had upset her at first. Under any other circumstances, she would have ignored it, but she knew his presence at the Chapel Royal would wreck the entire escape plan. She had to get him away from the cemetery—and then had to listen to his self-deluding excuses for participating in Rizzio's murder. She had been polite but cool. In fact, as he spoke she felt she was seeing him for the first time—ambitious, easily manipulated, hypocritical and concerned not so much for her opinion but only her approval. She had no opportunity to offer either, however, for their meeting was interrupted as the news of the Queen's escape spread through the palace. When Will left he had attempted to take her hand, but Tarrill had merely stood in the doorway and bade him an aloof goodnight. For the first time in many years, Tarrill could honestly tell herself that she did not care if she ever laid eyes on Will Ruthven again.

MAGNUS WAS DELIGHTED to see his mother but less enthused about his new brother. The red fringe of hair made him hoot with derision; the intermittent crying elicited threats; and whenever Dallas picked Robert up, Magnus suddenly revealed he'd hurt himself or wasn't feeling well.

"He'll get over it," Ellen asserted. "What he needs is a father's strong hand. I fear the child is a bit spoiled."

Nodding distractedly, Dallas couldn't help but agree. If their life continued at the present rate, her boys would grow up with a father they scarcely ever saw. But if Fraser had succeeded in spiriting the Queen away, no doubt he would be forgiven and restored to his place at court. Rumor said Mary Stuart had reached Dunbar safely and Dallas prayed that this was so.

The following night, at least part of Dallas's prayers were answered. Fraser returned home, slipping into the town house under the cover of darkness. But the very stealth of his arrival let Dallas know that all was not well.

They sat up late as Fraser recounted the events of the past two days. When he told her of the Queen's decision, she flared up, denouncing Mary Stuart as a capricious jade. Fraser did his best to soothe her, trying to divert her wrath from the Queen to Lord James. Dallas then told him about her encounter with the Queen's half-brother. But she kept James's threat to herself.

"That bogus bond is worthless," Fraser declared. "The Queen would never believe I connived at Rizzio's death. But you're right, I'll wager that James encouraged Morton and the others all along."

"I'd like to prove it, by heaven," Dallas declared, beginning to simmer down. "Oh, Iain, I am so tired of you being away! I know, I agreed you should go to sea, but you're just never here!"

Fraser propped his feet up on the bed. Dallas was lying under a goose-down comforter; she was being very careful about making a full recovery. "Lassie, you know my absences aren't entirely my fault," he pointed out reasonably. "It's not my choice to be away so much."

Dallas shifted her body under the comforter. So many hours in bed were making her back ache. "I know, I know. But Magnus looked at you tonight as if he wasn't sure who you were. Sometimes I believe he thinks Cummings is his father."

Her husband didn't respond for a few moments but stared uncomfortably at his signet ring, which winked in the candlelight. At last, he cradled her face in his hands and kissed her lips very gently. "You know," he said, the hazel eyes as serious as she'd ever seen them, "I wondered the other day when I talked to Queen Mary if I'd ever be free to come back to Scotland. But I will, and when I do, I'm staying."

Dallas's first reaction was to disparage such a vow. Her restless husband could never remain in one place for long. Besides, he enjoyed plying his trade as a pirate, it made him wealthy, it satisfied his urge for adventure, his love of the sea. But something in his expression made her pause; he means what he says, she thought with wonder. So she made no comment, just nestled against him and felt the comfort of his body against her own.

FRASER WAS GONE before the week's end. He had spent three days inside the house while Cummings and the other servants kept a constant watch on the street outside to make sure no one came to seek out their master. Meanwhile, Fraser got reacquainted with his elder son, played cards with Dallas and Tarrill, marked his charts for the journey to Genoa, and wished he could make love at least once to his wife before he left Edinburgh.

A week after his departure, Mary Stuart rode into her capital at the head of eight thousand men. Radiant with triumph, she acknowledged the cheers of the citizenry and knew that she was the ultimate victor in the miserable Rizzio affair.

In early April the Queen moved her court to Edinburgh Castle. The great fortress loomed above the town like a brooding eagle perched on a rock. It was not a homey site for the royal babe's birth, but it was considered secure.

Tarrill and Donald rejoined the Queen's household a few days later. At first, Dallas was lonely without them, but slowly adjusted to passing the days with her children, checking over the household supplies, establishing a routine for her family and trying to do something about Meg.

The youthful wet nurse had plenty of milk for Robert and performed her task efficiently. One of twelve children, Meg had been barely fourteen when she was seduced by the chapman who lived on the floor below her family in the crowded tenement off Horse Wynd. Cast out by her irate parents, the months spent with her sister had been difficult. When her bairn was born dead, Meg was torn between sorrow and relief. Donald's invitation to Holyrood had terrified her, and the events which had ensued during her first few days of service with Lord and Lady Fraser had overwhelmed her. But once settled into the town house, Meg began to relax. Eventually, she overcame her shyness enough to tell Dallas about her background.

"You must learn to read," Dallas had said as Meg stammered in astonishment. Girls didn't read, she had protested, it was sufficient to know the rudiments of household chores and birthing bairns. "Twaddle," Dallas had snapped. "I could read and write before I could wield a broom."

So she began to tutor Meg, a difficult task at best, but finally the girl demonstrated progress. Meanwhile, Dallas drummed into her the necessity of bathing at least once a week and remembering to wash her hair, too. After two months of pushing, nagging and prodding, Meg began to blossom out of her drab cocoon. Dallas was proud of herself, and even prouder of Meg.

By that time, Dallas was getting outside, visiting Walter and Glennie, going on shopping jaunts, walking with Ellen and the children in the soft spring air. It was all very peaceful, reassuring and dull. Dallas burned for Iain Fraser.

On the first day of June, a message arrived from the Queen, asking Dallas to come to court for the royal birth. It was the third invitation Dallas had received, and though she was still angry with Mary Stuart for not reinstating Fraser, she softened a little and decided to go up to the castle.

The Queen received Dallas with genuine pleasure. She apologized for the way she'd behaved the night of Rizzio's murder, expressed regret for failing to grant Dallas an audience, and lamented the fact that Fraser was still outlawed. Had the Queen not been so far gone in pregnancy, Dallas would have dared to give a bold reprimand. But having so recently borne a child herself, she curbed her tongue and politely answered the Queen's questions about giving birth.

Mary Stuart was already lying-in, looking as if she were floating on the great sea of a bed hung with blue velvet and taffeta. The child would actually be delivered in a smaller chamber, but for purposes of state, the Queen would wait in the larger, more elegant room until her labor commenced.

For two weeks nothing happened. Court life was so curtailed that Dallas decided her existence in the town house had been exciting by comparison. Still, there was the castle to explore, and while Dallas had been raised just a few hundred yards from its massive bulk, she'd never been inside until now. Consequently, she took every opportunity to visit the many rooms, the tiny chapel erected by St. Margaret, the small but well-supplied library, even the esplanade which led up Castle Hill from the Lawnmarket.

The Queen had done her best to make the great fortress habitable. Tapestries, furnishings, carpets and other finely crafted household accoutrements had been transported from Holyrood or purchased specially for the period of residency. Naturally, Dallas was more intrigued by the library than any other room. Most of the books were Mary's own and in French. Dallas spent several hours in the library, working diligently on translating some of the histories.

One afternoon after struggling over a particularly difficult passage for half an hour, she was forced to give up. The syntax just didn't make sense. Annoyed, she slammed the book back into place on the shelf, only to hear an odd scrunching noise. Curious, Dallas pulled the book back out again. She could see nothing unusual but extracted the adjoining volumes to make sure. Then she noticed about a square foot of masonry which had sunk into the wall almost a full inch, apparently from the force she'd used to put the history volume away. Carefully, she prodded at the stone with her fingers; it swung about, revealing an opening some six inches deep. Dallas reached inside and felt something solid. Whatever it was, it had an irregular surface and wasn't secured to the rest of the wall. She lifted experimentally, felt the object move free, and eased it out into the open.

It was a jewel case, layered with dust and speckled with bits of loosened masonry. Dallas tried lifting the lid but it was locked. Overcome with curiosity, she searched through the desk to find something with which she could pry the case open. No useful tool was to be found. Dallas was wondering what to do next when she heard footsteps outside the door. Quickly, she shoved the case into a drawer, then replaced the books on the shelf just as James Stuart entered the library.

"Ah, Lady Fraser," he said coolly. "I've not seen you since your child was born. I assume you've recovered?"

Dallas recognized the double meaning at once. She also hoped her skirts were covering the debris on the floor. For some reason, she decided it was imperative that James not know about her discovery. Submissiveness seemed her best hope of getting him out of the library as fast as possible.

"Yes, indeed, my lord. Such notions new mothers get! I hardly remember your visit at all!" Dallas laughed merrily at her own apparent folly.

The faintest smile played at James's mouth. "I'm pleased to see you so well. Are you enjoying the riches of the royal library?"

"Very much," Dallas replied, wishing James weren't behaving so civilly. "It reminds me of my father's, in the house where I grew up."

James came over to survey the titles. "Ah, yes, your father was a renowned tutor, was he not? I take great pleasure in reading, too, when I have time. And just now, there's plenty of that while we await the royal heir's whim."

Dallas felt as if she were rooted to the spot in front of the secret hiding place. She hoped to heaven that James would find a volume he liked before she was forced to step aside. "So many French poets," he said with disapproval. "I prefer something less flighty. What would you suggest, madame?"

"There are the chronicles of the Austrian emperors and kings," she said, recalling that these volumes were on the shelf right in front of James.

He leaned forward to select a title. "This looks intriguing. The Austrian dynasties have always ...." But his words were cut off by the sound of alarm bells ringing outside the castle. It was the signal that Queen Mary's labor had begun. James leapt to his feet. "Come, we must attend Her Grace!" As Dallas hesitated James grabbed her arm. "Hurry, the entire court must be present for this momentous occasion!"

Reluctantly, Dallas fell into step beside him. There was nothing else she could do, and at least he was leaving the library, too. She'd just have to come back at the earliest possible opportunity.

Mary Stuart had not yet been moved out of the lying-in chamber. The midwife was already present, as were several lords and ladies. The Queen lay in the huge bed, pale but composed.

"Her pains started about fifteen minutes ago," Tarrill whispered. "She'll be moved when they come closer together."

"Poor lady, I know what she's going through," Dallas said in commiseration. "But at least I didn't have fifty people gaping at me in my misery."

But an hour passed and nothing happened. The Queen began to look apologetic. "A false alarm, I'm afraid," the midwife told the courtiers. "It often happens, nothing to worry about."

The lords and ladies began to drift out of the chamber. Dallas filed out with the others, not wishing to appear overhasty in her departure. She glanced around to see where James was, but couldn't find him. He must have left ahead of her, possibly to confer with some of the other lords on the council.

Once Dallas had left the others, she quickened her pace to the library. Hurrying to the desk, she opened the drawer and removed the jewel case, thanking the Virgin that it was still there. She could do nothing about the disturbed masonry in the wall except hope that the servants who cleaned the library were an uncurious lot.

Hiding the jewel case in the folds of her skirt, Dallas headed purposefully back towards her room. Tarrill was not there, but Flora was busily shining the silver buckles on a pair of her mistress's evening slippers. Though Dallas trusted Flora implicitly, she did not want her maid present while she opened the jewel case.

"I'm famished, Flora," Dallas exclaimed. "Waiting around the Queen's chambers for naught has given me an appetite. See if you can find some pears, will you?"

Flora obligingly left on her errand and Dallas rummaged through her dressing table for something that would pry open the lock. She found a metal nail file and was about to pry up the lid when she noticed fresh scar marks along the edge of the case. She was certain they had not been there before. Anxiously, she used the file to wedge the lid upwards. The lock sprung immediately and Dallas looked inside. As she had feared, the case was empty. But the red velvet cushion clearly showed the impression of a necklace. Not just any necklace, Dallas knew instinctively, but an amulet which had once been examined by her father, and before that, briefly kept in the possession of Iain Fraser's mother.

Breathlessly, Dallas closed the lid and wiped the top clean with a handkerchief. There were the raised initials "MdG," shining in the June sunlight. The case had belonged to Marie de Guise, the amulet must have been entrusted to her some twenty years ago by Daniel Cameron. And there was no doubt at all in Dallas's mind that Lord James had removed the amulet within the past hour.

Dallas puzzled over what to do next. James must have known about the amulet and the secret hiding place all along. Perhaps he himself had put the jewel case there many years ago. He would suspect her of having found it, but he might not realize how much she knew about the amulet's significance. Should she put the jewel case back in the library desk drawer or keep it as evidence? But the case itself proved little and its possession might put Dallas in even more danger than she was already. She would return it at once to the library and hope that James could never be sure that she was the one who had opened it.

Half an hour later, Dallas returned to her room where Flora presented her with a handful of pears. Dallas looked at the fruit without appetite; she had thought she would feel relieved after getting rid of the case, but instead, she was overcome with anxiety. James Stuart had yet another reason to wish both herself and her husband out of his way. And Dallas still didn't know why the Queen's half-brother waged such a relentless war against them.

FOUR DAYS LATER Mary Stuart was delivered of a prince. The labor was long and difficult. While the Queen lay abed too exhausted to even speak, all Edinburgh rejoiced over her fruitfulness in producing a male heir. The court, however, did not resume its round of activities: Mary Stuart was not regaining her strength but lay pallid and enervated for several weeks after the delivery. Her supporters began to worry.

Dallas stayed on at the castle, though she visited the town house more frequently now that the prince had arrived. One early summer evening, returning alone from Gosford's Close, Dallas stopped off to see Glennie and Walter. Marthe had just baked some special butter and nutmeg cakes which Dallas could not resist. They nibbled and chatted for much longer than Dallas had planned, and by the time she left her old home, it was almost dark.

"Walter will escort you," Glennie said as Dallas picked up her lace shawl and headed out through the entry hall.

"Nonsense," Dallas declared. "It's less than five minutes from here to the castle. I'll be quite safe."

Glennie had to agree; there were still a few people abroad and the light had not gone completely. Hugging her sister and Walter, Dallas set out for Castle Hill. From somewhere close by, an owl hooted as two bats fluttered across the wynd, disappearing like wraiths into the eaves of an adjacent house. She had just passed by Tod's Close when she saw three people walking with an unsteady gait, their arms clinging to each other. One of them was extremely tall and Dallas recognized Lord Darnley at once. He seemed to be holding his companions very intimately, but Dallas assumed that if he was drunk, he needed their support. But as she drew closer she realized that the two young boys accompanying Darnley were not holding him up, but allowing the consort to paw and fondle their strong young bodies. Aghast at such perverted public behavior and never before having guessed this particular vice of Darnley's, Dallas turned quickly into Blyth's Close and fled in a different direction towards the castle. She was still running when she turned a corner by the esplanade and collided with John Hamilton.

"Dallas!" Hamilton reached out to keep her from falling. "What on earth—is someone pursuing you?"

Dallas was so amazed to see Hamilton that she momentarily forgot about Darnley. "John! I didn't know you were in Edinburgh!" She disengaged herself and stepped back to see him more clearly. He was somewhat heavier, there was more grey in his hair and his moustache, but he looked as fit and handsome as ever. Involuntarily, she put a hand to her bosom to quiet her racing heart. The running, of course, she reasoned, that was why she was out of breath.

"I just arrived this afternoon," Hamilton responded, smiling broadly in his delight at seeing her. She had changed, too, he noted, grown more womanly, and, he thought with a pang, more desirable than ever. "My father wrote to me about the prince's birth. I thought I should come home for the christening."

"I'm glad to see you," Dallas said, thinking the words sounded totally inadequate. She tugged at her shawl, wondering why she felt so befuddled. Finally, she remembered Darnley and blurted out the reason for her flight up the esplanade. "Oh, John, I'm appalled! Lord Darnley is a pederast!"

Hamilton considered the allegation with his usual care. "I've heard some tales—yes, it's possible. But how do you know?"

"I saw him, drooling all over two young boys near Tod's Close. He was drunk, as usual, carrying on right there in the middle of town!" Dallas was beginning to regain her composure as she let Hamilton take her arm to lead her up towards the castle.

"It's unnatural, but some men are like that," Hamilton said in a voice that neither damned nor condoned. "Poor Mary, how much she's had to put up with!"

"And now she's not at all well," Dallas put in. "Have you seen her since you got back?"

"Just briefly." Hamilton frowned deeply as Dallas noticed how tan he had become from the Italian sun. "I'm much concerned about her. She told me she hopes to go to Alloa soon, to take the sea air." He shook his head, then paused to open a door decorated with a finely carved lintel.

"I was there the night Rizzio was murdered." Dallas shuddered at the recollection as she stepped inside the castle. Torches flared along the walls and a page scurried by carrying a tray of food. "But tell me about Italy. You must have seen many wonderful sights."

"So I did. The ancient Roman ruins, St. Peter's, the Colosseum—I went to Padua, Siena, Venice, Milan. Most people were friendly, though some would become distant when they learned I wasn't a Papist."

"I suppose a Protestant is a rarity in Rome," Dallas said. They had paused by a staircase, both increasingly aware that their conversation masked words that had yet been unsaid. It was Hamilton who finally jumped the gap between them:

"Fraser is still outlawed, I hear. But you and he are happily married, is that not so?" The brown eyes begged her to deny his question.

Dallas forced her gaze to remain steady. "Yes, we are. We were apart for a year, but finally we reconciled. We have another son now, named Robert. I love Iain very much, I always have." She swallowed and was surprised that there was a large lump in her throat.

"I see." Hamilton was silent for a long moment, then he reached out to touch her hair. "I went away to forget—and ended up remembering ...." His hand dropped to his side, and he smiled ruefully. "Damn, I vowed I wouldn't beleaguer you with such maudlin self-pity."

She knew he was angry with himself. She wished that just once he'd turn his anger on her. A violent quarrel might break the spell they had cast over each other. But it would be uncharacteristic of Hamilton to shift any blame from himself to her, and they would only end up forgiving one another.

"You once told me we should put what's happened in the past," Hamilton said, one hand fingering the clan brooch which held his plaid in place. "You were right. It's just damnably hard."

She sought in vain for a word of consolation that wouldn't sound trite and yet wouldn't raise his hopes. But he had already started to back away. Hamilton realized even more than Dallas that there was nothing more either of them could—or should—say. "Good night, Dallas."

She watched him turn from her. "Good night," she said softly. And then after he was safely out of hearing range, she added, "Good night, my dearest, dearest John."

SOMEONE WAS SCREAMING in pain, pistols exploded with sound and death, swords crashed together and smoke billowed from somewhere in the forecastle. Men seemed to be dying or wounded everywhere, the deck running with blood, and an acrid, sickening stench filled the air.

Iain Fraser rolled over onto his back and sat up with a jolt. The squalid little room in the Copenhagen inn was almost totally dark. The blond woman beside him mumbled in her sleep and tugged at the thin blanket. Fraser glanced down at her, made sure she was still asleep and got out of bed to pour himself a cup of ale. He'd had the same dream for five nights in a row but this time he had awakened before the usual climax, in which he found himself hanging in chains on the sands at Leith.

The *Richezza's* crew had attacked two merchant vessels in the past three months, one en route to Genoa, the other on the return voyage. Neither had offered resistance, nothing had happened for a long time to match the bloodthirsty mayhem of his dreams.

Never in the fifteen years he'd spent at sea had he been prey to such pernicious nightmares. In fact, Fraser seldom dreamed at all, or if he did, he could rarely remember what the dreams were about. He had told Dallas he'd stay in Scotland if and when he was permitted to return lawfully. He'd meant it at the time, but once he felt the decks of the *Richezza* roll beneath him and savored the salt air in his nostrils, he'd begun to hope that Dallas, sensible little wench that she was, wouldn't hold him to his promise. Yet the dreams of the last few nights troubled Fraser, though he wasn't an easy man to frighten. At the root of his thinking lay a far more realistic reason for keeping his word to Dallas: Whatever thrills he'd reaped during those fifteen years had begun to pall. One encounter was rather like the next, one cargo as profitable as any other but now devoid of surprises, and there wasn't a port in the civilized world he didn't know by heart. He was thirty-five years old, he had a wife and a growing family, and the dwindling excitement was no longer worth the risk.

The woman stirred again, one plump arm stabbing out in the direction of Fraser's side of the bed. He stood with the ale cup in his hand, watching her with disinterest while she settled back into a deep slumber. There was no adventure in the women he met, either. This one was like the rest, ultimately submissive and infernally dull. Nor did he give them more than mere physical satisfaction: There had been a time when he would woo them with words or a few gallantries, talk of his life at sea or draw out their own backgrounds and listen with attention. The last year or two, he realized that he'd ceased to have any contact with his bed partners except on the level of sheer lust.

The only window in the shabby little room was covered with horn. Fraser could see nothing through it, not even moonlight. He could hear the sea outside, however, slapping against the wharves of Copenhagen. From somewhere in the distance, roistering sailors hooted drunkenly into the night.

Fraser dressed quietly, tossed some coins onto his pillow, made sure he hadn't left anything in the room, and slipped outside. He had paid the innkeeper in advance, as the man had sullenly insisted. There was no reason why he should spend the rest of the night in that sordid place.

Looking in every direction, Fraser made sure he was not followed by footpads or other riff-raff which lurked about the waterfront. Hand on his dirk, he walked past the sailmaker's dingy doorway, down by the deserted fishmonger's stalls, and beyond a net-mender's shuttered windows. The sailors he'd heard while he was still inside the room had long since disappeared. The night was empty, only the sea was alive.

In less than ten minutes he could make out the masts of the *Richezza*, swaying gently at anchor in the summer breeze. The ship's longboat lay at the end of the wharf. He jumped down into it, picked up the oars and began to row out over the incoming tide. He'd made up his mind: He would turn the *Richezza* over to MacRae, a man of little imagination but enormous competence. He would say nothing until they reached the Isle of Lewes; he wanted no protests from the crew, no arguments, no doleful partings. When they dropped anchor in Scotland, he would simply, finally, walk away.

Chapter Twenty-Seven

During the month of August, Dallas returned home while the Queen and her court traveled to Alloa. Tarrill wrote from the seaside establishment, saying that Mary Stuart was feeling somewhat better.

Three weeks later, Dallas received two other messages, each arriving within an hour of the other. The first came from Donald, and was written in the neat, round hand Tarrill had taught him. It stated briefly and concisely that he had been promoted to the Exchequer's household and would be moving out of Holyrood within a week. Dallas was very pleased.

But the second letter pleased her even more. It was written from Beauly in Iain Fraser's surprisingly artistic but slanted hand. "I arrived here two days ago, my mission in Rome accomplished as well as could be managed under the circumstances," he wrote guardedly. "Meanwhile, I am touring my properties to make sure all is well for the harvest and to implement certain other plans I have herewith set out to do." Dallas puzzled briefly over this statement, then continued: "Sorcha sends her fondest greetings. I send my own to you and to our dear children, and expect to lie in your arms before summer's end."

Dallas gloated over the words like a rabbit who has just discovered a clump of clover. But how Fraser could enter Edinburgh without being detected caused her much worry. He'd managed it in March, but his luck couldn't hold forever. Nor was there the slightest hope that James Stuart might have softened in his attitude. Dallas folded the cherished letter carefully and tucked it away in a little carved cedar chest where she kept her greatest treasures.

Before summer's end, Fraser had said. Well, August was almost over. He'd be coming soon if he kept his promise. Anticipation overcame worry as Dallas smiled happily at her own reflection in the bedroom mirror.

QUEEN MARY WAS back in Edinburgh, making arrangements for the prince's christening. Darnley had joined her at Traquair, where Tarril said they had engaged in a shockingly tasteless quarrel. The King and Queen were said to be on extremely bad terms.

After Tarrill had played for a while with Magnus and cuddled Robert, she suggested that Dallas join her in a shopping expedition. To her astonishment, Dallas refused. "I'm a bit fatigued today, it's been warm," Dallas explained unconvincingly. She wouldn't admit even to her sister that she scarcely left the house these days in case Fraser should arrive and find her not at home.

Tarrill set off alone and had not gone more than a hundred yards beyond the thatched houses of Beith's Wynd when she saw Donald McVurrich's tall figure striding towards her.

"Donald!" she called out in greeting, quickening her step. He waved and hurried to take her hand. "Congratulations! Dallas told me about your new post. I'm so happy for you," Tarrill said with her warm smile.

"It's a goodly opportunity," Donald said modestly. "I'm learning much there, and my new employer is kind—though he has sent me to outfit myself in a manner more befitting my new situation." Donald pulled a wry face. "I've never cared much for fancy fripperies but must try to please him."

Tarrill had allowed Donald to steer her back in the direction she'd just come from. They both paused in front of the hatmaker's, where he fingered the plush velvet of a feathered bonnet.

"Are you going to buy that one?" Tarrill asked, nonplussed by Donald's sudden gaudy taste.

"Nay," he laughed, " 'tis too sumptuous for me. Serge, maybe, with the smallest of feathers."

Tarrill picked up another bonnet, also blue, but darker, with a small pair of swan's feathers tucked inside the band. "Like this one?" she inquired, turning the bonnet in her hands.

Donald considered the item carefully. "Aye, that's more like it." He removed his own worn beret and took the bonnet from her, adjusting it carefully on his blond hair. "Well?"

"Oh, I like it! It goes well with your eyes!" Tarrill nodded several times in enthusiastic approval.

The hatmaker had emerged from his shop, ready to exert his powers of persuasion. But before he could utter a word, Donald had produced some coins. "How much?" he asked the merchant.

"Four royals," the man replied, too surprised to remember the higher price he usually started out asking for such a model.

Handing over the money, Donald gave Tarrill his arm. They strolled along in companionable silence, past the Mercat Cross, St. Giles, the Tolbooth, and the meal and corn sellers' stalls. When they reached the canvas booths of the Lawnmarket, Tarrill decided that since they were so near Nairne's Close, she ought to call on Walter and Glennie.

"Join me," she urged as they stepped aside to make way for a top-heavy wagonload of peat. "They'll be glad to see you."

But Donald declined. "I should buy some shirts here, mayhap a new doublet, too." He glanced across the way to the fine houses of Riddell's Close. "I'm told the Queen is visiting the Exchequer's soon to go over the royal accounts and make arrangements for Prince James's guardianship. Will you be joining Her Grace?"

"I don't know," she replied. "I assume the Queen will only bring two or three ladies with her, since the Exchequer's residence isn't large. Whether I'll be one of them, I can't say."

Donald laid a hand on her shoulder. "I see you seldom these days. If it's possible, I'd be most pleased to have you join the Queen's party."

His formal speech startled Tarrill. It also made her glance waver slightly. Knowing Donald, he hadn't spoken without a definite purpose in mind. Tarrill thought she knew what that purpose was and felt a sudden surge of unprecedented joy.

ROBERT HAD LEARNED how to crawl; he was scampering across the nursery floor to torment Magnus's dog, Caesar. Magnus had learned to accept his new brother but still found him a nuisance. He was also impatient about how soon Robert could play with him, instead of just scrambling about on the floor, eating, sleeping and crying. Dallas assured him that before long Magnus would find his brother a most willing companion.

"You'll have to teach him, of course," Dallas said. "Big brothers are so important to little brothers, they must show them what to do with toys and games. I'm sure you'll be very good at that."

Magnus brightened momentarily, then raced off to rescue Caesar. Dallas smiled at her sons, looking away from them only when distracted by Ellen's arrival.

"Cummings says a message is waiting for you downstairs, madame." Ellen turned quickly as Robert began to howl. Magnus had given his brother a good clout for mauling the dog. The governess moved purposefully across the room to remonstrate with the older child.

For once, Dallas didn't interfere. She blew her sons a kiss and flew down the stairs, hoping the message was the one she'd been waiting for so eagerly.

Cummings was standing in the entry hall, a small piece of paper in his hand. “Some stranger brought this just now. He says it’s from Baron Fraser.”

Dallas snatched the paper from Cummings. “I’m at the Mermaid Inn by Burghers Wynd in Leith,” it read. “Come at once. Iain.”

“He’s back!” Dallas glowed as she handed the note over to Cummings.

“Hmmm.” Cummings frowned at the piece of paper. “I mislike the fellow who brought the message.”

“Oh, fie, Cummings, Iain is in no position to be choosy about whom he sends with a note. The man probably can’t read anyhow.”

Since Cummings had no logical reason for his misgivings, he made no further effort to dissuade Dallas. But he did suggest accompanying her to Leith. “The man’s waiting outside with two horses, I’ll go ’round and fetch a third.”

Before Dallas could assent, the Fraser cook came charging into the entry hall, swearing volubly in his native French. “*Quelle Flora! Elle est une dame terrible!*” He waved his arms wildly, waxing on into the usual tirade about Flora’s meddling, which always ended with his resignation and Cummings exerting sufficient flattery and threats to change the volatile cook’s mind. But such sessions took time and Dallas couldn’t wait.

“Don’t worry, it’s broad daylight, I’ll be quite safe,” she shouted at Cummings as the cook continued to vilify Flora. Dallas ran to get her light wool summer cloak and hurried out into the street.

The man waiting outside was about her own age, rather short but burly and dressed plainly in jerkin, shirt and boots. He pulled deferentially at his cap when Dallas walked towards him.

“Clark, madame, at your service.” He handed her up onto a docile grey mare. “ ’Tis not far but Baron Fraser thought you’d rather ride than walk.”

Dallas wondered why Iain hadn’t thought about her taking the new coach she’d purchased just before Robert’s birth. Perhaps he’d forgotten about it, since he’d never used it himself.

They made the short journey in silence up the High Street, through the Canongate, down Leith Wynd and across the arched bridge over the Water of Leith. Dallas was too excited to pay much attention to her companion; she found herself smiling several times as they walked their mounts through the busy thoroughfare connecting Edinburgh to the harbor town.

It was a bright, crisp September afternoon, with the first feel of autumn in the air. Summer’s end was officially a week away; Fraser had kept his promise. Dallas savored the blue sky, the smell of peat fires, and the occasional splash of heather growing in a well-tended close. But most of all, she thought about her husband.

The Mermaid Inn was just off the Paunch Market. A young boy came out to take their horses, but before they could enter the inn, a man with a deep scar across the bridge of his nose came to meet them.

"I'm sorry, my lady," he said, "your husband was forced to change the meeting place. But don't worry, it's close by, near the harbor."

Dallas fell into step with the two men. They turned at the King's Wark, just above the sands. "There," the second man said, pointing to a ramshackle house with broken shutters and a tumbledown chimney. "It looks a mean place," he added as he opened the battered door for her, "but Baron Fraser thought it would be safe."

Rats fled across their path as they entered the house, but Dallas didn't let them dampen her enthusiasm. She ascended a stairway which creaked beneath their feet and then turned into a musty corridor. The second man opened the door at the top of the landing, revealing a shabby little room with a table, two chairs, a fireplace that hadn't been used for a long time—-and no sign of Iain Fraser.

"Where's my husband?" Dallas turned to Clark, feeling the first spasm of fear.

Clark's hand propelled her into the room as the second man shut the door. "Sit, madame," Clark said, indicating one of the chairs. "Your husband is not here."

"Where is he?" Dallas demanded, anxiety mounting by the second. "What have you done with him?"

The second man chuckled unpleasantly. He was at least ten years older than Clark, somewhat taller, with pointed ears and a splayed black beard. "We haven't done anything to your lord. We don't know where he is any more than you do."

Dallas pulled the note from her little silk purse. This time she read it carefully. It *looked* like Fraser's writing—but then she noticed the reference to Burghers Wynd—the r's were identical, as they had been in the forgery of Fraser's name on the bogus Rizzio bond. So this was James Stuart's doing! Dallas cursed herself for being such a fool and shredded the note into tiny bits. "Who are you? What do you want?" She stood with her hands on her hips, hoping she looked more imperious than terrified.

"My name is Maclnnes, though that matters not," the second man replied. "As for what we want, be a good wench and sit down as you were told."

Dallas's temper had ignited, acting as an antidote to fear. "How dare you! I'll do as I ...."

But Clark had come up beside her, pulled her arms behind her back and shoved her down onto the chair. Maclnnes held her tight as Clark bound her hands to the chair back.

"Now let's see if you're in a more docile mood," Maclnnes said, unsheathing his dirk. "What did you find in the library at Edinburgh Castle?"

Dallas had found the jewel case in June; it was now September. James's inaction had lulled her into a false sense of security. But hadn't Fraser always told her that James Stuart was a patient man?

"I found a jewel case," Dallas replied tartly. James would know that much anyway. "By accident, I knocked a piece of masonry loose from the wall. The jewel case was lying inside."

"And?" MacInnes leaned back against the table, flicking the dirk against his dirty fingernails.

Dallas ran her tongue across her lips. They were going to kill her, no matter what she told them. James had tried to kill Fraser more than once; now he was after her. It would be simple enough to slit her throat, then wait until after dark and row her body out to sea. She wondered fleetingly if these were the same men who had killed Kennedy and thrown him into the Nor' Loch.

"And what?" Dallas responded, feeling the perspiration begin to dampen the back of her yellow lawn gown.

Clark was standing next to her. He grabbed a handful of her thick hair and pulled hard. Dallas winced but refused to scream. "Just answer the question," Clark said roughly.

"There's nothing to answer," Dallas declared. "The Queen went into false labor, I left with Lord James—" She paused at the name but neither man reacted. "Later, well, I didn't go back. The jewel case was locked anyway."

The two men looked at each other. Then MacInnes spoke again. "What do you know of your husband's father? Don't lie, don't evade me." He made a sudden slashing motion with the dirk.

What little Dallas knew, James must know even more. If the amulet was the key, then he had learned the answer long ago, probably after Marie de Guise died. "Iain was illegitimate, of course," she said, wondering if they could tell she was trembling. "He may have some inkling of who his father was, but he has never told me."

There was another exchange of glances between the two men. This time Clark broke the silence. "You mean your husband never confided in you at all? That's hard to believe."

"He had no proof. He felt it unwise to burden me with knowledge he couldn't substantiate." The reply was vague, but true. Yet Dallas refused to mention the amulets. But she knew her failure to provide further information meant that her usefulness to them had run out. It was time to take a desperate initiative. "See here, I know you're in James Stuart's employ. If you plan to kill me, I must tell you that I have the real bond that Lord James signed before the Rizzio murder. If it's made public, your master faces disaster. Let me go and I'll give it to you."

MacInnes frowned at Clark. There had been whispers of such a bond, but their master had never discussed it with them. How could the wench have gotten hold of it? But then, she had been at Holyrood the night Rizzio was killed. Fraser had been there, too, and had helped the Queen escape. If that fool Darnley had taken the bond and given it to the Queen, might she not have entrusted it to Fraser, who then had given it to his wife?

Clark gripped Dallas's chin in his stubby fingers. "We can make you tell us where, we don't have to bargain with you."

Dallas tried to pull away but failed. "You can do what you like, I'll die before I tell you!"

Clark let go. "Well?" He turned to MacInnes.

"I'll ride to Stirling," the other man said. Their master was not the type to let his underlings make independent decisions, especially one like this which could ruin his political future. "I'll be back by nightfall. You guard the wench." He shoved the dirk into its sheath and left the room.

Neither Dallas nor Clark spoke for at least five minutes after MacInnes had departed. Clark moved restlessly about the room, finally extracting a leather flask from his jerkin. He took one deep swallow, then spat onto the worn floorboards. "Drink?" he asked Dallas. She shook her head, wishing her hands hadn't gone numb. She'd bought a few hours but they'd go for naught unless she managed to get untied from the chair.

Clark was taking another swig. He turned to Dallas and surveyed her critically. "You won't drink with me, eh? Not good enough for your high-flown tastes?" He reached out to pinch one of her breasts. "Baron Fraser and Lord Hamilton can share your sheets, but not Archibald Clark!"

Pale with revulsion, Dallas averted her face. Of course he'd know her background; James would have filled his ears with every shred of scandal.

Clark was taking yet another pull at the flask. Dallas wished it were bigger: The wretched man might drink himself into a stupor. As it was, he had only grown bolder. Now he squeezed both her breasts hard, breathing whiskey into her face.

"They're lucky men, you're a tempting wench, by God. Why should such as they get the fancy cuts of meat while I eat the marrow?" One hand pulled at the high neck of the yellow gown, ripping it to Dallas's waist. Dallas kicked out at him, but he wedged his stocky body between her legs and laughed. "You can't stop me, my lady, don't exert yourself trying. I can be very ungallant, you know." To prove his point, he pinched her nipples so hard that she finally did scream.

"You see? Wouldn't you rather be nice to me?" His mouth savaged hers, the tongue thrusting against her teeth. Dallas jerked away violently, but not before she'd bitten his lip.

“Whoreson scum,” she gasped, “leave me be!”

His reply was a stinging blow to her face. Momentarily stunned, she was totally unprepared for the second swing of his fist, which struck her stomach and made the room spin.

“I warned you,” he muttered viciously, “you’ll not like it by the time I’ve finished with you.” Clark reached inside the waist of her skirt and ripped at the flowing material. “Ah,” he mumbled, “your charms don’t stop in the middle, do they?” He plunged one hand between her thighs, brutally pawing her tender flesh. His other hand grappled both her breasts, kneading them roughly, tugging viciously on her nipples.

Still winded and dazed from the blow to her stomach, Dallas thought she would faint and prayed that she might. All the fears of a man’s touch which she had banished with such difficulty now came surging back. It didn’t matter if the men killed her; if Clark raped her, she’d rather be dead anyway.

His teeth gnawed at her thigh, then he was mumbling words she couldn’t make out at first. “Your arse, I want to see if it’s as fair as the rest of you.” He got up, hurrying around to the back of the chair. Dallas felt the ropes being cut. Slowly, she moved her leaden hands in front of her, noting the deep red marks at her wrists. Clark was standing before her again, breathing hoarsely with desire.

“Stand up, stand up and turn around,” he ordered. Virtually naked, trembling from head to foot, Dallas obeyed.

Clark came up behind her, one hand touching her sore breasts, the other exploring her buttocks. “Aye, I guessed aright. You’re round and succulent as a ripe peach!” He pressed against her, the force of his weight plunging Dallas forward, to fall face down at the dingy hearth’s edge.

Then, with a strength which astonished even herself, she rolled over and began to fight him off, kicking, writhing, flailing away with her arms at his fierce attempts to hold her down. Already some feeling was coming back into her hands. She clawed ineffectually at his face as he tried to pin her to the floor. Finally he succeeded in trapping her arms against her sides with his knees, using his hands to spread her legs apart.

“Open as a barn door,” he breathed. “If you lie still, I’ll make it easy on you. If not, I’ll ride you like the untamed filly you are. Which will it be, eh?”

Dallas was deceptively quiet. As Clark eased up on her to undo his breeches, she lunged to one side, catching him off-balance. He dove at her, but she had rolled just out of his immediate reach, her eyes fixed on an old coal shovel lying against the fireplace. He grabbed for her again, this time clutching at her legs but she had already grasped the shovel by the handle. Clark reached up to stop her but stumbled over the hearthstone. Dallas swung mightily, the shovel crashing against his skull.

Clark dropped to the floor like a bundle of dirty wash. Dallas stared at him with horror and revulsion. Had she killed him? There was blood oozing from a place just above his ear, but she thought he was still breathing. Dallas dropped the shovel with a bang, snatched up her cloak and fled from the horrible little room.

Down the stairs she raced, out into the welcome fresh air, clutching her cloak tightly about her and trying to compose her raddled wits. She was afraid to go through the town; her bedraggled appearance would draw attention and she couldn't be certain that MacInnes might not have changed his mind and turned back. She walked instead towards the harbor, feeling the sea breeze whip her disheveled hair and the soft sands ooze around her bare feet.

Some strange animallike noises sounded in her ears; Dallas was puzzled at first, until she realized she was making them herself. Whimpering with pain, shock, fear and humiliation, she collapsed onto the strand.

It was still daylight when Dallas heard the voice from somewhere above her. Slowly, she looked up, one hand shielding her eyes from the sun.

"I said, are ye all right?" the voice asked. It belonged to a young man attired in fisherman's togs. Somehow, even in her muddled state, Dallas thought he looked familiar.

"Oh—I think so." Dallas struggled to get up, remembering to keep the cloak clutched closely around her.

The young man was helping her. "Ye look unwell. In truth, I thought ye were dead!" Suddenly his eyes widened. "I know ye, ye were with Lord Hamilton that day in Master Forbes's bookstall!"

Dallas tried to force her weary mind back through the fog of time. "Oh! Yes, yes, the bird! I remember now! You're .... I'm sorry, I don't recall ...."

"I dinna know if I ever told ye my name," the young man said with a smile. "It's Andrew Dalrymple. I've always been grateful to Lord Hamilton. I saved the money he gave me and finally made enough to buy a fishing boat. Now I have four of them that I sail with my men out of Pittenweem and we do right well." The smile turned sheepish as if he were ashamed of boasting, especially to a lady who appeared so unwell.

"I'm glad for you," Dallas said, wondering if her intention of smiling had actually succeeded. She ached from head to foot and her bruised mouth made speech difficult. "Andrew, is one of your boats nearby?"

Andrew gestured towards a small dock. "Over there. I fished late today, there's a good run this time of year just before sunset. I've only now returned from taking my catch into town."

Dallas surveyed the water and weather. The sun was dropping rather quickly, but the sky was still clear and the sea appeared calm. It was too dangerous for her to go back to Edinburgh. MacInnes might already be back at the ramshackle house and he'd soon have men in hot pursuit.

"See here, Andrew, I can't explain the whole story to you, but I'm in trouble." She watched the questioning look surface in his eyes. "I'm Lady Fraser, you've heard of my husband, Iain?"

"Aye, he's said to be a brave lord, though outlawed just now." Andrew nodded as if in approval of her husband.

"The same evil people who have sent him into exile are now trying to do me a mischief," Dallas explained, thinking that her tale was certainly oversimplified. "In any case, I must get away. I have a bit of money," she added, feeling inside her cloak to make sure the little purse was still in her pocket, "and I'd be so grateful if you could get me away from here in your boat."

Andrew looked at Dallas carefully. If this poor disheveled lassie was indeed Lady Fraser, she'd obviously been having a very bad time of it. Bruises were beginning to show up on her face, her lip was cut in two places, she was barefoot, and when the breeze picked up he could swear he saw her knees. "Don't fash yourself over the money," he said at last. "You're friend to Lord Hamilton and you were kind to me that day at Master Forbes's. Where do ye want to go?"

"Dunbar," Dallas replied.

PART FIVE

Chapter One

TARRILL STOOD ANXIOUSLY by the small door in the garden wall which connected the Exchequer's residence to the neighboring house owned by David Chambers, a close friend of Bothwell's. The September night was cool but refreshing after the overcrowded banquet room where the Exchequer had entertained the Queen and her party. Just before the company had been seated, Donald had approached Tarrill, asking her to meet him after supper in the garden Now growing impatient, Tarrill began to pace the enclosure, until the creaking of a door made her turn. But it wasn't Donald who came into the garden; it was the Earl of Bothwell, entering by the connecting gate from Chambers's house. Tarrill stood motionless, watching the Border Earl move quickly past the main doorway and around to a side entrance. He had not seen her, and there was something about his urgent yet stealthy movements which aroused Tarrill's curiosity.

She had no time to dwell on Bothwell's peculiar actions as Donald came out of the Exchequer's house just then, loping purposefully towards her. "Tarrill," he said low, taking her by the hand. "I was delayed, the Queen wished to take one of the ledgers up to bed with her."

"That's all right," she replied with a smile, forgetting her impatience now that he was here. She also forgot about the Earl of Bothwell.

Donald was wearing his new doublet, of deep burgundy velvet with plain gold trim at the neck and sleeves. His blond hair shone almost white in the moonlight and Tarrill thought she had never seen him look so handsome. But for all his new status and apparel, he appeared uncomfortable. She decided to say something to break the silence but her own wits didn't seem to be working properly either.

It was Donald who finally spoke. The grip on her hand grew tighter as he cleared his throat rather loudly. "You've taught me to read and write, for which I'm very grateful," he said somewhat stiffly. "But no one ever taught me to make pretty speeches. So what I have to say, I'll put plainly: Will you wed with me?"

Tarrill disengaged her fingers and put a hand on Donald's cheek. "I'll answer plainly then," she said with a radiant smile. "Yes, Donald, I will."

THE FOLLOWING DAY, Tarrill and Donald went to visit Walter and Glennie to tell them the news of their betrothal. Donald felt obliged to ask Walter, as head of the Cameron family, for Tarril's hand. But after the excitement had died down and Glennie had hugged Tarrill while Walter wrung Donald's hand, it became apparent to the newly affianced couple that something was amiss.

Tarrill asked Glennie point-blank what was wrong. "Probably nothing," Glennie replied, getting out wine glasses with which to toast the engagement, "but Flora was here earlier, saying that Dallas left yesterday afternoon to meet Iain in Leith. She hasn't come back since."

Tarrill was getting out a bottle of vintage Portuguese red wine from the cabinet. "Since Dallas hasn't seen Iain for several months, I'm not surprised she's still gone," she remarked somewhat dryly. "They're doubtless lingering over their reunion."

Walter gave Tarrill a hand with the cork. "That's what I told Glennie and Flora. Dallas will be back in a day or so, I'm sure. Meantime, none of us must mention Iain's presence in Leith to a soul."

"Of course not," Tarrill agreed, gazing at Donald over her wine glass. Dallas had certainly weathered an unconventional marriage, right from the start. Being wed to a turbulent, reckless man like Iain Fraser must be very difficult. She was glad Donald was a totally different type of person.

Walter raised his glass. "To the happy couple," he said, beaming at Donald and Tarrill and his own wife as well. "And to Dallas and Iain, wherever they may be."

DALLAS WAS IN Dunbar, lying in Annie and Oliver McVurrich's bed, suffering from the after-effects of shock, pain and a severe cold as well. Andrew Dalrymple had hesitated at first when she'd asked him to take her to Dunbar. It was a twenty-five mile journey, to be made at night in a small fishing boat. But, Andrew had reasoned, the sea was calm, they would keep close in to shore the entire way, and the wind was in their favor. Besides, anyone who looked as if she'd suffered as much as Lady Fraser appeared to, desperately needed his help.

The voyage had been uneventful, though they had not arrived at Dunbar until well after dawn. Annie McVurrich had been astonished to see Dallas and her companion but had immediately set about fixing breakfast and insisting that Andrew join them. When he'd left two hours later, Dallas had pressed some coins on him and wouldn't give in until he'd reluctantly accepted them.

"I hate taking money from ye," he'd told her as he unwillingly pocketed the coins. "If ye ever see Lord Hamilton, tell him Andrew Dalrymple is most grateful to him."

"I shall," she'd replied, thinking that the person she'd most like to see about now besides her husband was Hamilton himself.

So Andrew had left for the harbor to sail his fishing boat back to Pittenweem. Annie had ordered Dallas to bed at once. Oliver and his sons had already gone to the fields by the time Dallas and Andrew arrived, for it was harvest season with much work to be done.

"Och," Annie exclaimed when Dallas finally took off her cloak before climbing into bed, "you poor lassie! What bruises! Do ye want to tell me about it?"

Dallas was too exhausted by then to tell anybody anything. Nor did she want to reveal her humiliation to Annie. And for discretion's sake, the fewer people who knew about James's dastardly intentions, the better.

"Just let me sleep awhile, Annie," Dallas said. "I'll try not to be a bother."

Annie had blustered about the croft, deflating the notion that Dallas could possibly bother her, but her guest was already fast asleep. When she awoke late that afternoon, she asked Annie if one of the boys could take a message in to Edinburgh.

Annie hesitated. It was such a busy time, Oliver truly couldn't spare one of his boys. But she'd already expressed her willingness to do anything she could for Dallas. Then Annie brightened, thinking of an alternative solution. "The Lauder laddie, he always wheezes and breaks out in spots whenever he goes into the fields. He's nigh onto seventeen, trustworthy as they come and 'prenticed to a sail-maker. I'll ask him." Annie smiled soothingly, tucked the comforter around Dallas's legs and sallied forth from the croft.

Dallas put a hand to her aching head and wondered if she'd ever feel normal again. She would not send the message to the town house; it might be watched by James's men. Instead, she'd have the Lauder youth go to Glennie and Walter's.

The lad left the first thing the next morning. Dallas had fretted over the wording of her note, not wanting to involve her kin, yet trying to let them know something was sorely amiss so that they could warn Fraser if he arrived in Edinburgh within the next few days.

"The messenger who took me away lied," she had finally written. "It was a trick for a devious end I will recount later. The lad bringing this message will tell you where I am and how I am. I will come back when I think best."

Dallas hoped Glennie and Walter could read between the lines; certainly Fraser would be able to—if and when he returned.

DALLAS'S CRYPTIC MESSAGE both alarmed and puzzled her relatives. When the Lauder youth had gone, Glennie and Walter had puzzled over what, if any, course of action they should take. Cummings and Flora must be notified at once. But beyond that, they were bewildered.

Could Tarrill or Donald help? Perhaps Donald should ride to Dunbar and talk to Dallas at his parents' house. But before they could devise a solution, Iain Fraser returned to Edinburgh.

He had entered the city unmolested and hoped to exchange his efforts on Mary's behalf in Rome for permission to temporarily ward himself within the capital. But Cummings's news dealt him a stunning blow. After every detail had been elicited from the serving man, Fraser galloped off to the Cameron house.

"That whoreson James!" he exploded after reading Dallas's message. "Either he lured her to Leith to somehow entrap me or to find out something he thinks she knows. I've vowed vengeance on him for years, but this time I'll not hesitate for the Queen's sake or any other reason."

Walter and Glennie exchanged uneasy glances. Fraser was in enough trouble already without trying to murder the Queen's half-brother. "James isn't in Edinburgh," Glennie remarked in a tentative voice. "Some say he's gone to Stirling for the christening but Mistress Drummond says he's at Wemyss Castle."

Fraser's scowl had grown deeper with every word. "Never mind," he asserted, already striding towards the door, "I'm not going after James yet. I'm headed for Dunbar."

BY HER FOURTH day at the McVurrich farm, Dallas was up and dressed, physically if not emotionally stronger. Annie, whose own garments were much too large, had borrowed some clothes from a neighbor girl. Dressed in a simple white muslin blouse and a plain blue kirtle, Dallas made her first foray outdoors after the noon meal, walking with Oliver and his three sons as far as the edge of their barley field. Sitting down on the low stone fence, she watched them continue on, scythes over their shoulders, waist-deep in the swaying grain.

A few moments later, she saw a rider cantering from the opposite direction along the Dunbar road. Dallas jumped up, waving wildly. "Iain! Iain! Over here!"

Fraser spurred Barvas to a gallop, then slowed the horse down just a few feet from where Dallas was standing. “Lassie!” He leaped onto the narrow path and seized her in his arms.

“Oh, my love!” Dallas buried her face against the soft leather of his jacket. He felt her convulsive movements, uncertain if she were laughing or crying. Gently, he pushed her away to look at her face. The bruises around her mouth were turning a sickly green, the swelling on her forehead was beginning to subside. He noted that she was shaking violently and seemed unable to speak. Fraser lifted her off the ground and carried her to the nearby stable.

Two of the McVurrich horses lifted their heads with mild curiosity. Fraser put his saddle blanket down on a mound of freshly cut hay. “Lie here, Dallas, you poor lass.” He dropped down on one knee beside her. “Do you want to talk about it?” he asked softly.

Dallas put an unsteady hand over her eyes. “I don’t know—it was so horrible. Maybe some day ....” She lifted her fingers to fleetingly meet his gaze. “It was James’s doing, wanting to find out what I knew about your father.”

Fraser stared at her. “Christ! I didn’t spare you after all by not telling you the truth!”

“It wasn’t just that—you see, I found a jewel case in Edinburgh Castle this summer, walled up in the library. I was certain it held one of the amulets.” Dallas told him the whole story and then recounted the questions James’s henchmen had put to her in the ramshackle house at Leith. Fraser listened raptly, then shook his head.

“So your father gave the amulet to Marie de Guise,” he said at last. “Your instinct was right, I’d wager that.”

“But can’t you tell me now who your father was?” Dallas asked, struggling to sit up.

Fraser gently pushed her back onto the blanket. “No. If anything, what happened to you proves how dangerous that knowledge is.”

Dallas could only mumble a weak assent. Fraser reached out to hook his forefinger in the bodice of her blouse but was amazed when she seemed to recoil at his touch. “Lassie,” he breathed, “was it that bad?”

She nodded, her eyes wet with tears. Fraser sat motionless for a few moments, his hand still on her blouse. Then he slowly slid it down from her shoulders and saw the savage bruises which covered her breasts. Unresisting, she let him remove her skirt, and with increasing shock he examined the rest of her battered body.

“Jesus!” he whispered, his own voice none too steady as he noted the teeth marks inside her thighs. Then he gave voice to the question he felt compelled to ask: “Were you raped?”

Twin tears rolled down her cheeks. “No. I—I stopped him in time.” She heard his deep sigh of relief and somehow managed to look at him squarely.

"But I feel so—-so soiled, so degraded. I don't think I'll ever forget what it was like."

He lay down beside her, wrapping her in his arms. "I'll not forget it either, lovey. He's a dead man, you know."

"He may be already," Dallas gulped. "I hit him with a coal shovel."

At any other time, her declaration would have made him laugh. But Fraser's mood was far from lighthearted. He understood the fragility of her emotional state and the terrible reaction she must still be suffering from such brutalization. The churls who had been responsible would suffer, too, he'd see to that. Yet he knew he must put aside thoughts of vengeance for now and devote himself to healing his wife's ravished spirit.

"I'm going to make love to you now," he said quietly. "I'll lock the door to make sure we're not disturbed." Fraser got up, went to the stable entrance, shot the bolt and came back to the mound of hay. Dallas was lying rigidly beneath him, the tears brushed away, her big eyes apprehensive. He was reminded painfully of their wedding night.

"Dallas," he said gently, stripping off his leather jacket, "you must remember that what happened to you had nothing to do with love. What happens between us has everything to do with it. Whatever that unspeakable animal did to you can't ever touch what we have together."

Dallas watched him undress in silence as she contemplated his words. Then he was next to her, cradling her body against his own. For almost a full minute he merely held her close, until at last she reached out and entwined her arms around his neck. Her lips trembled slightly as his mouth claimed hers; she sensed his unexpected gentleness and knew that he was trying not to hurt her. The hands which caressed her breasts were just as restrained. Dallas appreciated the tight rein he must be keeping over his usual intensity and guided one of his hands between her thighs. He smiled at her, a ghost of his mocking, crooked grin, and rested his head in the curve of her shoulder.

"Is my touch so loathesome now?" he asked, the long fingers tenderly plying the soft, moist flesh.

She shook her head. "But I do hurt-all over."

"Then I'll be very careful. Sit up. Here, I'll help you." He put his arms around her and pulled her close. " 'Tis a bit tricky, but you won't have to bear all my weight this way."

Dallas looked faintly bewildered but straddled his lap when she saw how hard and ready her husband had become. Fraser held her around the waist and she clung to his shoulders. Cautiously, he penetrated her body, and, locked together, they moved back and forth in an increasingly passionate quest of mutual fulfillment.

"Jesu!" Dallas breathed, as at last she slumped back in Fraser's arms. "I feared I'd never feel so again!"

Fraser kept hold of her as they both fell back on the straw. "Did I hurt you, lassie? I can't quite seem to get the hang of being restrained when you're in my arms."

She smiled at him lovingly as she pulled some pieces of straw from his dark hair. "You did right well, for a pirate. But," she added, propping herself up on one elbow, "this isn't the most comfortable bower I've ever lain in."

He reached out to run one long finger along her cheek. "Not as pleasant as the lake at Falkland?"

Dallas smiled dreamily at the memory. "No—but much more so than that first night—and those damnable pomegranates."

Fraser laughed aloud. "I could have been more sensitive. But you were so maddening and willful—and I thought to distract you."

"Distract me!" It was Dallas's turn to laugh—and she realized it was the first time she had laughed in days. "You distracted me all right, but to think I could ever have compared what you did to me then with what almost happened with that foul beast at Leith ...."

"Don't think about it." Fraser held her close again and kissed the tip of her nose. "Think instead, how far you and I have come since the pomegranates."

Dallas pressed close to her husband, ignoring the pain her bruises evoked. "Oh, yes, my love, we have indeed."

That night, when they walked hand in hand along the edge of the McVurrich farm, Fraser told Dallas that he had given up the *Richezza*. She was stunned, in spite of what he'd told her before leaving for Rome. Indeed, she actually tried to talk him out of it at first, fearing that he would eventually regret his decision and blame her for holding him to it.

But Fraser was adamant. "I've thought about it for some time and it's not just for you that I quit the sea. I won't say I walked away without a few pangs, especially for the crew, but that phase of my life is over." He paused as a cat crept up over the low stone wall, eyed them suspiciously, and zipped away into the evening fog. Fraser recalled the stunned reaction of his seamen who had not learned of his departure until he was actually ready to disembark. MacRae and Corelli had both been told the last night out. Stupefied, they'd argued with him for some time until they realized his mind was made up. MacRae was overwhelmed at the idea of captaining the *Richezza* but even more distraught at losing Fraser. Corelli, who would become first mate, mumbled a great deal in Italian and was still shaking his head in disbelief when their captain saluted the crew and walked away for the last time. From somewhere up in the forecastle, a lone piper had played a mournful sea chanty as Fraser rowed off in the long boat.

Dallas huddled into her cloak, for the September night was damp and chill, with a brisk wind coming off the North Sea to send the fog swirling over the partially harvested fields. "I never thought you'd really do it," she said. "All those handsome things in your cabin—you left them aboard?"

Fraser grinned at her. How like Dallas to concern herself more with the valuable possessions than with any of the other factors. "Aye, they belong there." He took her arm, steering her back towards the McVurrich croft. "One thing I took, though. I brought back the fur coverlet from the bunk to Beauly—I wanted that, to always remind me of how you shivered under it, scheming to marry me and making your strange bargain."

"It turned out to be stranger than I ever dreamed," she said, squeezing his arm. "All I wanted was to provide for myself and my family, to live a quiet, secure life. But look what happened instead!"

"It's not been tranquil, I'll admit. But for now, I think it best you stay here indefinitely," Fraser said, pausing at the door to the croft. He felt her bristle and continued speaking before she could protest. "It's not safe for you to go back to Edinburgh until I take care of a few matters. I'll remain with you here for a few days, though Annie and Oliver won't relish the idea of giving up their bed to us."

"We could always sleep in the stable." Her suggestion was not entirely facetious, but Fraser dismissed it with a kiss on her forehead.

"Nay, lovey, you need a comfortable resting place. When I'm gone, you can use Donald's old bed, and I'll leave money so that the McVurrichs aren't out of pocket having to keep you." He started to open the door, but Dallas put her hand on his arm.

"Iain, are we going to be poor?" she asked plaintively.

He raised one dark eyebrow at her. "I was wondering when you'd get around to asking me that. Nay, Dallas, we won't be poor, I've still got my estates in the Highlands, unless James figures out some way to steal them. But we won't be as well-off, that's just a fact."

Dallas wrinkled her nose, considering the prospect of reduced circumstances. "Isn't there some other type of work you might be interested in?" she finally asked.

Fraser stared at her for a few seconds, then threw back his head and roared with laughter. Dallas, obviously, was beginning to recover.

FOUR DAYS LATER he returned to Edinburgh. The city's mood was peaceful, with the court in residence at Holyrood. Fraser would have to see the Queen in order to report on his mission to Rome, but first, there were two items he had to take care of.

One of his serving men discovered MacInnes at the Thistle Tavern in Hackerston's Wynd. Fraser waited outside in the chilly October air for almost an hour. When MacInnes emerged, the duel to the death was conducted with dirks, and ended before more than a handful of onlookers could gather or the watch could be summoned.

Archibald Clark was tracked down in a brothel near Candlemakers' Row, lying with a scrawny whore. Clark's head was encircled with a dirty bandage and the whore fled when Fraser ordered her out of the room.

Fraser made certain his victim understood why the ultimate penalty was being extracted. Clark's death was neither as quick nor as clean as MacInnes's. Fraser was not a cruel man, but his inbred Highland code of justice could not always be subjugated to fit his conscience. He had given both men a fighting chance; it was more than they had given Kennedy, more than they had intended to give Dallas.

Fraser still had to deal with James Stuart of Moray.

JAMES DID NOT go from Wemyss to Stirling. The christening date had been delayed by the Queen and the elaborate preparations were temporarily put in abeyance, so he decided to return to his house in Edinburgh.

Shortly before James came back to the capital, Fraser made a surreptitious call on the Queen, who seemed happy to see him, eager for his news about the divorce proceedings. He carefully explained that while Pius the Fifth had agreed to consider the matter, he'd expressed concern over Mary's failure to suppress Protestantism in Scotland.

"I've practiced tolerance in order to keep peace," the Queen asserted petulantly. "Misguided though they may be, the majority of my subjects prefer the new religion."

"I personally sympathize with your approach," Fraser said calmly. "But His Holiness feels otherwise."

The amber eyes flashed angrily as the Queen picked up a silver-edged missal from her desk and threw it down in disgust. "I know how long papal dispensations take, and frankly, I don't care to wait for the Pope! Are you about to offer me more of your meddlesome advice?"

Fraser leaned his hands on the desk and faced Mary. "You asked me to go to Rome, which I did. I asked you to see that my wife was protected—which you did not do. In my absence, Dallas came close to being raped and murdered." He saw the expression of astonishment on the Queen's face and realized she'd probably not heard any of the details. "But all that is past," he went on, "and now I'm asking permission to ward myself in Edinburgh. My days at sea are over."

Distractedly, the Queen's hand fluttered at the silken veil which hung down from her pearl-edged coif. "I—I hadn't heard your wife was endangered. Tarrill should have told me."

No doubt Tarrill had thought it best not to prate her sister's horrendous experience about the court. Nor did Fraser have any intention of disclosing the details to the Queen. "You haven't granted my request yet," he reminded her with growing impatience. "Am I free to remain unmolested within the city?"

It appeared that Mary had to take a moment to comprehend his words. But she nodded jerkily and gave him her promise. A formal safe conduct would be drawn up for him that very afternoon. "I'll see that it's sent to your town house," she declared, one hand gripping the edge of the desk. Her white skin had suddenly turned chalky and she gritted her teeth in pain.

Fraser moved swiftly around the desk. "Lassie, are you ill?"

The drawn face regarded him uncertainly. "It's nothing, these attacks come and go. Send for my ladies on your way out."

He hesitated, unwilling to leave her in misery which was clearly both emotional and physical. The Queen had changed greatly since the spring; her behavior during this interview indicated some great erosion of spirit that Fraser couldn't yet fathom. But he'd been dismissed and knew that the Queen would be relieved to see him go.

JAMES STUART HAD built a small three-storied house next to Holyrood Palace. The wan October light was fading over the slanting gables and steep roofs as Iain Fraser dismounted by the hedge which surrounded the cobbled close.

A gaunt-cheeked serving man answered the front door. When Fraser gave his name, the man looked momentarily startled, but moved off immediately to inform his master of the newcomer's presence. As Fraser had half-expected, the serving man returned a few minutes later, saying that Lord James could not be disturbed.

"I'll wait then," Fraser said calmly, easing down onto a brocade settee.

"I'm sorry, sir, you don't understand ...." The serving man was not used to dealing with someone like Fraser. "His Lordship may be unavailable for the rest of the day."

Fraser surveyed the settee critically. "Not much room to stretch out .... Still, I could doze sitting up."

The serving man pressed his palms hard against his snow-white apron. "That's impossible, you must come back later on ...."

"Or not at all?" Fraser cocked an eyebrow at the man. "Don't fash yourself,

I know James would just as soon see a plague-carrier as me. But you might as well tell him I have no intention of evaporating like some misty Highland kelpie."

Thinking that anyone less like a water sprite would be hard to find, the serving man reluctantly scurried back to his master. Five minutes later, James himself appeared, regarding Fraser warily from his hooded eyes. "I'm quite busy with state matters," he said abruptly. "I understand you were outlawed and I have a good mind to call the watch to arrest you."

Fraser reached inside his jacket and pulled out a piece of parchment. "My safe conduct, signed by the Queen. Would you like to read it?"

James frowned at the parchment but waved it aside. "I've been away, I had no idea how misguided my sister had become in my absence. I shall have to speak to her in the morning."

"I hope you'll still be able to speak by morning," Fraser commented dryly. "I didn't come here just to listen to you prattle about your own self-importance, James."

Impassive as ever, James brushed a piece of lint from his plain black doublet. "Then I suggest you have your say and be gone," he declared, ignoring Fraser's veiled threat.

Fraser had risen from the settee. "Actually," he said with an indolence that masked his violent intentions, "I came to kill you. But this space is confining, so I suggest we move outside."

James's facial muscles tightened imperceptibly. "I always knew you were reckless, Iain," he said with a contemptuous little laugh, "but I never thought you were daft until now." He appeared to be unconcernedly stretching his arms but instead, his right hand had shot towards a bell cord next to the drawing room entrance. Fraser, however, was too quick for him. His sword unsheathed, he lunged at James, pinning the other man's sleeve to the wall.

"That was shabby, James, a trick unworthy of you. You're wearing a sword, I'll venture you can't even go to sleep without it. Now let's go outdoors and see if you can use it." Abruptly, he pulled his own weapon out of the wall to free his opponent's arm.

James's eyes glinted under their drooping lids. He seemed about to say something, then turned on his heel but made sure Fraser wasn't behind him. Throwing the door open, he let his unwelcome guest precede him into the close.

"Oh, no," Fraser said as James stopped. "Not here, where half of Edinburgh will be our audience and your household will race to the rescue. In back of Holyrood, on the level ground below Arthur's Seat."

"As you will," James shrugged. He didn't like it; he wished it weren't almost dark, with only a cleft of moon riding high in the autumn sky. But he'd never let

Fraser accuse him of cowardice. The two men trooped off around the house, skirted the palace gardens and halted on the damp grass of the meadow.

Though Fraser favored the dirk for close-in fighting, he knew James usually wore a sword. Consequently, he had decided to use the longer, slimmer weapon. He'd not want it said that he'd killed the Queen's half-brother without giving him every possible advantage to defend himself.

James moved back a few paces, trying to gauge Fraser's most vulnerable areas of defense. Though six inches shorter, James's compact frame and physical stamina made him a worthy foe. It also made him a smaller target.

He let Fraser move in first but was able to parry the thrust easily enough. They both made several probing feints, then James went high for Fraser's neck. It was a near miss, momentarily breaking Fraser's concentration. James moved in closer, but his opponent recovered quickly, parrying a second thrust and retaliating with a lunge that ripped the black doublet's shoulder padding. A subsequent attempt caught James in the upper arm. Retreating hastily, he sought time to regain his poise.

"I say you're daft, Iain," James asserted, trying to keep from sounding out of breath. "The Queen is unwell, and if she dies and you kill me, Darnley will rule!"

The threat was not a hollow one, Fraser realized. But Mary was not fatally ill, as far as he could tell. And Fraser had sworn to let nothing stop him from wreaking vengeance on James Stuart.

"I'll chance that," he replied, advancing on his foe. "I've so many scores to settle with you, I can't begin to count them all. But you know each one as well as I do."

James seemed to be considering Fraser's words but the apparent shift in his attitude was only a diversion—he lunged swiftly at the other man, grazing his left forearm. Then their swords clanged together as they fought toe to toe, neither daring to give the other an opportunity to break free. The proximity of their struggle prevented Fraser from seeing James draw a smaller dagger from the sleeve of his doublet. But he did catch the weapon's glint as it came thrusting up towards his ribs. Fraser whirled away and fell sideways in one furious motion. The impact knocked the swords from both men's hands.

But James fell upon Fraser, the dagger still clutched in his hand. Fraser swung sharply with his right fist, catching James on the temple. Grabbing his foe's wrist, he twisted it until James dropped the dagger. Then Fraser hurled James off of him and grasped him by the throat.

"Swords and such are too neat for you, James," Fraser grunted, using his knees to pin down his enemy's arms. "I'd rather kill you with my bare hands."

For once, James's eyes were wide open. "Killing me solves nothing! You'll die for it, you know!" He was dripping with sweat, struggling for breath, desperation oozing from every pore.

But Fraser was heedless of logic or consequences. His long fingers began to tighten around his victim's neck while James started to turn a hideous shade of purple. The voice which called Fraser's name had to repeat itself several times before being heard.

"Iain, for Christ's sake, leave him be!" Hands gripped at Fraser's shoulders in a vain attempt to break the stranglehold. At that point, James lost consciousness.

The Earl of Bothwell raised his fist and brought it crashing down against Fraser's skull. Stunned, Fraser released his prey abruptly and fell sprawling onto the grass. One hand rubbing his head, he sat up slowly, his fierce gaze turned on Bothwell.

"You meddling whorehound, why did you stop me?" Fraser yelled, struggling to his feet to confront the Border Earl and the four moss-troopers who stood alertly behind their lord.

"For God's sake, Iain, I know James has wronged you heinously, but killing him would mean disaster!" Bothwell stooped to pick up James's dagger, lest Fraser be unconvinced. The moss-troopers had already retrieved the combatants' swords. Bothwell lowered his voice, steering Fraser away from the others: "Queen Mary has been unwell since she gave birth. Even her mental state is unbalanced. If anything happens to her and James isn't around to protect the prince, Darnley will rule Scotland. And don't think he'd be strong enough to keep this realm out of Elizabeth's greedy hands. We'll all be dead men then!"

Fraser was getting a rein on more rational thought. He, who had always vowed to put his country's welfare above personal grievance and internecine feuds, was being put to a severe test. James had tried to kill him, had had him imprisoned, and though he'd had no part in putting him to the horn, had refused to lift the outlaw ban. He'd had Kennedy murdered and had almost succeeded in killing Dallas as well. Even Fraser's concept of loyalty to crown and country had its limits.

But there was one thing he hadn't considered. The crumpled man with the purple face who lay on the meadow grass was the only other person in the world who knew the identity of Fraser's father. If neither amulet was ever found, if no other proof could be unearthed, James Stuart was the only man who could offer witness. Though Fraser realized that James would only do so under the most severe duress, he had to stake his future on that frail, seemingly impossible chance.

He glanced at James's motionless form. "Maybe having his death on my conscience isn't worth it anyway," he growled. "His life is sin enough."

Bothwell let out a deep sigh of relief and clapped Fraser on the shoulder. "Now you're talking sense! If Scotland is going to be well governed, those of us with ability must keep our wits about us."

Fraser gave Bothwell a curious sidelong glance. Such a comment was out of character for the turbulent Border Earl! Obviously, Fraser thought, much had transpired during his absence.

One of the moss-troopers had hurried to join Fraser and Bothwell. "What about Lord James?" the man inquired.

"Go tell his servants to fetch him," Bothwell answered. "They know where to find him, they were the ones who told me about the fight in the first place. And give Baron Fraser his sword."

"But, sir," the man persisted, "is Lord James dead?"

Fraser broke in before Bothwell could reply. "Christ, no," he snorted contemptuously. "The puny-livered swine only fainted."

Chapter Twenty-Nine

FRASER WAITED A week for any repercussions from his fight with James. But nothing happened. Though rumors of the encounter trickled out into the Netherbow and down the Vennel and through the West Port, no one could be certain what really had happened. James's servants knew the value of discretion; so did Bothwell's loyal moss-troopers.

But Fraser was not deluded by James's inaction. Though Fraser moved freely about the capital, at least two of his men always kept close by. James, after all, was a very patient man.

The days passed by quickly enough for Fraser. He sought information about the Queen, about Bothwell, about all that had occurred during his sojourn abroad. The Queen wasn't herself and Bothwell now had great influence in state affairs, having leapt into the breach left by Rizzio's death and Darnley's estrangement from the Queen. Darnley himself, despite numerous attempts to reconcile with his wife, was in virtual exile in Glasgow, bullying his servants and drinking constantly.

To lighten the burden of politics, Fraser turned to his sons for company. He delighted especially in Magnus, who displayed a lively imagination and unbridled curiosity. But one of his most frequently asked questions was a very basic, "Where's Mother?"

Upon learning that the Queen had left for the borders to attend the annual assizes in the company of James, Bothwell and Maitland, Fraser sent Cummings to fetch Dallas.

She arrived at the town house on a blustery day in late October, wearing her too-thin summer cloak, a heavy serge blouse of drab brown and a wool skirt hitched up at the waist so that she could ride her horse astride. After

Fraser had greeted her with a resounding kiss and the boys had hugged her excitedly, she unwound the fusty plaid scarf from her tangled hair and kicked off her wet, ill-fitting shoes.

"By heaven, farm life isn't for me! Six weeks of hauling milk pails, thumping away at Oliver's damnable loom, and listening to Annie jabber about the cows' indigestion!" Dallas gazed around the supper room with renewed appreciation, then collapsed into an armchair. "I'm starving, but first I want a bath. Where's Flora?"

"She eloped with John Knox," Fraser said, leaning over the back of Dallas's chair and nuzzling the nape of her neck. "I once offered to give Meg a bath but you gainsaid me. Surely you won't again refuse me the privilege of assisting at a lady's toilette?"

Dallas leaned back to look up into her husband's hazel eyes. "Get the big tub," she said. "There's room for two."

THE NEWS FROM the borders was ominous: Bothwell had been seriously wounded in a typical border foray and lay near death at Hermitage Castle. A few days later word reached Edinburgh that the Queen had ridden with James to visit Bothwell and, upon her return to Jedburgh, had fallen dangerously ill. Churches in the capital were crammed with ordinary citizens praying fervently for their sovereign's recovery.

By All Saints' Day, the latest reports were more optimistic. Dr. Arnault had worked a miracle and the Queen appeared to be improving. Bothwell was said to be definitely on the mend. Even the very fog which enshrouded the city seemed to sigh with relief.

On a frosty evening in mid-November, Fraser looked up from the list of improvements he'd been writing down for the manor house at Beauly and asked Dallas if she'd consider going to Craigmillar Castle. "The Queen is being brought there by litter to recuperate," he explained. "I must abide by my word to remain in Edinburgh, but too much has gone on lately that I don't understand. If you agree to go, I'll send several men to protect you."

Dallas put aside the copy of Herodotus and frowned. "The rumors about the Queen and Bothwell are distressing. They're also confusing—some say he is wooing her and others say he uses threats and witchcraft."

"The only witchcraft Bothwell uses with women is in bed, but whatever means he exercises to gain control of Mary Stuart and the government, his rise must signify James's fall." Fraser had gotten up to throw another log on the fire. Outside, the wind had picked up, rattling the shutters and blowing snow clouds down from the north. "However amicably Bothwell and James may cooperate now, they hate each other, they always have. There's bound to be a confrontation, with the Queen caught in the middle."

Dallas pulled the skirts of her pale blue peignoir away from the hearth as the dry wood sent out a scatter of sparks. "Mind the carpet, Iain, you'll put holes in it yet."

"It's the wind, blowing straight down the chimney." Fraser knelt down to shove the logs back further. Dallas's mouth curved into a fond little smile as she watched her husband cope with the fire. For almost a month she had lived in relative, unfamiliar peace with her husband. He made only occasional protests about his confinement to Edinburgh, and she had begun to feel as if the secure, stable life she had so long desired was within her grasp.

"I'll go to Craigmillar if you wish," she said after he had stood up and was wiping his sooty hands with a napkin. "I've no mind to leave you and the children, but if you think it necessary, I'll be your eyes and ears at court."

Fraser leaned down to kiss her nose. "I think it is. And though you'll be well guarded, you're safe now. Whatever James thinks you know about the jewel case or the forged bond, he is certain you would have told me, too. There'd be no point in persecuting you further."

"How tactfully you put that," Dallas commented dryly. "Yet I'm not sorry you didn't kill James. Is that simple-minded of me?"

"Nay, lassie," Fraser assured her. "You're soft-hearted, as I've often told you. And," he added, stretching out on the floor in front of the fire, "I love you for it." She would never have to know about MacInnes and Clark; his own conscience would bear the burden for both of them.

Dallas managed to put off returning to court for several days, and by the time she left, the Queen and her retinue had moved to Stirling for the royal christening. On a cold, grey morning in December, she rode out of Edinburgh with Flora and six of Fraser's men.

While Dallas unpacked with Flora's help, Tarrill greeted her sister with a puzzling tale. "Donald came to Craigmillar for a few days in order to go over the christening expenditures," Tarrill began, sitting on the bed while Flora frowned at the wrinkles Dallas's gowns had accumulated during the brief journey. Neither sister had any qualms about talking freely in front of Flora; over the years, she had proven herself as discreet as she was loyal.

"After supper one night, Donald and I slipped away, to explore the castle. Donald remembered that he'd left a ledger in an anteroom just off the Queen's audience chamber. As he intended to recheck his figures before meeting in the morning with the prince's guardian, Lord Erskine, he had to retrieve the ledger at once."

Tarrill had gone with him, both moving noiselessly into the anteroom in case the Queen had retired for the night. But they realized immediately that Mary Stuart was not only still up, but conferring with her most important nobles. The door to the audience chamber was ajar just an inch or two, but

Tarrill and Donald could hear the earnest, conspiratorial voices without much difficulty.

"Donald motioned that we should leave at once," Tarrill said, a fine crease appearing between her dark brows. "But I was curious, I knew they were talking about Darnley, and though I shouldn't have, I insisted we stay."

" 'Twas natural, go on," Dallas urged. "What did you hear?"

Maitland had alluded to divorce, if the Queen would permit all the Rizzio assassins, especially Morton, to return from exile. Mary consented somewhat reluctantly but pointed out that the divorce must in no way jeopardize her son's legitimacy. Bothwell and George Gordon had begun to talk among themselves, apparently questioning how long such legal maneuverings would take. Sir James Balfour, the only lawyer in the group, pointed out that both Pope and Parliament would have to consent. Maitland interrupted at this point, suavely mentioning "other means."

"Then he said something strange, to the effect that 'James would look through his fingers' at whatever method was employed to rid the Queen of Darnley." Tarrill paused to see what effect this statement had on her sister. But Dallas merely frowned a little and said nothing. "The Queen protested that they must do nothing to dishonor her," Tarrill continued, "and Maitland assured her that whatever happened would meet with Parliament's approval. Argyll got up then, saying something about getting parchment and quills. Donald and I feared he might come into the anteroom as such writing materials are usually kept there, so we hurried out as quickly as possible." Tarrill sighed and tucked her legs up under her taffeta skirts. "We discussed it all at great length but didn't know what conclusions to draw."

Dallas toyed idly with her pearl and ruby bracelet. "Treason, I'll wager," she declared at last. "They'll arrest Darnley, charge him and execute him. After all, didn't King Henry in England do the same with two of his consorts?"

"That's so." Tarrill picked up a fox muff Flora had just unpacked and absently stroked the soft fur. "Yet Donald thinks they have no solid charge."

Rising from the bed, Dallas gathered up an armful of petticoats to store in the garderobe. "Darnley connived at Rizzio's murder and many still think the real target was the Queen. A miscarriage at that stage would have killed her."

But Tarrill remained uneasy. Dallas's ready acceptance of a treason trial puzzled her. She could not guess at how much her sister longed for a continuation of tranquil domestic life with Fraser and the children. To Dallas, Darnley's arrest and execution would be a neat, legal means of eliminating the man who had originally been responsible for sending her husband into exile. A more sinister means of ridding the Queen of Darnley might mean disaster.

PRINCE JAMES'S CHRISTENING was held with great pomp on December seventeenth in the Chapel Royal at Stirling. While many Protestant lords refused to enter the chapel itself, James Stuart, Bothwell and Argyll all attended, but one person's absence was noted with mounting speculation: Darnley was not present.

He was at Stirling, however, pouting in his chambers. Mary made excuses for him and allowed Bothwell to act as surrogate host. During the festivities, the Queen appeared more like herself, laughing, dancing, exuding her special charm to all, including the eighty nobles sent by Elizabeth to grace the occasion.

One evening while the courtiers muffled themselves against the cold winter air, fireworks were set off from the Carse of Stirling below the castle. Dallas stood with the others along the battlements, watching with wonder as spectacular bursts of color illumined the distant Ochils against the winter sky.

"It's a shame the prince is too young to enjoy such sights," John Hamilton commented as he edged in between Dallas and his sister, Barbara. "Though it seems grown-ups delight in fireworks as much as children do."

"True enough," Dallas replied, huddling into her miniver-trimmed cloak, "but they smell so!"

Hamilton smiled down at Dallas. They had seen each other casually during the fortnight since she'd come to court. On the surface, their relationship seemed to have resumed the pattern which had existed between them before their flight from London. If Hamilton still longed for Dallas, and if she herself had never quite understood her feelings for him, they kept these thoughts to themselves.

Barbara was gasping in wonder at an explosion of goldfish-shaped fireworks. Dallas, however, was gasping in wonder at something quite different: James Stuart had just strolled out onto the esplanade with Delphinia Douglas on his arm.

"What's this?" she whispered to Hamilton. "Has that snake James taken up with Delphinia?"

Hamilton glanced surreptitiously at the pair. Delphinia wore a magnificent purple cloak trimmed in swansdown; James was not as somberly clad as usual, since Queen Mary had personally selected a handsome new green doublet for him to wear during the christening festivities.

"James has many vices, but none as interesting as adultery," Hamilton said and then wished he hadn't for he saw Dallas stiffen and Barbara scowl. "No," he went on rapidly, "if James and Delphinia are going about arm in arm, it isn't because of any romantic notions—Lady Agnes is at Wemyss, suffering from the early stages of pregnancy, so it's possible that James is merely squiring the widowed Delphinia about for the festivities."

It was possible, Dallas admitted; but Delphinia had looked smugly suspect when she'd swept by on James's arm. "Those two are like a pair of cobras, ready to strike. I mislike their connivance."

"Don't let it spoil the evening," Hamilton said, not wanting to alarm Dallas further. But he realized as much as she that any conspiracy between Delphinia Douglas and James Stuart boded ill for Dallas and Iain Fraser.

TWO DAYS BEFORE Christmas, Dallas returned to Edinburgh just in time for a whirlwind shopping tour of the Lawnmarket and the High Street. She told Fraser about Delphinia and James, but though he was intrigued, he did not appear overly concerned.

"Delphinia is a born schemer," he said. "Who knows, she may be using James to help her find a rich husband." As for Tarrill's account of the meeting at Craigmillar between Mary and her nobles, Dallas's abbreviated, sketchy description left Fraser puzzled. "If they pardon the other lords for their part in the Rizzio murder, then I can't see how they can charge Darnley with his role in the tragedy."

"You know how things can be twisted," Dallas said blithely, holding up a toy sword she'd purchased for Magnus. "Do you think he could hurt himself on this?"

"Hmmmm?" Fraser was deep in thought, one long leg slung over the arm of the chair. "Nay, but keep him away from Robert."

The preparations for Christmas continued at a hectic pace; this would be the first time Dallas and her own brood would spend the holiday with her other relatives. They gathered together at the Cameron house on Christmas Eve, with Glennie and Walter and the boys, with Marthe and Tarrill and Donald. As new snow drifted down outside and the old carols reverberated within, Dallas thought the night seemed perfect. Donald had never quite overcome his awe of Fraser, and Walter had always felt a trifle uncomfortable in his brother-in-law's presence, but after several refills of the wassail bowl, the company grew increasingly congenial.

On Christmas day itself, the family joined together once more, this time at the Fraser town house. Dallas had festooned the walls with pine boughs and red satin ribbons; great swatches of fir stood in tall vases and garlands of holly decorated each of the fireplaces. Dallas herself wore a new gown of red silk trimmed with silver and a matching silver ribbon was entwined in her dark hair. Fraser declared she was the bonniest Christmas package he'd ever seen.

That night, when they were replete-with drink, food and each other, Dallas curled up against Fraser in the big bed and laughed over the antics of the children. "Jamie and Daniel are so grown-up these days," she said, "but they were scamps this afternoon, shredding their presents and fighting with each other over who got the best ones."

"Magnus should have been punished for taking away Robert's gifts," Fraser declared. "I'll be glad when Robbie is old enough to defend himself."

"I couldn't punish Magnus today," Dallas said, clasping Fraser's hand against her stomach. "At Christmastime, I suppose we must "look through our fingers,' as Maitland said of James Stuart."

Dallas felt her husband tense. "What do you mean, "look through our fingers'? I don't understand."

"Oh," Dallas replied, shrugging drowsily, " 'twas something Tarrill overheard that night at Craigmillar. If the nobles used other means to get rid of Darnley, then James would look through his fingers and not make trouble." She yawned elaborately and nestled into the pillow.

But Fraser had released her and was sitting up. "Dammit, Dallas, you didn't tell me everything! You mentioned Parliamentary approval, divorce and treason charges, but not this!"

"It's late, Iain, I'm tired," Dallas said peevishly. "We'll talk about it in the morning."

Fraser grabbed Dallas by the wrist, jerking her up into a sitting position. "You'll tell me now," he commanded. "You should have told me in the first place." He struck off a piece of flint, to light the one taper by the bed. Dallas blinked against the sudden brightness and pulled the comforter up around her shoulders. Annoyed, she launched into the entire story but was careful this time not to omit any of the details.

"I can't see that I left much out," she grumbled. "What difference does it make if they put Darnley in a barrel and sail him off down the Firth?"

Fraser was propped up on one elbow, rubbing the bridge of his nose. "Your judgment has deserted you of late," he commented at last. "Domesticity has softened your brain."

"Twaddle, Iain, that's not so!" But Dallas had to admit to herself that perhaps she had concealed the more sinister aspects of the Craigmillar meeting from her husband. As long as Fraser was not allowed to leave Edinburgh, Dallas could keep him securely in her arms.

"Legal methods are one thing," Fraser was saying, as if to himself, "but when Maitland talks of James looking through his fingers, he refers to something quite different—and illegal. Such schemes smack of intrigue which could only bring ill to the Queen."

"I told you, they said they'd do nothing to dishonor her," Dallas insisted as her eyes grew accustomed to the candlelight.

"Don't you realize by now that those self-seeking, ambitious cutthroats will do anything—anything at all—to serve their own purposes?" Fraser swung out of bed, his dark lean body outlined against the draperies. "I've told you often before that Scotland signifies little to them compared to their personal aggrandizement. They regard their country as I used to regard a merchant vessel—something to plunder, to use for one's own gain."

"Well, there's no point in staying up half the night fretting over their petty plots," Dallas averred. "Come back to bed, it's cold as a North Sea herring."

But it was at least five more minutes before Fraser blew out the candle and climbed back in bed. Dallas snuggled up against him, but for once he lay motionless beside her, staring up into the darkness.

FOUR INCHES OF new snow covered Edinburgh by morning. Fraser was up early and the prints of his calfskin boots were among the few tracks yet made along the High Street. The boots were new, a Christmas present from Dallas, and felt stiff as Fraser headed for Bothwell's town house in the Canongate.

The Border Earl was in his bedchamber, just getting dressed. Not waiting to be announced, Fraser pushed open the door and strode into the room. Bothwell stared in surprise at his unexpected guest but held out a welcoming hand.

"Jesu, Iain, you're abroad early! Will you breakfast with me?"

Fraser declined as he dropped into a chair, resting one leg on the other knee. "Being barred from court and warded in Edinburgh has put me out of touch," he said casually. "I come to find out what's happened in my absence."

Bothwell paused, his arms halfway into his shirt. "I thought your wife had been at court for a fortnight or so." The Border Earl pulled the shirt down and tucked it into his breeks. "What's the matter, Iain," he grinned, "haven't you given her a chance to talk since she got back?"

Fraser's mouth twisted into the familiar half-smile. "My lassie talks enough, but she can hardly learn in two weeks what's happened in five months."

"It's the same old story," Bothwell said, shrugging into a leather jerkin trimmed with lambskin. "Darnley is estranged from the Queen and mutters about getting revenge. Poxy little troublemaker." He picked up a decanter and two elaborately cut glasses. "Whiskey?"

Fraser nodded absently. "You've managed to secure a prominent place for yourself in his absence," he said mildly. "I would have thought you'd be better informed."

Bothwell's red brows drew together. "You sound a mite acerbic, Iain. Or," he queried with the faintest hint of malice, "is it envy?"

Fraser took his first swallow of whiskey and shrugged. "I've never sought power, you know that. You can make yourself King of Scotland, for all I care—as long as you don't hurt either Queen or Crown in the process."

Bothwell's laugh was forced and overhearty. "Christ, you're in a peculiar mood this day!" He sat down opposite Fraser and took a great gulp of whiskey. "One thing I will tell you, Her Grace pardoned the Rizzio conspirators on

Christmas Eve and will permit those who have been in exile to return."

"Morton, too?" Fraser queried over the rim of his glass.

"Aye, all of them." Bothwell lounged in his chair but Fraser thought the effort at looking relaxed came with difficulty.

"That's a mistake," Fraser said bluntly. "They should be punished, not pardoned. I can't imagine the Queen permitting it. Who influences her to countenance such misguided clemency?"

Bothwell offered Fraser another drink, but his guest declined. "Oh, she's a merciful lass," he said, refilling his own glass. "She hates bloodshed as most women do."

"She didn't hate it when the Gordons were her quarry," Fraser noted dryly. "No," Fraser said with a little shake of his dark head, "you must give me a better motive than mercy."

"I know of none," Bothwell said abruptly. He stood up, turning his back on Fraser, opening the draperies and peering out into the Canongate. "More snow," he said after a long pause.

Fraser had also risen and put down his empty whiskey glass on a side table. "You know," he said with an indolence which barely masked the threat in his eyes, "I don't meddle much in politics. But I would consider it, if I thought serious harm might befall the Queen and endanger the throne."

Bothwell had turned around. His skin seemed to merge with his red beard. "You talk in riddles," he muttered. "You have been out of touch too long."

"I think not." Fraser eyed the other man squarely and was amazed to see Bothwell actually flinch. "You've been a good friend to me," he said quietly as he picked up his heavy cloak from a peg by the door. "You could be a good friend to Scotland. Consider that."

Bothwell, the whiskey glass in his beefy hand, stood staring as Fraser left the room.

DURING THE NEXT few days, Dallas saw an unfamiliar facet of her husband's character. Fraser was extraordinarily quiet, spending much of his time sitting and brooding into nothingness or going out alone in the snow-covered city on long walks. Occasionally, he roused himself to romp with the children and at meals he asked Dallas about her day but scarcely seemed to hear her replies. Even in bed, he was detached, making love to her only once during that time and then in an aloof, almost absent-minded manner.

By turns, Dallas was annoyed, worried, and finally afraid. And on the last day of the year when she awoke to find him gone and his side of the bed cold to her touch, real panic set in.

Flying out of the bedchamber with her hair in disarray and her furred night-robe tied loosely at the waist, she accosted Cummings at the head of the stairs. "Where's my husband?" she demanded, dignity cast to the wind.

Cummings arched an eyebrow at her disheveled state. "His Lordship rode out early this morning, madame. He didn't inform me of his destination."

Dallas uttered a filthy one-word oath. Cummings twitched slightly but otherwise maintained his decorum. He should, he reminded himself sternly, be accustomed to Her Ladyship after all this time.

Dallas questioned everyone in the household that morning, from Flora to the stable boy. Fraser had left just before dawn, she learned, riding out with his retainer, Simpson.

As evening approached, Dallas paced the supper room, refused to join Glennie and Walter at the Cameron house to toast the new year, and even insisted that Ellen keep both boys out from under foot. When the city's church bells finally chimed in 1567, Dallas stalked up to bed. She lay awake for hours, finally falling into a restless slumber as the last sounds of the revelmakers died along the High Street.

Chapter Thirty

HENRY DARNLEY ARRIVED in Glasgow only forty-eight hours ahead of Iain Fraser. The consort had left Stirling on the thirtieth and Fraser cantered through the city gates late in the afternoon of New Year's Day. Glasgow lay in the heart of Lennox Stuart country, an ideal retreat for the apprehensive Darnley.

The Earl of Lennox received Fraser coldly. He had never forgiven the bastard Highlander for his outspoken opinions regarding Darnley's unsuitability as a royal bridegroom. "You are scarcely a visitor I would have expected," Lennox remarked, offering Fraser neither a chair nor a drink. "I was of a mind not to admit you."

"I was of a mind not to come," Fraser retorted, leaning against the carved mantelpiece of Lennox's handsome drawing room. "Where is His Grace?"

"Abed." The earl stood in front of a long Venetian mirror, his thickening body flanked by twin sconces set into the wall. "He's not feeling well."

"If I stay, will he be feeling well later?" Fraser asked wryly.

Lennox moved away from the mirror, a deep frown creasing his brow. "I can't say. I'm not putting you off, he's truly ill."

"In that case," Fraser said, pausing briefly to admire a portrait of the countess which hung above the mantel, "I'll say what I must and be on my way. I can trust you to deliver the message. Your son is going to be murdered."

The earl's face sagged with shock; he and Darnley had been expecting treachery but nothing as extreme as this.

"You lie!" he cried, advancing on Fraser, his hands clutched in front of him like beefy claws. "You hate my son! Why would you give me such a warning?"

Fraser held his ground, calmly regarding the earl with his cool, steady hazel gaze. "I don't hate your son. He's an unprincipled and dissolute young fool unfit to rule Scotland." Lennox's florid complexion turned an unhealthy purple at the blunt words, but Fraser continued: "My opinion of him has nothing to do with my reason for being here. If your son is assassinated, the Queen will bear the blame and Scotland will be thrown into turmoil. I won't stand by and see that happen. I've given it much thought these past days, weighing my own personal prejudices and well-being against the good of the realm. I finally decided I had to come and warn your son."

The empurpled skin was beginning to pale as Lennox lowered himself into a chair. "God's blood!" he whispered. "My poor laddie!" He sat with his chin almost resting on his chest, staring down at the tiled floor. Then he looked up at Fraser, who still stood by the mantel. "Who? Who plots this terrible crime?"

But Fraser would reveal no names. "The warning is sufficient. I've broken ward to come here, I've gone against my own interests. You'll have to be satisfied with what I've told you and take your own precautions."

Still stunned, Lennox remained immobilized in his chair as Fraser walked towards the door. "Can I believe you?" the earl muttered. "You may have tricks of your own."

"Nay," Fraser replied, "my word is good. You and your countess saved my lassie's life once. Though there's little else I like about you or your son, I could never forget that. Now we're even."

FRASER HAD GROWN so accustomed to moving about the city unmolested that he was surprised when two armed men hailed him just west of the Calton Burial Ground. They were dressed as moss-troopers and Fraser recognized them as Bothwell's men.

"Who are ye? Where do ye go?" the taller of the two men demanded.

"Iain Baron Fraser of Beauly," Fraser responded. "And this is my man, Simpson. I'm returning to ward myself in Edinburgh."

The two Borderers looked at each other. They had both seen Fraser at Hermitage with Bothwell in years gone by. But they had their orders.

"You are an outlaw, Iain Fraser," the taller man said. "The Queen has ordered that you be placed in the Tolbooth until your case can come before Parliament."

"The Tolbooth is where I'm headed," Fraser replied easily. He dismounted, signaling for Simpson to do the same. "I have a letter from Her Grace. Would you like to see it?"

Neither of the men could read a word beyond their own names but they would not admit that to Fraser. Their eyes were wary but both of them nodded. They could pretend to read the letter, and then hustle the Highlander and his companion off to the Tolbooth, confident of having performed their duty.

Fraser started to reach inside his jacket with his left hand; but his right fist flew out, catching the first man squarely on the jaw. Simpson fell on the other Borderer, knocking him to the ground. Both the moss-troopers had gone for their dirks. Fraser's leg swung up, catching the taller man on the forearm. A sickening crack sounded upon impact and the man's arm fell uselessly to his side, the dirk falling to the ground. The second man had been pinned down by Simpson, who wrenched the weapon out of the Borderer's hand and threw it into a snowbank.

Fraser and Simpson leapt back onto their horses. The man with the broken arm was crying out with pain. A handful of peddlers and farmers were coming up from the New Port, but Fraser could not spot any more moss-troopers among them. He put his spurs into Barvas's flanks and galloped away from the city.

THERE WAS NO mistaking Fraser's handwriting this time, though obviously the message had been written in haste. Dallas had received a parcel that morning which contained a finely woven shawl in the Fraser tartan. The note from her husband had been tucked inside the material.

"I've gone north for a short time since it appears my welcome in Edinburgh has worn thin. Wrap this shawl around you until my arms can take its place."

Dallas glared at the sprawling signature, then whirled on Glennie, who had stopped off for a visit on her way from the Grassmarket. "Devil take him!" Dallas screeched, flinging away the shawl and kicking at it in mid-air. "Devil take his ugly shawl, too!"

"I think it's rather lovely," Glennie commented placidly. "At least he sent you a present."

"Fie, Glennie, he wouldn't rest until he could be off somewhere, skulking about like a common criminal! Why didn't I marry someone peaceable like Walter or Donald?"

"You'd have perished from boredom," Glennie said drolly as she watched her sister stomp up and down the supper room. "But it mystifies me that Iain is said to be under penalty of arrest if he returns to Edinburgh. Why did he leave in the first place?"

Dallas plopped down onto the divan. "You think he told *me*? A fortnight ago I woke up one morning and discovered he wasn't there." She folded her arms across her bosom and thrust out her lower lip in a full-fledged pout.

"Maybe he'll send for you," Glennie suggested, trying to mollify her sister. "Though I hope you wouldn't leave before Tarrill's wedding."

"I most certainly won't," Dallas avowed. "Just because he beckons a finger at me, don't think I'll race off like a simpering country maid! Yet," she went on, waggling a finger at Glennie, "these marriage arrangements upset me mightily. The Queen has all but given her blessing to those pesky Protestants and their stiff-necked faith. Now Tarrill and Donald can't even find a priest to marry them!"

Glennie smiled sadly. "That won't bother Donald, since I think he'd have balked at being wed in the old faith. But Tarrill is upset, so am I. Yet what can we do?"

"Listen to Knox rant and rave, I suppose," Dallas said sourly. Glennie had to agree, but though she sympathized with her sister, she decided it was pointless to stay any longer and endure Dallas's ill temper. "I'd best be going, dearest, since Walter should be home with the boys soon. He took them sledding by the Nor' Loch."

"How nice," Dallas remarked in a tone which indicated she didn't much care if Walter had taken the boys to Peru. In fact, she thought angrily, for all she knew, that was where Iain Fraser might have gone, too.

A SHORT TIME LATER the Queen left for Glasgow amid much rampant speculation. Darnley had been very ill with smallpox, though some uncharitable souls said his disease stemmed from more sordid causes. To speed his recovery, his wife wished to take him to Craigmillar to bathe in the adjacent mineral springs. But Darnley refused: He'd been warned, he'd not walk into a trap.

But ultimately lured by promises of a reconciliation with Mary, Darnley decided it was safe to leave Glasgow, as long as he could choose his place of residence. He mulled over several possibilities, finally selecting a small but pleasant house in Edinburgh recommended by Sir James Balfour. Situated on a slope overlooking the Cowgate, the house had originally been connected with the old collegiate Church of St. Mary's and was known as Kirk o' Field.

Darnley traveled by litter, arriving in Edinburgh on February first. During the next few days, the Queen and members of her court moved back and forth between Holyrood and Kirk o' Field to visit the royal convalescent. Mary even spent several nights there in a room directly below her husband's.

Neither Dallas nor Tarrill joined the court that week; both women were occupied with the wedding, scheduled for February seventh. The ceremony would be held in the West Kirk, known before the Reformation as the Culdee Church of St. Cuthbert. From there the wedding party would proceed to a banquet at the Exchequer's house. The Exchequer had graciously offered his home for the festivities and insisted that Donald and Tarrill spend their wedding night under his roof. Though the couple had leased a flat in Blackfriars Wynd, they accepted the invitation. Since the Queen and many of the courtiers would attend the postnuptial festivities, Tarrill decided that after such a wearying day, it would be as well to stay on at the Exchequer's house rather than going to their own flat.

While Glennie helped Dallas and Tarrill with the trousseau and other preparations, Marthe and Flora fell back into their familiar pattern of bickering, and Walter and Donald tried to keep out of the way. It was a hectic week, almost busy enough to keep Dallas's mind off of her husband.

Iain Fraser, in fact, was not as far from Edinburgh as she imagined. Heavy snows had prevented him from going as far as Beauly, and though he had spent a few days on the fringes of Fraser country, he turned south again by the end of January. While Dallas rushed between her old family home and the town house, Fraser was at Callander, some twenty miles northwest of Stirling. It was there, in a small but tidy inn, that Fraser was approached by a Gaberlunzie man.

"I'll tell you a tale for a shilling," the man said, leaning on his staff and looking at Fraser with clear, sea-green eyes.

"I've not got a shilling," Fraser replied truthfully. His last few pennies would pay for this meager breakfast and he was already wondering if the poaching talents of his youth had grown rusty over the years.

The Gaberlunzie was not easily put off. He wore the ragged, flowing gown of his kind, and had a long, pale face with a greying beard. "You wear a fine cloak though it be somewhat soiled and torn. Your boots are of Spanish leather and look quite new. I'd say you are a man of means, though fortune may have turned her fickle face from you just now."

Fraser grinned at the Gaberlunzie. "If she doesn't have a change of heart soon, I'll be going about like yourself, telling stories for my supper."

"I'll tell you my tale for nothing, Baron Fraser." A whimsical smile touched the Gaberlunzie's face.

Fraser paused in the act of picking up the last bite of kippered herring from his plate. "You know me then?"

"Aye. From Edinburgh. I've seen you often, in the High Street and the Canongate Your man Cummings once bought me new shoes." He put a foot out, displaying the tattered leather bindings that now made up his footgear. "That was long ago, I'm afraid," he said ruefully.

"Sit then, mayhap some day I can reward you properly. I travel light these days and have naught to offer." He glanced down at his sole piece of adornment, the signet ring with the stag's head. Since it had been the only possession willed him by his mother, he could not part with that.

A perceptive man, the Gaberlunzie seemed to understand. "No matter, my story is short. Lord Darnley has been brought to Edinburgh by the Queen. He is recuperating from the pox in a house called Kirk o' Field."

Fraser had lifted both dark eyebrows at this piece of news. "Why would Darnley allow himself to be removed from Glasgow?"

The Gaberlunzie shook his head slowly. "Strange are the ways between man and woman. Often an army can't accomplish what one winsome lassie can. But there it is, Darnley returned, and Her Grace paying him much fond attention." He hesitated, watching Fraser consider this latest development. After a minute or two, the Gaberlunzie recognized that the other man had made a decision. "You'll be heading for Edinburgh, then," he said knowingly. "Mayhap I can ride with you as far as Stirling."

"As far as the outskirts," Fraser said, rising from the bench. "I find certain towns a mite risky these days." The Gaberlunzie nodded. "Edinburgh will be risky, too."

"I know that," Fraser conceded, heading for the courtyard where Simpson was readying the horses.

The Gaberlunzie rode behind Fraser that day and they talked of many things. Fraser never asked the man why he'd imparted his news; no one ever asked a Gaberlunzie such questions.

PROTESTANT OR NOT, the marriage ceremony had been beautiful, Glennie declared, her eyes rimmed red from joyful weeping. The banquet had been splendid, too, Walter chimed in, with plenty of his favorite oysters and some exceptional partridge.

"I thought the quail overcooked," Dallas declared, "and how the Exchequer thought to stuff most of the court into his banquet hall, I'll never know. It's stifling in here!"

"Hush, Dallas," Glennie admonished. "The Queen is just entering for the masque. Oh, doesn't Tarrill look marvelous!"

Tarrill and Donald were making their obsequies to Mary Stuart, who had arrived late from Kirk o' Field, where she'd spent the earlier part of the evening with Darnley.

"Tarrill and Donald both look marvelous," Dallas said, mimicking Glennie's voice, "the Queen looks marvelous, even Annie and Oliver look marvelous—for a pair of rustics." She was plainly put out with her sister's redundant comments about the wonders of the wedding day. She was also exhausted—the busy week, the long day and the anxiety over Fraser all finally coming together in the oppressive atmosphere of the Exchequer's banquet hall had made her more sharp tongued than usual.

"Dallas," Walter put in gently, "perhaps you should go away for a bit to rest. I'm sure the couple who rents my house in Earlston would be glad to take you in."

Feeling a pang of remorse, Dallas gave Walter a rueful smile. "Thank you, no, I'd rather stay in the city until Iain returns. That is," she added, with the note of asperity reappearing in her voice, "assuming he ever does."

Glennie was about to make a comment, but Mary Fleming was motioning for the masque to begin. Dallas tried to pay attention, caught herself dozing off several times, and never did quite get the gist of the performance except that it was something to do with True Love in Ancient Greece, and Jon Sempill seemed to be dancing a great deal in a sheep's suit.

A round of toasts followed, including the usual bawdy jests which Tarrill and Donald did their best to accept good-naturedly. The guests seemed to sense that the bride and especially the groom were not as receptive as others might be to such gibes, and when it came time for the couple to retire, the courtiers grew somewhat subdued. Donald allowed them to follow as far as the bedchamber door but stopped there with a protective arm around Tarril's shoulders.

"You've seen beds and you've seen newlyweds, so there's nothing new for you in what happens next," he announced in his low, deep voice. "But since it is new for us, I'll thank you to leave us to find out for ourselves." A few courtiers gasped, several chuckled, but all kept their places as Donald escorted Tarrill into the bedchamber and firmly closed the door.

"A good man," John Hamilton said, smiling in approval. "Your sister chose well."

"They chose each other," Dallas replied, turning to go back to the banquet hall for a final round of cheer. The Queen was already leaving, returning to Holyrood since it was closer than Kirk o' Field and the church bells had already chimed midnight.

"Will you join me in a toast to the happy couple's future?" Hamilton asked. "I've hardly seen you tonight."

"I'm very tired, John. I should leave …."

As if it were a reflex action, Hamilton put his fingers on her cheek. "You look weary, I'll admit, sweetheart." Abruptly, he dropped his hand to his side, closed his mouth tightly and glanced away. "Actually, Dallas, I wanted to speak privately with you. Might I escort you home?"

Dallas looked at him in alarm. She couldn't possibly let Hamilton see her home, not with Fraser away from the city. "I don't think so," she said, tugging at the long silver chains which adorned her dark green grown. "It wouldn't—I couldn't." She blushed and cursed herself for behaving like a silly chit.

"I'm not playing the importunate seducer," Hamilton asserted in a low, earnest voice as he steered Dallas out of the other guests' hearing range. "This may be very important. If I can't take you home, will you join Claud and my sisters at our cousin's house?"

Dallas was now cursing herself for wounding Hamilton. She wished she weren't so weary, that her wits were sharp and clear. If he said the matter was important, then that was the truth; Hamilton would never lie. And surely in the company of his relatives, there would be ample chaperones.

They walked quickly through the frosty night, along the Canongate, past the Netherbow Port and into St. Mary's Wynd. "Our sovereign lord must be asleep," Claud Hamilton noted snidely, gesturing to the nearby house of Kirk o' Field. "I hope he dreams ill."

"Enough, Claud," Hamilton said quietly. Claud frequently vexed him, but over the years he had tried hard to see his brother's better points and ignore the rest.

Gavin Hamilton apparently had retired for the night, too. As the little group, which also included Barbara, Jane and her husband, Hugh of Eglinton, entered the house, a servant came out into the hallway to offer a hushed welcome.

"Lady Fraser and I will be in the drawing room," Hamilton announced. "You may bring us something hot to drink." He turned to the others, bidding them good-night. Though Claud smirked, Barbara smiled pleasantly and asked Dallas to convey additional good wishes to her newlywed relations.

While waiting for the serving man, Hamilton broached the subject which had been disturbing him. "It's very late, so I'll say what I must. You recall that night at Stirling when Delphinia and Lord James came walking up the esplanade?" Dallas nodded as she made herself comfortable on a handsome cut-velvet settee. "I didn't want to cause you any unnecessary anxiety then, Dallas, but Delphinia had been trying to get information from me about your relationship with Iain. She had started pestering me as soon as I returned to court."

Hamilton paused as the serving man entered and placed a tray on a small table inlaid with marquetry. "Delphinia knew Fraser was outlawed," Hamilton continued after the servant had left. "Perhaps she thought—or hoped—your marriage was on precarious ground as well."

"Wishful thinking," Dallas said contemptuously.

Hamilton smiled wryly and sipped at his wine before he spoke again. "On another occasion, she bluntly asked how I felt about you." He paused again as a pained expression crossed his face. Dallas said nothing but regarded him with compassion and fervently wished she could throttle Delphinia.

"I was very discreet," he said at last, "but Delphinia is no fool. Would I marry you if you were free? The question caught me off-guard—I told her I was not the sort to speculate about filling a dead man's boots—or his bed."

Dallas looked away from Hamilton and felt her cheeks grow warm. "Brazen bitch," she muttered. "If she cares for Iain, why would she want him dead?"

"That was her point—she didn't. She said rather that it was a matter of ending your marriage, and that grounds for divorce were sometimes too strong to ignore."

Now Dallas riveted her eyes on Hamilton's face. "That's absurd! Delphinia sounds as if her wits have been addled!"

Hamilton refilled their wine mugs. "I think not. There is something afoot between her and James, mark my words. They're concocting a plot to undo you and Iain. But how—I don't know."

"It makes no sense!" Dallas rubbed at her forehead and frowned. "Delphinia wants Iain alive, James wants him dead. Their goals are directly opposed, and the mention of divorce is daft!"

"The very lack of logic is what worries me," Hamilton declared, putting his wine mug down on the inlaid table. The fire had almost gone out and the candles were burning low on the mantel. "But Delphinia and James met again this morning, before going their separate ways. I know, I saw Delphinia leave his chambers looking exceedingly smug."

Dallas sat in silence for a moment, watching the fading firelight reflect off her wedding ring. It occurred to her that Hamilton's concern actually worked against his own interests. And something else occurred to her as well—from out of nowhere came Delphinia's long-forgotten words about never giving up the game. The memory helped steel Dallas's resolve: "Delphinia can scheme from now until Doomsday, but the Nor' Loch will go dry before she has her way!"

Hamilton had gotten out of his chair and come to sit next to Dallas. "Nor will James ever get away with all his malevolent intrigues. I vowed some time ago that he would pay for what he's done to you." He saw the questioning look in her eyes and nodded. "Oh, yes, I know what happened in Leith. Tarrill told Barbara, and Barbara told me. There will come a time when the Hamiltons will put an end to James's sinister doings, you have my family word on it."

"Please, John, don't ever endanger yourself because of me! I couldn't bear it if I thought you might do something to bring about your own downfall!" The big eyes fastened on him as her fingers pressed together in a pleading gesture.

He took both her hands in his and kissed them gently. "I always do what I must. Though," he added with a rueful shake of his head, "I seem to take my time doing it." He let go of her hands and took her in his arms. "Stay with me tonight, Dallas. I need you. I've never stopped needing you."

Dallas was startled by his suggestion; she was even more startled by her own reaction. She wanted to stay, she felt secure and cherished in his embrace. "I mustn't," she muttered dreamily as he kissed her temple and the hollow of her cheek. "The servants will talk ...."

"We'll think of something to tell them," Hamilton said into the masses of her hair. Gently, he tipped her face up to his; Dallas stared into the brown eyes and felt herself move back in time to the inn at Durham. It would be so easy, so blissful to surrender to Hamilton again. Yet, she reasoned, she must not, she had almost lost husband and child for her previous indiscretion ....

But Hamilton's kiss blotted out logic and resistance. Dallas held him fast, her lips parted under his, and she felt his hands on her breasts. The years of controlled desire seemed only to heighten their mutual passion and Dallas made no protest when he began to pull the green court gown from her shoulders.

"Sweetheart," Hamilton sighed as he touched her nipples with loving, tender fingers, "there is not a woman in Scotland—or Italy either—to compare with you!"

"Oh, John," she whispered, leaning back in his arms so he could kiss her neck and throat, "you are my undoing—and I can't seem to stop you from whatever you intend to do."

Hamilton laughed delightedly, then pulled her down on top of him on the settee. "I didn't intend to do anything at first—but what is happening now seems inevitable."

With a sigh of pleasurable anticipation, Dallas started to help him unfasten the overskirt of her gown. "You are certain the servants won't ...."

A sudden wall-shaking explosion cut off her words. The night had come apart in a blinding flash, like thunder and lightning combined.

"Jesu!" cried Dallas, attempting to jump up, but finding herself even more tightly imprisoned in Hamilton's arms. "What was that?"

"I don't know, but it sounded as if it were just outside the house. Are you all right?" He looked down into Dallas's white face and felt her tremble slightly in his embrace.

"Yes, yes, but such a sound! John, we must see what's happened!"

Slowly, Hamilton released her and got to his feet. "Stay here, where it's safe." But Dallas was pulling her gown around her, curiosity overcoming caution. Hamilton was in the entry hall before she caught up with him. Several servants, Lord Hugh of Eglinton and Gavin Hamilton were already hurrying outside in their nightclothes. Just beyond the wall which separated the Hamilton residence from Kirk o' Field, they could see a bright red glow light up the winter sky.

From all up and down St. Mary's Wynd, people poured down towards Kirk o' Field. Some thought it was the end of the world; but within minutes they discovered the truth. Darnley and one of his servants lay dead in a corner of the garden.

Great murmurs of shock ran through the crowd. "It was black magic!" one woman cried. "The whole house rose up in the air!"

"The poor long laddie!" a man wrapped in a quilt lamented. "God rest his soul!"

Several onlookers had been joined by the nightwatch in making a wary inspection of the smoldering rubble which surrounded Kirk o' Field. Claud Hamilton had emerged, wearing a lapin-trimmed dressing gown. "We must see what's happened," he declared, but his older brother put out a restraining hand.

"Wait up, Claud," Hamilton cautioned. "We want no part of this. The whole world knows how little a Hamilton loves a Lennox Stuart."

Gavin agreed. It was bad enough that the King had been blown up in a house which adjoined their own. But now the family must keep together and attract as little attention as possible. Dallas, still shaken from the terrible shuddering blast, stood next to Hamilton, who had a protective arm around her shoulders. "Was it gunpowder?" she whispered.

Hamilton shrugged. "I suppose so. Yet it's strange—if the explosion killed Darnley and his manservant, why are their bodies so far from the house?"

"Ugh," Dallas grimaced, burying her face against Hamilton's chest. "Let's not dwell on it!" Much as Dallas had despised Darnley, she was repulsed by his manner of death. And then she remembered the conversation Tarrill and Donald had overheard at Craigmillar. Was it possible that this was what Maitland had meant by "other means"?

By now, the crowd had grown so large that the Hamilton group had been pushed back to the front stairs of their house. "We might as well go back inside," Gavin said, "we'll learn no more tonight."

"True enough," Hamilton agreed. "Come, Dallas, you're exhausted. You ought to be in bed."

"Not your bed, Hamilton!" Iain Fraser had one hand fingering his dirk, the other on Hamilton's arm.

Dallas broke free from Hamilton and hurtled towards her husband. "Iain! Where did you come from?"

"Never mind," he replied grimly. "The pertinent question is, what are you doing here?" The hazel eyes raked Hamilton, whose three kinsmen had formed a tight circle behind him.

Weary as she was, Dallas was not going to permit an ugly scene with half of Edinburgh as witness. "There's been enough mayhem for one night," she asserted, planting her hands on her hips and eyeing her husband head-on. "If you'd care to come inside, we can speak like civilized human beings."

Though only Gavin had picked up a weapon on his way outdoors, Fraser realized he was badly outnumbered. And if he had been astounded and angered to find his wife leaning on John Hamilton, he was not quite the same man who had tried to kill his rival at Strathmuir some three years earlier. Neither had seen the other since. Mutual antagonism flared up between them like a tangible thing, yet the horror of the night seemed to diminish their enmity. Surrounded by evil and treachery, Fraser and Hamilton accepted their animosity without seeking to resolve it. The proud nobleman and the arrogant Highlander wordlessly signaled a truce.

Nonetheless, Fraser refused to step over a Hamilton threshold.

"We'll talk here or not at all," Fraser affirmed, moving aside to let a half-dozen youths get closer to the murder site.

"This bedlam is hardly conducive to conversation," Hamilton said, raising his voice to make himself heard over the shrieks of some women who had gotten their first glimpse of the corpse.

Dallas shifted her gaze back and forth between the two men. She was thoroughly alert now, but still on edge from the shock of Darnley's murder and the tumult of the crowd. Out of the corner of her eye, she saw Claud and Gavin Hamilton watching her with bemused curiosity. "Then we'll go somewhere else. Tarrill and Donald's flat is just a few doors away in Blackfriars." Not waiting for any further argument from either man, she almost ran towards Our Lady's Steps, shoving aside several onlookers as she headed into Milk Row.

Hamilton signalled for his kinsmen to remain behind. Dallas was almost to Blackfriars before Hamilton and Fraser had made their way through the noisy crowd to catch up with her. She had been to the flat several times, helping Tarrill furnish her new home. But the door was locked and the landlord was gone, apparently roused out of bed by the explosion.

"Christ." Fraser regarded the gloomy corridor with annoyance. He stood with his arms folded across his chest, one booted leg slightly in front of the other. The old familiar stance made Dallas soften slightly but she remained silent.

"All right," Fraser sighed with resignation, "at least it's quiet. Well?"

Instead of answering Fraser's question, Dallas opted for counterattack. "I see you arrived too late for your sister-in-law's wedding, but made it in time for the King's murder!"

"God's blood, Dallas!" Fraser rounded on her. "You don't think I had a hand in that? I came back to Edinburgh to prevent such a thing, not to take part in it!"

"You? You wanted to spare the King?" Dallas stared incredulously at her husband. "But how did you know?"

"Never mind that now," Fraser retorted, prowling along the corridor and trying to keep his voice down in case some of the inhabitants had managed to sleep through the tumult. Hamilton was standing behind Dallas, one hand resting on the wall. "I've answered your question," Fraser glared. "Now you answer mine."

Hamilton put a hand on Dallas's shoulder, ignoring Fraser's grimace. "I can answer you."

"I'd prefer to hear it from my wife." Fraser's tone was dry. A draft from somewhere blew at his cloak and he slapped impatiently at the billowing fabric. "I trust you can still speak for yourself, Dallas?"

Dallas ignored the barb. As concisely as possible, she told him what Hamilton had said about Delphinia and James, sparing none of the details. As she spoke, her words were occasionally interrupted by chattering residents who were returning from Kirk o' Field. They paused to stare at the trio but made no comment. The night had already been filled with enough mysterious shocks.

Fraser had listened to Dallas's account with a growing sense of acceptance. He knew Delphinia well enough to realize she could be dangerous; as for James, his continued intrigues were an old story by now. Yet being grateful to Hamilton was extremely difficult. Then he noticed something which had never occurred to him before: Hamilton's stance in back of Dallas was more than protective, it was proprietary. Fraser knew his wife too well not to be aware that the other man's attitude was not only accepted by Dallas but somehow necessary to her.

"Jesus," Fraser breathed, forgetting momentarily about James and Delphinia, about Darnley's body lying just a hundred yards from Blackfriars. What he had just perceived astounded him, yet explained much that had long puzzled him about his wife. "You love this man, don't you?"

Dallas's hand flew to her bosom. Then she took a deep breath, gazed thoughtfully from one man to the other, and moved between them with unaccustomed dignity. Dallas had spent too many years fending off love to deny what she had ultimately won. "Yes," she answered simply. "I love John. I must have always loved him—but only in admitting it now to you have I admitted it to myself."

"Oh, Christ!" Fraser banged his fist against the wall, then wheeled on Dallas and Hamilton. "Then why in God's name didn't you marry him in the first place!"

"Oh, Iain!" Dallas was infuriated. Hamilton was gazing uncomfortably at them both. While the revelation might have come as a shock to both Dallas and Fraser, he was not surprised; despite her apparent uncertainties, Hamilton had always been certain that Dallas loved him.

And Dallas was confessing as much. "It was natural enough for me not to face the fact that I loved John. It was also natural that it would take me a long time to realize it. My God, it took me forever to recognize how much I loved you!"

Fraser had started to prowl the passageway, muttering angrily under his breath. Hamilton put a hand on Dallas's shoulder. "What can I say, Dallas? Your candor pleases me as much as it disturbs your husband."

"I suppose I can't expect it to make him feel elated," Dallas retorted in a vexed tone. "Really, Iain," she said as his pacing brought him within a couple of yards, "this is hardly the place for a domestic denouement. You seem to forget we have a murdered King lying just a few steps away."

Fraser's heavy cloak swooped like a huge bat as he turned abruptly. "What do you want me to do? Offer you your damned annulment after all?"

Dallas gasped. Her husband looked furious, miserable and confused all at once. "Of course not! I'm your wife, I love you, I refused to even think of an annulment when other women might have leaped at the opportunity." She clasped Fraser by the shoulders and her sheer force of will seemed to immobilize him. "I love you! I love you more than ...."Her voice trailed off as she glanced at Hamilton.

"More than you love him?" Fraser spoke sharply, one thumb gesturing jerkily in Hamilton's direction.

Dallas sighed. "Oh, fie! Yes. Yes, I suppose I do. But," she added, turning to Hamilton, "that takes nothing away from my feelings for you, John."

Even had the passageway been well lighted, it would have been impossible to tell which man looked more perplexed. Dallas stood between them, wondering how men could be so dense. "Iain," she said at last, "you must get away from here. It isn't safe, you may be suspected of complicity in Darnley's murder. And you, John, everyone knows the rivalry between the Hamiltons and the Lennox Stuarts."

Fraser swore softly, Hamilton sighed resignedly, but they both followed Dallas out of the passageway and into the wynd.

DALLAS HAD ASSUMED they would seek sanctuary in the town house, but Fraser swiftly relieved her of that notion. "Your reaction to my sudden appearance is one all Edinburgh will share. I must leave the city at once."

The crowd had begun to disperse, realizing there would be no more excitement or revelations that night. Fraser and Dallas had mingled with the others, moving south to the Cowgate. Rumors were rampant: A henchman of Bothwell's had been arrested; Darnley had actually been strangled; a woman swore she had seen a nobleman in court dress flee Kirk o' Field just before the explosion.

"If you race off again, I go with you," Dallas declared firmly. "I made up my mind after you left without a word this last time that from here on, we take flight together."

They had paused by St. Mary's Wynd Port, which led out of the city and into the adjacent farmlands beyond the new wall. "That's rather impractical," he said testily. Fraser still had not recovered from his recent insight and Dallas's frank admission. "Damn, I lost Simpson in all the commotion. If he were here, he could take you home."

Dallas was leaning against the stones of the city wall. "I'm not going home, I'm going with you. Didn't I just say that?"

Fraser swore under his breath and grasped her by the arm, all but pulling her through the portal. No one stopped them; apparently the guards were still at the murder site. They moved quickly down the snow-powdered lane, towards an abandoned stable where Barvas was tethered. Just as Dallas climbed up behind Fraser, Simpson cantered towards them.

"Go to my town house," Fraser commanded. "Tell Cummings that Her Ladyship and I are leaving the city. We'll try to let them know where we've gone later."

Simpson saluted Fraser, attempted a bow from the saddle to Dallas, and galloped back towards Edinburgh. Wheeling Barvas around, Fraser spurred the horse southwards as the moon began to set over the distant River Tyne.

TARRILL AND DONALD had drifted off to sleep in each other's arms when they were awakened by the explosion at Kirk o' Field. Donald had wanted to rush out to learn what had happened but Tarrill had urged him to remain with her. A half hour later, the Exchequer's servants brought them the news of Darnley's death.

For what remained of the night, the newly married couple slept little. Every time one of them began dozing off, the other would suddenly come up with a new piece of speculation. When dawn finally spread out across the February sky, Tarrill got up and announced she should leave for Holyrood to be with the Queen.

This time it was Donald's turn to protest. "The Queen has ladies aplenty to help her grieve," he said, kissing the curve of Tarril's neck as she began brushing her long black hair, "but I only have one wife."

Tarrill found his argument irresistible, but she did go to Holyrood later that day. Mary Stuart was astonishingly composed, behaving like a stiff, inanimate puppet.

"Has she cried?" Tarrill asked Barbara Hamilton.

"Not to my knowledge." Barbara critically surveyed a bolt of black serge, the first of the mourning materials delivered to the palace. "Her initial reaction was fright—she was certain the assassins aimed not for Darnley but at her."

"Oh!" Tarril's hand flew to her cheek. "I'd not thought of that! But of course, the Queen has been staying frequently at Kirk o' Field. It was only because of my wedding that she went to Holyrood instead last night."

"That's right," Barbara said with a sage nod. "You may be responsible for saving Her Grace's life."

"A coincidence," she said, wondering how soon she could impart these new facts to Dallas. Later, however, when she stopped off on her route from Holyrood to her new flat in Blackfriars, Tarrill discovered that her sister had fled the city.

FRASER HAD RIDDEN Barvas hard over the frozen ground to Dunbar. Dallas had suggested going to the McVurrich croft since the entire family was spending several days in Edinburgh following the wedding. But her husband didn't want to implicate anyone else in their turbulent affairs. Since Dallas still wore her dark green court gown, he thought it best to purchase something less ostentatious. Following a noon meal at an inn on the outskirts of Dunbar, he rode alone into town to obtain more suitable clothing for her and a change of gear for himself.

"A good thing I had some money with me," Dallas said when Fraser returned to their room at the inn. "You seem to have spent all yours in doing God-knows-what these past weeks."

"Aye, extravagances such as food and shelter," Fraser retorted. "I'd no plan to be gone more than a few days when I left." In bits and snatches, he had explained what had happened to him since his departure on New Year's Eve Day. She had been confounded by his determination to warn Darnley and his subsequent vain efforts to prevent the consort's death. But Fraser's persistent ideals about Queen and country had always mystified her; there was no point in arguing with him at this late date.

"Oh, Holy Mother," Dallas exclaimed in disgust as she unwrapped the blouse and kirtle her husband had purchased. "Orange! I detest orange! And this drab olive skirt! Would you make me into a crone?"

For the first time since being reunited with his wife, Fraser smiled faintly. "I'll admit men won't swoon when you walk past, but then we don't want you attracting every eye, do we?"

Dallas was pulling the elegant court gown over her head. "The way you've been acting of late, I don't think I could even attract yours anymore," she said in a muffled voice.

"I was preoccupied before I went to Glasgow," Fraser said with uncharacteristic defensiveness. "I had important decisions to make."

Carefully hanging her green dress inside the tiny wardrobe, Dallas gave

Fraser a questioning look from over her shoulder. "That was six weeks ago. You don't seem any more ardent now."

Fraser slammed his hand against the back of a chair. "Dammit, Dallas, how should I behave after you've coolly acknowledged you love another man? I think I found your going to bed with Hamilton easier to understand than that!"

"Fie, Iain, you know that's not so!" Dallas tossed her tumbled hair out of her eyes and smoothed down the folds of her petticoat. "If that were true, you'd have slit poor John's throat on the spot!" Advancing on him, she waved a finger in his glowering face, "At least now you know why I succumbed to him in the first place, and that's more than I knew myself at the time!"

He moved away from her, prowling about the room until he sat down on the bed. "I realized that last night," he conceded, draping one long leg on the faded counterpane. "I should have known all along that you, of all women, would never bed with someone you didn't love."

"But I love you more," Dallas declared with considerable vigor. She had come to the bed and flung herself down beside him. "For God's sake, Iain, I had ample opportunity to bed with John last summer while you were away. Yet I never permitted him the slightest familiarity," she averred, somehow managing to dismiss the previous night's near indiscretion from her mind. "You must remember, until I met the two of you, no man had ever made me feel like a woman. John showed me another side of myself, a tenderness, a sense of peace, a desire to give of myself. If I'd never loved him, I might not have made that discovery, and you and I both would have been the poorer for it."

"Jesus," Fraser muttered, "now I'm supposed to be grateful to the whoreson for making love to you?"

Dallas shook her head in exasperation. "Of course not. But it took both of you, being so different, to break down the barricade I'd built around myself. When that finally happened, I found out about love, and that it wasn't always the same. My love for you, my love for John, my love for the bairns, for Tarrill and Glennie and all the rest—all are unique kinds of love. Now I'm part of you, just as you're all part of me. Oh, Iain, am I making any sense?"

Fraser lay on his side, his head on his hand. "Perfect sense, since most people figure that out by the time they're twelve. Nay, Dallas," he said quickly, seeing the angry hurt spread across her face, "I didn't mean that in reproach. We all learn about life at our own pace. Until I met you, I wasn't open to love, either. Making love was easy, loving was the hard part. And then you came along, rebuffing the least of my advances, forcing me to deal with you in a completely different way than I'd ever dealt with a woman before. It was the first time I'd felt the need of wooing the heart along with the body."

Touching his thick new growth of beard, Dallas smiled. "You did it well. I love you, Iain."

"Hmmmm. I know you do, lassie. But I still can't quite take your feelings for Hamilton in stride."

"No," she said, moving her fingers to trace the outline of his ear, "perhaps you can't. But then I've never gotten used to wondering whose embrace you're lying in when we're apart, either."

"That's different," he asserted, rolling over to take her in his arms. "I never loved any of them."

"No. But pain, like love, may be different, yet it's still pain." She winced suddenly as the beard rubbed her cheek.

"Maybe pain is love," he replied, kissing the corner of her mouth.

"Maybe. At least it will be for me, until you shave off that damned beard."

THROUGHOUT EDINBURGH, THE whispers grew: Bothwell had murdered the King. The most blatant placards appeared along the High Street, accusing the Border Earl of regicide and implicating the Queen as his whore. Darnley was no longer the spoiled, contemptible fool, but a hapless victim whose blood had been spilled to make way for the illicit lovers.

Mary responded not with prudence but with collapse. By late March, she had taken to her bed and a new rumor spread: The Queen was carrying Bothwell's child. As she lay weak and melancholy at Holyrood, pressures mounted for Bothwell's arrest and trial. Ultimately, it was not Mary who acted but the Earl of Lennox who, through private petition, demanded that the Border Earl be brought before Parliament.

According to Scottish law, both accuser and accused could bring no more than six followers to the Tolbooth. Lennox felt compelled to comply with the stricture, but Bothwell, whose moss-troopers had filled the city for some time, showed up in the company of Morton, Maitland and four thousand Borderers.

Faced with such awesome numbers, Lennox did not confront his son's alleged murderer. The trial went on, however, lasting some seven hours before Parliament acquitted Bothwell.

When the news reached Dunbar the following day, Fraser mulled over the possible courses of action he might take to ameliorate the situation. He and Dallas had managed to lease a small farmhouse near the sea, using Dallas's jewelry as collateral. They had not made the deal themselves but had Oliver McVurrich handle it for them. Though Fraser had been loath to involve Oliver, the other man had insisted. He'd enjoyed pulling the wool over old Farquharson's eyes and telling him how he'd inherited a small fortune of jewels while in Edinburgh. Dallas had been surprised at the usually staid McVurrich but decided that a fortnight in the city had made him light-headed.

Posing as chicken farmers recently come from the Highlands, Dallas and Fraser moved into the sparsely furnished croft at the end of February. "Do you know anything about chickens?" she asked her husband. "I suppose we'll have to get some."

Fraser assured her that his bucolic background at Beauly would put him in good stead. Dallas had rolled her eyes at this pronouncement but once the chickens were installed, she was amazed at her husband's knowledge.

"Highlanders seldom make good farmers, but they love the land," he told her. "I'm an exception, since I love the land enough not to want it wasted. You forget, my sole source of income now derives from my farmlands."

Dallas was sitting on an overturned bucket, watching her husband candle the eggs. "It's just that I've never seen you in such a capacity before. Every so often I feel as if I don't know you as well as I thought."

"Man of multiple talents am I," Fraser grinned, placing the basket of eggs on the hen house floor. "But," he added, kneeling next to her and lifting the drab olive skirt, "essentially, the same simple bridegroom you married all those years ago."

"Not here, Iain!" Dallas protested as he slipped his hand between her legs. "This place smells!"

Fraser sniffed experimentally. "A bit. But you smell good, lassie, like clover."

"More like chicken droppings if we stay here," Dallas retorted, finally pulling away and knocking over the bucket in the process. "Besides, we have to get our eggs to market."

With an exaggerated sigh, Fraser picked up the basket. "A farmer's life is hard. So much sacrifice is required just for survival."

Their life during those weeks at Dunbar was filled with tension and tenderness, laughter and love, quarrels and quietude. Dallas did the cooking and cleaning, grumbling all the while. They both wished the children could have come, too, but didn't dare send anyone to fetch them from Edinburgh. Indeed, the message Fraser had dispatched to Cummings did not pinpoint their hideaway, lest it should fall into the wrong hands.

The folk they met in the Dunbar marketplace regarded them with curiosity. Newcomers were always treated thus, but the tall man with the hawklike profile and the indolent arrogance wasn't like any chicken farmer they'd ever seen before. As for his spouse—well, even dressed as badly as most of the other local women, she seemed both too lush and too refined for a farmer's wife. Yet Oliver McVurrich had vouched for the couple and all Dunbar knew what an honest man he was.

BUT THE NEWS of Bothwell's acquittal shattered the idyll. Fraser had already made up his mind to see the Queen when a new report reached Dunbar: James Stuart had left Scotland, ostensibly to make a leisurely tour of England and the Continent.

"Bothwell and Mary are steering their craft straight into the eye of the storm," Fraser asserted. "Didn't I tell you this would happen?"

"You're prescient, Iain," Dallas said, half-jokingly. Arguments or attempts to keep him at Dunbar were doomed to failure, as she recognized from experience. As for Fraser, he did not delude himself into thinking he could dissuade either his Queen or the man who had been his friend from their heedless course; still, his deeply ingrained loyalties required that he at least try.

Dallas knew it was pointless to remind Fraser of the dangers he would face upon his return to Edinburgh. With unwonted stoicism, she kissed him good-bye on the third morning of April, stifled one last urge to insist he let her come with him, and watched until he and Barvas cantered out of sight along the coastline road.

The Queen was in Edinburgh, somewhat recovered and making ready for the official opening of Parliament. The session called to sit upon Bothwell's murder charge had been a special one and not attended by the sovereign.

Fraser entered the city the morning after he left Dunbar, coming up through the long, steep Vennel and mingling with the usual influx of tradesmen, peddlers and farmers. Dressed in his rustic clothing, no one noticed him leading Barvas between several other far less magnificent specimens of livestock. He headed directly for the Cameron house in Nairne's Close.

Glennie was astonished to see him on the front stoop, though whether his appearance or his presence amazed her most, he could not tell. "I almost didn't recognize you with that beard!" she exclaimed, after he'd stepped into the hallway. "Where's Dallas? Is she all right?"

"She's out gathering eggs right about now," Fraser grinned as Glennie's blue eyes grew even wider. "Didn't you know your sister always longed for the rural life?"

Walter and Marthe both appeared before Fraser could offer any detailed explanations. After they had recovered from their own surprise, he became serious, impressing upon them the need for keeping his visit secret. "I must see Tarrill," he said, between mouthfuls of Marthe's cornmeal cakes. "Is she at court?"

Glennie told him that she was, but returned most nights to the flat in Blackfriars. Fraser asked if she could get a message to Tarrill, requesting her to stop at the Cameron house. Hesitantly, Glennie agreed. "Donald usually escorts her to their place since the Exchequer is so near Holyrood. You won't do anything to endanger Tarrill, will you, Iain?"

Fraser cocked an eyebrow at his sister-in-law. "We're all in trouble just now," he said dryly, "whether we know it or not."

The message which Daniel and Jamie guilelessly carried to Holyrood not only invited Tarrill to stop off at the Cameron house but to bring the two Fraser boys with her for a cousinly visit. A second message was enclosed with the first, addressed to Cummings but to be delivered by Tarrill. Fraser would need a change of clothes and some money.

Tarrill, Donald and the two small boys arrived shortly after seven. Magnus climbed all over his father with delight and Robert demonstrated his ability to walk. Fraser promised them both special treats since he had missed their birthdays.

"You always do," Magnus said bluntly. "Why don't you and Mother stay home?"

Somewhat guiltily, Fraser explained that he and Dallas did not want to go away, that certain evil people had forced them to leave, and that he hoped some day soon they could be together for always.

"In most families like ours the children don't live with their parents anyway," Fraser pointed out. "They are raised by their guardians. It's a custom among the wellborn, but one which your mother and I don't favor."

Magnus allowed that he was glad, told his father he thought his beard looked funny, and ran off to play with his big cousins. Fraser then sat down with Tarrill and Donald to work out a way to see the Queen.

"Maybe," suggested Donald, "it would be easier to get the Queen out of Holyrood than to get you in."

Ultimately, they agreed. In happier times, Mary Stuart had delighted in dressing as a peasant girl or even as a young lad and going about the city incognito. It was an avocation she'd inherited from her father, who traveled the country in many guises, even that of a Gaberlunzie. Tarrill would suggest that the Queen take her mind off her troubles by dressing as a simple burgher's wife and going to Blackfriars to visit the McVurrich flat.

"I'll tell her that I know we could never entertain her royally there, but that I want so much for her to see our first home," Tarrill said ingenuously. "You know how she is about love and romance—the idea will be irresistible."

Fraser agreed the plan might work. "Your lass is as cunning as she is fair," he grinned at Donald. "I'd watch out for her, if I were you."

"Aye, I do that," Donald beamed, gazing proudly at his wife.

Mary Stuart, attired in a homespun skirt of grey muslin and a simple blue bodice laced in with a darker blue stomacher, arrived with Tarrill in Blackfriars late the following afternoon. The Queen had opened Parliament that day and the idea of going from elaborate robes of state to the homely garb of a burgher's wife had instantly appealed to her.

Tarrill was dressed in a similar costume and both women were giggling when they ascended the stairs to the McVurrich flat. Outside in the close, two royal retainers waited, having followed the Queen from Holyrood at a discreet distance.

"To think I traveled from the palace to the Tolbooth this morning surrounded by hackbutters and men-at-arms!" the Queen exclaimed as Tarrill turned her key in the lock. "But now, I go like the breeze, virtually free of encumbrance."

Iain Fraser, still bearded, but wearing his own clothes, stood waiting by a tall window which looked out into the street. When Mary Stuart came through the door, he made a deep bow.

"Welcome, Your Grace. Circumstances have reduced me to becoming the McVurrich valet."

But the Queen did not find his remark amusing. Her expression froze and she turned abruptly to Tarrill. "You knew he was here?"

Flushing slightly, Tarrill nodded. "It was prearranged. My brother-in-law has been most anxious to see you privately."

"You tricked me!" the Queen railed at Tarrill. "You lied! I'll not have you attend me again!"

Tarrill began to protest, but Fraser interrupted. "It was my doing, Your Grace. Tarrill behaved as any loyal kinswoman would. If she'd told you the truth, would you have come?"

Mary Stuart held a long white hand against her throat.

"No. You broke ward, you're an outlaw. I don't deal with criminals." Haughtily, the Queen swept towards the door.

"If," Fraser remarked coolly, "criminals offend you, why does my lord Bothwell stand so high in your esteem?"

The Queen stood stock-still, then turned slowly to look at Fraser. "I don't understand you. Lord Bothwell was acquitted."

Fraser picked up a china comfit dish and examined the pattern of cherry blossoms around the rim. "No one believes he's innocent, least of all Edinburgh's good citizens." He set the dish back down on the sideboard and forced the Queen to look directly at him. "No one who was at Craigmillar one night last November would believe it either."

Tarrill had uttered a little gasp but the stunned Queen didn't notice. "You?" Mary Stuart breathed. "You were at Craigmillar?"

Fraser carefully avoided the anxious gaze of his sister-in-law. "I'd hardly admit it if I had been. That would mean I'd broken ward not once, but twice."

"Laws, rules, restrictions mean nothing to you!" the Queen cried, taking the offensive and advancing angrily on Fraser. "You've lived outside the law so long you don't know the meaning of integrity or honor!"

If Mary Stuart had been a man, Fraser would have struck her. As it was, his mouth tightened in the black beard and the hazel eyes turned as hard as onyx. "Do you mean to tell me," Fraser demanded between clenched teeth, "that though all other malcreants in this realm are forgiven their sins, real or imagined, I am not?"

The Queen could not help but glance at Tarrill, who looked as helpless as she was confused. "I mean you are still an outlaw," Mary Stuart said with unwonted harshness. "You are fortunate you haven't landed in the Tolbooth long before this. You put yourself above crown and council, Iain Fraser. You always have, in typical, arrogant Highland fashion."

His dark face blazed with a fury which only the greatest effort at self-control kept in check. "You'd cast old friends aside to go your heedless way? You will see injustice done to me and no justice at all for those who are guilty?"

The nerves which throbbed so close to the surface almost gave way in the face of Fraser's onslaught. But Mary Stuart was committed, body and soul, to her course of action. "I have finally found someone in whom I can put total trust," she asserted in a voice that trembled. "Someone who not only cares for the realm but for me as a woman. I willingly put my fate in Bothwell's hands!"

"You are as unjust as you are misguided, madame," Fraser said coldly. "For the sake of a man, a man I once called friend, you would throw away Scotland!"

"Scotland!" The word was spoken with startling scorn. "I, who have been Queen of France, who could be Queen of England, I can hold onto a poor country like Scotland with little effort!"

Sorrow filled the hazel eyes. "Oh, madame," Fraser said softly. "You have made a terrible mistake! You are guilty of great misjudgment, but not so great as mine for serving you as sovereign." This time it was Fraser who turned away, walking slowly back to the window. Outside, the chilly spring haar filtered down Blackfriars Wynd.

"UNLESS YOU PREFER being a chicken farmer's wife forever, I suggest we go to France." Fraser sat at the scruffy little table in the croft's tiny kitchen, trying to sort out their future. He was also trying to figure out what Dallas had cooked for supper.

"Kail brose, with barley bannocks," she informed him crossly, after deciphering his puzzled countenance. "It's what people in the country are supposed to eat."

Fraser grimaced slightly but realized this was no time to chide Dallas about her haphazard efforts in the kitchen. He'd already explained to her what had happened in Edinburgh. The Queen would no longer keep to her agreement not to confiscate his properties. Before long, he and Dallas would be landless. Even the town house would be taken, rumored to fall as booty to Morton for one of his Douglas adherents.

Dallas's initial reaction had been predictable. She'd stormed about the croft, berating the Queen, cursing Bothwell, damning Morton, reviling Lord James.

"James is sulking in London," Fraser reminded her.

"He's still at the bottom of all our troubles, mark my words." She waved a wooden ladle at him and managed to almost tip over a pitcher of cream in the process. "As for that swine Morton, I think he's always had his eye on the town house, either for himself or one of his loathsome kin. It better not be Delphinia!"

"She has a fine house already."

"And don't think I don't know how she got it!" Dallas could not resist the barb but Fraser did not react. He was still dwelling on his disillusionment with Mary Stuart and the wreck of his own dreams for Scotland.

He had remained in the capital for only two days, hiding out at the Cameron house while making arrangements through Walter Ramsay for Cummings to sell off the treasures in the cellar and as many of the household furnishings as possible. As soon as these matters were taken care of, Fraser would return to collect the children. It was risky but he would not entrust their safekeeping to anyone, not even Cummings.

Their household staff would be dismissed, Fraser told Dallas, except for Cummings, Flora, Ellen and the French cook. Meg could come, too, but she was being courted by a young lad from Colinton and preferred staying in Edinburgh.

"*I* prefer staying in Edinburgh," Dallas snapped, her chin on her fist. "How long will our money last once we get to France?"

Fraser dropped his napkin beside the plate. "A year, maybe more. I'll find some way of providing for us, lovey, don't worry."

But she did. Most of all she worried he might return to piracy. "When do we go?"

"Before the first of May. We'll take ship from Leith. You'll go with me when I return to Edinburgh, we won't stay more than a few hours."

Dallas was on her feet, banging plates, kettles and pans together in a noisome, full-blown rage. "I'm trying to be gallant about this, Iain, but it's damnably difficult! My whole life is bound up in Edinburgh—I never went more than thirty miles outside the city until I married you. All my kin are there, my old home, our own home." She dumped the cooking gear into a tub of water by the hearth and turned back to her husband. "To think I was ever foolish enough to believe that marrying you would solve all my problems!"

Fraser had not been listening; after much experience with his wife's tirades he had schooled himself to turn a deaf ear when it suited his mood. Still, he understood why she was so angry and he was not unsympathetic. "I don't much like surrendering property I've risked my neck to get in the first place," he said reasonably. "But if I don't leave the country my neck won't be worth a ha'penny. Though I've been outlawed for some time, until now I've always felt that the Queen would make sure no serious harm was done to me or my properties. But times have changed, most of all, the Queen has changed."

Her fury temporarily spent, Dallas sank back down into her chair. "Addlepated slut," she muttered. "Mary Stuart has all the brains of a poached egg. To think I actually cared about her, that I found Bothwell good company."

"I feel the same—they were both close to me for a long time." He reached across the table and gave her hands a squeeze. Dallas was slumped in the chair, the orange blouse turning her skin sallow, the thick hair more unruly than usual, the sensuous mouth petulant, and the hands Fraser held were scratched and reddened.

"Maybe that tenement in the Cowgate wouldn't have been any worse," he said with a wry grin.

But Dallas only stared at him. "Maybe," she said.

LATER THAT NIGHT, lying next to her sleeping husband, Dallas fixed her gaze on an open space in the thatched roof and tried to imagine what life would be like away from Edinburgh. The experience in London was no means of comparison; no matter what might have happened, she had known her stay would be temporary. The same was true with her sojourn to the Highlands—Dallas had planned on being there but a fortnight, and even when she had realized she could not flee Beauly with her son, she had still counted on an early return to Edinburgh.

But this was different. Perhaps she'd never walk up the High Street again, never climb Our Lady's Steps, never sniff the wood smoke in Peebles Wynd, never haggle over prices in the Flesh Market. And never walk up to the front door of the elaborately carved house in Gosford's Close and feel the pride of possession

Dallas turned over, to see the outline of her husband's dark head against the pillow. She was poignantly reminded of the night they were married when he had slept after taking possession of her unwilling body. Even then she had felt something stir deep within her and it suddenly occurred to her that the tears she had shed that night had welled up out of a sense of love. Her brain had not known what her heart did—that she already loved Fraser and was afraid of losing him.

Her mouth curved in a bittersweet smile as she moved closer to her husband and slipped an arm around his chest. He stirred slightly and murmured her name, just as he had done on their wedding night at the town house in Gosford's Close. Dallas had come close to losing him so many times, in so many ways. She vowed to herself that she would not lose him now.

Chapter Thirty-One

BOTHWELL'S MOSS-TROOPERS HAD infiltrated every part of Edinburgh. From Johnston Terrace to the west, from Potterrow Port in the south, to the Girth Cross in the east and the Lang Dykes on the north, they swaggered about the city, evoking resentment and enmity.

Fraser had decided they should enter the city as he had the previous fortnight: boldly in daylight, along with other visitors. If he were arrested, there was a good chance Dallas would not be apprehended with him. If necessary, she could still get away with the boys and sail for France. She'd fight it, of course; but she'd have to understand that there was no choice.

Yet, as they headed through the city gates on a mild April morning, no one stopped them. Fraser was perplexed, for he was certain that one of the moss-troopers who guarded the Cowgate Port knew him well from visits to Crichton and Hermitage. Neither the rustic clothes he'd resumed wearing nor the heavy beard were sufficient disguise, Fraser reckoned, and yet the man never gave him a second glance.

Uneasily, he guided Barvas along the roundabout way to the town house, up past the Corn Market, through the Upper Bow Port and into the West Bow, by the Butter Tron, along the Lawnmarket, and skirting Fisher's Close to come up behind his own residence. If they had not been riding Barvas, he would have taken the old back stairs through the Temple Lands, which would have been a shorter and perhaps safer route. But they were not stopped and no soldiers lurked in the vicinity of Gosford's Close.

A great commotion greeted them when they arrived. Cummings turned a deep red with scarcely concealed excitement and Flora exclaimed how thin Dallas looked. The children squealed with delight and the French cook announced that a sumptuous meal would be served for supper.

There was one jarring note, however: Cummings informed Fraser that the French vessel which would take them abroad needed repairs and would not sail for another two days.

"We'll have to take our chances," Fraser declared, holding Robert aloft while Magnus tootled on a toy horn passed on to him by his cousin, Daniel. "As long as we weren't stopped coming here, we should be safe for that long."

Dallas was already taking inventory of the house. Gone were the elegant tapestries, some of the carpets and much of the fine furniture. Her elation at being reunited with the children was wiped away by the stripped atmosphere of the place she'd called home.

"Maybe it's just as well I've seen the house this way," she said at supper. At least the little table and two chairs were still there, though the divan had been sold to one of Atholl's kin. "Mayhap it won't hurt so much to leave."

"I don't like it any better than you do," Fraser remarked, frowning at the half-bare little room. "When I think back on the chances I took and the ships we plundered to get so many of those things ...." He shook his head, the lean mouth twisted in regret.

"Cummings got good prices, I'll say that," Dallas commented, pushing her plate away. "Though the idea of Morton's relations living here fair turns my stomach."

"Something must have," her husband responded, eyeing her half-filled plate. "You hardly touched the best meal we've had in months."

The allusion to Dallas's own culinary efforts failed to upset her. "I'm not hungry. I wish there was some way to see Glennie and Tarrill before we go."

"You can send them notes, to be delivered after we sail." Fraser was about to call for dessert when Cummings came to the door. His blue eyes were wary and the high forehead was creased in a deep frown.

"You have a visitor, my lord, heavily muffled and unwilling to give his name, though I can guess it without much trouble." He coughed slightly. "I believe it to be the Earl of Bothwell."

"Christ!" Fraser threw down the carving knife he'd been using to slice off another filet of salmon. "I should have known."

"Shall I leave?" Dallas asked, already on her feet.

Fraser was surprised at the offer. Ordinarily, his wife's curiosity would have rooted her to the spot. "It would probably be just as well," he told her. "You look weary."

"I am," said Dallas, gathering the folds of her flaxen-colored peignoir about her. "It's been a tiring day." She leaned down to kiss his temple. "At least I can't mourn over losing the town house while I'm asleep."

As soon as she was gone, Fraser told Cummings to let Bothwell in. The Border Earl greeted Fraser effusively, apparently unperturbed by his host's lack of warmth. He threw his heavy cloak onto the chair Dallas had vacated but did not sit. "News travels fast, Iain," he said jovially though his eyes were restive. "I learned just a short time ago that you'd returned to Edinburgh."

"Illegally," Fraser noted dryly. "Have you come to arrest me in person or is there a contingent of moss-troopers on the doorstep?"

Bothwell chuckled and picked up the glass of wine Dallas had only sampled. "I came alone. And," he added, gazing squarely at Fraser, "in peace. You've suffered greatly in the past, though God knows we all have at one time or another. Daft, isn't it, how we Scots seem to spend more time on the run than at home?"

"Daft is putting it mildly," Fraser replied. "Why don't you stop fidgeting about and sit down? The salmon is excellent."

The Border Earl sat but refused the offer of food. "I've never been a man to hedge, so I'll come to the point." He took a long drink of wine, all but finishing it off. "It's craziness for us to be opposed to one another, Iain. We've been friends for too long. I'd like to see you reinstated."

The hazel eyes were steady. "That would be appreciated. What price respectability?"

Bothwell chuckled again, but this time the sound was forced. "You don't hedge either, Iain, that's another thing I've always admired about you. The price comes cheap, as a matter of fact." Bothwell drained the wine and reached for the decanter to pour out a full glass. "Tomorrow night there will be a grand supper at Ainslie's Tavern. The most important lords of the realm will attend. I'd like you to join us."

Fraser's expression was impassive. "Ainslie's Tavern serves up a good meal. But I fail to see how a satisfied digestive system will result in my reinstatement. Have you omitted something?"

Bothwell carefully smoothed his short-cropped red beard. "With so many influential men present, we'll discuss the Queen's future. She's edgy these days, she needs strong guidance. If some of us can take on the burden of her responsibilities, her health should improve."

Fraser selected a date from a plate of dried fruit Cummings had brought in. "Strange," he commented, placing the pit in a small porcelain bowl, "I would have thought Parliament a more appropriate arena for such discussions."

Tiny beads of perspiration were breaking out on Bothwell's forehead. "You seem to be deliberately avoiding my meaning," he said with a trace of impatience. "This is to be no general debate, but a specific course of action. The Queen should not govern alone."

"Elizabeth does," Fraser said, debating between an orange slice and a fig. "Nor would I know whom to suggest as a possible consort." He glanced up from the plate and stared fixedly at Bothwell. "You might not do badly yourself, but of course you already have a wife."

The Border Earl's skin flushed darkly. "We'll not discuss personal matters just now," he said gruffly. "The question is, are you coming to Ainslie's Tavern or not?"

There was no doubt in Fraser's mind. Bothwell intended to divorce Jean Gordon and marry the Queen. And he planned to act as swiftly as possible, though his predecessor had been dead for less than three months. Bothwell had not plotted Darnley's murder alone, Fraser was certain of that. But Bothwell was going to make sure he would profit the most. Had the Queen known about the murder plot? Or had she merely been used to get Darnley away from Glasgow? Whatever the answer, Mary Stuart was acting imprudently. The Highlander swore allegiance to his chief because the chief had earned it; the same applied to his sovereign.

Bothwell mistook Fraser's deep silence for a change of heart. The earl leaned forward, his eyes bright. "You see now, Iain? You need us, we need you. 'Tis simple enough."

Fraser straightened up in the chair and looked long at Bothwell. "You might need me, though I doubt it. But," he said with solemn finality, "I don't need you."

Bothwell's reaction was at first incredulous, then it hardened into bitter acceptance. He got to his feet without another word, picked up his cloak and went to the door. Fraser sat without moving, listening to Bothwell's tread fade down the hallway. He remembered small fragments of days gone by, of hunting in the park at Holyrood, of dicing at Crichton, of wenching in Edinburgh, of galloping through the Border country. It all seemed like a very long time ago.

PARLIAMENT ADJOURNED THE following day. For Fraser and Dallas, the hours passed slowly, with tension filling every nook and cranny of the town house. Dallas remarked that it felt like limbo; Fraser, who had spent many hours waiting for ships to sail, was more resigned.

He had sketchily described Bothwell's visit but hadn't gone into details for fear of worrying her. Yet Dallas sensed something was sorely amiss. But, she told herself, maybe it didn't matter much, since they would be away from Scotland within a few short hours. The sooner the better, she thought bitterly—not just for safety's sake but because every long minute spent in the town house would make the leave-taking all the more painful.

While Fraser and Dallas made love for the last time in their bedroom, a different kind of wooing took place at Ainslie's Tavern. Bothwell sat at the head of the table, plying his guests with drink upon drink. When the nobles finally dozed in their chairs, the Border Earl produced a bond. It not only pledged to defend Bothwell against all slander and accusations but promised to promote his marriage with the Queen of Scotland. Only one man did not sign; Hugh, Earl of Eglinton, bolted from the table, leaped out a window and fled to Gosford's Close.

"I COULD NOT sign," Eglinton explained dismally to Iain Fraser. Though the earl was John Hamilton's brother-in-law, he was also a staunch Catholic. As such, he had instinctively sought refuge at the nearest Catholic lord's house, which happened to be Fraser's. He knew the Highlander was outlawed but hoped the servants would let him in. His surprise at seeing Fraser was great, as Eglinton had not laid eyes on the other man since the night of Darnley's murder.

Fraser stood by a window, glancing from time to time between the heavy drapes. He had been half-asleep when Flora had announced the earl's arrival and had dressed hurriedly, leaving Dallas with her stream of questions unanswered.

"You were brave, Hugh," he said, "but probably foolish."

"I tried not to drink as much as the others—I feared something like this might happen." Eglinton sighed, the narrow, rather boyish face filled with despair. "I'm devoted to Her Grace, but I won't be a party to this scandalous marriage. She flaunts her faith, makes a mockery of the Church itself." He slumped into a chair and put his head down on his folded arms. "Jesu, how can she wed him? He's still married to the lady Jean."

"He'll find a way." Fraser came away from the window, one foot braced on a small damask-covered stool Cummings hadn't yet sold off. "You'd better flee, Hugh. They may have followed you and I'm not considered respectable company these days."

Eglinton looked up at him. "Why are you here then? Are you not in danger, too?"

"I'm not planning an extended visit, I assure you," Fraser answered with his twisted smile. He turned to see Dallas in the doorway, her hands waving in agitation. "Well, lovey, is the house afire?" he demanded.

Giving Eglinton hardly more than a glance, she rushed to clutch at her husband's arms. "Cummings is trying to fend off a dozen men at the door. They've come to arrest you!"

Eglinton leaped to his feet, but Fraser remained as he was, soothing Dallas with his hands. "On what charge?" he asked.

"Outlawry. And harboring a traitor." Now she did look directly at Eglinton, angry at him for seeking sanctuary under their roof, yet holding her tongue because he was Hamilton's kin.

Fraser moved quickly, releasing Dallas, giving orders to Simpson, who had entered the room. "Go back to Cummings. Tell him to say I'll be there as soon as I get my clothes on, I'm in bed with my wife. Hugh, wait here. I'll be back as soon as I get my boots and cloak."

Simpson thumped off down the corridor. Fraser took the stairs three at a time. From the open window of his bedchamber he could hear voices below. "Surround the house!" one of the men shouted in a thick Border accent. Fraser threw his cloak over his shoulder and pulled on his boots. His dirk, as ever, was in place. He flew down the stairs and back into the supper room. Both Cummings and Simpson were speaking in loud voices: "Can ye not wait for a man to get decent?" Simpson was shouting.

Dallas, big eyed and tense as a cornered doe, stood at the bottom of the stairs. Fraser gripped her shoulder and spoke rapidly: "The plan to leave here at dawn still holds. I'll meet you and the others aboard the ship." He gave her a short, hard kiss. "Be careful, lassie."

"You be careful!" She started running after him. "Don't go, they'll catch you the minute you go outside!"

"Your memory fails you," he called out over his shoulder. "We're not going outside. Come, Hugh, into the cellar!"

The earl followed him without question, down the corridor and through the kitchen. Behind them they could hear Dallas joining the group at the door, her virulent reproaches rising above the other, deeper voices.

The two men ran down the first flight of stairs, then Fraser made for the trap door which led to the second cellar. How long had it been since the underground passage had been used? A year, maybe more? Fraser wondered if the passage was still safe but knew he had no choice.

It was completely dark in the second cellar. "Hang onto my cloak," Fraser ordered Eglinton. The other man obeyed, stumbling a little but keeping up. Fraser felt for the secret entrance with his foot. Even in the dark, he knew the stone formation well. He paused to light the taper he'd snatched up from the supper room. "Hold this," he said and gave Eglinton the candle. Then he pried at the heavy flat stone and felt it move under the force of his hands. "Don't speak—and walk very carefully," he cautioned Eglinton, taking back the candle.

The cobwebs were thicker than ever, the walls of the passage ran freely with muddy water, the earth beneath their feet made sucking sounds with each step. They would head for the entrance by the Nor' Loch outside the city walls.

A clump of wet dirt fell down on Fraser's shoulder. He cursed silently but kept moving. He figured they must be under the Lawnmarket. Eglinton was breathing heavily, more from excitement than exertion. They turned around a little bend in the passage as several bats rushed out to greet them. Eglinton gasped but kept apace, his eyes riveted on Fraser's back.

They were past the Cameron house now. Fraser calculated that they were two-thirds of the way out and was reassured by the increasingly steep grade of the tunnel. The ground was more slippery now and Eglinton's deep blue velvet court slippers were muddied beyond recognition.

Pattering noises echoed behind them as they descended further and further down through the hillside. At first Fraser wondered if the soldiers could have followed them, then he realized that the sounds came from particles of earth dislodging from the tunnel walls. He had just started to glance over his shoulder when something in front of him caught his attention: One of the timbers was lying diagonally across the passage.

Fraser stopped and Eglinton almost ran into him. The timber had fallen in such a way that a man could neither go over it or under it. Some of the dirt had cascaded down with the timber and lay in a foot-high pile on the ground. Motioning to Eglinton, Fraser approached the barrier with great caution. An experimental tug told him that it was securely embedded in the floor; it must have fallen down some time ago, possibly during the heavy December snows.

Bending low, Fraser edged his shoulder under the beam. It didn't budge. He tried again and this time felt it give a little. Out of the corner of his eye, he saw Eglinton watching him nervously, his hands in front of him, the candle held out like a votive light. Fraser pushed repeatedly at the timber; it creaked and shuddered, then finally gave way.

And then a torrent of mud and dirt began to tumble down on their heads. "Run!" he called. But no feet followed his through the hail of wet earth and the passage was suddenly plunged into darkness. Fraser turned back and felt along the ground until he touched Eglinton's sprawled form.

"Hugh," he breathed, "are you all right?" There was no reply. Fraser put his hand up over his head to ward off another fall of mud. Then he grasped Eglinton under the armpits and pulled him along, backing towards the Nor' Loch entrance. More timbers crashed around them, chunks of wall disintegrated and caved in. But some twenty yards further, Fraser bumped into the rock which closed off the entrance. Here the passage was made out of more stone than dirt. Pebbles were falling down like giant hailstones and Fraser took a fair-sized rock full on the head but managed to throw his cloak over Eglinton and then rolled his weight into the boulder. It gave at the first lunge and went tumbling down a little slope. Fraser picked Eglinton up and carried him over his shoulders out into the cool night air just as a tremendous volley of rocks and dirt came hurtling down to reseal the entrance.

The sound died away as he struggled down the bank to the loch's edge.

Carefully, Fraser laid Eglinton down on the marshy ground. Then, he too, fell full length onto the rushes.

FRASER LAY MOTIONLESS at the edge of the water for nearly a quarter of an hour. Nearby, he heard the splashing sounds of the River Tumble as it ran full spate into the Nor' Loch. He knew they were safe for the time being. Certainly no one could follow them through the tunnel. But it was possible that the outskirts of the city would be searched. He and Eglinton would have to make for the Lang Dykes as soon as possible.

It was a cloudy night with no moon and Fraser was grateful for that. He stood up and walked the few feet to the loch to take a deep drink. Then he cupped his hands and filled them with water, returning to Eglinton's side where he splashed the other man's face and washed the bloody gash on his forehead. The wound was only superficial, though it was a good three inches long. Fraser was not surprised to see the earl's eyes flicker open and stare vaguely up at him.

"You're all right," Fraser reassured him. "You got hit with a falling timber. But we're outside now, by the Nor' Loch."

The vague expression began to fade from Eglinton's blue eyes. He raised his head to look around, taking in the dark bulk of Edinburgh Castle, the still waters of the loch in front of them and the quiet countryside beyond. "I thought we walked for miles!" he said in amazement. "But 'twas no distance at all!"

"The passage winds a bit," Fraser said. "An old smuggler's route used by a previous owner." Even at this late date, he'd rather Eglinton didn't know the truth. "Can you stand?"

Eglinton flexed his limbs. "I think so." He let Fraser give him a hand to help him to his feet. A bit shakily, he walked around in a circle. "Aye, I can walk. Maybe moving will keep my mind off my aching head."

"Good man." Fraser picked up his cloak and threw it to Eglinton, who had left his own at Ainslie's Tavern. "You wear this. A chill could be fatal in your condition." Eglinton started to demur but Fraser was already walking away from him, heading along the loch's edge towards the Lang Dykes.

"Where are we going?" he called out in a low voice.

"Where's Lord John?" Fraser asked back.

"He planned to leave Edinburgh for Arbroath as soon as Parliament adjourned," Eglinton replied, breathing with some difficulty. "He didn't come to Ainslie's Tavern."

Fraser grinned in spite of himself. "Good for Johnny," he murmured. "Then I suggest you make for Arbroath, too," he said in a slightly louder voice. "Can you manage alone?"

"I can try," Eglinton declared with a weak smile.

"I'll go with you as far as Leith. Mayhap you can get a boat to row you across the Firth tonight."

Eglinton accepted Fraser's decision without further comment. The earl took a deep breath of cool April air and set off through the marshy ground toward the lonely fields above the loch.

CONFRONTED WITH A dozen moss-troopers, Dallas stood her ground in the hallway. Dressed in a violet peignoir which revealed a tantalizing glimpse of bosom, her thick hair falling over her shoulders and the brown eyes snapping with self-righteous wrath, she berated the men with a voluble spate of invective. The moss-troopers gaped at her, as much taken aback by her salty language as her provocative appearance.

"Intruding upon husband and wife at such a time!" she went on. "Is there no privacy left in Scotland? And get your filthy feet off my clean floor!"

One of the men was no ordinary moss-trooper but Bothwell's henchman, Black Ormiston. "You waste our time, madame," he announced rudely. "Where is your husband?"

"Probably asleep," Dallas retorted. "He was rather fatigued."

Ormiston's crowlike eyes swept Dallas from head to foot. "I'll not doubt that," he muttered. Motioning to the mosstroopers, Ormiston commanded them to search the house. "Nay, madame, we have orders. Stand aside."

Dallas refused to budge. Behind her, Cummings and Simpson exchanged apprehensive glances. Flora was on the stairway, clutching her apron. Ormiston glowered at Dallas, then picked her up bodily and set her down by the drawing room door.

"Whore's spawn!" Dallas shrieked. "You dare lay hands on me!" But the men were moving swiftly through the hallway, forcing both Cummings and Simpson to step aside.

As the men dispersed into the various rooms, Cummings sidled up to his mistress. "It's been ten minutes," he whispered. "They should be well into the passage. Don't fret, madame."

"What if these churls find the passage?" Dallas hissed back. "Now that everything has been removed from the cellars, the entrances are exposed."

The thought had not eluded Cummings, but he was counting on the time factor. It should take Fraser and Eglinton no more than twenty minutes to make their way through the tunnel. Assuming, of course, that it was passable ....

Dallas seemed to read his mind; she had wondered the same thing. "The men who are still outside will know they haven't gone out by any regular door," she said. "If Iain is trapped down there ...." She stopped abruptly as Ormiston and three of his men tramped down the stairway.

"Your husband is not in your bedchamber, madame," Ormiston declared, his dark visage glowering at her. "Now where are he and that traitor Eglinton hiding?"

Dallas lifted her little chin defiantly. "Who knows? St. Giles, in Knox's pulpit?"

Ormiston considered using force on the obstinate wench but thought better of it. Lady Fraser and Bothwell had been on good terms over the years. He had a feeling his master might not want her mishandled. As for the two children upstairs in the nursery with their terrified governess, Ormiston had no stomach for threatening them either. Confident that his prey still must be somewhere within the town house, he announced they would continue the search if it took all night. As Dallas glared after him he stalked off towards the kitchen with his men.

A few moments later, she heard them open the door to the cellar. "Jesu," she breathed to Cummings, "we must stop them."

"No, madame," Cummings protested. "If you go after them, you'll only call attention to the trap door!"

But Dallas was already hurtling down the corridor and into the kitchen. They'd see the trap door anyway; but at least she could detain them for a few more precious minutes.

"Fools!" she called out, racing down the stairs. "Can't you see this place has been cleaned out? Where would anyone hide down here?"

Ormiston was in the act of lighting a candle. "We'll make sure they didn't," he retorted. But Dallas flung herself at him, knocking the candle from his hand. It fell to the floor, rolled just a few inches away from the trap door and sputtered out. Ormiston grabbed Dallas by the arm, swinging her away from him. "God's eyes!" he cursed, "you'll make me do you a mischief yet!"

Dallas's hands reached out to scratch at his face, but with one great thrust, he pushed her away. She fell, stumbling over the edge of the trap door, and crumpled to the floor.

"Fetch another candle!" Ormiston roared to one of his men. "And get this troublesome slut out of here!"

One man raced back upstairs while another came over to pull Dallas to her feet. But Dallas didn't move. The man pulled at her arm, then hesitated as she moaned aloud.

Ormiston hovered over her, his temper raging. "Enough tricks! I swear I'll arrest you along with your husband, if you don't get up!"

Dallas rolled over just enough so that Ormiston could see her face in the half-light which filtered down from the kitchen. "I can't move," she gasped. "I'm losing my babe!"

Half-stunned, half-suspicious, Ormiston knelt down warily. "You're lying!

Get up!" But then, as the mosstrooper he'd sent to fetch the candle reappeared and held the light by Dallas's face, Ormiston saw that she was ashen and in obvious pain. "Bring that maid down here!" he commanded, fervently wishing Bothwell had never sent him to Gosford's Close.

By the time Flora came charging anxiously down the stairs, Dallas had fainted.

JOHN HAMILTON HAD not left for Arbroath that evening. He had gone from Parliament to Gavin's house to await word of the Ainslie's Tavern meeting. Hamilton did not think it wise to leave Edinburgh until he found out what had transpired between Bothwell and the other lords.

When her husband, Hugh, had not returned by midnight, Hamilton's sister Jane grew anxious. "I wish he had stayed away, as you did," she told her brother. "We should all have left the city as soon as Parliament adjourned."

Hamilton said nothing. He had thought Hugh unwise but refused to meddle with another man's conscience. A few minutes later Black Ormiston pounded on the door with word that the Earl of Eglinton and Baron Fraser were on the run.

"His Lordship fled from Ainslie's Tavern, angering Lord Bothwell," Ormiston declared, resettling his helmet in place. The past hour or so he had spent at the Fraser town house had gotten on his nerves, with an unconscious ladyship, an outraged maid and a hysterical governess to contend with.

"So my brother-in-law and Fraser escaped together?" Hamilton inquired, carefully concealing his distress. Jane had just come into the hallway where she rushed up to grasp her brother's arm. "It's all right," he soothed her, "Hugh is apparently safe."

"It's not all right with Lord Bothwell," Ormiston said sharply. "The two culprits left the house before we arrived, though the others there let on that both men were still inside. They wanted to play for time."

"I'll not have the Earl of Eglinton referred to under this roof as a culprit," Hamilton asserted, with a menacing gesture of his right arm. "I must ask you to leave."

"And I must ask to search the house—sir." Ormiston wasn't keen on ruffling a proud Hamilton's feathers. He silently damned his new set of orders and waited for Hamilton to step aside.

"Let them search!" Jane urged. "Let them waste their time! Oh, dear God, where is my poor Hugh?" She buried her head against her brother's shoulder.

After Ormiston and his men had made their desultory search, they left the house grumbling among themselves. Hamilton, sitting alone in the library, had insisted that Jane go to bed. He hadn't known that Fraser had reentered the city. Was Dallas there, too? For the better part of an hour, he mulled over his course of action. If Hugh were apprehended, he might not be punished severely since until this evening his loyalty to the Queen was above reproach. Fraser's case was different: He was an outlaw already and rumored to have quarreled bitterly with the Queen. If Fraser were captured there was little doubt in Hamilton's mind that the Highlander would face execution. He would be sacrificed as John Gordon had been, to show all Scotland that Mary Stuart could act decisively when challenged by arrogant lords who refused to offer total obeisance. And if anything happened to Fraser, Dallas would be left a widow ....

Hamilton got up from his chair, grabbed his cloak and went out into the night.

Chapter Thirty-Two

THE FRENCH BARQUE was to sail at nine o'clock. When Dallas and the others had not arrived by eight, Fraser began to pace the decks. The ship was unfamiliar to him and he was relieved that she had never been one of his victims during his days as a pirate. Only a handful of other passengers were aboard, mostly Frenchmen, and so far he had attracted no special attention.

But now the captain, Romain LeClerc from La Rochelle, noticed the newcomer's apparent anxiety. "There are others in your party, I understand," he said with a friendly smile. "I assume you are wondering if they'll arrive in time for our departure."

"If they don't, I won't be sailing either," Fraser asserted. "You needn't worry, you can keep the passage money."

But the Frenchman seemed genuinely offended. "No, monsieur, I'm not concerned about that. It's just that I sensed your distress. It is your family you await, is it not? Under the name McKim I have some eight passengers listed."

Cummings had secured their passage under the maiden name of Fraser's mother. He himself had been very careful about making the arrangements, sending a trusted friend who would not be recognized by Bothwell's men.

But it was Cummings who now came hurrying up the gangplank. Fraser turned quickly from the captain, scouring the pier for Dallas and the children.

"Sir," Cummings called out, gesturing for Fraser to come by the rail out of the captain's hearing range, "if you please."

Before Fraser could start asking questions, Cummings recited his story as quickly as possible. "Her Ladyship has miscarried," he said low, not pausing for Fraser's stunned oaths, "but she is all right. Of course she cannot come with you, though she has insisted you sail without her. We will join you as soon as she's recovered." Cummings had spoken as if by rote, following Dallas's instructions to the letter.

"Christ!" Fraser exclaimed between clenched teeth. "I had no idea the lassie was with child! Why didn't she tell me?"

Cummings cleared his throat and clutched at his cap as a brisk wind picked up off the Firth. "She was afraid her condition might hamper your escape, sir. I understand also that until this past week she herself wasn't certain about, um, her impending motherhood."

Fraser stood with his hands on the rail, staring down into the deep water between the ship and the dock. Abruptly, he turned to Cummings. "The moss-troopers—did they harm her?"

There was the smallest pause before Cummings replied. "A small scuffle, provoked by Her Ladyship, occurred in the upper cellar. She fell over the trap door, and as it turned out, Ormiston and his men never did find the secret entrance in all the confusion."

By accident or design, Dallas had managed to conceal the means of his escape. Fraser shook his head ruefully, thinking that her effort was hardly worth the price she'd paid.

"Wait here, Cummings," Fraser said suddenly and moved to the foredeck where Captain LeClerq was talking with his first mate. Cummings watched as Fraser and the Frenchman exchanged a few words, then saluted each other.

"Let's go," Fraser called to Cummings, as he strode towards the gangplank.

"My lord!" Cummings exclaimed, "you can't go ashore! I promised Lady Fraser I'd see that you left for France!"

But Fraser was already heading for the dock. "She won't blame you," he said over his shoulder as Cummings hurried to catch up. "I'll not leave without her and that's that."

Huffing a bit, the serving man drew abreast of his master. "But you dare not enter the city! The moss-troopers are everywhere! I only got through Leith Wynd this morning because Bothwell was riding out to join the Queen at Seton and his Borderers were cheering him on."

They had left the dock area and were heading into Leith. The local citizens had started another day, pushing carts through the streets, carrying produce in large baskets, chasing geese into the fowlers', moving wagonloads of furniture, lumber, bricks, straw, peat and all the other necessities to keep life going. Scotland might tremble on the verge of civil war, but her people went about their business in an isolated sea of routine.

Cummings stopped trying to dissuade Fraser from his reckless course. He had no idea what his master planned to do. The tunnel was impassable; he'd found that out for himself when he'd tried to leave the town house by that route earlier in the morning.

Leith Wynd was even busier than the town itself. The day had turned sunny as the wind blew the threatening rain clouds out to sea. The two men passed by Holy Trinity Church, then slowed their pace as the wynd grew steeper and more crowded. Cummings realized that Fraser intended to brazen his way into Edinburgh and groaned inwardly at such recklessness.

As Cummings feared, the plan was doomed to failure. At first, Fraser was more curious than alarmed, for the men who blocked the city gate weren't moss-troopers but private retainers.

"This way," Fraser said, steering Cummings towards an adjoining wynd. But two more of the armed men stood in their path, and as Fraser glanced around him he realized they were surrounded. He also saw that the men wore the badge of Hamilton.

"You're under arrest," called a voice just a few feet behind Fraser. John Hamilton, flanked by his retainers and a gawking crowd of onlookers, stood with a cocked pistol in his hand.

"Christ!" Fraser gazed bemusedly at the other man, wondering if Hamilton were serious. He knew Hamilton had not attended the meeting at Ainslie's Tavern. He also knew that Hamilton and Bothwell were old adversaries, going back to the scandal over Alison Craik. But Hamilton had never veered in his loyalty to the Queen. And he did not look like a man playing a prank.

"Take him," Hamilton commanded, motioning to his men. At least twenty retainers surged forward, hemming in Fraser and Cummings. The first instinct was to fight, to take one last heedless chance at escape. But the sheer numbers were too much, even for Fraser, and he was still unsure of Hamilton's true intentions.

When they entered the city gate, a half-dozen mosstroopers ordered the group to halt. "Is this Baron Fraser?" a heavily bearded Borderer demanded.

"It is," Hamilton replied, stepping up to the man. "He is my prisoner. As a member of Parliament and a loyal supporter of Queen Mary, I have a right to take him into custody."

The bearded man frowned. His legal knowledge was scant but he recognized Lord Hamilton. While he had no wish to gainsay such an important noble, he also had orders from Bothwell. "Then let us accompany you to the Tolbooth," the man said. "We'll make sure Baron Fraser is secured."

Hamilton stood with his arms crossed, the pistol held in his right hand. "I need no help. I've waited five years for this moment. The enmity between Baron Fraser and myself is long-standing and deep. I'll brook no interference."

Instinctively, the Borderer stepped back a pace. Hamilton towered above him, proud as any prince, royal as any personage in Scotland except the Queen herself.

"As you say, my lord," the man replied deferentially. Then he added nervously, "I fear my lord Bothwell might think his own followers have failed him."

"Dammit, man, let us pass! What matters who captures this Highland devil as long as he's made to pay for his crimes?" Hamilton deliberately let the pistol stray towards the Borderer's chest. "Now move!"

The moss-troopers shuffled off to one side as Hamilton led his men and their captives towards the Netherbow Port. Many Onlookers followed along, excited over the spectacle of seeing one important lord lead another to the Tolbooth.

Hamilton turned to Fraser as they progressed up the High Street. "You've always thought me a fool," he called out, "a rival not quite worthy of your Highland bravado. You underestimated me, Fraser. I'll claim your wife yet!"

Fraser suddenly had no further doubts about Hamilton's designs. Surprising his captors, he lunged forward and hurled himself against Hamilton's back. The other man staggered but didn't go down. Swinging the pistol, he cracked it across the side of Fraser's head. It was a stunning blow, sending Fraser sprawling onto the cobbles. The Hamilton men drew their weapons as their lord swung out a booted foot and kicked Fraser in the groin. "Get up, you swine, I'm not ready to kill you yet!"

Fraser got slowly to his feet, angrily shaking off the retainers who had tried to grab him. "Whoreson!" he yelled. "You'd send twenty men to do what you could never manage alone!"

If the taunt rankled Hamilton, he gave no sign. They were in front of the Tolbooth now, its dark bulk filling the middle of the High Street. But Hamilton motioned his men to keep moving. "Not yet," he asserted in ringing tones. "I want Lady Fraser to see him first, subjugated at my hand. And I want this bastard cur to see me take his woman as my prize."

Fraser clamped his mouth tightly shut but the look he hurled at Hamilton's broad back was murderous. The crowd still followed along, growing in size and abuzz at such a thrilling turn of events.

As they approached the town house, Hamilton moved at a brisker pace. The others followed suit until they reached the front door. "You four," he said, gesturing to the men who flanked Fraser and Cummings, "bring them inside." The rest of his men would stay in the close to keep order. Hamilton let the others precede him into the house, then banged the door shut.

"Jesu!" he breathed, shoving the pistol into his belt. "I can't believe we made it! Get upstairs, Iain, before Dallas does herself a mischief and climbs out of bed to see what's going on!"

Fraser stared at Hamilton, speechless for the first time in years. Then he flung himself at the other man and grabbed him by the shoulders. "Sweet Christ, John, you're right!" he grinned. "I did underestimate you after all!"

Then he dashed down the hallway and mounted the stairs three at a time.

Dallas was indeed wondering what all the commotion was about. She sat up in bed, about to call Flora, when Fraser burst into the room.

"Iain!" she gasped, "you're supposed to be on your way to France!"

Fraser wrapped his arms around her and kissed her lips. "Lovey, I wouldn't leave you here. Are you all right?"

"Are *you* all right?" Dallas countered, taking in the fresh smear of blood at his temple and the numerous bruises he'd received during the flight through the tunnel. His clothes were filthy and torn, his hands were scratched in several places, and there was a small cut across the bridge of his nose. Dallas herself was pale and there were dark circles under her eyes, but otherwise she showed no visible signs of her ordeal.

Fraser shrugged off his damages. "I'll mend. But why didn't you tell me about the bairn?"

Swiftly Dallas explained her reasons: During the weeks at Dunbar, Dallas's appetite had dwindled steadily but she'd attributed it to the change in diet and to her own inept cooking. She'd not felt ill as she had with the first two pregnancies, and though she tired more easily, she thought that was because she'd grown unaccustomed to domestic chores. She'd also lost track of time; the routine on the chicken farm had made one day seem like another. It was only while Fraser was in Edinburgh that she'd realized she was pregnant again, probably some two and a half months along.

When her husband returned from the capital with his unsettling news, Dallas had not felt it was the right time to reveal her condition. His plans were made and much as she dreaded leaving Scotland, she'd do nothing to change his mind.

"But what's going on below?" she asked after he had absorbed her explanation and expressed dismay at her unwillingness to confide in him. "How did you get back here?"

Burying his face in the curve of her neck, Fraser momentarily put the immediate past out of his mind. "Are you certain you're all right?" he asked, finally pulling away enough to scrutinize her closely.

"Yes, yes, Dr. Wilson was here and assured me I'd be fine. He said it might have happened under any circumstances, such things do, you know." Her tone was impatient. "Now tell me, Iain, what's going on?"

Fraser got up and went out into the corridor to call down to Hamilton. Dallas was almost as surprised to see him as she had been to see her husband. As Fraser sat back down on the bed, holding Dallas's hand, Hamilton pulled up a chair and recounted his own story. After going over the events which had taken place at Gavin's house, he told them how he had come to Gosford's Close in the middle of the night and spoken with Cummings.

"Your man was like a clam at first," Hamilton said, "but I finally convinced him that he had to trust me, that my kin was as involved as you were. Then he opened up, giving me the details of your misfortune." Smiling gently at Dallas, he paused for a moment. He had been certain that when Fraser learned about the miscarriage, he'd come back to the town house, no matter what the risks. Hamilton himself would have done the same.

"I didn't know you were here last night, John," Dallas said in amazement. "No one told me."

"I asked Cummings not to," he answered, draping one booted leg over his knee. "If my plan was to work, I had to keep it a secret. Indeed, I didn't tell Cummings—he must have thought I was a damnable traitor."

Hamilton continued telling Dallas what had happened after he and his men had taken Fraser into custody. He glossed over some of the details which he thought Dallas might find distasteful, but Fraser wouldn't let him off the hook completely.

"The crack on my skull, I'll excuse," he said to Hamilton with a twisted grin, "but that kick in the groin was overdoing it a mite."

Hamilton cocked his head to one side. "Oh, I think not. If one must play a part, one ought to play it well."

Dallas gazed from one man to the other. "It's all quite remarkable, but I still reckon it would have been better if you'd used that pistol to make Iain leave Scotland, John. Now you're both in danger. What are we going to do?"

Hamilton had already thought that part of the plan through. "I'm afraid Iain will actually have to spend some time in the Tolbooth." As Dallas started to protest he held up a hand to silence her. "Don't worry, no harm will come to him. Bothwell and the Queen have left the city, Parliament is adjourned, and no legal action can be taken for some time. Besides, I have a feeling that Her Grace and her evil genius have other matters on their minds."

"Doubtless," Fraser put in, getting up from the bed to pour himself some claret. "Bothwell will act swiftly since the other lords signed the bond to support his suit for the Queen's hand."

"How soon can you travel, Dallas?" Hamilton inquired as he accepted a glass of claret from Fraser.

"A week, ten days—if I go by litter. I asked Dr. Wilson since I wanted to know the earliest moment I would be able to join Iain in France." She turned to look at her husband, her lower lip thrust out. "I still say you should have gone, I wish Cummings had never told you! And don't I get any claret?"

AN HOUR AFTER Hamilton had brought Fraser to the town house, the two men reappeared in the close. As they moved on to the Tolbooth, scuffles broke out in the crowd, as men of Highland ancestry traded insults with those who had Hamilton ties. Even some of the goodwives exchanged heated comments with one another, arguing over whether Lady Fraser was worth such a pack of trouble.

While Dallas regained her strength, Fraser bribed his gaolers into providing him with a decent cell, palatable food and a jug of whiskey. He briefly considered having them provide him with the bailiff's niece as well, thought about his wife lying ill and alone at the town house, felt that pang of conscience which he was beginning to accept with only a passing regret, and dismissed the idea. In any event, the girl had a frightful complexion.

On the fifth day of Fraser's confinement, the guards brought him a strange report: The previous day, Mary Stuart had been on her way back to Edinburgh, in the company of Maitland, George Gordon and James Melville. As they approached Gogar Burn, Bothwell, who had been with the Queen briefly at Seton, suddenly rode across the Bridge of Almond at the head of eight hundred men. Laying his hand on her horse's bridle, the Border Earl announced that there had been trouble in Edinburgh—great turbulence set off by Lord Hamilton and Baron Fraser. Her Grace might not be safe in the city, he warned, and suggested that she seek refuge in his castle at Dunbar.

There were only about thirty members in Mary's party. Several of them disagreed violently with Bothwell's plan but the Queen urged them to behave peaceably. Since they were overwhelmed by numbers, Mary attested that she wanted no blood shed on her behalf. Submissively, she rode off with Bothwell to Dunbar

" 'Tis said that Bothwell has abducted the Queen," one of the guards told Fraser. "That means one thing—if such was his intention, he must now marry her to right the wrong."

"Canny," Fraser commented, fingering his cleanshaven chin. "I suspect the abduction was prearranged."

Two days later, word reached Edinburgh that Bothwell had raped the Queen. Arguments raged throughout the city: The sickly, widowed sovereign had been ill-used by the ruthless Border Earl .... Queen Mary had been a willing victim to Bothwell's aggressive advances .... There had been no such rape at all, since the enamored monarch had been lying with the earl for months, probably even before Darnley's death.

It mattered little who was right. The fact that both Bothwell and the Queen freely admitted that a sexual act had taken place between them meant that they must either marry or else the earl would have to pay the penalty for rape. Bothwell's marriage to Jean Gordon was summarily dissolved. The people of Edinburgh began to publicly express their outrage at what they construed as the Queen's wantonness.

The following Monday, John Hamilton went to Gosford's Close. Dallas was up and feeling quite well, if occasionally given to spells of weakness. She wore a tawny gown embroidered with spring flowers as she greeted Hamilton in the entry hall.

"Do sit, John, if you can find a chair," she said, showing him into the drawing room. More of the furniture had been sold during the past week by Cummings. A Douglas servant had visited one day, insisting that his master wished to take possession by May first, which was now only three days off. "I'll not leave so much as a cleaning rag for that pestiferous Morton and his scruffy kin," Dallas declared, realizing that there were only some packing crates remaining in the drawing room. Dallas perched on one while Hamilton decided to stand.

"I've little time, sweetheart," he said, noting that her color was much improved. "I'm removing Iain from the Tolbooth tomorrow, if you're able to travel."

"I'm feeling almost well again," she asserted as their glances interlocked at the memory evoked by the situation. "We must go slowly, of course ...."

Hamilton brushed his hand at a fly which had alighted on a tall oak garderobe. "I wouldn't let you go at all if I thought your health might be jeopardized. Never, never again would I put you through that sort of danger—not in any way."

Dallas understood and nodded solemnly. "Of course you wouldn't. But Dr. Wilson has pronounced me all but recovered and as long as I act carefully and—uh—circumspectly for the next few weeks, all will be well. But where are we going, John?"

"Hamilton Castle. It's suited for defensive purposes, should the need arise." Noting Dallas's look of alarm, he placed a comforting hand on her .shoulder. "It won't be necessary, I'm sure, but I want to take every precaution."

"But," Dallas asked, looking up at him, "do you have the right to take Iain there? Won't someone under Bothwell's command try to stop you?"

Hamilton shook his head. "We're most fortunate that Bothwell and his followers have other priorities. I've heard he and the Queen plan to marry within a fortnight. But they'll return to Edinburgh for the ceremony, so we must get Iain out of the city before they do. I'm afraid," he said, darkening slightly, "that you will have to enact the role of my captive booty."

Dallas's eyes widened and then she laughed delightedly. "What a bizarrely amusing idea! Don't fret, if I must be a captive, I'd rather be yours than anyone else's!"

Her candor disarmed him. "Oh, sweetheart," he exclaimed ruefully, "to think I have the rest of my life to regret being so proud and cautious! It's no wonder people say the Hamiltons can never make up their minds!"

Sliding down from the packing crate, Dallas put her hands on his face.

"Regrets never changed a life nor saved a soul, dear heart. We both did what we thought right at the time. Stop making yourself miserable over that which you can't mend!"

Hamilton pulled her close and kissed her with a ravenous hunger that left them both breathless. Neither spoke for a moment afterwards, Hamilton still holding her, Dallas's hands pressed against his doublet. "I should apologize, sweetheart," he finally said, releasing her slowly and reluctantly. "Yet I'd compound the wrong with hypocrisy if I did."

Pushing her hair out of her eyes, Dallas shook her head. "Then don't, John. Your honest ardor suits you well. Unfortunately," she added with a wistful smile, "it has always suited me, too."

THE ATMOSPHERE IN Edinburgh had changed during the past few days. The city was tense, with an almost vicious aura seeping out of the wynds and closes. Placards sprang up along the High Street and the Canongate, denouncing Mary Stuart as a whore and Bothwell as her leman. If and when the Queen returned to the capital, the local citizenry would make certain that she understood their displeasure.

The onlookers' mood was surly when John Hamilton led his prisoner out of the Tolbooth and down the Lawnmarket towards the Salt Tron. Fraser had been Bothwell's friend; the House of Hamilton had consistently supported the Queen. Neither man evoked much sympathy from the crowd on this overcast spring morning.

Lord Claud Hamilton, riding at the head of over a hundred of his kinsmen, bestowed a contemptuous smile on the people who lined the West Bow. He was enjoying the farce tremendously. His older brother was usually much too staid for his own perverted tastes, but at least John was now acting with a bit of flair.

Claud turned in the saddle to glance at his brother. One thing about Johnny, Claud had to admit, he always cut an impressive figure. A pity that wretched Arran had been the eldest, otherwise Mary Stuart would have undoubtedly married John.

But instead of riding beside Mary Stuart, John Hamilton walked his horse next to the litter which carried Lady Fraser. A beddable wench, Claud conceded, but much too high-spirited for his own taste. He had the definite feeling she'd not submit docilely to some of his more exotic approaches to lovemaking.

Whether she submitted to his brother was something Claud didn't know and thought best not to ask. Whatever John's reasons for concocting this elaborate hoax, Claud hoped his brother would be well rewarded.

Reclining in the litter, Dallas tried to turn a deaf ear to the taunts of the crowd. She could have closed the curtains but felt she'd serve Hamilton's purposes better by letting herself be seen. Her flame-colored traveling costume was banded with pheasant feathers, as was the matching high-crowned hat. The bold color had been chosen intentionally, to emphasize her state as a fallen woman.

"Is Iain all right?" she asked Hamilton in a low voice. Her husband was riding several yards behind them, his wrists shackled together.

"He's fine," Hamilton responded as they passed through the Grassmarket. "I wish he'd try looking a bit more abject."

They did not reach Hamilton Castle until well after dark. Though they passed through stretches of unpeopled landscape during their journey, the pretenses were maintained at all times, since Hamilton had not fully confided in the majority of his followers.

Dallas was exhausted by the time they rode through the arched entrance of the castle. Cummings and the children had ridden on ahead with the rest of the Fraser household since Dallas was adamant that the boys not see their father suffer any sort of indignity. They couldn't possibly understand what was happening and would only remember that their sire had been a prisoner.

Flora was the first to appear in the courtyard, insisting that her mistress come straight to bed. "Not yet," Dallas asserted, allowing Hamilton to help her out of the litter. "I must see Iain."

But Hamilton deterred her. "Wait till morning. My men are trustworthy but I prefer they remain in ignorance awhile longer. If I show your husband too much hospitality too soon, word might leak back to Edinburgh before I can marshal the rest of my forces."

"Will you put him in the dungeon?" Dallas asked in alarm.

"Nay," Hamilton laughed, "he'll go to a tower room, secure but comfortable."

Dallas glanced around the courtyard just in time to see Fraser being led inside the castle. His wrists were still shackled, but he moved with his characteristic pantherlike walk and his dark head was held high. He looked in Dallas's direction and winked. She put a gloved hand over her mouth to cover the smile she couldn't control, then let Hamilton escort her into the castle entrance hall as Flora walked briskly behind them.

The castle had been built for war but furnished for peace. It was far from elegant, yet there was a homely atmosphere which Dallas found consoling. The Duke of Chatelherault lived there most of the time but had left that morning with his duchess and their son Arran for one of their smaller residences. The duke, into whose custody Arran had been entrusted the previous year, felt that the excitement of so many men and so much activity might unduly disturb his poor son.

Dallas found herself the center of a great commotion when she reached the rooms Flora had selected. The children, both keyed up from the long journey, raced to meet her, Ellen burst into tears, and Meg, who had decided to come along after all, clutched at her mistress's arm.

"Where's Father?" Magnus demanded. "Have they killed him yet?"

"Hush, you little beast," Dallas commanded, annoyed that Magnus obviously knew more than he should about what was going on. "Your father is quite well and getting ready to eat supper."

Dallas, however, ate sparingly from a tray Flora brought in after her mistress had taken a soothing bath. Within minutes of blowing out the candle, Dallas was fast asleep. She had no idea what time it was when she awoke to find John Hamilton standing next to the bed, clad in a plain dark nightrobe.

"Jesu, John," she whispered, struggling up on one elbow "you mustn't come here!"

"The rest are sleeping soundly in the next room," he said quietly. "If, as everyone thinks, I've gone to all this trouble to sleep with you, that's what I intend to do. Move over, sweetheart, you're smack in the middle of the bed."

"No!" she cried and immediately lowered her voice. "The miscarriage ... you know what happened to me when we ...."

"Be still, Dallas, I know all that." He kept the night-robe on and slipped between the covers. "I wanted to make love to you the night Darnley was killed—and you wanted me to, despite the consequences had we been found out. But tonight we can't, so it's quite safe for us to be together. Now stop hissing at me and let me hold you."

"Oh, fie, Johnny," she mumbled and rolled over into his arms. "You smell like pine and leather."

"And you feel like heaven. Good God, Dallas, have you any idea how much I've wanted to sleep in your arms again all these years?"

Locked in the security of his embrace, warmed by their enduring mutual feeling, Dallas sighed into his shoulder. "Yes, John, I do. There have been many times when ...." She broke off abruptly, afraid to say more.

His arms tightened around her. "It's all right, sweetheart, I know. There's nothing you could tell me that I don't understand already." His lips brushed the top of her head. "Now before I discover I'm a weaker man than I thought, we'd better go to sleep."

Dallas did just that, her head against his chest, one arm curled around his waist. But Hamilton lay awake for some time, savoring the softness of her body through the thin lambswool shift and deeply touched by her perfect trust in him.

Chapter Thirty-Three

TARRILL PAUSED ON her way from the Butter Tron as she noticed a wagonload of possessions being maneuvered into Gosford's Close. The furnishings looked bulky and ugly, a far cry from the elegant pieces they replaced.

Clutching her parcels tightly, she moved closer for a better look. Morton himself was talking to the kinsman who had taken over the town house. Tarrill knew the shifty earl slightly; she turned away, not wanting to speak to him. She'd seen enough; it upset her to watch the Fraser residence fall to the Douglases.

As she headed towards the fowler's to pick up a capon for supper, Mistress Drummond hailed her from a grainseller's stall just off Foster's Wynd. Tarrill wasn't in the mood to chat, but the confrontation was unavoidable.

"Och, marriage has made ye bloom! I dinna see ye much of late, though Glennie tells me ye've not been at court for a bit."

Tarrill juggled her parcels and hoped Mistress Drummond wasn't in the mood for a long gossip. "That's so," she replied noncommittally. The royal dismissal had been final but Tarrill had no regrets. She felt she was well out of the turmoil which raged around the Queen. "Donald and I visit occasionally with Glennie and Walter, but keep much to ourselves these days."

A slow wink closed Mistress Drummond's left eye. "Ah, 'tis the way it should be with newlyweds! That laddie ye married is a braw one!" Moving closer to Tarrill, Mistress Drummond lowered her voice. "But the Queen! Such an outrage! One husband dead but three months and doubtless dispatched by the new bridegroom himself! And did ye ever see a marriage dissolved as hastily as Lord Bothwell's!"

It was true. Jean, Countess of Bothwell, had been granted a divorce by the Protestant commissary court on May third; within four days a Catholic annulment had been arranged. A week later, Mary Stuart had married the Border Earl in the great hall at Holyrood—under Protestant rites.

"I hope they're happy," Tarrill said, though without much conviction. Only a fortnight after the wedding, she'd heard that the Queen was more distraught than ever and had even threatened to kill herself. Whatever passion had burned between Mary and Bothwell seemed to have been extinguished like a candle in a sharp draught.

Mistress Drummond was forging onward, berating the royal couple for a multitude of sins. "Topsy-turvy," she declared in summation. " 'Tis what I call Scotland these days. But there, I've run on so, I've not asked about your other sister—never was I so shocked in my life over what happened when Lord Hamilton—I used to think so much of him—carted her and her husband away!"

Tarrill herself had been shocked. Eventually, she and Donald, along with Glennie and Walter, had deciphered their sister's cryptic message enough to figure out that the situation was not exactly what it seemed. Yet at the time they had been stunned and infuriated by the stupefying turn of events.

"It's all politics," Tarrill said vaguely. "I don't understand it myself. If you'll excuse me, I must be going, I have to get to the fowler's and ...."

"Ah, ye won't want to not be there when that Donald of yours comes home!" Mistress Drummond nodded with a faint leer. "Run along now, and give him my best." She chuckled as Tarrill hurried up towards St. Giles. "Politics, indeed!" she said to herself and chuckled again.

AFTER THE FIRST few days at Hamilton Castle, Iain Fraser was given virtual liberty. If he went outdoors to ride or hunt, a nominal guard was sent along, but inside the castle, there were no such restrictions. He was released from the tower room to join Dallas and the children in their suite. Some of the Hamilton followers were puzzled but raised no questions. It was not uncommon for titled prisoners to receive such generous treatment. Then again, perhaps Lord Hamilton had merely changed his mind; indecision had been a way of life with his father, the duke.

The real change, however, had occurred in the relationship between Hamilton and Fraser. In their younger years, the two men's paths had not crossed frequently. It was only after Mary Stuart's return to Scotland that both men were drawn into the court circle, and then Fraser's longstanding friendship with Bothwell made him an enemy of the Hamiltons. His natural contempt for kin and clan feuds might have prevented him from carrying the antagonism further, but Hamilton's obvious attraction to Dallas had made that impossible. Then, when Fraser had discovered their betrayal of him, hostility flamed into hatred.

On that heart-shattering afternoon at Strathmuir, Fraser had hoped he had killed Hamilton. Afterwards, he was relieved that he hadn't. Later, when he'd learned that Hamilton was in Italy, nursing his wounded heart, Fraser had actually felt a pang of compassion for his rival. And when he'd encountered Hamilton with Dallas on the night of Darnley's murder, Fraser had seen him in an entirely new light—not as Dallas's lover, but as a man who loved Dallas and an honorable man at that.

The mock arrest in Leith Wynd momentarily destroyed any such charitable notions. While Fraser walked out of Leith and up into Gosford's Close, he loathed Hamilton more than he'd ever hated any man, even James Stuart himself. And then, in a cataclysmic moment of revelation, Fraser understood Hamilton's true motives—and Hamilton himself. This was not only an honorable man, but a selfless one, a man who loved a woman so much that he would sacrifice his own happiness for hers.

It had not been easy for Fraser to accept Hamilton's sacrifice, preferring at first to think the other man had acted out of gratitude for Eglinton's safety. Ultimately, however, Fraser had forced himself to recognize the extent of Hamilton's actions, and their peculiarly awe-inspiring implications. Hamilton, on the other hand, true to his innate generosity of spirit, had neither asked for nor expected Fraser's gratitude. He had done what he thought was right and that was sufficient.

But now Hamilton and Fraser were facing a crisis of another sort. Both men had been surprised the previous day when Maitland of Lethington had ridden into Hamilton Castle. When the Secretary of State's arrival had been announced, their first concern was whether or not Fraser should be sent back to the tower room to underscore his role as captive. But after a brief discussion, they came to the conclusion that if any one had seen through the deception, it would be the clever Maitland.

The Secretary, however, was too absorbed in his own dilemma to show much interest in what was happening at Hamilton Castle. He looked haggard and disconcerted as he came into the chamber where Fraser and Hamilton were playing chess.

"I was forced to flee Edinburgh," he declared, gratefully accepting a cup of whiskey. "God knows I've served the Queen faithfully over the years, but a man can only endure so much."

"Such as?" Fraser inquired, lifting an eyebrow. Maitland gave a short, bitter laugh. "An attempt on my life." The usually suave gaze flickered with anger. "Bothwell tried to murder me at Dunbar. In the Queen's presence, no less."

Hamilton picked up a pawn and set it down again. "Why? You've supported him thus far."

"I've supported the Queen thus far, you mean," Maitland countered, pulling off his riding gloves and tossing them onto a side table. "I've always despised Bothwell for the brute that he is. But he, he who murdered Darnley, had the gall to accuse me in front of the Queen of conspiring to assassinate Rizzio."

Hamilton looked away from Maitland to the chessboard, but Fraser merely grinned at the secretary. "Come, come, William, let's not be coy. You had a hand in that, and the Queen knew it well."

Maitland flushed slightly. "I'll admit I was involved, but I took no active part as Bothwell did in Darnley's murder. The man laid the gunpowder himself!"

From all that they had heard, there was little reason to doubt Maitland. Bothwell, along with some of his henchmen and several of the Douglases, was said to have been the actual assassin, though no one knew for sure who had strangled Darnley.

"In any event," Maitland sighed, "when Bothwell attacked me, it was the Queen who intervened. God knows I'm grateful for her intercession, but I could hardly stay on serving her when at any moment some rascally Borderer might stab me in the back."

Fraser and Hamilton agreed that Maitland had cause to take flight. Yet there was something terribly pathetic about his defection. Somehow, it symbolized the Queen's own precarious position. Though Maitland's loyalty over the years had not been flawless, he had been more steadfast than most. If he had abandoned her, how many others would follow?

Later that day, Maitland rode out, towards his country home in the west. Less than twenty-four hours later, another important visitor arrived at Hamilton Castle.

George Gordon had come not to hinder the Queen but to help her. He had ridden hard from Edinburgh that morning, and sweat poured down his ruddy face as he dismounted in the courtyard.

"George?" Dallas inquired uncertainly as she held onto the reins of the pony Magnus was riding around in a circle. "Jesu, you're more lathered than your mount!"

"Where's Lord John?" he asked peremptorily as a groom led Gordon's weary horse away.

Dallas motioned for Magnus to stop hopping up and down in the pony's saddle. "He went fishing," she replied. "He'll be back in an hour or so." Dallas noted that Gordon had added yet more weight and that his jowls were beginning to sag under the golden beard. She had to bite her lip to keep from smiling at the folly of her youth.

But Gordon was making his own appraisal: The tutor's daughter, with her head stuffed full of more learning than any woman had a right to know, had somehow managed to end up in the middle of an outlandish scandal involving two of Scotland's most important lords. The irony was that in her elegantly tailored plum-colored riding habit and matching high-crowned hat, she looked every inch the part of a woman men would fight over. The trim but voluptuous body, the big, dark eyes, the thick hair tucked up under her hat, and the full, sensuous mouth made him wonder why he had virtually ignored her ten years earlier.

But Gordon could not afford to let such distractions deter him further. He had come to see Hamilton—and Fraser—on urgent business. "Your husband, madame—where is he? I assume you still have him."

Gordon's tone was insinuating, but Dallas paid little heed because Magnus was trying to pull the leading strings out of her hands. "No, you cannot ride alone!" she told her son firmly and ignored his petulant expression. Dallas turned back to Gordon. "Oh, he went fishing, too. But," she added hastily, realizing the implications of what she'd just said, "he's not allowed to keep what he catches."

"A most peculiar sort of punishment," Gordon remarked dryly. "In what manner of captivity does Lord John hold your husband?"

But Claud Hamilton's arrival spared Dallas having to make a reply. Claud greeted Gordon effusively. Antagonism between the two powerful families had long been smoothed over, partially through the peacemaking efforts of Gordon's wife, Anne Hamilton.

Dallas purposely turned her back on the two men and gave her total attention to Magnus. A few moments later, Gordon and Claud went inside the castle. Let Claud make the explanations, she thought, he's slippery as a wet step and twice as dangerous. It always amazed Dallas that the old duke could have sired three sons so totally unalike.

And it had amused her to see the expression on George Gordon's face as he had eyed her in a fleeting moment of masculine appreciation. She had long ago forgotten the sound of his derisive laughter; indeed, she had virtually forgotten George Gordon completely.

GORDON'S PROPOSAL WAS simple enough. If Fraser and Hamilton pledged to support the Queen, there would be no repercussions from their own felonious deception. Gordon was no fool; he had discerned for himself what was going on at Hamilton Castle after watching Lord John and Fraser ride into the courtyard, obviously enjoying a certain measure of camaraderie,

Hamilton said he'd have to think about the matter. He was torn much in the same way as Maitland; he supported the Queen personally but could not abide Bothwell's treacherous ambition. He'd also prefer to discuss the matter with his father, who, after all, was still nominal head of the Hamilton house.

Fraser's attitude was skeptical. He'd quarreled with the Queen in a most bitter, antagonistic manner; he had also broken openly with Bothwell. Only a few weeks ago both were eager to put him in the Tolbooth and probably condone a sentence of execution. "The idea sets ill with me, George," Fraser said as he slit open one of the salmon he'd caught that morning in the nearby river. "It's not as if I can provide several thousand troops as John can. Not being my clan's chief, I could only offer a couple of hundred. And somehow," he added, dumping the fish's innards into a bucket, "I don't think that's enough to pay for my alleged past sins."

"Neither of you realize how desperate the Queen's position is," Gordon asserted. "Had you been in the capital these past weeks, you'd know that her prestige has all but evaporated. No epithet is too vile for the ordinary citizen to hurl against her. And meanwhile, her former supporters desert her day by day."

"I pity poor Mary," Hamilton acknowledged as he gestured for a servant to haul their catch away into the kitchens. "But it may be that her cause is already lost. Who is the actual leader of the opposition?"

Gordon leaned on the edge of the water trough and loosened his jacket. The June afternoon had grown warm. "No one lord leads them. Morton, Lindsay, Atholl, Argyll, young Ruthven, some others. Oh, yes, Kirkcaldy of Grange."

"Kirkcaldy!" Fraser expostulated. "The rest are of negligible character. But I'm surprised at Kirkcaldy. He's a sound man—and a doughty soldier."

Gordon nodded. "I know, I was amazed to hear of his defection. And Maitland's. It leaves the Queen and Bothwell with inferior captains, mainly Border men who are more used to raids than to battles. But if she could count on you two, it would help immeasurably."

"And you?" Fraser raised an eyebrow at Gordon. "You are committed to her cause?"

"I wouldn't be here if I weren't," Gordon replied with obvious indignation. "I put Corrichie Moor behind me long ago."

John and Claud Hamilton rode over to consult with their father later that day. They returned at dusk, no more enlightened than they had been before they left. The duke had given them at least a dozen sound reasons why the House of Hamilton should support the Queen; then he'd given another dozen why they should not.

But Claud's mind was made up. "Mary Stuart is our kin," he told his brother. “She is also our Queen. And unless she is actually deposed and not merely defeated, we will be considered traitors for not offering our support.” The two Hamiltons argued far into the night. By morning, they had agreed to take their men into Edinburgh. Claud’s reasoning was far from selfless, but it was sound. As they mustered their forces outside the castle, Fraser strolled under the arched entrance, swinging a riding crop against his hip.

Gordon, who was riding back to the capital with the Hamiltons, walked over to meet Fraser. “Well? What of you, Iain?”

Fraser scanned the well-ordered ranks of Hamilton men. “They don’t look as fierce as our Highlanders, do they, George? But I suppose they can put up a fight.” He signaled for a groom to bring Barvas. “I’ll go along, if only for the ride.”

When Fraser went back into the castle to bid Dallas farewell, she flew into a monumental rage. “After all the Queen has put you through? After what Bothwell’s done, too! God’s eyes, I’ll never understand men!” She flung a jam jar across the room, its contents spattering the wall. “Here we are, with only Gordon’s word standing between you and the Tolbooth. Yet you’ll ride off to risk your life for that brainless Mary Stuart! Oh!” Boiling with frustration, Dallas snatched up a heavy pewter water jug and aimed it at her husband.

“Enough, lassie,” Fraser commanded, “I’ve no time for tirades. The men are starting to move out.”

But Dallas paid no heed and let fly with the water jug. Fraser ducked and came to the bed where his wife had been eating her breakfast. “I tell you, I must leave at once. Now becalm yourself and bid me good-bye.” His tone was impatient as he put a hand under her chin.

Dallas jerked away, flinging herself halfway across the bed. “Don’t touch me! One way or another, you’ll end up dead! You don’t care what happens to me or the children, you’d rather play the braw gallant!”

Fraser froze with one foot on the floor, the other propped up on the bed rail. “So that’s it,” he said in tight-lipped wonder. “I should have guessed your true concern would be for yourself, for how impoverished you’ll be without me.”

Dallas stopped pounding her fists into the mattress and turned just enough so that Fraser could see the defiant outline of her profile. “Twaddle, you self-centered ape! Don’t justify your ....”

Her words were drowned out by the clatter of Fraser’s sword, helmet and chain mail dropping onto the floor. He moved swiftly around to the side of the bed and grabbed a handful of Dallas’s thick hair, pulling her around to face him. Rage and rejection waged war across his face as he pinned her thighs down with his knee.

Flailing uselessly with her fists, Dallas sought for words to calm her husband. "Wait, Iain! You mistook what ...."

But Fraser had gone beyond reason. He shredded the lambswool nightshift from Dallas's body in one fierce gesture. Instinctively, she raised her hands to fend him off but saw the cold, obstinate look in the hazel eyes, realized she had goaded him into fury, and knew that resistance would be as futile as it had been on their wedding night.

Fraser, however, did not recognize her surrender. He pinioned Dallas's arms behind her and hurled himself on top of her. His knees forced her legs wide apart and the hands which squeezed her breasts were harsh.

"Please, Iain, you're hurting me!" But Fraser paid her no heed. A moment later, she felt him thrust inside her, plunging with a ferocious intensity that she had never before experienced. His riding boots chafed her legs, the heavy belt buckle cut into her flesh, and her arms ached behind her back.

Dallas bit her lips to keep from crying out in pain; all she could think of was that at least she must be fully recovered from the miscarriage by now. And if she were not .... she closed her eyes tight at the memory of Strathmuir.

As her husband relentlessly plundered her body as savagely as any ship he'd ever captured, she vowed not to take pleasure from his brutal act. But Dallas could not keep rein over her own response. When Fraser's final thrust surged inside her, she cried out—with fulfillment instead of relief.

"Oh, Iain," she gasped as he stood up and put his clothes back in order, "you are an impossible beast!"

Fraser did not catch the loving note in her voice. Indeed, he did not seem to hear her at all. He picked up his gear, stalked from the room and banged the door shut without a word.

At last Dallas sat up slowly and groped for her peignoir. She remained sitting on the bed, feet dangling over the edge, until well after the sounds of men and horses had died away in the distance.

Damn the man, she thought, hadn't he realized her anger had been inspired by fear? Impoverishment! She could face it with him, but not alone. In fact, there was nothing she cared to face without Fraser: How dare he take her love so lightly as to put himself in mortal danger for such an unworthy cause!

"Damn!" she said aloud. If he'd just let her explain instead of resorting to virtual rape .... Dallas paused, catching her disheveled image in the faintly warped mirror on the dressing table across the room. Her fingers flicked lightly over her naked body, which was aching more every minute. She should be outraged, she told herself, revolted by her husband's violent behavior. But now, regret suffused any other emotion. He'd ridden off, to God only knew what fate, and she'd not had a chance to say she loved him.

GLENNIE AND WALTER were unprepared for the arrival of Dallas and her entourage at Nairne's Close. "But, Dallas, where will we put them all?" Glennie exclaimed, blinking rapidly in agitation.

"I promise, we won't stay for long," Dallas said, beginning to feel the first twinges of guilt. "I'll find a house or a flat as soon as possible. I have money from the sale of our furnishings which will tide us over—at least for a while," she added grimly and wondered if security of any sort would ever come her way.

ON THE DAY before the Hamiltons rode into Edinburgh, Bothwell and the Queen left for Borthwick Castle, twelve miles to the south. Though Mary Stuart had expected to find some peace in the country, her hopes were soon dashed. Several of the rebel lords besieged the fortress while Bothwell escaped to seek help.

Inside Edinburgh Castle, Fraser and Hamilton were unaware of this new turn of events. The Queen had sent a message to George Gordon, but it had fallen into Morton's hands. So as June moved into its second week, the Hamiltons remained encamped at the castle, wondering if a confrontation would actually occur, or if the Queen and Bothwell were merely enjoying a honeymoon at Borthwick.

Dallas had quickly found out where Fraser and the others were quartered. Every time she left Nairne's Close to house-hunt, she saw the bulk of the castle rising up out of the hill and wondered if her husband was still angry with her. She had considered going to see him but learned that no one was allowed inside except for military purposes. She had started several notes to him but shredded each one as awkward or inadequate.

But Iain Fraser assumed his wife was still at Hamilton Castle, cursing her fate and smashing up the furniture. He was therefore much surprised when George Gordon came bearing a message from Delphinia Douglas.

"Your wife is at her former home just down the hill," Gordon said, repeating what Delphinia's messenger had told him. "At four o'clock this afternoon, Delphinia will arrive there with some important news. She urges you to join her."

Fraser paused in the act of shining his helmet. There was little to do in the castle these days except drink, dice, and make sure that all the military equipment was kept at the ready. "Delphinia? At the Cameron house? Do you really think my wife will let her in?"

Gordon shrugged and laughed hollowly. "Under the circumstances, yes. Delphinia is most resourceful. You see," he said, gazing directly at Fraser, "she has found out who your father was."

Chapter Thirty-Four

BOTH MEN HAD predicted Dallas's behavior accurately. Upon seeing Delphinia with her hand on the tirling pin, Dallas had gone to the door and threatened to push the other woman off the stoop. When Delphinia made her announcement, Dallas's eyes had widened in astonishment, then turned dubious, but curiosity won out. Only as she jerked the door open did she notice the Earl of Morton coming up the stairs behind Delphinia.

But Dallas had just closed the parlor door when Marthe called out that Baron Fraser had also arrived. Dallas tried to conceal her further surprise at this announcement as she went back into the entry hall.

"Iain!" She stood motionless in the middle of the hall, willing herself not to rush into his arms.

"I just learned you were in the city," Fraser said formally. "I understand you're expecting a guest."

"Guests. They're already here. Iain, what's going on? That wretched Delphinia says it's about your father!"

Fraser brushed past her and started into the parlor but paused with his hand on the doorknob. "Guests? Who else?"

"Morton, the pig. He came with her." Dallas wished Fraser would stop looking so damnably reserved.

"Christ." Fraser pulled open the door with a violent motion and strode into the room. He moved swiftly to Delphinia, took her hand and kissed it perfunctorily, then whirled on Morton. "I wasn't told you'd be here. I mislike finding myself under the same roof with your ilk."

Morton chuckled malevolently. "Are you more riled over my politics or losing your charming town house? Oh, don't glower so, Iain, we Scots change sides as we change our clothes."

"Some do," Fraser said, pulling out a chair for Delphinia, who threw him an inviting smile. "Now let's get on with this business. I've no time for word duels."

"Of course not," Delphinia said in dulcet tones. "Morton has been kind enough to escort me and act in Lord James's absence."

"James!" Dallas spat the name. "What does he have to do with this?" But Dallas already knew; this was the apparent consummation of the conspiracy between Delphinia and Lord James.

Plying her fan with one hand, Delphinia reached into her voluminous damask skirts to produce a small silver box. "Take this, Iain. What's inside will answer a question which has plagued you for many years."

Warily, Fraser took the box from her and worked at the catch until the lid sprung open. Inside lay an amulet, set with rubies against an intricate gold background. Fraser carefully extracted the piece, turning it over slowly in his hands. On the back was an inscription. He walked to the window, to hold the amulet under the late afternoon sunlight. Dallas followed him, leaning over his shoulder, breathless with curiosity.

"What does it say?" she demanded. "Can you read it?"

Fraser turned to face her. He was visibly shaken, his dark skin faintly sallow. "It says," he read with some difficulty, " 'To my beloved Catherine, the love of my heart and the mother of my child.' " The hazel eyes pierced Dallas's own anxious gaze. " 'From your devoted Daniel Cameron.' "

Dallas was immobilized for several seconds before she flung herself at Delphinia. "It's not true! It's a lie! Where did you get this bogus trinket?"

The other woman smirked in triumph. "From James. And it's not bogus but was put by your father into the safekeeping of Marie de Guise many years ago. It's a pity, Lady Fraser—excuse me, you're not Lady Fraser at all—you're Iain's half-sister."

But Fraser had snapped out of his apparent trance. He grabbed Delphinia by the arm and pulled her to her feet. "This is a sham! I know the truth! Daniel Cameron told me!"

Delphinia instinctively flinched from the rage in Fraser's eyes. "A dying man ... his wits raddled ... perhaps he *wanted* to tell you the truth, but he was confused, his mind befogged by death."

"Rot!" Dallas all but spat on Delphinia and had to press her hands at her sides to keep from doing the other woman a lethal mischief. "At the very end my father was quite lucid!"

"Will Ruthven was there that night," Delphinia went on in a composed, reasonable voice. "He says Master Cameron rambled constantly. Perhaps, Iain," she said in a soothingly sympathetic tone, "you wanted to believe what Daniel Cameron told you. It would be natural enough, under the circumstances."

Fraser was glowering fiercely at the amulet. "None of this makes sense. Why would James give this to you? Why tell me now?"

"No mystery there," Morton commented with a shrug of his thick-set shoulders. "James never knew who sired you, either—until last summer when someone—" He paused to cast his piglike gaze in Dallas's direction. "Until someone dug the amulet out of a wall in Edinburgh Castle."

"It took some time for James to figure out its significance," Delphinia explained smoothly, "but at last he decided it must have something to do with you, Iain. Before he left Scotland, he entrusted it to me, knowing I would do what I could to set matters aright."

Feeling sick at her stomach, Dallas walked shakily to her husband. Tremulously, she put a hand on his shoulder. "My love," she whispered, her annoyance with him long vanished, "we'll prove it's a lie! I swear we will!"

But Fraser responded neither to her words nor to her touch. He stood by the window, staring unseeingly into Nairne's Close. One hand rested heavily against the casement, as if the wall itself were his sole means of physical and emotional support. "It's mad," he muttered fiercely, "it's impossible! I can't accept this!"

Delphinia was plying her fan again and moving briskly around the room. "You'll adjust to the idea in time, Iain. I understand it's a shock, but once your marriage is annulled and you can face life anew, you'll come to appreciate the peace of mind I've given you."

As Dallas edged away from Fraser, Delphinia came to stand behind him. She snapped her fan shut and addressed his rigid back. "I would guess that Daniel Cameron met Catherine McKim before he ever came to Edinburgh. Naturally, their families would have disapproved of such a match. Even before Blar-na-Leine, there was deep enmity between the clans. But Daniel must have continued his affair with Catherine even after her marriage to Malcolm Fraser. Later, it was obvious why Cameron was sent for by his kin to get the amulet, since it was inscribed with his own name."

"How did you know about that?" Dallas cried, holding onto a chair for support.

Delphinia shrugged her wide shoulders. "Lord James and I did some investigating. Your Cameron kin will do almost anything—for money."

Dallas ignored the barb and sunk slowly into the chair. The most horrible part was that the story fit together so well. Her father would have wanted to right the wrong, as he'd put it, to have his illegitimate son know the truth. But why had he waited so long? Clan hatreds or not, surely he could have acknowledged Iain.

Dallas stood up again, groping her way across the room in search of the wine decanter. The familiar surroundings blurred in front of her so that when the door flew open she scarcely recognized Marthe's chunky form.

"Dallas, dear child," the serving woman wheezed, "you look faint!"

Rallying slightly, Dallas put out a hand to fend Marthe off. "Please—don't meddle. I'll be all right!"

But Marthe paid no heed. "Of course ye will," she soothed, "as soon as I've had my say. Turn 'round, Iain, cease storming like a November day, and look upon your old nurse, Moireach!"

NEITHER DALLAS NOR Fraser ever put together a coherent sequence of the events which followed. Someone had screamed—Dallas wasn't sure if it was Delphinia or herself. Morton had tried to propel Marthe from the room but was stopped by somebody—Fraser himself, perhaps. Glennie and Walter had come racing into the parlor at some point, totally bewildered by the commotion. As Fraser gaped at Marthe, the serving woman's thick lips quivered and tears rolled down the withered cheeks.

"Moireach is the Gaelic for Marthe, as well ye know, Iain," she declared between gasps for breath. "Och, I knew ye'd never recognize me. But I alone know the story of your birth, as a true witness, and what this one"—she paused to glare venomously at Delphinia—"has told you isn't worth a bag o' beans."

"The old dame is out of her head," Morton snapped. "You've seen the amulet's inscription. Send the raddled harridan away!"

But Fraser had stepped up to Marthe's side and placed one arm firmly around her plump shoulders. "I told you at the outset, it didn't sound right. That amulet is a fraud, and so is your malicious tale, Delphinia. I suggest you both leave at once."

No one could ever accuse Delphinia of giving up easily. "Not until I've heard her story," she exclaimed, waving her fan at Marthe. "She's only trying to protect her precious Dallas!"

Marthe, however, averred stoutly that as she'd kept her secret for thirty-seven years, she wasn't about to babble it away in front of people who couldn't be trusted. Delphinia exchanged irate glances with Morton, then haughtily swept by Walter and Glennie, took the earl's arm, and started for the entry hall door.

"Hold on, Delphinia," Dallas cried. "You forgot something." Her spirits revived, she picked up the silver box and the amulet, and flung them both in Delphinia's face.

"Now," Dallas said, banging the door behind her, "tell us the truth, Marthe, before I burst!"

Still, the serving woman hesitated. "I can only tell ye, Iain—well, mayhap

Dallas, too, since ye be man and wife. But, Glennie, I'm afraid ye and Walter must go outside."

"It's all right," Glennie said with a reassuring pat on Marthe's arm. "You must abide by your conscience—though I'm sure Walter and I don't have the vaguest notion of what's going on anyway."

For the first time since Fraser had read the amulet inscription aloud, he looked directly at Dallas, but there was no time to speculate about his wife. Marthe's story was what mattered most at the moment.

The serving woman had composed herself in a chair by the hearth, plump hands folded over her apron, the florid cheeks redder than usual. As her narrative unfolded, the years fell away like leaves in an autumn wind.

Marthe, or Moireach, as she was called then, had come to Beauly when Catherine McKim was a bride. Moireach herself had recently been married to one of Malcolm Fraser's tenants. Shortly after Catherine and Malcolm were wed, the new bridegroom went to Inverness for a few weeks to make arrangements for the spring sowing. While he was away, a group of nobles arrived at Beauly to hunt stags.

"They were loath to tell us who they were, but we knew them to be fine lords," Marthe recalled. "One in particular carried himself so well—he was no more than twenty, but the others seemed to defer to him. He paid great court to your mother and they would ride off alone or go strolling through the woods together."

The party had remained for almost three weeks, leaving the day before Malcolm returned. Life went on as before, until some two months later when Moireach found her mistress sobbing wildly. "I asked what troubled her and finally she said she was going to have a bairn. I laughed at her tears, told her to be happy—I, too, was expecting a babe. But she confided that the bairn she carried was not Malcolm's but the handsome nobleman's, and she feared her husband greatly, for he had already shown her his cruel side."

Marthe paused and passed a hand over her face. "If she thought to fool Malcolm, she was mistaken. He was canny, in his way. Still, the time passed peaceably enough. My wee one was born about two months ahead of ye, Iain. So when Malcolm took Catherine to the convent, I did not go with her. But when her hour came, she sent for me, and my man and I traveled through the dark night to be at her side. You had just come into the world when we got there and Father Beathan was with your poor mother. She was so weak." Marthe paused, pressed her lips together and shook her head at the sad memory. "She asked that we be left alone. And then she told me who the nobleman was, who your father was. Oh, Iain, my poor bairn, you were sired by Jamie himself, our good King!"

The silence which followed appeared to immobilize all three of them.

Marthe seemed to be holding a deep breath; Dallas's unblinking stare was fixed on her husband's shadowy face. He sat with his hand resting on his knee, his eyes boring into the well-trodden carpet. Daniel Cameron had been right after all. Fraser had never doubted the dying man's words, it was the only explanation for James Stuart's deep antagonism .... James, his half-brother ... the Queen, his half-sister ... and if he had calculated rightly, he was some months older than James, if he'd been legitimated as James himself had been, he, not James, would have fallen heir to all those perquisites and powers ....

Fraser laughed aloud, shaking his head in wonder. How could he have had even the most fleeting of doubts? But Delphinia's story *had* been well contrived; Daniel Cameron *had* been a mortally ill man who had been incoherent until Fraser arrived in Nairne's Close.

Fraser stopped abruptly and looked at Dallas. She was staring dumbly into space, the hint of a frown playing about her eyes. "Well?" He reached over and grabbed her wrist, making her head jerk forward. "Don't you have anything to say to your royal bastard of a husband?"

Slowly, her free hand encircled the wrist which held hers. "I don't know what to say—except that at least it explains where Robbie got his red hair."

Fraser let go of her wrist but held onto her hand. "I'd expect more jubilation from you, madame," he said in a tone that was only half-teasing. "You wanted to know the truth all these years. Now you've found out that one great secret your father—and I—had to keep from you."

"True enough." Dallas nodded, displaying more of her usual animation. "Maybe I just can't take in all that's happened this afternoon. Or maybe I always knew that you didn't spring from the loins of some vagrant caird or plundering reiver. Truly, Iain, I marvel that it never occurred to me before."

"I wonder how long James knew," Fraser mused with a shake of his head. "Even when I first met him at the university at St. Andrews he was unfriendly. But he couldn't have known then, Marie de Guise was still alive. What happened, I wonder, to the second amulet the priest told you about, Dallas?"

"Och," interposed Marthe, "wonder no more." She reached inside her bodice and drew out a gold amulet, set with a ruby, not unlike the one Delphinia had displayed earlier that day. "Here," she said, pulling the chain over her head, "this is the mate to the one Master Cameron gave to the Queen Mother. Your own sweet mother entrusted it to me before she died."

Fraser took the necklace from her and turned it over in his brown hands. "Jesu." He pressed the side and the circular top clicked open to reveal a lock of red hair and an inscription in French. "To dearest Catherine," it read, "in devoted remembrance—James Rex."

"You mean you've worn it all these years and no one ever knew?" His tone was incredulous as he gave the amulet to Dallas so that she could study it more closely.

"Och, of course no one knew!" Marthe said indignantly. "I don't go about with my dresses like so, the way some women do nowadays."

Fraser laughed and leaned over to kiss her cheek. "You are a remarkable woman, Marthe—or should I say, Moireach? But what happened to you after you left Beauly?"

Marthe pulled a handkerchief from her apron pocket and wiped the perspiration from her forehead. The late June afternoon sun had made the parlor uncommonly warm. "I had lost both child and husband within a span of six months. Your aunt and uncle, the ones who took ye in after Malcolm drowned that wild night on Beauly Firth, said I could stay on with them, but there was so much sadness there for me. I misliked leaving ye but decided to go south, where my man had kin. I ended up working for a MacKintosh family whose daughter was soon to wed and move to Edinburgh. That was your mother, Dallas, and she was the one who insisted I be called Marthe. She said, dear lady that she was, the Lowlanders would never be able to pronounce the Gaelic name. So on to the city I went, leaving my past behind me. Strange, how very strange that I served both your mothers, and tended the two of you as bairns."

"Strange indeed," Fraser drawled. "What a shock it must have been when I showed up as Dallas's prospective husband!"

Marthe's eyes went round with remembrance. "Och! That it was! I could scarce believe it! But it seemed right somehow, almost as if the two of ye belonged together from the very start. But though Master Cameron told you the truth, I still couldna break my own vow of silence. Oh, I knew ye needed proof and I had it—but I knew, too, I'd pass on afore ye and leave the amulet to Dallas as the safeguard for your futures. But today—well, I had to speak up to spare ye both a terrible heartbreak."

It was Dallas's turn to kiss Marthe. She hugged the serving woman close, repeating her name over and over. "And you did spare us! I can't imagine what might have happened if you hadn't spoken out!"

After Dallas had released Marthe, the old serving woman got to her feet. "Whether ye tell all or not, 'tis your business now, Iain. In truth, I'm glad to be rid of the secret, it's been a terrible burden all these long years." She paused to give them one last fond look. "Now I must amble on to the kitchen, I've a supper to make!"

When Marthe had gone, Dallas and Fraser stared at the amulet which was resting on the little oak table. "I can't help but think Marthe might have saved me a lot of trouble if she'd revealed her secret a long time ago," he said wryly. "Though God knows, I hold a vow as sacred as the next man."

"James still would have tried to get you out of the way, I'll wager," Dallas asserted, putting her arms around Fraser. "And if there had been no secret, if my father hadn't mentioned your name on his deathbed, I might never have gotten to know you."

"Hmmmm." Fraser nodded his head once in assent. "I'd like to get reacquainted. It's been over a week since we parted at Hamilton Castle. Can you lock that parlor door?"

"No," Dallas murmured into his chest. "There's no key and as you may have noticed, this is an easy room on which to eavesdrop. Marthe's been doing it for years."

Fraser sighed as he let his hands stray down her back and over her hips. "I'm still poor, you know, king's son or not. If there's any place in this overpopulated house that's private, would you consider surrendering yourself to a royal pauper?"

"I was dreadful that morning before you left," Dallas murmured, forgetting the first part of his question and nibbling on his ear. "You know I didn't really mean it, don't you?"

"I'm never sure what you mean and what you don't," he said low, working rapidly at the hooks on her gown. Fraser kissed her once, twice, three times before his weight finally forced her down onto the carpet by the hearth.

"You were most ungallant at Hamilton Castle," Dallas declared as she felt his hands fondle her buttocks.

"So I was," Fraser admitted readily enough as he took off his own clothes. "But you are an aggravating little wench."

"Oh?" Dallas held his face between her hands. "Still, you seem capable of putting up with me."

Fraser laughed and shook his head. "I can't seem to *not* put up with you. How did a carefree libertine like me end up doting on the impossible likes of you?"

Dallas answered him by pulling his head onto her breasts. "At least you don't find me tiresome," she said as her hands slid down to capture his firm manhood in her slim fingers.

"True," Fraser replied in a muffled voice.

"Mmmmm," murmured Dallas and squirmed with delight as his hands and mouth made havoc of her senses. They made love in the little parlor for over an hour and no one disturbed them until Marthe announced it was suppertime.

Chapter Thirty-Five

FRASER RETURNED TO the castle after supper. Though resigned to his political position, Dallas had urged him to stay on at the Cameron house. The house might be crowded, she argued, but she had her old room to herself.

"Nay, lassie, I must remain at the castle with John and his men," he'd told her. "All seems quiet enough, but no one is sure what will happen—or when."

She walked with him as far as the entrance to the close where he kissed her good-bye. There was still a tinge of light between the tall houses, and over in Blyth's Wynd they could hear children calling to each other. After Fraser disappeared, Dallas remained in the close, pacing the cobbles until darkness settled in over the rooftops. She knew she ought to be exhilarated by finally learning the truth about Fraser's parentage. But now, with time for reflection, she began to speculate about what effect having proof of his royal parentage would have on their lives. Would he become obsessed with a vaulting ambition? Would he attempt to usurp James's place, since the man Fraser could openly acknowledge as his half-brother had left the country? Would he compete with Bothwell for a share of Mary's power? Most of all, would his royal blood exact the ultimate price: Was it possible that she would finally lose Fraser forever?

Dallas leaned on the curving stair rail and peered into the night, wishing that it were the future and that she might see what it held for all of them.

DRESSED AS A man, Mary Stuart had fled Borthwick Castle and ridden to meet Bothwell at Cakemuir. From there they went to Dunbar, where they called for their troops to rally 'round them outside Musselburgh.

"How many men does she have with her?" Hamilton asked Gordon as the clang of weapons and mail resounded from the castle esplanade.

Gordon perused the message a third time. "About six hundred," he replied, fingering his blond beard. "I keep thinking there is a mistake in the number written down, but that's what it says."

"That's madness!" Hamilton exclaimed. "Even with our reinforcements, we can't match the rebels by half!"

"Do you mean to tell me, George," Fraser said as he paused in fastening his chain mail, "that Bothwell and the Queen have not been joined by supporters along the way?"

Sitting down heavily on a wooden bench, Gordon sighed. "I'm afraid so, Iain. None of the ordinary people a Stuart sovereign can usually rely on have rallied to her standard."

An ominous silence enveloped the room. The three men seemed wrapped deep in their own thoughts, and there was little doubt among them that each was contemplating the same decision.

Fraser was the first to speak, throwing his helmet across the trestle table with a gesture of disgust. "By God, they're doomed. The Queen and Bothwell are finished."

Gordon got to his feet. "Hold on, Iain. If we go, there will be a fighting chance. At best, we might create a stalemate—at worst, the Queen and Bothwell may escape to raise more troops later."

But Fraser shook his head slowly, definitely. "Nay, George, that's not the worst that could happen. And that's not the point, either." He placed one spurred and booted foot on the bench and looked from Gordon to Hamilton. "If the people aren't willing to support the Queen, then it is pointless for us to do so. In my opinion, when any ruler falls so far as to lose the confidence and loyalty of his—or her—subjects, then that person has surrendered the right to rule. You're a Highlander, George, you know the truth of what I say. Where you and I come from, the chief has to earn and keep the clan's respect."

Gordon rubbed at his forehead, eyes closed, his pained expression clearly showing the uncertainties which racked him. "You speak well enough, Iain, but we're talking of the Queen, not some fierce Highland toiseach."

"It's the same thing," Fraser asserted. "Think it through, George. A good clan chieftain serves his people, his land. When Mary Stuart first came to Scotland, I hoped she would do the same. Young and naive as she was, I saw in her a hope for the future, the healer of old wounds and the benefactress of a sickly nation. But through her own fault or that of others, she's failed. I, at least, will not offer my sword—or my life—to a sovereign Scotland neither wants nor deserves."

For a moment, Gordon said nothing, then looked at Hamilton. "What of you, John? Do you agree with Iain?"

A small, sad smile touched Hamilton's mouth. "In a sense, I do. But I've not the vision of Scotland that Iain has. I see this wretched mess as Bothwell's doing, more than Mary's. If I could fight for her, and her alone, I'd do so without a qualm. But because of Bothwell, she has lost her people, and I see no other course than to remain here with my men."

"Damn!" Gordon banged his fist on the trestle table, toppling an ale tankard onto the floor. "Why did I ever talk my sister Jean into letting Bothwell go so easily?"

Fraser was taking off his chain mail and stretching the neck muscles which had grown tense during the last painful quarter of an hour. "Don't blame yourself, George. Maybe we shouldn't even blame Bothwell or the Queen. We Scots have always put ourselves above our country. Mayhap, in the long run, we're all guilty."

THE CASTLE ESPLANADE was deserted while the evening breeze from the Firth scattered the dirt in little grey clouds. Iain Fraser walked along the battlements, pausing by Mons Meg, the giant cannon cast in Belgium to defend Edinburgh from the English.

Hamilton and Gordon were still inside the castle, drinking a great deal and reassuring each other that they had made the right decision. But Fraser had left them, realizing that all the whiskey in Edinburgh would not assuage his sense of guilt.

Neither of the others could imagine the difficulty of his decision. If Mary Stuart had become less to him as a sovereign, she was much more to him as his sister. His longstanding concern and affection for her had to be reassessed in a new light. It was as if the affirmation of their kinship had stripped Mary of her monarchy and permitted Fraser to see her for the first time as a human being: charming but unstable, generous to those she loved but easily swayed where her heart was concerned, born to reign but not to rule, and incapable of putting her country's needs above her personal desires.

Watching the shutters close one by one on the houses which marched down Castle Hill, Fraser wondered if he would have reacted differently if he'd not known of his own royal ancestry. No, he decided, rivalry played no part. Being able to verify his knowledge made him feel curiously detached, as if he were viewing the world around him through new eyes.

To his right, he could see the steep roofs of the house in Nairne's Close. A light still burned behind the window Fraser adjudged to be Dallas's. She was probably reading in bed, the thick hair tumbling over her shoulders, the small, slim hands turning the pages, the full, pouty mouth changing in expression from disagreement to pleasure. His obstinate, loyal, perverse little lassie had taught him a few things over the years: Wild as a Highland glen, canny as a

Lawnmarket merchant, she'd bound him to herself with ties stronger than country or kin. If her love for him had been flawed, so was his for her. Perhaps that was the greatest lesson he had learned from her, that love was as imperfect as the people who offered it to one another.

The long summer twilight had slipped into darkness but the light in Nairne's Close still glowed like a beckoning star. Fraser moved away from the castle battlements and headed down the esplanade towards the haven of his lassie's arms.

STANDING IN THE long shadow of the Tron Kirk, Dallas moved closer to Iain Fraser as the noise of the crowd grew more deafening and venomous. "I can't see around all these people," she said nervously, "though I'm not sure I want to."

Fraser, being at least half a head taller than most of the other onlookers, had a clear view of the High Street. Slowly, picking their way through the clamorous throng, the soldiers and their horses moved towards the Black Turnpike, a large timber-fronted house owned by the Provost of Edinburgh.

Near the front of the procession, the Queen of Scotland rode between two insolent guards who seemed to be laughing at her expense. Mary Stuart wore a simple red and blue goodwife's outfit, hastily borrowed in Dunbar since she'd been unable to bring any of her own clothes with her when she'd flown from Borthwick.

There had been no battle that day at Carberry Hill. The rebel lords had merely waited until what few troops Bothwell had under his command melted away. He'd demanded that one of the enemy nobles meet him in single combat, but no challengers had come forth. At last, after a parley, it was agreed that if Bothwell withdrew from the field, the Queen would be escorted back to Edinburgh. Fearing not for herself, but for him, Mary had urged him to acquiesce. Reluctantly, he had embraced her for the last time and ridden off, while the Earl of Morton had signalled for his men to take the Queen as their prisoner.

While the mob hurled taunts and invectives, Mary rode with her head high, shoulders rigid, eyes staring straight ahead. Despite the homely garb, Fraser thought she'd never looked more regal.

"What's happening?" Dallas asked as the crowd's noise reached an unprecedented pitch.

"They're taking her into the Black Turnpike. Jesu," he muttered so that Dallas could barely hear him, "did I do right after all?"

"I wish we'd never come," Dallas cried, her hands over her ears to block out the obscenities of the mob. "Please, let's go back!"

But they were trapped by the crowd, their backs to the Tron Kirk. Even after the Queen had been led away inside the Black Turnpike, the vindictive citizenry remained, as if in a body they formed a single guard to hold her prisoner there.

"I don't think this lot would take kindly to me hacking our way out," Fraser told his wife, grimly surveying the ugly expressions on the onlookers' faces. "We'll have to wait a bit, just hang onto me."

Dallas did just that, her head resting against her husband's chest. The light was fading and the crowd had begun to quiet, though no one seemed ready to leave. "Remember," she said into Fraser's open shirt, "how we met that first night the Queen rode into Edinburgh? How different it all was then!"

Fraser's arm tightened around her waist. "Aye. A lot of things were different then."

They stood clasped together in silence for a long time, detached from the crowd by a mutual surge of memories: Dallas, prickly as a hedgehog, learned but naive, had trooped up the High Street, heartbroken over her father's impending death, yet eager for a glimpse of the bonnie young Queen; Fraser, arrogant, self-contained, half-pirate, half-royalist, all Highlander, ready to offer his services to the new sovereign, hopeful of a bright future for Scotland. And somehow, through it all, they had found neither the security Dallas had sought nor the vision Fraser had pursued, but instead, they had found each other.

Their twin reveries were broken by a sudden hush which engulfed the crowd. It was dark now, but torches lit up the night in front of the Black Turnpike. From a window above the street, Mary Stuart could be seen, no longer regal, her composure shattered by defeat and humiliation. The auburn hair streamed down her shoulders, the plain blue bodice hung open to reveal most of her white breasts, the long graceful hands clawed at the air.

"Oh, God, oh, my God," she shrieked, "come to my defense! I have been betrayed! Oh, help me, somebody, help me!"

The crowd turned breathlessly silent. In the glare of the torches, Fraser could see faces change from malevolence to pity. Then the Queen was gone from the window, and slowly, quietly, her subjects moved away from the Black Turnpike.

FOR JAMES STUART, the feel of Scots soil beneath his horse's hooves felt satisfying. How long he'd waited for this day, a virtual lifetime: He alone would now assume total power in Scotland. Indeed, for once in his life, he'd not been patient; after leaving Berwick, he'd spurred his horse to a gallop, leaving his retainers far behind. He cared not for riding into Edinburgh surrounded by faithful minions. To ride into the city by himself was triumph enough.

Of course he'd have to act the faithful brother and visit the deposed Queen at Lochleven where the Douglases had imprisoned her. But that was of little consequence—Lochleven was well fortified, isolated in the middle of a lake, and rumors that the irksome Hamiltons planned a rescue attempt worried him little.

He was feeling so full of himself that he almost started to hum, but his Protestant upbringing would not permit such unseemly behavior, even here, alone on the tree-shaded road between Restalrig and Edinburgh.

And then he realized with a shock that he was not alone after all. Just a few yards ahead of him, a horse and rider moved out from behind a massive oak tree. James cursed under his breath as he recognized Iain Fraser.

"Welcome home," Fraser called out, leveling his pistol at James. "I trust you've time to chat?"

It never occurred to James that his adversary would not use the pistol. He slowed his horse to a walk, then dismounted in front of Fraser, who was now standing next to Barvas. "How did you know I was coming?" he demanded, hoping he looked as impassive as usual.

"It seemed the most likely route." The shafts of sunlight filtering down through the trees made the muzzle of Fraser's pistol gleam like mellow gold. "Besides, I've been scouting these byways for the past week."

"You are persistent, I'll say that." James was breathing more rapidly, almost in tune to the deep, snorting wheezes of his weary horse. "Speak then, I'm listening."

"How generous you are." Fraser waved the pistol with an exaggerated carelessness that made James grit his teeth. "It appears you are going to be regent, James. You've coveted that position for a long time, even before Mary ever left France." He knew James's hackles were rising but paid no heed. "You'll need some help, though. The Gordons aren't pleased about deposing the Queen. The Hamiltons are furious at the prospect. And Bothwell is still at large."

"You would bargain with me for your support?" James laughed scornfully. "I'm surprised at you, Iain. If I'm willing to take on all the Hamiltons and Gordons put together, not to mention Bothwell and his Border ruffians, I can deal with you as well."

Fraser raised an eyebrow. "Can you now, James? I don't think you quite get my meaning. It's not support I'm offering, it's hindrance—or the lack thereof." He reached inside his dust-stained jerkin and pulled out the amulet. The ruby caught fire in the sunlight, momentarily dazzling James. "This isn't the one you gave Delphinia, of course. But I'm sure you have its mate."

James's heavy-lidded eyes opened wide. He gazed at the amulet for a drawn-out minute. "How long have you known?" he said at last, his voice very low. "How long have you been certain?"

"Long enough," Fraser replied. He stuffed the amulet back inside his jerkin. "By my reckoning, I'm the elder by seven months. Do you suppose the people of Scotland might consider me a better candidate for the regency than you? After all, I bear nowhere near the stains and stigmas of the past as you do. I never intrigued to murder Rizzio or Darnley, either. I may be Catholic, but I've always let a man follow his own conscience when it came to religion. Oh, I've some enemies here and there, but they don't total anywhere near the number you've acquired over the years. I just might make a damnably good regent myself, James."

"You would not dare!" James seethed. "I've earned the regency, I've waited all these years, I've had experience ...."

"Come, come," Fraser taunted, allowing himself to be fascinated by the workings of James's face, "you sound as if you were applying for some post as butcher's apprentice. I'm not saying I actually want your treasured prize. I could be appeased, after all."

"What do you want?" James growled, his eyes once more hooded but wary.

Reaching out with his right hand, Fraser playfully poked at James's chest with the pistol. But there was no laughter in the hazel eyes as he answered the question: "Now you're being sensible, James. I want my lands restored immediately. Morton must settle in cash for the town house, my lassie insists upon that. Of course, it is understood that I am no longer outlawed. And I will be legitimated when Parliament meets next."

"I shall tend to all your requests, but the last," James said, trying not to let his shoulders slump in relief. "I'm afraid your legitimization would be inappropriate. There is no one left in Scotland capable of doing that."

Fraser shoved the pistol into James's chest so hard that the other man gasped. "Lucky for you it didn't discharge," Fraser said mockingly. "You forget, I studied some law at St. Andrews. With proof and witnesses, both of which I now have, any court of law in the country is empowered to legitimate me. Though I would prefer that Parliament act in my case, as it did in yours."

James took a deep breath, trying to control his rampaging thoughts. If Fraser were made legitimate, he would always present a threat. Yet James knew that outright refusal would doubtless mean death. If he acquiesced now and reneged later, Fraser himself could go before Parliament. Of course, it might be possible to put Fraser out of the way before that happened. But others must know the truth by now—the redoubtable Lady Fraser, for one, and God only knew who else. If Fraser died mysteriously, all Scotland would know who was responsible. And such an accusation could jeopardize the regency, an unthinkable possibility.

"You're quite right, it could be worked out," James said, with something of his customary blandness. "It merely seemed rather late in time to act on the matter."

"Never too late when it means the difference between my sons inheriting my property one day or letting it revert to the Crown." The pistol remained pointed at James, and Fraser looked quite solemn. "Oh, James," he said softly, "how easy it would be to kill you! I owe you so much vengeance, for what you've done to me, to my wife, to the Queen!"

Even James's mount seemed to sense the danger. He snorted, pawed the ground, and James had to steady him with a hand that was none too sure.

"But for all that," Fraser went on, "you are Scotland's best hope to prevent civil war and to secure the succession. After all, you've always been Elizabeth's pet, and if anyone can persuade her to name a successor, it will be you." Fraser lowered the pistol and stuck it into his belt. "And," he added with a rueful shake of his head, "you are my brother. That's meant nothing to you, but much as I hate to admit it, it does mean something to me." Then he jumped into the saddle, wheeled Barvas around, and galloped off through the shadowy forest.

For the past month and a half, the Fraser entourage had been encamped in George Gordon's town house at Johnston Terrace. Dallas had gone there grudgingly, none too pleased at sharing Gordon's roof and wary of meeting Catherine. But Gordon behaved civilly enough and Catherine never made an appearance. It was a more commodious arrangement than sharing quarters, at least that was what Dallas kept telling herself. But as the summer dragged along she began to wonder. She'd found two acceptable houses, one in the High School Wynd, the other near the Water Port. But Fraser had dismissed them both. Dallas suggested, somewhat sarcastically, that if her tastes didn't suit him, perhaps he should go house-hunting on his own. The comment had not rankled him in the slightest; he'd merely grinned, paused for a moment to fondle her bottom, and ridden off towards Restalrig.

When he returned to Johnston Terrace that night, he told her about the confrontation with James. Ecstatic, Dallas fairly jumped into his arms. "We aren't poor! You have your lands back, you'll be legally recognized as the King's son! Oh my love, you finally bested that odious James!"

"Not precisely," Fraser said, shaking off her enthusiastic stranglehold. "But I suspect James may see my shadow across his path for a long time to come."

Dallas clapped her hands in triumphant glee. "He's lucky you didn't shoot him as he so richly deserved. Oh, Iain," she exclaimed, the dark eyes shining, "tomorrow, first thing, let's make arrangements to get the town house back!"

Firmly, he took Dallas's hands in his. "Nay, lassie, I'm afraid we can't. We're not staying in Edinburgh." His hazel eyes held no mockery now as he looked directly into her questioning face. "We're going home. To the Highlands."

FRASER EXPECTED DALLAS's resistance to come in the form of a shrieking tirade. Instead, she turned cold, obdurate and logical. With Fraser no longer an outlaw, she pointed out, there was no reason to leave Edinburgh. Her kinfolk were all in the city, she'd seldom see any of them if she lived in the Highlands. Besides, Tarrill was expecting a baby at Christmastime. Then there was James—would her husband turn his back on that villain and let him govern with a free hand? And what of the Queen, held captive by Morton and the rest of the despicable Douglases? Misguided as Mary Stuart might have been, her tragic state must surely touch Fraser's heart—wasn't she his half-sister?

"Everything you say is true," Fraser acknowledged, pulling off the jerkin and carefully depositing the amulet in Dallas's little cedar chest. "But I've finished with all that. James will do no worse by Scotland than his predecessors. I grieve for Mary, I care about her, but she chose her own path. As for your personal inclinations," he continued, stripping off his white cambric shirt, "you can come with me or stay here." He was washing his face and hands in a big silver basin. His back was turned to Dallas and for some moments he heard no sound out of her.

"I suppose," she finally said, somewhat testily, "I could always while away the hours teaching some of those illiterate clansmen of yours to read. At least I'll have Sorcha for company. The boys will probably like it there, with all those peculiar poachers and wondrous woodmen and whatever else crawls around the Highlands."

She'd come up behind him, pressing her body against his back, wrapping her arms around him, letting her fingers stray across his chest and down towards his midsection. "Ugh, I mustn't distract you from washing," she said, dropping her hands, "you've been in the saddle so much lately, you smell like Barvas!"

But he'd already swung around, reaching out to lift her up in his arms. "You're too late," he grinned. "If you insist on molesting a gentlemen at his toilette, you'll have to pay the price. Besides, I always thought Barvas smelled rather good—for a horse."

"Barvas may smell better than some of the feckless wenches you've bedded," Dallas retorted as he dumped her on the bed. "Oh, Iain, I'd go with you anywhere. What could be worse than that chicken farm at Dunbar?"

He had unbuttoned her bodice and freed her breasts, teasing the nipples with his tongue. "Actually," he said, pausing to slip the rest of her dress over her hips, "we won't be living at Beauly, at least not for long. I have a surprise for you." He traced the outline of her waist, her hip, her thigh with his finger.

"Remember last summer I wrote to you and said there was something I couldn't tell you yet?"

"Vaguely." Dallas shivered with delight as he put his hand between her legs.

"I'm building you a house, on property near Inverness." He looked up to watch her expression of pleasure over this new, grand acquisition. But Dallas only sighed and pulled him down on top of her.

"Tell me about it—later," she said and kissed him hard on the mouth.

Fraser could not help but regard his wife quizzically; nose to nose, he tried to read her reaction. "Is this the same lassie who once lusted after a certain house in Gosford's Close?"

"Oh, aye," she answered between kisses, "but since then ... I've discovered I lust ... only after you."

If Fraser was even faintly skeptical, he did not let Dallas know it. Women, he had decided a long time ago, always believed precisely what they wanted to believe. And the lush curves of Dallas's body definitely befuddled Fraser's analytical processes. As he kissed her stomach and the dark, curly hair between her thighs, he heard Dallas sigh with pleasure; but her question caught him off-guard:

"Did you ever make love to Catherine Gordon here?"

Fraser looked up, his chin resting on her hip. "Catherine? Well, no." He paused, and the crooked grin was sheepish. "I mean not in this bed."

"But in this house?"

Fraser tried to shrug nonchalantly. "Well, it *is* a Gordon house."

To Fraser's surprise, Dallas laughed and pushed his head back between her legs. But when she spoke again, her voice was serious. "It's strange," she said, "but I don't care any more about Catherine ... or Delphinia ... or the rest of them."

Fraser was straddling her, his hands clasped behind her head. "Nor," he asserted, "do I."

As he possessed her body and Dallas moved to the pinnacle of ecstasy, she felt that Fraser was with her not just for the moment, but for always.

JOHN HAMILTON HAD come to say good-bye. He had hoped to see both Frasers before they left Edinburgh, but only Dallas was in when Hamilton called at Johnston Terrace.

"Iain's out with Cummings, seeing a furnituremaker about some special pieces he wants for the new house. Do sit, John. George and Anne are out, too—in fact, they left Edinburgh several days ago." Dallas gestured in the direction of a handsome leather-covered chair in the Spanish style. During the Gordons' absence, she seemed to have taken over the whole house.

"I can't stay long," Hamilton replied, sitting down and trying to make his large frame comfortable in the narrow, straight-backed chair. "I just wanted to wish you both well in your new home."

"That's very kind ...." Dallas halted in mid-sentence. "See here, John, I'll not mince words. What can I say? How can I thank you for all you've done for Iain and for me?"

He shook his head with an unaccustomed air of impatience. "Say nothing. It's better that way. I'm just pleased that you and Iain have had things work out so well."

Dallas wasn't sure how much he knew about the confrontation between her husband and James Stuart. Rumors of their meeting had run rampant throughout the city during the last few weeks. For all Dallas knew, Fraser might have already confided in Hamilton. But even though the whole world would know eventually of Fraser's birthright, she felt obliged to hold her tongue. "It is only fair that Iain be reinstated," she commented evasively. "Tell me, what news of the Queen?"

"You heard she is recovering from her miscarriage of Bothwell's twins?" He saw Dallas nod. "It's all so damnably tragic. Bothwell still on the run, the Queen forced to abdicate, the little Prince crowned in his mother's stead and tales of escape attempts from Lochleven abound."

"One such story mentioned that the Hamiltons had tried to stop the Douglases from taking Mary there in the first place." She eyed him speculatively but it was his turn to be evasive.

"You hear all sorts of rumors these days." Suddenly he smiled. "One amusing tale, though—Will Ruthven is said to have fallen under the Queen's spell and has been dismissed as her gaoler."

"Will! Always the weathervane, blowing on the winds of romance or ambition—or are they one and the same to him?" Dallas shook her head ruefully. "But what of James? Will he be named regent as Iain says?"

Hamilton was rearranging the gold chain which gleamed against the deep purple of his doublet. "I'm afraid so, probably before the week is out. It seems," he went on, casting an all-knowing glance at Dallas, "there is no other choice."

He knows, she thought, and looked away for a moment, apparently scrutinizing a bowl of dahlias which had begun to wilt in the heat of the August afternoon. "I've never wished any man dead, yet sometimes when I think of all that James has put us through ...." She made an outflung, hopeless gesture with her hands. "Oh, fie, John, what's the use? Iain could have killed him like a cat gobbling up a mouse. But he didn't."

Hamilton moved towards Dallas and took her hands in his. His brown eyes were solemn and his voice was so low and intense that it seemed to vibrate the very walls of Gordon's sitting room. "You have my word, Dallas, as your friend and as a Hamilton that there will come a time when James will trouble you no more."

Her big eyes conveyed both shock and fear. "Nay, John, I told you once before you mustn't ever do anything on my—on our—account which would endanger you."

His grip on her hands grew tighter. "I'll do what I must. I'll take my time, I always do—for better or for worse." Hamilton's smile was tinged with irony. Dallas would have argued with him further but Iain Fraser came into the room before she could speak.

If he was upset to find Hamilton holding his wife's hands, he gave no sign. Fraser greeted the other man with a clap on the shoulder, kissed Dallas on the cheek, and called to Cummings to fetch some of Gordon's best whiskey.

"I hate to refuse a good drink," Hamilton said with a smile, "but I must be going. Greet George and my sister, Anne, for me." He shook Fraser's hand, wished him good fortune, and then turned back to Dallas. There was an awkward silence as they faced each other with a bemused Fraser looking on. Then Dallas reached out and embraced Hamilton tightly. They clung to each other for several moments until the sound of Fraser pushing at the Spanish chair with his foot jarred them apart.

Hamilton did his best to appear composed. "God willing, you'll visit Edinburgh some day," he said, moving towards the door.

"It's possible," Fraser answered noncommittally. "Meanwhile, come to Inverness. The stag hunting is plentiful and the fishing is superb."

Hamilton paused on the threshold, one hand on his hip. "Aye," he replied, grinning at Fraser and casting a quick glance at Dallas, "I'd enjoy such sport." The Hamilton plaid swung from his broad shoulders as he turned away and walked out into the August sunshine.

It was six years to the very day that Mary Stuart had returned to Scotland.

DALLAS AND FRASER rode up to the building site on a clear, autumn day with the morning mist still clinging to the tall grass. The workmen were busy, putting the final touches on the native blue-grey stone walls. It would be a large house, but not, Dallas calculated, unmanageable. Fraser had gone over the drawings with her, pointing out the second story gallery, the new-fashioned perpendicular windows which would allow a maximum of light in the dreary Highland winters, and the various rooms which they would furnish together.

"It's going to be beautiful," Dallas said, careful not to stumble over a timber which had been discarded in the tall grass.

"I always wanted to build my own home up here," he said, gazing off towards the heath-covered hills. "There will be a good view of the farmlands from this direction and you can see the river and Inverness itself from the back."

"We'll have to plot out the gardens before spring," Dallas said, trying to envision how they might look. "I'd like a pond somewhere, maybe one of those Italian fountains ...."

But Fraser wasn't listening. He looked from the unfinished house out to the fields and finally back to his wife. For a long time, he had perceived Scotland through his sovereign, seen his homeland embodied in the personage of Mary Stuart. How wrong he had been—this was Scotland, this land, the house, and most of all, his wife and children. A king's son he might be, but he was still a Highlander. Fraser reached out and put an arm around Dallas's shoulders.

"You like this place, lassie?" he asked, rubbing her little chin with his fist.

"I think so," she said, lengthening her strides to keep pace with him. "It's not Edinburgh, but," she added, turning to look at his lean, dark face, "it is our home."

"Aye, lassie," he agreed, holding her close, "and we'll call it Gosford's End."

About the Author

Seattle native Mary Richardson Daheim lives three miles from the house where she was raised. From her dining nook she can see the maple tree in front of her childhood home. Mary isn't one for change when it comes to geography. Upon getting her journalism degree from the University of Washington (she can see the campus from the dining nook, too), she went to work for a newspaper in Anacortes, Washington. Then, after her marriage to David Daheim, his first college teaching post was in Port Angeles where she became a reporter for the local daily. Both tours of small-town duty gave her the background for the Alpine/Emma Lord series.

Mary spent much of her non-fiction career in public relations (some would say PR is fiction, too). But ever since she learned how to read and write, Mary wanted to tell stories that could be put between book covers (e-readers were far into the future and if she hadn't seen her daughter's iPad, she might not know they exist). Thus, she began her publishing career with the first of seven historical romances before switching to mysteries in 1991. If Mary could do the math, she'd know how many books she's published. Since she can't, she estimates the total is at least 55. Or something. See below—count 'em if you can.

At the time of her husband and mentor's death in February 2010, David and Mary had been married for more than 43 years. They have three daughters, Barbara, Katherine and Magdalen, and two granddaughters, Maisy and Clara. They all live in Seattle, too. Those apples don't move far from the tree...literally.